The 1300 Year's War

The 1300 Year's War

The Evolution of Judeo-Christianity and Islam and their Associated Warfare

(Volume 1)

ROBERT MADDOCK

Illustrated by Raija Pönkänen

urlink
PRINT & MEDIA

1603 Capitol Ave., Suite 310 Cheyenne, Wyoming USA 82001
1-888-980-6523 | admin@urlinkpublishing.com

URLink Print and Media is committed to excellence in the publishing industry.

Published in the United States of America

ISBN 978-1-64367-518-3 (Paperback)
ISBN 978-1-64367-517-6 (Digital)

17.05.19

DEDICATION

We stand at the brink of a moral cliff. We are ignorant, haughty and selfish. Many families are broken; many ignore religious beliefs, morality and eternal truths. We steal our children's and grandchildren's inheritance and perjure for political advantage. We give in to harmful addictions that destroy mind and body. Many kill the unborn while many more kill the living vicariously in violent games. We look to the state, politics, and the philosophies of man for succor despite their flaws rather than to our religious eternal truths. Have we strayed so far from the truth that our freedom is in jeopardy (John 8:31-47)? "*Is it any wonder then, that our children no longer know what democracy, free speech, ethics, and Western culture are, much less where they came from and how they are to be preserved?*" [Hanson, VD & Heath, J. *Who Killed Homer?* The Free Press, New York, 1998 p. 157.]

Only a moral, well educated, industrious people can tolerate the freedoms and limited government that our founders sought for us. Man does not tolerate chaos within society and will have the government needed to maintain order. We must repent or face the consequences of the government we deserve.

This book is dedicated to my fellow countrymen and especially to my wife, Raija, who illustrated it and encouraged me in this 10 year project. It is dedicated also to my children, relatives, their children and peers. The war in which we are engaged is like many of the past. It is about ideas – religious ideas – theirs and ours. To understand it we must forget "revisionist" theories of history that teach that all history is based on "class struggle" – haves vs. have nots. Most warfare has been between tyrannical kings, dictators, their wannabes and cronies. This war has been ongoing for a little over 1300 years and is about ideas, culture and religion. To understand it, we must know our own beliefs and those of *Islâm*. Only in this way can we hope to make sense of today's events. May we avoid the errors of historical ignorance?

PREFACE

Jihād, a Religious War

> "*But the recompense of those who fight against GOD and his apostles, and study to act corruptly in the earth, shall be, that they shall be slain, or crucified, or have their hands and their feet cut off on the opposite sides, or be banished the land. This shall be their disgrace in this world, and in the next world they shall suffer a grievous punishment;*" (*Korân* **5:33**). "*Kill the idolaters wheresoever ye shall find them, and take them prisoners, and besiege them, and lay wait for them in every convenient place*" (*Korân* **9:5**). "*Wherever they are found they shall be taken, and killed with a general slaughter,*" (*Korân* **33:61**).

On the morning of September 11, 2001, I turned on the morning news. It was 9 AM in New York City. I watched in horror as the television repeatedly showed one of the Twin Towers of the International Trade Center, 110 stories high, rammed at high speed by a large airliner. Earlier, not caught on film, another airliner had struck the other tower. These were United Flight 175 and American Flight 11. The smoke and flames shot through the upper stories of one building while black smoke poured from the upper part of the other. TV news showed men and women leaping to their deaths from the upper floors to escape the flames and smoke. Within an hour, each of the buildings had crashed to earth with tons of steel and concrete squashing thousands in the rubble. Dense smoke cascaded downward like a volcanic pyroclastic flow to the streets below. The collateral damage was horrific with several other large buildings destroyed by the collapse of these two giants. Later that morning we learned that another plane, American Flight

77, had hit the Pentagon. In a fourth hijacked airliner, United Flight 93, passengers attempted to retake their plane. It crashed in Somerset County, Pennsylvania killing all aboard. Its target had been either the White House or the Capitol Building. In all 29731 were known dead (including 19 hijackers) and 24 were missing and presumed dead. It could have been much worse. 10,000 men and women worked in each of these buildings. **Osama Bin-Laden**'s al Qaeda group claimed responsibility.

The press never mentioned the significance of the date September 11. On September 11-12, 1683 (63 years after the Plymouth and 74 years after the Jamestown colonies were established), the siege of Vienna was broken by an army of 70,000 men under King Jan III Sobieski of the Polish-Lithuanian Commonwealth, fighting against an Ottoman army of 138,000 under the Grand Vizier Merzifonlu Kara Mustafa Pasha. It was the high watermark of the Islâmic Ottoman Empire. From here it would be a slow retreat until the Empire was broken up in 1922 following World War I. Islâm's Holy War of the 7th Century had never stopped. It had had quiet periods when it was unable to fight, but oil money changed that. Islâm was on the march again. Strife was in progress in East Timor (3.9°S,129.3°E) the Philippines (Mindanao), the Spice (Maluku) Islands of Indonesia 8.39°S,125.34° E), Thailand, Xinjiang Province in China, Kashmir, Sudan, Somalia, Ethiopia, Nigeria, Ivory Coast, Mauritania, Caucasus, Bosnia, Albania, and parts of Central Asia. A migratory invasion brought many millions of Muslims into Europe and North America. Osama bin Laden (1957-2011) declared the *jihād* at the end of 1996, but few in the West paid any attention. The document is long and rambling.[2] But on September 11, 2001 an opening salvo was fired. It was Bin-Laden's way of saying that Islâm was back – "*taste the punishment.*" (**3:106**)

Then commentaries by press, pundits and politicians began. The act was committed by an Islâmic Arab "terrorist" group, a small group of "crazies;" surely most of Islâm was not that way. New York cops and FBI could handle it; armed force was unnecessary. This was not a "religious war." Revisionist history teaches that "class struggle" causes all wars, but news pictures from the Arab world showed many dancing in the streets. They showed "terrorist" training camps. Most important, there was no outrage from Muslim clerics. In fact, there was the opposite. Many Imams spewed hatred towards the Western, Indian and Asiatic Infidels, but their voices went unreported in the Western press. The voice of Islâm has remained silent about numerous atrocities. Suicide bombers continued their attacks and many families received compensation for their loss. Not all Islâm is involved, but much is.

When the United States struck back at the Afghanistan Tāliban who were supporting bin-Laden, there was outrage in the Islâmic press and parts of the Western world. Clerics castigated America. Why? Clearly these events could be explained in the context of a "religious" war. Nonetheless, Marxist dogma and political correctness of our time held that wars were only fought over economics – proletariat (oppressed) vs. bourgeoisie (oppressors). Despite the sorry history of the world that has documented many past religious wars, a "religious" war was impossible. The media made efforts to blame the United States for economically oppressing the Arab states. But that did not square with the mountains of cash Western countries were paying them for oil and the opulent life-style apparent in many of their larger commercial centers. The hijackers were mostly from Saudi Arabia, an allegedly friendly state. When Arab terrorists' statements were analyzed, however, it was clear that they had repeatedly warned "*USA Crusader military forces*" for 5 years or more that they were declaring a holy war against us.

The attack was true to the *Korân*. Aircrews had their throats cut. Fire destroyed many in the Twin Towers. The attack had occurred in the morning. As the wars in Afghanistan and Iraq progressed, a number of captives were beheaded by masked men on TV – the press ignored it. These events sparked my interest in Islâm. At one time Islâm had conquered most of central Europe from the Mediterranean to Austria, Hungary and the Ukraine, but had been relatively quiet and in decline for several centuries.

These events excited my curiosity and began me on a 10 year Odyssey. To understand a people, understanding their religion is primary. This began my study of the *Korân* and the development of a topical guide, attached to these volumes. This permitted me to know the context of many key words and phrases. It allowed me to study their history with greater understanding. My hope is that this work will stimulate others to do the same and dig deeper into the history of Islâm and its religion and its people. Despite popular impressions, Islâm and Judeo-Christianity are not the same; the nature of our God differs.

This work is about a war that has lasted over 1300 years. Like the war in heaven (Rev 12:7-9; Isaiah 14:12-13) it has been fought with religious fervor. At first it was over which tyranny would prevail, but more recently over the principles of Islâmic *predestination* against Judeo-Christianity's democratic *free will* or *choice* (Gen 2:16-17; Josh 24:16; D&C 101:77-80). Neither side admits it.

CONTENTS

Koran Scripture Key: Early Mecca (chapter:verse); Mid Mecca (chapter **verse**); Late Mecca (**chapter** verse); Medina (**chapter verse**)

INTRODUCTION

It is risky to write about *Islâm*, but religious and secular beliefs of leaders are important. This work contains recurring themes. This introduction covers many of these and will assist your understanding. This volume makes comparisons between Christianity and *Islâm* and follow their historical evolution and the wars between them.

The Mind of Man

Sociobiology[3] is a field of science that arose in the mid-20th century. It began with the assumption that social behavior arises from genes acting under Darwin's theories of survival. Among the first studied were the Hymenoptera (ants, bees, wasps). They form societies in which individuals (workers, soldiers, drones and queens) sacrifice themselves for the good of the "hive." Their instinctive, "***predestined***" behavior depended on a genetically predetermined "hard wired" primitive central nervous system. Next, higher animals' mating, courting, territorial fighting, and pack hunting behaviors were studied. Man had similarities, but did not seem to fit a definite mold. He was more complex, yet did all these things. He could "change his mind." He had "***choice***." From his beginnings he organized himself into families, tribes, and nations, governed by different societal and religious doctrines. Civil law controls behavior within society to benefit the group. Religious doctrine free of nation-states benefits families and individuals. This book follows the history of nations and two major religions. Are we accidents of nature; predestined pawns to be the way we are; or choice driven inheritors of God's kingdom? These are the three choices offered to us from the secular and religious world. Which is it? In my opinion, our lives consist of trial and error, success and failure, sin and ***repentance***. Is this not choice driven and part of a grand design?

Most ancients believed that thought and feelings came from the heart or breast, not the head. Hippocrates (460 – 370 BC) believed it was the brain, but he was ignored. Neuroscience was unknown until the 19th century when powerful microscopes, fixing and staining techniques allowed study of the brain and its systems. Paul Broca (1824-1880) discovered the speech area of the brain giving rise to theories that assigned various functions to specific parts of the brain. This was strengthened by observations that illness or injury to parts of the brain changed personality and inhibited or destroyed a person's ability to do certain tasks. Electrophysiology demonstrated that nerves responded to and transmitted electrical and magnetic impulses. Despite the wisdom of the ancients found in texts such as the Bible, many believed our behavior was "natural" / predestined by genes or at least that we were fixed by the onset of adulthood. These ideas began to change in the latter half of the 20th Century with better imaging techniques – computerized axial tomography (CAT), magnetic resource imaging (MRI), and positron emission tomography (PET) scans. These could be modified by combining several techniques to get a better idea of function and its anatomical location in the brain. Molecular biology discovered neurotransmitters important in various parts of the nervous system and correlated this with careful observations of persons with central nervous system and mental illness. The 21st Century has opened with improved knowledge of brain function, but our knowledge remains incomplete. Neuroscience continues to advance rapidly.[4]

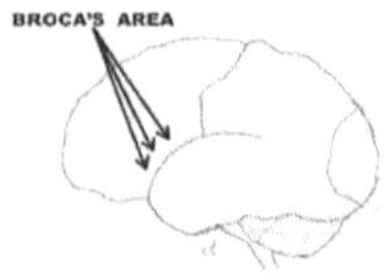

Human brain and nervous system development begin in embryo. Man is born with about 1 billion neurons (nerve cells). Each neuron has many connections (dendrites) with other neurons. By the time of birth the mid-brain 5 is almost fully developed, but the forebrain is not. The first part to develop is the limbic system.[6] This lies beneath the cerebral cortex in the midline and includes the hypothalamus, amygdala, septal nucleus, cingulate, and hippocampus. It perceives hunger, thirst and emotions including social contact. Without development the person has great difficulty with learning and memory. A few decades ago we found that the adult brain could change; we really could "change our mind." It was not fixed. Repentance, an old religious concept of change in attitude and

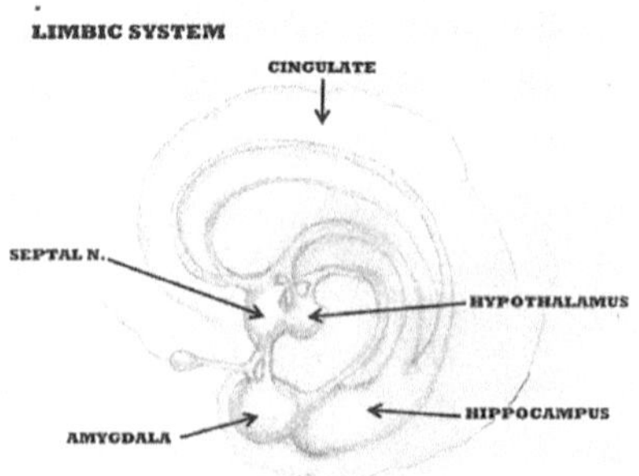

behavior, is demonstrable. This is due to **neuroplasticity**. [7] The brain modifies itself based on environmental factors and neural signals from other parts of the brain and body throughout life. Change becomes more difficult with time, but remains possible.

Brain function can be damaged in embryo by various toxins, resulting in illness such as fetal alcohol syndrome that causes mental retardation and inability to learn from experience and anticipate consequences. [8] Amblyopia can lead to blindness in one eye through lack of stimulation of its neurons.[9] During childhood and adolescence millions of neurons are pruned away on a "use it or lose it" basis. As we age, we normally lose neurons, but it is through dendritic formation and attrition that specific neural networks are sculpted and formed. This fine-tunes our perception, selective attention, learning, memory, and cognitive development, which accounts for the unique learning and survivability of man. We can change ourselves from within. Our brains "defrag" and "reprogram" themselves.

An infant requires emotionally sensitive maternal contact. The amygdala causes an infant to seek indiscriminately stimulation from everyone.[10] This increases opportunities for further stimulation needed for the developing limbic system. Without it, death can result. Neglected infants develop passivity, apathy, attention deficits, shyness and bizarre behavior. Some develop repetitive, obsessive, stereotypical movements such as rocking, head banging and tearing at the flesh. The amygdala is responsible for memory, attention, arousal, and experiences of love, fear and pleasure. It promotes social interaction and leads to our facial expressions and reactions to others. By 6 months, the amygdala is responsible for fear reactions. Between 6 and 12 months the cingulate and septal nucleus develop. Infants begin to discriminate between mother and others. They fear maternal separation, bond to their mothers, and fear strangers, often their father. This fear can cause an outburst when they suddenly recognize a stranger; only the mother can calm the infant. Disease or damage to this part of the brain causes severe withdrawal, and emotional blunting. This part of the limbic system is "experience-expectant" and leads to neuroplastic changes in such cases with loss of neurons.

Reduction of the cingulate and septal nuclear functions diminishes its counterbalancing purposes and allows the amygdala to predominate. Maternal depravation during this critical stage can lead to bizarre behavior and explosive emotional outbursts. When the amygdala malfunctions such as can occur with earlier maternal depravation, the individual becomes emotionally deprived, shy and withdrawn. They have difficulty feeling love and affection. They can engage in extreme oralality, self-stimulation (septal release) and avoid contact with others, preferring to sit alone in isolation. When the "terrible two's" is over, limbic development quiets down until adolescence.

Between the age of 3 and early adolescence the septal nuclei develop. They inhibit the indiscriminate weariness of strangers of the amygdala and contribute to a narrowing of social contacts. While the amygdala is responsible for the oral stage of exploration, the septal nuclei seem to be responsible for the phallic or psychosexual stage of development. Each child is different. Some need more attention than others, but males suffer more than females for lack of it. A well-functioning limbic system with all its emotionality is responsible for the developing intellect that starts about the age of 3. Elegant imaging studies show that in the first 18 months of life gray matter is overproduced. This is followed by a period of steady decline in gray matter. There is a second spurt of gray matter production in the prepubertal period which is followed by a steady decline in gray matter on a "use-it-or-lose-it" basis during adolescence. The first areas to mature are those at the very front and back of the brain involved in processing senses and movement. This is followed by areas in the parietal lobe involved in spatial orientation and language. More complex or advanced functions of the pre-frontal regions such as integrating information from the senses, reasoning and other executive functions mature last. In illness such as Alzheimer's disease the last to mature are the first to disappear. In schizophrenia there seems to be an exaggerated loss of the gray matter during and following puberty. In autistic children there appears to be an abnormal back-to-front wave of gray matter increase instead of decrease. [11]

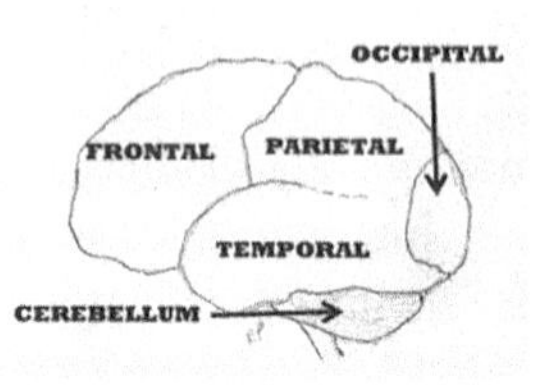

The adolescent period of brain pruning correlates with a time when youngsters begin to recognize their freedom to choose. Many become defiant, select friends not particularly good for them, and engage in risky behaviors (dare-devilishness, drug use and sex). This is another period of limbic system development which peaks between age 13 and 17 and quiets down by 21. Parents must understand this and reduce nurturing and increase monitoring. Children will not begin to develop judgment until about 21-22 and insurance companies won't trust them with an automobile until age 26. What goes in the mind is important – garbage in means garbage out. Political theory and religious doctrine have contended over the question of whether man is predestined to be the way he is or whether he has choice within himself – **predestination or freedom of**

choice. Predestination goes with tyranny, strict laws and control. Free choice promotes freedom to choose (representative government), change and repentance.

Education

During the pre-adult period education is man's most important activity. Very early in our lives we develop the ability to fit together sight, sound, smell, taste, touch and the emotional content associated with them. Without a normal limbic system learning is difficult to impossible. Language is one of our first skills. Some animals have rudimentary language and can obtain a human vocabulary of a few to about a hundred words. Some have their own language of various cries, growls, howls, squeaks, purrs, clicks, tweets, and whistles, but only man seems to think in terms of present past and future and develop conscience tracts that allow him to delay gratification for the purpose of achieving better outcomes. This allows him to bypass pleasure of the moment and experience joy in the future (3 John 1:4). Once language has developed to the point that a child can grasp basic concepts, other learning takes place. Reading readiness occurs anywhere from age 4 to 8. Girls' brains tend to mature a year or two ahead of boys', especially in language. The brains of men and women reach parity about age 21-22. The old one-room school house had the advantage of allowing each child to progress at his own pace. Learning language is easiest before the age of 12. A multilingual family is best advised to pass along all its languages to their children early in life. This sets up multiple pathways for "logical thinking." In the ancient world the educational philosophies of Plato (Greek) and Marcus Aurelius (Roman) described education they thought best. Marcus Aurelius (AD 121-180), Emperor of Rome and Stoic philosopher advised in *Meditations* that a child not attend public schools, but rather learn from tutors at home even if it meant to "*spend liberally.*"12 Following this he outlined what each of his home tutors had taught him. In opposition to Marcus Aurelius, modern "politically correct" theories of education promote the concept that children should be taught in public institutions to indoctrinate them in ways not based on "class." 13 Karl Marx wrote:

> "*we destroy the most hallowed of relations, when we replace home education by social ... The Communists ... seek to ... rescue education from the influence of the ruling class. The bourgeois claptrap about the family and education, about the hallowed correlation of parents and child, becomes all the more disgusting, ...*"

Until the late 19th Century home schooling was common. Depending on the ability of the child and parents, home school could teach elementary reading, legible writing, and simple arithmetic. This was usually successful until the child reached ages 8 or 9 (3rd grade). The basic reader was often the family Bible. In the 18th century the *New England Primer* and in the 19th century the *McGuffey Readers* provided the lesson plans and materials for language training. *McGuffey Readers* sold more than 120 million copies in the 19th Century; it still sells 30,000 per year. With simple instruction and lesson plans most children got a 3rd grade education at home. The mothers nurture and meaningful household and farm chores with the father further bonded the child to his parents, taught life's skills, and emphasized their necessity.

In the U.S. Pre-school and kindergarten were developed in the latter half of the 20th Century as more mothers worked outside home. Their value remains under study. As children mature individually, their attention spans increase and they begin to learn. Social interaction with peers, often highly touted as a benefit of public schooling, is frequently detrimental especially if the peers have unchecked destructive behaviors and the school lacks discipline.

Some children are naturally curious and intelligent. These will profit from private instructions – schools or tutors. Under our current public education systems, bright children tend to become lost, then bored and disruptive which is disadvantageous to them and their schools. Intelligent children must be challenged often to the limit of their capabilities. Good private schools attract good teachers that can substitute for the tutors advocated by Marcus Aurelius. Today private schools are often less expensive per pupil than public schools, but they are not subsidized.

During the 20th Century's rush to progressivism (socialism-lite) education in America underwent a revolution. Public schools replaced home education. By the mid-20th Century much public education dumbed down students by eliminating grades, competition and recognition of good scholarship. Many schools became undisciplined laboratories of social change. Some students could not read their diplomas and a high school degree that was a mark of accomplishment 100 years earlier became nearly worthless. Even the universities began to follow this lead and much of what is taught at the undergraduate level outside the sciences is fluff. In the 1970s mandatory classes on Western Civilization were dropped in most universities and politically correct, "Revisionist," speculative, social sciences replaced tough history. The result is that well thought out, planned and monitored, home-schooling is again becoming a necessity.

An informed electorate is capable of managing representative government. Those motivated by the passions of the day are not. A solid education based on fact, is needed. This means study of the hard subjects and real learning. It means separation of truth from propaganda and ferreting out the false. It means pragmatic testing of ideas, not debating them. If it doesn't work; it may be false. It means making judgments about good and evil. By 1500 the European printing press invented in 1450 had most of its practical problems solved. One printer replaced thousands of scribes. The Bible became the first book to be printed in large numbers. This made it available to many Europeans. It also made possible the rise of larger modern states to replace principalities and city-states. It brought about the Reformation, which required biblical understanding and Age of Reason that depended on scientific advancement. The Bible became the household reader that promoted literacy in most of Protestant Europe and North America. Besides teaching Judeo-Christian morality, the Bible contained the world's first linear history. By the late 16th Century literacy had become so common that the English masses paid good money to enjoy Shakespeare's plays that used a vocabulary of up to 29,000 words. This is far more than the average working vocabulary of 5,000 words found among most people today. [14]

A word of warning – education without moral training is dangerous. There is nothing worse than a smart crook. Many intelligent people have done horrible things. Too much esoteric education can lead to feelings of self-importance and arrogance. Many nations have fallen into the trap of seeking an elite "intelligentsia" to rule. Scholar bureaucrats of the Ming (1368-1644) and Qing (1644 – 1911) Dynasties were a disaster. China turned in on itself and permitted foreign powers to take it over by use of one of its own principle inventions – gunpowder. Many state bureaucracies around the world rely on academic examinations to determine who will get the "select" positions. Book learning does not guarantee wisdom, "street smarts," moral behavior, or a practical approach to problems.

Marcus Aurelius, despite his philosopher king status, stoic philosophy, and ideas on education abandoned the adoptive process of choosing Roman emperors and turned to the dynastic method. He chose his son, Commodus, to succeed him. Commodus was only 17 at the time. He had been instructed by the best tutors, but turned out to be a weak narcissistic emperor with many self-destructive habits. Gibbon traces the fall of the Roman Empire back to him. The dynastic formula was supposed to lead to greater political stability; it didn't.

Beware of the Narcissist

Narcissism is common among power seekers. It is often a secondary manifestation of major mental disorders. It is defined as a pattern of behavior characterized by "grandiosity, need for admiration, and a lack of empathy." According to the DSM IV 15 such individuals will have five or more of the following traits: 1) grandiose ideas of self-importance ; 2) preoccupation with fantasies of unlimited success, power, brilliance, beauty or ideal love; 3) belief they are special and can only be understood by or should associate with people or institutions that are also special or of high status; 4) require excessive admiration; 5) have a sense of entitlement; 6) are interpersonally exploitative; 7) lack empathy; 8) are often envious of others or believe others are envious of them; 9) show arrogant haughty behaviors or attitudes. Humility is not one of their characteristics. It is thought that about 1% of our population is afflicted with this disorder. These are often people who believe that they are so special that the usual rules of society and moral behavior do not apply to them. When such people achieve power, they are dangerous. Many of the world's most treacherous tyrants have been narcissistic. They frequently espouse the philosophy that the end justifies the means and will step on anyone in their way to wealth and power. Their lack of empathy is so complete that exploitation, murder and theft is no barrier. The Ten Commandments have no meaning for them.

The cause of narcissism is not understood. Many believe it has to do with upbringing as children. Whatever the cause, it does not seem to respond to psychotherapy or medication. The desire to change must come from within; in religious terms, repentance is the only cure. Whatever it is, it is important for people living in a democratic society to recognize such people and keep them from public office or rid them from it as soon as the telltale traits are recognized.

They can be recognized by their continuing immoral personal behavior, "showboating," and the need for much "press." They are constantly "bending the rules." Tax avoidance, alcoholism, drug addiction, and sexual laxity, are common. Their accouterments often betray them – gold chains, gaudy diamond rings, Rolex watches, fancy automobiles, expensive sharp clothing, excessive attention to extravagant personal grooming. Their behavior around people subservient to them will often demonstrate rudeness and lack of consideration. They can make a show of "caring for others," but to them, people exist for their benefit. Such people should never be trusted to hold political office or positions of power.

Government

The type of government selected by a people makes a major difference between war and peace liberty or enslavement, and prosperity or poverty. One of the most cogent arguments against despots and kings is found in the Bible in 1 Samuel 8. Samuel was approached by the people because of the corruption of judges, especially Samuel's own children and demanded that they have a king like other nations (Sam 8:5). The Lord counseled Samuel in detail what would happen to them if they had a king, but the people resisted his advice and insisted on a king. The Lord told Samuel to let them have their desires and that their rejection of Samuel's advice was not a slap at him, but a slap at the Lord, Himself. Everything predicted happened. Saul, David and Solomon all had their fatal flaws. Over taxation, the division of the kingdom into North and South, and a series of wicked kings led to the demise and conquest of first Israel then Judah.

We are warned that power corrupts and absolute power corrupts absolutely. Elections and popular support during uprisings often have dire consequences. **Adolf Hitler** received enough of a plurality in Germany to allow him to become Chancellor, then dictator. Mussolini was also a popular leader of Italy. Lenin and Stalin received their power through a popular uprising in Russia as did Mao in China. All of these individuals were responsible either for the destruction of their countries or the slaughter of millions of their own citizens and those of their neighbors. The greatest enemy of a people can be their government. The founding fathers of the United States devised a Constitution and Bill of Rights that protected the public from its own government. It combined separate states into a national government for their defense. It is based on a republican model in which popularly elected bodies indirectly represent the citizens in a system of checks and balances. Frequent elections allow for changes, but the system was not intended to make radical change. The founders were aware of the tyranny of the majority (democracy) and the danger of the minority (Kings, Despotic rulers, Oligarchs and royalty). The greatest fears at the time were loss of state's rights, an imperial executive, and courts with too much power. All occurred in the 20th Century. A careful reading and thorough understanding of the Constitution and Bill of Rights by the student should be part of all our children's education.

In the English colonies the American Dream that a man was free to make of himself what he wanted through hard work was primary. However, there were two groups that suffered. Native American Indians were placed on "reservations" and became wards of the Federal Government. Slaves, brought to the English colonies by colonial powers although not initially discriminated against, were designated chattel / slaves by the mid-17th Century. The Constitution and Congress attempted to correct the situation by 1808, but plantation economics was too strong. A horrible war resulted in their freedom, but not without popular prejudice. This has been slow changing. The class structure of Europe (nobility / clergy, bourgeoisie, peasantry / common people) described by Marx was not present in the United States; there was no "first estate" of royalty and clergy. Poor and middleclass could change positions. A person might be born rich, but die poor and vice versa. One might make several fortunes in a life time after losing several. Our Founding Fathers attempted to prevent government controlled social immobility. Having property, "skin in the game," entitled one to vote. Amendments and legal interpretations of the Constitution and bureaucratic regulations beginning in the 20th Century have eroded some of the checks and balances that kept society classless. Since 1900 we have experienced greater democratization of our institutions. It created "strong" presidents, concentrated power in the Federal government, degraded the power of the states and reduced individual freedom. We are developing a nobility of political elites – federal politicians, top bureaucrats and their cronies.

Our founders were educated in history, philosophy, languages, and religion. Their par has rarely been equaled. Government was to secure our rights. After that it is up to the individual. Many politicians are unrealistic utopian liars. Utopia derives from the Greek meaning "no place." They promise everything and the ignorant gullible swallow it hook, line and sinker. Daniel Webster (1782-1852) warned that our danger as a nation lay within ourselves. Our inattention, carelessness, and negligence by placing too much confidence in government and by failing to scrutinize its conduct and thus becoming dupes of designing men would lead to our ruin. [16] Corruption in politics is as old as history. In a representative republic or democracy, the most important job of the electorate is to elect competent, honest people. Selection of leaders can be difficult. In weeding out corrupt individuals we must remember that all make mistakes especially in their youth. By the time they reach "maturity" they should have learned from their mistakes and taken steps to correct their errors. The mistakes of youth and early adulthood should never be held against a repentant individual. Those critical of others corruption are often more corrupt than those they criticize (Matt 7:1-2; Luke 6:37; John 7:24).

War & Peace

War and Peace are poorly understood. There are ironies that puzzle many. The greatest involves how to maintain peace. Evil exists in this world. According to Christian thought peace cannot endure in the presence of evil. Evil results from our choices and actions. *Islâm* believes evil results from God and the disposition of men, predestined by God to be evil. According to Judeo-Christian thought evil men violate the Ten Commandments in a number of ways, primarily by murder, adultery, theft, slander, and coveting the possessions of others. They attempt to obtain and maintain power and often engage in all the "Thou shalt nots" of the Ten Commandments. In the case of *Islâm*, peace is present where there is Sharia Law. War is present where it is not. Sharia Law includes Hammurabi's Lex Talionis or law of revenge – "an eye for an eye, etc. The teachings of Christ abolish the Code of Hammurabi (Matt 5:38-41).

World history shows that the best way to maintain peace is through a credible military force and the will to use it under righteous situations. A "credible force" depends on the technology of the day. The best military force is the one that no one dares fight. It is too terrible and determined.

War is a brutal method of conflict resolution. It is destructive and there is no way to prevent its misery. War is hell. Wars occur when one people believe they can obtain the upper hand over another. Thus a "credible force" prevents wars. In war fighting there are few or no restrictions. Deuteronomy Chapter 20 and parts of 21 lay out certain restrictions, most of which pertain to civilians not directly engaged in war fighting. There are no rules in the Oriental / Middle Eastern ideas of war fighting. Civilians who get in the way are slaughtered, raped and enslaved. For both those who win structure the peace which tends to outlast diplomatic solutions. Despite popular hopes, there is no war that will or can end all wars. So long as man inhabits the earth and is in charge of what goes on here, there will be war. For Islâm, God is in charge (**10**:11, 24; **8**:42-44; **9:2; 5:14** (See God Topical Guide). For Judeo-Christianity it is man (Gen 1:26, 28-30).

The 20th Century taught us that "rules of engagement" can lead to a prolongation of conflict. This erodes the will of people to fight. **Sun Tzu** (544-496 BC) warned, "*There has never been a protracted war from which a country has benefited.*" 17 He also warned that able generals should not be constrained by civil government. [18] The U.S. was engaged in WWII for only 3

⅔ years – December 1941 to August 1945. It was very destructive and bloody. It resulted in a peaceful Europe ever since. It was maintained by the military might of the U.S, Britain, and Soviet Union who although adversaries during the Cold War period (1946 – 1989), never came to major conflict. The Collapse of Soviet military credibility led to Islamic uprisings in much of the Middle East and Central Asia. The presence of ¼ the world's oil production and transport through this region makes it a strategic center of great concern to all industrial nations.

World War I lasted from 1914 to 1918 and was called off when the Central Powers found that they were unable to continue. It ended in an armistice and then a "peace" that led to the economic ruin of Germany. While the victors placed their trust in disarmament and a League of Nations, the League was unwilling to act when needed and Germany re-armed and began taking surrounding Germanic territories. This led to Word War II. Our Korean War was from June 1950 – July 1953. It also ended in a stalemate armistice that brought about a stable South Korea still threatened by the North. Viet Nam lasted nearly 20 years (November 1955 to 30 April 1975) and ended in a U.S. defeat. It was fraught by impossible rules of engagement that made quick victory impossible. Despite this the military did not lose any battle; the American public would not sustain the effort and gave up. The Gulf War (Aug 2, 1990 to Feb 28, 1991) was a victory that re-established the boundaries of Kuwait. However, it did not solve the primary problem of Iraq's aggression or terrorism from the Middle East. The Iraq War began March 20, 2003 coincident with the Afghan War (begun Sept 11, 2001), both continued with the armed services hampered by "rules of engagement," most of which are aimed at limiting inevitable civilian casualties. Terrorism is a method in Phase IV warfare directed primarily against civilian targets. All war is won when one side destroys the other's will to fight.

Economics

Economics are poorly understood by most. In the ancient world it was simpler. Everything was sold at a market where the producer was face to face with the consumer. Both understood the bargaining process. Weights and measures had to be standard so as to level the playing field. It was barter. There were no banks or credit for most. The concept of money came about 3000 BC in Mesopotamia when a specific weight of barley (Shekel) was said to have a specific value. Other valuable trade items appeared such as gold and silver bars. Tokens or coins were used about 700 BC in the

Greek Aegean. [19] From then on, weights, measures and money became responsibilities of government in the regulation of fair trade. Manipulations of the currency became one of the major frauds of government and rulers.

Money was made from 3 basic metals – gold, silver, or copper alloy. Smelted metal such as Iron could not be trusted. Although kings tried to manipulate markets, debase currencies and fool their people, this led to assayers, expert in telling the difference between good and bad coin. If manipulations of the market went too far the system would break down in mistrust, shortages, black markets, or famines. The system might relapse to barter or even popular revolt, but would eventually straighten out. Paper was first a product of the Papyrus plant. It came from the ancient Egyptian and Greek world. The invention of paper from plant fibers and rags occurred about AD 105 by Ts'ai-Lun of China. Paper manufacturing was brought to the west by the Arabs in about 700, but the development of pulp paper from wood fibers did not occur until 1838 first described by Charles Fenerty of Halifax in Great Britain. [20]

1795 $10 NGC MS60

During the economic boom of the Tang Dynasty (618-907) bank notes made from paper were first used. In 960 the Song Dynasty issued the first generally used paper money because of a copper shortage. During the late Southern Song in the 13th Century, the currency was backed by gold coin. The notes were complex with different colors and other devices that frustrated counterfeiters. Banking for princes and kings of Europe was introduced by the Knights Templar in the 12th Century AD. By the 14th Century *nota di bancos* reached Italy. In Europe the Bank of Sweden was the first to put out a general issue of bank notes in 1660, but a run on the bank 4 years later for specie (coin with value) put a halt to operations. In 1696 the Bank of Scotland was the first to issue paper currency that has been redeemable ever since. The first bank notes in America were issued in the Massachusetts Bay Colony in the 1690s and may have sparked the first industrial growth in that part of the U.S. During the Revolutionary War the Continental Congress issued paper currency called "Continentals." Inflation made it almost worthless. Following the Constitution of the U.S, the government chartered the First Bank of the U.S. to issue notes in 1789; it closed in 1811 and was replaced by the second U.S. bank in 1816. The second bank's charter expired in 1836, but continued operation under a charter of the Commonwealth of Pennsylvania. The first copper coin backing U.S. notes was minted in

1793. The first silver came in 1794 and the first gold in 1795. [21] Coin's disadvantage is weight and wear. Notes have the problem of counterfeiting and excessive government printing. Coin is difficult to counterfeit on a mass scale and can be assayed for weight and value.

Credit card purchasing did not become common until the mid-20th Century. This involved the concept of "buy now, pay later." If you lend money you expect to receive "interest." If you borrow it, you expect to pay "interest." Interest is like a two edged sword – only a fool grabs the blade. Many know little about credit and other important matters in family finance. Why do the rich get richer and the poor get poorer? What is an asset and what is a liability? Knowing the difference is what makes the rich richer. According to *Rich Dad Poor Dad* by R. Kiyosaki assets put money in your pocket; liabilities take money out. Your home is not an asset. It usually is a bank's asset. You pay principle and interest on it. Even if you own it, you are taxed and make repairs. This takes money out of your pocket. Assets put money into your pocket. An asset might be a profitable business, an interest-bearing note or bond, or your skill that allows you to earn money. What is the behavior of millionaires? *The Millionaire Next Door* by TJ Stanley and WD Kanko describes this. First marry a very, very, frugal person. Millionaires' marriages usually last; divorces cost money. They are most often moral people. Immorality costs money. Next is to learn to spend conservatively and own what you buy. If you can't afford it, don't buy it. Millionaires don't pay interest, they collect it. They do not live in big houses on the hill. They usually live in middle-class neighborhoods – thus the name of the book. They drive good second-hand cars; they let the other guy take the hit on the first 3-year's depreciation. Their kids don't have cars, but they are well educated. This means hard classes that lead to personal production and satisfaction. They do not subsidize their children after they leave home; this reduces the child's potential income. The most common vehicle is a pick-up truck used in business. They purchase good, but not fancy clothing, shoes and watches. They love to work and "mind their business." They do not own lots of "toys." 90% become millionaires by their own efforts; only 10% inherit it and these often do not have the habits of the other 90% described above. An old adage is, "shirtsleeves to shirtsleeves in three generations."

Plan a family. The best retirement plan is 4 self-sufficient children (Psalm 127:3-5). In marriage husband and wife must be equal partners with different primary functions. Mothers are best suited for the nurture and education of their children. As managers of the home, they must be frugal and have a plethora of skills. Fathers are specialists. They provide the necessities and protect their families. Fathers should not expect their wives to earn money. This additional duty will wear her out and short change the children. The father's income must be sufficient to allow his wife to stay at home. For both, this means education with a purpose.

Home economics are a microcosm of national economics. The same principles apply when considering what make the rich, richer and the poor, poorer. Assets, put money in your pocket. Liabilities take it out. The difference is that in a family the mother and father either work together or the family falls apart quickly. In the case of governments, it takes longer. Many politicians attempt to tax away the assets and become more powerful at the expense of the productive. The structure and function of the government must be designed to protect and promote the productive individual. Without surplus, the poor are defenseless.

Business depends on honesty. "Sharp dealing" often leads to bankruptcy. If you can't trust it, don't buy it. Advertising attempts to get you to forget this principle. This is not new. "*Caveat Emptor*" was the ancient advice in the Roman market place – "Let the buyer beware." It still applies. This advice is good for material items, business matters, marriage, and political philosophy. If you are involved in a Ponzi scheme, you will be cheated whether it is run by an individual or a government. None are sustainable. A Ponzi scheme is an investment fraud that relies on a continuous flow of money from an ever-increasing number of investors to pay the expenses of the business and dividends of the older investors. When the numbers of investors drop, the money stream dries up. The system collapses and all lose their money. Most governmental social systems are Ponzi schemes. If their population decreases, the money collected decreases. Benefits are unsustainable if the money collected has not been wisely invested or used as a tax to fund other purposes. Birth control, abortion and selfishness resulting in falling birth rates, means fewer workers and a lower tax base.

The first two permanent English North American colonies (Jamestown, Virginia and Plymouth, Massachusetts) were founded on the principles of "common stock" (everything held in common by common consent). Following the "starving time" and near abandonment in Jamestown of 1609-10, the common storehouse was abandoned in favor of free markets. Plymouth learned more quickly. Utopian concepts did not die easily. Many experiments, especially in the 18th and 19th Centuries sprouted in Europe and America, but all died despite their best efforts.

Under the influence of Marx, state-wide socialist experiments began in the late 19th Century in Bismarck's Germany and spread rapidly throughout Europe and many other parts of the world. Great Britain and North America became more fully invested in socialist schemes after World War II. Environmentalism began at the same time. It suffered from flawed research and led to environmental and economic disasters. *The Arrogance of Humanism* by David Ehrenfeld chronicled this. During the Great Depression of the 1930s America tried to spend its way to solvency with public works and printed money.

Other countries in the West that did little except rely on market forces to make the corrections got out in 2 to 10 years. It took America World War II and inflation to get us out in 20 years (1930 – 1950). **John Maynard Keynes**' theory of centrally controlled economies claimed to prevent depressions, popular from 1920 to 1970s, failed in "stagflation." It was replaced by **Friedrich von Hayek**'s and **Hernando De Soto**'s theories of free market economics. Free markets are the only way a "price" on anything can be realistically determined. Markets move as fast as women bargaining in a bazar or as fast as the "electronic herd" watching the ticker-tape. Bureaucrats, planners and legislators can't keep up with it.

Rome's corruption at the top, deficit spending, debased currency, periodic wage and price controls and continuous warfare led to their economic ruin, political failure, barbarism, and finally serfdom that lasted over 1000 years in much of Europe. Bottom line – don't mess with the currency or the market!!!

The welfare state based on a theory that "liberty" relies on an equal redistribution of wealth to make men free rather than on the freedom to allow individuals to provide for themselves has led many to unsustainable social programs, dependency on government, indebtedness, inflation, and destruction of families. Fiat currencies, without intrinsic value, replaced specie with intrinsic value. In 1933 an executive order by President Roosevelt made it a crime to own more than $100 in gold and the "New Deal" abandoned the "gold standard." Gold went underground or overseas, but most was melted and redeemed for paper backed by silver. [22] Johnson's "Great Society" abandoned the "silver standard" in 1964. Silver coin disappeared in a year. This illustrated an ancient principle put into words more recently by Gresham (1519-1579) and Copernicus (1473 – 1543): "*Bad money drives out good if their exchange rate is set by law.*" Specie is unnecessary as currency, but its lack encourages inflation. Our founding fathers knew this and put simple protections in the Constitution against fiat currencies. See Article 1 Section 8 in which Congress has the power to coin money while States do not. Section 10 says that the States cannot "*make any Thing but gold and silver Coin a Tender in Payment of Debts.*" This was ignored in 1964; inflation followed for the next 15 years.

The rise of socialism in the 18th and 19th Centuries led to confusion in what constitutes wealth. According to most modern economic texts, wealth is equated with natural resources and its equitable distribution. This is simplistic Marxism. It does not take into account the technology that defines the resource or changes it into useful products. Countries that stifle the freedom of their citizens remain in or progress to poverty. John Locke said, "*the products of the earth useful to the life of man, ... we shall find that in most of them ninety-nine hundredths are ... on the account of labor.*" 23 Pilzer's formula of wealth, $W = P\ T^n$ illustrates this. Wealth (W) is the result of the efforts of people (technology = T) on physical resources (P). Technology defines natural resources. The rapidity with which information is shared promotes technology (T^n) and its effect on natural resources.[24] Land is not a resource unless you can farm it or otherwise use it. Likewise, copper has little value without hardening it by alloying it with other metals. Iron ore has little value unless you know how to smelt and forge it into a hard non-brittle substance. Sand can become glass and microchips, if you understand the technology to make and use these products. Oil is a pollutant unless you can refine it. The printing press and now the Internet make a difference in the speed with which new techniques can be learned and turned into useful products. Human ingenuity or technology and the rapid flow of knowledge are far more important in the creation of wealth than the physical resources themselves. Ask yourself, "What countries have the most resources?" Answer – Russia & Brazil. "Which country has little?" Answer – Japan. Which country has more wealth? Theories that teach that natural resources alone account for wealth and that equitable distribution is the key are false.

5-20% of all people are incapable of caring for themselves. They require the charity of the rest of us to sustain them. Without a surplus there can be little support for the needy and they die. The "80-20 rule" will be discussed later. Taxation that funnels wealth into government impedes and dilutes this effort. The 80% can find themselves in a needy condition; however, this is usually temporary. They either die or get better. The question of how to support the needy is important. The most efficient has been found to be small communities and churches that know who within their midst is needy. They seem to be able to do a more effective less expensive job than large government. Aside from major catastrophes national governments should probably get out of the business. In fact, government hardly does anything more efficiently than the populace. Even in war fighting there is tremendous waste and inefficiency. In the days of sail, letters of marque and reprisal were often more efficient and less of a diplomatic problem than national navies in the protraction of maritime warfare. [25] Benjamin Franklin wrote to his sister, Jane, in 1787, "*An army is a devouring monster, and, when you have raised it, you have, in order to subsist it, not only the fair charges of pay, clothing, provisions, army, and ammunition, with numberless other contingent and just charges to answer and satisfy, but you have all the additional knavish charges of the numerous tribe of contractors to defray, with those of every other dealer who furnishes the articles wanted for your army, and takes advantage of that want to demand exorbitant prices. It seems to me, that if statesmen had a little more arithmetic, or were more accustomed to calculation, wars would be much less frequent.*"[26]

The false concept that natural resources equal wealth remains at the core of much economic teaching just as it was preached by Marx. The Soviet Union collapsed in economic ruin in 1989 and much of the Western world appears to be following her example. How did this happen?

The "Enlightenment"

Many thinkers of the Enlightenment did not believe in work. They preferred to philosophize in a vacuum and let someone else do the work. They didn't want to leave Eden (the Ivory Tower) and consequently had little respect for learning the difference between good and evil. They became relativists. Everything was relative – no black or white, good or evil, morality or immorality. Many have adhered to this drivel. Their ideas were appropriate for college sophomoric bull sessions, but little else. Like "silly women," "*Ever learning, and never able to come to the knowledge of the truth.*" (2 Tim 3:7) many of their followers disparaged and ignored their Judeo-Christian heritage. Instead they questioned and advocated abolition of "*religion, and all morality, instead of constituting them on a new basis*" as later advocated by Marx. [27]

The rogue skeptic, intellects of the 18th Century managed to infect Europe and much of the world with their anti-clerical heresy, eventually called "higher criticism," promising to change the world for the better. Jean-Jacques Rousseau, "*an interesting madman*" began the slide.[28] Karl Marx, who stayed close to library stacks without ever putting boots on the ground, went about "*howling gigantic curses.*" [29] Modern intellectuals have used their ideas to push "political correctness" into the 20th and 21st Centuries.

Much of today's social thinking, "Social Marxism," is firmly rooted in Part II of *The Communist Manifesto.* Go to any website giving a text of *The Communist Manifesto.* Cut and paste Part II into a word processor then use the search engine to find, "*abolition of the family.*" Start reading and you will find: "*abolition of the family,*" "*replace home education,*" "*an openly legalized system of free love,*" "*abolish countries and nationalities,*" and finally abolition of "*all religion, and all morality, instead of constituting them on a new basis.*" This is the basis of all modern "political correctness." It is nothing more than failed 1848 philosophical thinking.

The motivation for "Revisionist history," commonly taught in today's public schools and universities is an effort to prove Marx's theory of history – "*class struggle.*" Anyone who has seriously studied history knows this is bogus. It completely ignores the entire history of Islâm that includes government based on religion. It ignores the religious influence of popes and their political toadies in many wars that devastated Europe for centuries. Common men can be stirred up to fight by the rhetoricians and propagandists of their leaders and then used as cannon fodder. However, when left to their own devices they behave in the far more peaceful ways of the market place. They don't have enough money to raise armies, are scared to death by real combat, and are too busy bargaining and trying to put food on the table.

Modern education and politics have been influenced by despotic reprobates whose motivation was to change or re-make society. First a scapegoat class is identified – the "bourgeoisie" or "middle class" (Marx, Lenin, & Stalin), "the Jews" (Hitler), or "the rich" (modern America). It is accomplished first by ridiculing the despised group or "scapegoat." This is done with propaganda from mass media. Once enough anger has been aroused against this group, laws are passed that deny them their freedoms and livelihood. Then their property is confiscated. The leaders keep theirs. This transfer of wealth can be accomplished by theft, legal taxation, bureaucratic regulation, licensing, and deliberate inflation or other monetary manipulations by state-controlled banks. Finally, the group is slaughtered so as to remove their influence on society and make it possible to "re-make" society according to the planners' designs. This is done gradually at first, then more quickly by confiscation of food resulting in starvation, concentration (re-education) camps / gulags, machine guns and gas chambers. ["Scapegoat" is a poor analogy; it is released and allowed to live. See Leviticus 16:8-10.] Lenin and Stalin set out to accomplish these goals in the 1920s in the Soviet Union and Ukraine. This became the game plan for tyrants who followed such as Mussolini, Hitler, Mao, and a host of petty tyrants. It continues to this day.[30]

In the U. S. Mark Twain (1835-1910) observed in Pudd'nhead Wilson's New Calendar, "*It could probably be shown by facts and figures that there is no distinctly Native American criminal class except Congress.*" Confiscation of private property literally kills the goose that lays golden eggs. Most new enterprises in the western world are begun when a free man mortgages his property to borrow money from a bank to start a business.[31] The 20th Century showed the results of Marxist-Socialist thinking in steel, blood and horror. Hitler, the Nazi (National Socialist Worker's Party) killed millions. Europe was left in ruins. Stalin and Mao killed tens and maybe hundreds of millions. Europe was rebuilt with initial efforts by the United States and then the Europeans themselves, but it remains addicted to social and economic Marxism.

Jean-Jacque Rousseau (1712 – 1778)

Rousseau was the first principal thinker of the "Enlightenment. He promoted environmentalism: the country cottage, open air, and exercise for its own sake. He criticized urban life.[32] He criticized the Age of Reason and its early scientific discoveries and slow progression of material benefits. He taught that in man's evolution from pure nature of the "Noble Savage" to his urban society, he became corrupted by the love of self and what he thought was proper. This included vanity, self-aggrandizement and what others thought important especially money, physical strength, and native intelligence. Competition in acquiring these attributes tended to separate man from his fellows and lead to their exploitation. All this tended to destroy man's natural communal nature. Rousseau had obviously not studied primitive tribal society that was in constant competition motivated by loot, women, and feuds; and resorted to atrocities against neighbors. It was easy to identify the skeletal remains of the "noble savage" from other species by their bashed in skulls. According to Rousseau the culprit was private property and Capitalism and all that it engendered. Money does not hop off a table by itself and injure anyone. It is man's use and love of it that causes problems. (1 Tim 6:9-10) Rousseau ignored powerful individuals (princes, kings, and dictators) working themselves into a frenzy over perceived insults and the need for revenge and / or their grasping for power, riches and sex. Most of Rousseau's ideas had been previously discussed by others before him, but he cataloged and incorporated them into a unified philosophy.

Although brought up a Calvinist among the favored classes in Switzerland, his father was a violent man who likely mistreated him. Jean-Jacque had little respect for family. He spent his life failing at various occupations and living off women, Madame de Warens and Thérèse Levasseur. He eventually turned to the aristocracy. Denis Diderot, an avowed atheist, the editor of the *Encyclopédie*, was his friend for a time. Rousseau was not anti-religion, but used Calvinism and Catholicism to his own purposes. He had a superb intellect, but used it to exploit the guilt of the well-to-do with eccentric rudeness, ingratitude, and quarrelsome, uncouth, paranoid behavior. Rousseau's relationships with women were reprehensible. He used them and treated them with ingratitude. He shared Madame de Warens with her gardener and seems to have preferred masturbation to real relationships. Some believed him to be a latent homosexual. Although he had five children with Thérèse Levasseur, all were abandoned by leaving them without identity at the Hôpital des Enfants-trouvés, a foundling home. He never recorded their names, birthdates or took any interest in them. For her part Thérèse allowed Bosworth, one of Rousseau's associates, to seduce her. This "free love" abandonment of the 7th commandment infected many of the intellectuals who were to follow in Rousseau's footsteps. Eventually, "the end justifies the means" became the morality of the 20th Century that led to the banishment of the Ten Commandments from the court-house lawn in America and one of the bloodiest centuries in world history – 160 million deaths according to some. [33]

It was part of Rousseau's philosophy that the state, not parents, should educate children. His *Emile* influenced many educators. How would he know? He abandoned all his children at the time of their birth. Although he made much about being truthful, his *Confessions* were crafted to promote sympathy and much of it turned out to be unsubstantiated. Rousseau hated the great people of his day, but he also abhorred revolution. Rather he preferred replacing the rich and famous with an authoritarian state with everyone on an equal basis. He wanted an impersonal dictator to do the dirty work. There is no such animal. He despised "patriotism." The state would derive its authority through the collective will of the citizens. Rousseau's state was totalitarian; it provided for every aspect of human existence. He defined this as "liberty." This kind of state sponsored "liberty" became part of the French Revolution's cry for "liberty, equality, fraternity." It is not the same as John Locke's Scottish "life, liberty, and property," or Thomas Jefferson's American "life, liberty and the pursuit of happiness."

The state that Rousseau envisioned was outlined in his ideas for Corsica. See *The Social Contract* 1762. Rousseau believed extensive education would be required to get men to accept it. Experience has taught us that it requires tyrants who are willing to rob and kill to force it down our throats. Eventually it was tried in the 20th Century by a host of notorious dictators. This resulted in the devastation of their countries and the murder of their countrymen. Those who knew and attempted to help Rousseau eventually ended up hating him and what he stood for. Modern intellectuals, who had no personal experience with him, overlook his faults and ape his ideas.

Karl Marx (1818 – 1883)

Karl Marx plagiarized much of what we consider to be his ideas.[34] Although he claimed them to be "Scientific," he never studied science, had no idea of its meaning, and never tested his precepts using the scientific method. Marx is best described as a mad scholar. His father was a lawyer and his grandfather a rabbi. His mother was the daughter of a rabbi. Laws discriminating against Jews caused his father to become a Protestant in 1824. Although Karl had a doctorate, he could not find an academic post. He became a journalist, poet and essayist. His father studied Rousseau and Marx distorted his ideas to develop his theory of the proletarian revolution and its ultimate outcome. His theory spawned the socialist slave states of 20th Century under Hitler, Stalin and Mao.

Marx never had enough money; this may explain his views on capitalism and usury which he despised and blamed on the Jews and the "bourgeoisie" or entire "middle-class." He never earned a living from his reporting. He lived off his wife's (**Jenny von Westphalen**) inheritance. With her he fathered 7 children. Only 3 daughters survived adulthood; two of them committed suicide. The evidence that Marx had an illegitimate son, Frederick Demuth (1851-1929) with his wife's housekeeper, Helene Demuth is uncertain. [35]

Marx theorized that violent revolution would change the system, but he had no real life experience. He never served in the military and did no investigative reporting. He wrote of the plight of workers, but never worked in a factory, visited their workshops, or interviewed them or their bosses.

He spent most of his time in libraries. He wrote of finance and industry without practical experience with either. He took Hegel's dialectic (thesis, antithesis, synthesis) and applied it to a theory of history, but instead of carrying it out logically, he hypothesized that it would no longer apply when the "proletariat" achieved control. If "the proletariat" were to gain control as a "synthesis", Hegel would have said they would be the new "thesis" against which another "antithesis" would develop. The collapse of the Soviet Union and events that followed is evidence in favor of Hegel and against Marx. The problem with intellectuals is that many think themselves into ridiculous impractical positions.

In contrast, the founding fathers of the United States knew Plato's *Republic* (380 BC) and his philosopher king. They knew More's *Utopia* (1516) and its prince, and Hobbes' (1588-1679) *Leviathan* and the Sovereign. All described tyranny. Instead they favored the writings of Cicero (106-43 BC), John Locke (1632-1704) and his Christian based ideas, and Charles de Montesquieu (1689-1755). The Declaration of Independence is nearly a paraphrase of Locke. The Constitution is based on Montesquieu's political philosophy of separation of powers. The complete separation of religion from government, a Jeffersonian concept, was not seen as possible by Rousseau or a reality to Marx. The society envisaged and ultimately achieved in North America was based on the protection of the "individual" and truly became "classless." There were rich and poor, but in America today's millionaire can be tomorrow's pauper and vice versa. Until the New Deal, Fair Deal and Great Society, there was no aristocracy, or "first estate" as in Europe. To become "super rich" often requires help from government. Many politicians in U.S. history have been well to do, but most made, married, or inherited their money before achieving political office. J. F Kennedy was probably our wealthiest President. [36]

Only recently have special perks reserved for the President, Congress, judges, and other top government officials made our politicians rich. These need to be eliminated. Term limits are not needed. Forbes says half our congressmen are now millionaires. [37]

The founders knew tyrants targeted the pulpits, free speech, and arms of its citizens. Rome had disarmed its citizens and the British had attempted to disarm the American colonials from 1768-77. The Battle of Lexington & Concord occurred when citizen soldiers of a hastily organized ad-hoc colonial militia, Minutemen with their own arms, faced British regulars attempting to disarm them. On July 6, 1775 General Gage seized the arms of all Bostonians. There were other well-known and hated excesses of the Crown. The Bill of Rights protected citizens against tyrannical government and were added to insure passage of the Constitution.

Religion

Religion is not the opiate of the masses as described by Marx. It is powerful doctrine that directs the action of individual believers who take the time to read and ponder it. Primitive man lived in tribal communities usually lead by a headman / priest. The tribe worshiped spirits in nature, including sun, moon, stars, animals, plants, and earth. Appropriate sacrifice to these gods was important to get them on the tribe's side especially during any conflict. Fertility and cohesive families were important in the maintenance and growth of the tribe. Without both, the tribe could not survive. As men became organized into communities, of many families and multiple tribes their political structure and religions reflected greater complexity and became interconnected. When empires developed, their leaders achieved god-like status. Church and state were bound together and preachers or imams influenced the masses.

Ancient Israel was different. God was represented as a person apart from the politics of the state. The Bible demonstrates this dichotomy with prophets frequently castigating and warning political leaders. When Jesus came and Rome was all powerful, His advice was, "*Render therefore unto Caesar the things which are Caesar's; and unto God the things that are God's.*" (Matt 22:21; Mark 12:17; Luke 20:25) – a clear separation of church and state. Our founding fathers drew further conclusions from Judeo-Christian ethic: *"We hold these truths to be self-evident, that all men are created equal, that they are endowed by their Creator with certain unalienable rights, that among these are life, liberty and the pursuit of happiness."*[38]

In the Diaspora Israel maintained aloofness from states and was and is frequently persecuted by them. From the time of the "patriarchs" (Adam, Noah, Abraham, Isaac, Jacob and Joseph) Israel had been corrupted by local gods. Moses, Joshua, and the Judges through Samuel had tried with God's help to redirect the Israelites away from the local gods, but their efforts were frustrated. Solomon, allegedly wise, began the next major decline, but despite efforts of numerous prophets, Israel and Judah divorced themselves from their God and were conquered and scattered. Even the remnant of Judah that returned from Babylon was soon corrupted through

the influences of Greek philosophy following the conquests of **Alexander the Great**. Their conquerors from Greece and Rome proved too much. Christ came to try to lead them back, but they would not. (Matt 23:37; Luke 13:34) The Jews to this day continue to struggle under Rabbinic Judaism and the philosophies of men (Deut 4:27-29). Jerusalem fell in AD 70. The

Apostles were dead by AD 100. For the next 200 years Christian apologists tried to fend off vicious Roman persecutions by incorporating Greek philosophy into Christianity. When Rome finally offered Christianity the position of state religion at the Council of Nicaea (AD 325), Christianity rushed into the arms of the State. When Rome fell in the 5th Century, Christianity in the West remained tied to various kings and princes of Europe. Popes placated the barbarian princes to keep good relations with them and tried to take their power at times. In the East Constantinople became tied to Byzantium and finally Russia under Prince Vladimir in 988. In the 17th & 18th centuries Christianity in North America lost its ties with sectarian Europe where religion was tied to the state. Many fled Europe for religious freedom; the Reformation had failed them. As dispersed American farmers many became non-sectarian and interpreted the Bible for themselves and some looked for a true "restoration." Following the American Revolution all sectarian Christianity in the U.S. was freed from the power of the state, but with the Great Awakening of the early 19th Century there was a rush back to sectarianism. In Europe the "Enlightenment" began to take hold along with a general disillusionment of religion in the late 19th Century. There was a trend towards the anti-morality and the secular doctrines of Marxist Communism that eventually led to the bloody 20th Century. Paul's warning became a reality for all time, "*Beware lest any man spoil you through philosophy and vain deceit, after the tradition of men, after the rudiments of the world, and not after Christ.*" (Colossians 2:8)

Christianity led to the moral betterment of millions over two millennia, but its corporate association with state politics led to such horrors as the Inquisition, the Crusades, and an excuse for colonialism in less developed parts of the world. The corruption and break up of European Catholicism led to numerous brutal internecine wars such as the 30 Years' War (1618-1648). Religion can incorporate secular philosophies as well as theological ones. My family crest and shield carry a motto from the early 18th Century or Age of Reason that states, *Sic ratio vestra dux* – "Let reason be your leader." A century earlier it might have read, *Sit Deo vestra dux*, but the thinkers of the Enlightenment changed the way mankind approached both history and religion. Much of Christianity had become "the arm of flesh" (2 Chron 32:7-8).

The *Bible* states, "*And the LORD God said, Behold, the man is become as one of us, to know good and evil: … Therefore the LORD God sent him forth from the garden of Eden, to till the ground from whence he was taken.*" (Gen 3:22-23) If individuals are to advance we cannot lie around Eden and allow the fruit to fall into our mouths or sit around all day naming animals. We must experience life –get our hands dirty – learn the difference between good and evil. Yet we must be in the world, but not of it. This became the North American destiny.

The Modern Study of History

Most people no longer learn history in schools. When asked about history, many say they hated the subject, but without facts how can anyone love history? Most learn prejudices from current events in newspapers and other mass media and are assured this is history. From the time of the invention of the printing press these sources expressed opinions, hidden agendas, and the religious and cultural bias of their editors and press owners. [39] Newspapers and TV news are motivated by sales and sensationalism; "if it bleeds, it leads." In his Orders to the Mayor and City Council of Atlanta (12 Sep 1864), General William T Sherman warned: "*You have heretofore read public sentiment in your newspapers, that live by falsehood and excitement; and the quicker you seek for truth in other quarters, the better.*"

My history professor at Stanford, Anatole G. Mazour (1900 – 1982), also a Ukrainian veteran of the Russian Revolution, did not permit his undergraduates to study history less than 100 years old because state archives are closed for at least this long. He emphasized the importance of knowing the culture and religion of people under study. Chronology of events was important if one were to understand how one event might lead to another. He taught about conflict between leaders and peoples and the rationale behind it. War is the great mix-master, motivator, and disrupter of civilizations. Religions and philosophies of leaders were important. We were expected to render judgments in our analysis as to whether or not leaders and their actions were good or evil and why. Marxist doctrine by which academicians now evaluate history states there is no good or evil. Everything is relative – no black or white, just shades of gray. In my early training I found that the study of archival documents, well researched biographies and diaries were important sources in the study of history. It was also important to follow the sex and money trail of the "movers and shakers." It is important to know their attitudes, beliefs, their unrepentant personal behavior and even their psychiatric and physical state that influence their actions. All this can determine who might blackmail them, threaten their power through exploitation of personal weakness, and what they might do to hide their personal secrets. Marxist dogma tries to force all conflict into a "class struggle." This simplistic theory is behind the *Revisionist* history taught in many schools and universities today. This work is a history of warfare between the two major religions of the Middle East and West and should present enough evidence to demonstrate the fallacy of Marx's "class struggle" theory of history.

Today history can use hard sciences that add precision and proof for major historical events. Archeology, biology, climatology, volcanology, numismatics, carbon dating, dendrochronology, genetics, and forensic pathology can add to our understanding of events and the people who shape them. Chemical analysis of plants, tooth enamel and other substances allow us to know more about the person's remains, environment and even where he was born. Forensic pathology can determine causes of death. Other branches of medicine including PCR (polymerase chain reaction) and DNA (Deoxyribonucleic acid) analysis have added to our understanding of events. It can determine family members, track mass migrations, and identify epidemic diseases. Recent advances in the neurosciences are important. An example of how PCR data helped understand the demise of **Napoleon**'s Grand Armeé in 1812-13 was published in *J Infectious Dis* 2006: 193:112-120. An analysis of remains from French soldiers in a mass grave in Vilnius with the observations of the British military attaché to the Russian army indicates that disease rather than the Russian Army, scorched earth or the winter led to his catastrophic casualties. It found that typhus (a Rickettsial disease), trench fever, pneumonia and diarrhea (bacterial and viral diseases) were principle causes of death and contradict Napoleon's report to the French government, "*My army had had some losses, but this was due to the premature rigors of the season.*" Some losses!! Some rigors!! 265,000 French troops began the foray into Russia in 1812. 95,000 left Moscow before the first snows fell. By 1813 only 3000 veterans remained. There were only 36,000 battle casualties in Napoleon's army.[40] No one won except disease.

The body of President **Zachary Taylor** (1784 – 1850) was exhumed in the late 1991 on suspicion that his death from a gastrointestinal illness might have been from arsenic poisoning. There were several close associates who wanted him dead. Examination of skin, nail and hair at the Oak Ridge National Laboratory for arsenic by neutron activation analysis demonstrated some arsenic, but far too little to be implicated in his death. [41]

A recent elegant history by David Keys[42] presents a plausible theory based in part on dendrochronology (dating by tree ring analysis) and ice-core data as to why numerous ancient civilizations collapsed within a 100-year period and why the "Dark Ages" separated the Ancient World from the Modern. Keys found evidence of a 20 to 30-year climatic cooling starting in 535 that also brought the plague epidemics to Europe after 540. He theorized that this and severe crop failures caused the collapse of many ancient civilizations creating power vacuums that paved the way for the emergence of a host of new centers of power including Islâm.

Spencer Wells[43] used Y-chromosome DNA evidence to plot the migration of man from his origins in Africa to his global spread. It also supports an interesting theory that modern man has been on the planet for no more than 200,000 years (mitochondrial DNA data) or as recently as 59,000 years (Y-chromosomal data). If mankind existed before this it is conceivable that most of it was wiped out by climatic change caused by a super volcano Toba on Sumatra 74,000 years ago. Studies remain in progress. [44]Three of the earth's known 6 super volcanoes are in the Western U.S – Yellowstone (WY), Long Valley (CA) and Valles (NM). The others are in New Zealand, Sumatra, and Japan.

Abbas Sadeghian[45] carefully analyzed ancient records found in the Hadiths for evidence of Muhammad's long suspected complex partial seizure disorder and then used modern medical information to back up the theory that Muhammad suffered from temporal lobe epilepsy. See Appendix II. This work presents the plausible cause of Muhammad's physical and mental deterioration – a left temporal lobe meningioma. This is based on modern medical information and observations not available until the 20th Century. Nassir Ghaemi, MD uses the disciplines of modern medical evaluations, medical student instruction (the clinical pathological conference or CPC) and psychiatry to analyze the mental state of dead historical figures. It is described in his introduction to *A First-Rate Madness* pages 1-19. These methods are used in this work in the analysis of Muhammad's illness.

Many basic history books ignore these tools. Those who write history for secondary schools don't seem to know how to make it interesting. I have been appalled by the ignorance of most students of these fundamentals, but I am reminded that even in my day there was little understanding of the history of the Middle East, India, and Asia; we tended to concentrate on the history of Western Civilization, but we had to start somewhere.

The Current Conflict

The conflict has been in progress for nearly 1300 years. To find out why, study of the *Korân*, especially those chapters from the Medina period is important. In 1784, the year following our successful Revolution, the infant, pre-constitutional United States of America confronted its first foreign war. Like the present, it was undeclared and was against part of the Islâmic world. It will be taken up in detail later in this work. From the start of U.S. tribute payments in 1784 until its end in 1816 took 32 years. Islâm does not go away easily and it doesn't respect weakness.

This war is not simple. It is about oil – theirs not ours. Had we developed our own energy resources we would not be facing our current problems. We would be stronger economically and militarily and they would be weaker. About ¼ of the world's oil comes through the Persian Gulf. Protecting that trade route and eliminating terrorist threats are essential for the industrial world's economy. Abandonment of Iraq at this time is dangerous. Sale of Middle East oil provides much of the money supporting the war against us. So long as we fail to discover our own oil and refine it we will remain in this predicament. Other solutions present major engineering problems that take time to solve. Toyota had to build nearly a million Prius in 6 years to work out the bugs and create a reliable automobile that gets 40 plus miles per gallon and deliver it to the public at a reasonable price.

This war is not a usual war. A recognized foreign country did not attack a military instillation of the United States. A small group, mostly from Saudi Arabia, a friendly state, attacked a civilian economic target. An attack against our government in Washington DC had been planned, but frustrated. We had not taken seriously numerous aggressive acts against us (See Appendix I, Acts of Aggression). A list of attacks such as this should cause concern, but the world continues its collective slumber. It is like the 1930s. Then there was little concern about Adolf Hitler in Europe, Benito Mussolini in Africa, and Tojo in Manchuria, China, and Southeast Asia. Now Islamic terrorists are spreading to Europe, Asia, Africa, and America with almost the same National Socialist (Nazi) tendencies mixed with *jihād*."

Somehow, we lost Osama bin Laden's *Declaration of Jihād Against the Americans Who Occupy the Land of the Two Holy Mosques*, issued on August 23, 1996.[46] It was straight out of a 1959 Hollywood farce, *The Mouse That Roared* (Peter Sellers) in which the State Department had lost a declaration of war against the US from a mythical tiny wine producing Alpine country between France and Switzerland, the Duchy of Grand Fenwick. California wine producers had ruined their business. The Duchy planned to declare war on the U.S., lose, and then be rehabilitated beyond their wildest dreams. However, it all went awry when a squad sized raid by the Duchy's medieval army went to New York City, captured the world's most destructive weapon, the Q Bomb, and returned in triumph with their prize. They had defeated the U.S. much to the consternation of the entire world and their own interests.

Even worse, we also failed to countenance the edict issued by Osama bin Laden on February 22, 1998: "*We – with God's help – call on every Muslim who believes in God and wishes to be rewarded to comply with God's orders to kill the Americans and plunder their money wherever and whenever they find it. … The ruling to kill Americans and their allies – civilians and military – is an individual duty for every Muslim who can do it in any country in which it is possible to do it, in order to liberate the al-Aqsa Mosque and the holy mosque (Mecca) from their grip, and in order for their armies to move out of all lands of Islam, defeated and unable to threaten any Muslim.*" [47]

The al-Aqsa Mosque is on the Temple Mount in Jerusalem under Palestinian control. None but Muslims are permitted to go to Mecca or the Ka'ba (Caaba), its holy mosque. Muhammad said lies were permitted during war if it suited Islâm's purposes. The *Korân* tells Islâm that the modern State of Israel or Palestine belongs to them, not the Jews. "*O my people, enter the holy land, which GOD hath decreed you, and turn not your backs, lest ye be subverted and perish.*" (**5:21**)

Terrorist Acts

Table I Shows the number of Acts of Islâmic Aggression listed in Appendix I that have occurred worldwide between 1904 and December 27 2007. These do not include acts of terrorism against citizens or Allied military forces involved in the on-going Arab Israeli War or related to the US involvement in Afghanistan or Iraq.

Table I Documented Numbers of Terrorist Incidents Unrelated to Arab Israeli, Iraq or Afghan War (See Appendix I Acts of Aggression)		
Time Period	Probable	Suspected
Before Jihad Declaration		
May 18, 1904 – Aug 29, 1969	9	1
Feb 21, 1970 – Nov 4 1979	10	3
Apr 30 1980 – Sep 1989x	36	7
May 30, 1990 – Jun 25 1996	28	0
Totals pre Jihad Declaration	**83**	**11**
Jihad Declared August 23, 1996		
Feb 1997 – Dec 1999	9	0
2000	6	0
2001	10	1
Total Pre 9-11-2001	**20**	**0**
2002	21	0
2003	20	0
2004	20	0

2005	29	0
2006	38	1
2007	81	1
Totals 1904 – Dec 2007	**231**	**3**

As stated above, many Americans then and now do not believe we are engaged in war. If we are, what kind of war is it?

THE CHANGING FACE OF WARFARE

Hijā or *Jihād*

A *hijā* is an insulting poem. It is a common form of speech used before one Arab tribe attacks another.[48] The Arab invective that begins with "May 1000 flies infest your, etc.," is a way of pronouncing a curse and once said is real to the one making it. The Bible includes several examples of a *hija.*

> *"And Balak the son of Zippor was king of the Moabites at that time. He sent messengers therefore unto Balaam the son of Beor to Pethor, ..., to call him, saying, Behold, there is a people come out from Egypt: behold, they cover the face of the earth, and they abide over against me: Come now therefore, I pray thee, curse me this people; for they are too mighty for me: peradventure I shall prevail, that we may smite them, and that I may drive them out of the land: for I wot that he whom thou blessest is blessed, and he whom thou cursest is cursed."* (Num 22:4-6)

A *hijā* can be very effective. *"And the Philistine* (Goliath) *said, I defy the armies of Israel this day; give me a man, that we may fight together. When Saul and all Israel heard those words of the Philistine, they were dismayed, and greatly afraid."* (1 Samuel 17:10-11) See also Psalm 109.

Besides the Arabs many ancient societies believed that words had great power. The *Kalevala*, the Finnish epic is full of "magical" words and statements. Once an insult finds its mark, it causes great damage. Arab societies before and since the rise of Islâm, believe that such magical insults have lasting consequences. The worse an insult, the greater its damaged. According to ***Raphael Patai (The Arab Mind),*** it was primarily when

Arabs fought Arabs that the emphasis was placed on oral invective, boasting, and the use of weapons that were less than deadly. Intertribal fighting most typically took the form of raiding in which armed clashes were avoided as far as possible. However, when it came to fighting non-Arabs, which in the heyday of Arab expansion meant non-Muslims, the religious fervor changed the concept of battle radically. It became a matter of kill or be killed. The only proviso was that if the pagan enemy submitted and accepted Islâm, his life was spared. The Arab heroic spirit in these wars was encouraged by the promise of paradise to all those who fell in a *jihād* – a holy war waged by Muslims against non-Muslims. According to Muslim doctrine the fate of man was *maktūu*b, "written," that is predetermined."[49] See also the *Korân*: **64:2; 2:186; 3:145; 57:22**.

The Twin Towers attack had all the earmarks of a *jihād* – very deadly force used against non-Muslims. It also included characteristics prescribed in the *Korân*: morning attack (**3:121**; 15:**73**; 54:**38;** 100:3) and death by fire (**2:24**; **35**:36; **16**:62). Yet, it wasn't taken that way in the West and in the minds of many it still is a criminal not a religious matter. Although *jihād* can mean a personal struggle, its use in the *Korân* is predominantly that of a holy war. In the University of Michigan on-line text it is used 13 times: (7:195), (**8:18, 72, 74, 75**) (**9:16**) (**16**:110) (**22:15**) (**40**:25, 37) (**49:15**) (52:46) (**61:11**). It means a personal struggle in only two 7:195 and 52:46.

"Spread out! One round can get you all!"

Anyone who reads the *Korân* will soon discover its war-like tone. Such verses as "*O true believers, fear GOD, and earnestly desire a near conjunction with him, and fight for his religion, that ye may be happy.*" (**5:35**) are immediately reminded of a World War II patriotic pop-song, "*Praise the Lord and Pass the Ammunition.*"

To understand terrorist attacks, it is necessary to understand how war and its battlefields have evolved. In October, 1989 *The Marine Corps Gazette* published an article "*The Changing Face of War: Into the Fourth Generation*" by WS Lind, K Nightengale, JF Schmitt, JW Sutton, GI Wilson.[50] They outlined three distinct transitions in the way battlefields had changed since the 17th Century – 30 Years' War and the common use of gunpowder. Throughout history all these phases of warfare were known. Those that predominated are described here; all depended on technological advances in warfare. The authors then surmised a fourth generation.

The first generation was characterized by use of the **smoothbore musket** and **line and column** tactics. **Drill** was necessary to **mass and**

move troops on the battlefield. **Direct artillery fire** broke up enemy formations. As he closed a high rate of musket fire killed many before the rest were killed with sword, pike / spear or bayonet. High ground, wind at your back, simple orders, luck, lack of disease, and personal courage carried the day.

The second generation came about with the development of **rifled muskets**, breech loaded repeating rifles, barbed wire, machine guns, and massed **indirect artillery fire.** Tactics depended on **massed fire**, but battlefields remained linear. Defense tried to prevent penetrations of the line by **digging in**. Successful attacks were characterized by a 3:1 advantage and rushes in small groups, not massed troop charges. The major change was reliance on indirect fire from artillery – "the artillery conquers, the infantry occupies." Thus, **massed firepower replaced massed manpower**. Heavy machine guns on fighter aircraft and bombers began to join the fray along with heavier artillery and accurate rockets. Command from the top of military units using **wire communications** allowed tactical change in the midst of battle. The number troops that could be concentrated on a battle field increased because of improved logistics, **railroads** and **medical services**.

The third generation came about because of increased battlefield firepower and mobility. Tactics went from linear to **non-linear tactics**. Units were spread out. Infiltration or bypass isolated and collapsed the enemy's forces. Closing with the enemy and overwhelming him was unnecessary. Go around him, cut him off, then kill or capture him became the objective. Defense had to be "in depth," but as the defense began to spread out with space between units, this invited **infiltration**, which in turn laid the groundwork for the **patrol** and **counterattack**. By the beginning of World War I most of these concepts were known. It was the advancing technology of weapons and the **introduction of motor vehicles and aircraft** that caused the changes on the battlefield. The success of tanks at the end of World War I brought about "blitzkrieg" (lightning war) at the beginning of World War II. This marked the end of 2nd generation war and the beginning of the 3rd Generation. This form of highly mobile warfare necessitated: 1. "Mission orders with **coded radio communications**," 2. Dispersion of supplies with increased speed of delivery, 3. **Increased mobility** and maneuver with dispersion of troop concentrations, 4. **Tactical close air support** of troops on the battlefield and s**trategic bombing** designed to weaken the enemy's will to fight while destroying his culture and munitions-making capacity. All this required correct identification of the enemy's strategic centers. The end of World War II necessitated the invasion of Italy, the death of Hitler, total destruction of Germany's major cities, and the credible threat of total annihilation of Japan with atomic weapons after demonstrating their power and the will to use them at Hiroshima and Nagasaki.

The authors believed that **fourth generation warfare** would be fought by widely **dispersed undefined small units**. The distinction between war and peace would blur to the vanishing point. **Definable battlefields and fronts would disappear**. The distinction between "civilian" and "military" might completely disappear. Actions would occur concurrently throughout the enemy's land. Targets would include their society, economy, culture, and religion, not just physical entities. Attacks against major military installations would be obsolete because of their ability to defend themselves. Instead, **civilian equivalents would be targets** – seats of government, corporate headquarters, power plants, industrial sites, major economic districts, and knowledge based and manufacturing industries. Success would depend on effectiveness in joint operations as lines between responsibility and mission became blurred. All these elements were present to some degree in **guerilla warfare** throughout history and third generation warfare with "Special Forces," but would become greatly accentuated in the fourth generation.

With new technologies a few highly trained soldiers could do as much damage as a brigade. **Robotics** using remotely controlled aircraft and ground vehicles and other forms of artificial intelligence could lead to tremendous destruction operated from afar by unknown entities. A few very intelligent soldiers with **high tech weapons** could wreak havoc on an enemy in a few weeks. The concept of "front" and "rear" would change to **"targeted"** and **"non-targeted."** In the 4th generation **targets would be almost exclusively "civilian."** The modern soldier might be working or going to school in an enemy country; he or she would live off the land. He would have at his disposal **high tech weapons that might be nuclear, biological, or gaseous**. He might possess **electronic capabilities** for disrupting communications and making massive thefts of banking institutions. He might have nuclear or other high explosives capable of great physical destruction of large buildings, and disrupting the life of cities for months. He might possess biological agents capable of inflicting epidemic illness and death. All of this would be caused by only a few individuals in each major location. In their **civilian disguise** with **legally issued visas, and legally licensed vehicles** or **taxis**, or **stolen aircraft** they could roam the country seeking targets of opportunity. The more freedom that society permitted the greater damage they could cause. Their targets would be large, fixed, soft, poorly guarded and "civilian."

"Terrorism" carried out by high-tech fourth generation warriors would have as its objective the collapsing of the enemy and destroying his will to fight.

Like a skillful judo-artist the "terrorist" would **use his enemy's strength, such as his freedoms, against him**. Like the forts and fortified frontiers, these legally mandated freedoms and courts of law would become the death trap of a society. A free society's greatest strength would become its greatest weakness. Its laws meant to protect its citizens would be subverted to protect the "terrorists" and permit them to gain access to our infrastructure for nefarious purposes. If we permit them to work within our laws, they receive our protection. If we gun them down, TV news gives them "victim" status. Thus, while they attack us, we protect them, but if we set aside our Constitutional protections, the terrorists win a different victory. Somehow, we must identify these 4th generation soldiers and treat them like prisoners of war outside the protection of our Constitution meant for citizens engaged in peaceful pursuits. This article was reprinted in the November 2001 issue of *The Marine Corps Gazette* along with three more articles by many of the same authors. All are valuable and available on line and are worth reading.

Four Generations of War in History

The four generations of war may also be understood within the context of history. First generation war – the massing of troops to close with an enemy – began in ancient times. Soldiers moved in columns and stood in lines or phalanx usually with cavalry on the flanks. Commanders typically picked battlefields where they could occupy high ground, survey most of terrain, watch the enemy's movement, and observe the progress of the battle. Wind at your back with dust blowing in the face of your enemy. Blinding him was greatly desired. Lines were rarely more than a mile or two in length. Cavalry commanders had to be smart and know what their general wanted. Orders were very simple. Changing orders in the heat of battle was hazardous. The will to fight depended mostly on the soldier, but the army had to have sufficient support from the country in order to field it.

Gunpowder originated in China in the 10th Century and was used in the form of bombs fired from catapults in the 11th century. Bamboo tube cannons were used in the 12th century. By the 13th Century the Chinese had developed shoulder firing matchlocks, but these were used sparingly. These weapons were known and imported to the Middle East and used by Egyptian forces against the Mongols at the Battle of Ain Jalut in 1260.

Gun powder was used in siege weapons to blast down fortifications and by selected musketeers in European armies until 1618. By the start of the 30 Years' War, Sweden's King, Gustavus Adolphus (1594-1632), then only 24 years-old, had redesigned his military formations based on the universal use of gunpowder. He developed horse drawn field artillery on wheels and used it as an anti-personnel weapon at the front of his line. He developed a conscript army to replace mercenaries and armed most of them with muskets. Column and line continued. The Swedish cavalry was used to butcher a fleeing army or attack its lines of supply. All European armies quickly followed Sweden's lead. Linear deployment of no more than a mile or so was typical since logistics could not supply more than 50,000 men arranged for battle. This gradually improved until the time of Napoleon's defeat at the Battle of Waterloo in 1815. Field artillery was still small bore, deployed in front and withdrawn when the enemy closed. Its effect was to kill and slow the enemy until the two lines finally met. An attack usually failed unless the attacker had a 3:1 advantage over his opponent. By the time of Waterloo (1815) the length and depth of battlefields had increased to about 5 miles in both directions. However, technology would change this.

As the Revolutionary War in America opened in 1775, rifled muskets used by the colonials were accurate at 200 yards while the usual infantry "Brown Bess" smooth bore musket was effective at 80 to 100 yards. After 1815 most military muskets had rifling. By the 1840s railroads improved logistics and made larger armies possible. With the improvements in rifles, artillery pieces and rockets, closing with the enemy became more hazardous during the Crimean (1853-6) and US Civil War (1861-5). This was especially true if an enemy was "well dug in." The "king of spades," Robert E Lee, became a master of defensive trench positions. By the time of World War I defensive warfare had become extraordinarily effective with the addition of machine guns, barbed wire, heavier breach loading, indirect firing artillery, and breach loading rifles. One of Lee's lieutenants, General James Longstreet, had resurrected the concepts of "fire and maneuver" from the principles of Gustavus Adolphus. [51] This would change the tactics that began in World War I and came to fruition in World War II. Small groups of men would rush the enemy while others concentrated their fire at the point of attack. At the end of World War I the tank became the surprise weapon and made it possible to overcome trenches, barbed wire, rifle and machine gun fire. Tanks could breach a trench line and the following troops could mop up. By this time the length of the line had become a country's entire frontier and the depth of the battlefield was 7 miles in both directions. Artillery was no longer deployed in the front, but was positioned in the rear with "forward observers" directing the artillery's fire. This was "indirect" fire. Massed fire power was rapidly replacing massed manpower. As the French observed, "artillery fire conquers and troops occupy." Public health and medical practices were important in keeping armies intact and reducing the non-battle deaths and returning casualties to the front.

Planning for future wars usually includes what worked in the last one. In modern times this is a common error in both military and civilian thinking. In the 1920s and 30s both Europe and America failed to look to the future. Despite the demonstration by Billie Mitchell that aircraft could sink a battleship with bombs, most countries continued to build battleships as the mainstay of their navies. Japan built aircraft carriers and Britain and the U.S. experimented with a few. In Europe World War II preparations included the fortifying of strong points along the borders of each country. The Siegfried Line guarded Germany and The Maginot Line guarded France. Both included a series of heavily fortified trenches and strong points. Belgium built an elaborate, "impregnable," fortress, Eben-Emael to protect them from Germany; the French didn't bother extending the Maginot Line across the Belgian border – a big mistake.

World War II began on 1 September 1939 when the Germans crossed the Polish border using the Blitzkrieg (lightning war) tactics. Tanks rolled through the front. Soldiers followed, encircled the front line and it surrendered. Poland was gone in 6 weeks. On 10 May 1940 85 glider-borne paratroopers landed on the top of Fort Eben-Emael followed by a German regiment. The fort surrendered the following day and 1200 Belgians were captured. By 13 May Belgium and the Netherlands were occupied. The Germans poured into France by way of the Ardennes Forest through Belgium, bypassing the Maginot Line and conquered France by 22 June. That was the end of fixed positions. "Digging in" was dying. "Fire and maneuver" were king. Indirect artillery fire and bombing made massed troop concentrations suicidal.

World War II was fought by coalitions. Historically coalitions are usually defeated unless one of the powers can carry the entire weight of the war. [52] The Axis powers were not successful with Germany and Japan failing to coordinate. The Allies were able to concentrate on defeating Germany first largely due to the coordination between Churchill, Stalin and Roosevelt. In the West the British American Coalition was kept together by Eisenhower as supreme commander, a general highly effective in settling political interests. Also available was a group of highly skilled, no-nonsense, battlefield generals exemplified by George S. Patton Jr. He was master of mechanized war, close air support, and student of military history. He stated, "*A good plan, violently executed now, is better than a perfect plan next week.*"[53]

Between 1943 and 1945 US forces in Europe used carpet bombing and massed artillery fire to open holes in the German defenses. Patton used the corridors to pour fast, light Sherman tanks supported by motorized infantry and fighter aircraft into the enemy's rear area wiping out command posts, communication networks and supply lines. **General George S. Patton**'s 3rd Army liberated more square miles of territory (81,500) in shorter time than any army in history; killed, wounded or captured 1.8 million Germans with only 300,000 men; and suffered fewer casualties than other allied armies at a rate of 13:1 when compared to enemy losses. He kept the Germans from regrouping until he ran out of fuel. Patton also spread his units out leaving gaps in-between. This gave him greater mobility. Ground and air patrols were used in the unoccupied spaces to keep enemy infiltration to a minimum. This was the beginning of real third generation warfare of the modern era. For lack of fuel he feared that the allied advance would slow to a halt and allow the Germans to re-group.[54][55][56] They did.

On 16 December 1944 an attack against the center of the Allied lines ("*Herbstnebel*" or Autumn Fog) was launched. It was the opening of a major German offensive, "*Wacht am Rheinübung*" or known by the Allies as, "*The Battle of the Bulge.*" It pushed a salient far into allied lines, but became a death trap for German forces when Patton's 3rd Army, spread out and deployed for rapid mobility, did the "impossible." It turned 90° and moved 160 miles to the north. In 2 days, it hit the German salient in the flank relieving the besieged city of Bastogne. Later the entire German salient (60 x 30 miles) was destroyed. This kind of mobility was impossible in linear formations, but not for Patton's spread out deployment.

Two military axioms came out of these experiences: ***"Spread out!! One round can get you all!!!"*** and ***"Fire and maneuver, it's got to be. Fire without maneuver is a waste of ammunition. Maneuver without fire is suicide."*** The spread-out mobile offense became the king of 3rd generation warfare. In the Pacific, the Navy and Marine Corps bombed and bypassed most Japanese fortified islands. The few that had to be taken ended up with enemy killed nearly 3 and 4 to 1 greater than the attackers. Although the "butcher's bill" at Iwo Jima was 6800 Marines killed in action and 22,000 wounded, Japan lost 22,000 killed. Strategic bombing did not cause either side to lose the will to fight, but destroyed much on both sides.

The Korean War, 1950-53 was inconclusive due to "**rules of engagement**" and **political / diplomatic considerations**. It was fought as a coalition under the U.N. banner and ended in an armistice with neither side benefiting. Disagreements between North and South Korea continue to fester with continued deployment of troops. Instead of allowing the generals to determine the tactics and strategy to be used, political considerations became paramount and hamstrung U.S. military forces. Since then several military efforts have ended also in costly stalemates or defeat.

Vertical envelopment, the landing of large units by helicopter behind enemy lines was first demonstrated in 1957. [57] This became common practice in Vietnam, the battlefield extended out to 100 miles deep and units became even more widely dispersed. American troops suffered no major military defeats in Vietnam despite "rules of engagement," but the home front caved in under constant anti-war propaganda and "rules of engagement" prevented a conclusive victory. The US was forced to leave Vietnam. This is the classic example of military success on the battlefield, but loss of a war. The Vietnam and World War II experiences should have taught us that Sun Tzu was correct, "*For there has never been a protracted war from which a country has benefited.*"58 The best strategy is "neutralize" the enemy, win, and get out without pussyfooting around. World War II for the U.S. lasted from December 1941 to August 1945 – 3 ½ years and resulted in decisive victory; Vietnam lasted from 1959 to April 1975 – over 15 years and dragged on without eliminating the enemy's will to fight. Third Generation warfare reached its peak in the Gulf War of 1991 with wide dispersal of military units and helicopters operating up to 400 miles to the front. Its effectiveness against the Iraqi Army, still married to 2nd generation linear warfare was phenomenal. The usual 3:1 advantage needed by an attacker proved unnecessary. It achieved its limited objective of freeing Kuwait, but lacked a strategic victory in the mid-East because of political considerations.

As previously mentioned all the various generations of war have always existed. Genghis Khan (1162 – 1227) used many of the principles of 3rd generation warfare to defeat larger armies. Every soldier was a cavalryman with a minimum of 3 horses. Fresh mounts were always available. The Cavalry was broken down in multiples of 10 – 10 men to a squad, 10 squads to a company, 10 companies to a regiment, up to Tumens of 10,000 men – the largest unit. Leaders were selected based on skill, not on family or tribal ties. Tribalism was outlawed so that the army was a single cohesive unit. The Mongolian bow was capable of accurate fire in the hands of cavalrymen at 200 to 300 yards and from moving horseback at 50 yards. Half his army consisted of light cavalry with bowmen. Half were heavy cavalry armed with light armor, lances and swords. His army moved upwards of 70 miles per day while other armies at that time moved only 10. An army was usually no more than 40,000 troops in a single unit, but he could mass as many as 250,000 at one time. When not engaged and spread out, his troops in smaller units lived off the land. The extra horses carried what little additional logistical support he needed. He made extensive use of spies and mobile scouting parties that would search out the enemy, estimate strengths and assist in picking weaker enemy concentrations to attack first.

When attacking cities, his forces carried portable catapults that could be packed on animals. Genghis Khan's ability to encircle and shoot at enemies from a distance made him capable of beating armies 2 and 3 times his size. He could divide his forces into task groups and be assured that he could escape any enemy if the need arose and regroup with a larger force. His army was always moving and never static. His "take no prisoners" policy caused most potential enemies to give up without a fight. If they chose to fight, he butchered their army, tortured the captives first, and then impaled them on stakes. He took only selected female prisoners and prepubescent youth to be used by his troops. His conquests were greater than any other conqueror in world history extending from Poland in the West to the Pacific Ocean in the East and from the arctic south to Vietnam in east and from Polish Baltic south to include all of the Middle East and Persia. This did not include the Indian Subcontinent.[59] The 13th Century was also very bloody.

On 11 September 2001 Osama Bin-Laden's irregulars, 19 in all, knocked a hole in the Pentagon, blew up two of the tallest buildings in the U.S., did billions of dollars in physical damage, and killed 2973 with 24 missing and presumed dead. This was only the immediate cost of the attack. The Center for Contemporary Conflict tallied the actual cost as follows: Lower Manhattan lost approximately 30 percent of its office space and a number of businesses ceased to exist. Close to 200,000 jobs were destroyed or relocated out of New York City, at least temporarily. The destruction of physical assets was estimated at $14 billion for private businesses, $1.5 billion for state and local government enterprises and $0.7 billion for Federal enterprises. Rescue, cleanup and related costs have been estimated to amount to at least $11 billion for a total direct cost of $27.2 billion."60 This is 4th generation warfare. Suppose there were 1000 well placed soldiers in sleeper cells? The "battlefield" is our entire country "from sea to shining sea." Regular warfare as most know it from historical record, (1st & 2nd Generation) is over. Bin-Laden's lieutenants are well trained and motivated "irregulars" or knights. Make no mistake, they were and are a formidable enemy and masters of 4th generation warfare. We must still be prepared for 3rd generation.

The 9/11/ 2001 attack was just as predicted by the 1989 article referenced above. The first line of defense in 4th generation war is to know where every alien in the country is at all times. This means securing borders and carefully identifying every alien inside the country. We must know where they are whether or not they are living according to the restrictions of their visas. This is an immigration problem. The second task is military. Potential 4th generation enemy soldiers must be found and wiped out wherever they are. They must not be permitted to get close to the country. If caught inside, they must be denied Constitutional protection and treated as prisoners of war if foreign or traitors if native. Legalized border sovereignty only provides a cover for enemy training camps and must be disregarded. Intelligence must have the ability to monitor all electronic communications between potential enemies and their "sleeper cells."

Newer high-tech weapons such as **unmanned air reconnaissance vehicles** and **predator drones** can be highly effective. The Geneva Convention, based on 1st and 2nd generation war, is obsolete. Aliens must understand that they do not have the rights of citizens protected by the Constitution. Military strikes against terrorist sleeper cells may be necessary. For those captured, military tribunals are more appropriate than the civilian courts. Although they are not wearing uniforms and appear to be following "civilian" pursuits, these are real enemy combatants. The information they possess is sensitive and would be damaging to our military effort were it publicized in a civil trial. "Terrorists" have used open border policies and guest worker programs to infiltrate Western Europe and North America. Fourth generation warfare has been known throughout history. Any group within a country that foments rebellion against existing authority has engaged in various forms of fourth generation warfare. Modern technology is what makes this form of warfare more dangerous than ever.

Islâm's objective under Arab control has always been the replacement of all the world's religions with Islâm and worldwide establishment of Sharia Law. Historically this has been accomplished with conquest associated with murder, rapine and plunder. Recent history from several African countries confirms the continuation of this policy. Despite some ill-informed political rhetoric in the West, we face a clash of civilizations and we either fight now while we have the upper hand or wait until later when they possess nuclear weapons. The objective of any war is the same as it has been since Sun Tzu wrote it in

The Art of War, and Carl von Clausewitz (Prussian military philosopher 1780-1831) expressed it in *On War* – the destruction of the enemy's will to fight not necessarily his physical forces. The tactical military maxim to remember is – "Spread out!! One round can get you all!!" Disperse your resources. Massing them creates a target. Large businesses and civil governments need to learn this principle or face the possibility of their annihilation. "*Everything in war is very simple, but the simplest thing is difficult.*" [61]

The Will to Fight & a Novel Approach

Once you have read the *Korân* and learn of the "X-rated" paradise promised for martyrs, you will understand why so many males in their late teens and early 20s are eager to sign up. To counter this we must make the martyr's sacrifice so horrible that most will be discouraged. A more secular and less Arab influenced Islâm would be desirable. This will decrease Islâm's desire for jihād. As long as their populations remain largely illiterate or subject to Wahhabist imams' teachings, their will to fight will continue. Islâmists do not adhere to the Judeo-Christian ethic and the Geneva Convention or other rules of war. Most central Asiatic and Middle Eastern cultures adhere to more oriental and brutal rules of war that simply state, "To the victor go the spoils." They do not respect life, free will or "agency." Consequently, they will use suicide bombers and kill or torture male prisoners as they desire. The spoils of war include your wives, daughters, and young pre-pubertal boys. According to the *Korân* these will fall under Sharia Law as "those whom the right hand possesses" or "gifts of the right hand."

A novel approach to discouraging a Muslim's will to fight was allegedly used by Col. **John J Pershing** and Col. Alexander Rodgers of the 6th Cavalry during the Spanish American War in the Philippines. American troops faced the fierce Muslim Moros, who were eager to fight the Yankees to the death. The prompt and swift action in completely surrounding their forces at Bud Dajo and cutting off all supplies discouraged them. Rodgers instituted the policy of burying all Muslim dead soldiers in a common grave with the carcasses of slaughtered pigs. Pershing told the Muslims in his area of operation that he would, splatter pigs' blood on their homes if anyone from their village attacked his troops. Those killed fighting his troops would be buried in pig-skins. It is said that Pershing had no further trouble from Muslim Moro insurgents. Wrapped in pig skins, you can't go to paradise and get the virgins. [62]

To Those Who Desire War

Soldiering, probably the second oldest profession is a deadly business. To be good at it requires constant study and combat experience. **General W T Sherman** warned, *"I am tired and sick of war. Its glory is all moonshine. It is only those who have neither fired a shot nor heard the shrieks and groans of the wounded who cry aloud for blood, for vengeance, for desolation. War is hell."*[63] Armies are trained to kill people and break things. If the country is prepared to go to war and commit her armed forces, it must be prepared to step aside, support the effort, and allow its generals to be victorious without "rules of engagement." General George Patton was a veteran of the Mexican Incursion, commander of tanks in World War I, and probably the most famous general of World War II. He knew commanders win battles, but lead men prepared to fight. "Unfortunately, war means fighting and fighting means killing." Soldiers had to learn "to be able to fight anywhere, any time, and to do it better than our opponents." As his biographer quoted him, "The intense desire for physical contact with the enemy rather than the threat of armed force alone produced victory. Offensive, mordant troopers imbued with the fierce desire to destroy the enemy by always attacking him, will beat troops who … are more desirous of escaping alive … than of remaining victorious surrounded by slain opponents. … The fierce-frenzy of hate and determination flashing from bloodshot eyes squinting behind glittering steel is what wins. … Ever since man banded together with the laudable intention of killing his fellows, war has been a dirty business. … Wars are fought with weapons, but they are won by men."[64] As general, he saw himself an actor to imbue his troops with this state of mind. He knew that "a coward dressed as a brave man will change from cowardice" and become a hero. It explains the ivory handled pistol, his use of profanity, the over-sized stars on helmet, shoulders and command car, the constant wearing of a steel helmet off the battlefield and attention to detail in planning and dress that Patton exhibited.[65] In his younger years he was far more mild mannered. Although he suffered many horse accidents, I do not buy the theory of head injury causing a personality change for a number of medical reasons. His military planning and logic were too precise for a person suffering from concussion caused brain deterioration.

Without victory, there is no decision. Once victory is achieved politicians and the public can re-enter the arena and help clean up the mess from the devastation created. For those, especially diplomats and politicians without or with minimal combat experience who believe they are experts about how war should be waged the following ancient advice is good for all time.

"*Commanders should be counseled chiefly by persons of known talent, by those who have made the art of war their particular study, and whose knowledge is derived from experience, by those who are present at the scene of action, who see the enemy, who see the advantages that occasions offer, and who, like people embarked in the same ship, are sharers of the danger.*

If therefore, anyone thinks himself qualified to give advice respecting the war which I am about to conduct – let him not refuse the assistance of the State, but let him come with me into Macedonia. He shall be furnished with a ship, a tent, even his traveling charges will be defrayed, but if he thinks this is too much trouble, and prefers the repose of a city life to the toils of war, let him not on land assume the office of pilot. The city in itself furnishes abundance of topics for conversation. Let it confine its passion for talking to its own precincts and rest assured that we shall pay no attention to any councils but such as shall be framed within our camp." [66] (General Lucius A Paulus 229-160 BC – Rome)

For those whose zeal compels them to war General William T Sherman offered this advice on the eve of the American Civil War to Prof. David F Boyd, Louisiana State Seminary 24 December 1860.

"*You people of the South don't know what you are doing. This country will be drenched in blood, and God only knows how it will end. It is all folly, madness, a crime against civilization! You people speak so lightly of war; you don't know what you're talking about. War is a terrible thing! You mistake, too, the people of the North. They are a peaceable people but an earnest people, and they will fight, too. They are not going to let this country be destroyed without a mighty effort to save it… Besides, where are your men and appliances of war to contend against them? The North can make a steam engine, locomotive, or railway car; hardly a yard of cloth or pair of shoes can you make. You are rushing into war with one of the most powerful, ingeniously mechanical, and determined people on Earth—right at your doors. You are bound to fail. Only in your spirit and determination are you prepared for war. In all else you are totally unprepared, with a bad cause to start with. At first you will make headway, but as your limited resources begin to fail, shut out from the markets of Europe as you will be, your cause will begin to wane. If your people will but stop and think, they must see in the end that you will surely fail.*" [67]

The U.S. Civil War was fought from 1861 to 1865. It was the bloodiest in U.S. History with 618,000 total deaths (Battle deaths: 110,070 Federal & 94,000 Confederate – Disease deaths: 250,152 Federal & 164,000 Confederate). [68] It resulted in terrible material loss to the Confederacy in destroyed industry and railroads. Many youths left and migrated to the Western U.S. It took nearly 90 years before it was completed. The South remained bitter and segregated for the same length of time.

William T Sherman was a brilliant military leader who suffered the blessing and curse of bipolar disorder. [69] After watching the carnage of battle under old Napoleonic principles, he realized the need for "total war," to destroy the will and means of people to fight. His devastating march through Georgia and South Carolina worked. In a matter of weeks, Lee was cornered and the South surrendered.

Table II Generations of Warfare

	G 1	G 2	G 3	G 4	Time
	personnel	intelligence	operations	logistics	
Ancient	Infantry Cavalry Catapults Siege Size 100K	Spies Cavalry Rhetoric	Line & Column Battlefield 1x1 mile High ground Wind at back Military Targets Simple	Horse Ships Live off land Camp followers	Until 1618 30 Years. War
1st	Infantry Field Artillery Cavalry Size 250K	Spies Cavalry Press use	Line & Column Battlefield 5x5 miles Artillery forward High ground Wind at back Simple Smooth bore – 100 yds. Military Targets	Horse & Ships Live off land Less Camp followers	1618 – 1853 Crimean War
1st	Infantry Field Artillery Cavalry Size 250K	Spies Cavalry Press use	Line & Column Battlefield 5x5 miles Artillery forward High ground Wind at back Simple Smooth bore – 100 yds. Military Targets	Horse & Ships Live off land Less Camp followers	1618 – 1853 Crimean War
2nd	Infantry Field Artillery Cavalry Armor Airborne Aircraft Medical Size – 1-2M combat	Spies Patrols Motorized Air Radio Com Press & Media	Line & Column Battlefield Artillery rear Frontier x 40 miles High ground Fire & Maneuver Rifles 200-500 yds. Military Targets Gen Staff–Complex	Horse & RR Ships Trucks Local camp follow	1853-1943 World War II

3rd	Infantry Artillery Armor Airborne Aircraft Medical Missiles 500 k–combat	Spies Air Patrols Motorized Satellites Press & Media	Battlefield – 400 x 400 miles Non-linear Artillery protected Fire & Maneuver Military Targets Gen Staff–Complex	Complex – ships RR – aircraft – trucks Tec Weapons	1944 – 2000 Desert Storm
4rth	Small units Special forces Task Forces 1-5 k sleeper 500 k–combat	Same as 3rd Drones Satellites Press & Media	Battlefield – Enemy Country Dispersed sleeper cells Civilian Targets Use Enemy Country's resources & laws Gen Staff–Complex	Live off enemy land High Tec Weapons	2001 – 21st Century

Treatment of the Conquered – Genocide; kill all men of fighting age, enslavement and / or intermarriage with women and children; leave in ruins to fend for themselves; rehabilitation / nation building.

ISLÂM & WAR

Oriana Fallaci (1929-2006), an anti-fascist partisan, Italian journalist, political interviewer and author, wrote several books attempting to warn Europe about Islâm. In *La Forza della Ragione*, 70 she interviewed **Yasser Arafat** (1929-2004) in Amman, Jordan. The Nobel Peace Prize laureate told her that **Islâm and National Socialism (Hitlerism) were similar.** Following this interview, she traveled to Beirut, Lebanon to meet his rival, George Habash (Marxist / Eastern Orthodox 1926-2008), head of the Popular Front for Palestinian Liberation. In the presence of a bodyguard, who held a pistol to her head, Habash stated, "*Our revolution is but a moment in a worldwide revolution. It is not limited to the re-conquest of Palestine. We need to be honest and admit that we want to arrive at a war like the war in Vietnam – that we want another Vietnam; and not only for Palestine, but for all Arab Countries. The Palestinians are part of the Arab nation. It is therefore necessary that the entire Arab nation unleash a full-out war against America and Europe. May America and Europe know that we are just at the beginning of the beginning, that the best is yet to come. That from now on there will not be peace for them. (We intend) to advance step by step, millimeter by millimeter, year after year, decade after decade, determined, obstinate, patient. This is our strategy, a strategy moreover, that we will enlarge.*"

Habash's predictions were accurate. On March 20, 2003 Iraq was invaded and "conquered." Saddam Hussein was captured on December 13. The occupation of Iraq and Afghan war degenerated into a "politically correct," Vietnamized war of attrition between our troops and their mostly foreign "insurgents / terrorists" or guerillas. On the morning of 7/7/05 the London subway and a double-decker bus were bombed. 52 civilians and 4 terrorists died and 700 were injured. There has been no report on the collateral economic damages. All 4 suicide bombers were Islâmic. The press reported that "cults" cause "criminal" attacks. The London Police called them "terrorists" or "bombing suspects." Bulana Shahid Raza, head of the Leicester Central Mosque declared, "There should be a clear distinction between the suicide bombing of those who are trying to defend themselves from occupiers [probably referring to bombers killing American soldiers in Iraq], which is something different from those who kill civilians, which is a big crime." Raza called for "planners of last week's atrocity being brought to justice." Other British imams called it, "utterly criminal," and declared that the *Korân* forbids killing "innocent" civilians. [This contradicts the *Korân*; see **9:5**.] Many imams fumed over the usual litany of causes: "Islâmophobia, racism, unemployment, economic deprivation, social exclusion, alienating our children, driving them to anger and desperation." Raza declared they needed *"understanding, not bashing."* He added that killing an innocent person was tantamount to killing all mankind (**5:32**), but neglected to quote **5:33**, hoping that our ignorance of the *Korân* would bamboozle most. For us, Jews or Christians, who allegedly *"spread disorder in the land"* we should *"be put to death or crucified or have* (our) *hands and feet cut off on alternate sides, or be banished from the country."* Christians in the Sudan had been subjected to this kind of punishment. He did not disclose that "love" does not apply to "Infidels" or that Muhammad said, "*War is deceit.*" (Sahih al-Bukhari, Vol.[4] Book 52, #269) For those not of Islâm it is convert or die.

Tony Blair saw it differently and came under criticism because of his views. "The terrorist cause is not founded on an injustice ... it is founded on a belief, one whose fanaticism is such that it cannot be modified, it cannot be remedied." Since 11 September 2001 many have asked the question about how a "peaceful religion" such as Islâm can accept the dastardly attack on the World Trade Center towers that killed innocent civilians engaging in their daily occupations. Why is it that Muslim clerics have not condemned this frightful act and distanced themselves from it? The real question is whether Islâm is really "peaceful?"

A "Religion of Peace?"

"*Beware of false prophets, which come to you in sheep's clothing, but inwardly they are ravening wolves. Ye shall know them by their fruits.*" (Matt 7:15-16)

The Arab Mind by Raphael Patai describes harsh discipline imposed on boys and women. It would be called "abuse" in our society. The level of violence in Arab feuds is also unusual. According to Patai, you cannot take the Arab out of Islâm, but history has shown that Arab influence can be lessened. Arab oil revenues reached phenomenal levels in the mid-1970s. The Saudis and others chose to devote much of this wealth to the restoration of and the building of new mosques. Since the Saudis built or repaired them, they claimed the right to populate them with their imams, Wahhabists.

An analysis of wars around the world by Samuel P Huntington (1927-2008) 71 showed that Islâm has "bloody borders." 72 The difference between militarism of Muslim and Christian Countries was striking. According to Ted R Gurr between 1993 and 1994 quoted by Huntington, "Muslims were participants in twenty-six of fifty ethnopolitical conflicts. Note that these data were collected before bin-Laden's declaration of jihād.

Table III Intracivilization and Intercivilization Warfare in 1993-4

	Intracivilization	Intercivilization	Total
Islâm	11	15	26
Others	19	5	24
Total	30	20	50

There were three times as many intercivilizational conflicts involving Muslims as there were conflicts between all non-Muslim civilizations. In 1993 the *New York Times* identified 48 locations involving fifty-nine ethnic conflicts. In half, Muslims fought with other Muslims or non-Muslims. Thirty-one of the fifty-nine were between groups from different civilization and 21 of these were between Muslims and others; three times as many intercivilizational conflicts involved Muslims as opposed to others.

Table IV Ethnic Conflicts 1993 – *New York Times* data

	Intracivilization	Intercivilization	Total
Islâm	7	21	28
Others	21	10	31
Total	28	31	59

In 1992, according to Ruth Leger Sivard there were twenty-nine wars in progress. Nine of twelve intercivilizational conflicts were between Muslims and non-Muslims and the Muslims were fighting more wars than people from any other civilization.

The tendency of Islâm towards violence is also suggested by the degree of militarization of society. A "Force Ratio" involves the number of soldiers per 1000 of the total population. "Military effort" is the percent of public revenues devoted to military activity. In the 1980s Muslim countries had military force ratios and military effort indices far in excess of other countries.

Table V Force Ratios & Military Effort

	Average Force Ratio	Average Military Effort
Muslim (n = 25)	11.8	17.7
Other countries (n = 112)	7.1	12.3
Christian countries (n = 57)	5.8	8.2
Other religions (n = 80)	9.5	16.9

The difference between militarism of Muslim and Christian Countries is striking. The table shows the average force ratios and average "military effort". In 25 Muslim countries the average force ratio was 11.8 and the military effort was 17.7. In 57 Christian countries the force ratio was 5.8 and the military effort was 8.2. The author states that Muslim states have had a tendency to resort to violence in international crises. Between 1928 and 1971 they used violence to settle 76 crises out of a total of 142 or 53.5%. In contrast during this time the rate for settling crises with violence was 11.5% for the United Kingdom, 17.9% for the U.S., and 28.5% for the Soviet Union. Only China's rate was higher at 76.9%. [73]

A recent KFN study by the German Interior Ministry and the Institute for Criminology Research of Lower Saxony 74 found violent tendencies among young devout Muslim immigrants in Germany. It concluded: "***the more devout young Muslims become, the more prone to violence they get.***" They interviewed 45,000 14-16-year-olds in 61 cities across Germany between 2007 and 2008. 10,000 had immigrant background. It found that the best adjusted Muslims came from nonreligious families. These went to school and 41% were interested in obtaining a high school diploma, about 63% had German friends and 66% considered themselves Germans. Among those "practicing" Muslims only 16% were pursuing a high school diploma, 22% had German friends and about 22% considered themselves German. They also concluded that the problem lay with the teaching by non-German Imams. Most did not speak German and were temporary residents. The opposite was true among Christian immigrants into Germany. "*The willingness to commit violent crimes, such as armed robbery or assault and battery, among young Catholics and Protestants decreases with religious fervor, the KFN study revealed.*"

This is not to say that Muslims never live peacefully with their neighbors because during parts of history they have. Recently apologists have cited various excuses for their violent behavior. Some note the rapid increase in numbers of children among Muslim peoples and believe this may be the root causes of clashes in the countries along the southern Russian border and in the Balkans. Others point to the population explosion among Muslim groups and the lack of employment of males may also be part of the problem. [75] Although crowding tends to make certain species more aggressive and neurotic, mankind adjusts. Many peoples in this world live under very crowded circumstances without too much difficulty; the Japanese are a classic example. Some ascribe this aggressiveness to a lack of financial means. However, according to FBI Uniform Crime Reports during the great depression in America, there was less personal criminal activity than there was after the 1960s when personal wealth rose. Some societies seem to regard theft as a right of conquest. This has been especially true among peoples of the Middle East and the North African Coast. It was a practice used by Muhammad. Strength through humility, a great Christian virtue, tends to keep many from theft, disrespectful treatment of others, and gossip. The *Korân* does not promote these virtues when Infidels are involved.

Others say that from the beginning Islâm has been "a religion of the sword" and glorifies the virtues of war. Even a casual reading of the Korân should convince the skeptic on this point. However, despite their doctrine not to fight among themselves – *fitna* – their initial *jihād* against the Infidels of the 7th and 8th centuries rapidly degenerated into internal squabbles. The *Korân* contains few prohibitions against violence. The doctrine of *lex tallionis* or retribution – "an eye for an eye," is approved. (**2:178, 194**) (**5:45**). Contrast this with Christ's teachings (Matt 5:38-39). There is also the tendency to convert by the sword. Again, Christ counseled against this (Matt 26:52). Conquered peoples who convert to Islâm are spared. As an absolutist faith, Muslim majorities have a great deal of trouble living in the same country with other minorities while other religions have little difficulty with Muslim minorities. Islâm also tends to merge religion and politics more than others. By necessity politics and religion are not separated. The *Korân* contain the roots of Sharia Law which developed over time after Muhammad's death and have evolved ever since. The *Korân* does not recognize equality of people before God (**2:90**) (**5:54, 64**) and does not recognize the free agency or free will of individuals (**2:186**) (**65:3**). Without agency and faith (Heb 11:1) progress and secular invention are discouraged (D&C 104:17). For a Muslim cleric to denounce the attacks made against the U.S. (a mostly Christian and Jewish country of unbelievers) would be to renounce a significant part of the *Korân* that predicts and promotes the destruction of Infidels at the hand of believers. It also owes much of its militancy to Wahhabism and the Muslim Brotherhood as will be mentioned. Although the state of Israel is often cited as the principal reason for modern Islâmic warfare, the Muslim Brotherhood established in 1928 and Wahhabism beginnings in the 18th Century invalidate this assertion. Israel was formed in 1948. These two organizations are devoted to Islâmic law and terrorism to enforce it. Their targets include the "lukewarm" of Islâm as well as the Infidels. (**2:191**) (**4:89**) (**5:33**) (**8:39**) (**9:29**) The *Korân* is a religious work that advocates the destruction or conversion of all unbelievers. Many past monarchs and dictators motivated by religion and lusting for riches and power waged horrible war. There is no need to invoke Marx's convoluted logic of "class struggle" as a cause. The dogma of the *Korân* makes it clear that Infidels must convert or die. Fundamentalist Islâm perceives "the West" as morally weak and without nerve. Now that much of the Arab world is flush with oil money, this is an ideal time to rid the world of Infidels and the "less active" of their own faith and make the whole world bow to Islâmic law. Now is the time for *jihād*. According to Bin-Laden this is a religious or "holy war."

Peace and Sharia Law

Islâm's definition of peace differs from the West's. "Peace" to us is: "*l. freedom from war or civil strife 2. a treaty or agreement to end war, 3 freedom from public disturbance or disorder; public security; law and order. 4. freedom from disagreement or quarrels; harmony, concord. 5 an undisturbed state of mind; absence of mental conflict; serenity. 6 calm; quiet; tranquility.*" 76 A discussion on the Dar al-Islâm, or 'House of Islâm,' and Dar al-Harb, or 'house of War' is noted below. The *Korân* discusses this topic in **6**:127-133. Anyplace where Sharia Law is in force, by definition, is in a state of "peace." Any place where Sharia is not is in a state of "war." To Islâm, "peace" means the establishment of Sharia Law.

There are many faithful adherents to Islam and Christianity who will find this history difficult to believe. However, the *Korân*, the Hadiths, ancient and modern resources are what they are. There are many who do not know the written doctrines of their faith or their history. They rely on what they are told by political and church leaders. As for the war-like characteristics of both sides and to all those faithful and honest of heart who do goodness in the name of both religions, we must consider the characteristics of many of their present and past leaders who sought power in the name of their religion.

What are Arab, Islâm, & the *Korân*?

Who Was Muhammad?

To understand "Arab" and "Islâm" requires knowing about their culture and religion. Islâm is serious about religion. It guides its politics, law, personal beliefs and conduct. This is foreign and confusing to us in the relativistic, secular West. In the *Bible* Jeremiah described Arabs as people who polluted the land with whoredoms and wickedness (Jer: 3:2) and as a "mingled people" who "dwell in the desert." (Jer 24:24) Isaiah said they were nomads who pitched tents. (Isaiah 13:20) In 1 Kings 10:15 they are depicted as wealthy merchants who traffic in spices. In 2 Chron 9:14 their kings bring gold and silver to Solomon. Ezekiel also described those from Sheba as merchants in lambs, rams, goats, and in "*all sorts of things, in blue clothes, broidered work, in chests of rich apparel, bound with cords, and made of cedar*" (Ezek 27:19-24). Matthew described three "wise men" from the East who paid homage to Jesus at his birth by bringing gifts associated with temple worship – gold, frankincense, and myrrh (Matt 2: 1-12). Paul describes the Arab's position with regards to the blood lines of the priesthood, "*For it is written, that Abraham had two sons, the one by a bondmaid, the other by a freewoman. But he who was of the bondwoman was born after the flesh; but he of the freewoman was by promise. Which things are an allegory: for these are the two covenants; the one from the mount Sinai, which gendereth to bondage, which is Agar (Hagar). For this Agar is mount Sinai in Arabia, and answereth to Jerusalem which now is, and is in bondage with her children. But Jerusalem which is above is free, which is the mother of us all.*" (Gal 4:22-26) Like all of us, the Arabs of the ancient world received mixed reviews.

Arabs cannot be described as a single people. There are nomadic Bedouin tribes, pastoral Arabs, and settled Arabs. Those who settled founded great civilizations along the Tigris and Euphrates Rivers in Assyria (Kurdistan), Babylon (the middle section around Baghdad) and Sumeria in the delta and lower reaches of the twin-rivers. There were also the settled Arabs of Saba / Sheba whose empire included much of African Abyssinia. All these Arabs were heavily invested in agriculture, trade and mining, especially gold in Abyssinia. Strategic control of the Bab el Mandeb, "*the gate of tears,*" at the southern end of the Red Sea and the Strait of Hormuz that opens into the Persian Gulf, meant control of sea trade with Africa, China and India in the ancient western world. To a large extent, it still does.

The pastoral Arabs settled in towns and villages in the Arabian Peninsula especially near the western mountains. Mecca and Medina are examples. These were near water sources such as mountain streams, oases and developed wells where herding and agriculture was easier. The Bedouin had less water, were mostly herders and hunters. For lack of water they could not wash often and were known as "black" Arabs by some. They were the least "civilized." Pastoral Arabs and Bedouins tended to remain in a tribal society.

In the modern era Raphael Patai offers helpful insights. He quotes the philologist all-Tha'alibi (died 1038), "Whoever loves the Prophet (Muhammad) loves the Arabs, and whoever loves the Arabs loves the Arabic language in which the best of books was revealed ... whomsoever God had guided to Islâm ... believes that Muhammad is the best of prophets ... that the Arabs are the best of peoples ... and that Arabic is the best of languages." [77] Patai defines an Arab as one who speaks Arabic as his native language and thus "feels" Arab. [78] See also (**2:143**) (**3:110**) (**62:2**) (**41**:3) (20:**113**) (43:**3**). Patai makes further important observations.

Arabs believe they are the basis of Islâm and therefore other Muslim nations. They founded Islâm and spread it throughout much of the world. From their point of view the world is divided into an inner and outer circle. The inner one representing Islâm is the *Dar al-Islâm*, or "House of Islâm;" the outer, represents the rest of the world – *Dar al-Harb*, or "house of War." Islâm which includes the concept of *salaam* or "peace" indicates that wherever there is Islâm, there is "peace." [79] This is not unlike the Mormon concept of Zion – a place where the Saints dwell. However, we must consider these concepts hypothetical because as we know, man is man and there is no perfect or completely peaceful society on earth where man lives.

Patai continues his discussion by drawing an analogy of a fruit with three parts. The seed or Arab world is its most valuable part. The flesh of the fruit represents a protective covering. It is the Muslim world that derives its strength from the inner core. The skin is the world of Infidels who demonstrate "the inscrutability of the ways of Allah." Patai criticizes a book by the Syrian scholar, Muhammad Kurd 'Alī (1876-1953) *Islâm and Arab Civilization* because he uses the words, Arab, Muslim, and Bedouin interchangeably and does not distinguish between "Arab" and "Bedouin." In addition, he does not discriminate between "Arab," and "Muslim." [80] My own observations are the same as Patai's. Distinguishing the difference between Arab and Bedouin and Arab and Muslim is difficult. You can't take the Arab or his idealized Bedouin culture out of Islâm and you can't take Islâm out of the Arab. However, the Arabs seem to make a distinction between themselves and their somewhat second class Islâmic brethren of South East and Central Asia and the Indian sub-continent.

The *Korân*

The scriptural basis for Islâm is the *Korân*. Like much scripture it is difficult for many in the secular modern world to read. It is not in chronological order and its chronology has been determined by experts. Such an arrangement is not unusual. The Pauline Epistles as they occur in the *New Testament* are also not in chronological order. Much like the *Korân* they are placed according to length except for *Hebrews*, which appears at the end and may have been written by Timothy. The chronology of the sūras has been worked out by the several academics cited in this work. Their conclusions are close, but not exact. They all agree on which sūras were from Mecca (610-622) and Medina (622 – 632).

Islâmic doctrine found in the *Korân* comes from five sources: 1 Ancient Arab paganism, 2. Persian Zoroastrianism, 3. Judaism 4. Christianity and 5. Muhammad's revelations and interpretations of these sources. A number of criticisms of Muhammad and Islâm have been made; many are found within the *Korân* itself. These can be summarized as follows:

1. Muhammad may have had trances or epilepsy to explain his revelations; there is evidence of a progressive central nervous system disorder that explains his revelations, his increasing libido and militancy in the last 22 years of his life (610-632).
2. Some of the *Korân* appears to be borrowed from Christianity, Zoroastrianism and Judeo-Christian mythology / apocryphal sources.
3. Militancy against infidels is mild in the early sūras. God will take care of this problem. In the later sūras it becomes harsh with the believers responsible for blotting it out. Thus, God is inconsistent.
4. Muhammad suffered from sexual urges probably part of his illness. These may have colored his visions of Paradise. However, these practices were common in the ancient world and are found in the revelations of the early Meccan period.
5. Muhammad did not preserve his revelations in a cohesive permanent record. This permitted those that followed to make additions and alterations.
6. Muhammad believed he was only a prophet in a long line of others whose duty was to correct the religion of Christians, Jews and pagan Arabs. He was not interested in establishing a religion with structure and priesthood that could keep doctrine pure. He

described himself as an Apostle of God and "warner" to society. In the final 10 years of his life he built an army of supporters that engaged in power politics and military conquest.

7. Muhammad's life style and behavior portrayed in the *Korân*, Hadīths, and history weakens his claim as a prophet.
8. There is ample evidence that the *Korân* has been altered. The *Korân* mentions changing concepts (**16**:101) and one of the later sūras (**2:106**) introduces the doctrine of abrogation that validates changes made later. The concept of an unchanging God that can only speak the truth is not supported in the *Korân*. God is also the best layer of plots (**3:54; 8:30**)
9. Conversion to Islâm is often carried out under duress by the sword.
10. The *Korân* contains many stories from Judeo-Christian scripture and mythology. Despite challenges to the contrary, the *Korân* could be fabricated in part by a person who knew this material.
11. The *Korân's* major flaw is that recorded revelations were not kept under close observation or published early. Publication took place years after Muhammad's death. Alterations, interpretations, and additions were possible.
12. The oldest validated *Korân* is either in Tashkent dating from 651 or in the British Museum dating from 790. In either case it comes to us years after Muhammad's death. Ancient Jewish and Christian scripture have the same problem.

In the George Sale translation of the *Korân* Muhammad's name appears in 46 verses, Jesus in 35 and Mary in 31. The *Korân* also refers to itself 149 times. This varies from translation to translation depending on the use of pronouns. The *Korân* includes many references to parts of the *Old Testament*, the *New Testament* plus other materials from the Jewish and Christian culture in the Middle East (Arabia); these are outlined later.

Evolution of Scriptures

During the pre-Islamic 5th and 6th centuries AD, there was warfare between Christian and Jewish communities in Arabia. Muhammad expected help from the Jews in proclaiming monotheism. (Deut 6:4), and expected them to convert to Islâm. Jews were at odds with Christians who held to a more traditional concept of God. The *Torah* refers to God the creator / planner, the Spirit of God and "Jehovah God" or "Jehovah" the "builder" and "law giver." These are discussed in detail elsewhere. The *Spirit of God* is associated with the prophets, but is not mentioned in the Old Testament after Ezekiel 11:24 (about 598 BC – beginning of the Babylonian Captivity). He is identified in Christ's baptism (Matt3:16) as a "dove" and later in the New Testament in many places as the Holy Ghost (1 Cor 2:9-14).

Early Islâm prayed in the direction of Jerusalem; this is discussed later. When the Jews would not convert, Muhammad became angry with them and seems to have turned more to the Christian communities, but later he fought Byzantium. 'Uthman's burning old scripture rather than preserving it makes study of Islâm's religious evolution in the 70 years following Muhammad's death (632) difficult. This is the critical period when the *Korân* may have evolved under 'Uthmān, an Umayyad or even those that followed. The *Korân* is silent on its proper disposal; this is a matter of scholarly opinion.

The Septuagint, a translation of the Old Testament into Greek from the original Hebrew was written by scholars in Alexandria sometime before 132 BC. This was necessary since many of the Jews had come under Hellenistic influences following the conquests of Alexander the Great (356-323 BC) and spoke only Greek. This translation was used extensively by many Christians following the death of Christ. Greek was an easier language than Hebrew.

The validation of the *Old Testament* goes back to 200 BC to AD 60 in the form of the *Dead Sea Scrolls*. Jesus left no personal written scripture although he is alleged by Eusebius to have received a letter from King Agbarus and replied to him. [81] Others wrote what He did and said, but out of a 3-year mission we have only the events of 31 days. Early Christian sources also have an extensive history with almost all of the *New Testament* validated by direct quotations from early church fathers within 150 years of Christ's life and by actual documents and fragments that occurred earlier. Deliberate destruction of sources makes the *Korân* a more difficult study.

The concept of linear history was uncommon in the ancient world. History was more circular and was dated based on the life of kings during their rule. This continued through the Roman Period. The *Bible* contains the first well known linear history. It begins in the Pentateuch and continues in Joshua, Judges, Samuel, Chronicles and Kings. It is carried forward in many of the Prophets and in much of the Apocrypha. Titus Flavius Josephus (AD 37-100) followed it closely in his *Antiquities*. It was only towards the end of the Roman Empire that A.D. and B.C. were used in dates. There are Christian, Jewish, and pagan sources of information about Islâm during the 7th Century, but these are sparse.

There were Christian communities in parts of Arabia. Paul reported this in Galatians 1:17 written sometime from AD 48-58. *"Neither went I up to Jerusalem to them which were apostles before me; but I went into Arabia, and returned again unto Damascus.* Galatia was in the central Turkish highlands. It is likely that later the Eastern and Syriac branches of Christianity such as the Nestorians (5th Century AD) and Monophysites (6th Century AD) sects were present in the Arabian Peninsula. Tradition says that Muhammad heard Christian preaching at the fair of Ukaz, and he probably heard more when he conducted caravans for his first wife, Khadīja. Gospel stories derived apparently from non-canonical works, such as the *Gospel of the Nativity*, occur in the *Korân*. A mistaken notion of the Trinity as defined by the Nicene Creed was sharply attacked in the *Korân* (**5:72-77**).

Alexander Stille states in *Scholars Scrutinize the Korân's Origin* that there is no evidence for a written *Korân* before 691 [82] when the Dome of the Rock was built. He also states that *Korânic* inscriptions written in the Dome of the Rock differ from those in the *Korân*. He suggests that the *Korân* was undergoing revision between then and the earliest complete texts that exist. The George Sale translation of the *Korân* refers to itself 149 times; however, it then contradicts this "*O true believers, inquire not concerning things which, if they be declared unto you, may give you pain; but if ye ask concerning them* ***when the Korân is sent down****, they will be declared unto you:*" (**5:105**) Chapter 5 is either the last or second to last chapter of the *Korân* and thus (**5:105**) abrogates all previous references to the *Korân*.

Much of what we know about Islâm comes from the Hadiths that were written 130 to 300 years following Muhammad's death. Professor Roy Mottahedeh of Harvard University states that many Muslims accept that Islâm came from monotheistic thought prevalent in the Middle East. Monotheism in this part of the world probably originated from the Greek philosophical writings of Plato (about 428 – 347 BC). These influenced Judaism following the conquest of the region by Alexander the Great and influenced Christianity following the death of the Apostles during the period of Roman persecution. The *Korân* 18:**83-98** includes a curious mention of Alexander the Great (Dhu'lkarnein) that is alleged to have come from the Haggadah, a Jewish source of Biblical Myths. [83]

There is evidence of some early stylistic studies of the *Korân;* however, these are not freely available on line. Scholars such as Gerd Puin and Christoph Luxenberg at Saarland University in Germany comment that the earliest known copies of the *Korân* include no vowels or diacritical marks that modern Arabic uses to clarify what is meant. Those that came later may have been guessing about ambiguities. This is not unlike the problems faced by translators of ancient Hebrew. Early Aramaic texts may more accurately describe what is meant in the Arabic texts of the time. However, early Aramaic texts about the *Korân* have not been found.

According to professor Luxenberg the passages in the *Korân* that describe paradise can be traced to a Christian text known as *Hymns of Paradise* by Ephraem of the Syriac School (AD 306-373). Paradise was derived from the Aramaic word for garden and all the descriptions of paradise described it as a garden of flowing waters, abundant fruits and white raisins, a delicacy in the ancient Middle East. The word *hur* means white raisin. Professor Luxenberg states that this word might have been mistranslated into *huris*. Martyrs may be disappointed to have traded their lives for white raisins instead of virgins. The Hadiths support virgins.

Professor Andrew Rippin, an Islâmic scholar at the University of Victoria in British Columbia, Canada states that when he teaches history, students are surprised about the amount of independent thought that existed in the early centuries of Islâm when compared with the tendency to restrict such thinking in more recent times.

The *Korân's* book of Joseph (sūra 12) contains materials found in Thaʿlabīʿs collection of traditional stories from descendants of Jewish refugees to Persia following the destruction of Jerusalem by the Romans in 70 AD. According to Hugh W. Nibley[84] this book was written before 1036, the year Thaʿlabī died. An analysis of this chapter is found in Appendix III.

The *Korân* also includes references to "crucifixion" as a punishment in ancient Egypt. (**12**:41) Roman style crucifixion using a cross was not used in Egypt; however, prisoners of war and criminals were impaled on stakes and then hung from trees as an example to those who considered rebellion. Exactly how this word is used in the *Korân* is unknown. Likewise, it is unknown how stories in Thaʿlabī 's collection of the 11th Century found their way into the *Korân*. Chances are that they came from common traditional oral or written sources.

At first glance one might believe that the *Korân's* description of Paradise was ready made for young soldiers urged to sacrifice themselves for the cause. However, these revelations originated during the Meccan period and not the Medinan period when conquest was being pursued.

Laws relating to women in the *Korân* are typical of many tribal societies. Some claim that they were more liberal than those before. The Bible gives a different picture for the House of Israel. Bible stories include many names of women and many stories about them. Within the first 30 chapters of Genesis these names Eve, Milcah, Sarai (honored along with Abram with a new name, Sarah), Hagar, Keturah, Rebekah, Leah, Rachael,

Bilhah, Zilpah, and Dinah all appear. All this was 1000 years before the revelations of the *Korân*. The *Korân* mentions only one other woman besides Mary, mother of Jesus – 'Ā'isha in **24:11**, Muhammad's first or second harem wife, when she is accused of infidelity.

Korânic fragments have turned up over the years indicating that the *Korân* has undergone alterations. A careful honest look at the *Korân* should include stylistic analysis. The progressive militancy within its pages during the Medina period may be the result of corruptions, glossing, notations, and misinterpretations added later by others for other than religious purposes. These are unlike the more tolerant poetic verses of the Early-Mecca period.

The chase after "the historical Jesus" has been popular for the past 150 years. He gets brief mention by Josephus. [85] *"Now, there was about this time Jesus, a wise man, if it be lawful to call him a man, for he was a doer of wonderful works – a teacher of such men as receive the truth with pleasure. He drew over to him both many of the Jews, and many of the Gentiles. He was Christ; and when Pilate, at the suggestion of the principal men amongst us, had condemned him to the cross, those that loved him at the first did not forsake him, for he appeared to them alive again the third day, as the divine prophets had foretold these and ten thousand other wonderful things concerning him; and the tribe of Christians, so named from him, are not extinct at this day."* There is some dispute over the validity of this passage, but all copies now in existence of *Antiquities* include it regardless of their origin. Josephus also mentions Jesus as brother of the martyred James in *Antiquities* 20.9.1. He is also mentioned by Tacitus (AD 54-119) as founder of the Christian religion and that he was put to death by Pontius Pilate during the reign of Tiberius. He is mentioned by Suetonius (AD 75-160), by Pliny the Younger (61-115) in a letter to Trajan. The Catholic Encyclopedia mentions other sources from pagans, Jews and Christians. [86]

Investigation into the historical evidence of Muhammad is also frustrating. "Muhammad" is mentioned in a number of verses in the *Korân*; see the Topical Guide. However, this may not be the name of a person; it is also a title meaning "The Blessed One." Muhammad is mentioned as a person in *The Life of Muhammad,* (A translation of Ishāq's Sīrat Rasül Allāh) written about 700 and in the *Sīra* by Ibn-Hisham, about 200 years after his death. Problems with the history of Islâm are outlined in two online references. [87] [88]

The Dome of the Rock is another enigma. Muslims claim it commemorates the night Muhammad spoke with Allah in Heaven or the Mi'raj. However, it is not designed as a mosque. It is octagonal and has no *Qibla*. Inscriptions in the dome date from 694. Most are neither from the

Korân nor in Arabic. There is no mention of the Mi'raj; most are in a Syro-Aramaic calligraphy that speaks of a dispute over the divinity of Christ between Syrian and Hellenistic Christians. Nestorian Christians did not believe in the virgin birth or the resurrection of Jesus. It is possible that the building was originally a Nestorian church that became an Islâmic Mosque.

Saint John of Damascus (670-753), Mansur ibn Sarjun Al-Taghlibi, a credible source, was Arab born and reared as a Christian in Islâmic Damascus. He received both a Muslim and Christian education. His father, despite his Christianity, served the Umayyad Caliphs supervising taxes for the Middle East. Saint John of Damascus later held a similar position of trust. Afterwards he sought orders in the Syriac Christian Church and wrote *On Heresies*, a book that claimed the Ishmaelites were Umayyad Christians and this is why there is a "Jesus Minaret" at the Umayyad Mosque in Damascus. Umayyad Christians claimed that Jesus would return there when He came again. Even coinage of Arabia in the 7th century immediately following Muhammad's death depicts Christian symbols. All this suggests that early Islâm had a strong Christian beginning. This may be why Islâm paid no attention to a religious structure, clergy or a hierarchy and instead concentrated on civil law, government and conquest. Paul Johnson does not agree. [89] He traces Islam back to Jewish influences rather than Christian and describes it as a heterodox movement within Judaism which diverged to become a separate religion and sites a long presence of Judaism in Arabia dating back to 600 BC or earlier. According to Johnson Muhammad accepted the Jewish God and their prophets, the idea of fixed law embodied in scripture, many of their dietary restrictions, a reluctance to commit oral law to writing, but eventually did. Both submitted points of law to their rabbis or muftis. In my opinion it is not an either / or proposition. As will be shown later, the *Korân* contains the influences of both Judaism and Christianity blended with a dash of Zoroastrianism plus the concepts of Allah, and the other ancient beliefs from Arabia.

Another major question considering the emphasis that Jesus and his mother, the virgin Mary receive in the *Korân* is whether or not the title, "Blessed One" or "Muhammad" refers not to the prophet of the movement, but rather to Jesus the Messiah. A later inscription in the Dome of the Rock gives the Islâmic Creed mentioning Muhammad.

The *Korân* is arranged in chapters with some idea of theme; however, many see it only as a collection of disconnected ideas. Although there is mention of faith, the attributes of God and his mercy do not extend to all of mankind, but only to "believers" (**2:130; 5:29**). The greatest problems in the *Korân* is the doctrine of abrogation (**2:106**), its concept of God, and its progressive militancy. This will be demonstrated later. Christianity and Judaism consider God to be "changeless." The militancy of the *Old Testament* against 7 specific tribes, living in the "promised land" and engaged in abominable practices that could corrupt the morals of the faithful is understandable. This is not the same as a universal world-wide militancy that the *Korân* levels at those who do not accept its teachings (**3:152**). Initially, the *Korân* leaves management of the Infidels to God. Later, believers are tested by having to cleanse the earth of them (**9:29, 123**) (**5:33**) (**47:4**).

Many Islâmic schools teach that Sūra 9 abrogates all previously tolerant attitudes towards unbelievers. If Allah is changeable, he is unlike the God of the *Old* and *New Testament*. "*For I am the LORD, I change not;*" (Malachi 3:6) and *"Till heaven and earth pass, one jot or one tittle shall in no wise pass from the law"* (Matt 5:18). According to the *Korân* Allah leads some astray into wickedness and takes part in plots and deceptions. In the *Old Testament* we read, "*Thou hast redeemed me, O LORD God of truth.*" (Ps 31:5). In the *New Testament* we find: "*Grace be with you, mercy, and peace, from God the Father, and from the Lord Jesus Christ, the Son of the Father, in truth and love*" (2 John 1:3). In Mormon Latter-day scripture we see: "*And truth is knowledge of things as they are, and as they were, and as they are to come; And whatsoever is more or less than this is the spirit of that wicked one who was a liar from the beginning. The Spirit of truth is of God. I am the Spirit of truth, and John bore record of me, saying: He received a fulness of truth, yea, even of all truth;"* (D&C 93:24-26).

If this is so, God does not and cannot change his mind about revelations given in truth. It is outside his nature. Earlier (**6**:115) denied the possibility of change in the *Korân*, but the law of abrogation (**2:106**) abolished (**6**:115). The *Korân* does not express the idea that Allah loves mankind but hates their sins (**6**:39). In this sense the *Korân* preaches a *"hell fire and damnation"* akin to fundamentalist Protestantism. Islâm's paradise is materialistic and highly sensual. The presence of (pederasty) with "pleasure youth" or [*ghilunan*] (52:17-28) (56:11-26) (76:**5-22**) goes against the Judeo-Christian teachings found in the *Old* and *New Testaments*. Muhammad honored father Abraham as he is described in the *Old Testament*. It was also the classic religion of the Patriarchs that Christ attempted to restore among the Jews, but they rejected it (Matt 23:37; Luke 13:34). According to the *Old Testament* it is through families that the Abrahamic Covenant will bless the earth. God promised Abraham, *"And thy seed shall be as the dust of the earth, and thou shalt spread abroad to the* *west, and to the east, and to the north, and to the south: and in thee and in thy seed shall* ***all the families of the earth*** *be blessed."* (Gen 28:14) Families are not described in the Islâmic paradise.

There is no acknowledgment of the *Old Testament's* many predictions of Christ. Although the *Korân* honors Christ and his virgin mother, His divinity and mission as Savior are denied. He is only an apostle sent by God (**5:72, 75**). There is no atonement, no constancy of doctrine, no priesthood, no church structure with apostles, priests, or divinely inspired hierarchy that might allow for further revelation and guidance. There is no reclaiming of the lost tribes (gathering), no plan of salvation or advancement towards perfection, no love of all mankind, and no marriage for eternity as described for Adam and Eve in Genesis and Matthew (Gen 2:22; Matt 19:6).

There is little free agency or free will (**13**:8). "Men" are not all equal in the eyes of Allah. The believer women are inferior to the believer men and seem to have a different heaven. Non-believer women can be used in any way by male believers if they are "slave girls" or booty taken in war. As such believer men, even those who are married, may have relations with them at any time they desire without it being sinful in the eyes of Allah (**4:24**) (23:**1-11**) (70:29-30). Believers may kill infidels, if they do not convert to Islâm, with throat cutting (**8:12**) (**47:4**) or burning by fire (**3:131**) (**9:14, 68**) (**33:64**). God is a respecter of persons. When one accepts Islâm, Allah is merciful; and this was predestined by God (**64:2**; 21:**101**; 74:31).

Islâm's lack of specified religious leadership (apostles, bishops, pastors, etc.) has left Islâm open to theocratic dictatorships or caliphates, often brutal and warlike. From its beginning it has been mired in politics and government. It has never been separate from a state. In this environment, Wahhabism and the Muslim Brotherhood flourish. In fact, even before the *Korân* was finally put together in written form under the caliphate of 'Uthmān about 30 years after Muhammad's death, a major schism occurred between Sunni and Shia. The *Korân* decries schisms in true religion (**2:137; 3:7**; 21:**92-93**; **30**:31-32). The feud between Sunni and Shia continues unabated. The *Encyclopaedia Britannica* [90] lists 96 sects within Islâm. Sects invalidate modern *Islâm* according to the *Korân*. (**30**:32), (**22:53**), (43:**65**), (**3:105**), (**2:256**), (**6**:159).

When the *New Testament* was finally put together about AD 360, the non-canonical texts that were excluded remained available for examination and discussion. The *Korân* refers to some. The same cannot be said for the *Korân's* origins. All sources and texts of Muhammad's sayings that predated 650 were destroyed according to Islâmic history. Some recent findings indicate this may not be true.

Apostasy & Change

Both Christianity and Judaism underwent apostasy immediately following the death of Christ and the sacking of Jerusalem in AD 70. Paul predicted it for Christianity in 2 Thessalonians 2:3. Christian doctrine became infected with Greek Philosophy, especially that of Plato and his concept of God. Despite efforts to make Christianity better understood and more palatable to the Roman Empire, persecutions lasted about 300 years and congregations were scattered and in hiding. Following the destruction of Jerusalem Temple in AD 70 Judaism evolved into a rabbinic form constantly on the move. During the rule of kings, Judaism underwent a fundamental change in its concept of God even to the point of paganism despite the efforts of numerous prophets. It is likely that Islâm underwent revision in its early years. Following Muhammad's death caliphs were the religious, military and state leaders. There was little peace. We have minimal knowledge of how the *Korân* came about and what may have been included, added, modified or deleted.

The floor plans of early mosques show that Islâm was undergoing considerable change in its first 100 to 200 years. According to the *Korân* Islâmic prayers were supposed to be offered towards Mecca. *"Many a time have We seen you (Muhammad) turn your face towards heaven. We will make you turn towards a quiblah that will please you. Turn your face towards the Holy Mosque; wherever you (believers) be, turn your faces towards it"* (**2:144**). These instructions are repeated twice more in **2:149-150**. Yet, archaeological evidence shows that many pre-8th century mosques had their sanctuaries aimed closer to Jerusalem than Mecca. The Qibla in the Kufa mosque built in 670 points west instead of southeast. [91] Two Umayyad mosques also in Iraq (650-750) show an orientation north of Mecca. The Wasit mosque and Baghdad mosques are off by 33 and 30°. The Amrb al 'As mosque near Cairo pointed too far north; it was corrected later. Jacob of Odessa, a Christian traveler, wrote a letter dated AD 705, now housed in the British Museum that Arabs in Egypt prayed facing east towards their patriarchal land (Palestine). Arab desert travelers were highly adept at navigating across desert landscapes. This was how they were able to move caravans and trade. It is inconceivable that they were confused about the way to Mecca. All this indicates that until the early 8th century, prayers were not directed towards Mecca. Between 705 and 715 the Caliph Walid I ordered the demolition and enlargement of all mosques. This may have marked the change when prayers were directed towards Mecca. Were **2:144, 149**, and **150** added later to make sure mosques of the future would face Mecca instead of Jerusalem?

This may also answer questions about Mecca itself. According to Islamic orthodoxy Mecca was founded about AD 400, but even this is controversial. Profane history of the time does not mention Mecca until the end of the 7th century. It was not on any international trade route. The claims of its founding in AD 400 will require independent study, but since unbelievers are prohibited entry into Mecca and Medina, [92] this is unlikely for now.

Arabic rock inscriptions of the Syro-Jordanian and Negev deserts, studied by Yehuda Nevo of Jerusalem University are useful to our understanding of the period from non-Muslim sources. It is always best to obtain evidence from direct sources when possible, but Muhammad said, "*War is deceit.*" Consequently, verification is necessary.

Arab religious texts of the late 7th century note a monotheistic creed with no reference to Muhammad. His name is found on inscriptions after 690. Muhammad as God's prophet appears first on an Arab-Sassanian coin about 690 struck in Damascus. The first appearance of the Tawhid appears in the Dome of the Rock dated 691. Before that the Muslim confession of faith cannot be found. Thus, it appears that Muhammad's status as prophet was not confirmed until after 684, 52 years after his death. Between 680 and 685 the Caliphate was in a state of constant change [Yazid I (680-83); Muawlyah II (683-684); and Marwan I (684-685)]. This was the time when the descendants of Abu Sufyan ibn Harb lost power as Caliphs.

As for the *Korân*, Islâmic history indicates that 'Umar, Abū Bakr, Zaid ibn Thābit (Muhammad's scribe born 610), Hodhaifa (a general) and Hafşah (Muhammad's 5th harem wife and Umar's daughter) all had a hand in its original compilation. From this source we believe that it came about in the midst of warfare and assassination occurring about 650-1. Although early texts and fragments of early texts may exist, none have apparently been studied in any great detail. The claim that the *Korân* fell from the sky and is the pure word of God is not validated by the textual, historical, or archaeological evidence. More will be said later. Islam has a history that has yet to be told. A quote from one of Sir Winston Churchill's radio talks in 1939 seems apropos – "*a riddle, wrapped in a mystery, inside an enigma.*" Like Russian historians, Islâm's greatest historians are those who can predict the past.

Islâm's Message

What is the message of Islâm and the *Korân*? The *shahadah* or Islâmic creed is simple: "God is One and Muhammad is His prophet." Part of Islâmic doctrine includes:

1. God is the creator of all things. He is responsible for the good and ill that befalls mankind. He has no sons or daughters. There is no Savior; He doesn't need one. He may change verses in his revelations as He sees fit, but will always replace them with better ones before voiding the old ones.
2. A woman who believes is worthy to be one of four wives for a believer man, but is worth only half a man in inheritance. She is like a field to be ploughed; believers are to go to their fields when they please (**2:224**). A woman must hide her attractive features from men not of her immediate family. If she is obedient and good, she is entitled to a non-descript paradise. Wives and children are a distraction from Allah. "*O true believers, verily **of your wives and your children ye have an enemy***" (**64:14**):
3. Islâm's laws are strict and just. Those who do not believe in Islâm must be destroyed so that the whole world can come under Islâm and enjoy the peace of Sharia Law. Our government follows Sharia Law. Muhammad is our Prophet. Follow his example.
4. If an Infidel truly converts to Islâm, he becomes one of us. Otherwise, it is no sin to kill an Infidel or fornicate with his women. Kill, ambush or maim all Infidel men wherever you find them; plunder their property; rape their wives, daughters, and pre-pubertal youth. Keep the best of their women and youth for your personal purposes, kill or enslave the rest. Islâm will give all *that your right hand possesses* for your pleasure here on earth.
5. If you are a man and die in the cause, you will be rewarded in Paradise with riches, food, plenty of cool water, shade, wine and fruit. You will never lift a finger. You will have endless sexual pleasure. As a believer you will eat, drink and be merry in this life, for tomorrow you will do the same in paradise. If you find all this hard to believe, you can find it in the *Korân.*

Readers of this work should understand that getting history right is a very difficult task. There can be many blind alleys and wrong turns that lead to erroneous conclusions. The fact is that Islâm has been in physical conflict with the rest of the world for much of its history. Muhammad stated that "war is deceit." War exists where ever Sharia Law is not. The *Korân,* itself, is full of abrogations. Consequently, anything we get from Islâmic sources during a declared *jihād* is suspect. My hope is that the information in this work will stimulate legitimate science and scholarship to investigate the first 200 to 300 years of Islâm and give us a documented, accurate portrayal of events that brought it into being. Whatever it is, Islâm seems to preserve the most restrictive features of Protestantism combined with the Roman Catholic Crusades and Inquisition.

Some Doctrinal Differences

Many believe that the God of Islam is the same God that Christians worship. This is claimed by some politicians, preachers, and much of the public. Nothing could be further from the truth. Their characteristics are different. There are also different concepts about the Christian God among Christians and between Christians and Jews. Christians depend on both the Old and New Testament for their beliefs; Jews depend on the Old.

According to the Christian concept of the Godhead, Father and Son work together for the same purpose. Some believe in a separation of the three persons while others combine them as a single spiritual being, but characteristics, combined or separate, are similar. Citations from the 4 Gospels attest to God's characteristics: (Matt 11:27; 28:19; Mark 13:32; Luke 10:22; John 1:14, 18; 3:35; 5:19, 20, 26, 30, 36, 37, 45; 6:27, 37, 44, 57; 8:16, 18, 28, 29; 10:15, 36, 38; 12:49, 50; 13:3; 14:6, 9, 10, 11, 13, 26, 28, 31; 15:9, 16, 26; 16:15, 16, 17, 23, 28, 32.).

The Jews do not believe in Christ as the Son of the Father. For the Christian, what can be said about Jesus Christ can be said about the Father (John 5:19, 30; 8:28). The God of the Jews and Godhead of Christians according to scripture have the following characteristics:

1. *Jehovah God* (Gen 2:4) formed the world and is everlasting to everlasting. He was God before the world was created, and the same God that he was, after it was created.

> "*Before the mountains were brought forth, or ever thou hadst formed the earth and the world, even from everlasting to everlasting, thou art God.*" (Psalm 90:2)

> "*But the mercy of the Lord is from everlasting to everlasting upon them that fear him, and his righteousness unto children's*

> *children, to such as keep his covenant, and to those that remember his commandments to do them.*" (Psalm 103:17-18)

> "*IN the beginning was the Word* (Jesus Christ), *and the Word was with God, and the Word was God. The same was in the beginning with God. All things were made by him; and without him was not any thing made that was made.*" (John 1:1-3)

Muslims and Christians agree that both God (a unified spirit) and Allah created the earth and heavens (**6:**73; 7:54; 7:185; **2:29**), but there the similarities end.

2. Jews and Christians believe God is merciful and longsuffering, abundant in goodness and truth. He executes righteousness and judgment for the oppressed. His mercy is from everlasting to everlasting and He is slow to anger.

> "*And the LORD passed by before him, and proclaimed, The LORD, The LORD God, merciful and gracious, longsuffering, and abundant in goodness and truth,*" (Exodus 34:6). "*The Lord executes righteousness and judgment for all that are oppressed. He made known his ways unto Moses, his acts unto the children of Israel. The Lord is merciful and gracious, slow to anger and plenteous in mercy:*" (Psalm 103:6-8). See also Nehemiah 9:17; Psalms 145:8; Joel 2:13; Joel 4:2; Nahum 1:3.

Although the *Korân* states that God is merciful this is not a universal form of mercy. He loves those who give alms, those who bridle anger and forgive men (**3:134**); those who are humble (**4:36**) and the repentant (**3:134-6**). He does not love "transgressors" (7:55), "every perfidious unbeliever" (**22:38**) or "wicked doers" (**3:57**). This is not as a Christian might say that God loves the man, but not the sin.

3. Jews and Christians believe that God is a God of truth and does not lie. "*God is not a man, that he should lie; neither the son of man that he should repent*" (Num 23:19). "*In hope of eternal life, which God, that cannot lie, promised before the world began*" (Titus 1:2); "*He is the Rock, his work is perfect: for all his ways are judgment: a God of truth and without iniquity, just and right is he*" (Deuteronomy 32:4).

In the case of Allah, "*GOD laid a plot against them; and GOD is the best layer of* plots" (8:30).

Also, "The hypocrites act deceitfully with GOD, but he will deceive them; and when they stand up to pray, they stand carelessly, affecting to be seen of men, and remember not GOD, unless a little, wavering between faith and infidelity, and adhering neither unto these nor unto those: and for him whom GOD shall lead astray" (4:142-143). He also advises, "take not the Jews or Christians for *your friends;* they *are friends the one to the other; but whoso among you taketh them for his friends, he is surely one of them: verily GOD directeth not unjust people*" (**5:51**). In addition, he also causes men to err or make mistakes: (**6**:39), (7:186), (**13**: 33), (17:**97**), (18:**17**), (**30**:29), (**35**:8), (**39**:23), (**40**:33), (**42**:44, 46), (74:31).

4. For Christians and Jews God does not change; there is no variableness with Him; He is the same

> "*Of old hast thou laid the foundation of the earth: and the heavens are the work of thy hands. They shall perish, but thou shalt endure: yea, all of them shall wax old like a garment; as a vesture shalt thou change them, and they shall be changed: But thou art the same, and thy years shall have no end*" (Psalm 102:25-27). "*For I am the LORD, I change not*" (Malachi 3:6);
>
> "*Jesus Christ the same yesterday, and today, and for ever*" (Heb 13:8). "*And, Thou, Lord, in the beginning hast laid the foundation of the earth; and the heavens are the works of thine hands: They shall perish; but thou remainest; and they all shall wax old as doth a garment; And as a vesture shalt thou fold them up, and they shall be changed: but thou art the same, and thy years shall not fail*" (Heb 1:10-12). "*Every good gift and every perfect gift is from above, and cometh down from the Father of lights, with whom is no variableness, neither shadow of turning*" (James 1:17).

In the earlier Meccan chapters of the *Korân*, God does not change (**10**:63-64). Towards the end of the Meccan period there seems to be doubt about whether or not God can abolish or confirm what he pleases (**13**:39). About the same time abrogation of previous words is considered possible (**16**:101), but then in the early Medina period the doctrine of abrogation is stated (**2:106**). Nowhere is this more apparent than in Allah's attitude toward people of other religious beliefs. Allah began as the ancient pagan Moon God of War and continued according to Muhammad's revelations.

Although there are many peaceful verses in the Koran especially in the Meccan period, the law of abrogation allows all these to be wiped away by such verses as **2:216; 47:4-6; 9:5, 29; 8:67; 5:33**.

5. Christians believe that God is no respecter of persons; but in every nation he that fears God and works righteousness is accepted of Him.

> "*Then Peter opened his mouth, and said, Of a truth I perceive that God is no respecter of persons: But in every nation he that feareth him, and worketh righteousness, is accepted with him.*" (Acts 10:34-35)

The Koran indicates that God is a respecter of those that he pleases. The phrase "*as he pleases*" occurs numerous times throughout the *Korân*. He cleanses (**24:21**), confirms (**13**:39) creates (**3:47; 5:17**; **28**:63; **30**:54; **35**:1; **42**:49; 82:8) *that which he pleases*. He curses many *as he pleases*: (**2:88, 89, 159, 161**) (**3:61, 87**) (**4:46, 47, 52, 93, 118**) (**5:13, 60, 64**,) (**9:68**) (**24:23**) (**33:61, 64, 68**) (**47:23**) (**48:6**) (**63:4**) (7:38, 44) (**11**:18, 99) (**13**:25) (**28**:42) (**40**:52) (15:**35**) (17:**60**) (38:**78**) (51:10). Others he delivers from danger and grief (**6**:63-64); however, he destroys unbelievers or Infidels and has mercy on believers (meaning those who follow Muhammad) *as he pleases*. (**3:141**), (**3:152**), (**5:17**), (**8:8**), (**8:54**), (**22:45**), (**47:10, 13**); (**6**:6) , (**6**:133), (7:4), (**14**:13), (**14**:19), (**16**:33), (**28**:43, 58, 59, 78), (**29**:31, 38, 39, 40), (**32**:26), (**42**:34), (**45**:24), (**46**:25, 27); (15:**60, 79**), (17:**7, 16, 58**), (18:**59**), (19:**74, 98**), (20:**61, 128**), (21:**6, 9, 95**), (23:**48**), (25:**36, 39**), (26:**139, 172, 208**), (27:**51, 57**), (36:**31**), (37:**136**), (38:**3**), (43:**8**), (44:**37**), (50:**36**), (54:**34, 51**); (51:41, 46), (53:50), (77:16), (91:14). Allah directs *as he pleases*: (**2:142**), (**2: 213**), (**2: 272**), (**6**:88), (**10**:25), (**16**:93), (**22:16**), (28:**56**), (**35**:8), (**39**:23); he does *what he pleases*: (**3:40**), (**14**:27), (**22:14**), (**22: 18**). He enriches (**9:28**), effects (**11**:107), (85:16) elects (**42**:13), extends his hand to (**2:245**) *whom he pleases*. He forgives and punishes *whom he pleases* (**2:284**), (**3:129**), (**5:18**), (**5: 40**), (**6**:133), (7:30), (7:155), (7:156), (17:**54**), (**48:14**), (**5:98**). He forms in the womb *what he pleases* (**3:6**), (**42**:49), (**42**:50): He frees you from what you ask of him *as he pleases* (**6**:41) and gathers his tribunal whenever he wants (**42**:29). He gives to and provides for *whom he pleases* (**2:90**), (**2:105**), (**2:212**), (**2:247**), (**2:261**), (**3:37**), (**3:73-74**), (**5:54**), (**5: 64**), (7:128), (**10**:107), (**13**:11), (**13**:26), (17:**30**), (**24:38**), (**28**:82), (**29**:62), (**30**:37), (**34**:36), (**34**;39), (**39**:52), (**42**:12), (**42**:19), (**2:27**), (**42**:49), (**57:21**), (**57:29**), (**59:6**), (**62:4**). He makes gardens *at his pleasure* (25:**10**). He is gracious *to those he pleases* (**12**:100) and he justifies (**4:49**) *whom he pleaseth*. He bestows knowledge *as he pleaseth* (**2:255**). He leads astray *those he pleases* (**4:88**), (**4:142-143**), (**6**:35), (**6**:39), (**6**:125), (7:178), (7:186), (**13**:27), (**16**:93), (**42**:8), (**42**:8), (**48:25**), (76:**31**). He gives mercy (**3:74**) and ordains (**5:1**) that *which he pleases.* He will confer mercy on *whom he pleases*; for God is endued with great beneficence. He sends to paradise *whom he pleases* (**57:21**) and pardons *whom he pleases* (**4:48**), (**4:116**). He protects *whom he pleaseth* (23:**88**) and punishes likewise (**11**:32-33), (**29**:21), (**33:24**). He sends hail (**24:43**), the spirit (**40**:15), thunderbolts (**13**:13) and wind and rain (**30**:48) *on whom he pleases.* He spares, withholds or bestows goods *on those he pleases*: (17:**30**), (**28**:82), (**29**:62), (**30**:37), (**34**:36), (**34**:39), (**39**:52), (**42**:12). He will strengthen (**3:13**), turn to (**9:15**), (**9:27**), grant success (**30**:5) and wisdom (**2:269**) to *whom he pleases.* Finally, he gives revelations through angels to his servants *as he pleases* so long as they say "*there is no GOD, except myself, therefore fear me.*" (**16**:2)

6. Christians believe that God is love.

> "*But God, who is rich in mercy, for his great love wherewith he loved us*" (Ephesians 2:4).
>
> "*Beloved, let us love one another: for love is of God; and every one that loveth is born of God, and knoweth God. He that loveth not knoweth not God; for God is love*" (1 John 4:7-8).
>
> "*Herein is love, not that we loved God, but that he loved us, and sent his Son to be the propitiation for our sins.*" (1 John 4:10) "*No man hath seen God at any time. If we love one another, God dwelleth in us, and his love is perfected in us*" (1 John 4:12). "*And we have known and believed the love that God hath to us. God is love; and he that dwelleth in love dwelleth in God, and God in him. Herein is our love made perfect, that we may have boldness in the day of judgment: because as he is, so are we in this world.*" (1 John 4: 16-17). "*If a man say, I love God, and hateth his brother, he is a liar: for he that loveth not his brother whom he hath seen, how can he love God whom he hath not seen*" (1 John 4:20)?

According to the Koran Allah does not love transgressors, infidels, wicked doers or the ungodly: (7:55), (**22:38**), (**3:57**), (**2:276**). Again, his dislike of people is extended towards persons and not the act itself.

Like Nestorian Christians, Muslims do not believe in the divinity of Christ or His Atonement to save mankind. He was neither crucified nor killed (**4:157**). He was another apostle or prophet (**5:75**) sent to and rejected by the Jews. The Nestorians also did not believe in a virgin birth, but the *Korân* does and devotes an entire chapter to Mary (Sura 19 Mary), His mother and part of another **sūra 3** (Imran). Islâm is strictly monotheistic; Allah needs no son. Jesus is nothing more than an apostle like Muhammad, but Muhammad is more important since he was the one to be sent after Jesus by the Father to bear good tidings (**34**:28) and (**3:81**). In other words, Muhammad was the Paraclete or Comforter, the Holy Ghost. Christ is mentioned in 35 verses of the Sale version of the *Korân*. There is no mention of him in the early Meccan period. In the mid and late Meccan period there are 7 verses mentioning Jesus (**6**:85), (**42**:13), (**19**:34, 37), (36:**13** (43:**59, 63**); however, 28 verses in the Medina period mention Him (**2:87, 136, 253**) (**3:45, 52, 55, 59, 84**) (**4:156, 157, 162, 171,172**) (**5:17, 46, 75, 78, 110, 111, 112, 114, 116**) (9:30, 31) (**33:7**) (**57:27**) (**61:4, 13**).

> Christians are mentioned in 17 verses of the Sale translation of the *Korân*. Only 2 are in the Meccan period (18:**22**) (21:**93**), the rest are in the Medina period: (**2:62, 111, 113, 120, 135, 140**) (**3:67**)(**5:14,18, 51, 69, 82**) (**9:30**) (**22:17**) (**22:17**). As you read further, keep differences between the revelations of the Meccan period (650-622) and that of the Medina period (622-632) in mind. Those of the Medina period may abrogate earlier ones.

Evil

The existence of Evil in God's world has puzzled man almost from the beginning. The Book of Job, considered by some to be the oldest book of the Bible written about Abraham's time 2000 BC [93] is devoted to this subject. Other Bible chronologies place it following Genesis 1-22 [94] or later about the time of David and Solomon. [95] Job presents us with 3 propositions:

1. God's power causes everything that happens and nothing happens without his willing it.
2. God is good and just – the good prosper and the wicked are punished.
3. Job is a good person (Job 1:1, 8).

The modern understanding of evil is made fuzzy by many belief systems current in our world not the least of which is Marxist socialism, which is regarded by many as a religion even though its proponents stoutly deny it. The *Manifesto of the Communist Party – Part 2* advocates the abolition of religion, morality and eternal truths. To the relativist there is no such thing as "good" or "evil" just shades of grey. This common philosophy blinds many. Many Christians and Jews contend that at least one of the three propositions in Job must be in error. The Lord never answers Job's question, but gives this final rebuke to him, "*Shall he that contendeth with the Almighty instruct him? he that reproveth God, let him answer it.*" (Job 40:2). In other words, do we have enough knowledge or power to tell God how to run the universe? However, the book of Job assures us that all three propositions are correct. God is good, just, and is powerless to do evil. He can prevent evil if he wishes, but he doesn't. God allowed the Devil to have his way with Job other than killing him (Job 2:6). Job is a good and faithful man who does not curse the Lord for his misfortunes. The Book of Job gives us a clue about the source of evil. If it cannot come from God, the only other creature capable of it in the story is man.

The problem of evil depends on an understanding of man's pre-existent state, his ability to act for himself, and his ultimate goal. Mark and Paul alluded to this information among the "mysteries" in the New Testament. See Mark 4:10-11; Rom 11:25; Rom 16:25-26; 1 Cor 2:7; Ephesians 1:9-10; 3:9; Colossians 1:26-27; 4:3; 2 Thessalonians 2:7. The Greek text from which "mystery" or *misterion* (μυστῆριον) was translated meant a religious refer to ceremony or doctrine revealed only to the initiated. In modern terms this may refer to ordinances and covenants.

> Both Old and New Testament attest to a pre-existence: "*God of the spirits of all flesh.*" (Num 16:22; 27:16) "*Where wast thou when I laid the foundations of the earth? ... When the morning stars sang together, and all the sons of God shouted for joy?*" (Job 38:4-7) "*the spirit shallreturn unto God who gave it.*" (Eccle 12:7) *let this child's soul come into him again* (1Kgs 17:21).
>
> "*Before I formed thee in the belly I knew thee*" (Jer 1:5). *Lord ... formeth the spirit of man within him* (Zech 12:1) *who did sin, this man, or his parents, that he was born blind* (John 9:2) *poets have said, For we are also his offspring* (Acts 17:28) *For whom he did foreknow, he alsodid predestinate* (Rom 8:29).

[There is a subtle but distinct difference between "predestinate" and "predestined." Predestinate means to have been chosen, but given the choice not to fulfill the calling. Predestined means chosen without chance to deny the calling.] *Chosen us in himbefore the foundation of the world* (Eph 1:4); *subjection unto the Father of spirits* (Heb 12:9); *angels which kept not their first estate* (Jude 1:6); "*And there was war in heaven: Michael and his angels fought against the dragon; and the dragon fought and his angels,*" (Rev12:7).

Most believe that our ultimate goal is to return to our Father in Heaven. There are many Biblical passages that refer to this. There are also many verses that give us responsibility for our agencyto act as we will. Both Adam and Eve were placed in the Garden as immortal and innocent beings in direct communication with the Father and the LORD. Genesis 2:16 states, "*Of every tree of the garden thou mayest freely eat.*" It was in the "*midst of the garden*" (Gen 3:3)." God warns man in Gen 2:17 about becoming mortal if he eats of the *tree of knowledge of good and evil;" "thou shalt surely die."*

Sin is considered disobedience to our Father's commandments. If fallen man repents of his sins and has faith in his Lord and Savior, Jesus Christ, he will be saved by the LORD's grace (power). Through Christ man can achieve his ultimate goal by returning to his Father in heaven.

Satan came to Eve and persuaded her to eat the fruit of the tree so that she would be as "*wise asThe Gods,*" but promised her she would not die. Eve persuaded Adam to eat. They were now mortal and subject to death. God sent them from Eden (out of his presence). Eve was to bear her children in "*sorrow*" (work) and Adam was to till the ground for his food, also in "*sorrow*" (work). The ground was cursed "***for his sake***." (Gen 3:17) As they were leaving the Garden, the Lord God complimented them, "*the man is become as one of us to know good and evil."*

Many interpret the "Fall" as a punishment; however, it was more an opportunity than a punishment. In order to know good from evil we must live and work in the world. Living in Eden did not permit us to progress. All of us commit evil acts. This is how evil comes into the world and this is frequently how we are taught the difference. It may be through Satan or on our own (Gen 4:1-8). The Cain and Abel story, shows that evil is the result of man's disobedience through Satan's urging. There are also many examples of evil committed by individuals of their own free will that adversely affect innocent people. Chronicles and Kings give specific examples of many evil leaders of Israel and Judah. There will also be natural disasters that pour down on the just and the unjust (Mat 5:45). This is how bad things happen to good people.

Genesis 3:22 is often criticized and said to be preposterous for supposing that man can become like God. However, we are told that the just and unjust will be resurrected (Acts 24:15) and John suggests perfection in 3 places: "*And this is life eternal, that they might know thee the only true God, and Jesus Christ, whom thou hast sent. ... That they all may be one; as thou, Father,art in me, and I in thee, that they also may be one in us: that the world may believe that thou hast sent me. And the glory which thou gavest me I have given them;that they may be one, even as we are one: I in them, and thou in me, that they may be made perfect in one; and that the world may know that thou hast sent me, and hast loved them, as thou hast loved me.*" (John 17:3; 21-23) "*Beloved,now are we the sons of God, and it doth not yet appear what we shall be: but we know that, when he shall appear, we shall be like him; for we shall see him as he is. And every man that hath this hope in him purifieth himself, even as he is pure.*" (1 John 3:2-3) "*To him that overcometh will I grant to sit with me in my throne, even as I also overcame, and am set down with my Father in his throne.*" (Revelations 3:21) When this may happen will not likely be on this earth, but will come later. The degree of glory will likely be what we desire.

Does God the Father have more in mind for us than we give him credit? Do we live in this world as cynics without realizing our own potentials or what may lie in store for us after this life? As noted above John's revelations appeared to have another view. Early on he wrote, "*For God so loved the world, that he gave his only begotten Son, that whosoever believeth in him should not perish, but have everlasting life. For God sent not his Son into the world to condemn the world; but that the world through him might be saved. He that believeth on him is not condemned: but he that believeth not is condemned already, because he hath not believed in the name of the only begotten Son of God.*" (John 3:16-18) If we believe Christ's words, that He can be our Redeemer or Savior, then we are more likely to follow His commandments which gets us closer to His Father.

"Islam differs from Judeo-Christianity in the responsibility for evil and the free will or agency of man. The *Korân* considers Eve as an enemy of Adam and never mentions her name (**2:36**) (7:24) (20:**117, 123**). In general wives and children are also considered distractions or enemies of men (**64:14**). According to the *Korân* we are predestined to be good or evil. (**3:145**) (**9:51**) (**10**:99-100) (**13**:8) (19:**84**) (20:**50**) (21:**101**) (23:**43**) (**28**:68) (37:**96**) (**39**:62) (51:56) (**57:22**) (**64:2**) (87:1-3) To further this end God also deceives unbelievers (**2:26-28, 213, 257**).

There are a number of verses in the Koran that express a determinist philosophy. "*I [GOD] choose that thou [Cain] shouldest bear my iniquity and thine own iniquity; and that thou become a companion of hell fire; for that is the reward of the unjust*" (**5:29**). "*It is he who hath created you; and one of you is predestined to be an unbeliever, and another of you is predestined to be a believer; and GOD beholdeth that which ye do*" (**64:2**). "*The devil replied, O LORD because thou has seduced me, I will surely tempt them to disobedience in the earth; and I will seduce them all, except such of them as shall be thy chosen servants*" (15:**40**). Allah is thus responsible for both good and evil in the world. It is our lot to be chosen for good or evil by god.

BASICS IN ISLAMIC DOCTRINE

The Korân & Al-Hadīth

It has been frustrating for me to listen to high-level government officials quote the *Korân* (**5:32**) out of context, in an attempt to convince the public that Islâm is peaceful. It is not by our definitions. (See **5:33.**) To understand the current conflict requires an understanding of the *Korân* and the *Hadiths*, the two main sources of Islamic teaching.

The *Korân* contains Muhammad's revelations as given to him by the Angel Gabriel. They were either written by him and / or recited to others. They were not placed in final form until at least 30 years after his death after passing through a number of hands. Almost as important are the *Hadī*th*s*. These are traditions about the words and deeds attributed to Muhammad. Many in Islâm consider it second only to the *Korân* as a sacred work. It is an important tool in determining the way of life, interpretations of the *Korân* itself, and the Sharia Law of an Islâmic state or the "House of Islâm." A discussion on the House of Islâm is below. Some Islâmic scholars do not agree with the *Hadiths* especially in the interpretation of the role of women. These hold to an idea that the *Korân* indicates men and women are equal. More modern translations of the *Korân* do not agree.

The *Hadīth* were passed down by oral tradition beginning about 100 years after Muhammad's death or starting about 732 AD. The Caliph 'Uthmān, Muhammad's last secretary urged that the *Korân* and traditions of Muhammad be put into writing about 656, but before he could begin the project he was assassinated. Muslims began their first civil war at this time. Following the assassination of the 4th caliph, the Umayyad Dynasty took control in 661. A second civil war followed. The Umayyad Dynasty ended in 758. The Abbasid Dynasty followed and lasted until 1258. *Hadīth* collections began during the first civil war and continued through the Umayyad dynasty. Beginning in the Abbasid period *Hadīths* were first recorded. By the 9th Century there were 600,000 such sayings. Scholars then had to determine which of the conflicting stories were valid and extensive editing took place to reduce them to about 25,000.

Those who disagree about the importance of the *Hadiths* cite **6**:115 as a rebuttal. "*The words of thy LORD are perfect in truth and justice; There is none who can change his words: he both heareth and knoweth.*" However, this verse was abrogated by **2:106**. Muslim scholars classify the *Hadīth* into three parts – what Muhammad said (qawl), did (fi'l) and approved (taqrir). Isnads accompany each *hadīth*. This is a form of referencing: A heard it from B, who heard it from C, who heard it from Muhammad. Sunni, Shia, and Ibadi, have different views of this collection. Their validity remains questionable because of the length of time between oral tradition and written tradition plus the apparent need to edit conflicting *hadīth*s. Some ignore the *Hadīth* in preference to the *Korân* alone. A discussion about verses **6**:115 and **10**:63-64 as they regard the Doctrine of Abrogation **2:106** occur below. There is a website that can assist the reader in finding key words and various *hadīth*s to which they are connected. [96]

"War Is Deceit"

This concept is attributed to Muhammad. Its origin is ancient dating back to the Greeks and is part of the philosophy of consequentialism. A modern version is "the end justifies the means." It is important to remember that Islâm's definition of war is where there is no Sharia Law.

The following are examples from the Hadīth that illustrate that War is characterized by deceit or lies. In Islâm it is necessary to tell a lie if it protects Islâm, your army, your family, or you. This is one reason why it is impossible for the Judeo-Christian West to make treaties with the leaders of Islâmic countries. Lies, especially with infidels, are an acceptable part of such treaties.

Volume 4, Book 52, Number 268: Narrated Abū Huraira: Allah's Apostle called, "War is deceit" ***Volume 4, Book 52, Number 269***: Narrated Jabir bin 'Abdullah: The Prophet said, "War is deceit." ***Volume 4, Book 52, Number 271***: Narrated Jabir: The Prophet said, "Who is ready to kill Ka'b bin Ashraf (i.e. a Jew)." Muhammad bin Maslama replied, "Do you like me to kill him?" The Prophet replied in the affirmative. Muhammad bin Maslama said, "Then allow me to say what I like." The Prophet replied, "I do (i.e. allow you)."

Jihād

In the *Korân jihād* is described primarily as a holy war against infidels, non-believers, etc. Although it can mean "personal struggle", it is rarely used in the *Korân* in this context. The following *Hadīth* ranks *jihād* among other virtues. ***Volume 4, Book 52, Number 41***: Narrated 'Abdullah bin Masud: I asked Allah's Apostle, "O Allah's Apostle! What is the best deed?" He replied, "To offer the prayers at their early stated fixed times." I asked, "What is next in goodness?" He replied, "To be good and dutiful to your parents." I further asked, what is next in goodness?" He replied, "To participate in Jihād in Allah's Cause." I did not ask Allah's Apostle anymore and if I had asked him more, he would have told me more."

Volume 4, Book 52, Number 42: Narrated Ibn 'Abbas: Allah's Apostle said, "There is no Hijra (i.e. migration from Mecca to Medina) after the Conquest (of Mecca), but Jihād and good intention remain; and if you are called (by the Muslim ruler) for fighting, go forth immediately."

Volume 4, Book 52, Number 45: Narrated Abū Said Al-Khudri: Somebody asked, "*O Allah's Apostle! Who is the best among the people?*" He replied, "*A believer who strives his utmost in Allah's Cause with his life and property.*" They asked, "*Who is next?*" He replied, "*A believer who stays in one of the mountain paths worshipping Allah and leaving the people secure from his mischief.*" ***Volume 4, Book 52, Number 50***: Narrated Anas bin Malik: The Prophet said, "A single endeavor (of fighting) in Allah's Cause in the forenoon or in the afternoon is better than the world and whatever is in it."

Hadith Volume 4, Book 52, Number 53 The Prophet said, *"Nobody who dies and finds good from Allah (in the Hereafter) would wish to come back to this world even if he were given the whole world and whatever is in it, except the martyr who, on seeing the superiority of martyrdom, would like to come back to the world and get killed again (in Allah's Cause)."* [97] This applies also in questions about suicide.

Volume 1, Book 1, Number 6: Narrated 'Abdullah bin 'Abbas: "Just Issue orders to kill every Jew present in the country."

Chronology & the Law of Abrogation

The Doctrine of Abrogation is a baffling concept for those of Judeo-Christian belief because to them God represents only truth. According to the Doctrine of Abrogation Allah can change his mind about a scripture previously given and replace it with another that is "better." This makes it necessary for students to know the chronology of the *Korân.* There are two main sections of the *Korân*, those given in Mecca before Muhammad's migration to Medina (610-621) and those given in Medina (622-632 / 1-10AH). The Islamic calendar begins on 622. Those after Hijra (migration to Medina) are designated as AH. A number of scholars have further broken down the Meccan period into early, mid, and late. In this work sūras and verses from the early Meccan period are given in regular black print. Those in the mid-Meccan period note sūras in regular print with **verses** in **bold face.** Those in the late-Meccan period have **sūras** in **bold face** and verses in regular print. Those from the Medina period have both **sūra and verse in bold face**. To complicate matters further, the chapters in the *Korân* are not in chronological order. They are arranged according to the numbers of characters or words. The earlier chapters are found mostly at the end of the work. This will be discussed later in specifics.

Muhammad began having revelations in 610 and migrated to Medina in AD 622. He died in AD 632 or 10 AH. God first indicated that his words were final. "*The words of thy LORD are perfect in truth and justice; **There is none who can change his words**: he both heareth and knoweth.*" (**6**:115). "*When our evident signs are recited unto them, they who hope not to meet us at the resurrection, say, Bring a different Korân from this; or make some change therein. Answer, **It is not fit for me, that I should change it at my pleasure: I follow that only which is revealed unto me**. Verily I fear, if I should be disobedient unto my LORD, the punishment of the great day*" (**10**:15). "*They who believe and fear GOD shall receive good tidings in this life and in that which is to come. **There is no change in the words of GOD.** This shall be great felicity*" (**10**:63-64). "*If GOD pleaseth, he will seal up thy heart: and GOD will absolutely abolish vanity, and **will establish the truth in his words**; for he knoweth the innermost parts of men's breasts*" (**42**:24). Note that all these verses occur in the late Meccan period.

The years AD 619 to 621 were a period of transition. During these years Muhammad was not welcome in Mecca. His wife, Khadīja, and protector uncle had died. Muhammad left Mecca and began preaching to Arab groups outside of Mecca. In the process he recruited men of arms that pledged their support to him. This presented the possibility of vengeance against his Meccan tormentors and towards the end of the Meccan period there was indication that change might be possible. ***"GOD shall abolish and shall confirm what he pleaseth**. With him is the original of the book*" (**13**:39). "***When we substitute in the Korân an abrogating verse in lieu of a verse abrogated, (and GOD best knoweth the fitness of that which he***

revealeth,) the infidels say, Thou art only a forger of these verses: *but the greater part of them know not truth from falsehood*" (**16**:101).

Following his move to Medina the Doctrine of Abrogation was laid down, "***Whatever verse we abrogate, or cause thee to forget, we will bring a better than it, or one like unto it.*** *Dost thou not know that GOD is almighty?*" (**2:106**). By now Muhammad had begun raids against the Meccans and opposition Jewish and Arab settlements in addition to acquiring numerous wives. Changes or exceptions to previous rules in the *Korân* were needed. In 620, when Muhammad was 50 years old he acquired two wives, Sauda bint Zam'a then in her early 50s and 'Ā'isha bint Abū Bakr, then about 7-years old; he did not consummate the marriage until she was 9 according to most sources. Following his move to Medina in about 624 he married two more women, Hind bint Abi Umayyah, a 24-year-old widow, and Hafsah bint 'Umar, an 18-year-old widow. Clarification was needed regarding marriage; no more than 4 marriages were permitted (**4:2**). In December 626 he married Juwayriya bint al-Hārith b. Abū Dirār al-Khuza'iya, a 19-year-old captive taken during a raid against the B. Muşţaliq of Khuzā'a. In 627 he fell in love with Zaynab "Barrah" bint Jahsh his stepson's wife. Muhammad had him divorce her so he could marry her. She was reputed to be a very beautiful 34-year-old. This required scriptural changes (**33:36-39**). The fires of libido were not yet quenched. In April 628 he married Umm Habība or Ramla bint Abū Sufyān, former wife of a Muslim who converted to Christianity and daughter of an arch enemy; she was 34. In June 628 he married Safiyya d. Huyayy b. Akhtab, a "gift of the right hand," She was a 19-year-old Jewess beauty, taken at the Battle of Khaybar following the torture death of her husband. Mary the Coptic Christian and her sister, Sirin were gifts from the Governor of Alexandria sent in 628. Muhammad kept Mary because of her beauty and gave her sister to another. In most lists she is classed as a concubine, not a wife. Her age is not known, but presumably she was young. Mary bore a child, Ibrahim, whose parentage is in some doubt, but is considered to be Muhammad's child. Although Mary was not quartered in the harem, Hafsa caught Mary and Muhammad in her (Hafsa's) bed. Muhammad told Hafsa he would never do it again if she kept it secret. However, Hafsa told 'Ā'isha and word spread causing an uproar in the harem. Hafsa was threatened with divorce and all the wives were ignored for one month while Muhammad visited Mary exclusively. The *Korân* memorializes the incident (**66:1-3, 5**). While in a state of ritual purity during a pilgrimage to Mecca in March 629, he married Maymūna bint Hārith b. Hazn; she was 34. The *Korân* lists an exception in this case for Muhammad (**33:50**), but forbids him further marriages (**33:52**). There are other wives noted later. See the Section on Muhammad's wives.

According to Islamic scholars, the final two books of the *Korân* are 5 and 9. These contain the "last word" on all doctrine. The implications are critical. The militant verses in these sūras abrogate the more peaceful verses in the *Korân* given earlier. This creates a justification to allow Islâm to attack others on religious grounds. Ever since the death of Muhammad Islâm has continued this policy–it is scripture. The doctrine of abrogation also allowed Muhammad license in his marriages by creating scriptural exceptions to the limitations set down for other believers. To understand the *Korân* it is necessary to know not just that a verse was given, but when it was given and whether or not it was changed later.

An example of abrogation is a comparison of **2:256** written in AD 214 and **9:5** compiled at the end of Muhammad's life. Both have to do with attitudes toward Idolaters, Infidels or unbelievers. The verse of tolerance: **2:256** "*There is no compulsion in religion; truly the right way has become clearly distinct from error; therefore, whoever disbelieves in the Shaitan and believes in Allah he indeed has laid hold on the firmest handle, which shall not break off, and Allah is Hearing, Knowing.*" Even though Sūra 2 was allegedly written after the capture of Medina it was one of the first. This verse is trumped by **9:5** written even later known as the verse of the sword: "*So when the sacred months have passed away, then slay the idolaters wherever you find them, and take them captives and besiege them and lie in wait for them in every ambush, then if they repent and keep up prayer and pay the poor-rate, leave their way free to them; surely Allah is Forgiving, Merciful.*" Since **9:5** was revealed after **2:256**, we can ignore **2:.**[256] and replace it with **9:5** just as we did above with verses **6**:115 and **10**:63-64.

Another example of abrogation occurs between **22:39** "*Permission is granted unto those who take arms against the unbelievers, for that they have been unjustly persecuted by them.*" Compare this with **2:190-195** that commands attack and slaughter of the Infidels even during holy months. Compare it with **5:33** that commands a dire punishment for those who oppose Muhammad: "*But the recompense of those who fight against GOD and his apostles, ... shall be, that they shall be slain, or crucified, or have their hands and their feet cut off on the opposite sides, or be banished the land.*"

Contrast this to the Judeo-Christian doctrine of an unchanging or unchangeable God. "*Thou laid the foundation of the earth: and the heavens are the work of thy hands. They shall perish, but thou shalt endure: yea, all of them shall wax old like a garment; as a vesture shalt thou change them, and they shall be changed: But thou art the same, and thy years shall have no end*" (Psalms

102:25-27). This is paraphrased later in Hebrews 1:10-12. "*The earth also is defiled under the inhabitants thereof; because they have transgressed the laws, changed the ordinance, broken the everlasting covenant*" (Isaiah 24:5). "*For I am the LORD, I change not*" (Malachi 3:6); "*Professing themselves to be wise, they became fools, And changed the glory of the uncorruptible God*" (Romans 1:22-23). The Doctrine of Abrogation is the Achilles' heel of Islâm. Suppose God speaks again through another prophet that comes later. This might nullify much of the *Korân*, especially its more militant verses.

Islâm & Suicide

Suicide is also said to be forbidden for members of Islâm. *"Do not destroy yourselves. God is merciful to you, but he that does that through wickedness and injustice shall be burned in fire. That is easy enough for God"* (**4:29**). However, this does not apply to martyrs for Allah (**4:66, 69**). *"Verily GOD hath purchased of the true believer their souls and their substance, promising them the enjoyment of paradise; on condition that they fight for the cause of GOD: whether they slay or be slain, the promise for the same is assuredly due by the law, and the gospel, and the Korân. And who performeth his contract more faithful than GOD? Rejoice therefore in the contract which ye have made. This shall be great happiness"* (**9:111**). Sūra 4 was written in the early Medina period. Sūra 9 trumps it. See also ***Hadith Volume 4, Book 52, Number 53*** cited above.

The Sword, Expansion, and Islâm

The history of Islâm is replete with expansion by conquest. The *Korân* of the Medina period urges war against the Infidels. Sūra **9:5** has been quoted above. Sūra **2:216** states, *"War is enjoined you against the Infidels; but this is hateful unto you: yet perchance ye hate a thing which is better for you, and perchance ye love a thing which is worse for you: but GOD knoweth and ye know not."* Sūra **8:67** proclaims, "*It hath not been granted unto any prophet, that he should possess captives, until he had made a great slaughter of the infidels in the earth. Ye seek the accidental goods of this world, but God regardeth the life to come; and GOD is mighty and wise.*" Sūra **9:29** says, *"Fight against them who believe not in GOD, nor in the last day, and forbid not that which GOD and his apostle have forbidden, and profess not the true religion, of those unto whom the scriptures have been delivered, until they pay tribute by right of subjection, and they be reduced low."*

Paying the tribute was often so severe that it was impossible and subjugation often meant kowtowing while being struck on the back of the neck or head or even torture. "*When ye encounter the unbelievers, strike off their heads, until ye have made a great slaughter among them; and bind them in bonds: and either give them a free dismissal afterwards, or exact a ransom; until the war shall have laid down its arms. This shall ye do:* ***Verily if GOD pleased, he could take vengeance on them, without your assistance; but he commandeth you to fight his battles, that he may prove the one of you by the other.*** *And as to those who fight in defense of GOD's true religion, God will not suffer their works to perish; he will guide them, and will dispose their heart aright; and he will lead them into paradise, of which he hath told them*" (**47:4-6**). Sūra 47 was one of the last to be written.

Alliances with Infidels or Unbelievers

A commonly expressed belief by many in the West is that if we could make friends with Islam, all would be well and there would be no need for war. The *Korân* does not permit this. Believers may have associations with unbelievers out of necessity, but, "*Let not the faithful take the infidels for their protectors, rather than the faithful: he who doth this shall not be protected of GOD at all; unless ye fear any danger from them: but GOD warneth you to beware of himself; for unto GOD must ye return. Say, 'Whether ye conceal that which is in your breasts, or whether ye declare it, GOD knoweth it: for he knoweth whatever is in heaven and whatever is on earth: GOD is almighty*'" (**3:28-29**). Lying about your feelings or intentions with unbelievers is sanctioned. Consequently, negotiations and alliances are impossible under conditions of Jihad.

The House of Islâm is not like anything in the Judeo-Christian U.S. In Islâm, church and state are one and Sharia law must be obeyed because it is the word of God. There is no questioning or amending it. Most is from the Medina period. In addition, you must know Arabic, your dress must be in accordance with prescriptions; your women are treated in a specified manner; marriage and sexual relations with slaves are ordained; how you deal with government, military, dietary habits are all specified. In the House of Islâm, believers are first-class citizens; the rest are subjugated and subdued as second-class citizens or "*demi*" peoples who are meant to serve the believers. If Muslims are in the minority in a society these feelings are not displayed, but once they achieve majority status, Sharia Law is not far behind. "***Afterwards we appointed thee, O Muhammad, to promulgate a law concerning the business of religion: wherefore follow the same, and***

follow not the desires of those who are ignorant. *Verily they shall not avail thee against GOD at all: the unjust are the patrons of one another; but GOD is the patron of the pious.* ***This Korân delivereth evident precepts unto mankind;*** *and is a direction and a mercy, unto people who judge aright. Do the workers of iniquity imagine that we will deal with them as with those who believe and do good works; so that their life and their death shall be equal? An ill judgment do they make"* (**45**:18-21).

How are Christians, Jews, and for that matter, all other religions viewed? *"Verily those who believe not, among those who have received the scriptures, and among the idolaters, shall be cast into the fire of hell, to remain therein forever. These are the worst of creatures"* (**98:6**).

Muhammad, as an Example

The *Korân* advises all to look to the Prophet Muhammad as an example of good behavior. *"**Ye have in the apostle of GOD an excellent example,** unto him who hopeth in GOD and the last day, and remembereth GOD frequently"* (**33:21**). What about Muhammad's propensity for warfare? *Volume 5, Book 59, Number 285:* Narrated Abū Ishaq: *"Once, while I was sitting beside Zaid bin Al-Arqam, he was asked, "How many Ghazwat* (battles) *did the Prophet undertake?" Zaid replied, "Nineteen." They said, "In how many Ghazwat did you join him?" He replied, "Seventeen." I asked, "Which of these was the first?" He replied, "Al-'Ashira or Al-'Ashiru."* [98]

According to *The Life of Muhammad* page 461-466, Muhammad had put away his weapons when Gabriel visited him and told him that he, Gabriel, was not finished and that he and his angels were headed for the B Qurayza and that God commanded Muhammad to go. Muhammad laid siege to their forts for 25 nights. When desperation set in among the besieged, Muhammad offered them 3 options: 1) accept Islâm and Muhammad as prophet and save your lives and property; 2) kill all the women and children and come out with weapons until God decides between the two forces; 3) mount a night attack on the Sabbath against Muhammad's army and possibly surprise and get the best of them. None of these were acceptable and they decided to surrender and be at Muhammad's mercy. Muhammad's decision was to kill all the men, take all their property and sell the women and children as slaves after keeping the best of them for use by his troops. 600 to 900 men from the Qurayza were taken in batches to the Market of Medina. Trenches were dug and the men were beheaded, and their decapitated corpses buried in the trenches while Muhammad watched in attendance. Women and children were sold into slavery, a number of them being distributed as gifts among Muhammad's companions, and Muhammad chose one of the Qurayza women (Rayhana) for himself. The Qurayza's property and other possessions (including weapons) were also divided up as additional "booty" among the Muslims, to support further jihād campaigns. [99] If Muhammad's example is followed in the modern world, it would be called "terrorism." Muslim men don't have to be martyrs to get *houris*, or the "dark-eyed beauties." They can have Infidel women now, on this earth, in the form of slave-girls as "gifts of the right hand."

The House of Islâm

There are two States according to Islâmic doctrine, the House of Islâm where Islâm is established and Sharia Law is enforced. Peace reigns here by definition. This is the "peace" that Islâm talks about. It has nothing to do with the Western concept of "peace" as an absence of conflict. There is also the House of War, where unbelievers reside in a state of *Jahiliyyah*, a condition of confusion or ignorance of the *Korân* and Sharia Law. Here, by definition, there is no peace. It existed for everyone in pre-*Korân* times.

The House of Islâm, although it may be a place of "peace" is a very serious place according to the Ayatollah Khomeini, "Allah did not create man so that he could have fun. The aim of creation was for mankind to be put to the test through hardship and prayer. An Islâmic regime must be serious in every field. There are no jokes in Islâm. There is no humor in Islâm. There is no fun in Islâm. There can be no fun and joy in whatever is serious." [100]

Islâm & "Peace"

Throughout its history conquest has been a way of life in Islâm. It has been from the beginning regardless of what more secular and "peaceful" Muslims might say or quote from the *Korân*. Since deceit is part of war according to Muhammad, it is impossible to trust what a Muslim might say or allegedly feel during a time of war. The purpose of *jihād* is to establish Islâmic Sharia Law and either kill or subjugate unbelievers. Conversion follows because if you live in a "protected," "*demi*" status within an Islâmic country you are restricted from certain occupations. Your houses of worship may not be repaired or built and you will slide into degeneracy. The law of abrogation makes Sūras 9 & 5 the last word. They replace all the peaceful verses in the *Korân*. Since peace only reigns in the House of Islâm under Sharia Law, all the rest of the world is in the House of War where, by definition, there is no peace. Thus, Islâm is a "religion of peace."

Islâm, the Restored Religion of Abraham

Islâm claims to be the original religion of Abraham and his family down to and including Moses. It is strictly monotheistic. However, the *Korân* does not included the covenant making between the Lord God and Abraham (Genesis 12:1-3; 15:18; 17:9; Exodus 2:24; Leviticus 24:42; 2 Kings 13:23; 1 Chron 16:13-19; Psalms 105:9). It also does not include the tripartite God of Abraham, Isaac, and Jacob outlined in Genesis 1:1-2; 2:4). Allah is all powerful. He controls everything on earth and must be considered the God of this world (See 2 Cor 4:4). He is responsible for both good and evil, and we are all predestined to be good or evil. Many Apostles in the *Korân* are found in the Bible and the New Testament. According to Islâm, Jesus Christ was not crucified or resurrected. (**4:157**) He was taken up by God after having received perfection through the Holy Spirit **(2:253)**. He is not a God. This is a Nestorian Christian belief of the 7th Century AD proselytized in the Arabian Peninsula 100 years before Muhammad's birth. Nestorian Christians did not believe in the virgin birth, crucifixion, or resurrection. However, Islâm holds to Christ's virgin birth (21:**91**; **66:12**). Heaven and Hell are Persian Zoroastrianism. See **2:124-140; 22:78**. Allah assumes the position of the Judeo-Christian equivalent of God the Father as the only – monotheistic – god. He is the creator. He is responsible for everything on earth – good and evil. He has no children or helpers (**2:107; 4:123; 9:116**). He made man from nothing (19:**9**), not from the dust of the ground (Gen 2:7; 3:19). The Christian doctrine of *Creatio ex nihilo* is credited to Basilides, later developed by Tatian (AD 110 to 172), teacher of Clement of Alexandria). [101]

For 1000 years or more before Muhammad's time Allah was the Arabian's chief god, the Moon God of War (74:36) and the Lord of the Dog Star (53:49). His consort, Shams, the sun goddess, had three daughters, Alatt, Al-'Uzzā, and Manāt. See the heading of Sūra 53 to see how all this ties to the "Satanic verses." The old symbols of crescent and star continue to this day to represent Allah. It adorns all mosques and many flags. Sūra 56 is entitled The Moon and Sūra 86 is known as the Star. Allah's characteristics are reviewed in the Topical Guide under "God."

Alms

Alms are gifts that all practicing Muslims pay to Islam for its support. These gifts are not only for the poor, but are for the support of the Islâm in its peaceful and warlike pursuits. In this sense they are different from alms given in Christian and Jewish charities. They are mentioned with prayers as a necessary part of worship in Islam (**2:3, 43, 110, 272; 9:60**). Prayer and alms are a requirement for mosque attendance / *Hajj* (pilgrimage to Mecca) participation (**9:18**).

Apostles

Apostles are sent by God to warn people on earth. A number are mentioned in the *Korân* including Jesus Christ. Muhammad is the last. Any time a religion says it is "the last," it denies the power of God it allegedly supports. Both Christianity and Islâm fragmented into sects within a hundred years of their foundation. Muhammad Ibn Abd-al-Wahhab, a contemporary of George Sale, who became the imam for the Saudi royal household in the 18th Century attempted to revive Islâm by use of terror and his movement persists to this day. The billions of dollars in oil money that flows into Saudi Arabia fund most of this effort. Although it is called radical / fundamentalist by many, it attempts to restore Islâm to its former glory and continue the conquests of old.

Believers & True Believers

These are the bedrock of Islâm. They oppose hypocrites (lukewarm believers), infidels, unbelievers, non-believers, disbelievers, Christians, Jews and those of Islâm who apostatize or do not practice the true religion.

Family

Family is referred to mainly in a historical context such as the Family of Abraham, Moses, Aaron, etc. Family in a contemporary sense is referred to as part of law, but not as part of any heavenly plan. Missing from the *Korân* is one of the basics of life, the concept of the basic family unit, mother and father working together in a mature partnership of love within the family. Sharia Law itself, diminishes women to second class status. Although Islâm claims to be based on the religion of the family of Abraham, it seems to mean the tribe of Abraham and its male dominated warrior power structure. The female component, Sarah (Gen 17:15-16) is left out. As mentioned elsewhere, the *Korân* includes the name of only two women, Mary, the mother of Jesus and 'Ā'isha, Muhammad's child harem wife when she is falsely accused of sexual indiscretion (**24:11**). Adam is without Eve, Abraham without Sarah or even Hagar, Isaac without Rebekah, Jacob without Leah and Rachel. Even Muhammad's first faithful wife, Khadīja, is not mentioned. The *Korân* skips over one of the major concepts of the entire Abraham story, "*And I will bless them that bless thee, and curse him that curseth thee:* ***and in thee shall all families of the earth be blessed***" (Gen 12:3). When it comes to women and wives, the emphasis is purely sexual. "*Your wives are your tillage; go in therefore unto your tillage in what manner soever ye will*" (**2:223**); "*O true believers, verily of your wives and your children ye have an enemy: wherefore beware of them*" (**64:14**).

Fighting for God's True Religion

Fighting for God's True Religion is emphasized in the *Korân*. Much of this is directed against the Meccan idolaters. However, the faithful are also directed to fight against those who have been given the scriptures (Jews & Christians) until "*they pay tribute by right of subjection, and they be reduced low*" (**9:29**). True believers are told to "*strike off their heads*" and make "*a great slaughter among them.*" They are then advised that God "*could take vengeance on them, without your assistance, but he commandeth you to fight his battles, that he may prove the one of you by the other*" (**47:4**). The faithful are also told not to "*invite your enemies to peace, while ye are the superior*" (**47:35**). They are assured that "*GOD loveth those who fight for his religion*" (**61:4**). As for negotiations with Islâm this question is posed by the *Korân*: "*How shall the idolaters be admitted into a league with GOD and with his apostle; except those with whom ye entered into a league at the holy temple?*" (**9:7**). It then answers the question: "*It is not fitting that the idolaters should visit the temples of GOD ... The works of these men are vain; and they shall remain in hell fire for ever...* " (**9:17**). The *Korân* then drives the point home again and also tells the believers that they need not worry about sanctions: "*O true believers, verily the idolaters are unclean; let them not therefore come near unto the holy temple after this year* (631). *And if ye fear want, by the cutting off trade and communication with them, GOD will enrich you of his abundance, if he pleaseth; for GOD is knowing and wise*" (**9:28**). It is against Saudi law for any non-Muslim to enter Mecca, let alone the temple. Even if we wanted to negotiate, we would be unable to do it in an environment acceptable to Islâm, unless we have a Muslim leader.

Free Will & Free Choice or Agency

There are several words and phrases found in the *Korân* that describe determinism and predestination as Islamic doctrine. Allah is responsible for all good and evil in the world. Christians and the *Torah* state that the God of Israel created heaven, earth, but unlike Allah, God planned the universe (Genesis 1); all was "good" (Gen 1:4,10,12,18,21,25,31). This included creating man in the pre-life image and likeness of God. (Gen 1:26, 28-30). Jehovah God, or LORD God, put the plan into action (Genesis 2:4). This included making man a living soul (Gen 2:7). In Genesis 2: 9 we learn that the LORD God / Jehovah God placed the "*tree of knowledge of good and evil*" "*in the midst of the garden*" and warned man that he would die, if ate its fruit (Gen 2:17). The serpent found Eve alone, tempted her to eat the fruit claiming she would become as wise as the Gods (pleural), but lied that she would not die, become mortal (Gen 3:5). The fruit "*was pleasant to the eyes, and a tree to be desired to make one wise, she took of the fruit thereof, and did eat, and gave also unto her husband with her; and he did eat.*" (Gen 3:6). At this point the *Korân* departs from both the story of Genesis and its basic point. In the *Korân* Eve becomes an enemy (**2:36**) along with Satan. Adam is thrown out of the Garden with her. In the Genesis story, the LORD God begins their instruction. In Eden where all is provided, they have no chance to learn. First, God places enmity between Eve and the serpent (Gen 3:15). Next, He tells Eve, "*in sorrow* (work) *thou shalt bring forth children; and thy desire shall be to thy husband, and he shall rule over thee.*" (Gen 3:16). He tells Adam, "*cursed is the ground* ***for thy sake****; in sorrow* (work) *shalt thou eat of it all the days of thy life; Thorns also and thistles shall it bring forth to thee; and thou shalt eat the herb of the field; In the sweat of thy face shalt thou eat bread, till thou return unto the ground; for out of it wast thou taken: for dust thou art, and unto dust shalt thou return*" (Gen 3:17-19). Note these things, are considered curses by the *Korân* (**2:38-39**). In the Old Testament they are done for Adam and Eve's education and benefit – "*for thy sake.*" Then the Lord God gives them the ultimate compliment as he clothes (Gen 3:21) and launches them into mortality with its physical death, "*Behold, the man* (male & female) *is become as one of us, to know good and evil:*" (Gen 3:22). Even so the LORD God does not limit man's freedom to make choices and do what he will. This brings both good and evil into the world. The Cain and Abel story shows us that the source of good and evil is man and his choices (Gen 4:1-8). The *Korân's* version of the Cain and Abel story is found in **5:27-34**. The rest of the Old Testament provides us with the history of man through the Children of Israel and the writings of the prophets. The salvation of man or his ability to return to God lies with the LORD God / Jehovah God, who becomes known as the "redeemer" (Job 19:25; Psalms 19:14, 78:35; Proverbs 23:11; Isaiah 41:14, 43:14, 44:24, 47:4, 48:17, 49:7, 26, 54:5, 8; 59:20; 60:16; 63:16; and Jeremiah 50:34). Unlike the *Korân* we have choices; we are not directed by God into evil; however, by our nature and choices, evil comes into the world. Early verses in the *Korân* seemed to give man some freedom of choice (75:5; 79:38; 91:8; 68:**38**) However, all this is abrogated later. According to the *Korân* we are predestined to be either good or evil and have little choice in the matter (**3:145**)(**5:29**) (**9:51**) (**33:36**) (**57:22**) (**10**: 49, 99-100) (**13**:8) (19:**84**) (20:**50**) (21:**101**) (23:**43**) (**28**:68) (37:**96**) (**39**:62) (51:56) (**64:2**) (87:1-3). Allah even severs the wicked from the good (**3:179**).

As Jews or Christians we learn, we can change our minds, "repent," and reshape our lives. Even modern neurophysiology documents this possibility. We are not, as expressed in the *Korân*, predestined or predetermined to be good or evil and we are not directed as pawns of God who does with us what he pleases. In the Topical guide under free will and free choice are examples of how these words are used in complete sentences so that you might see the difference between Biblical and *Korânic* teachings. According to the *Korân*, Allah would never grant the political freedoms of "*life, liberty, and the pursuit of happiness*" to man. Allah would remain in charge – Sharia Law.

Freedom of Speech

Many of us in the West are puzzled by Islâm's sensitivity to criticism in any form. Cartoons portraying the prophet Muhammad in a bad light and written works such as *The Satanic Verses* by Salman Rushdie have prompted riots and death threats with the real possibility of assassination by terrorists and pronunciamentos or "*fatwas.*" In his time Muhammad ordered the assassination of a number of critics that included several locally famous poets. James Arlandson has called this group, *Muhammad's Dead Poet Society.* [102]

In the Judeo-Christian tradition the only prohibited speech is damaging slander, libel, and perjury or bearing deliberate false witness. Satire, sarcasm and other forms of written or spoken material, although frequently inappropriate and considered ill-mannered or unwise are not crimes. The Western press engages in it on a regular basis especially when politics are involved. Such invective is usually not tolerated in totalitarian dictatorships or oligarchies, but becomes almost an art form in the West. In

Arab society, both past and present, the *hijā*, an insulting personal poem, is also an art form and examples can be found in the *Korân* (**6**:10 19:**77-80**; 21:**98-100**; 104; 108; 111). Since the 1960s "politically correct" speech has been promoted to avoid "offending" certain ethnic groups. This has always been part of "good manners," but to others it has always been a part of great humor not to be taken seriously. "Dumb Blond" jokes are classic. In Islâm critical speech or writing is not tolerated.

The justification is found in the *Korân*. Initially Muhammad was advised to bear insults with patience: "*Ye shall sure be proved in your possessions, and in your persons; and ye shall bear from those unto whom the scripture was delivered before you, and from the idolaters, much hurt: but if ye be patient, and fear God, this is a matter that is absolutely determined*" (**3:186**). After the siege of Medina or Battle of the Trench (627) several Jewish settlements were ravaged (**33:26-27; 59:1-17**). Because of the great wealth obtained Muhammad's power markedly increased. He put his wives in their place (**33:28-33**). Next, he received special permission to marry his step-son's wife (**33:37-39**). Finally, he is given permission to strike back against criticism: "*As to those who offend GOD and his apostle, GOD shall curse them in this world and in the next; and he hath prepared for them a shameful punishment. And they who shall injure the true believers of either sex, without their deserving it, shall surely bear the guilt of calumny and a manifest injustice*" (**33:57-58**). Sūra **58:7-10** prohibits "clandestine" speech. Notes #1-2 by George Sale in his translation of the *Korân* on page 525 state that in Medina "Jews and hypocritical Moslems" who met each other in private would make "signs to one another when they saw the true believers" despite this being a serious crime. Regardless of the danger they would greet each other with "*Al sâm aleica*" instead of the usual greeting "*Al salâm aleica*" "Mischief on thee" instead of "Peace be upon thee."

The Life of Muhammad and Arlandson list the following 9 people killed for their ideas expressed in speech, song, or writing. Details of their deaths are recounted later.

1. Al-Nadr bin al-Harith – prisoner of war, Badr; beheaded by Ali on Muhammad's command, March 624
2. Uqba bin Abu Muayt – prisoner of war, Badr; beheaded at Muhammad's command, March 624
3. Asma bint Marwan – poetess, assassinated on Muhammad's command, March 624
4. Abu Afak – old poet in Medina, assassinated by Salim b. Umayr at Muhammad's request, April 624

5. Kab bin al-Ashraf – poet of Medina stabbed by Abu Naila and 4 others following Muhammad's request, September 624
6. Ibn Sunayna – Jewish merchant of Medina killed by Muhayyisa b. Masud after orders to "Kill any Jew that falls into your power" September 624
7. A One-eyed Bedouin – killed by Amr bin Umayya sent to assassinate Abū Sufyān. He failed, but on the way home met a one-eyed Bedouin who recited anti-Muslim verse. While the Bedouin slept, Umayya rammed the end of his bow through the Bedouin's good eye driving it through his skull.
8. July-Aug 625. Abdullah bin Katal and one of his singing-girls – Abdullah was a poet of Mecca and the girls sang satirical verses about Muhammad. These three individuals were on Muhammad's list of those who were to be killed after Mecca's fall; one of the singing girls escaped; January 630.

Friendship with Unbelievers

True believers are not to be friends with Infidels. Since Muhammad declared that War is deceit and a state of War exists anywhere unbelievers are, Islâmic friends can be deceitful in their overt attitudes and statements to unbelievers and be true to their religious beliefs. God is an enemy to unbelievers (**2:98**). True believers are advised against making friends with infidels or those who have previously received the scriptures (Christians & Jews). In fact, God is incensed against unbelievers. Even non-believing family members are to be shunned (**5:57, 80**) (**9:23**).

GOD

The characteristics attributed to Allah are not those of the Judeo-Christian gods. Allah is strictly monotheistic (**4:36**) and responsible for everything that occurs on earth – good and bad. He does what he pleases (**13**:39), he abrogates scripture previously given (**2:106**), he causes men to make errors (**6**:39); he controls the weather producing rain and plenty or drought and death (**10:**24); in war he kills the enemy and Islâm acts as his instrument (**8**:17). He is the lord of all (1:1) (**5:28**) (**13**:16) (26:**28**) (114:1); He loves the obedient (**3:57**), but not the Infidel (**22:38**). He gives to whom he pleases (**5:64**) and causes "bad luck" to befall others (7:131). He creates and he destroys. He stirs up enmity among Christians (**5:14**). He gives life and causes death (**7**:158) and sends favors to those he pleases while punishing those who do not believe (**2:90**). He punishes with his own hands or with those of the faithful (**9:52**) and takes vengeance out on people (**5:95**), and even leads people astray (**4:88**). Much of the ritual and symbolism that attends the Allah of Islâm is the same that attended him as Lord of the dog-star (**53**:50) and the old Moon God of War from Pagan times (74:36).

Contrast this with the Christian Doctrine of Christ – faith in Him (Jesus Christ), repentance, baptism and the gift of the Holy Ghost. See Hebrews 6:1-4; 11:1; and 2 John 1:9. Also, contrast this with the Christian concept of God the Father who loves all of mankind and sent "*His only begotten son*" as our Savior (John 3:16). He also gives us our freedom by removing us from Eden so that we might experience the difference between good and evil and learn from it and then provides us a way back to Him through Christ's atonement, death and resurrection. It is in this learning process that evil occurs – not by His hands. We are not predestined to be good or bad. We are given the opportunity to learn the difference.

The Godhead is tripartite (John 1:1-14) and even the Godhead of Abraham and Moses is described as tripartite – God the planner of Genesis 1- Genesis 2:3. The Spirit of God (Gen 1:2) later known as the Holy Ghost, influenced the prophets of the Old Testament. God the builder and creator of Genesis 2:4 (the Hebrew "Jehovah God" or the King James "LORD God") who clearly uses the pleural form to liken man to God *"And the LORD God said, Behold, the man is become as one of us, to know good and evil:"* (Gen 3:22). Islâm claims in (**3:81**) that Muhammad was sent by God as the promised "comforter" / Holy Ghost.

Love

The God of the Bible is love. He loves his children even when they sin. He gives them a chance to repent and sent his son to be a propitiation for our sins. However, in the Korân, "*GOD loveth not every perfidious unbeliever*" (**22:38**); and the LORD, "*loveth not those who transgress.*" (7:55) God "*loveth not*" the sinner, but he seems to revel in the fact that they sin. He will "*disgrace the unbelievers*" (**9:2**) and "*will lead into error whom he pleaseth, and whom he pleaseth he will put in the right way*" (**6**:39). Since God did not have a Son, he could not send him because he loved the world (John 3:16). God commands the destruction and /or torture of the Infidel, not their quiet conversion or opportunity for repentance, "*Those who fight against GOD and his apostles, and study to act corruptly in the earth, shall be, that they shall be slain, or crucified, or have their hands and their feet cut off* *on the opposite sides, or be banished the land. This shall be their disgrace in this world, and in the next world they shall suffer a grievous punishment;"* (**5:33**) Loyalty to the prophet Muhammad is on a par with loyalty to God.

"Love" is used in several principal ways in the *Korân*. The *Korân* speaks of what God loves in people. In summary God loves those who do good; repent; are clean; keep covenants; fear and trust in Him. He loves those who give alms; bridle their anger; and forgive others. He loves those who fight for his cause; persevere patiently; and act in the cause of justice. Muhammad is counseled to forgive, be patient and consult with his men in matters of war, but not necessarily his wives apart from a sexual context. God loved Moses and protected him (**2:195, 222**) (**3:76, 134, 146, 148, 159**) (**5:13, 18, 42, 54, 93**) (**49:9**) (**60:8**) (**61:4**) (**16**:23) (**42**:23) (19:**96**) (20:**39**).

The *Korân* speaks of what God does not love in people. In summary God does not love those who fight against believers, transgressors, Infidels, ungodly people, the wicked, those who act corruptly or work iniquity, or those that destroy crops. He does not like the proud or vainglorious, the deceiver or the unjust. He does not like speaking ill of anyone in public. However, He curses the Jews for what they have said. God increases their transgression and infidelity, until the day of resurrection. Jews are corrupt doers and He hates them for it. He dislikes gluttony or being "profuse". He hates treachery, but advises believers to be treacherous with enemies. GOD will frustrate the plans of infidels because he does not love the unbeliever. He does not like those who rejoice in their riches "immoderately." He wants you to show kindness to parents, relatives, orphans, the poor, your neighbor who is your kin, and to your neighbor who is a stranger. He wants you to be kind to "your familiar companion," traveler, and "captives whom your right hands shall possess." He wants you to call upon Him in secret. He wants you to seek riches, but be bounteous with them. Retaliation against evil ought to be "an evil proportionate thereto" (**2:190, 205, 276**) (**3:32, 57, 140**) (**4:36, 107, 148**) (**5:64, 87**) (**8:58**) (**9:4,** 7) (**22:38**) (**57:23**) (**6**:141) (7:31, 55) (**28**:76, 77) (**30**:45) (**31**:18) (**42**:40).

The *Korân* speaks of people's love for God: (**2:165**) and (**3:31**); and then what they usually like or love. In summary people often like what is worse for them, especially war, even when war is good for them. In matters of religion people avoid scripture designed to help them and tend toward schismatic beliefs. Men will spend hours admiring their wives, children, horses, cattle, land, and riches. Those who are patient and love truth are the alms givers and those who pray for pardon. Men love the present life and give little thought of the after-life. They often prefer blindness to true direction

(**2:216**) (**3:7, 14, 17, 92, 119**) (**9:108**) (**24:19**) (**59:9**) (**14**:3) (**16**:107) (**28**:79) (**41**:17) (21:**90**) (38:**32**) (76:**27**) (75:20) (89:20) (100:8). It also talks of what people don't like or love. Many don't like even good advice and love infidelity over faith. Many will have to give up their close relatives, because they are unbelievers (**9:23**) (**58:22**) (7:79). Finally, it alludes to the love of women. Men should separate themselves from them when they are having their menses. After they are cleansed, then they may return. Marriage is good for men and they should marry whom they can afford. Adultery is a punishable offense (**2:222**) (**4:25**) (**12**:30, 51) (**30**:21) (56:37).

In all there are 43 verses devoted to what God likes and doesn't like about people. These are guides to personal behavior. Man's likes and dislikes are covered in only 22 verses. His relationships with women are found in 6 and his love of God in only 2. The tone and message of these verses is not that of the Sermon on the Mount (Matt 5, 6, 7) where Jesus would have his followers follow the golden rule and not the law of retaliation. He would have us love our enemies, not hate them and would have us demonstrate our love by actions not words. Comparing these verses with those found in the Sermon on the Mount will demonstrate one of the principal differences between the Christianity of the West and the belief in Christ as a God and Savior and that of Nestorian Christianity and its first cousin, Islâm, that deny the divinity of Christ. Since all men engage in evil, there can be no return to God without a Savior.

In the *New Testament* types of love are described in terms of the Greek words for love. Ῥως (eros) lust or erotic attraction is one type. Φίλωσέ, (filios) or the term for brotherly love or comradery is a higher type of love. Αγαπας (agapae), translated as "charity" in the King James Bible is equated with the love of God. An illustration of the use of these last two forms of love is found in John 21:15-17. *"So, when they had dined, Jesus saith to Simon Peter, Simon, son of Jonas, lovest thou me more than these? He saith unto him, Yea, Lord; thou knowest that I love thee. He saith unto him, Feed my lambs. He saith to him again the second time, Simon, son of Jonas, lovest thou me? He saith unto him, Yea, Lord; thou knowest that I love thee. He saith unto him, Feed my sheep. He saith unto him the third time, Simon, son of Jonas, lovest thou me? Peter was grieved because he said unto him the third time, Lovest thou me? And he said unto him, Lord, thou knowest all things; thou knowest that I love thee. Jesus saith unto him, Feed my sheep."*

Why was Peter "*grieved because he said unto him the third time, Lovest thou me?*" The answer lies in word for "love" used in this exchange between the Lord and Peter. The original text was written in first century AD Greek. The first time Christ asks if Peter loves him, he uses the word ἀγαπας (agapae); however, when Peter answers and says "you know that I love thee," he uses the word φίλωσέ, (filios) or the term for comradery. Christ repeats his question as before using the word ἀγαπας and again Peter answers using the word φίλωσέ." The third time Christ asks the question; however, he uses φίλωσέ when he asks Peter if he loves him. This is what grieved Peter since this is a step down in the form of the word for love. However, Peter continues to use the word φίλωσέ when he answers the Savior about his love for him. Peter had not yet gotten the picture. You may recall that a month earlier, before his death and resurrection at the last supper the Lord said to Peter, "*Simon, behold, Satan hath desired to have you, that he may sift you as wheat: But I have prayed for thee, that thy faith fail not: and **when thou art converted**, strengthen thy brethren*" (Luke 22:31-32). Peter eventually gets the point when he receives the Holy Ghost and the witness of Christ at Pentecost. Then Peter is converted.

Muhammad

The *Korân* refers to Muhammad numerous times. The George Sale translation cites him 46 times by name. Other translations name him fewer times, but use pronouns to indicate him. The *Korân* lists many duties about preaching. Some verses, especially those of sūra **5** should replace or abrogate all the others. These indicate that he is "only" or "no other than" a preacher (**3:20**) (**5:92, 99**) (7:184) (**11**:12) (**13**:7, 40) (**16**:35, 82) (**22:49**) (**24:54**) (26:**115**) (**29**:18, 50) (**35**:23) (36:**17**) (**42**:48) (**64:12**). Other verses mention the fact that he is a preacher and does preach without adding anything else (**2:119**) (**3:103, 193**) (**5:109**) (**6**:51) (**9:6**) (**10**:101) (15:**89**) (**16**:2) (21:**45**) (25:**1, 7, 51**) (26:**137**) (**28**:46) (**32**:3, 12) (**35**:42) (38:**70**) (50:**2**) (74:2). Others assure us that he asks for no "recompense," "compensation," or "reward" for his preaching (**6**:90) (**11**:29, 51) (23:**72**) (25:**57**) (26:**109, 127, 145, 164, 180**) (**34**:47) (38:**86**) (**42**:23) (52:40) (68:**46**). This is inconsistent with his taking whatever he desired of the spoils of war or more commonly a "fifth part" (**8:1, 41**). We are also told that he received the *Korân* so that he might preach it to his people (**6**:92) (7:2) (26:**192-195**) (36:**10**) (**46**:29). In one verse we are assured that he also has the power to forgive sins (**46**:31). Other apostles have been sent to preach to their respective peoples: (**11**:25) (26:**208**) (**35**:24, 37) (**40**:12, 34, 70) (43:**23, 24**) (**46**:21, 23). Muhammad is also said to consult with his people in matters of war (**3:159**), and about women (**4:127**). Muhammad has only the limited powers of "a preacher." This is emphasized in **35**:22-23: "*Neither shall the living and the dead be held equal. GOD shall cause him* *to hear whom he pleaseth; but thou shalt not make those to hear who are in their graves. Thou art no other than a preacher.*" As such he does not have nor can he claim the various powers of the priesthood described in the Bible.

An X-rated Paradise for Men Only

The early suras of the *Korân* show a fascination for the worldly opulence and sexual possibilities of heaven. This may reflect the prophet's unusual mounting libido suffered as he entered his 5th and 6th decades of life. Muhammad refers to this kind of heaven in seven Suras from the Meccan period: 37, 44, 52, 55, 56, 76, and 78. Paradise is not described in the Medina period.

The claim that Islâmic martyrs in a jihād get 72 virgins is found in the Book of Sunan (volume IV, chapters on *The Features of Paradise as described by the Messenger of Allah,* Chapter 21: "About the Smallest Reward for the People of Paradise," Hadith 2687). The Tafsir of Surah Al-Rahman 55, verse 72: states, "It was mentioned by Daraj Ibn Abi Hatim that Abu-al-Haytham 'Abdullah Ibn Wahb narrated from Abū Sa'id Al-Khudri, who heard the Prophet Muhammad saying: 'The smallest reward for the people of Paradise is an abode where there are 80,000 servants and 72 wives, over which stands a dome decorated with pearls, aquamarine, and ruby, as wide as the distance from Al-Jabiyyah [a Damascus suburb] to Sana'a.'" [103]

However, the number of *houris* a Muslim man may have is not limited to 72. In fact, it may be unlimited. Furthermore, the *Korân* does not tell us how the "seventy-two" like being the consorts of martyrs or even tell us where they come from. The *houris* are there waiting for the martyrs. Paradise also includes "young boys" for those of that preference. It also has wine, water and fruit in abundance plus riches. The phrase "eat, drink, and be merry for tomorrow ye die," has special significance. For the faithful it is: "tomorrow we die so we can eat, drink and be merry." Although all quotes below are from the early and mid Meccan period, none are abrogated later.

The propriety of former times comes out in George Sales' translation of the *Korân,* where he attempts to "clean up" heaven. He softens the place by adding a more Christian moral twist. In 37:**48** Sale translates, "*And near them shall lie the virgins of paradise, refraining their looks from beholding any* ***besides their spouses****, having large black eyes.*" Modern translations do not include "*besides their spouses.*" In 55:74 the Sale translation reads, "*Whom no man shall have deflowered,* ***before their destined spouses****, nor any genius (genii).*" "*Before their destined spouses*" does not appear in modern translations. In 56:37 Sale translates, "*and we have made them virgins,*

beloved by their husbands *of equal age with them;*" "*Beloved by their husbands*" is not in the modern translations.

Korân 37:40-49 "*But as for the sincere servants of GOD, they shall have a certain provision in paradise, namely, delicious fruits: and they shall be honoured: they shall be placed in gardens of pleasure, leaning on couches opposite to one another: a cup shall be carried round unto them, filled from limpid fountain, for the delight of those who drink: it shall not oppress the understanding, neither shall they be inebriated therewith. And near them shall lie the virgins of paradise, refraining their looks (…), having large black eyes, and resembling the eggs of an ostrich covered with feathers from the dust.*" The parenthetical expression removed does not appear in any of the modern translations.

> *Korân* 44:51-55
>
> "*But the pious shall be lodged in a place of security; among gardens and fountains: they shall be clothed in fine silk and in satin; and they shall sit facing one another. Thus shall it be: and we will espouse them to fair damsels, having large black eyes. In that place shall they call for all kinds of fruits, in full security:*" Modern translations use the word "*wed*" rather than espouse.
>
> *Korân* 52:19-20
>
> "*And it shall be said unto them, Eat and drink with easy digestion; because of that which ye have wrought: leaning on couches disposed in order: and we will espouse them unto virgins having large black eyes.*" "Unite" is used instead of "espouse" in the more modern translations.
>
> *Korân* 55:46-78
>
> The phrase: "*Which, therefore, of your LORD'S benefits will ye ungratefully deny?*" is repeated numerous times below and is removed wherever you see (…)
>
> "*But for him who dreadeth the tribunal of his LORD, are prepared two gardens: (…) Planted with shady trees. (…) In each of them shall be two fountains flowing. (…) In each of them shall there be every fruit two kinds. (…) They shall repose on couches, the linings whereof shall be of thick silk interwoven with gold: and the fruit of the two gardens shall be near at hand to gather. (…) Therein shall receive them beauteous damsels, whom no man shall*

> *have deflowered before them, neither any genius (genii). (...) Having complexions like rubies and pearls. (...) Shall the reward of good works be any other than good? (...) And besides these there shall be two other gardens. (...) Of a dark green. (...) In each of them shall be two fountains pouring forth plenty of water. (...) In each of them shall be fruits, and palm-trees, and pomegranates. (...) Therein shall be agreeable and beauteous damsels, (...) Having fine black eyes; and kept in pavilions from public view. (...) Whom no man shall have deflowered,* ***before their destined spouses****, nor any genius (genii). (...) Therein shall they delight themselves, lying on green cushions and beautiful carpets. (...) Blessed be the name of thy LORD, possessed of glory and honour!" "Before their destined spouses*" is not in modern translations.

Korân 56:7-40 includes a lush description of paradise for those most favored: those "*to the fore*" and "*those on the right hand.*" "Those on the left hand" are the damned. Those "to the fore" are described: *"These are they who shall approach near unto God: they shall dwell in gardens of delight."* We are told that many will be the earlier martyrs of Islâm, but there will be fewer from later generations. Those of the highest degree will have the added advantage of being served by ageless youths (verse 17). This is an allusion to "youths of pleasure" or *ghilunan* that inhabit paradise according to Hindu lore with whom pederasty is permitted. Pederasty was common in the ancient world and is still practiced in many countries without "age of consent" laws. There will also be the "black-eyed" fair damsels found in verse 22. Verse 27 begins a description of rewards for others of the right hand that include virgins, but no youth.

In verses 41-56 we find what awaits those on the left hand – black smoke, scorching winds and scalding water.

> *Korân* 78:31-34
>
> *"But for the pious is prepared a place of bliss: gardens planted with trees, and vineyards, and damsels with swelling breasts, of equal age with themselves, and a full cup."*

The Hadiths go further and describe a market where, like fruit, a man may select either a *houris* or a young boy to enjoy. Homosexuality, being "gay," is prohibited. However, sexual domination over another man and pederasty is still practiced in some Islamic countries.

Al Hadis, Vol. 4, p. 172, No. 34 "Alī reported that the Apostle of Allah said, "There is in Paradise a market wherein there will be no buying or selling, but will consist of men and women. When a man desires a beauty, he will have intercourse with them." [104] This is further confirmed in the *Korân*. In Paradise houris and *youth* (pre-pubertal young boys) will be available according to the following verses in Sūras 52, 56, and 76:

> *Korân* 52:22-24
>
> "*And we will give them fruits in abundance, and flesh of the kinds which they shall desire. They shall present unto one another therein a cup of wine, wherein there shall be no vain discourse, nor any incitement unto wickedness. And youths appointed to attend them, shall go round them: beautiful as pearls hidden in their shell.*"
>
> *Korân* 56:17
>
> "*Youths which shall continue in their bloom forever, shall go round about to attend them,*"
>
> *Korân* 76:11-19
>
> "*Wherefore GOD shall deliver them from the evil of that day and shall cast on them brightness of countenance, and joy; and shall reward them, for their patient persevering, with a garden, and silk garments: therein shall they repose themselves on couches; they shall see therein neither sun nor moon: and the shades thereof shall be near spreading above them, and the fruits thereof shall hang low, so as to be easily gathered. And their attendants shall go round about unto them, with vessels of silver and goblets: the bottles shall be bottles of silver shining like glass; they shall determine the measure thereof by their wish. And therein shall they be given to drink of a cup of wine, mixed with the water of Zenjebil* (ginger)*, a fountain in paradise named Salsabil: and youths, which shall continue for ever in their bloom (Dawood renders this "graced with eternal youth"), shall go round to attend them; when thou seest them, thou shalt think them to be scattered pearls:*" See this sūra in the translation of the *Korân* by George Sale and the Index & Topical Guide on homosexuality among the Arabs of Muhammad's time. This will be discussed further under Euphemisms below.

Women & Paradise

If this is Paradise for men, what about the paradise for women? As one wag put it, the women in paradise get 72 eunuchs. There are websites that claim there is equality of men and women in Islâm. These are not well documented and do not agree with statements in the *Korân* or Hadiths.

It is also alleged that more secular Islâmic believers do not rely on the Hadīth which place women below men. Rather, they rely on the *Korân* that elevates women to near equality with men. It is important to understand that sūras written after 622 or AH 1 supersede verses from sūras written during the earlier, Meccan *Korân*ic period of 610 to 622. Those suras noted in **boldface** are from the Medinan or late Meccan periods. Women in the ancient world with rare exceptions including the Jews were little more than chattel. They were valued only for their general labor and household work.

According to the *Korân* women have half the value of men. Quotations below are from the George Sale translation. Sūra **2:282** describes court witnesses where one man equals two women,

1. *"and call to witness two witnesses of your neighboring men; but if there be not two men, let there be and man and two women of those whom ye shall choose for witnesses;"*
2. In matters of inheritance sūra **4:11** teaches, "*GOD hath thus commanded you concerning your children. A male shall have as much as the share of two females.*"
3. Sūra **3:14** teaches that women are like goods: "*The love and eager desire of wives, and children, and sums heaped up of gold and silver, and excellent horses, and cattle and land, is prepared for men.*"
4. Women must veil outside the home: Sūra **24:31**, *"And speak unto the believing women, that they restrain their eyes, and preserve their modesty, and discover not their ornaments, except what necessarily appeareth thereof."*
5. The Hadīth quotes Muhammad's teachings, "I have not seen any one more deficient in intelligence and religion than women." Al Bukhary Vol. 2:541. "Bad omen is in the women, the house and the horse." Al Bukhary Vol. 7:30. "After me I have not left any affliction more harmful to men than women." Al Bukhary Vol. 7:33.

The *Korân* further places men in a superior position to women.

1. Islâm allows polygamy up to 4 wives (**4:2**)

2. A man may divorce his wife simply by saying it twice (**2:229**). If he says it three times, she cannot come back to him until she has married another man and been divorced by him. (**2:230**)
3. A husband may punish his wife by beating her and by withholding sexual contact with her. (**4:34**)
4. Women are considered sex objects, *"Your wives are your tillage; go in therefore unto your tillage in what manner soever ye will:"* (**2:223**)
5. If an unbeliever woman marries an Islâmic man, he has rights of custody of children if there is a divorce and all children must be reared as Muslims. (**3:19; 4:144**).

The same is true in matters of inheritance. A wife who has not converted to Islâm gets nothing when her husband dies. It reverts to other family members. If she has converted, she gets ¼ and the family gets the rest. If there are children, she gets 1/8th. If the woman dies childless, the husband inherits ½ of her estate. If there are children, he gets ¼ (**4:12**).

Paul, in his day found it necessary to warn women contemplating marriage outside Christianity, *"Be ye not unequally yoked together with unbelievers: for what fellowship hath righteousness with unrighteousness? and what communion hath light with darkness?"* (2 Cor 6:14)

In regards to Paradise and women the *Korân* teaches,

1. *"By another sign He gave you spouses from among yourselves, that you might live in peace with them, and planted love and kindness in your hearts. Surely there are signs in this for thinking men."* (**30**:21) A similar statement occurs in **9:71**.
2. A *Hadīth*, Vol. 7 No 120 by Abū Hurairah / Bukhary states, "A woman should not fast except with her husband's permission.

In this statement men and women appear to have equal status and will go to paradise if they have sacrificed themselves and suffered for the cause through martyrdom, exile or move to Medina.

1. *"Their LORD therefore answereth them, saying, I will not suffer the work of him among you who worketh to be lost, whether he be male or female: the one of you is from the other. They therefore who have left their country, and have been turned out of their houses, and have suffered for my sake, and have been slain in battle; verily I will expiate their evil deeds from thee, and I will surely bring them into gardens watered by rivers; a reward from GOD: and with*

GOD is the most excellent reward" (**3:195**). Similar sentiments are expressed in **4:124**.

2. *"Whoso worketh righteousness, whether he be male or female, and is a true believer, we will surely raise him to a happy life; and we will give them their reward, according to the utmost merit of their actions"* (**16**.97). *"Whoever worketh evil, shall only be rewarded in equal proportion to the same: but whoever worketh good, whether male or female, and is a true believer, they shall enter paradise;"* (**40**:40). Note, they must be a true believer. Infidels don't count.

There is no clear statement about the nature of the paradise that women get. As noted in the verses from the *Korân* above, Paradise for men is full of trees, fountains, water, wine, fruit, meats of your choice and riches consisting of fine couches, carpets, silks, fine brocade, jewels, and gold and silver eating utensils and other benefits. No one even has to leave his couch to go to the bathroom according to one of the Hadiths.

Sahih Muslim Book 39, Number 6798: Narrated Jabir ibn Abdullah: *I heard Allah's Apostle (PBUH) as saying that the inmates of Paradise would eat and drink but would neither spit, nor pass water, nor void excrement, nor suffer catarrh. It was said: Then, what would happen with food? Thereupon he said: They would belch and sweat (and it would be over with their food), and their sweat would be that of musk and they would glorify and praise Allah as easily as you breathe."*

Resurrection

Resurrection of the dead is one of the principal doctrines of Islâm (**2:85**). Many other references are found in the Topical Guide under Resurrection. For believers this means paradise and for martyrs even more. The *Korân* has a great deal to say about "paradise" and "gardens," and "virgins." These sections should also be searched. For unbelievers it means "hell" and perpetual burning along with punishments both in this life and in the life to come (**3:56**). It is mentioned in the *Korân* in 338 verses. Believers are given Allah's permission to begin carrying out the punishments against unbelievers in this life (**5:33, 38; 9:14**).

Vicarious Work for the Dead

Paul's statement, "*Else what shall they do which are baptized for the dead, if the dead rise not at all? why are they then baptized for the dead*" (1 Cor:15:29) hints about the power to do vicarious work for the dead in the name of the LORD. The *Korân* comments on this, but the power to do it is denied to Muhammad and to Islâm by implication. "*Neither shall the living and the dead be held equal. GOD shall cause him to hear whom he pleaseth; but thou shalt not make those to hear who are in their graves. Thou art no other than a preacher*" (**35**:22-23).

Scriptures & Censorship

Scriptures, usually meaning those given to Jews and Christians, are mentioned frequently in the *Korân*. The *Korân* is also mentioned frequently; in the Sale translation it is mentioned in 149 verses mostly in the Mid-Meccan and Late-Meccan periods. In other translations it is referred to as a "book" and specifically as a "perspicuous book" (5 verses). References to "scripture(s)" occur in the Medina period (72 verses) and Late-Meccan period (22 verses). The Early-Meccan period includes only 1 and Mid Meccan period 7 verses.

Several specific books are mentioned in the *Korân*: "Day of Resurrection" (9 verses), "Book of the Law" possibly the "Pentateuch" (22 verses), "Book of God" (10 verses), "Book of Decrees" (6 verses), the "Gospels" (1 verse) and "Psalms" (3 verses). There is also a generic reference to sacred books (11 verses). The word "religion" also has a similar distribution in the *Korân* as does "scriptures" with about 2/3rds of the citations occurring in the Medina period. This may reflect the escalating militancy against Jews and Christians during the Medina period.

During the Medina period censorship became a policy of Muhammad; he ordered the assassination of several of his critics. After his death Islâmic armies are credited with destroying the Alexandrian Library, the repository of much of the ancient world's knowledge.

Terror

Terror against Islâm's enemies is doctrinal. Four verses from the Medina period make this point (**8:60**) (**33:26**) (**59:2, 13**). The *Korân* even prescribes the methods. "*Strike off their heads, and strike off all the ends of their fingers*" (**8:12**); "*strike off their heads, until ye have made a great slaughter among them*" (**47:4**). "*But the recompense of those who fight against GOD and his apostles, and study to act corruptly in the earth, shall be, that they shall be slain, or crucified, or have their hands and their feet cut off on the opposite sides, or* *be banished the land. This shall be their disgrace in this world, and in the next world they shall suffer a grievous punishment;"* (**5:33**). "*O true believers, the law of retaliation is ordained you for the slain: the free shall die for the free, and the servant for the servant, and a woman for a woman:"* (**2:178**). "*Kill them wherever ye find them,"* (**2:191**). "*If they turn back from the faith, take them, and kill them wherever ye find them; and take no friend from among them, nor any helper"* (**4:89**). "*Kill the idolaters wheresoever ye shall find them, and take them prisoners, and besiege them, and lay wait for them in every convenient place"* (**9:5**). "*Wherever they are found they shall be taken, and killed with a general slaughter,"* (**33:61**). This is opposed to Christ's denial of the code of Hammurabi and "turn the other cheek," (Matt 5:39; Luke 6:29) or his warning that "*all they that take the sword shall perish with the sword*" (Matt 26:52).

Women are not immune from the wrath of an Islâmic army. "*Ye are also forbidden to take to wife free women who are married, <u>except</u> those women whom your right hands shall possess as slaves*" (**4:24**). "Those whom the right hand possesses" is a euphemism for female captives. The following verse was quoted by Muhammad to give license to his troops to begin a mass rape of women prisoners following a battle. "*The Jews say, the hand of GOD is tied up. Their hands shall be tied up, and they shall be cursed for that which they have said. Nay, his* (meaning God's) *hands are both stretched forth; he bestoweth as he pleaseth:"* (**5:64**). The "bestowal" of women and children to the Islâmic conquerors at the Jewish settlement of the Banu-Qurayza (April-May 627 near Medina) led immediately to the beheading of all the men the rape of all the women and children and the confiscation of all their property. This same scene was repeated at another Jewish settlement of the Banu Sa'da tribe near Medina Feb 628 and again at the Battle of Khaybar August 628 when another Jewish tribe, Banu Nadīr, was despoiled and annihilated. During the general rape that followed, Muhammad spotted a very pretty Jewess, Safiya bint Huyai/Huyayy, being raped on the battlefield by one of his chieftains. He claimed her for his own, raped her, and married her when she agreed under duress to become Islâmic. This created a near rebellion in the harem and required two special verses in the *Korân*: "*O Prophet, why holdest thou that to be prohibited which GOD hath allowed thee, seeking to please thy wives; since GOD is inclined to forgive and merciful? GOD hath allowed you the dissolution of your oaths: and GOD is your master; and he is knowing and wise*" (**66:1-2**).

Allah Uses Islâmic Soldiers to Execute His Will

The *Korân* assures us that Allah executes these punishments through Islâm. Although the believers do the killing and raping, it is all by the will and hand of Allah. "*Ye slew not those who were slain at Bedr yourselves, but GOD slew them. Neither didst thou, O Mohammed, cast the gravel into their eyes, when thou didst seem to cast it; but GOD cast it, that he might prove the true believers by a gracious trial from himself; for GOD heareth and knoweth*" (**8:17**). If you live or die in battle, the great rewards of paradise are yours. "*Let them therefore fight for the religion of GOD, who part with the present life in exchange for that which is to come; for whosoever fighteth for the religion of GOD, whether he be slain, or be victorious, we will surely give him a great reward*" (**4:74**).

Works

"Work(s)" and other cognates are used 148 times in the Sale Translation. Most of the emphasis is found in the Late-Meccan, 55, and Medina periods, 50. In contrast the word is used only 35 times in the Mid-Meccan and 8 times in the Early-Meccan periods. Good works among the faithful are an insurance plan for paradise (18:**103-107**) (37:**39**).

Euphemisms in the *Korân*

The use of a delicate phrase or word to mean something that may be crude to most people is common in all languages. This is especially common when the topics are crime, sex and violence. Words that have a straightforward meaning in one era may take on a crude meaning and require substitutes in later writings. The *Korân* is no exception. I have used several texts of the *Korân*. These have included *The Korân: Translated into English from the Original Arabic* by George Sale, Frederick Warne & Co., London & New York 1734, reprinted 1764, 1825, and 1877. Other texts include the *Korân* (Penguin Classic translated by NJ Dawood, translated in 1956; now in its 5th revision, 1993) and the *Quran, An English Translation* by Malmud Y Zayid assisted by a committee of Muslim scholars; approved by the Supreme Sunni and Shii Councils of the Republic of Leabanon, 1980, Beirut Lebanon. Pickthall, M. *The Meaning of The Glorious Qur'an Text and Explanatory Translation,* Jajarmia Publications, Tehran, Iran, ISBN

964-6766-01-3. I have also used on-line texts from the U. of Michigan [105] and U. of Virginia. [106]

As one progresses from earlier to later translations this becomes apparent. Straight forward words found in the Sale translation are noted in column 1. The number of times it is used in later translations is noted in the parenthesis. The current euphemistic phrase and number of citations are noted in column 2 and 3. For example, "Maid-servant" is found in two verses pertaining to the marriage of believers with righteous captives in the Sale translation. This becomes "*whom the right hand possess*" in later versions. "Infidels" used in the Sale translation, is not used in later translations where "unbelievers" and "those who disbelieve" are used in later translations.

There are a number of references to sexual activity, but "sex" or "sexual intercourse" does not appear commonly in the newer versions. "Intercourse" appears once and "fornication" five times while "indecency" occurs 18 times in the newer versions. The term "homosexual" is not used in the Sale translation or in newer versions of the *Korân*. Euphemisms include *two who are guilty of indecency from among you.* (U. of Michigan text) or *commit the like wickedness* (Sale Translation); **4:16**.

This is in contradistinction with adultery which is termed *indecency from among your women* (**4:15**) – "*Guilty of whoredom*" in the Sale Translation. Notice that men are not responsible for adultery.

Table VI Searches performed at University of Michigan Web Site:[107]

Word (# of times it appears)	Euphemism	*Korân* Citations
Booty (0)	acquisitions	**48:15,19,20**
Spoils (0)	accession	Chapter heading
	"Allah restored"	**59:6**
	"Allah has restored"	**59:7**
	"It"	**59:8**
People of the Book" (0)	"followers of the book"	32 total citations
Infidel(s) (0)	"unbelievers"	125 total citations
	"those who disbelieve" etc.	168 total citations
Adultery (0) Fornication (5)	"indecency"	18 total citations
Maid-servant (2) **24:32, 33**	"whom the right hand possess"	14 total citations

There are several phrases used for homosexual relationships (**7**:81; 26:**165**; 27:**55**; **29**:29) and there is unusual attention paid to Sodom and Gomorrah in the *Korân*. Lot or "Lut," whose daughters lay with him to conceive children, is considered an "apostle" and cited 27 times. "*And Lot* *was also one of those who were sent by us. When we delivered him and his whole family, except an old woman, his wife, who perished among those that remained behind:"* (37:**133-135**). The story of Sodom is retold in varying detail in 8 sūras: 7, 11, 15, 26, 27, 29, 37, and 54.

There is also a fascination with Lot's wife (not mentioned by name) and her demise (**66:10**) (**11**:81) (**29**:32, 33) (15:**60**) (26:**171**) (27:**57**) (37:**135**). Homosexuality is prohibited.[108] Pederasty, *bacha bazi*, is not. [109] See Abu-Nuwas (756-814) *Perfumed Garden*.

The original translation by Sale does not use the phrase "slave girl(s)." It does use "maid-servant" in connection with marriage. It appears infrequently in the Dawood, and other on-line translations. Sale uses the more delicate phrase: "*slaves whom their right hands possess.*" These are the spoils of war that Muslim men may have at their will. Since a state of war exists in any part of the world where Sharia Law is not recognized, many have interpreted this to mean that sex with unbelievers living outside of Sharia Law is sanctioned without any implication of fornication or adultery (23:**1-11**; 66:1-2; 70:29-31). Muslims who achieve sexual conquests in Infidel nations are soldiers in the current *jihād*. Women combatants captured on a battlefield are clearly covered by the *Korân* as "gifts of the right hand" (**33:52**). The problem of "slave-girls" or "*whom the right hand possesses*" is fraught with multiple interpretations. In general, "slave-girls" don't count as legal wives. The faithful man can have 4 legal wives. (**4:2**) Any Islâmic man who receives one or more "slave girls" may have them as a bonus. Islâmic scholarly literature has many comments about slave-girls or "*whom the right hand possesses.*" In short, they have no rights. Those taken in war are to be sent first to higher authorities who either exchange them with the enemy for their prisoners of war or keep the ones they want and distribute the rest to the soldiers. Rules are cited on line. [110]The use of women in combat roles against Islamic enemies has increased risks for them and should be prohibited.

Contrast this with the relatively simple statement about the treatment of adult female captives according to the rules of war for ancient Israel. The captor had to allow a desired woman a full month of mourning before marrying her as a legitimate wife. However, if she proved to be undesired, he was obliged to let her go and was forbidden to sell or prostitute her.

> *"When thou goest forth to war against thine enemies, and the LORD thy God hath delivered them into thine hands, and thou hast taken them captive, And seest among the captives a beautiful woman, and hast a desire unto her, that thou wouldest have her to thy wife; Then thou shalt bring her home*

> *to thine house; and she shall shave her head, and pare her nails; And she shall put the raiment of her captivity from off her, and shall remain in thine house, and bewail her father and her mother a full month: and after that thou shalt go in unto her, and be her husband, and she shall be thy wife. And it shall be, if thou have no delight in her, then thou shalt let her go whither she will; but thou shalt not sell her at all for money, thou shalt not make merchandise of her, because thou hast humbled her."* (Deut 21:10-14)

Why is the phrase about the "right hand" used to mean a captive? In ancient times when armies lined up in a phalanx formation, all men carried the sword in their right hand and the shield in their left. This created a solid front without gaps. However, "lefties" were highly prized because of their ability to wield a sword or dagger with their left hands and thus be a complete surprise to another in single combat. The Bible uses "left handed" to mean *assassin* because of this skill. (Judges 3:21)

A common belief is that all major religions advocate restrictions against killing, stealing, and forcible fornication or adultery. For Islam there are exceptions when it comes to treatment of unbelievers especially during war. **2:175, 3:131**, **9:5, 9:110, 47:4** are extermination orders against unbelievers. **5:3** orders mutilation of non-believers often likely to kill them. Female captives can be raped (**4:24**) (**33:52**) (70:30). Spoils in war are sanctioned. (**3:153**) (**4:94**) (**8:1, 41**) (**33:19, 50**) (**48:15, 19, 20, 21**) (**59:6,** 7) (**29**:67).

Those in the West have trouble understanding this concept, however, that is why rape has become common in countries such as Sweden, where Sharia Law is not. Once the population contains upwards of 7-8% Islamic refugees. Attitudes of the Islamists change. A state of warfare exists and all Swedish women are thus, "fair game" for the Islamic men. See The Sīra: *TheBook of Campaigns* later in this book that describes how Islamic conquest of Infidel nations is to take place.

MODERN CONCEPTS

"Terrorism" Today

The "war on terror" is a misnomer. It fails to personify the enemy and what he stands for. It does not explain why we fight, which makes it difficult for people to remain focused. There is no enemy. It is not personal; there is nothing to worry about. "Terror" is a "technique" of war.

World War I was personified by the "Kaiser;" World War II by "Hitler," "Mussolini," and "Emperor Hirohito" or "Tojo." In both these wars people remained focused. World War I ended in an unsatisfactory armistice that led to Word War II. The only wars we actually won in the 20th Century were World War II, Grenada, and the Gulf War. In WWII Italy folded after a successful invasion. Japan and Germany were more difficult. Despite the slaughter caused by fire-bombing raids on their cities, it was necessary to use two atom bombs to convince Japan to quit. Conventional "terror bombings" on German cities failed. They did not give up until Hitler committed suicide, their infrastructure was wrecked, their army beaten, their major cities in ruins, and their country overrun with allied troops. Korea ended in an armistice, but with South Korea preserved. In Grenada we defeated a Communist coup (1979). In 1983 the U.S. supported a popular uprising by sending in troops and defeated the local militia aided by Cuban Special Forces in a few days. In the Gulf War (1990-91) we either killed or captured the Iraqi army occupying Kuwait; the aerial bombardment lasted about 3 weeks and the ground action about 1 week.

Both Grenada and the Gulf were led by General "Storm'n" **Norman Schwarzkoph** (1934 -); they were quick. Other wars of the 20th Century should have convinced us that the only solution is victory. This requires the enemy to lose his will to fight. Consequently, if we are to commit our military in a war, we must desire to win and fight as rapidly as possible to a successful conclusion. This is why we were unsuccessful in WWI, and Vietnam. The Gulf War was successful in liberating Kuwait, but did not convince Iraq to cease funding, equipping and training terrorists. Another war became necessary to complete the job. If it fails, it will be the result of political interference that prolongs the conflict.

Carl von Clausewitz (1780-1831) and Sun Tzu (544-496 BC) were correct. To win, you must destroy the enemy's will to fight and do it quickly. We must realize our current adversary is patient and fights with religious zeal. The *Korân* advocates destruction of unbelievers, infidels and Islâmic backsliders. They will not quit until Sharia law governs the entire world. For us to win, we must have a will to win that is stronger.

A response to an editorial by Aziz Junejo in *The Seattle Times* February 17, 2006 stated that President G.W. Bush was "right to go after those people, wherever they are, but he is wrong to call them *terrorists.* They are "imperialists of tribe, clan and race. The West has had to make a valid distinction between *Muslims* as a group and *tribal/clan/racial imperialism* that was fronting for Islâm in general. ...Terrorism is a misnomer, tragically missing the reality of those individuals and groups. ... They are driven by Muslim-sourced petrol, trading and construction dollars."

These observations are accurate. In all warfare it is important to know and identify the enemy with precision. *War on Terror* does not. *Police Action* used during the Korean War implied that it was a matter that required "police" not armed forces. Without a clear definition, there is confusion that dilutes the war effort. Regardless of what we want to call it, we are in the middle of a *jihād* or war with many of Islâm who use their "holy book" as justification and seem to have as their goal world domination. We ignore this at our peril.

Wahhabism

"Radical Islâm" is a mystery to many. Its tactics are based on Wahhabism or Salafism, "fundamentalist" Islâmic movements. [111] The number of Muslims who adhere to Wahhabism and tactics is unknown, but it does not include all Muslims. Many are just as frightened of it as we are. It targets all including the "lukewarm" of Islâm. It began as a small Saudi Arabian sect under the Islâmic theologian, Muhammad ibn Abd-al-Wahhab (1703-92). [112] He was unpopular and unaccepted during his life, but he allied himself to the Saud Royal family. Wahhab was offended by the soft, secular trends of the Ottoman Empire. He believed that pictures of human beings, praying at tombs, women not wearing burqas, skipping prayers, invoking any prophet, Sufi saint, or angel in prayer, celebrating annual feasts for Sufi saints, wearing charms as part of healing, practicing magic and other new forms of worship were corruptions of original Islâmic beliefs. He longed for glory-days of the 7th and 8th Centuries of a heroic, conquering, jihādist, Islâm. From the beginning Wahhab reformers used brutal, often lethal tactics in their attempt to reform "corrupt" Muslims, but remained relatively powerless and obscure until the Saud family began receiving mountains of oil money in the late 20th Century.

After WWI, the Ottoman Empire was divided into protectorates with Britain controlling Palestine, Jordan, Egypt and Iraq; the French got Lebanon and Syria. Of the two major Islâmic sects, the Shiites controlled in Iran, but the Sunnis were more influential in Iraq, Afghanistan, and Saudi-Arabia. All religions were respected in oil-poor Jordan. Sunnis were in the majority, but despite this, Wahhabism had little influence. In return for Saudi promises of unlimited oil supplies the British kept them from becoming a protectorate. The Saudis used their independence to take over Mecca and control the *hajj*. In 1933 they signed a contract with Standard Oil of California to allow oil exploration and development. [113] Despite little success Texaco purchased 50% of the concession. In 1938 oil was discovered. In 1944 the company became Aramco – Arab American Oil Co. **U.S. Gold (Philadelphia mint)** was used to pay the workers from1945-47. Using their share of the profits, the Saudis purchased complete ownership by 1980; oil revenues became huge.

OPEC, The Organization of the Petroleum Exporting Countries, headquartered in Vienna, Austria, was formed in Baghdad in September 1960. Its five founding members were Iran, Iraq, Kuwait, Saudi Arabia and Venezuela. Since then Qatar (1961); Indonesia (1962); Socialist People's Libyan Arab Jamahiriya (1962); United Arab Emirates (1967); Algeria (1969); Nigeria (1971); Ecuador (1973–1992); Gabon (1975–1994) and Angola (2007) have joined. [114] In 2011 the top three oil producers in the world are Russia 10,120,000 bbl/d, Saudi Arabia 9,764,000, and the U.S. 9,053,000 bbl/d. Canada is #6 with 3,289,000. Mexico is #7. [115]

In 1945 Michel Aflaq (1910-1989), a Greek Orthodox, and Salah al-Din al-Bitar, a Sunni, formed an Arab nationalistic party with socialist leanings known as Baath Party. They joined with the socialists in 1952 and after political turbulence took control of Syria and Iraq in 1963. It was controlled by Sunnis in Iraq and by the Alaouite (a subdivision of Shiites) in Syria and was a "hard line" Marxist party. In the 1970s the Baathists in Iraq and Syria separated. The Baathists took over during a coup in 1968 in Iraq with Saddam Hussein, a party loyalist, as dictator in 1979. As a secularist, he brutally suppressed the Shiites and would not follow the practices of the Sunni Wahhabis. He was respected and feared as an Arab leader, but was a controversial Muslim. [116]

As oil income increased in Saudi-Arabia, it was used to build mosques and spread fundamentalist Wahhabism throughout the Middle East. As the wealth increased and migration of Islâmic peoples spread into Europe, mosques and Wahhabism followed. Ridding the world of all infidels, not just "corrupt" members of Islâm became a goal. Since the 1970s they have expanded into Lebanon taking over that country. Most religious minorities in Iran fled or were slaughtered.

War with Israel began with its independence and two decades later with the West. At first it was characterized by multiple isolated attacks. The first major war came with the Soviet Afghan war of 1979 to 1989. The invasion of Kuwait by Iraq in 1990 led to the Gulf War with the U.N Coalition, primarily the U.S. Recent refusals to adhere to U.N. policies created a war between the U.S. coalition and Iraq. The Wahhabis follow the *Korân's* prescription for dealing with enemies – morning attacks, beheading, throat cutting, and incineration with explosives. Targets are civilians, their churches and economic structure. The message is clear – non-Islâm will convert or die. Those in the West are mostly Judeo-Christian. Without fighting back, our culture and religions will be exterminated. If we know history, none of this will be a surprise.

The Muslim Brothers

In 1928 **Hasan al-Banna**, a 22-year-old elementary school teacher, founded an organization that has been called by a number of names. It happened as a result of the fall and division of the Ottoman Empire and the ban of the caliphate system of government. Its motto was *"Allah is our objective. The Prophet is our leader. Qur'an is our law. Jihād is our way. Dying in the way of Allah is our highest hope."* 117

Al Banna followed the tenants of Wahhabism. This regarded Islâm as a religious observance, a way of life, and an educational system that included training in *jihādia* for young males. Its political arm was called the Party of the Muslim Brotherhood, Hizb Al-Ikhwan Al-Muslimoon. It should be noted that this group was organized 20 years before the establishment of the Jewish State in Palestine. However, when Zionism began to gain power, it opposed the Egyptian government's tolerance of Zionism. On December 28, 1948 a Muslim Brother assassinated the Egyptian Prime Minister, Mahmud Nokrashy Pasha. Al Banna was killed by Egyptian agents in February 1949. In 1954 the Brotherhood was banned in Egypt because it insisted that Egypt become governed by Shari'a Law and an attempt was made to assassinate President Nasser. [5] were executed and 4000 fled to other Middle Eastern countries. In 1964 President Nasser granted amnesty to the Brotherhood, but then suffered three more assassination attempts and in 1966 the top leadership of the Brothers were executed. Anwar-as-Sadat who succeeded Nasser pardoned the imprisoned Brothers, but was assassinated by the Brotherhood in 1981, 2 years after he had signed a peace agreement with Israel. Since then the Brothers have created numerous financial networks that fund the jihād and have spawned a number of jihād groups.

The *Korân* states, *"Verily those who believe not, among those who have received the scriptures* (People of the Book in more modern translations), *and among the idolaters, shall be cast into the fire of hell, to remain therein for ever. These are the worst of creatures. But they who believe, and do good works; these are the best of creatures: their reward with their LORD shall be gardens of perpetual abode, through which rivers flow; they shall remain therein for ever. GOD will be well pleased in them; and they shall be well pleased in him. This is prepared for him who shall fear his LORD"* (**98:6-8**).

"Moreover, the complete number of months with GOD, is twelve months, which were ordained in the book of GOD, on the day whereon he created the heavens and the earth: of these, four are sacred. This is the right religion: therefore deal not unjustly with yourselves therein. ***But attack the idolaters in all the months, as they attack you in all****; and know that GOD is with those who fear him."* (**9:36**). God states further, *"**Unless ye go forth when ye are summoned to war, God will punish you with a grievous punishment**; and he will place another people in your stead."* (**9.39**). *"Go forth to battle, both light and heavy* ***(unarmed or armed)****, and employ your substance and your persons for the advancement of GOD'S religion. This will be better for you, if ye know it."* (**9:41**). Those who claim to be believers, but who do not join the fight are proven to be unbelievers and of them it is stated, *"But hell will surely encompass the unbelievers."* (**9:49**).

The State of Israel is not the reason for the current Jihād. It is one of many excuses. Wealth due to oil makes possible the training and equipping of armies. The history of Islâm is that of armed conflict whenever it had the means and will to carry it out. It began in the 7th Century AD. 1300 years ago, Islâmic armies threatened all of Europe and the Mediterranean and required Charles Martel of the Franks (732) and Byzantium to keep them at bay. The Crusades of 1100 – 1300 attempted, but failed to push them back. With the collapse of the Ottoman Empire in 1922, most of Europe except for the Balkans was temporarily cleared of Islâm. According to the *Korân Jihād* against Christians and Jews is a matter of faith.

Are Negotiations Possible?

Many suggest that we "negotiate" with Islâmic terrorists. This has been discussed above under the heading of "War is Deceit." However, this concept is also handled specifically in the *Korân*. Treaties that are valid must be made in the Sacred Mosque. ***"How shall the idolaters be admitted into a league with GOD and with his apostle; except those with whom ye entered into a league at the holy temple*** [the Ka'ba in Mecca]. (**9:7**).

Agreements were made by Muhammad for strategic advantages during the early days of Islâm. "*So long as they behave with fidelity towards you, do ye also behave with fidelity towards them; for GOD loveth those who fear him. How can they be admitted into a league with you, since, if they prevail against you, they will not regard in you either consanguinity* [family / tribe] *or faith? They will please you with their mouths, but their hearts will be averse from you; for the greater part of them are wicked doers. They sell the signs of GOD for a small price, and obstruct his way; it is certainly evil which they do"* (**9:7-9**). True alliances with Infidels are no longer permitted nor can they be. Neither unbelievers nor infidels are permitted to enter Mecca or Medina, let alone a sacred mosque. ***"It is not fitting that the idolaters should visit the temples of GOD, being witnesses against their own souls of their infidelity. The works of these men are vain; and they shall remain in hell fire for ever"*** (**9:17**). Furthermore, Islam is forbidden to make treaties of friendship against any that have borne arms against them.

"***But as to those who have borne arms against you on account of religion, and have dispossessed you of your habitations, and have assisted in dispossessing you, GOD forbiddeth you to enter into friendship with them: and whosoever of you entereth into friendship with them, those are unjust doers.***" (**60:9**) Christian countries and Islâm have been at war with each other off and on since the 7th Century.

Will "Sanctions" Work?

Trade "Sanctions" are cited as a way to force Islâmic nations into negotiations or as an alternative to war. They won't work; the *Korân* says so. It is tough to enforce sanctions if your opponent sits on resources everyone wants. "*O true believers, verily the idolaters are unclean;* ***let them not therefore come near unto the holy temple after this year***. (632 AD) *And* ***if ye fear want, by the cutting off trade and communication*** *with them, GOD will enrich you of his abundance, if he pleaseth; for GOD is knowing and wise* (**9:28**). ***Fight against them*** *who believe not in GOD, ...,* ***until they pay tribute by right of subjection, and they be reduced low***" (**9:29**). This passage of God's "holy scripture" demonstrates the enmity of Islâm with all other beliefs except Islâm In the next section we will visit the pre-Islamic world and the fall of Rome.

Much of its fall was due to inflation, corruption and war. Ancient Israel dealt with indebtedness every 50 years with a "*jubilee.*" (Lev: 25). There was one who tried in vain to warn the Romans – Marcus Tullius Cicero (106-43 BC), "*Freedom does not mean the freedom to exploit law in order to destroy it. It is not freedom which permits the Trojan Horse to be wheeled within the gates and those within to be heard in the name of tolerating a different point of view! He who is not for Rome and Roman law and Roman liberty is against Rome. He who espouses tyranny and oppression and the old despotism is against Rome. He who plots against established authority and incites the populace to violence is against Rome. He cannot ride two horses at the same time; He cannot be for lawful ordinances and for an alien conspiracy at one and the same moment! One is a Roman or not a Roman!*" (Probably a composite from Cicero's speeches.) [118] Cicero was murdered.

HISTORY OF ISLÂM

The Pre-Islâmic World AD 306–570

At the time of Muhammad's birth his world was in transition, decline and chaos. Most sources state that Muhammad was born about 568-570 and died in 632. About 125 years preceding his birth the almost simultaneous collapse of the two world super powers, the Roman and Persian Empires occurred. There are many theories as to why western Rome failed. Among them was the ruin of its economy by a series of corrupt emperors who raided the treasury to benefit themselves and their cronies and maintain their power. They were also usually engaged in warfare. The exhaustion of the Eastern Roman Empire came from nearly 150 years of war with the Persian Empire, the Avars and Slavs. Another recently recognized factor was the climatic catastrophe of 535 that resulted in famine, plague and depopulation that followed. Although the climate had begun to resolve into a more normal pattern about the time of Muhammad, the plague was still much in evidence. Starvation, war, and the plague beginning in the 6th Century had decreased the peoples of the Mediterranean coastal regions by as much as 50%. All these factors were to play into the hands of Muhammad and the Arab Armies of the 7th Century. Christians living then would have thought that the end was near. The four horsemen of the apocalypse (Rev: 6) had come. The white horse bore a false prophet, wearing a crown and carrying a bow and arrow. The red horse and rider brought constant warfare with his sword. The black horse and rider had empty scales – severe famine. The horse and rider with deathly green pallor brought death. He visited the land with pestilence, famine, and war that for a time seemed never ending. Even the moon had cooperated by turning blood-red in 536. For Islâm and Muhammad's chieftains this meant opportunity.

Fall of the Western Roman Empire

Since the downfall of the Roman Republic and the beginning of the Empire, Roman mobs had demanded more and more "bread and circuses." Circuses in those days were sports arenas with a circular track where chariot racing, personal contests of strength and speed, and gladiatorial contests were held. This distracted the mobs and helped the emperors maintain power. However, it also meant inflation and devaluation of the currency with base metals.

Inflation

Inflation is like drug addiction. It feels good in the beginning, but with time it swindles the most productive members of society. A modern formula created from the works of John Maynard Keynes (1883-1946) and Milton Friedman (1912-2006) was simplified by Jens O. Parsson. [119] He states that the cost of goods or price level is equal to the total quantity of money and other forms of credit times the turnover rate of this money / money velocity (the length of time a given quantity is held before spent) divided by the real assets or value of a country's goods and services.

$$\textbf{Price level} = \frac{\textbf{money quantity X money velocity}}{\textbf{Country's real assets}}$$

This looks easy, but the calculations are nearly impossible. Money velocity can be determined in retrospect after a year or so, but "real assets" as opposed to spurious ones are impossible to determine with modern accounting practices. Often total salaries paid are equated with a country's real assets. However, salaries paid for bureaucracy (private or public), luxuries and non-essentials do little to produce real wealth or assets. Remember, assets "put money in your pocket." Land value fluctuations are also unpredictable. However, experience shows that money velocity and real assets often cancel each other and so price level is equivalent to the money quantity. When money quantity increases, inflation will occur if assets are static or fall.

Typically, politicians blame price increases (inflation) on "speculators," "greedy merchants," "foreign exchange rates," and a host of bogeymen. However, the fault lies with those who control the currency. Increasing money supply without a real increase in the nation's assets makes the original money worth less and prices will rise since the real value of goods and services remain static. This is inflation. The rise in prices often lags for several years while the markets readjust to the new amounts of money and its appearance in general circulation.

At first any inflation will look and feel good. The money supply expands, government spending increases, but the deficits are often not paid, stock markets or the value of industries generally increase, a period of spectacular general prosperity occurs while prices temporarily remain stable. However, much of the prosperity is spurious. It takes the form of increasing governmental and private sector bureaucracy disproportionate to the population and growth of national assets. These activities produce nothing except "paper pushing." It can also take the form of "consumption" activities (vacations, resort living, villas, estates, restaurants). These produce no real wealth and are most vulnerable. Continuing the inflation in bits and pieces can continue the prosperity while prices continue to lag behind. In the later stages of an inflation the prosperity falters, money tightens, investments cease, stock markets or industries lose value and some collapse. Taxes rise, government deficits often continue while money expansion continues to accelerate with rising prices. Unemployment occurs as businesses close or move to escape the financial chaos, increasing taxes and bureaucratic regulation.

The government has its choice as to how to stop the inflation. It can default or repudiate its debts by massive inflation. This can disrupt the value of money causing the loss of all fixed assets based on the old currency such as personal savings, life insurance cash value, pensions and other property. In the private sector debtors win and the frugal lose. This may stop the inflation and restore what is left of the currency and allow for a period of readjustment. This is often very painful. The producer's trust in the consumer is lost and credit becomes difficult to obtain. This slows the growth of new businesses. The government can continue with more inflation, but this makes the ultimate disaster that much more prolonged and painful. In some cases, revolts occur or the entire civilization collapses in rebellion and slaughter.

Inflations of the past 100 years have occurred with similar consequences. One of the most notable was the German inflation following World War I that ended in 1922 with a burst of hyperinflation. It was cured very rapidly by eliminating all previous money with the new Mark worth 1 trillion of the old Mark. Its issue was specific and not permitted to increase. The government was able to pay all its debts with worthless old Marks. However, it had to balance its budget, which eliminated 400,000 jobs in the bureaucracy. The productive citizens lost their pensions, savings, life-insurance (all based on the old worthless Mark) and the debtors ended up with no debt at the expense of the productive. There was temporary massive private sector unemployment with the collapse of many paper pushing businesses not engaged in producing real value. About the only things that maintained value was gold, productive farm land, and industry making needed products. Political upheaval occurred. The country was preserved and started over within a year. 10 years later the cheated middle class supported Hitler who promised "change," became chancellor, and led them to war and ruin. Following World War II Germany survived, prospered, but fell again into the trap of socialism and a Ponzi, unsustainable welfare state.

Note that the type of money does not make any difference when considering its supply. It can be fiat having no intrinsic value or specie with intrinsic value. So long as the amount remains proportionate to the national wealth, there is stability. National wealth includes the value of stocks in companies rooted in real production – mining, manufacturing, food producing, building, transportation, energy production and distribution, and legitimate banking. Gross domestic or national product (GDP or GNP) figures do not substitute for "real assets." Politicians have found specie based on gold and silver very difficult to manipulate and fiat easy.

Two quotations by Thomas Jefferson are worth remembering when discussing the merits of fiat (money with little or no intrinsic value) and specie (money with intrinsic value). "*Specie is the most perfect medium because it will preserve its own level; because, having intrinsic and universal value, it can never die in our hands, and it is the surest resource of reliance in time of war.*" [120] "*Paper is poverty ... it is only the ghost of money, and not money itself.*" [121]

Inflation is caused by excesses of government. Payment of obligations using cheaper currency may seem smart and feel good at the time. However, today's ecstasy brings tomorrow's baby. The leadership that starts the problem is often absent when trouble hits and leaves others to clean up the mess. This was seen as a problem in post-World War I Britain. Then Chancellor of the Exchequer, Winston Churchill, after consultation with many including John Maynard Keynes, returned Britain to the gold standard in 1924. His "dear money" policy cost him much political capital, but in response to those who said it was unrealistic, he said, "*I will tell you what it* [the return to the Gold Standard] *will shackle us to. It will shackle us to reality.*" He later considered this a mistake as inflationary pressures and labor unrest were high at the time. [122] Politicians responsible for inflation should pay the price of treason; it is a crime against the country. Assets from the earth and man's labor are intimately bound to the Lord's laws of consecration and purpose (Gen 3:17, 22; Lev 27: 30, 32; Malachi 3:8-9). Any person, institution or government that is unable to manage assets well will lose them, their sacred honor, and their destiny (Matt 16:25-26; Mark 8:35-36; Luke 9:24-25).

Aurelianus

Currency tinkering was overt during the reign of Emperor **Lucius Domiius Aurelianus** (214-275). He reigned only 5 years. He fought several major wars to bring the Palmyrene (Middle Eastern) and Gallic Empires into submission and re-unite the Roman Empire. He chose inflation to pay the Empires debts. The scheme was to pay debts with cheap money for expenses incurred with "hard" money. He attempted to recall all the old silver *denarius* and replace them with the *antoninianii* that contained only 5% of the silver of the *denarius.* He claimed that the Roman mint workers were stealing the silver and not minting with the specified amounts of silver. So, he recalled all the old "bad money" and replaced it with even worse after executing the mint workers.

The quantity of silver or gold used in minting coins does not determine whether or not inflation occurs. It is the total amount of money factored by the value of the nation's net worth that determines inflation. See the above formula. However, it is also true that if the coins contain a specified amount of gold or silver, it is worth at least the price of its precious metal. It is more difficult for a government to inflate currency without first having the gold or silver required to issue its specie. If politicians inflate the currency as happened under Roosevelt's "New Deal" that got rid of the "gold standard" in 1933 and LB Johnson's "Great Society," which got rid of the "silver standard" in 1964 without an increase in the nation's value, inflation occurs and fiat rapidly replaces specie. U.S. silver coin disappeared by the end of 1965.

Diocletian

Gaius Aurelius Valerius Diocletian (244 – 311) ruled from 284-286 (alone) then as emperor of the East until 305 when he abdicated. He died an unusual "natural death" in retirement. He is noted for his splitting the Empire into East and West, establishment of an eastern capitol in Byzantium away from chaotic Rome, expansion of the Roman bureaucracy, fighting wars, and persecuting Christians. From AD 211 to 285 numerous emperors died by assassins and revolts. Diocletian tried to put a stop to this chaos by re-establishing hereditary rule. It didn't work. Neither did his monetary "reforms."

Until AD 235 the Roman Empire paid its debts with gold or silver. Despite excesses by emperors, there was enough to satisfy debt from the conquests of other lands, but even this source eventually dried up. Debasement of the coinage starting with Aurelianus had progressively removed the amount of gold and silver in circulation and the government now relied on "requisition" (theft) to supply its armies and governmental functions. The new money was not acceptable to merchants and farmers. True to politicians, Diocletian decided that a tax would be a better alternative. He took a census of people, productive businesses and land and taxed them. The previously exempt Italian peninsula now came under taxation except for Rome, where the politicians lived and held most of their wealth.

Diocletian re-established the coinage based on gold, silver and copper, mostly the latter. However, inflation of the currency continued with naturally occurring price increases. In 301 he issued two edicts. The first was the *Edict on Coinage* that devalued the *nummi*, the most common base-metal coin, to ½ of its previous value. Then when prices threatened to spiral out of control a few months later he followed with an *Edict on Maximum prices*. This edict fixed the prices on about 1000 goods and services without regard to provincial differences, transportation costs or local conditions. Violations were punishable by death. The immediate effect was shortages and "black market." Within a year or so, the unworkable edict was abandoned, but inflation continued. Later many emperors returned to a price control strategy to keep the Roman mobs happy, but had to abandon them as being too destructive of the economy.

Farmers found it impossible to plant, grow and harvest crops for legal prices. Many abandoned their farms and joined the Roman mobs. Famine resulted. Eventually it was impossible to sustain the army with provisions. To solve this problem, Constantine the Great made it illegal in AD 322 for the farmers to leave their lands. As usual the penalty was death. Worthless currency forced farmers and skilled tradesmen to barter. Although clumsy, this worked for a time. Within 150 years the Empire was in its death throes.

Roman Empire Divided AD 303

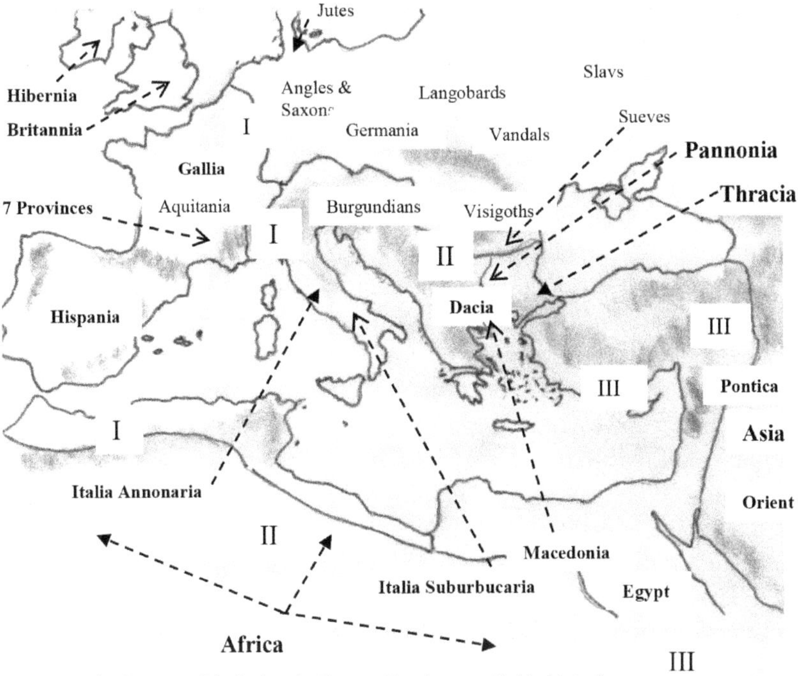

In 303 under Emperor Diocletian the Roman Empire was divided into three Prefects: I) Gallia, II) Illyricus, Italia & Africa III) Orient. Its 15 major divisions are given in **bold face.** Outlying tribes and some provinces are noted in smaller regular type. With the exception of the hot springs areas of southern Germany, highly prized by the Roman bath culture, the dividing line between Gual and Germania was the Rhine River.

Barbarian Invasions of Rome

In AD 370 Hun armies crossed the steppes of central Asia and reached the Don River. This exerted pressure on the primitive tribes of Central Europe. Visigoths who fought as Roman soldiers demanded protection within the Roman Empire's borders against the invading Huns. Broken promises to the Visigoths led to the Battle of Adrianople in AD 378. The Visigoth Army killed the Roman emperor, Valens, and wiped out 2/3rds of his Army. Visigoths were now permitted to enter the Italian peninsula. In 406 Vandals, Alans, Suevi and Burgundians overran Gaul. To resist this move, all Roman troops were pulled out of Britain in AD 407. The defeat at Adrianople was so complete that Emperor Theodosius, who succeeded Valens, found it necessary to reorganize the army of the Eastern Empire along lines of the victorious Visigoth heavy armed cavalry. Until this time Roman Legions were typically heavy infantry, but it was now clear that they did not stand a chance against heavy cavalry that "rode them down." Infantry and its organization became secondary in the East. The Western Roman Empire was more resistant to change. [123] In 387 Gauls under Brennus routed the Romans and entered Rome, but were forced out after fierce fighting.

As the 5th Century AD opened collapse of the Western Empire was imminent. The Visigoths, Balkan branch of the Germanic Goths, were at the gates of Rome. Roman Legions were pulled out of the provinces to defend the heartland. Roman soldiers deserted in droves to the barbarian armies for hard money pay. Farmers in Vandal held North Africa and on the Iberian Peninsula, the "bread basket" of the Roman Empire revolted. They found local corrupt princes with armed retainers who agreed to accept 35% of their crop in return for protection against marauding bands of Roman soldiers sent out to "requisition" crops. The farmers kept 65%. Thus, began serfdom. Over the next 50 years serfdom spread rapidly into the remaining parts of the Western Roman Empire from the Mediterranean to the Barbarian inhabited Baltic Coast; it lasted more than 1000 years and was finally abandoned in 1861 in Russia. Without food and money, what remained of the Roman army deteriorated rapidly and northern barbarians who had been grafted into the Roman legions and learned the Roman art of warfare turned their talents against Rome.

Rome also fell as a result of officious bureaucracy and hyper-legalism. Hugh Nibley described a meeting in AD 448 between the Roman ambassador, Priscus, at the Court of Attila, the Hun and a former Greek citizen of Rome who lived in Scythia, along the northern coast of the Black Sea. Following its conquest by Attila he elected to become a Hun to save his business. He stated that the Huns had a far better way of life than that which he had experienced under Rome. He was now free to manage his business and his personal affairs far more easily than previously. He had several complaints. As a Roman his chance of death in a war was greater because Roman citizens were prohibited from bearing arms for their own defense. They had to rely on "*incompetent and cowardly commanders*." There was also "*the intolerable load of taxation and tribute, the insults and injuries of rascally officials, the unequal application of the laws, by which an offender if he was rich enough got off scot-free, but if he was poor felt the full weight and majesty of the law for even the slightest unintentional slip; and if he lived long enough to see his case through the courts, would find himself utterly ruined by long, drawn-out, and expensive legal proceedings. The most disgusting thing about the whole business, he said, was that law and justice were strictly for sale.*" [124] [125]

Rome was sacked in AD 410 by the Visigoths under Alaric. Suevi swept west into Spain in AD 409 and Vandals into North Africa in AD 429. They established kingdoms in these regions from AD 429-431. In AD 435 the Emperor of Byzantium recognized the Vandal Kingdom of North Africa which extended its kingdom to Carthage in AD 439. In AD 446 Attila became the undisputed leader of the Huns with the death or possibly assassination of his brother. He then forged an alliance with the Franks and Vandals and launched a campaign into Gaul in AD 451. After successfully pillaging many towns he was met by the combined Roman and Visigoth armies and forced back behind the Rhine River. In AD 452 Attila attempted an invasion of Northern Italy. He moved his armies from his capital in Budapest to the northern Adriatic and thence into northern Italy. He pillaged successfully across the northern part of the Italian Peninsula from Padua to Milan, but he was unable to take Ravenna, the new Western Roman capitol surrounded by swamps. He retreated home and died in AD 453. In AD 455 Rome was sacked by the Vandals under Genseric; this time the plundering lasted 14 days instead of the 3 days in AD 410.

Following the 407 Roman abandonment of the British Isles, the Saxons from northern Germany, as Roman mercenaries living in England, attacked the natives. Britons fled their homes in England for the safety of Wales, Cornwall, Scotland, and across channel into Brittany. The Anglo-Saxons now occupied East Anglia, Kent, Sussex (South-Saxon) and Wessex, but an alliance of the natives occurred sometime around 490 and drove the invaders out of Kent and Sussex under a general known as "The Bear," Artus, or Arthur. The King Arthur legends date from this period. [126] As Christian Britain became more vulnerable to attacks, the pagan Irish increased raiding Christian seaports for child slaves. In AD 401 a 16-year-old Christian by the name of Patricus was kidnapped and taken to Ireland where he worked for 6 years as a sheep herder for a local tribe. A voice told him that a ship was waiting for him. He walked 200 miles to a port on the south eastern coast of Ireland, boarded a ship and within hours was on his way to Brittany. He was eventually made a priest and Bishop and returned to Ireland to convert the Irish population. St Patrick's work was highly successful by the time he died in AD 461 at the age of 72. In the 6th Century an Irish monastery system was developed by St Columba / Columcille (521-597) and St Columbanus (543 – 615). This became a sanctuary for what remained of the intelligentsia of Europe who fled to

Ireland with as much of their libraries as they could carry. Columba also established a bible college in 563 on the Scottish Island of Iona that was to last for 700 years. The students were known as the Culdees, a secret society, who were the progenitors of much non-Catholic biblical teaching that attempted to keep alive remnants of "true Christian faith" and were the forerunners of the Protestant Reformation. John Wycliffe was a Culdee. For many years, both religious and profane works from the ancient world were copied by the monks in Irish monasteries; these were relatively free from attack by barbarian hordes. As Europe began to stabilize in the 8th and 9th centuries AD, the Irish spread their monasteries into Europe and eventually back to Italy itself. Much of what had been lost returned to Europe. [127]

Frankish Power & Lombards

With the collapse of the Pax Romana 5th century Germany was thrown into chaos and ruin. In AD 455 the Franks of south-central Germany (around the modern city of Frankfurt) challenged Rome for control of Germany. By AD 457 both Roman and Frankish authorities were competing for control of Germany; however, Rome's army had deteriorated with many going over to the Frankish side. Goths and Saxons invaded. Wholesale desertions of Roman legions strengthened Barbarian forces and Rome's power evaporated in Northern Europe. In AD 455 Rome was sacked a second time by Vandals under Gaiseric.

Europe in Chaos AD 500

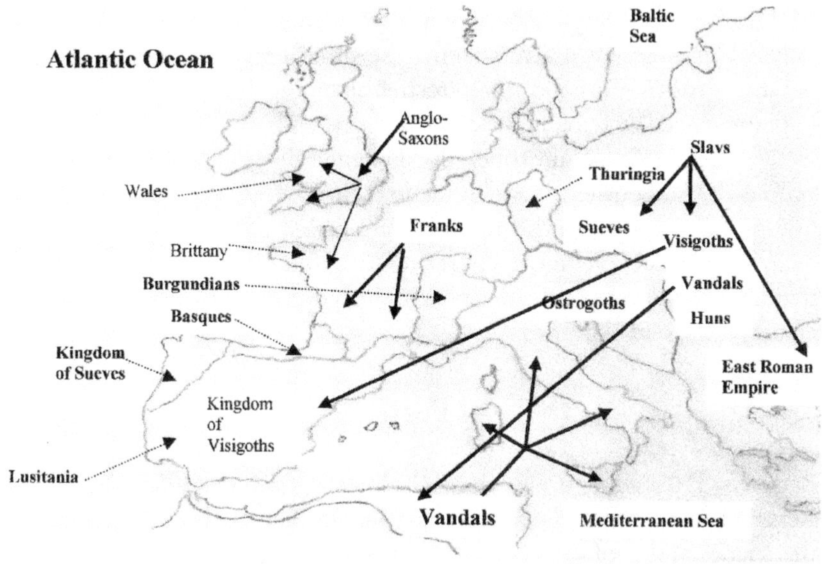

By 500 AD the Western Roman Empire had collapsed under the onslaught of Barbarian invasions. Pressure came out of the East from Slavs, Vandals, Huns, & Visigoths. This forced the movement of Anglo-Saxons to the west, Burgundians to the South and transplantation of the Sueves and Visigoths far to the west. Vandals moved all the way to N. Africa. From here they sacked the islands and heartland of the Roman Empire. The Britains fled west into Wales and south into Brittany. War is the great mix-master of civilizations. The Eastern Roman Empire was able to hold out despite invasions from the north.

The end came in AD 474 when Julius Nepos (AD 430-480) fled to Dalmatia and barbarian generals took over and established Romulus Augustus as the Emperor of Rome.

The rise of Frankish power and the change from Gaul to France began with Clovis (466-511). Clovis subjugated the Thuringians and Alamanni and dominated the peoples southeast of the Rhine. When he defeated Syagrius, the last Roman governor of the region in 486, Clovis took control of most of northern Gaul. The Merovingian Dynasty was founded in 481 and lasted until 751; it was centered in the area of modern Belgium. In 496 Clovis was baptized by Saint Remi (Remigius) into the Roman Catholic faith; this led to the fall of Arian Christianity held by most of the Goths. In 507 Clovis defeated Alaric II and forced the Visigoths back into Spain, pushing them against the Vandals. When Clovis died in 511 he divided his kingdom with his four sons who unlike most brother rulers got along and further expanded the Frankish kingdom. They and Clovis' grandchildren continued their cooperation until the Frankish kingdom extended to the Middle Danube regions controlled by the Burgundians and Ostrogoths. When Clovis accepted Christianity, the official religion of this vast area became Roman Catholic. Despite the changing fortunes of Rome, the Popes managed to remain on tolerable terms with the barbarian tribes.

Another barbarian tribe, the Langobards or Lombards, (bearded peoples) from Southern Sweden made their way into Northern Italy from 568-572 and colonized this region over a period of several hundred years. They were never able to overcome Frankish military power, but seemed to maintain their independence and style of government until the Norman conquests several centuries later.

Persia

Between 550 and 330 BC the Achaemenid Empire under Darius and Xerxes, the enemy of Greece predominated. Cyrus the Great displaced the Medes and took much of the Arabian Peninsula including Babylon, Phoenicia and Lydia. His son, Cambyses II took Egypt. Under Darius I the Persians extended their empire from the Indus Valley into Thrace (southern Bulgaria, northeastern Greece and European Turkey) in Europe. The Greeks held him back at the Battle of Marathon (490 BC). His son Xerxes I again attacked the Greeks, but was defeated at Plataea in 479 BC. Darius divided his realm into provinces, each of which was ruled by satraps (governors). He expanded the postal system of the Assyrians and developed secret agents, "the eyes and ears of the King." He improved the roads that improved commerce and included the "silk road" into China. The Zoroastrian religion became prominent at this time.

The Persian army's weakness against the Greek / Spartan phalanx and Athenian navy explained its repeated failures. In 401 BC Cyrus the Younger employed Greek mercenaries and took the throne. Philip II of Macedonia unified the Greek City States and his son, Alexander the Great rapidly took the Mediterranean provinces away from Persia and defeated Darius III at Gaugamela in 331 BC. The capital Susa fell and Alexander ruled Persia. Alexander founded many cities that extended Greek culture into most of the Old Persian Empire. Following Alexander's untimely death, his generals began taking over various pieces of the empire.

Seleucus I Nicator tried to control Persia, Mesopotamia, Syria and Asia Minor; however, Ptolemy Keraunos killed him in 281 BC before he could take Greece and Mesopotamia. Under the Ptolemies Greek culture continued its expansion into old Persia. Zoroastrianism expanded west to influence Judaism, while Buddhism came in from the East. The Seleucid reign declined as the eastern provinces broke off and challenged Persia itself. Antiochus III kept the Parthians at bay and his probes against Greece, caused the Romans to react against Persia. The revolt of the Maccabees in Judea and other problems finally permitted Parthia and Rome to take over the Old Persian Empire.

The Parthians under the Arsacid Dynasty overthrew the Seleucids in 238 BC but the whole of the empire was not consolidated until Mithridates I who took over in 170 BC. Rome and Persia now shared a border in Armenia, but the Persians had found a military formula that successfully competed against Roman foot soldiers – cavalry supported by mounted archers. Wars between Rome and Persia became frequent. Wars with Rome drained the treasury and Arsacid Dynasty collapsed as provincial governors failed to obey.

This gave rise to the Sassanid Empire under the Sassanian Dynasty from AD 226-651 began with Ardashir I who defeated the last Arsacid king, Artabanus IV (ruled AD 216 – 224) and became the Shah of the new Persian Empire. Society was now organized into a caste system and Zoroastrianism became the official state religion. Eastern Orthodox Christianity and its belief in Christ as God and Savior was persecuted, but the Nestorian Christians who did not were tolerated. The Sassanid Empire was fatally weakened in a war with Byzantium under Heraclius (575-641) who sent armies into Asia Minor and attacked Persia from the rear. The *Korân* mentions this as a victory for believers because the Byzantine Christians were considered monotheists in contrast with Zoroastrian paganism (**30**:2-6). When the Persians lost its struggle with the Islâmic Caliphate in 651; this was its end. Its riches poured into the Caliphate treasury permitting a huge buildup of the Arab armies that swept both east and west.

Zoroastrianism

Zoroastrianism was the predominant religion of Persia from 559 BC to AD 651 when it was displaced by Islâm. It influenced Islâm and some of the mythology surrounding Judaism and Christianity. It came from the teachings of Zarathustra known by the Greeks as Zoroaster. The exact time of his birth and death are unknown, but some believe he lived about the time of Moses between 1500 and 1000 BC. Tradition is that he was born near the Araxes River near Mount Ararat in the highlands of Armenia and came from the Ahura Mazda or "wise lord." Its major tenants are expressed in a group of 17 hymns known as the *Gathas* that are part of a general scripture known as the *Avesta*. The *Avesta* consists of 22 books. Zarathustra believed he was a prophet of Ahura Mazda who created the world, its people and all that is good. There remain 140,000 worshipers in mostly India with some in Iran that adhere to this faith. 5000 live in North America. Some of the tenants of Zoroastrianism are found on-line. [128]

Some Zoroastrian beliefs are expressed in the *Korân*. These include the Night Journey described outside the *Korân* and doctrines of Paradise and Hell. [129] These are also not unlike those found in Norse mythology concerning the resting place for brave slain warriors: Odhin, Valhalla, the "Hall of the Slain" and the Valkyries. The Zoroastrianism paradise includes fair female spirits that appeal to men. These are described as light or sunshine. *Hur* is used in the Pahlavi dialect of Persian to designate them and is not unlike the Arabic *houris*. [130]

Chaos in the Far East & the Americas

From AD 317 to 589 the Dynasties of the North and South ruled China. It was a period of chaos. Finally, in 580 the Sui Dynasty that lasted until 618 re-united China and engaged in improving the canal system. This occurred parallel with Muhammad's life. It was succeeded by the Tang Dynasty 618-907 that included stability, more improvement of the canal system and invention. With the privatization of land, wealth, power, commerce, agriculture and invention blossomed and China entered a golden age that lasted until the Mongolian conquests.

For many years archeologists have dated the collapse of the Mayan Civilization to about 800. More recent data reveals a double collapse of the Mayans. During the mid-6th Century AD a 30-year period of drought and crop failures with famine occurred in the Americas. [131] Ice core evidence from Peru and dendrochronology (the study of tree rings) from the Americas and many other parts of the world including Europe and Asia showed that severe drought conditions persisted in the Americas from 535 until about 565 to 575. [132] The presence of high levels of sulfuric acid in the ice core samples of about 535 suggested the cause as a massive volcanic eruption that altered the earth's climate during this 30-year period. The city of Teotihuacan (19.41°N, 98.50°W) began its demise about then. Recent anthropological data showed that people began dying at earlier and earlier ages. [133] The cause was probably famine and infectious diseases. Religious frescoes became military. Finally, a layer of ash in the ancient city and the shattered skeletons of people likely to have been rulers indicate that it was destroyed by fire and rebellion about the year 662. [134] A later or Classic Mayan resurgence recurred and lasted until about 750 when it was replaced by the Aztecs.

Byzantium & Persia, Justinian I & Theodora

The major powers in the Western World were Byzantium, the inheritors of the Eastern Roman Empire and Persia. These had been locked in an intermittent struggle for control of the eastern end of the Mediterranean and the profitable overland trade routes from Damascus south to the Indian Ocean, Saba (Yemen) and to the east and China. The most notable of the early Emperors of the Eastern Roman Empire was Flavius Petrus Sabbatius Iustinianus (AD 482 – 565) otherwise known as **Justinian I**. His mother Vigilantia was sister to Justin, a general in the Roman Imperial Guard. In 523 / 525 Justininian I (age 43) married Theodora, a vibrant beautiful actress (age 23). Most of what we know about her was written by Procopius, who had no use for her. The relationship between Theodora and Justinian I rank among the greatest love stories ever told.

Theodora's background was not auspicious. She was born in Cyprus about 502; Cyprus was a backwater of the Empire. Her father was a bear and animal keeper at the hippodrome in Constantinople. He died when Theodora was about 12-years-old leaving her initially with her mother, an actress who died soon after. This left Theodora on the streets to fend for herself. She turned to the life of a cheap prostitute and comic actress. Within 4 years she had clawed her way to the top of her profession as a high-priced courtesan. At the age of 18 she became the mistress of Hecebolus, the governor of Cyrenaica, an African coastal province from Al-'Alamayn in western Egypt to Qsar al-Burayqah in eastern Libya. Hecebolus had no idea that his good fortune resulted from Theodora's flight from Constantinople to escape the law. As Hecebolus's wife, with whom he soon lost interest, she took the opportunity to educate herself in his library. When John of Cappadocia, the Prefect of Constantinople discovered her whereabouts 3 years later, he ordered Hecebolus to banish her. She was taken to the western border of his province and told to start walking. She was in early pregnancy at the time from an illicit affair. She survived likely certain death in the Sahara by hiding out in a caravan headed east. She met up with a caravan headed east and made her way to Alexandria where she delivered a girl, gave her up for adoption, and returned to Constantinople. When Justinian met her, she had been "spinning" for 4 months; the prescribed method for getting out of the world's oldest profession. To make extra money she used her talents as a comic actress to perform as a dancer in a cabaret; she was stunning.[135]

[136] **Theodora** was the best choice Justinian could have made. She was 22, loyal, "street savvy," politically mature, intelligent, beautiful, knew all the tricks of her old trade, and ambitious. Justinian soon found her his intellectual equal and his most able political and diplomatic advisor. She could talk diplomacy with diplomats, religion with bishops, and did. After being his mistress for about a year, Justinian had the law against patricians marrying actresses repealed. He married her in 523. When Justinian I ascended the throne in 527, he did the unexpected making her joint ruler or co-equal. At about the age of 27 Theodora found herself the Byzantine Queen. The people whispered that they had seen many Queens become whores, but never a whore become a Queen. Despite her reputation, she lived up to her responsibilities.

A popular uprising, the Nike Riots occurred in 532. [137] When the royal household was about to flee Constantinople in the face of the revolt, she allegedly said, "*In a crisis like the present we have not time to argue whether a woman's place is the home, and whether she ought to be meek and modest in the presence of the lords of creation. We have got to get a move on quick. My opinion is that this is not time for flight – not even if it is the easiest course. Everyone who has been born has to die; but it does not follow that everyone who has been made an emperor has to get off his throne. May the day never come when I do! If you want to make yourself safe, Emperor, nothing stops you. There is the sea over there, and boats on it and money to pay your way. But if you go, you may presently very much wish that you had not. As for me, I stand by the old saying, that the best winding sheet is a purple one.*" [138] She stayed as did Justinian and his generals. Theodora saw to it that military forces were used effectively to quell the rebellion. Byzantium lasted nearly 1000 years more because of her.

Theodora's importance in history is her sponsorship and guidance of a lawyer, Tribonian, to codify Roman civil law and create a new constitution for Byzantium. These laws have influenced the entire Western legal system. Theodora's stamp can be seen throughout. It included abolition of the death penalty for adultery and making rape a capital crime. Women could own and inherit property. Married women had the same rights as married men. She created laws for the establishment of houses of prostitution, but passed laws against forced prostitution. She was unsurpassed at diplomacy and could quickly see through plots especially by the Persians. She died in 548 probably of breast cancer; she never lost her beauty and Justinia never remarried.

His interests later in life turned towards the Christian religion, but Theodora's passion was diplomacy and government. She ran the Byzantine Empire during her adult life. She saw to Justinian's wishes and engineered them. She championed the Monophysite Christian faith. She was the most powerful monarch of her era and certainly one of the most powerful women ever.

Justinian's and Theodora's reign were devoted to war. Justinian inherited a war with the Persians from his Uncle Justin I. In 530 Byzantine armies defeated the Persians at Daras, but in 531 they were defeated at Callinicum. When the King of Persia died, Justinian and Theodora concluded an "Eternal Peace" with his successor in 532. This allowed them to concentrate on Justinian's objective, the retaking of the Western Roman Empire. In a

campaign similar to the Allies of World War II under Generals Eisenhower and Patton, General Flavius Belisarius, who had quelled the Nike Riots for Theodora, attacked and took Vandal North Africa in 533-4. This served as an amphibious base of operations from which he invaded and conquered Sicily in 535. Another amphibious invasion (more successful than Anzio in WWII) took Naples in 536 and Rome later that year.

Belisarius (505-565) is considered one of the world's greatest generals. He reorganized his army into task force units or *comitatus* of various sizes so as to confuse the enemy. These consisted of light infantry/archers, heavy cavalry, and horse archers. The heavy cavalry was after the German model and were heavily armored and fought with lance and sword. They were used much as the German Tiger Tanks of World War II, to break up front line troop concentrations. The horse archers were like those of Central Asia and Persia. They were used much as Patton used his light, fast Sherman Tanks of World War II. They were a rapid strike force used to attack the flanks and get behind the lines and break up command, communications and logistics leaving the front headless. They were lightly armored and could shoot accurately from a gallop. Of great importance was his cavalry's secret weapon, the stirrup. This gave the riders more stability and accuracy from the back of a horse. They were armed with a small shield and also carried lance and sword. Belisarius also hired his own personal body guard from sources outside the army. These were known as *buccellarii* and used by generals who followed.

In 537-8 the Ostrogoths besieged Rome, but could not take it. Belisarius attacked Milan, but could not hold it. Then the Ostrogoth Capital at Ravenna fell in 540 and the Ostrogoth King, Vitigis and his wife were taken to Constantinople. Belisarius was recalled to take on the Persians who had broken "the Eternal Peace." In 540 the Persians had made considerable headway against the Roman armies, but now the campaigns of both armies were threatened by the plague that broke out in the region in 540. Finally, after jockeying for position for a number of years a 50-year truce was agreed upon by the Persians and Byzantium for the price of 400 to 500 lbs of gold in tribute per year ($11,000,000) to be paid by the Romans.

The Climatic Catastrophe of AD 535 & Plague of AD 540

Weather commentaries were rare in the ancient world. However, in 536 John of Ephesus wrote about the climate of the preceding 18 months, "*There was a sign from the sun, the like of which had never been seen and reported before. The sun became dark and its darkness lasted for 18 months. Each day, it shone for about four hours, and still this light was only a feeble shadow. Everyone declared that the sun would never recover its full light again.*"[139] The weather turned cold, crops failed, and a severe famine followed. It was little better in 537.

In 535 the Byzantine historian Procopius, wrote, *"And it came about during this year that a most dread portent took place, for the sun gave forth its light without brightness like the moon during this whole year, and it seemed exceedingly like the sun in eclipse, for the beams it shed were not clear, nor such as it is accustomed to shed."*[140]

According to a Chinese History of the Southern Dynasties written in Nanjing, the text states that in February 535, *"There twice was the sound of thunder."* The fact that thunder was not generally reported makes this report significant. [141] In China during 536 drought and famine occurred as "*yellow dust rained down like snow.*" Real snow occurred in mid-August. [142]

In an Indonesian Chronicle, *The Book of Ancient Kings* is noted, *"There was a furious shaking of the earth, total darkness, thunder and lightning. Then came forth a furious gale together with torrential rain and a deadly storm darkened the entire world. A great flood then came from Mount Batuwara and flowed eastwards to Mount Kamula."* It goes on to state that the land sank creating an ocean passage separating Java and Sumatra. [143] There are a number of problems with this source, [144] but what is described here could easily fit the 535 event. David Keys postulates that the cause of climatic change and the plague that followed was the result of a massive eruption by the world's most notorious volcano, Krakatoa.

To add to the misery, in the year 539 the plague struck Saba / Abyssinia and in 540 it arrived in the Mediterranean world hitting Pelusium in Egypt first. From here it spread to Alexandria then to Constantinople where nearly 50% of the population died. The historian Evagrius wrote,

"With some people it began in the head, made the eyes bloody and the face swollen, descended to the throat and then removed them from Mankind. With others, there was a flowing of the bowels. Some came out in buboes (pus-filled swellings) which gave rise to great fevers, and they would die two or three days later with their minds in the same state as those who had suffered nothing and with their bodies still robust. Others lost their senses before dying. Malignant pustules erupted and did away with them. Sometimes people were afflicted once or twice and then recovered, only to fall victim a third time and then succumb."[145]

John of Ephesus wrote, *"God's wrath turned into, as it were, a wine-press and pitilessly trampled and squeezed the inhabitants* (of many cities) *like fine grapes."* And, *"Homes, large and small, beautiful and desirable, which suddenly became tombs for the inhabitants and in which servants and masters at the same time suddenly fell* (dead), *mingling their rottenness together in their bedrooms."*[146] He continued, *"Corpses which split open and rotted on the streets with nobody to bury them." "There were those who perished falling in the streets to become a terrible and shocking spectacle for those who saw them, as their bellies were swollen and their mouths wide open, throwing up pus like torrents, their eyes inflamed and their hands stretched out upward and over the corpses, rotting and lying in corners and streets and in the porches of courtyards and in the churches."*[147]

John tried to flee, but, *"we saw desolate and groaning villages and corpses spread out on the earth; staging posts on the roads full of darkness and solitude filling with fright everyone who happened to enter and leave them."* There were *"cattle abandoned and roaming scattered over the mountains with nobody to gather them."*[148] There were fields, *"abundant in grain which was becoming white and stood erect* (yet no one) *to reap or gather it in."* There were *"flocks of sheep, goats, oxen and pigs which had become like wild animals, having forgotten life in a cultivated land and the human voice which used to lead them."* While in Constantinople John observed, *"It happened that 5,000 and 7,000, or even 12,000 and as many as 16,000 of them departed this world in a single day. Since thus far it was only the beginning, men were standing by the harbours at the cross-roads and at the city gates counting the dead. Thus the people of Constantinople reached the point of disappearing, only a few remaining, whereas of those only who had died on the streets – if anybody wants us to name their number, for in fact they were counted – over 300,000 were taken off the streets. Those officials who counted having reached the number of 230,000 and seeing that the dead were innumerable, gave up reckoning and from then on the corpses were brought out without being counted." "The city stank with corpses as there were neither litters nor diggers, and corpses were heaped up in the streets."*[149]

There are more descriptions. The land was decimated. The plague reduced harvests, taxes, and wealth of all sorts. It was a wonder that the armies of Rome or Persia could function. The Plague rapidly spread around the Mediterranean and reached the southern coasts of the British Isles a few years later. Those that traded with Rome such as the British were more affected than those who traded with northern Europe such as the Anglo-Saxons. To Christians who lived through this horror, it seemed that the world was coming to an end as described in Revelations.

The plague probably originated in Africa in regions north and east of Lake Victoria. When weather cools blood sucked by fleas coagulates creating a sensation of hunger. Increased vegetation through heavy rain favors the increase in animal populations. Although drought followed the initial cold weather, weather patterns then became much wetter for a few years and washouts followed droughts. All this favored the spread of plague. As the fleas' stomachs filled with coagulated blood and plague bacteria, they went into a feeding frenzy jumping rapidly from one animal to another spreading the disease. In Africa the first animals to be affected were the gerbils. It then spread to mice and other animals including the Black Rat. With famine, there is little food in the dumps of cities and the rats and mice move indoors or aboard ships with humans where there is food. Humans then get the disease from fleas abandoning the dying mice and rats. In tracing its spread, the plague originated in the coastal cities below the horn of Africa and was associated with the Ivory trade. It went to Yemen (Saba), then Egypt and thence to Constantinople in 540. It then spread into Persia from the Roman soldiers. It took 2 years to spread throughout the Mediterranean, 4 years to reach the trading ports in Britain, but about 40 to 50 years to find its way to China. [150]

The Immediate Fallout of the Climate and Plague

The Persian threat in the East plus the plague and serious climatic changes weakened the Roman forces in Italy and the Ostrogoths quickly retook most of the Italian Peninsula. In 544 Belisarius returned to Italy, but had insufficient troops to retake any territory. Between 544 and 550 Rome changed hands 3 times. The Ostrogoths raided Sicily and the Greek coasts, but they too had difficulties. Eventually Narses (AD 478-573) was sent with an army of only 30,000, mostly cavalry. Narses was a eunuch who had also helped Theodora with the Nike riots. He had further refined the tactics employed by the heavy horsemen by having them dismount and form an old Greek phalanx with spears facing outward as a barrier to cavalry charges by the enemy. In 551 his Eastern Roman Empire army retook Visigoth Spain. He took Ravenna in 552 and then defeated the Ostrogoths a month later. The Ostrogoth king was slain and their armies shattered. This became the high watermark of Justinian's conquests. When compared with the armies of Imperial Rome that numbered nearly 400,000 according to Edward Gibbon or that included all the Foederati troops of 650,000 to 700,000 men according to Antonio Santosuosso, Narses force of 30,000 that retook the Italian peninsula and Spain was pathetic by numerical comparison.

Throughout his campaigns in Italy and other parts of Western Europe and North Africa, he attempted to keep good relationships with the Popes of Rome. Justinian I died in 565, 5 years before Muhammad's birth. The results of the famine, 30 years of cold weather, the plague, and marauding armies had so reduced the population of these regions that entire towns were abandoned. Wild animals lived where people had once lived. Thus, the size of an army required for conquest was miniscule by comparison to those of times just a hundred years earlier.

The Avars and Continuation of Plague

About 558 when Khadīja bint Khuwaylid, Muhammad's future first wife was 8-years-old, a group of fierce nomadic tribesmen, the Avars from mountainous eastern Mongolia, arrived in Eastern Europe to the North of Byzantium. Their origin is controversial. Keys hypothesizes that the climatic change of 535 brought about drought conditions in Mongolia favoring the cattle of the Turks rather than the horses of the Avars. Horses cannot graze as close to the ground as cattle and they cannot digest the poorer forms of forage because they lack a rumen. Like the Mongol hordes that were to come in the 12th Century AD, the Avars were cavalry warriors and relied on horse power. As the climate worsened their horses died leaving them at the mercy of their Turkic vassals. [151] By 555 the Turks who had seasoned infantry threw them out of Mongolia and for the next 3 years the Avars headed west along the steppes of Central Asia while their horse herds gradually recovered. By the time they reached Central Europe they were back to strength and ready for war. In 568 they conquered the Huns and Slavs in the Ukraine and moved into eastern Hungary and Western Romania Slovenia, Moravia (Eastern Czech), Bohemia (Czech) and eastern Germany. The Lombards fled into northern Italy because of the Avar invasion. The Avars and their Slavic allies were brutal conquerors. They tortured their captives by impaling them on stakes or stripping their flesh off and roasting them slowly over an open fire on a spit. [152]

The Avar goal was booty. They used their Slavic vassals to get it. Word of their tortures spread and few cities fought. They gave up and paid up.

The Slavs now clients of the Avars attacked Byzantine settlements in the Balkans and demanded gold from the Byzantine government to keep the peace.

Between 572 and 622 the historical period lived by Muhammad (AD 570-632); this pattern repeated itself many times. [153] In all Byzantium paid over 70,000 lbs. or 35 tons of gold to the Avars to keep peace on the northern border. In today's money this amounts to 1.7 trillion dollars and is 3 times the alleged current U.S. gold reserves. [154] At first it was 80,000 gold solidi per year, but as time passed, the protection money continued to increase. Each solidus is slightly larger than a U.S. quarter eagle ($2.50) piece that included .12094 oz. of gold. [155] Year after year, the Eastern Roman empire was forced into more negotiations with the Avar *kagan*, king. Little by little through repeated acts of appeasement, it lost more treasure, valuable land, and people. For the next 50 years the Romans paid. Like so many countries before and since, Byzantium had blundered. Instead of building up their armies and fighting the Avars, the Eastern Roman Empire had chosen appeasement. Appeasement is akin to blackmail, which must eventually lead to more and more payment and end in violence.

The suffering of the Mediterranean world from pestilence prompted Evagrius, the church historian to write in 593, [Muhammad was 23.], *"I believe no part of the human race to have been unafflicted by the disease.* (for it occurred in some cities) *to such an extent that they were rendered empty of almost all their inhabitants. ... And during the course of the various visitations, I lost to the disease many of my children and my wife and much of the rest of my kin ... For now, as I write this, I am 58 years old and it is not quite two years since the fourth outbreak of plague struck Antioch and I lost my daughter and the son born to her in addition to those I lost earlier."* [156] After 540 the plague returned in waves for the next 180 to 210 years. This may account for the remarkable success of Islâmic armies following the death of Muhammad in 632 as they moved west across North Africa into Egypt and into the Eastern Mediterranean coastal states, Mesopotamia, Assyria and Persia.

The Weakening of Persia and Byzantium

Flavius Mauricius Tiberius Augustus, otherwise known as Maurice was born in 539. He ruled Byzantium from 582-602. In 579 he was commander in chief of the armies fighting the Persians. Following a great victory in 581 he married Constantina, the Persian Emperor's daughter and succeeded his father–in-law. He inherited a bankrupt Empire because of war with Persia and appeasement of the Avars. Under pressure of the Persians and Avars, the populace of Constantinople revolted and Phocas came to power after killing Maurice and his entire family. Phocas ruled from 602 to 610. This precipitated a war with Persia in which Persian military forces successfully invaded the Roman Empire. See sūra **30** of the *Korân*. A revolt that began under Heraclius, the Governor of the African Province and his son Heraclius (575-641) in 608 finally spread to the Capital. Heraclius Jr. went to Constantinople in 610, the year that Muhammad began having his visions. Phocas was delivered to him and Heraclius Jr. personally decapitated him. Heraclius abandoned the policy of tribute and appeasement and drove the Avars and their Slavic vassals out of the northern part of the Empire. He destroyed most of the Persian army in 627 at Nineveh but it was a pyrrhic victory. [See also sūra **30** *Korân*.] Both sides had exhausted each other in combat. In 631 Muhammad's troops sought a battle with a Persian outpost at Tabūk; the Persians abandoned the city. The general failure of the Persian army permitted the Arabs to move into Persia without much effort and brought them into direct contact with Byzantium. In 634, just 2 years after Muhammad's death, Arab armies swept into Syria. Heraclius was then old and feeble possibly from prostatic disease, and sent Theodore with a force to oppose them, but his army was defeated and the Arabs began their conquests of Syria, Armenia, and Egypt. [157]

The Arabs

Reference to a map of the Arabian Peninsula and surrounding territories will help your study of Arabian history. The Mediterranean Sea lies to the northwest where the modern states of Israel, Lebanon and Syria are located. These countries have some arable land and have the benefit of the humidity coming from the sea. To the north and north east lie the mountainous Anatolian Peninsula bordered on the north by the Sea of Marmara, Dardanelles, and the Black Sea. The modern country of Turkey occupies the Anatolian Peninsula. The Taurus Mountains extend west to east along its southern border and include two large volcanoes. Mount Erciyes (12,851 feet) in the center and Mount Ararat (16,853 feet) at the eastern end. The modern states of Georgia (north) and Armenia (south) are to the east between Turkey and he Caspian Sea.

ARABIAN PENINSULA

To the south of the Taurus Mountains and Caspian Seas lie the modern states of Syria, Iraq, and Iran going west to east. The Anatolian Peninsula is an active earthquake zone. The western geological border of the region is the Rift Valley. It divides two major tectonic plates that include the Sea of Galilee, Jordan River, and the Dead Sea whose surface is 377 m or 1237 ft. below sea level. The Rift Valley enters the Bay of Aqaba, which divides the costal countries and the Sinai Peninsula from the Arabian Peninsula. The Sinai Peninsula is a land bridge between the Arabian Peninsula and the Nile Delta region.

The Rift Valley enters the Red Sea and splits the African continent from Khartoum along the White Nile and along the western border of Uganda and Tanzania. The modern country of Jordan lies to the east of the Rift Valley and borders Israel. The northeastern part of the Arabian Peninsula is dominated by two great rivers, the Tigris and Euphrates, arising from the Taurus Mountains. The region of the Twin Rivers spawned the ancient states of Assyria in the north, Babylonia in the center and Samaria in the south at the northern end of the Persian Gulf. This territory includes the modern state of Iraq.

Most of the Arabian Peninsula is desert. There are oases here and there until one reaches the ancient Kingdom of Saba (Sheba – modern Yemen) in the southwestern corner. During the summer day time temperatures in the desert can reach 140°F. A man traveling through this region will require many gallons of water per day to stay alive. There is high hilly / mountainous country that borders the Red Sea in the southwestern corner of the Arabian Peninsula which is the location of ancient Saba. This region is blessed with mountains and a tropical coastal climate. It controls the Bab-el-Mandeb strait or "strait of scars," the passage between the Red Sea and Indian Ocean. In ancient times Saba, one of the largest empires, often controlled Abyssinia (Somalia & Ethiopia). It was rich in gold and expert mercenary archers. In Saba's interior the people learned to dam rain water from the mountains and irrigate crops. They built the Mārib Dam which supported one of the largest communities of settled Arabs in the ancient world, 30-50,000. Mārib (15°25'N 45°21'E) lay on the main overland trade route in the desert plateau region about 4000 feet in elevation and 250 miles north and slightly east of Aden (12°48N 45°02'E). Aden was the terminus of the major 1800-mile overland trade route between Aden and Damascus. Aden is strategically positioned in the northwest corner of the Indian Ocean on a peninsula. It was the principal port connecting the Mediterranean cultures with East Africa, the Far East, and Indus Valley civilizations.

Low hills border much of the peninsula's eastern coast along the Persian Gulf region. Oman occupies the southeastern corner of the Arabian Peninsula and has mountains that border it. The Straits of Hormuz separate the Persian Gulf from the Indian Ocean. Persia or modern Iran lies to the east of the Persian Gulf. The Zagros Mountains extend along the western border of Persia and border the Persian Gulf. A large navigable river, the Karūn, comes from these mountains and empties into the Persian Gulf at its southern end near the Iranian port cities of Abadan and Khorramshahr.

During much of the Ancient World the Red Sea was connected to the Mediterranean by a canal which made the Red Sea a popular overseas trade route. This canal has been dug in two directions. The modern Suez Canal runs north to south directly into the Red Sea. A more common canal in the ancient world ran from the northwestern branch of the Red Sea to the west through the Reed Sea to connect with the Nile at the southern end of the Nile Delta. The ancient and modern city of Cairo (30°.03'N, 31°13E) lay at its western terminus.

A trail borders the eastern shore of the Red Sea. However, its climate is intolerable because of its suffocating heat and humidity. The overland, inland trail that followed the eastern side of the Hejaz Mountains along the western edge of the Arabian Peninsula had numerous springs and mountain streams and followed a high desert plateau. It was more hospitable. Although hot and dry by day, the nights are cool, clear and star-lit. Night was a preferred time for travel. This made the 1800-mile trip from Damascus (33°51'N 36°29'E) to Aden far more comfortable than the sweltering Red Sea route. The overland trail began at Damascus, headed south to Petra (30°19N 35°26'E), then to Tabuk (28°23'N 36°35'E), Badr, Mecca, Marib, and finally Aden.

The Red Sea port of Jeddah (21°32'N 39°10'E) was connected by a mountainous 50-mile trail to Mecca (21°25'N 39°49'E), which occupied the half-way point on this trail. Jeddah became an important port for pilgrims visiting Mecca and the Ka'ba (Caaba–temple). It still is.

The town of Medina (24°28'N 39°36'E) is 180 miles or 10-11 caravan days, further north and east about a third of the way from Mecca to Petra. It was not on the main north-south trail or for that matter on the main east west trail to Baghdad (33°32N 44°42'E); however, it was close enough to both to be strategically important. Medina is located near a number of oases and wells. It was an agricultural center rather than a trade center. It included a number of old Jewish-Arab tribal settlements.

Water in this part of the world is life itself and worth more than gold. The Arab pastoralists settled among the larger oases and mountains and hilly countries adjacent to the Persian Gulf, Red Sea and Indian Ocean, where rain was more common. Settled Arabs were found in larger cities along the Tigris and Euphrates Rivers and in the South West corner of the Arabian Peninsula in Saba. The nomadic or Bedouin, "black" Arabs occupied the oases of the desert hinterlands and dug wells whenever possible. These were of necessity smaller tribes that herded small flocks from one watering place or small oasis to another and survived by hunting. Less water meant fewer animals and people within a tribe. The pastoral Arabs could have larger flocks and often had some arable ground for planting crops. However, it was only in the first millennium BC that some of the more powerful Bedouin tribes were able to become pastoralists and even these were little better than their nomadic cousins up to the 6th and 7th century AD.

At the dawn of the 6th Century, the pastoral Arabs living at the major points along the Aden to Damascus trail found their numbers and power increasing while their more civilized neighbors suffered from famine and the recent onset of the plague. Deserts are an effective barrier to rats and armies. The civilizations along the Tigris and Euphrates Rivers and in Saba had enough water to become urbanized rich and powerful nations that could afford sizable armies. These also attracted other peoples thus creating more of a mixture of groups. Neither the pastoral Arabs nor the Bedouins could compete militarily with Mesopotamia or Saba – unless some unfortunate catastrophe weakened these two cultures.

Tribal culture was the earliest form of human society. Protection relied on the young men, all of whom were expected to be hunters and warriors. They honed their fighting and hunting skills, became expert trackers and were leaders of families and eventually of the tribe itself. The Book of Numbers in the Bible emphasizes the importance of soldiers and men in each tribe. Women were not counted. "*Take ye the sum of all the congregation of the children of Israel, after their families, by the house of their fathers, with the number of their names, every male by their polls; From twenty years old and upward, all that are able to go forth to war in Israel: thou and Aaron shall number them by their armies*" (Num 1:2-3). Specifics for each tribe were given: "*Those that were numbered of them, even of the tribe of Reuben, were forty and six thousand and five hundred*" (Num 1:21). Many believe that word "thousand" is a mistranslation of the word for "fully armed soldier." Thus, in the tribe of Ruben among the men 20 years of age and up there were 46 fully armed soldiers and 500 other male heads of household.

Women did all the domestic work and reared the children until the age of 8 when the youth were turned over to the men to begin their training. The girls remained with the women to learn their duties. Women were important. They represented the labor pool of the tribe and loss of one or several meant more work for everyone else. Consequently, they were closely held within the tribe unless an alliance was necessary to bring two tribes together for protection. Then the chief's daughter or sister would be sent as a wife to the other tribe usually in exchange for a woman from the chief's family of the other tribe. She would be married to one of the chiefs in the receiving tribe. It is difficult to fight the husband of your sister or daughter. Marriages within the tribe were usually determined by the parents and were often with first or second cousins. This meant greater protection for the women within a family. The patriarch of the family would be the grandfather or great-grandfather of these women and would see to their protection. In some cases, especially involving princes or kings, sisters were often married as being more trustworthy and loyal to their husbands; there was less of a risk of assassination especially when cousins were contending for the position of chief. However, this kind of inbreeding also led to increased viciousness when fighting another tribe that did not include a close relative. When the Lord wished to make Israel a nation, He sent down instructions to Moses found in Leviticus 18 that prohibited marriage to close relatives – cousins, uncles, aunts, etc. However, he also prescribed marriages only between the tribes of the children of Israel and took great pains to prohibit marriage to outsiders of seven specific tribes residing within the land of Canaan.

Women are the teachers of their children, the guardians of their culture, religion and language – the "mother tongue." A civilization that permits "license" among its women is one generation from disaster. This is expressed in Exodus 34:10-17. In Deuteronomy 7:1-8 and Deuteronomy 20:16-18. The Canaanite tribes practiced fertility rites that included infant sacrifice. Any possible intermarriage with them was to be avoided.

Arabic Religion of Muhammad's Time

The pagan religions of the Middle East included the worship of a moon god in Sumer, Babylon, Assyria, Akkadia, Egypt and throughout the entire Arabian Peninsula. He had many different names. [158] These included Nanna, Suen or Sin, Asimbabbar, and Kusuh. The crescent moon was the symbol used to represent him. The name Sin was used primarily by the Semitic peoples, but his title was Al-ilah that was shortened to "Allah" in pre-Islâmic times. As previously noted, Sin was married to the sun goddess, Shams, and they had three daughters one of whom one was called Ishtar in other cultures. Their Arab names are al-Lat, al-'Uzzā and Manāt. Al-Lat is a moon goddess, al-'Uzzā is a fertility goddess and is represented by the planet Venus (a "wandering" star / planet), while Manāt is best represented by the goddess Fortuna. She held the cords of life; when they were cut you died. They were represented by the stationary stars and considered intermediaries between the people and Allah. Archeologists have uncovered many temples built in these regions to the moon god and there is much ancient statuary and idolatry representing this god.

Early Arabian History

The history of the Arabs is sometimes divided into several parts. The first is a time in which most functioned as nomads or Bedouins. Following the decline of the Greeks after Alexander the Great, Arabs expanded as pastoral tribes along the mountains and hills bordering the Red Sea from Petra in the North to Najran (on the Saudi-Yemen border in the South. They were still hemmed in by the Babylonians, Persians, Sabaeans and Romans. As Arab tribes increased and their towns became better established, they became vassals of their more powerful neighbors: Byzantium, Persia, and Sabaeans. At this time Christianity and Judaism spread into the Arabian Peninsula making Arab converts. In 500 the Quraysh became the dominant tribe and Mecca became a religious center with the Ka'ba (Caaba) as its temple. With further growth, military power in and about Mecca many Arab tribes in the region joined their circle. Arabic became the uniting language. The Bedouin culture of manliness became a guiding principle. Muhammad and his secular and religious beliefs brought most of the remaining Arab peoples together and ushered in an age of conquest in the 7th Century AD. This was aided by the final collapse of the Western Roman Empire and the exhaustion of Byzantium and Persia through nearly 150 years of warfare.

The climatic catastrophe of 535 added famine and the plague to the formula afflicting what was left of the barbarians of western Europe and the more developed civilizations of the eastern Mediterranean and the Middle East. Although life in the desert regions of the Arabian Peninsula was hard, it offered protection from rats, plague and armies. Napoleon's first maxim states, "*The frontiers of states are either large rivers, or chains of mountains, or deserts. Of all these obstacles to the march of an army, the most difficult to overcome is the desert; mountains come next, and large rivers occupy the third place.*" [159]

The inhabitants of Saba did not escape the catastrophe. Following the droughts of 535-36 torrential rains came in waves for the next 30 years. Silt began to pile up behind the Mārib Dam (53 feet high, 2046 feet in length and 200 feet wide at the base). Finally silt and massive flows of water breached the dam probably in the 540s and famine in addition to plague struck the southwestern Arabian Peninsula. [160] *"But they turned aside from what we had commanded them: wherefore we sent against them the inundation of Al Arem, and we changed their two gardens for them into two gardens producing bitter fruit, and tamarisks, and some little fruit of the lote-tree."* (**34**:16) According to the *Korân* these people were totally dispersed because of their wickedness. (**34**:19). Then sea trade in 539-40 from Abyssinia probably brought the rats and mice from Africa (possibly the Ivory trade). Plague which now combined with famine spelled the end of Saba. [161] Efforts to repair the dam were frustrated by silting-in and washouts. By 590 the population around Mārib was reduced from 50,000 to fewer than 10,000 people. Over time many attempted to escape up the trail towards Mecca, Medina, and Damascus, but the plague came with them and many perished. [162] The *Korân* may reference this: *"the tribe of Thamûd, and the people of Lot, and the inhabitants of the wood near Madian, accused the prophets of imposture before them: these were the confederates against the messengers of GOD. All of them did no other than accuse their apostles of falsehood: wherefore my vengeance hath been justly executed upon them. And these wait only for one sounding of the trumpet; which there shall be no deferring. And they scoffingly say, O LORD, hasten our sentence unto us, before the day of account"* (**38**:13-16).

The pastoral Arabs and Bedouins faced famine, but not plague. Famine hit Mecca probably in the late 540s when Muhammad's great-grandfather, Amr lived. Amr was credited with saving the people of Mecca by bringing in caravans loaded with wheat from Damascus at his own expense. This earned him the nick-name of Hāshim, "to crumble," meaning the breaking of bread. [163] This is how al-Hāshim, "the crumbler" became incorporated into the family name. The Koran memorializes this event: *"For the uniting of the tribe of Koreish; their uniting in sending forth the caravan of merchants and purveyors in winter and summer: let them serve the LORD of this house: who supplieth them with food against hunger, and hath rendered them secure from fear."* (106:1-2)

The Life of Muhammad describes the arrival of an Army of Abyssinians, Arabs from Saba / Yemen. [164] Their leader Aswad b Mafsūd was bent on destroying the Ka'ba at Mecca. If the Meccans would not permit destruction of the Ka'ba, he would destroy it and them. Abraha sent his Abyssinian cavalry commander Aswad b Mafsūd up towards Mecca on a foraging raid. 'Abdu'l-MutTālib b Hāshim, grandfather of Muhammad, owned 200 camels and represented the Quraysh as the principal chieftain. Two-hundred camels belonging to the Quraysh were seized. Abraha sent a message to 'Abdu'l-MutTālib giving his intentioons. When 'Abdu'l met with Aswad, he noted the superior forces of the Abyssinians. 'Abdu'l offered him a third of the cattle of the lowlands, if Aswad would withdraw and not destroy the Ka'ba. In response Aswad returned the 200 camels, and prepared for war.

'Abdu'l resorted to common Arab tactics. He ordered the Meccans to abandon the city and take up defensive positions in the mountains surrounding the town and block all the passes. On the morning of the attack Aswad's elephant would not obey its masters and head into Mecca. The story goes that Allah then sent swallows and starlings to pelt the Abyssinians with pebbles. Walking around the Ka'ba and throwing pebbles at the devil is a custom that survives to this day. All who were hit died. Ibn Ishaq describes the fate of the Abyssinians and their king, Abraha: "they died miserably falling by the wayside and at every well. Abraha's fingers fell off one by one and exposed purulent, bloody sores. He allegedly died when his heart "burst from his body." [165] Almost certainly this is a fanciful description of the plague. Although the inhabitants of Mecca were fearful of being struck by the "pebbles," they were spared. This historical incident is also remembered in the *Korân* Sura 105, The Elephant: *"Hast thou not seen how thy LORD dealt with the masters of the elephant? Did he not make their treacherous design an occasion of drawing them into error; and send against them flocks of birds, which cast down upon them stones of baked clay; and render them like the leaves of corn eaten by cattle?"* It was from this incident that the Quraysh gained both political respect and religious power in Mecca. They were known as the guardians of the Ka'ba. This may have made them reluctant to abandon their gods so soon after defending them. Muhammad's grandfather Abdu'l MutTālib also had religious duties in Mecca. Guided by a vision, he had dug a well, Zamzam, which supplied pilgrims to the Ka'ba with water. Upon its discovery he had cried, "Allah akbar!" [166] Abdu'l MutTālib's well was very successful. If it was successful, he promised to sacrifice one of his sons. When lots (arrows with words on them) were cast at the Ka'ba, the lot fell on his youngest son, 'Abdullah, who would be Muhammad's father. Many persuaded MutTālib that it would not be wise to kill his own son. It would be appropriate to continue casting lots and add 10 camels for each throw that went against 'Abdullah until the lots finally selected the camels. 100 camels were eventually sacrificed. [167] 'Abdullah b. Abdu'l MutTālib b Amr al-Hāshim married Amina d. Wahb b. Abdu Manaf b. Zuhra.

"The Hosts of Heaven"

Muhammad was raised as a pagan worshiper of Allah and was known for his faithfulness to Allah and his participation in the rebuilding of the Ka'ba (Caaba). Muhammad's pagan father and uncle had "Allah" as part of their names. The Ka'ba in Mecca housed 360 idols representing lesser pagan gods. The crescent and star date back to ancient times. They are seen on every mosque, even today, and the flags of most Islâmic states include these symbols. Arab worship of the moon god included giving alms to the poor, fasting for a month beginning and ending with the appearance of the crescent moon, circling the Ka'ba, praying towards Mecca, making annual pilgrimages to Mecca, sacrificing animals to the moon god, kissing the black stone in the Ka'ba, and throwing stones at the devil while walking around the Ka'ba. In the *Book of Abraham* of the *Pearl of Great Price* there are 5 references to a god named "Korash" (Abraham 1: 6, 13, 17, and twice in the Facsimiles).

The *Old Testament* contains a number of warnings about the worship of these gods often referred to as ***"the host of heaven."*** These are not to be confused with the Heavenly Hosts that glorify Jesus Christ. Deuteronomy 4:19 states, *"And lest thou lift up thine eyes unto heaven, and when thou seest the sun, and the moon, and the stars, even all the host of heaven, shouldest be driven to worship them, and serve them, which the LORD thy God hath divided unto all nations under the whole heaven."* Deuteronomy 17:2-3 states, *"If there be found among you, within any of thy gates which the LORD thy God giveth thee, man or woman, that hath wrought wickedness in the sight of the LORD thy God, in transgressing his covenant, And hath gone and served other gods, and worshipped them, either the sun, or moon, or any of the host of heaven, which I have not commanded;"* Other references to the "*hosts of heaven*" are noted in 2 Kings 21:3; 23:5; Jeremiah 8:2; 19:13; Zephaniah 1:4-5.

JUDAISM & CHRISTIANITY, BACKGROUND OF ISLAM

"*To me it seems certain that the fatalistic teachings of Mohammad and the utter degradation of women is the outstanding cause for the arrested development of the Arab. Here, I think, is a text for some eloquent sermon on the virtues of Christianity.*" General George S Patton Jr. [168]

Scattering the Seed of Abraham

Islâm, Judaism, and Christianity follow a number of common lines. To understand Islâm it is necessary to understand the development of Judeo-Christian religious beliefs.

The Bible, especially the Old Testament contains a number of genealogical lists. This tells us that family lines are important especially for Abraham and his lineage. This is also important in Islâm. "*And I will bless them that bless thee, and curse him that curseth thee: and in thee shall all families of the earth be blessed.*" (Genesis 12:3)

Does the "blood of Israel" run through my veins? Most discount this possibility and fall back on the concept of "adoption." However, the math shows that all of us have the literal seed of Abraham and Israel within us. Assume 4 generations every hundred years. In 1000 years there will be 40 generations. If there is no cousinage in the family, very unlikely, you would have 240 ancestors in your family tree. This equals 1,099,511,627,776 individuals or more than 1 trillion people. In 1500 years the number is 260 or more than 1 quintillion individuals. This is way more than all who have ever lived. Go back 2500 years and the figure is 2100 or (1,267,650,600,2 28,229,401,496,703,205,376) or one nonillion plus. [169] It is safe to assume that you have the literal seed of Israel within your background especially because of the "scattering" of Israel.

There were three main scatterings. The first occurred 726–721 BC (Assyrian) and the second 598–587 BC (Babylonian), and the third in AD 64-70 (Roman). Since then there have been more and within our memories there have been terrible persecution and flight – Germany 1933 to 1945 and Russia 1917 and 1989.

Inheritance or "birthright," is important. It was usually, but not always reserved for the first legitimate son. With it came leadership and inheritance. In religious terms this meant priesthood. In the case of Israel, it meant the sons of Joseph, the first son of Jacob's favorite wife, Rachael. It should have gone to Reuben, but he "*lay with Bilhah his father's concubine.*" (Gen 35:22), so it passed to Joseph and his children: *NOW the sons of Reuben the firstborn of Israel, (for he was the firstborn; but, forasmuch as he defiled his father's bed, his birthright was given unto the sons of Joseph the son of Israel: and the genealogy is not to be reckoned after the birthright. For Judah prevailed above his brethren, and of him came the chief ruler; but the birthright was Joseph's:)* (1Chron 5:1-2).

Joseph's sons were Ephraim and Manasseh. They were adopted by Jacob who during his blessing of them placed Ephraim, the second born of the two, ahead of Manasseh (Genesis 48:18-19). These were part of the northern 10 tribes; most were slaughtered, but a few were taken into captivity by the Assyrians and scattered about 721 BC (1 Chron 5:3-26). Israel's individual tribes ceased to exist. With the rediscovery of scripture in the temple at the time of Josiah (640 BC) the worship of "one god" (Deut 6:4) may have been introduced.

Although Josiah "did that which was right in the sight of the LORD" (2 Chron 34:2) his reviews by the prophetess Huldah (2 Chron 34:24-28) were mixed and those of Jeremiah were not complementary (Jer 1-4).

In 587 BC most of Judah and what had remained in the Southern kingdom were killed or captured by the Babylonians under Nebuchadnezzar. Jerusalem was destroyed. Some that escaped populated Samaria. A few of those captured were released by Cyrus of Persia and returned after 50 years (2 Chron 36).

Jerusalem was rebuilt under Nehemiah's leadership (444–432 BC) and Malachi, the last of the old prophets gave his final warnings about 420 BC. In 320 BC Judah was subjected to the rule of the Ptolemies following the conquests of Alexander the Great. Most of the Jews spoke Greek. Legend has Ptolemy II ordering translation of Hebrew scripture into Greek – the Septuagint. The Torah was translated in the 3rd Century BC. Other scripture came later.[170] With the rise of the Seleucids in Egypt (198 BC), Antiochus IV (215-164 BC Epiphanies) raided the temple to fund a war against the Ptolemys. The religion of the Jews was banned in favor of the Greek gods. This included the philosophies especially those of Plato (424-347 BC) and his one god ideas.

From 167 to 160 BC the revolt lead by the Maccabees was successful. Jerusalem was liberated and worship in the Temple restored. The Maccabees ruled as the Hasmonian Dynasty with approval by the Roman Senate until 63 BC when Pompey of Rome took Jerusalem and Roman rule was established under the Herods (The Great 74-4 Bc; Antipas 20 Bc- AD39; Agrippa 10 BC – AD 44; Agrippa II AD27-100). As a family the Herods were full of intrigue and murder. In 30 BC Rome took Egypt, Cleopatra died and Rome established its hold on the Eastern end of the Mediterranean. Christ's mission to re-establish the religion of Israel (opposed by the Jews) ended after only 3 years with His crucifixion about AD 33. In AD 64 a second Jewish revolt began against Rome; Agrippa II remained loyal to Rome and assisted in crushing the Jews. The capture and destruction of Jerusalem followed in AD 70. The Romans "*made the whole city run down with blood, to such a degree … that the fire of many of the houses was quenched with these men's blood*" (Josephus, *Wars of the Jews*, Chapter VIII). The end came in AD 73 with the fall of Masada. Another scattering occurred as Jews fled in all directions. Those who stayed in Judea were enslaved or slaughtered. All of us have the literal blood of Israel within us.

The Tripartite God of Israel & Christianity

Christianity owes its existence to the God of Israel. Through history His memory has been dimmed on several occasions, but has been restored. The Bible teaches us that the children of Adam and Eve eventually became so wicked that God despaired of every having made man and threatened to destroy all except Noah and his family. It required revival again about the time of Abraham and his family. Again, after only 4 generations His memory became clouded with the sojourn into Egypt and was finally revived at the time of Moses during which His priesthood was restored. But once again the Children of Israel fell into paganism following Solomon. The Assyrians scattered the people of Israel and almost destroyed Judah, had it not been for disease. The Babylonians took the Jews captive then released some. After Malachi (430 BC) no further prophets were sent. Soon they had become corrupted by Greek thought and culture. Christ came to revive the true religion of His Father, but many Jewish leaders became hard-hearted and stiff-necked and killed Him as they had the prophets. This gave rise to Christianity.

Originally the God of Israel and the Christian God was a tripartite God. Sometime between Moses and Josiah's reforms and possibly later with Greek Platonic influence, the God of Israel went to a monotheistic god.

The Jews misinterpreted Deuteronomy 6:4 "*The LORD our God is one LORD.*" The Christian's made the same error during the period of the apologists following the death of the apostles. Both thought the tripartite god was one in person instead of one in purpose. Christian apologists came under the spell of the "one god," Platonic Greek philosophy, as did the Jewish rabbi, Phillo of Alexandria (20 BC-AD 50).

The *Torah* makes a distinction between God, the designer or planner of creation found in Genesis 1, and "Jehovah God," the builder of that creation found first in Genesis 2:3-7. The *Torah* states: "*which God had created to make.*"(Gen 2:3) [171] A paragraph-break separates verse 3 from 4-7 which demonstrates a clear distinction between *God*, the planner, and "*Jehovah God*" who carries out the plan. The Hebrew Torah continues: "*they were created in the day that Jehovah was making earth and heavens … And Jehovah God formed the man out of dust from the ground, and blew into his nostrils the breath of life: and man became a living soul.*" (See Gen 2:4-7) [172] The German *Luther Bible* also makes this same distinction. In Genesis 1, God is referred to as *Gott*. In Genesis 2:4 the terminology changes from *Gott* to *Gott der Herr*, "God the Lord."

The *King James Bible* renders the translation thus: "*And God blessed the seventh day, and sanctified it: because that in it he had rested from all his work which God created and made.*" (Genesis 2:3) "*These are the generations of the heavens and of the earth when they were created, in the day that the LORD God made the earth and the heavens, … And the LORD God formed man of the dust of the ground, and breathed into his nostrils the breath of life; and man became a living soul.*" (Gen 2:4-7)

Beginning in Genesis 4:1 the phrase "LORD God" no longer appears. It is replaced by "LORD" in capital letters. The word "LORD" seems ambiguous. Are the translators speaking of the "planner" or the "builder" of the universe? The *Torah* translates "LORD" as "Jehovah," the "builder." However, the King James Version of the *Bible* seems to make a change in the *New Testament* when the word "LORD" indicates "the planner," "Father," not the "Son." The King James translators, [173] began using two other terms for deity that assist us in knowing what part of Israel's tripartite God is meant. These are "word of the LORD" and "Lord God"

"*AFTER these things the word of the LORD came unto Abram in a vision, saying, Fear not, Abram: I am thy shield, and thy exceeding great reward. And*

Abram said, Lord GOD, what wilt thou give me, seeing I go childless, and the steward of my house is this Eliezar of Damascus?" (Gen 15:1-2)

The *Torah* renders these verses as follows: *"After these things the word of Jehovah came to Abram in a vision saying, Do not fear, Abram; I am your shield, your reward will increase greatly. And Abram said, Lord Jehovah what will You give to me, since I am going childless, and the son of the inheritance of my house is Eleazar of Damascus?"*[174]

It seems clear that we are still talking about Jehovah or Jehovah God, the "builder." Later on, the translators of the *King James Bible* further clarify the issue for English readers by demonstrating that "*word of the LORD*" and "*LORD*" are one and the same person: "*And the LORD spake unto Moses in the wilderness of Sinai, saying, Number the children of Levi after the house of their fathers, by their families: every male from a month old and upward shalt thou number them. And Moses numbered them according to the word of the LORD, as he was commanded*" (Num 3:14-16).

The *Torah* remains consistent rendering these verses thus: *"And Jehovah spoke to Moses in the wilderness of Sinai, saying, Visit the sons of Levi by their families, by their fathers' house. You shall number every male from a month old and* upward. *And Moses numbered them according to the command of Jehovah, as he had been commanded."* [175]

The phrase "word of the LORD" is used in the *Old Testament* by the King James translators 244 times starting in Genesis 15:1 and ending in Malachi 1:1. It is used in the *New Testament* 13 times. In the *New Testament* John 1:1-14 makes it crystal clear whom we are referring to when he defines "the Word" as Jesus Christ and makes a distinction between Him and God the Father.

IN the beginning was the Word, and the Word was with God, and the Word was God. The same was in the beginning with God. ... He was in the world, and the world was made by him, and the world knew him not. He came unto his own, and his own received him not. But as many as received him, to them gave he power to become the sons of God, even to them that believe on his name: ... And the Word was made flesh, and dwelt among us, (and we beheld his glory, the glory as of the only begotten of the Father,) full of grace and truth" (John 1:1-2, 10-12, 14). The King James translators of the *New Testament* often use "LORD" to mean the Father, but "Lord" refers to the Son. Acts uses the phrase "Lord Jesus" 18 times. Paul further makes this clear: "*peace from God our Father, and the Lord Jesus Christ.*" (Romans 1:7) The tripartite Christian God is further clarified when all individuals are described separately during Christ's baptism. (Matt 3:16-17; Mark 10:9-11; Luke 3:21-23; John 1:29-34)

The Spirit of God or Holy Ghost

The third member of the Godhead is "the spirit of God" for Israel or the "Holy Ghost" for Christianity. Genesis 1:2 reads, "*And the Spirit of God moved upon the face of the waters.*" The *Torah* reads, "*and the Spirit of God moving gently on the face of the waters.*" [176] This "spirit of God" is referred to a number of times in the Old Testament as being influential among the prophets (Ex 31:3; 35:31; Num 24:2; 1 Sam 10:10, 11:6, 19:20, 19:23; 2 Chron 15:1, 24:20; Job 27:3, 33:4; Ezek 11:24). For Christianity the "spirit of God" is clearly identified in the New Testament as the Holy Ghost: (Matt 3:16, 12:28; Rom 8:14, 15:19; 1 Cor 2:11, 14; 3:16, 7:40, 12:3; Eph 4:30; 1John 4:2.)

As a practical matter Jews and most Christians pay little attention to the third person in the Godhead, The Holy Ghost, even though he is mentioned in the Nicene Creed. Many in Islâm believe that the "Paraclete" is Muhammad, the one sent to bear witness of God. This interpretation is in error. When Christ spoke to His disciples at the end of the Last Supper, he promised them two "Comforters." "*If ye love me, keep my commandments. And I will pray the Father, and he shall give you another Comforter, that he may abide with you for ever; Even the Spirit of truth; whom the world cannot receive, because it seeth him not, neither knoweth him: but ye know him; for he dwelleth with you, and shall be in you. I will not leave you comfortless: I will come to you*" (John 14:15-18). Later Christ promised, "*If a man love me, he will keep my words: and my Father will love him, and we will come unto him, and make our abode with him. He that loveth me not keepeth not my sayings: and the word which ye hear is not mine, but the Father's which sent me. These things have I spoken unto you, being yet present with you. But the Comforter, which is the Holy Ghost, whom the Father will send in my name, he shall teach you all things, and bring all things to your remembrance, whatsoever I have said unto you*" (John 14:23-26).

There is no mention of the "Holy Ghost" in the *Old Testament*, but Christ makes the Comforter's purpose clear, "*when the Comforter is come, whom I will send unto you from the Father, even the Spirit of truth, which proceedeth from the Father, he shall testify of me*" (John 15:26); And "*for if I go not away, the Comforter will not come unto you; but if I depart, I will send him unto you*" (John 16:7; 7:39). John the Baptist promised people that Christ would baptize "*with the Holy Ghost, and with fire*" (Matt 3:11; Luke 3:16; Mark 1:8; John 1:33). After John baptized Christ with water, the Holy Ghost descended upon him (Luke 3:22; 4:1). Blasphemy against the Holy Ghost is an unpardonable sin (Matt 12:31-32; Mark 3:29; Luke 12:10). Christ told Peter, James, John and Andrew that in the end times,

His followers would be persecuted, *"But ... take no thought beforehand what ye shall speak, neither do ye premeditate: but whatsoever shall be given you in that hour, that speak ye: for it is not ye that speak, but the Holy Ghost"* (Mark 13:11). Christ's disciples were told the same, *"And when they bring you unto the synagogues, and unto magistrates, and powers, take ye no thought how or what thing ye shall answer, or what ye shall say: For the Holy Ghost shall teach you in the same hour what ye ought to say"* (Luke 12:11-12). *"But the Comforter, which is the Holy Ghost, whom the Father will send in my name, he shall teach you all things, and bring all things to your remembrance, whatsoever I have said unto you"* (John 14:26).

Christ's apostles continued to teach of the Holy Ghost. The Acts and Epistles describe him on numerous occasions. *"Until the day in which he was taken up, after that he through the Holy Ghost had given commandments unto the apostles whom he had chosen"* (Acts 1:2). The apostles were taught, *"For John truly baptized with water; but ye shall be baptized with the Holy Ghost not many days hence"* (Acts 1:5). *"But ye shall receive power, after that the Holy Ghost is come upon you: and ye shall be witnesses unto me both in Jerusalem, and in all Judæa, and in Samaria, and unto the uttermost part of the earth"* (Acts 1:8). This occurred on the day of the Pentecost, *"And they were all filled with the Holy Ghost, and began to speak with other tongues, as the Spirit gave them utterance"* (Acts 2:4). In the early Christian Church, the gift of the Holy Ghost was given to all who repented and were baptized. *"Then Peter said unto them, Repent, and be baptized every one of you in the name of Jesus Christ for the remission of sins, and ye shall receive the gift of the Holy Ghost"* (Acts 2:38). Later statements about the Holy Ghost indicate that the Apostles often spoke to others *"being filled with the Holy Ghost."* Stephen was said to be a man full of faith and the Holy Ghost (Acts 6:5). The gift of the Holy Ghost is bestowed by the laying on of hands (Acts 8:17). There are many more references to the Holy Ghost in the New Testament. The Holy Ghost bears witnesses to the divinity of Christ and gives those who possess it powers to bear witness of Christ and even the power to heal. At the end of his ministry, Jesus told his disciples, *"Go ye therefore, and teach all nations, baptizing them in the name of the Father, and of the Son, and of the Holy Ghost"* (Matt 28:19). We also learn that the gift of the Holy Ghost was given coincident with baptism in the early Christian Church (Acts 2:38; 10:47). It was given by the laying on of hands by apostles of Christ (Acts 8:14-20), and it could not be purchased. See also Acts 9:17; 19:6. In modern times members of the Church of Jesus Christ of Latter-day Saints who receive the Holy Ghost at the time of confirmation attest to all the powers described above – witness, revelations, warnings, and promptings.

The Position of Women in Jeduo-Christian Society

One of the most important differences between Islam and Judeo-Christian belief concdrns the treatment and position of women especially as a wife. In Genesis 1 after each day of the creation is found the words, "God saw that it was good." See verses: 4, 10, 12, 18, 25 of Genesis 1. However, following the creation of man there was no such statement. As the creation story continues in Genesis 2 we find the creation of "the man" was incomplete. The Lord God said "*It is not good that the man wshould be alone; I will make him an help meet for him*" (Gen 2:18). The King James translators described the woman as an "*help-meet.*" However, the Hebrew word from which they translated it was "ezer" רֶזֵע."[177] Literally translated this means "*savior*" not "help-meet." In Judeo-Christianity women have a special protected place in society. The change in common law was brought about by Queen Theodora of Constantinople, as previously described, supported this. In Islam women can be wives, concubines, slave-girls or "gifts of the right hand." They are subjected to polygamous relationships with men and when it comes to inheritance and trust, they are definitely second-class citizens. If we are to believe the Bible, women, especially as wives, are the "saviors" of their husbands and polygamist marriages are not permitted. In modern society, there has been a tendency to denigrate marriage and replace it with the "community of women" and "free love." [178] This will usually cause the quick death of societies that try to practice it as noticed in New Harmony, Nashoba, Davis House[179] , and many European countries with their collapsing populations.[180]

A Unification of Purpose or Plan of Salvation

> "*This is my work and my glory—to bring to pass the immortality and eternal life of man.*"
>
> (Moses 1:39)

The important doctrine of free agency or free will is found frequently in the Bible (Gen 2:16-17, 4:7; Deut 11:27, 30:19; Josh 24:15; 1 Kgs 18:21; Prov 1:29; Matt 26:39; John 5:30). These scriptures present the choice to do what is right or follow the good, or chose in error, and follow evil. In the beginning Adam & Eve chose to eat the fruit from the tree of the knowledge of good and evil. In so doing they chose mortality, but at the same time chose to be like the gods (Gen 3:5). After Eden children came, but many were trouble. Work and children are difficult, but give both man and woman as partners a chance to learn and change. "*And the LORD God said, Behold, the man is become as one of us, to know good and evil:*" (Gen 3:22). A loving Father / God also knew that in the process, His children would choose evil at times. If Justice were to prevail, this would permanently separate Him from his children, unless there was a Savior, Redeemer or Advocate who could effectively plea for mercy for His children. However, mercy could not rob justice, otherwise justice would cease and God would cease to be God. The price to pay for the atonement was severe. Just as it was played out in Ancient Israel with sacrifice of an innocent or pure animal without blemish or by the near sacrifice of Isaac by Abraham, the Savior would have to pay the price. "*God so loved the world, that he gave his only begotten Son, that whosoever believeth in him should not perish, but have everlasting life*" (John 3:16). Christ asks us to believe in his ability as Savior and repent of our sins and wickedness. "*If ye love me, keep my commandments. And I will pray the Father, and he shall give you another Comforter, that he may abide with you for ever;*" (John14:15-16). Receipt of the Comforter or Holy Ghost is known as "baptism with fire" or serious cleansing (Matt 3:11; Luke 3:16). Note that all 3 members of the Godhead are needed to bring this about.

God rarely interferes with man and his individual agency. However, sometimes we are shown the hand of God in specific events. "*And the LORD said unto Gideon, The people that are with thee are too many for me to give the Midianites into their hands, lest Israel vaunt themselves against me, saying, Mine own hand hath saved me*" (Judges 7:2). There are events in recent history that may demonstrate the Lord's interference in world events so great were the odds against them. The American Revolution (1775 – 1783), ratification of the Constitution of the U.S (1787-88), the Finnish Winter and Continuation wars of 1939 through 1944 against Russia, and the Battle of Midway June 1942 are such incidents.

The God of Israel and Christianity are not the same as the God of Islâm. Furthermore, Muhammad is not the Holy Ghost, Comforter or "Paraclete." Without atonement and a Savior, without a witness or Comforter, and without a pre-existence of souls, freedom to act on our own makes little sense. On the other hand, the Islâmic god bears the responsibility for everything that happens on this earth, good and evil. According to the *Korân* god participates in lies, plots, deceptions, murders, and wars much as did Al-Lah, the Moon God of War. He has no way of being merciful to his followers without destroying justice and picking favorites. By representing two conflicting principles, mercy and justice, good and evil, the Islamic God ceases to be God. This is a major doctrinal problem Islâm faces. In Judeo-Christianity, it is man who creates or does evil acts.

Apostasy & the God of Israel

When did worship of the God of Israel change? We see early evidence of it during the time of Moses. Major transgressions occurred during their sojourn in the wilderness. "*And the LORD said unto Moses, How long refuse ye to keep my commandments and my laws*" (Ex 16:28)? They spent 40 years in the wilderness eating manna (Ex 16:35). The Israelites demanded a king despite Samuel's warnings (1 Samuel 8) about the potential evil leadership by kings. Both Saul and David were guilty of disobedience, adultery and murder. Serious degradation of God's commandments continued with Solomon's desire to marry many "strange" (foreign) women of differing religions (1 Kings 11:1). All 19 rulers of Israel led the people into false worship as did 12 of Judah's 20 kings. King Josiah attempted a return to correct religious practices, but his efforts to clarify and simplify seemed to further corrupt temple worship and change the concepts of priesthood and God. Jeremiah gave serious warnings about the reforms and the calamities that would befall the Jews because of them. Following the Babylonian Captivity, prophets became fewer and died out with Malachi (430 BC). Malachi himself sent final warnings about polluted sacrifices, priests that led the people astray and corrupted the covenants with the Lord, robbing the Lord in tithings, and abandoning the Abrahamic Covenant by which all the families of the world would be blessed (Gen 12:3; 28:14; Exodus 33:6-11; Malachi1-4).

During the reign of Josiah (641-610 BC) a religious reformation occurred in Judah and in what had been the Northern Kingdom. The tripartite God of the earlier era, God, The Spirit of God and Jehovah God (Genesis 1&2) was likely lost because of Deuteronomy 6:4, "*Hear, O Israel: The LORD our God is one LORD*:" Details of his reforms are described in 2 Kings 23 and 2 Chronicles 34 and 35:1-19. In the process of restoring the Temple in Jerusalem, Hilkiah, the priest and father of Jeremiah, found a book, probably Deuteronomy. He took it to Shaphan, the scribe, who read it to King Josiah who *"rent his clothes"*- repented. (See 2 Kings 22:8-12.) The priestess Huldah was consulted. She prophesied of the temple, "*Thus saith the LORD, Behold, I will bring evil upon this place, and upon the inhabitants thereof, even all the words of the book which the king of Judah hath read: Because they have forsaken me, and have burned incense unto other gods, that they might provoke me to anger with all the works of their hands; therefore my wrath shall be kindled against this place, and shall not be quenched*" (2Kings

22:16-17). None the less Josiah made extensive reforms outlined in 2 Kings 23:1-24.

1. Josiah gathered the elders, had the book read and had them covenant to keep the Lord's commandments.
2. The vessels of Baal and the Hosts of Heaven were burned and pounded to powder.
3. He "*put down the idolatrous priests*" who had made offerings to Baal, and the Hosts of Heaven.
4. "*He brought out the grove from the house of the LORD, without Jerusalem, unto the brook Kidron, and burned it …*" (2 Kings 23:6) The word "*grove*" is best translated from the Hebrew as a "wooden object of worship." This could have been Aaron's rod or even the Ark of the Covenant.
5. He destroyed the homes of the sodomites that lived near the house of the LORD, where women wove hangings for the "*grove.*"
6. He defiled and broke down the "high places and places where human sacrifices to Moloch had been made.
7. He removed the horses of the sun and burned the chariot of the sun.
8. He destroyed the heathen altars of King Ahaz and King Manasseh in the upper chamber (Holy of Holies).
9. He destroyed the spots and their idols where the fertility rites of Ashtoreth were performed. Then he did the same at Beth-el built by Jeroboam.
10. He killed the priests of the high places.
11. He ordered the people to honor their covenant to keep the Passover.
12. He got rid of witches and wizards that were in Judah and Jerusalem.

2 Chronicles 34:3 to 2 Chr 35:19 describes similar reforms with some differences or additions below:

1. He burned the bones of the priests upon their altars and cleansed Judah and Jerusalem
2. He restored the ark to the Temple
3. He ordered a huge Passover feast.

King Josiah died at the age of 39 in combat against the Egyptian Pharaoh Necho. Following his death, the people installed his 23-year-old son, Jehoahaz as king, but Necho returned in 3 months, deposed him, hauled him off to Egypt and put his brother Eliakim on the throne after taking 100 talent of silver (3000 kg) and a talent of gold (33-50 kg) in tribute. Necho changed Eliakim's name to Jehoiakim (2 Chronicles 35:20–36:4). While King Josiah was said to have done good, the kings that followed him did evil according to the scriptures.

In 598 BC Nebuchadnezzar and the Babylonians invaded the land, raided the temple and installed Jehoiachin the 8-year-old son of Jehoiakim as king. He ruled for only 3 months when Nebuchadnezzar returned again, raided the temple a second time and installed Zedekiah as king. Zedekiah also did evil in the eyes of the Lord. He ruled for eleven years, revolted against Nebuchadnezzar who returned with his army and killed most of the people and burned everything to the ground. Those he did not kill he took as captives. The land then rested for 50 years (587 – 537 BC) until Cyrus' order to release the captive Jews and allow them to return to Jerusalem.

Old Testament scholar Margaret Barker, a Methodist, has written that during Josiah's reign, the ark, manna, Aaron's rod and the holy anointing oil disappeared. [181] The disappearance of the ark does not agree with the statement in 2 Chron 35:3. She has also asserted that Josiah's Deuteronomists did not recognize angels or revelations. She states that a number of Jewish sources state that the Josiah reforms so distressed devout Jews that many left for Egypt and into the Arabian Desert where they were not accepted and had to cross the ocean. [182] She also states that the menorah and the wooden pole, Asherah, representing the Queen of Heaven, were removed from the temple during the reforms. [183] One only need read Jeremiah to find that there might have been a great deal of distress among devout Jews.

The Prophesy of Jeremiah

Jeremiah, son of Hilkiah the priest, began his prophetic calling in the 13th year of Josiah's reign (628 BC) and continued his prophecies until his death in Egypt after the defeat of Judah by the Babylonians in 586 BC. Chapters 1-6 cover Josiah's reign up to 608 BC. Chapters 7-20 cover the reign of Jehoiakim (608-597 B.C.) and chapters 21-38 cover the reign of Zedekiah (597 – 586 B.C.) Chapters 39-44 cover events after the capture. 46-51 are prophecies against foreign nations and 52 is the historical conclusion. One of Jeremiah's first prophetic statements refers to the rod of Aaron which had sprouted almonds (Num 17:8) and possibly the sacred candle stick

(Exodus 25:33-34) that was in the temple and probably destroyed during Josiah's reforms (Jer 1:11-14). His prophesy has to do with temple worship conducted by the high priest and the lesser priests. It cites "the rod of an almond tree" [See Num 17:8; Exodus 7:19, 20; 8:5, 16, 17; 17:3, 6, 8; 20:8; and Hebrews 9:4.] and "a seething pot." [See Exodus 16:33; 38:3; Leviticus 6:28; 1 Sam 2:14; 1 Kings 7:45]. In the New Testament Paul refers to the worship of the old temple in Hebrews 9:2-8.

Jeremiah begins the second chapter by describing the old days of Israel (Jer 2:2-3). He recounts their delivery from Egypt, their sojourn in the wilderness and their arrival in the Promised Land. But the people and the pastors defiled the land and transgressed the Lord's Law (Jer 2:7-14). Jeremiah then wonders why Judah must run after Egypt or the Assyrians (Jer 2:18-19). He criticizes them for changing their religion and killing their prophets (Jer 2:28-30).

In Chapter 3 Jeremiah points out that both Israel and Judah have divorced themselves from the Lord. He becomes specific about the times of Josiah the king and accuses them of *backsliding,* and *playing the harlot.* This not only included Israel but "*her treacherous sister Judah*" (Jer 3:6-11). Jeremiah promises the return of Israel from a scattered condition (Jer 3:12-19). Despite the pleading of the Lord for the Children of Israel and Judah to return to right ways, it is no use (Jer 4:22). In Chapter 5 Jeremiah predicts judgments will be poured out upon Judah and blessings are withheld. A nation will be brought from far off (Jer 5:15). The cause is laid out in the rest of Chapter 5. In Chapter 6 Jeremiah prophesies the destruction of Jerusalem by a great cruel nation. In Chapter 7 he states this can be avoided if Judah will return, but then he laments of the Temple "*Is this house, which is called by my name, become a den of robbers in your eyes? Behold, even I have seen it, saith the LORD* (Jer7:11). In Chapters 8 to 20 he predicts the destruction and scattering of Judah and eventually its gathering.

Jeremiah was not impressed by the reforms of Josiah and how the people were behaving. Jeremiah speaks of the persecution he was subjected to by Pashur, the priest (Jer 20:2). He later notes his migration with some Jewish remnants into Egypt (Jer 43:2-7). Jewish legend indicates he was eventually stoned to death in Egypt.

Summary of the Apostasy of Israel

The scriptures tell us that the following basic beliefs were lost over the period of the Kingdoms of Israel and Judah.

1. The Jews came to worship a single god instead of their tripartite God
2. They lost the higher of the two priesthoods, the Melchizedek (Gen 14:18; Ps 110:4), while retaining only the Aaronic (Gen 14:18, Heb 5:6, 10; 6:20; 7:1, 10-11, 15, 17, 21). With it went the Abrahamic Covenant. *"And I will make of thee a great nation, and I will bless thee, and make thy name great; and thou shalt be a blessing: And I will bless them that bless thee, and curse him that curseth thee: and in thee shall all families of the earth be blessed"* (Gen 12:2-3). "Nation" as used here should be translated as "priesthood." See the meaning of the word "ethnos" in its earliest form in Greek and 1 Peter 2:9. See also Malachi 4:5-6. "Great" can also mean "high." Thus "high priesthood" (Gen 14:18-20; Psalms 110:4; Heb 4:14; 7:1-2; 14-17).
3. They lost the prophets and the spirit of revelation after Malachi (430 BC).
4. They corrupted their temple worship (See Matt 21:13; Mark 11:17; Luke 19:46).

Dispensation & Restoration

The concept of "dispensations" or a "restoration" of God's truth to the earth by authorized servants is not understood by many Jews and Christians. The Bible suggests these may have followed Adam, Enoch, Noah, Abraham, Moses and Jesus. One of Christ's missions was to bring the Jews back to the correct worship of earlier times (Gal 4:4-5), but the Jews, especially the leadership, resisted Him (Matthew 10.). The Old Testament, prophets, especially Isaiah gave references to the Lord as the redeemer of Israel (Isaiah 41:14-15; 44:6; 47:4; 48:16-19; 49:5-7; 54:5-6; 63:16). In this context the house of Jacob and Abraham are mentioned. Chapter 1 of Matthew begins with Abraham's genealogy that ends with Joseph, husband of Mary, "*of whom was born Jesus, who is called Christ*" (Matt 1:16). In the New Testament we find Christ called "King of the Jews" once at the beginning of His life when it is threatened by Herod and then in derision at the end of His life when he is under trial. It is found in all 4 Gospel accounts (Matt

2:2; Matt 27:11, 29, 37; Mark 15:2, 9, 12, 18, 26; Luke 23:3, 37, 38; John 18:33, 39; 19:3, 14, 19, 21). In his charge to his Apostles Christ told them to preach only to the Jews (Matt: 10:5-6). Zachiarias' blessing of his son John (Luke 1:67-79) also makes this clear. At the beginning of His Ministry Jesus commanded his disciples, "*Go not into the way of the Gentiles, and into any city of the Samaritans enter ye not: But go rather to the lost sheep of the house of Israel.*" (Matt 10:5-6). Christ's early journeys show Him going as far north as the regions of Tyre and Sidon. In John 7:1 it is said, *Jesus walked in Galilee: for he would not walk in Jewry, because the Jews sought to kill him* and he went to Galilee, but had minimal success here (John 7:5). After the Jews sought to kill him, he changed the instructions (John 7:1). Christ accused the Jews of corrupting their old religion (See Matt 13:15; 15:7-9; 23:13-39). This led to charges of blasphemy against Christ and to his crucifixion. Evidence of the Jews' apostasy is laid before them by Stephen before his martyrdom (Acts 7). Despite His efforts, the Jewish Leadership rejected, tried to trap and kill Him. He bemoaned their fate, "*O Jerusalem, Jerusalem, thou that killest the prophets, and stonest them which are sent unto thee, how often would I have gathered thy children together, even as a hen gathereth her chickens under her wings, and ye would not* "(Matt 23:37)! This is repeated with little alteration in Luke 13:34-35.

Following his crucifixion and resurrection He returned to the disciples leaving them with this final charge, "*Go ye therefore, and teach all nations, baptizing them in the name of the Father, and of the Son, and of the Holy Ghost*" (Matt 28:19). Similar instructions are found In Mark 16:15 and Luke 24:47. Luke's Acts of the Apostles further testify of this effort in detail. In John 21:15-17 He told Peter 3 times, "*Feed my sheep.*" Peter took the primary responsibility of apostleship to the Jews while Paul was given apostleship to the Gentiles. (Acts 9:15, Rom 11:13 and Gal 2:8). History indicates that Gentiles became the bulk of Christian converts (Acts 11:26; 26:28; 1 Pet 4:16).

Christ's Mission

Most important was the atonement, the bringing together, or the reconciliation between fallen, sinful, man and God. A similitude of this action included animal sacrifices from the time of Adam until the death of Jesus Christ. The word, "atonement" is used many times in the Old Testament in this regard. While in the Garden of Gethsemane on the Mount of Olives, Christ prayed earnestly for several hours while his disciples slept. He was then taken captive, tried, scourged, crucified, and resurrected. All these activities plus the example of His life brought about the atonement.

He had become the innocent, willing sacrifice for the sins of the world (Matt 26:30-46; Mark 14:26-43; Luke 22:39-46; Rom 5:11; 1 Cor 15:42-57; 2 Nep 9:7; Mosiah 16). The faith, repentance, baptism, gift of the Holy Ghost, and endurance to the end of individuals determined whether or not they could claim Christ as their Savior and Advocate with the Father. The good works and repentance of man were important, but insufficient to pay the debt. This could only be done through the grace (power) of Jesus Christ and was essential to His Plan of Salvation (Moses 1:39-42). These are outlined in the Articles of Faith 1:1-4 written in a letter (1842) by Joseph Smith in the Barstow and Wentworth letter.

In addition, it was important for the Jews to understand the Godhead as it had been portrayed in ancient times. There had to be a re-establishment of the high priesthood of Abraham, Melchizedek, and Moses in addition to the lesser priesthood of Aaron, which had remained. Baptism and the revelatory power of the Spirit of God or Holy Ghost had to return to the earth by way of the Apostles and given to the rest of the church. As many Christian Churches today even chant, "*As it was in the beginning, it is now and ever shall be, world without end. Amen.*" Even more important, the people would have to change their ways. What better way could there be other than for the Messiah (Hebrew word) or Christ (the Greek word) to return to earth, be an example, and demonstrate who He was with his power and love for mankind?

The New Testament tries to make these points clear. Mark 1:1 starts it with, "*THE beginning of the gospel of Jesus Christ, the Son of God.*" Mark 9:7-8 recounts events on the Mount of Transfiguration, "*And a voice came out of the cloud, saying, This is my beloved Son: hear him. And suddenly, when they had looked round about, they saw no man any more, save Jesus only with themselves.*" See also Matthew 17:5-8 and Luke 9:35. Jesus is identified clearly as the Messiah or Christ. Matt 16:15-17: "*But whom say ye that I am?... Thou art the Christ, the Son of the living God. And Jesus answered and said unto him, Blessed art thou, Simon Bar-jona: for flesh and blood hath not revealed it unto thee, but my Father which is in heaven.*" Christ does not deny his identity even when it means his life. See Matt 26:63-66; Mark 14:61-64. Devils were said to have identified Jesus as the Christ the Son of God. (Luke 4: 41) The twelve also bear witness of him, "¶ *From that time many of his disciples went back, and walked no more with him. Then said Jesus unto the twelve, Will ye also go away? Then Simon Peter answered him, Lord, to whom shall we go? thou hast the words of eternal life. And we believe and are sure that thou art that Christ, the Son of the living God*" (John 6:66-69). When Jesus arrived to comfort Mary and Martha over the death of Lazarus, Martha chided Jesus about his delay claiming that Lazarus would not have died had Jesus come earlier. Jesus assures her that Lazarus would live again. "*Martha saith unto him, I know that he shall rise again in the resurrection at the last day. Jesus said unto her, I am the resurrection, and the life: he that believeth in me, though he were dead, yet shall he live: And whosoever liveth and believeth in me shall never die. Believest thou this? She saith unto him, Yea, Lord: I believe that thou art the Christ, the Son of God, which should come into the world*" (John 11:24-27). Then Christ restored Lazarus to life.

Christ never argues with his opponents. Rather he gives straight answers or parables to make his points and performs miracles as acts of charity. "¶ *And many other signs truly did Jesus in the presence of his disciples, which are not written in this book: But these are written, that ye might believe that Jesus is the Christ, the Son of God; and that believing ye might have life through his name*" (John 20:30-31).

There are numerous testimonies of the Father, Son and Holy Ghost in the Acts and Epistles. This one by Paul might summarize them all: "*PAUL, a servant of Jesus Christ, called to be an apostle, separated unto the gospel of God, (Which he had promised afore by his prophets in the holy scriptures,) Concerning his Son Jesus Christ our Lord, which was made of the seed of David according to the flesh; And declared to be the Son of God with power, according to the spirit of holiness, by the resurrection from the dead: By whom we have received grace and apostleship, for obedience to the faith among all nations, for his name: Among whom are ye also the called of Jesus Christ*" (Romans 1:1-6). Other examples can be found in Acts:34-38; Acts 9:20-21; 1Cor 1:9; 2Cor 1:19-21;; Gal 2:19-20; 1Tim 1:2; 2 Tim 1:2; Titus 1:4. John also bears witness in 1 John 1:3, "*That which we have seen and heard declare we unto you, that ye also may have fellowship with us: and truly our fellowship is with the Father, and with his Son Jesus Christ.*" See also 1 John 2:22-23; 1 John 5:20; 2 John 1:3; 2 John 1:9.

The Great Christian Apostasy

The New Testament is full of warnings about an apostasy to come. John told of early apostasies (John 6:66). Before He died, Christ gave a number of warnings to his disciples (Matt 13:15; 15:9; 24:1-24). Afterwards there are a series of warnings by Paul of apostasy of the faithful in his time (Acts 20:29; 1Cor 11:18; Gal 1:6-7; 3:1; 2Thes 2:3; 1Tim[4]:1; 2 Tim 1:15; 2 Tim 2:18 and Titus 1:16). Paul's well-known warning of apostasy in times to come is found in 2 Tim 3:1-7: "*THIS know also, that in the last days perilous times shall come. For men shall be lovers of their own selves, covetous, boasters, proud, blasphemers, disobedient to parents, unthankful, unholy, Without natural affection, trucebreakers, false accusers, incontinent, fierce, despisers of those that are good, Traitors, heady, highminded, lovers of pleasures more than lovers of God; Having a form of godliness, but denying the power thereof: from such turn away. For of this sort are they which creep into houses, and lead captive silly women laden with sins, led away with divers lusts,*

Ever learning, and never able to come to the knowledge of the truth." Then later in 2 Timothy he states. *"For the time will come when they will not endure sound doctrine; but after their own lusts shall they heap to themselves teachers, having itching ears; And they shall turn away their ears from the truth, and shall be turned unto fables"* (2 Tim 4:3-4). What may surprise many are the warnings given by Peter, James, John, and Jude.

James said, *"FROM whence come wars and fightings among you? Come they not hence, even of your lusts that war in your members"* (James 4:1)? Peter, too, had strong words of warning: *"BUT there were false prophets also among the people, even as there shall be false teachers among you, who privily shall bring in damnable heresies, even denying the Lord that bought them, and bring upon themselves swift destruction. And many shall follow their pernicious ways; by reason of whom the way of truth shall be evil spoken of. And through covetousness shall they with feigned words make merchandise of you: whose judgment now of a long time lingereth not, and their damnation slumbereth not"* (2 Peter 2:1-3). Later he adds, *"beware lest ye also, being led away with the error of the wicked, fall from your own stedfastness"* (2 Peter 3:17).

John warns, *"and as ye have heard that antichrist shall come, even now are there many antichrists; whereby we know that it is the last time."* (1 John 2:18) John also tells how to recognize the false from the true. "*BELOVED, believe not every spirit, but try the spirits whether they are of God: because many false prophets are gone out into the world. Hereby know ye the Spirit of God: Every spirit that confesseth that Jesus Christ is come in the flesh is of God"* (1 John 4:1-2).

Jude warns, *"For there are certain men crept in unawares, who were before of old ordained to this condemnation, ungodly men, turning the grace of our God into lasciviousness, and denying the only Lord God, and our Lord Jesus Christ"* (Jude 1:4).

Finally, in the Revelations of John come more warnings to churches in Asia, south Turkey. *"I know thy works, and thy labour, and thy patience, and how thou canst not bear them which are evil: and thou hast tried them which say they are apostles, and are not, and hast found them liars:"* (Rev 2:2). *"I know thy works, that thou art neither cold nor hot: I would thou wert cold or hot. So then because thou art lukewarm, and neither cold nor hot, I will spue thee out of my mouth"* (Rev 3:15-16). *"And it was given unto him to make war with the saints, and to overcome them: and power was given him over all kindreds, and tongues, and nations"* (Rev 13:7).

The Rise of Christianity and the Arian Controversy

Buried in the *Korân* are found the vestiges of schismatic Christianity in its first five centuries. Jesus is mentioned frequently. Sūra **3**, the Imran refers to the Gospels of the New Testament and assures us that, *"The true religion in the sight of GOD is Islâm"* (**3:19**). The family of Imran is allegedly the family of the Virgin Mary (**3: 33**) according to the Protevangelium of James the Less, a non-canonical source. Sūra 19 is entitled Mary and again deals with the New Testament and the Virgin Mary. This chapter was used to convert the Nestorian Christian Negus or king of Abyssinia to Islâm. Another non-canonical source *The Miracles of the Virgin Mary* seems to provide information used in this chapter. Schism is mentioned a number of times in the *Korân* as an evil: (**2:137**) (**3:7, 105**) (**6**:159) (21:**93**) (23:**53**) (**30**:32) (**42**:13-14). According to many scholars Muhammad was tutored by Nestorian Christians and there were accusations from the Meccans that one of them even wrote the *Korân* (**16**:103) (25:**4-5**). Nestoriansism also influenced the Arabian Christians and their conversions to Islâm.

During Paul's second journey he and Timotheus of Lystra traveled to the regions of Phrygia and Galatia where they received a warning: "*when they had gone throughout Phrygia and the region of Galatia, and were forbidden of the Holy Ghost to preach the word in Asia,*" (Acts 16:6). ["Asia" is a region in S. Turkey and Syria.] Following this advice, they traveled to Troas on the Ionian (Turkish) coast where Paul had a vision that he should go to Macedonia. He did and afterward traveled to Athens where he preached of the "Unknown God" on Mars Hill (Acts 17:22-23) He then traveled to Corinth and across water to Ephesus then back to Caesarea by sea and then to Jerusalem. Thus, he avoided further proselyting in Asia. On his third journey Paul returned to Ephesus (in Asia), then the third largest city in the Roman Empire behind Rome and Alexandria. It was a huge port at the end of the ancient Silk Road. Here he confronted the idol makers of Diana and preached with some success (Acts 18 – 19). In his letter to Timothy he had the same promptings: "*That good thing which was committed unto thee keep by the Holy Ghost which dwelleth in us. This thou knowest, that all they which are in Asia be turned away from me*" (2 Tim 1:14-15). In contrast Peter states he was an apostle to Asia (1Peter 1:1). Despite the brief mention about warnings from the Holy Ghost, apostles preached in Asia-Minor. John later writes warnings to "*the seven churches which are in Asia*" (Revelations 1:4, 11): Ephesus, Smyrna, Pergamos, Thyatira, Sardis, Philadelphia, and Laodicea (Rev 2-3).

Besides Paul's efforts to build up Christian churches among the Gentiles, he spent a great deal of time dealing with heresy. Rather than warning, Paul preached a positive message. One of Paul's greatest sermons dealt with death, resurrection and faith. Parts of it are often used at modern Christian funerals. As in the typical writing technique of a chiasm the central question of 1 Corinthians 15 is posed in the middle where Paul lets slip one of the more obscure practices of the early church, "*Else what shall they do which are baptized for the dead, if the dead rise not at all? why are they then baptized for the dead*" (1 Cor 15:29)? Paul continues, "*And why stand we in jeopardy every hour? I protest by your rejoicing which I have in Christ Jesus our Lord, I die daily. If after the manner of men I have fought with beasts at Ephesus, what advantageth it me, if the dead rise not? Let us eat and drink; for tomorrow we die*" (1 Cor 15:30-32). In other words, if Christ and all of us are not resurrected we just as well *carpe diem* (seize the day or moment) and follow the common advice of the ancient world–*eat, drink, and be merry for tomorrow we die* (Ecclesiastes 8:15). It is only by faith in Jesus Christ and the power of the resurrection that propels men toward perfection. It was after the death of Christ that Christianity began. At first it was only a sect among Jews that believed Christ had come to save Judaism and mankind through his crucifixion and resurrection. He had restored Judaism to its correct form that included the lost worship of the Patriarchal era. The apostles who knew the Savior attempted to instruct new converts in the faith in Christ that was necessary for salvation. This meant understanding that Jesus Christ really did exist and who He was in relationship to the tripartite Godhead. John's Gospel hit this head on in Chapter 1:1-14. This offered a clear understanding of Christ's existence, his divinity, his relationship to God the Father, when it all started, and how we could obtain perfection through Him. In John's epistles he warned of deviations from this explanation: "*Even now are there many antichrists; whereby we know that it is the last time.*" (1 John 2:18) and "*Who is a liar but he that denieth that Jesus is the Christ? He is antichrist, that denieth the Father and the Son. Whosoever denieth the Son, the same hath not the Father:*" (1 John 2:22-23) and "*And every spirit that confesseth not that Jesus Christ is come in the flesh is not of God: and this is that spirit of antichrist,*" (1 John 4:3) and "*For many deceivers are entered into the world, who confess not that Jesus Christ is come in the flesh. This is a deceiver and an antichrist*" (2 John 1:7). Paul cautions Timothy, "*The time will come when they will not endure sound doctrine; but after their own lusts shall they heap to themselves teachers, having itching ears; And they shall turn away their ears from the truth, and shall be turned unto fables*" (2 Tim 4:3-4).

Despite warnings converts still had doubts about Christ's virgin birth, his divinity, his death by crucifixion and resurrection. When the apostles were gone and the Roman persecutions heated up, a series of apologists attempted to explain Christ in such a way as to make Him more understandable and acceptable to the Roman mind. Since Greek philosophy was well known in the Roman world, this was the vehicle they used as they attempted to explain Christ. [184] [185]

The leading cities in the early Christian Church were Jerusalem, Antioch, Rome, Alexandria, Laodicea and Cesarea. [186] Each had its "see" or district. Each had a school of religious teaching and each picked its own favorite texts from which to teach. There was no cannon of scripture. There was little recognition of the Holy Ghost, the Spirit of God, who inspired prophecy. Without prophets or leading apostles who could speak to the whole church, bishops and their clergy continued "interpretation" by their own wits. It was only natural that heresies developed. Some were minor. Others were serious. The greatest of these challenged the virgin birth, divinity of Christ, and His crucifixion, death and resurrection. Antioch and the churches of Asia Minor (the regions of modern Syria and Turkey) seemed to seethe in heretical ideas. The school at Alexandria leaned toward a Platonic, metaphysical (good spirit, evil matter) approach to understanding Christ's nature while the school at Antioch leaned more towards an Aristotelian concrete (man and works) emphasis.

The Early Scriptures

All of the Old and New Testament that we have today are copies of copies. By the end of the first century, much of what we know as the *New Testament* circulated as manuscripts or letters among Christian churches. In AD 172 Tatian (about 120-185), an Assyrian cleric and pupil of Justin Martyr (AD 100-165) was excommunicated by the Church in Rome for Gnosticism. Before his excommunication he wrote a popular version of the 4 gospels, a "harmony" of all four called the *Diatesarron* (a Greek musical term for a four-part harmony). It was a continuous narrative of the 4 gospels that left out only 56 verses (Christ's genealogy and John 8:1-11, the woman taken in adultery). [187] It was also known as the *Evangelion da Mehallete* (Gospel of the Mixed). *Diatesarron* texts are available on-line. For about 200 years it was popular in the West, but was rapidly replaced by the four Gospels as we know them. These were called the *Evangelion da Mepharreshe*

(Gospels separated) and were accepted in the Bibles of Rome and later Constantinople. In Antioch the *Diatesarron* and the *Gospel of the Hebrews* was included in the Antioch version of the New Testament known as the *Old Syriac*. The Peshitta that eventually replaced the *Old Syriac* was a revision written about AD 400, but did not begin to replace it until about AD 500. Despite this the *Old Syriac* remained popular in many places until 800-900. Arabic versions were still in use as late as 800. The *Gospel of the Hebrews* exists only in fragments.

The oldest complete collection of the 27 books of the New Testament dates from about AD 315. Although scraps of much of the New Testament are available numerous early Church Fathers had quoted virtually the entire New Testament before then. The development of the Bible as we know it did not begin until after the Council of Nicaea. Constantine ordered Eusebius of Caesarea to produce 50 Greek Bibles that included the Old Testament. He is not to be confused with Eusebius of Nicomedia, the Arian, of whom we will learn later. Two of the fifty AD 331 editions of Constantine's Bible known as the Codex Vaticanus (listed on the Vatican Library record since 1475) and the Codex Siniaticus, found in 1844 in a monastery at Mt. Sinai are available. These included the earliest known Old Testaments until the discovery of the Dead Sea Scrolls, which validate most of our current Old Testament except for the Book of Esther. Constantine's Bible differs from the Latin Vulgate of Jerome (AD 384) in that it does not include several important additions: 1) the last 12 verses of Mark; 2) the addition of the phrase "the Son of God" in Mark 1:1) the addition of "and carried up into heaven" in Luke 24:51. Included in the Constantine Bible, but missing from the Jerome Bible were *The Letter of Barnabas* and *The Shepherd of Hermes* (full texts are available on line). Both these Bibles were popular in Rome and Constantinople, but not elsewhere. In 367 Athanasius (AD 293-373), Bishop of Alexandria and champion of Nicaea issued a proclamation canonizing the New Testament much as we know it.

Jerome's Latin Vulgate (AD 384) included all the books of our current Bible and the Apocrypha. It continued to be translated into numerous languages until 600 when it was restricted to Latin only. All priests were required to know Latin by then and the possession of a non-Latin text was punishable by death. However, older texts and scraps continue to be discovered, preserved and studied. There has been no effort to destroy these or other manuscripts and codices from Christian and Ancient Hebrew sources. This is not the case in the development of the *Korân* where efforts were made from the beginning to destroy all original source material. The Latin Vulgate forms the basis of most modern Bibles today.

In AD 260 Paul of Samosata (AD 200-275)[188] was elected 15th Bishop of Antioch. His beliefs in the oneness of God and mortal birth of Jesus plus accusations of corruption and sexual liaisons with two sisters got him deposed in AD 269. However, his friendship with Zenobia, Queen of Palmyra in Syria allowed him to continue his popularity, power, and teaching. He taught that Christ after receiving the Holy Ghost was able to purge himself of all sin and coalesce with God. A branch of this school of thought continued among the Gnostic Paulicians in Armenia for about 100 years. A number of diverse teachings were also noted in the region.

Arius of Alexandria (AD 250-336) was a devotee of Paul of Samosata and received his education in the school of Lucian in Antioch. Paul of Samosata believed that the One God could not appear in substance on earth and thus could not become the person of Jesus Christ. He taught that God had filled Jesus with the Logos (power). Lucian tried to move Christ to a more divine position. He held that the Logos became a person in Christ. This was a second individual created by God before the world was made and came to earth and took on a human body. In this sense, Lucian's Christ was a perfect man with a divine spirit. God the Father and Christ were two different beings, thus different substances.

Arius experimented with a number of theological ideas. He was excommunicated because of his association with the Meletian schism by Peter, 16th Bishop of Alexandria (AD 300-311) Peter was martyred in the final Diocletian persecutions in November, 311. His successor, Bishop Achillas, lasted only 6 months in AD 311 and AD 312, but he re-instated Arius and placed him in charge of the Baucalis, one of the largest churches in Alexandria. Bishop Alexander (AD 312-326) who succeeded him was a patient man. He tolerated Arius, permitted him to remain at his post, but attempted to dissuade him of his heretical views. However, Arius continued to use his modifications of Lucian's ideas to explain the unity of the Godhead. He became very popular and many flocked to his church.

Arius believed that he had explained the Godhead correctly, an assumption that has led many to excommunication or "the stake" throughout Christian history. Alexander allowed the situation to smolder for a number of years, while Arius gained popularity and numerous followers. When Alexander could stand no more, he excommunicated Arius about AD 319. Other Bishops from the Lucian school backed Arius as did Eusebius of Caesarea for a time. A general conflagration of Arian belief threatened to envelope much of the Eastern Church. Word of this reached the Emperor Constantine by way of his sister, a Christian.

The Council of Nicaea

Constantine the Great (AD272-337) was a devotee of Apollo and a Mithras worshiper. He became Rome's undisputed emperor following his victory over Maxentius at Milvian Bridge in AD 312 during a civil war that united the Empire. Initially there were no reports mentioning any Christian influence that assisted Constantine's victory. [189] His victory arch (AD 315) in Rome bears no Christian symbols. [190] An inscription states "*Inspired by the Divine*," but this could just as easily refer to Apollo or Mithrias. Until AD 324 the commemorative victory coins depict the Sol Invictus, the Sun god, Apollo. Some of the figures on the Arch include priests of Mithras. Mithras was a Persian Zoroastrian Indo-Iranian sun god, popular among the Roman upper classes. [191] There is evidence that Christianity existed among the rank and file of the Roman Army (Mat 8:5-13; Mat 27:54; Mark 15:39; Luke 7:2-10; Luke 23:47; Acts 10:1-48; Acts 22:25; Acts 27:43). Its extent is unknown, but such symbols as the cross, "fish," and "**Ƨator Square**" have been found in areas where troops likely worshiped. [192] There is little evidence that Constantine was a Christian until his deathbed baptism. The myth of Christian influence on his victory probably originated about AD 325. Constantine saw in Christianity a unifying religious force for the Roman Empire, but dissention among Christians threatened his plans. He sponsored a council of Bishops to meet at Nicaea in Bithynia, a few miles from Nicomedia (hotbed of Arian support) in AD 325. 1800 Bishops with 2 presbyters and 3 slaves each were invited to the Constantine sponsored event, but only about 300 came; their retainers numbered in the thousands. [193]

Constantine's letter to the bishops was blunt, "*These questions are the idle cobwebs of contention, spun by curious wits … Who is capable of distinguishing such deep and hidden mysteries? … Seeing that our great and gracious God, the preserver of all, has given us the common light of his grace, I entreat you that my endeavors may be brought to a prosperous end, and my people be persuaded to embrace peace and concord. Suffer me to spend my days and nights in quiet, and may I have light and cheerfulness instead of tears and groans.*" [194]

Eusebius explained Arius' ideas thus: "*God has not always been a Father, and that there was a time when the Son was not; that the Son is a creature like the others; that he is mutable by his nature; that by his free will he chose to remain virtuous, but that he might change like others. He said that Jesus Christ was not true God, but divine by participation, like all others to whom the name of God is attributed. He added, that he was not the substantial Word of the Father, and his proper wisdom, by which he had made all things, but that he was himself made by eternal wisdom; that he is foreign in every thing from the substance of the Father; that we were not made for him, but he for us, when it was the pleasure of God, who was before alone, to create us: that he was made by the will of God, as others are, having no previous existence at all, since he is not a proper and natural production of the Father, but an effect of his grace. The father, he continued, is invisible to the Son, and the Son cannot know him perfectly; nor, indeed, can he know his own substance.*" [195]

Constantine opened the proceedings with a speech that included, "*When I gained my victories over my enemies, I thought nothing remained for me but to give thanks unto God and to rejoice with those who have been delivered by me. But when I learned, contrary to all expectations, that there were divisions among you, then I solemnly considered them, and praying that these discords might also be healed with my assistance, I summoned you here without delay. I rejoice to see you here, yet I should be more pleased to see unity and affection among you. I entreat you, therefore, beloved ministers of God, to remove the causes of dissension among you and to establish peace.*" [196] [197] He then dramatically threw all the petitions he had received into a blazing brazier and the conference began in a shouting match between the supporters of Arius and those of Alexander. Arius had put much of his philosophy to easily memorized chants. His supporters used them to drown out the forces backed by Alexander and his Deacon, Athanasius (AD 293-373). Athanasius had well thought out scriptural points to support their part of the controversy and has been recognized as the brains behind Bishop Alexander. It was like the pot calling the kettle black; one heresy versus another.

As the council progressed Constantine listened for a number of days to the wrangling. He then suggested that the controversy boiled down to this issue, Was Christ of the same or one substance with the Father or was he of a similar substance. Constantine suggested the word *homoousians* (same substance) as opposed to *homoiousians* (similar substance) as the heart of the problem. The words were different only by the smallest letter of the Greek alphabet, an iota "I" or "i" in the middle of the word. Thus, the ironical expression came about, "not an iota of difference."

Bishop Hosius of Cordova, the moderator of the Council, suggested that the best way to solve the problem was to write a creed that all could agree to. The Arians tried first. It failed. Then Eusebius of Caesarea suggested a creed from the Church of Palestine that he had first heard as a child. It was beautiful, poetic, and would ultimately form the basis of both the Apostle's Creed (AD 390) and the Nicene Creed finally adopted at the Council of Constantinople in 381.

"*We believe in one God, the Father Almighty, maker of all things visible and invisible, And in one Lord Jesus Christ, the Word of God, God from God, Light from Light, Life from Life, the only begotten Son, the Firstborn of every Creature, begotten of the Father before all worlds, through whom also all things were made. Who for our salvation was made flesh and lived among men, and suffered and rose again on the third day, and ascended to the Father, and shall come again in glory to judge the quick and the dead. And in the one Holy Ghost. Believing each of them to be and to have existed, the Father, only the Father, and the Son, only the Son, and the Holy Ghost, only the Holy Ghost . . . .*" [198]

The Emperor accepted it and the Arians probably would have because it did not destroy their position. However, it was not specific enough for the Alexandrian forces who wanted total annihilation of the Arians. Then Constantine suggested that Christ should be described as *homoousios*—one in essence with the Father—and this definition should be included in the creed. About 2-3 weeks into the Council, Bishop Hosius read a creed that was adopted by most present.

"*We believe in one God, the Father Almighty, maker of all things visible and invisible. And in one Lord Jesus Christ, the Son of God, begotten of the Father, only begotten, that is, from the substance of the Father, God from God, Light from Light, very God from very God, begotten not made, of the same substance as the Father, through whom all things were made, both things in Heaven and things in earth; who for us men, and for our salvation, came down and was made flesh, was made man, suffered and rose again the third day, ascended into Heaven, and shall come to judge the quick and the dead. And in the Holy Ghost. And those who say "There was a time when he was not" and "He did not exist before he was made" and "He was made out of nothing" or those who pretend that the Son of God is "of another hypostasis or substance" or "created" or "alterable" or "mutable," the Catholic Church anathematizes.* " [199]

This was adopted. Alexander the Alexandrian won and Arius the Antiochian lost. Ideas of Christ being created or subordinate to the Father were excluded. Arius and the Bishops of Marmarica and Ptolemais refused to subscribe and were excommunicated and banished. As it turned out that was round one. The decision did not stick. Eusebius of Caesarea accepted the decision, but later convinced Constantine to be conciliatory towards Arius and his followers. Alexander died shortly thereafter, but was succeeded by Athanasius, his Deacon. Constantine called upon Eusebius of Caesarea to put together 50 of the first official Christian Bibles in AD 331 noted above. Eusebius of Nicomedia who initially backed Arius accepted the Council's decision but was exiled to Gaul where he spread Arian ideas. He later baptized Constantine in 328 on his deathbed. In 336 Alexander received Arius back into the church. In general, the churches in the West held to the Nicene Creed. Ironically, most of the Bishops who attended the Council were from the Eastern cities and they continued to champion Arius' views. Eventually these splintered into other competing theories – Nestorian and Monophysites.

The Significance of Nicaea

Religious doctrine was anything but settled following the Council of Nicaea. Only about 1/6 of all Christian bishops attended, but the majority of bishops were Arians. There followed a period of great uncertainty and further religious discussions. The Arian ideas of the Godhead were that God the Father alone was self existant. The Son, Christ, was not. According to their critics this relegated Christ to a demi-god or "good man / philosopher" status having been created later. This made him incapable of an atonement or redemption of mankind since he was not totally divine. This idea was similar to that of Nestorian Christianity and Islâm that were to come.

Although Athanasius was the apparent winner at Nicaea, by AD 335 he found himself in hot water. He had been a zealot in favor of the Nicaea settlement, but at the First Synod of Tyre in AD 335 he was banished by Constantine for his divisive behavior. Then in AD 336 at the Synod of Jerusalem, Arius was readmitted to full fellowship, but he died the same year before he could take advantage of it. In AD 337, Constantine became severely ill. He called for Eusebius of Nicomedia, his advisor and an Arian, to be his baptizer. He promised to repent of his ways if God would allow him to live, but he didn't live. In the chaos that followed Constantine's death, the empire was divided into 4 parts. In the midst of this a Gothic convert was sent to the Goths north of Rome's borders to convert them. He turned out to be an Arian.

Constantine had 3 sons, Constantine II, Constans, and Constantius II. From AD 337 to AD 340 Constantine II and Constans ruled, but civil war between them resulted in Constantine II's death in AD 340. In the meanwhile, the religious differences between Constantius II, an Arian ruling in the East and Constans, a Nicean Christian ruling in Rome threatened to divide them, but eventually they agreed to disagree and let religious matters rest. Constans outlawed pagan worship, but there was no enforcement. In AD 350 a military mutiny led by Constans' chief general, Magnentius (AD 303-353), brought about the end of Constans' rule. He fled towards Spain, but was caught by Magnentius' agents and assassinated. Magnentius, a pagan, re-opened the temples for pagan worship. This did not please Constantius II, who bribed the barbaric tribes North of the Rhine to attack the Western Empire and take what they could. Magnentius counter bribed and mounted an invasion of the Eastern Empire. In AD 353 at the Battle of Mons Seleucus in France Constantius II defeated Magnentius, who committed suicide.

In AD 355 Constantius II became the sole ruler of the Roman Empire until his death in AD 361. Arians now held the places of power in the entire Christian world. When Constanius died in AD 361, the Emperor Julian came to power and immediately freed all exiled bishops. Julian, himself was a pagan who favored the Roman gods, but wanted religious freedom in the empire. However, Julian, the Apostate, as he was known in Christian circles, was killed in battle fighting the Persians in AD 363. He was succeeded by Jovian, elected by the army to be emperor. One of his first acts was to issue an edict making it punishable by death to worship pagan gods, but he lived only 8 months. Some believe he died of carbon monoxide poisoning in his tent that was equipped with a charcoal burning heater. Others believe it was from mushroom poisoning.

In AD 364 Valentinian I came to power in the West; he permitted religious freedom, but favored Christianity of the Nicene Creed. He died in AD 375 and was succeeded by Gratian, Valentinian I's son. He ruled until AD 383 without being Emperor. The succession was to go to Valentinian II, but he was only 4 years of age and died in AD 392 probably by assassination.

The Religious Reforms of Theodosius

In AD 364 Valens, Valentinian's brother, ruled in the East. He was also an Arian, but died fighting the Visigoths at the Battle of Adrianople in AD 378 along with 2/3rds of his army. Gratian promoted one of his generals, **Theodosius the Great** (AD 347-395), the last Emperor of the entire Roman Empire. Theodoseus had no sympathy for religious squabbles or any religion other than the Catholic Orthodoxy of Nicaea. In February AD 380, he decreed:

"*We desire that all peoples subject to Our benign Empire shall live under the same religion that the Divine Peter, the Apostle, gave to the Romans, and which the said religion declares was introduced by himself, and which it is well known that the Pontiff Damascus, and Peter, Bishop of Alexandria, a man of apostolic sanctity, embraced; that is to say, in accordance with the rules of apostolic discipline and the evangelical doctrine, we should believe that the Father, Son, and Holy Spirit constitute a single Deity, endowed with equal majesty, and united in the Holy Trinity.*

"We order all those who follow this law to assume the name of Catholic Christians, and considering others as demented and insane, we order that they shall bear the infamy of heresy; and when the Divine vengeance which they merit has been appeased, they shall afterwards be punished in accordance with Our resentment, which we have acquired from the judgment of Heaven. Dated at Thessalonica, on the third of the Kalends of March, during the Consulate of Gratian, Consul for the fifth time, and Theodosius." [200] The following year he issued this decree. "*Let no place be afforded to heretics for the conduct of their ceremonies, and let no occasion be offered for them to display the insanity of their obstinate minds. Let all persons know that if any privilege has been fraudulently obtained by means of any rescript whatsoever, by persons of this kind, it will not be valid. Let all bodies of heretics be prevented from holding unlawful assemblies, and let the name of the only and the greatest God be celebrated everywhere, and let the observance of the Nicene Creed, recently transmitted to Our ancestors, and firmly established by the testimony and practice of Divine Religion, always remain secure.*"

"Moreover, he who is an adherent of the Nicene Faith, and a true believer in the Catholic religion, should be understood to be one who believes that Almighty God and Christ, the son of God, are one person, God of God, Light of Light; and let no one, by rejection, dishonor the Holy Spirit, whom we expect, and have received from the Supreme Parent of all things, in whom the sentiment of a pure and undefiled faith flourishes, as well as the belief in the undivided substance of a Holy Trinity, which true believers indicate by the Greek word These things, indeed do not require further proof, and should be respected."

"*Let those who do not accept those doctrines cease to apply the name of true religion to their fraudulent belief; and let them be branded with their open crimes, and, having been removed from the threshhold of all churches, be utterly excluded from them, as We forbid all heretics to hold unlawful assemblies within cities. If, however, any seditious outbreak should be attempted, We order them to be driven outside the walls of the City, with relentless violence, and*

We direct that all Catholic Churches, throughout the entire world, shall be placed under the control of the orthodox bishops who have embraced the Nicene Creed. Given at Constantinople, on the fourth of the ides of January, under the Consulate of Flavius Eucharius and Flavius Syagrius." [201]

In November of AD 380 Theodosius handed over to Gregory of Naziaznus, the leader of the small Nicaean community in Constantinople all the Arian properties and banned all Arian worship.

In AD 381 the Council of Constantinople was held to modify the Nicene Creed. It no longer included the clause against other beliefs and added more detail about the Holy Ghost. It added a statement directed towards various Christian churches not of the "catholic and apostolic" belief and a statement about one form of baptism. Because of its origins, it retained the name of the Nicaen Creed and is still in use by the world's Catholic, Episcopal, and many Protestant Churches. There are other previous versions without any material changes in meaning.

We believe in one God, the Father, the Almighty maker of heaven and earth, of all that is, seen and unseen. We believe in one Lord, Jesus Christ, the only Son of God, eternally begotten of the Father, God from God, Light from Light, true God from true God, begotten, not made, of one Being with the Father. Through him all things were made. For us men and for our salvation he came down from heaven: by the power of the Holy Spirit he became incarnate from the Virgin Mary, and was made man. For our sake he was crucified under Pontius Pilate; he suffered death and was buried. On the third day he rose again in accordance with the Scriptures; he ascended into heaven and is seated at the right hand of the Father. He will come again in glory to judge the living and the dead, and his kingdom will have no end. We believe in the Holy Spirit, the Lord, the giver of Life, who proceeds from the Father and the Son. With the Father and the Son he is worshipped and glorified. He has spoken through the Prophets. We believe in one holy catholic and apostolic Church. We acknowledge one baptism for the forgiveness of sins. We look for the resurrection of the dead, and the life of the world to come. Amen. [202]

Religious Intolerance of Christianity

In AD 383 Theodosius took away the rights to make a will of Christians who returned to paganism: "*We deny to Christians and the faithful who have adopted pagan rites and religion all power of making a will in favor of any person whatsoever, in order that they may be without the Roman law; ... even of enjoying a will with the power of acquiring an inheritance.*" [203]

In AD 384 he ordered his Praetorian Prefect, Cynegius, in the East to use his troops in cooperation with the Bishops in northern Greece and Asia Minor to destroy all pagan temples. This began a systematic destruction of all pagan temples throughout the Roman Empire. Very few survived other than as ruins. They remain in ruins to this day.

In AD 389 Theodosius outlawed the old form of dating in preference of the use of AD – Anno Domini, in the year of our Lord. In AD 391 he forbad the use of Pagan shrines and ordered their destruction throughout the Empire. It was a crime to look at a statue. Such was the "Cultural Revolution" in China millennia later. The following year he decreed paganism to be a crime. Attacks against Jews, their synagogues, and citizen rights began despite their "protected" status in the Empire. They were banned from holding public office or positions of military leadership.

In AD 393 the pan-Hellenic or Olympic Games were banned as having classical or pagan roots; they had begun in 776 BC and would not begin again until 1896.

Theodosius also applied the power of the state to those who continued to adhere to Arian or pagan philosophies. The order "*to be driven outside the walls of the City, with relentless violence*" was taken seriously and many were killed. The exact numbers are unknown, but some estimates indicate that it may have been in the tens of thousands. By all these decrees and acts, the Roman Empire just before its total collapse succeeded in ridding itself of any worship other than Catholic (universal) orthodoxy. However, Arianism continued to persist among the Germanic Tribes in the North and in the churches of Asia-Minor.

The Significance of the Councils of Nicaea & Constantinople

The Council of Nicaea in AD 325 and Constantinople in 381 had far greater significance than just the acceptance of the Nicene Creed. It placed the Christian Church under the "protection" of Rome. Church and state were allied. Later kings and princes would become "defenders of the faith." Christianity and States continued in this fashion beyond the Reformation. Within a short time, popes and kings in the name of the Church pursued their quests for power and worldly treasure. Individual priests and nuns committed acts of immorality under the guise of vows for celibacy (no marriage) as opposed to chastity (no sexual activity). All this corrupted the sublime, peaceful doctrines of Christ. The Christian church was often used to rile up people in acts of murderous atrocities and war. Until recent times most Christian churches were supported by tax money. The Vatican still maintains diplomatic relationships. It was only in the United States of America where combination of church and state was broken first by distance from the "Mother Churches," and eventually by law. The Commonwealth of Virginia's law on religious liberty authored by Thomas Jefferson, a devout but non-sectarian Christian had its principles incorporated into both the *Constitution* and the *Bill of Rights* also under Jefferson's influence. Elective office would no longer carry a religious requirement (Article VI paragraph 3) and the state could not establish or sponsor a religion, "*Congress shall make no law respecting an establishment of religion, or prohibiting the free exercise thereof.*" It was the first time Christianity was liberated from state influence since AD 325. It also allowed a people unfettered by state-controlled religion to use their individual moral influences to guide a nation based on the principles of a representative republic and freedom of choice.

The Council of Nicaea (AD 325) ratified at Constantinople (AD 381) handled a number of State-Church relationships. It approved the use of pagan holidays with different names under church sponsorship. Even though Christ's birth and death were thought to have occurred in the spring, Christmas would be celebrated on Dec 25. This replaced pagan celebrations of the birth of Mithras and the Saturnalia, a drunken brawl. The resurrection of Christ would be celebrated on the first Sunday after the first full moon following the vernal equinox (lunar calendar). This would replace the spring fertility rites of Ishtar and be called Easter also set by lunar callendar.

Syriac Christian Influences

Most in the West think of Christianity as having two major branches, Roman Catholicism whose capitol was Rome and Greek Orthodoxy whose capitol was Constantinople. As mentioned earlier the schools of religion associated with the principal cities trained their own clergy and used their own scriptural sources. Because of the persecutions, general Church gatherings were impossible until Constantine's rule. Almost from the beginning there arose doctrines that tended to make Jesus Christ a mortal man and not divine. The school at Antioch encouraged debate about the divinity of Christ, his virgin birth, crucifixion, death and resurrection. This heresy is mentioned by John (1 John 4:1-3). Despite the development of Eusebius' Bible of AD 331 and Jerome's Latin vulgate in AD 384. *Old*

Syriac and other non-canonical sources continued in common use in Asia-Minor for several more centuries.

From the time of its legalization by Constantine, Galerius, and Licinius from AD 306 to AD 311 Christianity became a powerful force in the declining Roman Empire. With the establishment of Constantinople in 330, the Eastern Roman Empire and the Christian Church became split into East and West regions and became the predominant religion in the Roman Empire. As the power of Rome in the West diminished, its preeminence as a church temporarily declined. Efforts at Christianizing the Barbarians of Europe were successful and the Bishop of Rome maintained neutrality between the contending powers fighting for control in Western Europe. Besides Rome and Constantinople, the Christian Church had two other main bases of operation, Alexandria in Egypt that gave rise to the Coptic Christians and Antioch which spawned Syriac Christianity. Jerusalem, no longer a factor, had been in ruins since AD 70.

About 100 years before Muhammad's birth two major schisms affected churches in Antioch – Nestorian and Monophysite. Nestorianism was spread by monks throughout the Arabian Peninsula, Persia, India, Africa, especially Ethiopia, and even China. The differences between their views of Jesus Christ can be summarized as follows:

1. Catholic doctrine – Nicene Creed–states Christ is one person – same as God with one hypostasis (substance or essence – human and divine natures united) and two natures (God & Man).
2. Coptic beliefs are that the human and divine natures were separate more like the creed of the Church of Palestine above; they split from the Catholic position at the Council of Chalcedon AD 451.
3. Nestorians and Islâm believe that Christ is one person (Man) with two hypostases (Man perfected to God) and two natures (Man joined with God). [See *Korân* **4:153-158.**]
4. Monophysites (championed by Theodora) believe that Christ is one person (God) with one hypostasis (divine) and one nature (divine).
5. John 1:1-14 – Two divine Gods (Christ – The Word and God the Father; both coexisted in the beginning before the world was made – a pre-existence; all physical things were made by Christ). No creed expresses this relationship and activity precisely, but it closely resembles the modern-day LDS Church view.

Until 1054 the eastern and western branches of Christianity were united, but then split over the issue of papal authority. The Syriac Christian Churches arose from Antioch, the only major Christian Church noted in the *Korân* (36:**13-29**). A good review of Syriac Christian history is found on line. [204]

Nestorian beliefs of God and the Father were adopted by Islâm. Nestorius (AD 386 – 451) got his training in Antioch. His ideas were similar to the Arian concept of Christ. As with many Christians both ancient and modern, Christ's virgin birth, crucifixion and resurrection challenged their faith. Arius' efforts to explain it in doctrine had been rejected. In his early years Nestorius held the important post of patriarch of Constantinople where he could develop and spread his ideas. He taught that Christ was not a God in eternity. He did not derive his divinity through Mary and he suffered, but was not crucified. See *Korân* **4:157-158**. Rather he was a human being who progressed to perfection resulting in his resurrection / translation and symbiosis with God at the time of his death. Despite his beliefs, Nestorius became the Archbishop of Constantinople (AD 428-431). The Council of Ephesus AD 431 rejected Nestorianism as a heresy and deposed him as Archbishop. In AD 435 they banished him to the desert. The result was a schism between the Nestorian Assyrian Church and the Orthodox, Byzantine Church.

Simultaneous with these schools of thought was a movement towards asceticism. Some converts attempted to live a life based on Christ's ascetic beliefs noted in Matthew 19:11-12 (celibacy), 19:21 (poverty), and 19:29 (homelessness). Initially, these individuals lived as hermits in caves, but when "service" to others was emphasized, they began banding together in isolated villages and eventually monasteries so that they could work cooperatively for the benefit of those around them. These monks are referred to in the *Korân* (**5:82**).

Babai the Great (551-628) became head of the Nestorian monastic movement and sent numerous missionaries into Persia, the Arabian Peninsula, India and even China where the Emperor T'Ang-Tsung (627-649) became converted as did many Chinese. A Nestorian stele dated 781 remains today in the old imperial capitol Chang'an (modern Xi'an), but the Emperor Wuzong of the Tang Dynasty (840-846) persecuted all religions and suppressed Buddhism as well as Nestorian Christianity. Some say that Muhammad was taught much of his Christianity by Nestorians monks.

The *Life of Muhammad* [205] refers to a number of Christians by name and event:

1. Faymiyūn of Najrān (pages 14-16); Bahīrā (pages 79-81);
2. Salmān who became a Christian and later a Muslim (pages 95-98);
3. A deputation of Christians that accept Islam [206] (**28**:53-54) (**5:82-83**) (**6**:52-54); Jabr, "and they used to say, 'The one who teaches Muhammad most of what he brings is Jabr the Christian, slave of B. al-Hadramī.' Then God revealed in reference to their words, '*We also know that they say, Verily, a certain man teacheth him to compose the Korân. The tongue of the person unto whom they incline is a foreign tongue; but this, wherein the Korân is written, is the perspicuous Arabic tongue.*" (**16**:103) (page 180);
4. Waraqa b. Nafaul, Khadīja's cousin (pages 73, 83, 99, 103, 107, 144);
5. A deputation of Christians of Najrān (**3:49**) (19:**21**) (pages 270-277); and 'Adīy b. Hātim who converted to Islâm (pages 637-638).
6. See also George Sale's Translation of the *Korân* page 267 Note #2. This mentions Jabr (above) plus Jabar and Yesâr, slaves who made swords and read the Pentateuch and gospels (Al Zamakh, Al Beidâwi) and/or Aïsh, a man of learning who had become a Muslim (Al Zamakh, Al Beidâwi) and/or Kais, a Christian often visited by Muhammad (Jallalo'ddin) and/or Addas (Al Zamakh, Yahya); etc. This note is very long and covers nearly 2 pages.

The *Korân* states, "*And the unbelievers say, This Korân is no other than a forgery which he hath contrived; and other people have assisted him therein: but they utter an unjust thing, and a falsehood. They also say, These are fables of the ancients, which he hath caused to be written down; and they are dictated unto him morning and evening.*" (25:**4-5**) Most Christians in the Arabian Peninsula would have been Nestorians.

With the conversion of a number of powerful warriors to Muhammad's new religion, their assent to his personal body guards, and the progressive militancy of his visions along with the raiding of caravans and war against Jewish settlements, Islâm began to be a war-lord state and has remained as such throughout its existence. The *Korân* in the Medina Period makes many statements about war and its conduct especially against other beliefs. This is in contrast with the peaceful doctrine of Christ.

About 715 St John of Damascus (676-754) wrote *The Fount of Wisdom*. John was reared a Christian by his father despite living among Islâm. He was a brilliant man versed in mathematics and theology of his time. He became the chief financial officer of the 12th caliph Abdul Malik despite his Christianity, but eventually went to Jerusalem where he obtained the priesthood. The online *Catholic Encyclopedia* includes an extensive biography on John. [207] *The Fount of Wisdom* second edition included a section "On Heresies." The Ishmaelites were listed as one of the Christian heresies. He quotes from the *Korân,* the Hadiths (Muhammad's sayings) and the Sunnah (Islâmic traditions) and lists a number of contradictions to prove his point and show that Muhammad was not a prophet. He also criticized Islâm's treatment of women with their easy divorce and polygamy.

Eastern Orthodoxy might have been destroyed by Islâm had it not been for Russia's Prince Vladamir I, *fornicator maximus* (958-1015). [208] He noted that other states in Europe and the Middle East had a religion. It was time that Kiev and Novgorod (Russia) had one, so he went shopping. His ministers were sent to investigate the principle religions. They reported that the Roman Catholics were "too plain." not enough pomp; Islâm was "too dry" (they forbade alcohol and pork); and Judaism was "too small and weak and abandoned by God" to be of any use. However Eastern Orthodoxy had glitz and ceremony, so in 980 Vladamir invited the head of the Eastern Orthodox Church to come and baptize all his subjects.

Islâm's conquests of Africa, the Arabian Peninsula and Persia greatly reduced the influence of Alexandria and Antioch among Christianity. It wiped out most of what was left of the great Syriac missionary efforts in Persia, the Middle East and Africa so that only remnants held on as Coptic and Syriac Christians. When Islâmic armies arrived in Alexandria (654), it has been said that they destroyed the Library of Alexandria. The truth is that there was probably little left to destroy by then as it had undergone several previous destructions. It has been said that when the Moslem General asked the caliph Umar what to do about the library, he said of the books, "*If what is written in them agrees with the Korân, they are not required; if it disagrees, they are not desired. Destroy them therefore.*" [210]

MUHAMMAD'S BIRTH AND ADULT LIFE AD 570 – 610

The chronology of many events in Muhammad's life is disputed. Some will be outlined here, but for purposes of clarity, the dates that will be used are found in an official Sunni Islâmic site. [211] Muhammad was born on Monday, 12th Rabi'u'l-awwal, in the year of the elephant, [212] or about April 570. His father, Abdullah, died before his birth. His grandfather took him to the Ka'ba where he gave thanks to Allah for his birth. Eight days later he was given to a foster mother for nursing, Halima d. Abū Dhu'ayb. [213] She is known as Hadrat Halima Sadiyya. There was famine in the land and Halima was part of a Bedouin tribe, the B. Sa's b. Bakr that had productive flocks. When he was about age 6 Muhammad experienced what may have been a seizure; he was said to be standing with bluish red face. When asked what the matter was he stated that two men in white threw him on the ground, opened his belly and searched inside him. Another source indicates that the men washed his heart and body with snow and made him pure. [214] This is referred to in sūra **94:1-4**. "*Have we not opened thy breast; and eased thee of thy burden, which galled thy back; and raised thy reputation for thee?*" His step father declared he might have suffered a "stroke" and they sent Muhammad, to his mother, Amina in 577. Only a few months later Amina died and he returned to his grandfather, 'Abdu'l-Muṭṭalib (AD 497-578), who lived only 2 more years. He was now left in the care of his uncle, Abū Ṭālib ibn 'Abd al-Muṭṭalib (549-619). Abū Ṭālib was Muhammad's uncle, Abdullah's full brother from the same mother, Fatima d. 'Amr b. 'A'idh b. Abd b. Imran b. Makhzum.

His uncle put him to work as a shepherd caring for camels and cattle outside of Mecca. His lack of brothers and sisters, a natural father and minimal contact with his mother must have made a major impact on his life. The *Korân* mentions good care of orphans and protection of their property 21 times (**2: 83, 117,** [215]**, 220; 4: 2, 3, 6, 8, 10, 36, 127; 6: 152;**

8: 41; 17: 34; 59: 7; 76: **8**; 89: 17; 90: 15; 93: 6, 9; 107: 2). Muhammad continued to work as a shepherd, but Abū Tālib, a successful trader exposed him to the life of a businessman. Controversy about Muhammad's ability to read or write exists; however, a seasoned trader such as Abū Ţālib might have taught those skills to his young ward. The *Korân* claims he was illiterate (7:158).

When Muhammad was 12 years old in 583, Abū Ţālib took Muhammad on a trading mission to Busra, Syria.[215] While there a Nestorian Christian monk by the name of Bahīrā found that he had a mark between his shoulder blades described in Christian books. He also refused to swear by al-Lat and al-'Uzzā, but only by Allah. The monk told Abū Ţālib that Muhammad had a great future. He should take Muhammad back to Mecca quickly and guard him carefully from the Jews because they might do him harm.[216] In Mecca Muhammad grew up to be a kind, truthful, reliable, and moral neighbor. He was known as "The Trustworthy." During the rebuilding of the Ka'ba when he was 35, an unseen force reminded Muhammad to put on a shirt while he was carrying stones.[217] At that time that he suffered a falling spell and a brief period of unconsciousness. This may have been his first adult seizure.[218]

Muhammad's World AD 558 – 591

In 559 about the time of Muhammad's first wife Khadīja's birth the Avars arrived north of the Caucasus Mountains. The Avar *khagan* (king) Kandich negotiated a treaty with the Byzantine Eastern Roman Empire to attack the tribes in southern Russia and the Ukraine along the northern Black Sea coast. These had menaced the Empire's northern border and distracted their efforts against the Persian threat to the south and east. The Avars were to receive gold for their services. 2-3 years later Kandich reported that he had "wiped them from the face of the earth." Kandich died in 562 and the new kagan, Bayan, demanded land in the lower Danube basin in Scythia Minor (the Crimea) and Moesia (Romania / Bulgaria). He wanted more gold to maintain the peace. Justinian I refused their request and the Avars attempted to push further west across the Elbe River, but were stopped by Sigebert I (535-575), the Frankish King of Austria. The Avars returned to the lower Danube basin and "squatted" on the land. Following Justinian's death in 565, they demanded more gold from Justin II (520-578), who also refused them. In 565-66 the Avars attempted to push further south, but were stopped. Again, they tried to move west into Thuringia (Germany) and again Sigebert stopped them.[219] [220] To more fully understand the campaign that followed it is well to know the geography of Central Europe and as you read what follows, orient yourself with a map.

The modern states of Moldova, Romania, and Bulgaria lie to the west and south of Kiev, Ukraine and the Black Sea. The Carpathian Mountains with their dense forests is a formidable barrier. These mountains are shaped like a giant sickle with its mountain range handle beginning in the Greek Peninsula and extending north to form a barrier between the modern states of Bulgaria and Serbia. The concave blade of the sickle cuts east through the heart of Romania then heads north and then west. This divides the Upper Danube Plain in western Romania and Hungary from Lower Danube Plain shared by Romania and Bulgaria. Cutting along the southern part of the Upper Danube plain is another major river, the Sava which joins the Danube near Belgrade. These then wind their way through a canyon into Romania where it forms most of the border between Bulgaria and Romania and divides the upper and lower Danube plains.

The Danube arises in the northern Austrian Alps and forms the border between Slovakia on the north and Hungary on the South. It then turns south at Budapest and forms the border between Croatia and Serbia. It heads east again to Belgrade. Here it is joined by the Sava and becomes a huge river that flows through a narrow pass or strategic choke point, along the southern border of the Carpathian Mountains. It then runs through the Danube basin forming the Bulgarian / Romanian border, and heads east toward the Black Sea. Within 40 miles of the Black Sea it makes an abrupt turn north and travels about 100 miles through Romania where it reaches a delta region that empties into the Black Sea.

The Sava River arises from the southern Austrian Alps. From Austria it enters Slovenia and runs through its capitol, Ljubljana. It then enters Croatia heading southeast reaching Zagreb. It goes into Bosnia and Herzegovina where it forms the border between it and Croatia. It turns east, enters Serbia, and goes to Belgrade to join the Danube. The Sava River plain was the home of the Gepids who were under the protection of the Eastern Roman Empire and held the strategically important overland roadway between the Eastern and Western Roman Empires.

In 566 the Avars found themselves in a desperate situation. Their Turkish enemies who had run them out of Central Asia were approaching from the East. The only way out was through the "choke point" of the narrow Danube pass at the south end of the Carpathians, but this was held by Eastern Roman Empire forces. Not a moment too soon the Langobard (Lombard) king Alboin, Siegebert's brother-in-law, and probably Siegebert, met Bayan and formed an alliance to attack the Gepids occupying the plains of eastern Hungary around the Tisza River. At that time the Lombards occupied the territory in the modern Czech and Slovak Republics to the north of Hungary. If the Avars succeeded in getting rid of the Gepids, their land and fortune would belong to them. They would also be safe from the Turks by holding the Danube narrows and the wall of the Carpathian Mountains. Longobard guides now helped the Avars advance along the left bank of the Danube and the pass thus avoiding the Eastern Roman forces. Once on the plains of the Sava, they slaughtered the Gepids. [221]

Conquest by Avars or their Slavic allies was not a happy event. According to Procopius, "*Now they killed their victims, not with sword nor spear, nor in any other accustomed manner, but by planting very firmly in the earth stakes which they had made exceedingly sharp, and seating the poor wretches upon these with great violence, driving the point of the stake between the buttocks and forcing it up into the intestines. These barbarians also had a way of planting four thick stakes very deep in the ground, and after binding the feet and hands of the captives to those stakes, they would then assiduously beat them over the head with clubs killing them like dogs or snakes or any other animal.*" [222] When the Lombards had the nerve to ask for their share of the loot, the Avars threatened to turn against them. This caused them to flee into northern Italy, Moravia, Bohemia and Germany in 568. Next, the Avars, safe from the Turks, formed an alliance with the Slavs and turned their attention towards the hapless Eastern Roman Empire. The Eastern Empire had lots of gold and little stomach for a brutal enemy. Their will to fight lapsed into appeasement. Bayan now took his Avar army towards the junction of the Danube and Sava rivers. Holding this area would cut off the land route between the Eastern and Roman Empire and give him tremendous leverage. All Bayan and his military arm, the Slavs, had to do now was milk the cash cow, and he did. [223]

Meanwhile in the area of the old Western Roman Empire, in 572 the Visigoth's under King Leovigild took the Iberian Peninsula (Spain & Portugal). Following the withdrawal of the Romans in 410 England became a battle ground between the British Tribes and the Anglo-Saxons. The era between AD 460 and 520 has been theorized to have been the time of the mythical King Arthur. [224] The Anglo Saxons finally triumphed in 577 at the Battle of Deorham when they defeated the Welsh and took most of Britain. [225]

During the period of the Christian Apostles the Far East was beginning to experience prosperity. There were advances in astronomy and mathematics. The ship's stationary rudder was invented. [226] By then the armillary sphere was developed, [227] and planetary elliptical movement around the sun was surprisingly accurate for the visible planets from Mercury to Saturn. [228] From AD184-220 political infighting broke up the Eastern Han Dynasty into 3 parts (Cao Wei, Shu Han, and Eastern Wu). During the Western Han (206 BC-AD 9) a national monetary system was developed and a census recorded 58 million people. A gentry and scholar class arose and a period of invention that included paper followed. From AD 220 to AD 263 there was greater stability, but then civil strife dropped the population from about 50 million to16 million by the beginning of the Jin Dynasty (AD 265-420). The Jin was displaced by the Southern and Northern Dynasties (AD 420-589). Despite the continuing civil war during this period, the people continued to advance in culture and science. In military matters the stirrup was invented about AD 322 and was in widespread use in China by AD 477 giving cavalries more power. Medicine, astronomy and mathematics continued to develop. Buddhism became the predominant religion and painting and calligraphy developed.

The Sui Dynasty (581 – 618) existed during Muhammad's life. It combined the northern and southern dynasties, built the Grand Canal, and minted a unifying currency, thus promoting commerce and ushering in a new period of prosperity and relative peace. [229] Popular revolts over high taxation brought the central government down in 618. During Muhammad's later years, the Tang Dynasty (618-907) expanded far to the West along the Silk Road, dominated its trade and came into direct contact with Islâm. Military conquest with its Turkic allies included much of Central Asia in 640s and 50s. This was during the period of the 4 Caliphs. The capitol was Chang'an (modern Xi'an). With stability and relative peace within its borders, the population increased to 50 million. Poetry, cartography, wood-block printing and continuing progress in mathematics and astronomy were accomplishments. Economic prosperity accelerated rapidly with the development of a legal code and withdrawal of government controls. Civil service examinations were developed to select state bureaucrats from among the aristocratic families. Buddhism continued as the predominant religion initially, but Daoism was accepted and eventually eclipsed it.

Two years after Muhammad's birth, 572, the Avars began their "gold for peace program" with Byzantium. For the next 50 years the Avars demanded and got ever increasing amounts of gold until they had accumulated nearly 35 tons of it. Byzantium got neither peace nor security. The Avars continued to edge closer and closer to Constantinople. When Maurice tried to buy Bayan with an elephant and a gold bed, the kagan sent them back and said, "No. Send the cash." [230] When Maurice refused, Bayan took Sirmium and added the Sava and Danube Rivers to his kingdom. Whereupon, Maurice sent the cash and the Avars pulled back into Hungary, but their allies the Slavs didn't and proceeded to invade the region about 100 miles west of Constantinople. When Maurice refused another payment, the Avars and Slavs invaded Greece and sacked Corinth and Athens in 585.

By 587 the Avars had tightened the noose around Constantinople further by reaching the Sea of Marmara, the body of water connecting the Mediterranean and the Black Sea. All this happened during Muhammad's childhood and adolescence. More peace payments were made and the Avars withdrew. The Romans signed a peace treaty with Persia in 591 and moved troops to the northern borders; however, this did no good as the Slavs began another invasion of the Dalmatian coast (modern Croatia – upper Adriatic Coast). Muhammad was now 21 and was about to begin adult life with his first employment.

Predictions of Muhammad's Prophetic Life Muhammad Is the Alleged "Paraclete"

At this time a number of soothsayers predicted the arrival of a prophet to the Arabs. [231] The Gospel of John 15:23-16:1from a Syriac Bible was also used to convince Christians that Muhammad was the "Paraclete" (one who consoles, a comforter, an advocate or in the case of Christianity, the Holy Ghost) foretold by Christ himself. A Syriac Bible reads, *"He that hateth me hath hated the Lord. And if I had not done in their presence works which none other before me did, they had not had sin: but from now they are puffed up with pride and think that they will overcome me and also the Lord. But the word that is in the law must be fulfilled, 'They hated me without cause' (I.e. without reason). But when the Comforter has come whom God will send to you from the Lord's presence, and the spirit of truth which will have gone forth from the Lord's presence he (shall bear) witness of me and ye also, because ye have been with me from the beginning. I have spoken unto you about this that ye should not be in doubt."* [232]

The *King James Bible* reads as follows: *He that hateth me hateth my Father also. If I had not done among them the works which none other man did, they had not had sin: but now have they both seen and hated both me and my Father. But this cometh to pass, that the word might be fulfilled that is written in their law, They hated me without a cause.* [See Psalm 35:19; 69:4.] *But when the Comforter is come, whom I will send unto you from the Father, even the Spirit of truth, which proceedeth from the Father, he shall testify of me: And ye also shall bear witness, because ye have been with me from the beginning. THESE things have I spoken unto you, that ye should not be offended."* (John 15:23-16:1)

The Syriac text although not much different than that found in the Latin Bible was taken out of context. The statement above was part of Christ's personal instructions to his disciples just before his crucifixion. It tells them that He will send the Holy Ghost from the Father to them. This event is described in Acts 2. The Holy Ghost is sent from the Father, not the Son. This is also noted during the baptism of Christ (Luke 3:22; John 1:32-33; Matt 3:16; Mark 1:10). This is the baptism *with fire* noted in Matt 3:11, Luke 3:16; 12:49, and Acts 2:3. It is an event that had taken place shortly after Christ's death in AD 33. It can divide families and bring a sword upon the earth (Matt 10:34, 35). It has nothing to do with Muhammad or events that were to occur 600 years later.

When Muhammad was 40 the *Korân* states, "*We have not sent thee otherwise than unto mankind in general, a bearer of good tidings, and a denouncer of threats: but the greater part of men do not understand.*" (**34**:28) The *Korân* continues: "*And remember when God accepted the covenant of the prophets, saying, This verily is the scripture and the wisdom which I have given you: hereafter shall an apostle come unto you, confirming the truth of that scripture which is with you; ye shall surely believe on him, and ye shall assist him. God said, Are ye firmly resolved, and do ye accept my covenant on this condition? They answered, We are firmly resolved: God said, Be ye therefore witnesses; and I also bear witness with you:*" (**3:81**)

Muhammad's Early Manhood – Marriage and Children

A war between the Quraysh and Kināna tribes began when Muhammad was 20. [233] He did not participate as a soldier, but the outcome favored the Kināna. Following it his life changed in other significant ways. Khadīja was a woman of dignity and wealth who operated long-haul caravans out of Mecca. [234] She hired agents on a profit-sharing basis to manage trading of goods from her caravans. The exact reason she hired her distant cousin, Muhammad, to act as her agent on a trip to Syria in 595, is unknown. She also sent one of her trusted slaves, MaYasāra, to watch over her fortunes. While on the trip Muhammad rested under a tree. A monk came to Maysara and told him that only prophets rested beneath that tree. Maysara later told Khadīja about the incident and said he had seen two angels shading him. Trading went well and Khadīja doubled her profits. According to a few sources, Khadīja sent him south to Saba (Yemen) with another caravan. This trip also netted her profits and by this time she had fallen in love with Muhammad and proposed marriage to him through a friend and relative, Nufaysa bint Umayyah; he accepted. Greater detail can be found on-line. [235] Much of the history of Khadīja is controversial with claims and counter claims. *The Life of Muhammad* does not give the precise age, at which Muhammad married Khadīja, but most authorities state that he was 25 and she was 40; this is disputed by some.

Khadīja

Some claim that **Khadīja bint Khuwaylid b. Asad b. Abdu'l-'Uzza b. Qusayy b. Kilib b. Murra b Ka'b b. Lu'ayy b. Ghālib b. Fihr** was born in AD 565; others claim she was 15 years older than Muhammad which would make her birth 555. Some say she died in 623 while others claim she died in 619-620. For a number of reasons 619 seems more likely. Some claim she lived 58 years while others claim she lived 65 years. If Khadīja was born 65 years before 620, her birth would have been in 555. These dates are important because they permit us to determine whether or not Muhammad fathered any of his alleged children. Sūra 108 is a *hijā* or curse against Al As Edn Wayel. He opposed Muhammad's religious views and stated at the time of the death of Al Kasem, Muhammad's son, that Muhammad was "*abtar*," or one who has no children or posterity. This sūra is attributed to the early Mecca period. Khadīja's mother was **Fatima bint Za'ida ibn al-Asam of Banu `Amir ibn Luayy ibn Ghālib.** [236] Her father's name appears in her own above. "Bint" means "daughter of." Her father acquired vast wealth through trading. Khadīja inherited it and the business when her father died about 585. She ran caravans from Saba (Yemen) to Damascus, a distance of about 1800 miles. Mecca was midway on the overland trail. Her caravans were said to equal all the other caravans of the Quraysh put together. She earned two titles during her life, Ameerat-Quraysh, "Princess of the Quraysh" and al-Tahira, "The Pure One." She was virtuous and generous with her money. She fed the poor and provided for marriages of relatives who could not afford them. She was reputed to be the best born woman of the Quraysh, of the greatest dignity and the richest. All this favors the earlier birth date of Khadīja being 555 or thereabouts. It takes time to build a reputation and experience to manage a huge trading business. Such reputations are unlikely for a 20-year-old woman, but not impossible for a 30-year-old. Another source, *Encyclopaedia of the Orient*, favors a birth date in 555 and death in 619 at the age of 64. [237]

Waraqa b. Nafaul, Khadīja's Cousin & Christian Monk

Waraqa b. Nafaul b. Asad b. 'Abdu'l-'Uzzā b. Quṣayy was Khadīja's cousin and a Christian monk (probably Nestorian). He was a scholar who studied scripture and followed the Torah and Gospel. He is mentioned a number of times in the *Life of Muhammad*. He found Muhammad when he became lost from his foster mother and took him to 'Abdu'l-Muṭṭalib, his grandfather. [238] He also asserted that Muhammad was a prophet of his people. [239] He was mentioned as one of four men who participated in the polytheism of idol worship in Mecca. It was said he studied the scriptures and mastered them. [240] He composed an elegy for Zayd b. 'Amr b. Nufayl who sought the religion of Abraham, sampled Judaism and Christianity, but was unsatisfied with them. Following Muhammad's first vision, Khadīja took him to her cousin Waraqa who confirmed the onset of his prophetic life. "*Surely, by Him in whose hand is Waraqa's soul, thou art the prophet of this people. There hath come unto thee the greatest Nāmūs, who came unto Moses. Thou wilt be called a liar, and they will use thee despitefully and cast thee out and fight against thee. Verily, if I live to see that day, I will help God in such wise as He knoweth.*" [241] Early in Muhammad's ministry after persecutions had become severe and just before the exile to Abyssinia Waraqa b. Nafaul went to the persecutors and warned them that if they should kill Muhammad, he would make a tomb and shrine for him. [242]

Khadīja's Previous Marriages

One source states that Khadīja married a man from the Makhzumi clan in 570. She would have been only 5 if her birth date had been 565, but a more likely 15 if her birth date had been 555. Some sources state that his name was **Abū Halah Hind ibn Zarah** of the Banu `Adiyy. Some sources claim she was married twice before she married Muhammad. Her second husband was allegedly **Ateeq ibn `Aaith**. [243] Some claim both were killed in the frequent warfare of the region while others claim that one divorced her. She had a son by her first husband, Hind, who became one of Muhammad's most loyal supporters. He fought at Badr and Uhud, but was killed after Muhammad's death at the Battle of the Camel as one of Ali's troops. She also bore Abū Halah two other sons, al-Tahir and Halah. Neither is well known. In addition to her father's inheritance, she would have also obtained inheritance from her two previous husbands. Some sources deny knowledge of these husbands or their names.

Khadīja's Children

Khadīja had daughters by her second husband. Zainab married Abdul-`As ibn al-Rabee'. She accepted Islâm and with her husband moved to Medina with Muhammad. She died in 630 and her grave is still in existence. *The Life of Muhammad* page 83 states that Khadīja had several children by Muhammad: Al-Qāsim in 598; and Abd-Allah or al-Tāhir who died in childhood in 615. They also had 4 daughters: Zaynab (600-630), Ruqayya (603-624), Umm Kulthum (604- 630), and Fatima (605-633). Some say the first three may have been adopted daughters Ruqayya and Ummu Kulthoom married sons of Abū Lahab, one of Muhammad's uncles. Abū Lahab is cursed in sūra 111 for failure to accept Islâm. Following its publication, Abū Lahab ordered his sons to divorce these daughters of Muhammad and they did. Ruqayya married 'Uthmān ibn `Affan, eventually the 3rd caliph of Islâm and went with him to Abyssinia in 615. She returned with him and died in Medina in 624. ''Uthmān then married her sister Ummu Kulthoom in 625, but she died in 631 without having children.

The Sunnis believe that Ruqayya was born when Muhammad was 33 and was 3 years older than Zaynab. These two daughters were eventually married by 'Uthmān, the 3rd Caliph of Islâm. Shia scholars believe that the three earlier daughters were either the children of one of Khadīja's previous husbands or the children of Khadīja's deceased sister. Shia scholars argue that it would be impossible for Khadīja to give birth to children when she was past the childbearing years. This agrees with current medical information. After 40, pregnancy is uncommon. It is rare after 47. Before the advent of modern fertility clinics, the oldest known woman to deliver a child was 52 and the youngest was 5 ½. According to US vital statistics for 1948 there were 3,500,000 births in the U.S. Only 168 were to women over 50. In 65,000 deliveries at the Boston Lying-in Hospital, the oldest woman delivered was 49. [244]

Fatima's birth date is controversial. [245] Some say she was born when Muhammad was 35 (born 605), others state when he was 45 (born 615). Other sources claim she was 18 (born 614) when Muhammad died. Most favor a date after Muhammad began receiving revelations. However, if Fatima was born when Muhammad was 35, Khadīja would have been 50 and her giving birth at that age would have been unlikely. If she was born after the revelations began, Khadīja would have been about 60 – a physiologic impossibility for conception without modern fertility treatments or a miraculous conception. Khadīja's birth date of 555 is way too early for many of these children including Fatima to have been fathered by Muhammad. There are no claims that the birth of Fatima was miraculous. All of this becomes important in the arguments by Shiites over legitimacy by virtue of Muhammad's relationship to Ali, the 4th Caliph who married Fatima and the illegitimacy of the first three Caliphs who have no claim of direct ancestry within the family. Ibn Ishaq's *The Life of Muhammad* claims that al-Qasim (known as Abdu'l-Qasim), al-Tahir, al-Tayyib, were both boys who died in infancy and were children of Khadīja and Muhammad. [246] He also states that he and Khadīja had Zaynab, Ruqayya, Umm Kulthum, and Fatima. This appears to be the Sunni's point of view. The Korân sūra 108 (an early Mecca sūra) includes a curse against Al As Ebn Wayel who claimed that Muhammad had no posterity.

Khadīja's Religious Background

Khadīja was said never to have worshiped idols or believed in them. She had a cousin, Waraqa b. Nafaul (see above), who was a Christian monk. His belief in the unity of God ("same substance" definition at the Council of Nicaea) may have influenced her. In the Sale Translation of the *Korân* Jesus appears in 35 verses, Mary in 33, and Muhammad in 46. Other translations vary in these numbers depending on the translator's use of pronouns. In any event, there were a small number of Christians and Jews living in Mecca.

Muhammad's Young Adult Life

Best evidence suggests that Muhammad married this remarkable woman when he was 25 and she was 40. He had tremendous respect for her and complimented her to his other wives after her death. The only physical description of Muhammad that I have been able to find is in *Sword &* Seizure. [247] He was of a medium build with a large head. He was big boned and possessed a reddish face with full beard and body hair. When he walked, he leaned forward like a person going uphill. He had a very good reputation with the people of Mecca and must have been quite intelligent. He must have had an appealing personality to have been able to marry well and eventually gain followers. In addition, he was known for his negotiating skills and his pious nature.

Rebuilding the Ka'ba and First Seizure in Adulthood

When Muhammad was 35 years of age (AD 605). [248] The Quraysh, the clan responsible for maintaining the Ka'ba or Caaba decided to rebuild it. It needed to be razed, made more secure and be re-roofed. Timbers were obtained from a shipwreck near Mecca's port city of Jeddah. The building was destroyed to its foundation and then rebuilt according to new plans. During the rebuilding Muhammad and a companion assisted in carrying stones. "Abbas said to the prophet, 'take off and put your waist sheet over your neck so that the stones may hurt you.' [But as soon as he took off his waist sheet] he fell unconscious on the ground with both his eyes towards the sky. When he came to his senses, he said 'My waist sheet! My waist sheet' then he tied his waist sheet." [249] [250] This may be the first description of a seizure that recurred frequently after age 40 in association with Muhammad's visions. During the Ka'ba's reconstruction, Muhammad had the honor of acting as the judge to determine who would replace the "black stone" in the temple wall. Several clans of the Quraysh were competing for the honor. Muhammad solved the problem by having a member of each clan take the corner of a large cloak into which was placed the "black stone." It was then lifted to its place in the wall and Muhammad then, representing all the clans, put it in its place.

The Quraysh considered themselves special among all the Arab tribes. They declared they were the sons of Abraham, the people of the holy territory, the guardians of the temple, and the citizens of Mecca. No other Arabs had these rights. Mecca was within "sacred territory." They declared themselves Hums or "people of the sanctuary." [251] This was not unlike the designation of the Levites among the Children of Israel. A distinction was made between those born within and those born outside of the "sacred territory." They then made rules about those who were to make a pilgrimage to the Ka'ba. It was improper to use a tent made from camel-hair as a sun shield. Only a leather tent would do. They could not go around the Ka'ba except in garments of the Hums. If they did not possess such garments, they could go around naked or wear their regular clothing; however, these had to be thrown away so that no one else could use them. This was later simplified in the *Korân* 7:31-32. It was against this background that Muhammad began receiving revelations at the age of 40 (AD 610) and Islâm was born.

Muhammad's World AD 587 – 610

Following the death of Justinian I, his nephew, Flavius Iustinus Augustus (520-578), Justin II, became the eastern Roman emperor in 565. In 568 the Lombards invaded Italy and took much of the territory that had been conquered by Justinian I. One of Justin's first acts was to stop the "peace payments" to the Avars. This precipitated war which was unsuccessful for Justin II. Within a short time, the payments resumed. In 572 his refusal to pay the Persians their "peace tribute" led to war that lasted nearly 20 years. The Persians overran Syria and took the city of Dara. Justin II became insane for 4 years during which time Sophia, his wife and niece of the legendary Queen Theodora, and Tiberius, a general in her army became joint regents and ruled until 578 when Justin II died. The Ecclesiastic History of John of Ephesus (507-586), previously mentioned in connection with the climatic catastrophe of 535 and plague of 540, chronicled much of this part of history of the Eastern Roman Empire. Tiberius II (520-582) became the Emperor in 574; he is known as the first of the Greek Emperors and from this time forward the Eastern Roman Empire would be called Byzantine. Tiberius was not a good money manager and spent most of what was left in the treasury. He gave away 7,200 lbs. of gold per year as tribute until his death in 582.

Flavius Mauricius Tiberius Augustus (539-602) also known as Maurice began his reign from 582 to 602. He started as a military man who rose to commander in chief by 579. In 581 he humiliated the Persians and in 582 married Emperor Tiberius II Constantine's daughter Constantina and later that year succeeded him as Emperor. Maurice had some problems. There was no money in the treasury. The Dalmatian Coast, a formerly rich tributary of the Empire was overrun with Slavs. The Avars were demanding their usual annual gold tribute to keep them out of war, but the Slavs, although allies of the Avars paid no attention to any agreements made between Byzantium and the Avars. Despite the payments the Avars took the strategic city of Sirmium and the Slavs were pounding on the gates of Constantinople. In 587, Maurice came up with the cash, the Avar / Huns withdrew, and this permitted Maurice to go after the Slavs. By 602 he had forced them north of the Danube.

On the Persian front Maurice drove the Persians out of Dara in 586. The Persians began having internal problems. Prince Chosroes II and his military commander Bahram Chobin challenged the king Hormizd IV and overthrew him in 590. Following the coup, Chosroes II fled to Byzantium and begged assistance from Maurice to help him retake the throne. Maurice agreed and Chosroes dethroned Bahram Chobin in 591. This brought about peace and an alliance with Persia. To cement the deal Maurice's oldest daughter, Miriam, married Chosroes. This freed all Maurice's troops on the southern frontier to move north against the Slavs; however, not all was well at home.

In 582 Maurice had cut the army's pay by 25%. He increased taxes to pay for his campaigns and tribute to the Avars. He divided the Empire into east and west and placed his two sons in charge of each region, much as had happened under the tetrarch of Diocletian. In 599 the Avars captured 12,000 imperial soldiers and demanded ransom. Maurice could not pay and many of the captives were tortured and killed. A military delegation from the front led by Phocas, one of their commanders came to Constantinople to beg for the troops in the north, but was humiliated. The Byzantine "peace payments," appeasement policy, began to unravel.

At the beginning of 600 when Muhammad was about 30 Byzantium faced total collapse. It was surrounded by enemies and still weakened by the plague that had killed a third of her population. She had lost much productive territory and faced massive tributes to keep her enemies from the gates.

In the winter of 602, Maurice ordered the troops to continue their offensive and move to the north side of the Danube instead of coming home to winter quarters as usual. This infuriated the troops who now elected Phocas as their leader and revolted with demands that Maurice abdicate in favor of Theodosius, his son or General Germanus. These men were now declared traitors.

In 602 a popular uprising occurred first among Byzantine troops on the northern frontier, and then spread to Constantinople. Maurice (539-602) fled with his family. He was found and his entire family murdered. This included his queen, the daughter of the Persian King, who now refused to receive ambassadors from Byzantium. The result was an immediate resumption of the Persian war. This eventually wakened both powers creating a power vacuum later filled by Islâmic armies. Flavius Phocas Augustus, the Tyrant, was proclaimed emperor of Byzantium by the "Green" party. [There were 4 parties in Constantinople, **Red, White, Blue** and **Green** – the colors of sports fans in the hippodrome who championed various chariot racing teams. The "Blues" were bought off during the Nike Riots when Theodora saved her husband Justinian from abdication. The Reds and Whites had little political influence by then. Red, white, blue, and green are common flag colors throughout Europe today.]

We know little of Phocas' background including his birth date. However, he was very popular at first. He lowered taxes. He received praises from Pope Gregory I in Rome. Internal factions and strife further weakened the Empire and in 604 most of southern Anatolia (Turkey) fell to the Persians. Persia now turned its attention to The Middle East and Egypt where forces under tenuous control of the revolutionary Roman government still held sway.

Phocas removed the army from the Balkans in 605 which allowed the Avars and Slavs to renew their aggression and retake the territories gained by Maurice. The Persian army began pressing northward and overran Roman Mesopotamia. Phocas purged former leaders and their families in Constantinople while Persia overran Armenia in 606. In 608 the Exarch of Africa and his sons, Heraclius revolted against Phocas. This precipitated the execution of ex-Empress, Constantina and her daughters. Phocas sent an army to Egypt and was defeated. The Persians moved into the eastern Mediterranean Roman territories. When the youngest Heraclius arrived with a delegation near Constantinople in 610, Phocas' personal body guard defected and Heraclius personally beheaded Phocas, mutilated his body, dragged it through the streets and burned it. In the meanwhile, the Slavs took the Adriatic coast and left that once prosperous part of the Empire in total ruin. Most of the inhabitants fled to Italy while some built fortified towns and held off the Slavs. Byzantium was in the capable hands of Heraclius who ruled and triumphed until 641. However, in the Arabian desert a new power was rising in Mecca – Muhammad.

MECCA, THE BIRTH OF ISLÂM 610–619

About 610 Muhammad, now age 40 and still in Mecca, had his first revelation while meditating in a cave.[252] This experience was associated with depression, fear, and doubt. He had several more visions over an unknown period of time associated with worsening fears and depression. Muhammad "intended several times to throw himself off cliffs," but each time Gabriel appeared to him and said, 'O Muhammad! You are indeed Allah's Apostle in truth.' Whereupon he would become quiet, calm down and return home (90:11). At first, visions came at long intervals. This increased his doubt and he went to the mountains again with the intent of ending his life, but Gabriel reassured him."[253][254] "*The inspiration ceased to come to the messenger of God for a while, and he was deeply grieved. Muhammad went to the tops of mountain crags, in order to fling himself from them; but every time he reached the summit of a mountain, Gabriel appeared to him and said to him, 'You are the Prophet of God.' Thereupon his anxiety would subside and he would come back to himself.*"[255] See also Congealed Blood sūra 96 heading. Muhammad went home to his wife and reported his vision. According to Ibn Sa'd, translated by S. Moinal Haq, page 225 he was reputed to have said, "*O Khadīja, I see light and hear sounds and I fear I am mad*". It was during this period that the revelations stopped for a time until they began again with the sūra of the Morning (93). For three years he preached only to family and intimates.[256]

The reaction to commit suicide in the face of a true message from God is unusual in the experience of Judeo-Christian prophets and servants of God. It did not occur in the stories of Adam (Gen 2-3), Noah (Gen 6), Abraham (Gen 12-18), Moses (Exodus 3-34), Samuel (1Samuel 3), Isaiah (Isaiah 6), Mary (Luke 1), Paul (Saul) (Acts 9) or even Joseph Smith (*Joseph Smith History*). Those who see God often fear him, but then behave rationally. They often repent of their weaknesses and go about as peaceful servants true to the seriousness of their experience. Many describe repeated visitations for instructional purposes and many have been called upon to seal their testimony with their own blood as martyrs. Depression, anxiety, and suicidal ideations are not described. Many attribute it to his being a private man, but this reaction becomes important when we examine the illness that affected Muhammad in the last 30 years of his life.

Khadīja, Muhammad's faithful wife, was the first to accept Islâm in 610 about 6 months after the first revelation. [257] The first male convert was Alī b. Abū Ṭālib and the second was Zyad b. Hāritha, Muhammad's freed man. [258] Abū Bakr b Abū Quhāfa is listed as 3rd. [259] Abū Bakr became an early proponent and missionary. He brought many into Islâm including 'Uthmān b. Affān b Abdu'l-'Ās b. Umayya b. 'Abdu Shams b. 'Abdu Manāf b. Qusayy. Other early converts are also mentioned in detail. [260] Public preaching commenced and more converts followed, but it was not generally accepted, especially by the Quraysh. Sūra 15 was revealed and Muhammad was commanded *"Wherefore publish that which thou hast been commanded, and withdraw from the idolaters."* (15:**94**) *"The Meccans say, O thou to who the admonition hath been sent down, thou art certainly possessed with a devil: wouldest thou not have come unto us with an attendance of angels, if thou hadst spoken truth? Answer, We send not down the angels, unless on a just occasion; nor should they be then respited any longer. We have surely sent down the Korân; and we will certainly preserve the same from corruption."* (15:**6-9**)

The commandment to publish was not heeded as far as known. Publication of the New Testament was delayed 2 centuries. Muhammad was also warned: *"Invoke no other god with the true GOD, lest thou become one of those who are doomed to punishment. And admonish thy more near relations. And behave thyself with meekness towards the true believers who follow thee: and if they be disobedient unto thee, say, Verily I am clear of that which ye do."* (26:**213-216**)

Accusations Against Muhammad: Opposition Increases

In 615 Meccans were invited to become Muslims. At first many accepted. [261] However, once talk began in Mecca active opposition developed. One of Muhammad's major opponents was Al-Walīd B. Al-Mughīra who is mentioned in the note at the end of Sūra 15. [262] Some members of the Quraysh came to Al-Walīd giving their opinion of Muhammad. At first, they stated he was a seer, but Al-Walīd said he wasn't because he did not have unintelligible babbling and rhymed speech. Next Muhammad was accused of being possessed, but Al-Walīd disagreed; he did not have seizures characterized by choking and spasmodic movements. Next, they called him a poet, but Al-Walīd dismissed that theory as well. Finally, they accused him of being a sorcerer, but again Al-Walīd objected since there was no "spitting" or "knots." [See Sūra 113.] At a loss for an explanation the Quraysh asked Al-Walīd what he thought was wrong with him. He replied that sorcerer was closest because his message was dividing families. The Quraysh warned all travelers in the region to avoid Muhammad. Sūra 74:11-25 warned Muhammad about Al-Walīd. *"Let me alone with him whom I have created, on whom I have bestowed abundant riches, and children dwelling in his presence, and for whom I have disposed affairs in a smooth and easy manner, and who desireth that I will yet add other blessings unto him. By no means: because he is an adversary to our signs. I will afflict him with grievous calamities* [a hijā follows – an invective, diatribe or insulting poem] [263]*: for he hath devised and prepared contumelious expressions to ridicule the Korân. May he be cursed: how maliciously hath he prepared the same! And again, may he be cursed: how maliciously hath he prepared the same! Then he looked, and frowned, and put on an austere countenance: then he turned back, and was elated with pride; and he said, This is no other than a piece of magic, borrowed from others: these are only the words of a man."*

As the Quraysh endured Muhammad's preaching, they became more agitated. He was insulting their way of life, their religion, their forefathers and their gods. [264] When one of Muhammad's followers attempted to read the *Korân* at a conference of the Quraysh, they hit him in the face. When Muhammad read to them, they listened, but afterwards were critical and began persecuting believers especially those among the lower classes. [265]

Most Meccans refused to accept the *Korân* as the word of God. They resented Muhammad's complaints against their pagan traditions and the religion which they had defended. They were suspicious of his motives and the origins of the *Korân*, itself. No doubt his initial deep depression and suicidal ideations had been a topic of local conversation. They had heard of his visions which Muhammad refused to deny. Some had observed his trances as reported in later Hadiths. However, they had no way to interpret these observations as medical science was primitive. The Meccans knew it was abnormal, and consequently did not believe what he told them. The *Korân* reports their accusations:

Madness: *and when they privately discourse together: when the ungodly say, Ye follow no other than a madman.* (17:**47**) *Or do they say, He is a madman?* (23:**70**) *or rather he is distracted (mad)*. (**34**:8) *But he turned back, with his princes, saying, This man is a sorcerer or a madman.* (51:30) *In like manner there* *came no apostle unto their predecessors, but they said, this man is a magician or a madman* (51:52). *Wherefore do thou, O prophet, admonish thy people. Thou art not, by the grace of thy LORD, a soothsayer or a madman.* (52:29)

Bereaved of Senses, Possessed by the Devil, or Being a Soothsayer: W*hich of you are bereaved of your senses*? (68:**6**) *The Meccans say, O thou to who the admonition hath been sent down, thou art certainly possessed with a devil (insane)*: (15:**6**) *neither is it the discourse of a soothsayer: how little are ye admonished!* (69:42)

Being a poet: *But they say, The Korân is a confused heap of dreams: nay, he hath forged it; nay, he is a poet: let him come unto us therefore with some miracle, in like manner as the former prophets were sent* (21:**5**). *We have not taught Muhammad the art of poetry; nor is it expedient for him to be a poet. This book is no other than an admonition from God, and a perspicuous Korân* (36:**69**); *Shall we abandon our gods for a distracted poet* (37:**36**)? *Do they say, He is a poet: we wait, concerning him, some adverse turn of fortune* (52:30)? *and not the discourse of a poet: how little do ye believe* (69:41)!

Distraction: *Ye follow no other than a man who is distracted* (25**: 8**); *they answered, Verily thou art distracted (deluded)* (26**:153**): *they answered, certainly thou art distracted* (26:**185**): *he is distracted (mad)* (**34**:8). *They swell with arrogance, and say, Shall we abandon our gods for a distracted poet* (37:**36**)? *but they retired from him, saying, this man is instructed by others, or is a distracted person* (44**:14**)? *thou, O Muhammad, through the grace of thy LORD, art not distracted* (48**:2**). It *wanteth little but that when they hear the admonition of the Korân; and they say, He is certainly distracted* (68**:51**): *and your companion Muhammad is not distracted* (81:22).

Forgery and Lies: *but ye have forged lies concerning him* (**6**: 57). *Will they say, Muhammad hath forged it* (**10**:38)? *Will they say, He hath forged the Korân* (**11**:13)? Will *the Meccans say, Muhammad hath forged the Korân* (**11**:35)? *When we substitute in the Korân an abrogating verse in lieu of a verse abrogated, (and GOD best knoweth the fitness of that which he revealeth,) the infidels say, Thou art only a forger of these verses: but the greater part of them know not truth from falsehood* (**16**:101). *This Korân is no other than a forgery which he hath contrived …* (25:**4**). *Will they say, Muhammad hath forged it? Nay, it is the truth from thy LORD, that thou mayest preach to a people, unto whom no preacher hath come before thee; peradventure they will be directed* (**32**:3). *He hath forged a lie concerning GOD* (**34**:8), *and they say of the Korân, This is no other than a lie blasphemously forged* (34:43). *Muhammad hath blasphemously forged a lie concerning GOD* (**42**:24). *Will they say, Muhammad hath forged it* (**46**:8)? *He hath forged the Korân* (52:33)?

If Muhammad had forged any part of these discourses concerning us (69:44). [Most of these accusations occurred in the late Meccan period.]

Sorcery: *The unbelievers say, this is manifest sorcery* (**10**:2). *Verily this is manifest sorcery* (10:76). *The unbelievers will say, this is nothing but manifest sorcery* (**11**:7). *Is this Muhammad any more than a man like yourselves? Will ye therefore come to hear a piece of sorcery, when ye plainly perceive it to be so* (21:**3**)? *This is no other than manifest sorcery* (**34**:43): *and say, This is no other than manifest sorcery* (37:**15**): *This is a piece of sorcery; and we believe not therein* (43:**30**). *the unbelievers say of the truth, when it cometh unto them, This is a manifest piece of sorcery* (**46**:7).

Telling Fables: *This is nothing but silly fables of ancient times* (**6**:25). *This is nothing but fables of the ancients* (**8:31**). *They answer, Fables of ancient times* (**16**:24). *this is nothing but fables of the ancients* (23:**83**). *These are fables of the ancients, which he hath caused to be written down; and they are dictated unto him morning and evening* (25:**5**). *This is no other than fables of the ancients* (27:**68**). *This is no other than silly fables of the ancients* (**46**:17). *They are fables of the ancients.* (48:**15**) *fables of the ancients* (83:13).

The *Korân* assures us that these accusations are false. However, they reappear so commonly, that one must believe that not all the Meccans were mistaken in their observations. The longer criticism and persecution continued the more agitated Muhammad became. We know that initially there were long pauses between the earlier visions. This heightened his doubts, but within a year or so the visions were coming regularly. His wife and those close to him assured him that he was a prophet of God. Accusations against Muhammad recorded in the *Korân* tended to be specific depending on when they were recorded: "madness," "bereaved of senses," "possessed by the devil," "soothsayer," and "poet" were commonly used in the early and mid-Meccan period. "Distraction," "forgery," "telling lies," and "sorcery" were more common in the mid to late Meccan period. "Telling fables" seemed to be spread out in all periods, but this one may have come from one source.

A Secret Society & Conspiracy

According to *The Encyclopaedia Britannica*, for the next 3 years Muhammad gathered together a secret society of believers and that sometime between 613 and 616 Muhammad and his followers attempted to seize the government of Mecca, first through exhortation, then by diplomacy and finally by force. During this period Muhammad continued to receive revelations of the *Korân*. It was also said that parts were dictated to him by an Abyssinian

Christian "since the Christian technicalities of the *Korân* are mainly derived from the Ethiopic (Old Syriac) Gospels and Acts."

The Life of Muhammad does not speak directly about such a conspiracy, but does mention persecutions of Muslim members in various clans. Every clan of the Quraysh persecuted all who supported Muhammad. They attacked, imprisoned, beat, denied them food and drink and chased them into the desert in order to persuade them not to follow Muhammad. [267] Under this pressure some fell away, but others resisted. This kind of activity by the Quraysh would be unusual against their tribesmen, unless there was some kind of provocation outside of simply expressing religious beliefs. However, I have been unable to find anything that would include efforts to take over the civil government of Mecca at this time as alleged above in *The Encyclopaedia Britannica.*

Assassinations

The Life of Muhammad reported that after Muhammad moved to Medina, he ordered the assassination of several poets who wrote disparaging verses about him. These acts describe an anger and vengeance that may have disturbed the Meccans before 620. Most prisoners taken in Arab wars were ransomed. Only if the ransom was not paid were they killed. However, this did not apply to two prominent critics of Muhammad. In March 624 Al-Nadr b. al-Hārith b. 'Alqama b. Kalada b. 'Abdu Manāf was mentioned as mocking Muhammad. [268] See **6**:8, 21:**98-100**, 25:**6**, **45**:7-9 and 83:13-17. He was captured at the Battle of Badr and summarily executed by Ali under Muhammad's orders. Uqba bin Abū Muayt, one of Al-Nadr's close associates and critic of Muhammad was also taken prisoner at Badr and beheaded instead of ransoming. [269] [270]

James Arlandson's observations about a dead poets' society mentioned above are verified in the *Life of Muhammad.* In March 624, Muhammad ordered the assassination of Asma bint Marwan. 'Umayr b. 'Adiy al-Khatmi killed her with a sword while she slept. [271] Abū 'Afak had written an uncomplimentary poem about Muhammad. In April 624 Muhammad ordered his assassination and Salim b Umayr killed him. [272] In September 624 Muhammad ordered the assassination of another poet, Ka'b b. al-Ashraf, who had visited the Battle of Badr site and continued on to Mecca where he circulated a poetic lament over the slain Meccans. A volunteer assassin was Muhammad b Maslama. He returned after three days of fasting and told Muhammad that he couldn't do it because he would have to tell lies. Muhammad then stated, "Say what you like, for you are free in the matter." He went with several others and killed Ka'b by deception. [273] Muhammad had said, "Kill any Jew that falls into your power;" [274] as a result Ibn Sunayan was ambushed and killed. In July – August 625 Muhammad sent Amr bin Umayya and a companion to assassinate Abū Sufyān b. Harb in Mecca; they failed. This was to avenge Muslim missionaries who had been killed. However, on their way home they murdered Ibn Malik, and then fled into the hills. While hiding in a cave they found a one-eyed Bedouin sheepherder. He sang a ditty, "I won't be a Muslim as long as I live, Nor heed to their religion give." After he fell asleep Umayya killed him by pushing the end of his bow through his good eye socket until it came out his neck. The Bedouin died a horrible death. As Umayya continued home he found two Meccan spies. He killed one and took the other prisoner. On reporting his activities to Muhammad, he received Muhammad blessings. [275] In January 630 A.D. ten thousand Muslim warriors entered Mecca with orders to hunt down and kill any who resisted and a small number who had been special enemies of Muhammad.

On this list were 'Abdullah bin Sad, 'Abdullah bin Katal, an apostate Muslim and his two "singing-girls." A foster brother pled for the life of 'Abdullah bin Sad and he was allowed to leave. After 'Uthmān had gone Muhammad said to his companions that he had remained quiet, to see if one of them might behead him. One of the Ansār (Medina Arabs) asked why he had not given them a sign that he wanted the man killed. Muhammad told them that a prophet "*does not kill by pointing*." [276]

'Abdullah b. Khatal of B Taym b. Ghālib was a Muslim whom Muhammad had sent to collect the poor tax. An Ansār went with him. There was also in the party a freed slave servant, also a Muslim. When they stopped to rest 'Abdullah ordered his servant to kill a goat and prepare supper while he slept. When 'Abdullah wakened, his servant had done nothing, so he killed him and then apostatized. He had two singing-girls Fartana and her friend who sang satirical songs about Muhammad. Muhammad ordered that they should be killed with him. Al-Huwayrith b Nuqaydh had insulted Muhammad in Mecca; assassination was ordered. Miqyas b Hubaba had killed an Ansāri who had killed his brother accidentally. Afterwards he had gone back to the Quraysh and became a "polytheist." He was eliminated. One of the singing-girls escaped. [277]

A number of those critical of Islam in the modern world have been subject to execution orders and rewards for their deaths. Just as now, totalitarian dictators find it necessary to silence the opposition and institute favorable press in its place. In the ancient world, this meant control of scribes with a few well-placed assassinations. This was a far easier task than control of the modern press (radio, TV, print) or the Internet's blogosphere.

The Conversion of Hamza

One of the important early converts to Islâm was Hamza b. 'Abdu'l-MutTālib. He was Muhammad's uncle who liked to hunt with the bow and arrow. He was alleged to be "the strongest man of the Quraysh, and the most unyielding." [278] Muhammad was near the Ka'ba minding his own business. Abū Jahl approached and began insulting him. Muhammad said nothing, but went to the Ka'ba. Hamza arrived. He had been hunting and was told what had transpired between Abū Jahl and his nephew. Hamza found Abū Jahl, hit him and told him that he followed Muhammad's religion. He then challenged Abū Jahl to hit him if he could. At this point members of the B. Makhzum came to Abū Jahl's aid. They were told that he had insulted Muhammad. With Hamza's conversion, Muhammad had acquired a powerful protector and a prestigious convert. [279]

Hamza's conversion influenced others of the Quraysh to become Muslims, but the majority resisted. The tribes of the Quraysh in Mecca imprisoned and attempted to discourage as many as they could from becoming Muslims. Finally they decided to try negotiations with Muhammad again. They spoke to him frankly about his derisive comments about their pagan religion and again repeated their offers of money, honor, sovereignty, and treatment for "familiar spirits." Muhammad said that he wanted none of it and repeated that God had sent him as an apostle, announcer or warner to them with a revealed book. They asked him to intervene for them with God to make their life easier with more water and with other signs such as raising their dead. If he could accomplish such miracles, then they would believe him. This prompted him to quote the *Korân*: "*And they say, We will by no means believe on thee, until thou cause a spring of water to gush forth for us out of the earth; or thou hast a garden of palm-trees and vines, and thou cause rivers,* etc. etc. … (17:**90-97**) [280]

Persecutions of AD 615

According to Islâmic chronology, public preaching by Muhammad began in 614 AD, four years after his first revelation in sūra **96**. When Hamza accepted Islâm the Quraysh met in assembly with Muhammad. They had been unable to convince him to stop preaching and now resorted to bribery. 'Utba sat next to Muhammad, his nephew. After complimenting him as being one of the noblest of the Quraysh he stated that Muhammad had divided the community by ridiculing their customs, insulting their gods and religion, and by claiming their forefathers to be unbelievers. 'Utba then said that if he would cease and desist, the Quraysh would make him the richest among them if he wanted money. If he wanted honor, they would make him their chief and give him judgment power over them or even make him king. They would find a physician for him to cure him of his visions of Gabriel even if it meant exhausting all their means to do it. [281] Muhammad's response was to quote to them from the *Korân*: "*This is a revelation from the most Merciful, a book the verses whereof are distinctly explained, an Arabic Korân for the instruction of people who understand; bearing good tidings, and denouncing threats: but the greater part of them turn aside, and hearken not thereto. And they say, Our hearts are veiled from the doctrine to which thou invitest us; and there is a deafness in our ears, and a curtain between us and thee: wherefore act thou as thou shalt think fit; for we shall act according to our own sentiments.*" (**41**:2-6)

The Real Conspiracy?

'Utba b. Rabī'a b. 'Abdu Shams, one of Muhammad's uncles, reported to the council that Muhammad had said he had not used poetry, spells, or witchcraft. He advised them to leave Muhammad alone because if Muhammad continued his talk other Arabs would kill him and save them the trouble. If he convinced other Arabs to go along with him then Muhammad would rule, but the Meccan Council would eventually prosper from his conquests. When the council accused 'Utba of being convinced by Muhammad, he told them that was his opinion, but they would have to do what they thought best. [282] This buried tidbit of history, predicted here by 'Utba as reported in *The Life of Muhammad* may be more accurate than most wish to believe. The conspiracy will be mentioned later in greater detail.

By this time Muhammad's illness with its fetishes towards violence and insatiable libido had become a severe distraction. He must have become a prisoner of his desires and easily manipulated by his immediate associates, all of whom eventually became Caliphs of Islam. Two of them (Abū Bakr and 'Umar) sent their daughters ('Ā'isha & Hafṣa) to feed Muhammad's growing libido. 'Uthmān & Alī married Muhammad's daughters to cement their relationships to him.

The Councils response to Muhammad was to go ahead and let *"the heaven to fall down"* on them. Abū Jahl threatened to split Muhammad's skull with a large stone while he was at prayer, but when he tried, he was stopped by what he described as a large stallion camel that threatened to eat him. Ibn' Abbās ridiculed the *Korân* whenever it was read to him. [283] The *Korân* quotes him eight times. Whenever Ibn' Abbās heard it read, he would say, "*fairy tales of the ancients*" or "*fables of the ancients*" (**6**:25; **16**:24; 23:**83**; 25:**5**; 27:**68**; **46**:17; 68:65; 83:13; **8:31**). This phrase appears nine times in the *Korân* and is found from the earliest period to the last.

The Council consulted a Jewish rabbi. He advised that they ask Muhammad three questions: 1) What happened to the young men who disappeared in ancient days? 2) What about the mighty traveler who reached the confines of both East and West? And 3) what is spirit? If Muhammad could give satisfactory answers on all these subjects, he would have demonstrated his prophetic abilities. If he could not, he was a forger. The council asked Muhammad the three questions and he told them that he would have an answer in the morning. For 15 days, Muhammad went without a vision, but soon thereafter Gabriel brought him the vision on the cave and the answers. 18:**1-27**; 83-98 answered the first two. The third question about the spirit was given in 17:**85**. [284] Still the Quraysh would not believe and accused the prophet of being prompted by a man in al-Yamāma called al-Rahmān. 'Abdullah b Mas'ūd now offered to read the *Korân* loudly in the presence of the Quraysh Council, but when he did, they beat him in the face. [285]

Abū Sufyān b. Harb ibn Umayya (560-650 AD) plays an important role in Muhammad's history from inside Mecca from here on. He frustrated the Meccan's attack against Muhammad at the Battle of Badr. He raised the army that attacked Muhammad's forces at Medina in 625. Although the Meccans prevailed at the battle of Uhûd and could have killed Muhammad and destroyed his forces, but Abū Sufyān led the Meccan army from the field without exploiting its victory and returned to Mecca thus giving Muhammad a strategic victory. At the Battle of Al-Khandaq or the Trench in 627 the Meccan Army outnumbered the Muslims nearly 4:1. Abū Sufyān used the excuse of the wind that knocked down the Meccan's tents to pack up and go home. The Jewish allies, around Medina were left defenseless at Muhammad's mercy. Incredibly, Muhammad married Abū Sufyān's daughter as his 8th wife and possibly his ex-wife as his 12th wife. This was the same woman that mutilated the Muslim soldiers on the battlefield at Uhûd. Later Abū Sufyān's son, brother of Muhammad's 8th wife and son of his questionable 12th wife became the 5th Caliph and began the Umayyad Dynasty. The division of the two clans, Hāshim and Umayyad, lead to the deadly schism between Shia and Sunni over the Caliphate and leadership of Islâm.

Exile

The Life of Muhammad pages 130 to 148 covers the history of persecutions. It lists a number of references from the *Korân* in the foot notes: **41**:1, 37 ; 68:15 ; 19:**65** ; 18 all; **31**:26; 25:**8, 22**; 17:**31, 87, 92, 94, 110**; **13**:29 ; 34:46; 74:31 ; 53:1; 92:5-7. The Persecution that began in 615 forced 83 Muslim men and their families into exile in Abyssinia. The heads of households are recorded. [286] The Meccans feared that this might create an alliance between the Muhammad and the Abyssinia king. Envoys led by "Abdullah b. Abū Rabī'a and 'Amr b. al-'Ās b. Wāil went to Axum demanding that the exiles be sent home. 'Amr was to later distinguish himself in the cause of Islâm in the conquest of Egypt. Muhammad knew that Abyssinia was a Christian nation and sent envoys with Sūra 19, Mary. This sūra included an account of the birth of Christ with miracles found only in non-canonical scripture. It included material from a popular source, *The Miracles of the Virgin Mary*. The Abyssinian king (Negus) and his Christian priests thought that the exiles were persecuted Christians and took Muhammad's side. [287] The Negus and his bishops wept when the sūra of Mary was read to them. [288]

The Abyssinian Negus rebuked and sent home the Quraysh envoys. In 617 Muhammad's followers in Axum (Aksum) strengthened connections between him and Abyssinia. Axum included all of what are now Ethiopia, Djibouti and Yemen in the southwestern part of the Arabian Peninsula. Its highlands are bisected by the Great Rift Valley. It included the southern half of the Red Sea's western coast line and the interior of the horn of Africa. It was one of the first African countries to be Christianized and first to use the cross on its coinage. At the time of Christ and for several centuries it was considered one of the 4 great powers in the world that included Rome, Persia and China.

Worsening Persecution & the Boycott AD 615

The Quraysh were unable to stop Muhammad's preaching. If they could not bribe, cure or kill him they would have to isolate him and his followers. They prepared a legal document proclaiming that the tribes of Hāshim and MutTālib could not marry other women from the clan of Quraysh and that the remaining tribes / houses of Quraysh would not trade with them for any goods. They then took this proclamation and hung it on the Ka'ba. It is known as *The Document Proclaiming A Boycott.* [289] This began according to Sunni chronology on September 30, 615. [290] Other sources describe a boycott in 617 lifted in early in 619. [291] It lasted 2-3 years. Few details are given. [292]

Another source [293] tells us that those who remained in Mecca went to a mountain pass, shi'b Abi Tālib, outside of Mecca under the direction of Abū Ṭālib. They were not permitted to enter Mecca except during the seasons of pilgrimage (Umrah and Hajj) in the months of Rajab and Dhulhijjah. The area was defensible so attack by the Quraysh was frustrated, but it was subject to siege. Those who were there were cut off from commerce causing them to endure poverty, famine, and deprivation. However, the revelations continued declaring the wickedness of the Quraysh. When the Quraysh threatened to curse Muhammad's god if he continued to curse theirs, Sūra **6**:108 was revealed. *"Revile not the idols which they invoke besides GOD, lest they maliciously revile GOD, without knowledge. Thus have we prepared for every nation their works: hereafter unto GOD shall they return, and he shall declare unto them that which they have done."*

Some sources claim that the exile took place in stages. Early in 615 eleven men and four women slipped out of Mecca at night and headed for Jeddah where they caught two boats to Abyssinia. This group included Uthman and Ruquyyah bint Muhammad. It is said that these returned following the incident with the Satanic Verses later that year, but once the Meccans realized there was no change in Muhammad's preaching, the persecutions increased which led to the boycott and siege and caused a second migration of nearly 100 followers of Islâm back to Abyssinia in 616. [294]

The Life of Muhammad tells us that the *Korân* was probably written initially by Muhammad when the Quraysh accused him of being unable to create a better story than they and his stories were full of old fables that he had copied. [295] (See Table XXIX.) Muhammad responded, "*Say, He hath revealed it, who knoweth the secrets in heaven and earth: verily he is gracious and merciful.*" (25:**6**)

Despite Muhammad's protection he continued to be ridiculed. The Hāshim and MutTālib clans at shi'b Abi Tālib took advantage of their safe passage two months out of the year to return to Mecca for provisions and see former friends. Umayya b. Khalaf b. Wahb b. Hudhāfa b. Jumah slandered Muhammad whenever he saw him. Sūra 104 is a *hija* directed at him. [296] Despite the boycott Muhammad continued to preach to the Quraysh and meet with them on occasion. Al-Akhnas b. Shariq b. 'Amr b. Wahb al-Thaqafī was an ally of the clan Zuhra and was one of the Quraysh's leaders. He listened to Muhammad, but contradicted him. [297] Muhammad received (68:**10-13**) about him. Al-Walīd questioned why revelations were given to Muhammad and not to great men of the clan such as himself or Abū Mas'ūd 'Amr b. 'Umayr al-Thaqafī, chief of the Ta'īf and Mecca. [298] If it had, then the Quraysh would have received it (43:**31**). Two men of the tribe, Ubayy b. Khalaf b. Wahb b. Hudhāfa and 'Uqba b. Abū Mu'ayt were friends. When Ubayy discovered that 'Uqba was listening to Muhammad, he told him they could never be friends again unless 'Uqba spit in Muhammad's face; he did. In response Muhammad received (25:**27**). [299] 'Uqba further harassed Muhammad by taking an old bone to him and questioned whether or not God could resurrect it. He then crumbled it and blew the dust into Muhammad's face. Muhammad told him God, could and after he had resurrected 'Uqba He would send him to hell (36:**77**-**83**).

Another incident during this period occurred when Muhammad was walking around the Ka'ba (Caaba). Al-Aswad b. al-MutTālib b. Asad b. 'Abdu'l-'Uzzā, Al-Walād b. al-Mughīra, Umayya b. Khalaf, and al-'Ās b. Wā'il al-Sahmī came to him and proposed, that they would worship Allah, if Muhammad would worship their gods. Each could get a share of what was better. In response, Muhammad received (109:1-6) that told them, you keep your religion and I'll keep mine. [300]

The Satanic Verses

As persecutions increased and the conditions of the siege became intolerable, Muhammad was distressed by the attitude and aggressiveness of his tribe's people and attempted to get the Quraysh on his side. [301] If he could tie the old gods of the Arabs to his version of Allah, it might bring peace to the two factions and cause more converts. The first edition of Sūra 53, *The Star*, given in AD 615 according to Sunni chronology, made this attempt. The Meccan goddesses, Allat, al-'Uzza, and Menat were memorialized.

Sūra 53 originally asked the question, *"What think ye of Allat, and Al-'Uzza and Manāt, that other third goddess?* (53:19-20) Allat was equivalent to Minerva or Aphrodite. Al-'Uzza was the mistress of heaven or virgin warrior / star goddess of Saba and Mecca. She was also the fertility goddess, Venus or Ishtar. Manat was the goddess of fortune or luck – Fortuna. These three pagan goddesses were the daughters of the Moon God, al-Lah or Allah and worshiped by the Arabs in Mecca and Petra. The question was answered thus: "*These are the exalted cranes (intermediaries) Whose intercession is to be hoped for.*" The word used was Gharānīq – Numidian cranes said to fly at a great height. [302] The three goddesses, al-Lāt, al-'Uzzā and Manāt, daughters of Allah, would now intercede between man and Allah. We do not know how long this sūra remained in this form, but it was later abrogated to remove "the exalted cranes" verse and read the way it now reads regarding the three goddesses: "*Have ye male children, and God female? This, therefore, is an unjust partition. They are no other than empty names, which ye and your fathers have named goddesses. GOD hath not revealed concerning them anything to authorize their worship. They follow no other than a vain opinion, and what their souls desire: yet hath the true direction come unto them from their LORD.*" (53:21-23) When the Meccans found out about the abrogation, they became more antagonistic towards Muhammad and his followers. This incident is also referred to in sūra **22** from the Medina period.

The "Satanic Verses" temporarily reconciled the differences between the Meccans and Muhammad's concept of a single, Supreme Being in the form of their old Moon and War God, Allah combined with Jehovah, the Judeo-Christian God. This pleased the Quraysh and they began to listening more closely to Muhammad. When news of the reconciliation between the Quraysh and Muhammad reached the exiles in Axum, they returned home. However, at about the time of their return sūra 19 Mary or Marium that had been sent to Abyssinia became known in Mecca. It denied the value of the connection between Allah and his three daughters (19:**80-81**) Controversy again broke out and all but 33 men and their families went back to Axum. [303] As mentioned above, 'Umar who was to become the 2nd Caliph of Islâm was so impressed by this incident between the Quraysh and the Islâmic exiles that he became a Muslim in 616 AD. The exiles that returned to Mecca later went to Medina. [304]

Muhammad is later rebuked for the addition of the daughters of the Moon God / God of war. It was an error influenced by Satan. "*We have sent no apostle, or prophet, before thee, but, when he read, Satan suggested some error in his reading. But GOD shall make void that which Satan hath suggested: then shall GOD confirm his sign; for GOD is knowing and wise. But this he permitteth, that he may make that which Satan hath suggested, a temptation unto those in whose hearts there is an infirmity, and whose hearts are hardened: (for the ungodly are certainly in a wide disagreement from the truth:)*" (**22:52-53**) In the same sūra God gives permission for Muhammad and his followers to fight against the Meccans, "*Permission is granted unto those who take arms against the unbelievers, for that they have been unjustly persecuted by them; (and GOD is certainly able to assist them);*" (**22:39**)

Muslims generally claim that the crescent and star originated with the Ottoman Empire and that it has no meaning for Islâm. It is curious that the pagan god Allah was the moon god of war and that the *Korân* refers to Allah as Lord of the dog-star (53:49). The crescent and star appear on all mosques today, on the flags of modern Islamic states, and represents Islâm.

'Umar b. al-Khaṭṭāb Is Converted

In 616 'Umar, destined to be the 2nd Caliph, became a Muslim. 'Umar was strong and stubborn. No one dared attack his friends. At first'Umar had little use for Muhammad. At one point he put on his sword and determined to kill Muhammad. However, a friend, Nu'aym suggested that before he killed Muhammad, he should settle affairs within his own family who had become Muslims. His sister, Fātima, her husband, and nephew, Sa'īd, were all Muslims. Fātima had just been given the manuscript of Tā Hā, Sūra 20. 'Umar wished to see it. Fātima initially refused fearing what he might do with it, but then relented. It began: "*We have not sent down the Korân unto thee, that thou shouldest be unhappy; but for an admonition unto him who feareth God; being sent down from him who created the earth, and the lofty heavens. The Merciful sitteth on his throne: unto him belongeth whatsoever is in heaven and on earth, and whatsoever is between them, and whatsoever is under the earth. If thou pronounce thy prayers with a loud voice, know that it is not necessary in respect to God; for he knoweth that which is secret, and what is yet more hidden. GOD! There is not god but he: he hath most excellent names*" (20:**2-8**). [See also Matthew 6:5-6.] 'Umar read it, became impressed and determined to become a Muslim. News of the rejection of the Quraysh envoys in Abyssinia had recently arrived and this too impressed him. He went back to Muhammad and instead of attempting to kill him, offered himself as a believer. Muhammad now living with his uncle had three formidable body guards, 'Umar, Hamza and 'Alī, devoted to his protection. The addition of 'Umar served to make his defense and prestige more powerful. [305] This incident suggests that the *Korân* was being recorded as it was given.

Persecutions Continue in Mecca

Persecutions continued. When verses in the *Korân* mentioned the tree of al-Zaqqūm, Abū Jahl b. Hishām told the Quraysh, "*It is Yathrib dates buttered. By Allah, if we get hold of them we will gulp them down in one!*" Verses (44:**43-50**) were specifically directed towards him. [306] Muhammad attempted to convert Al-Walīd and spoke with him at some length. He was interrupted by a blind man, I. Umm Maktūm, who wanted Muhammad to recite the *Korân* to him. This distracted Muhammad so much that he frowned and walked away. (80:1-2)

When the 33 families re-entered Mecca after their exile, they either slipped into town and hid or sought the protection of powerful friends. The names of the 33 returnees are known. [307] 'Uthmān b. Maz'ūn sought al-Walīd's sanctuary, but soon rejected it. Abū Salama asked Abū Ṭālib for protection. This relationship remained solid despite objections from the Quraysh. When the exile first began, Abū Bakr left Mecca but shortly ran into Ibn al-Dughunna whose brother was chief of the Ahābīsh tribe. He offered Abū Bakr and his family protection and Abū Bakr returned to Mecca. When the Quraysh confronted al-Dughunna with their objections, Abū Bakr relieved him of his promise. Abū Bakr was then subjected to the insults of the Quraysh.

Muhammad had five principal antagonists in Mecca. [308] He pronounced a curse (hijā) against one: "O God, blind him and bereave him of his son." As the five were going around the Ka'ba Allah told Muhammad: *"Wherefore publish that which thou hast been commanded, and withdraw from the idolaters. We will surely take thy part against the scoffers, who associate with GOD another god; they shall surely know their folly."* (15:**94-96**) All suffered curses. Al-Aswad b. al-MutTālib went blind when Gabriel threw a green leaf in his face. Next Gabriel pointed at Al-Aswad b. 'Abdu Yaghūth's belly. It swelled and he died of dropsy (congestive heart failure or liver failure). When al-Walīd went by, Gabriel pointed at an old scar on his ankle; it opened and he died of it. Next Al-'Ās came along. Gabriel pointed to his instep. On a trip to Tā'if he tied his donkey to a thorny tree and a thorn entered his foot; he died of it. Finally, al-Hārith went by. Gabriel pointed at his head, which filled with pus and killed him (probably a random case of the plague). [309]

George Sale's *Korân* gives a different account of their fates: Al Wālid died of bleeding to death when in his pride, refused to bend over and remove an arrow that had caught in his lower garment. The arrow cut into a heel vein. Al 'Ās died with a thorn stuck in his foot, which then became infected. Oda died of a persistent cough. Al Aswad killed himself by running his head against a thorny tree. Another by the name of Al Aswad went blind. [310]

Despite the hard feelings, the boycott isolating Hāshim and Muttallib from the Quraysh was considered too inhumane and caused a number of the Quraysh to get rid of it. Principal in the effort to remove the boycott was Hishām b. 'Amr. He enlisted the support of four others to assist in lifting the boycott: 1) Zuhayr b. Abū Umayya b. al-Mughīra, 2) al-Mut'im b.'Adīy, 3) Abū'l-Bakhtarī b. Hishām, and 4) Zama'a b. al-Aswad b. al-MutTālib b. Asad. These 5 men then met and resolved to ask the Council to lift the boycott restrictions. Zuhayr presented their case and it was accepted. [311]

Following the lifting of the boycott, the Hāshim and Muttallib were free to return to Mecca, but persecutions continued. The Quraysh never tired of telling anyone they met that Muhammad had done them much harm by dividing their community and breaking up its unity. He was likened to a sorcerer who broke up families. [312] One man, Al-Tufay b. 'Amr Al-Dausi, a traveler, arrived in Mecca and was immediately seized by the Quraysh and told about Muhammad, but he decided not to listen to them. He found Muhammad at the Ka'ba, listened to him, and then followed him home. Muhammad explained Islâm to him and he accepted it. He then went back to his people, the Daus, and by the time of Khaybar he had converted 70 or 80 households all of whom eventually came to Medina. [313]

A similar story is told of 20 Christians who arrived from Abyssinia, found Muhammad and accepted Islâm before they could be propagandized. For this they were ridiculed by Abū Jahl and others who called them names and insulted them. Sūra **28**:51-56 refers to this episode. Part of Sūra **6**:52-54 tells the Meccans not to persecute these Christians. However, those who unknowingly do evil can repent of it and receive God's mercies.

Criticism continued to accuse Muhammad of receiving his "revelations" from Christians because he sat listening to Jabr, the Christian slave of B. al-Hadrami at a booth in al-Marwa. [314] In response God comforted Muhammad: '*We also know that they say, Verily, a certain man teacheth him to compose the Korân. The tongue of the person unto whom they incline is a foreign tongue; but this, wherein the Korân is written, is the perspicuous Arabic tongue*' (**16**:103). Most Arabian Christians likely spoke Arabic.

The Sīra: *The Book of Campaigns*

The *Sīra*, referenced in Introduction of *The Life of Muhammad* pages xiv-xli is known as "The Method of Muhammad." It is an outline of conquest and should be studied carefully as it is the way conquests are to be carried out. According to Mary Habeck, the author of *Jihādist Ideology* when the Prophet was in Mecca and relatively powerless, he held secret meetings with small groups to instruct them in the Muslim way of life. The first phase was the Dawa or the call to Islâm and was peaceful. The second stage or Hejira was the immigration away from Mecca. This represented a migration of the vanguard away from a non-Islâmic society to a place where one could develop without interference or where there is already an intact Muslim society. This is done in the guise of peace involving small cells of true believers. The next step occurred when Muhammad's followers assembled in Medina where a true Islâmic State developed. History shows that when

Muslims arrived in Medina, they became violent and ruthless in their treatment of Infidels and Jews. By this they gained a reputation for terror that would "persuade" others to join them or face death. Once successful with an ever-increasing number of Muslims, war was spread outward across the Arabian Peninsula and into the eastern Mediterranean coasts and northern African shores. Habeck states that the *Korân* includes both peaceful and violent verses which can be used as the situation demands.[315] This pattern appears to be occurring in both Europe and America.

Muhammad's World 610 to 619 AD

In 610 Flavius Heraclius Augustus (575-641) was crowned Emperor of Byzantium and began a rule that would last 31 years. He was the younger of two sons. Both were named Heraclius, of the Armenian Exarch of Africa who had been a general in Maurice's army that had fought the Persians in 590 A.D. In his youth Heraclius fought against lions as a gladiator. He was no stranger to hand to hand combat. In 608 his father disavowed Phocas as his emperor. His general, Nicetas invaded Egypt in 609 and defeated Phocas's forces. While this was underway, Heraclius Jr. sailed to Constantinople where he personally beheaded Phocas and was crowned emperor. Later he was crowned again in St Stephen's Church and married Fabia known as Eudocia; however, she died in 612. He then married his niece, Martina. The populace did not approve of her and she became a devisive factor as the two brothers attempted to rule the Empire. Phocas' policy of appeasement and withdrawal of troops had left an empty treasury and permitted the Slavs and Avars to retake the Balkans and further their conquests of Byzantine Greece and islands in the Aegean. They also began raids against the Anatolian (western Turkish) coasts. Avar troops began invading and looting the last vestiges of the Eastern Roman Empire.

King Chosroes II, also spelled Khosrau II, who had given shelter to one of Maurice's sons, Theodosius, insisted that Heraclius was just another pretender and that the throne did not belong to him. Taking advantage of the chaos in Constantinople, Chosroes launched an attack in northern Mesopotamia against Byzantine forces. When Heraclius responded, the Persians defeated him while taking Damascus, most of Syria in 613, and Jerusalem and Palestine in 614. Both cities were burned, thousands of Christians were slaughtered and many taken to Babylon as slaves. The Church of the Holy Sepulchre was destroyed and the holy cross carted off. This ignited conflict between Jews and Christians in the Arabian Peninsula about the same time Muhammad's followers were fleeing to Abyssinia.

The situation became so desperate that Heraclius considered moving the government to Carthage to avoid the carnage and chaos, but instead he reorganized it giving local governors more autonomy that included raising troops. The Persians were eventually defeated and thrown back to their original borders as were the Avars. Byzantium regained much of its lost territories. [316]

BETWIXT & BETWEEN AD 619 TO 621

The period between 619 and 621 was one of change for Muhammad. After 10 years he had only 100 loyal followers; some had found Islam too difficult and dropped out. 619 was the "Year of Sadness." His support and love of his life, Khadīja, died and his uncle, mentor and guardian, Abū Ṭālib had died within months or days of each other. However, important events that would lead to Medina and his ultimate rise to power were about to occur. Although the ruling tribe of Quraysh was not ready to kill Muhammad, persecution took on a more vicious form. [317] A sheep uterus was thrown at him while he prayed and another was thrown into his cooking pot as he was about to eat. Muhammad's fished it out and tossed it into the street. . *The Life of Muhammad* also clarifies the time line of this period stating that Abū Ṭālib died three years before Muhammad migrated to Medina at the same time the Quraysh became overtly offensive in their treatment of him. [318] We are assured that if Abū Ṭālib had been alive, these offenses would not have occurred. What caused the Quraysh real discomfort were the conversions of Hamza and 'Umar.

When the Quraysh found that Abū Ṭālib was gravely ill, they sent a deputation ('Utba and Shayba, sons of Rabī'a, Abū Jahl and Umayya b. Khalaf, Abū Sufyān plus others to him to see if some kind of compromise could be worked out. They wanted his uncle to persuade Muhammad to leave them alone. In return, they would leave him alone. Muhammad refused to budge. He insisted that the Quraysh state there was no other god besides Allah and repudiate worship of all other gods. Despite Muhammad's urging Abū Ṭālib had not accepted Islâm. [319] It is controversial as to whether he ever did. 38:**1-6** and **5:**77 refer to this incident.

Trip to al-Tā'if and Nakhleh

Muhammad's depression worsened. He traveled to al-Tā'if, a cool hilltop resort town where there is water, but he found no sanctuary. The chiefs, three brothers, one with a Quraysh wife, feared making the Meccan Quraysh angry and chased him out of town. Children threw stones at him and injured his leg forcing him to seek refuge in a nearby village, Nakhleh. Muhammad prayed and recited the *Korân*. Seven Jinns were there and heard his recitations and prayers and became interested and converted to Islâm (**46**:29-35). When they returned to their own city, the town became divided; half converted and the other half did not (72:**1-28**). Before returning to Mecca Muhammad tried finding another protector, but could not. Later that year he returned to Mecca, made a trip to the mosque and warned a number of his former friends. This did not set well with the Quraysh. Muhammad left Mecca again and traveled to Bedouin fairs where he tried to convert them; they were just as resistant as his own people. Sunni chronology indicates that he married Sauda / Sawda bint Zam'a / Zam'ah (571-644) a widowed Muslim loyalist of the Quraysh. She was to be his housekeeper and was said to be plump and happy. The same year he married Abū Bakr's 7-year-old daughter, 'Ā'isha bint Abū Bakr (613-678 AD); she would become his favorite. The marriage was consummated two years later when she was 9.

The "Night Journey and Ascent to Heaven" took place after his trip to al-Tā'if in 619 AD. This has a single line account in the *Korân* (See Sūra 17:**1**). *The Life of Muhammad* describes it in detail. [320] 'A'isha, allegedly said "The apostle's body remained where it was but God removed his spirit by night." [321] Muhammad also said, "My eyes sleep while my heart is awake."

Travels Among the Arabs

As Muhammad traveled to Arab encampments and fairs outside Mecca, his spirits began to rise despite his inability to find a "protector" in Mecca. One of his detractors, 'Abdu'l-'Uzzā b. 'Abdul'l-MutTālib, also known as Abū Lahah, followed him and warned the encampments not to obey or pay any attention to him. [322] Muhammad failed to convert the Kinda, the Kalb, the B. 'Abdullah or the B Hanīfa. The B. 'Āmir b. Sa'sa'a were interested only in who would control after he was gone. Muhammad told them, *"Authority is a matter which God places where He pleases,"* and they declined. However, when they returned home and consulted with their shaykh, he told them,

"O Banū 'Āmir, could it have been avoided? Can the past ever be regained? No Isma'īlī has ever claimed prophethood falsely. It was the truth. Where was your common sense?" Muhammad continued his travels among the Arabs. He also sought prominent visitors to Mecca with the same intent. Muhammad had two converts, Suwayd b. al-Sāmit from Medina and Iyās b. Mu'ādh, but both died. [323]

The Helpers

Despite failures Muhammad persisted. Finally, he met with members of the tribe of Khazraj who were allied with the Jews who lived close to them. Although they were pagans, they knew some Jewish scriptures that predicted the rise of a prophet. After listening to Muhammad, they believed he was the prophet predicted by the Jews. There were six men of the Khazraj who became Muslims and they invited more of their tribe to join them in Medina. In 620 Muhammad and 12 Helpers attended the fair at al-'Aqaba. Here he converted 3 from the B. al-Najjār; 2 from each of the B. Zurayq b. 'Āmir; B. 'Auf, B. Sālim, and 1 from the B. Salima, the B. Sawād, and the Aus. They pledged themselves to the prophet to associate nothing with God. They also pledged not to steal, commit fornication, kill their offspring, slander neighbors, or to disobey Muhammad in what was right. In return, paradise would be theirs. There was no pledge of warfare. They returned to Medina accompanied by Mus'ab b. 'Umayr b. Hāshim b. 'Abdu Manāf who was to be their spiritual instructor and read the *Korân* to them. [324]

The Ansārs

While in Medina As'ad b. Zurara accompanied Mus'ab b.'Umayr and conversed with the B. 'Abdu'l-Ashhal and B. Zafar tribes. When their chief, Sa'd b. Mu'ādh found they were using their territory to preach Islâm, he became angry and sent the other chief, Usayd b. Hudayr with a lance, to chase them out. However, when he arrived, he listened to Mus'ab b. 'Umayr preach and became converted. When he returned, Sa'd criticized him for not carrying out his orders, grabbed the lance and went back. Mus'ab repeated what he had told Usayd and converted Sa'd. This led to the conversion of all men and women of the B. 'Abdu'l-Asbhal. As'ad and Mus'ab returned to As'ad's home and converted most of the Ansār (Arabs of Medina) to Islâm.

Mus'ab and the Ansār went to al-'Aqaba where they met Muhammad. 73 men and 2 women attended the conclave. Muhammad read the *Korân* and called on the people to pledge their allegiance and protection to him. They did. In return Muhammad pledged that he was of them and they were to him. He would wage war against those who made war against them and be at peace with those who were at peace with them. When this group gathered together to support Muhammad, al-'Abbās b. 'Ubāda b. Nadla al-Ansārī told them that they were pledging their lives, property and nobility to support Muhammad and that this would likely mean war. [325] They pledged themselves to the prophet and then asked him what to expect in return. Muhammad said, "Paradise." The names of those at the second 'Aqaba are listed. [326]

This listing shows how rapidly Islâm had increased once Muhammad began gaining support from various outlying Arab tribes and clans. More important, armed fighting men pledged to support Muhammad in his wars. Up to this time he had not been given permission to fight. He had been ordered to preach, call men to Islâm, endure insults and forgive his persecutors. In the early Meccan and mid Meccan periods sūras were generally peaceful and tolerant. Muhammad was now developing an armed force ready to fight. Permission to fight would require an abrogation of all the peaceful verses in the *Korân*. These included some from the late Meccan period that urged continued tolerance, but it was conditional: "*Dispute not against those who have received the scriptures (People of the Book), unless in the mildest manner; except against such of them as behave injuriously towards you: and say, We believe in the revelation which hath been sent down unto us, and also in that which hath been sent down unto you; our GOD and your GOD is one, and unto him are we resigned.*" (**29**:46)

The *Korân* and Contradictions; Law of Abrogation

The problem of cancellation of verses previously given in the *Korân* came up in the late Meccan period. The unbelievers of Mecca had accused Muhammad of insanity, madness and deceit. He had been accused of copying fables of the ancients, perpetrating forgeries and telling lies. Changing verses previously given would only validate such claims. In anticipation of this, new revelations were received:

"When we substitute in the Korân an abrogating verse in lieu of a verse abrogated, (and GOD best knoweth the fitness of that which he

revealeth,) the infidels say, Thou art only a forger of these verses: *but the greater part of them know not truth from falsehood.*" (**16**:101)

GOD shall abolish and shall confirm what he pleaseth. *With him is the original of the book*. (**13**:39)

Verse **29**:46 quoted above urged tolerance UNLESS, those who had received scriptures injured believers. The definition of an injury is subject to interpretation. It is of interest that all our authorities on the chronology of sūras put **16** before **29**. There is another problem. How can the "peaceful" verses from the Meccan period be reconciled with the "fighting" verses of the Medina period? First, we might consider that God is a deceitful plotter.

"*And call to mind when the unbelievers plotted against thee, that they might either detain thee in bonds, or put thee to death, or expel thee the city; and they plotted against thee: but GOD laid a plot against them; and GOD is the best layer of plots.*" (**8:30**) AND "*The hypocrites act deceitfully with GOD, but he will deceive them*;" (**4:142**)

If there are contradictions in the *Korân,* how would anyone believe it? We already know that there are many contradictions, especially those verses regarding peace and tolerance as opposed to those advocating no tolerance and war. The *Korân* says it best: "*Do they not attentively consider the Korân? If it had been from any besides GOD, they would certainly have found therein many contradictions.*" (**4:82**)

Unless Allah is deceitful, the *Korân* could not come from God, because it contains many contradictions. This is what faced Joseph Smith when 116 pages of *The Book of Mormon* were lost. The Lord told him not to re-translate them, but rather leave them out, because the lost text had already been altered by wicked men. If it surfaced later, it would invalidate the entire work. (See *Doctrine & Covenants* 3 and 10).

Many have tried to create a parallel history of Joseph Smith and Muhammad and there are a number of parallels. The first large conversion to Mormonism occurred in Kirtland, Ohio prompting the church to move there – much like Mecca to Medina. In the Missouri War of 1838 Mormons were dispossessed of their property by mob action supported by the Missouri State Militia. Some decided to fight back under the leadership of Sampson Avard and the Danites. After a few skirmishes in which lives and property were lost, the Mormons fled from Missouri to Illinois. Joseph Smith and a few church leaders were imprisoned for instigation of violence, larceny, arson, murder, and treason. Those who came to trial were acquitted and the rest were permitted to escape after 6 months.

Unlike the *Korân*, the Doctrine and Covenants 121, 122, and 123 were given to Joseph Smith while he was a prisoner in the jail at Liberty,

Missouri. Here it is clear that Joseph was told not to fight, but rather use the legal system. Church representatives appealed directly to President Van Buren in 1839, but got no assistance. Sampson Avard was excommunicated in 1839. Later in Nauvoo, Illinois, the Mormons received a charter from the State that included developing the Nauvoo Legion, a force of 5000 men with cavalry and cannon, larger than any state militia then in existence in the U.S., plus a Lt. General commission for Smith. Even following the assassination of Joseph Smith in 1844, Brigham Young and the Quorum of the 12 would not permit its use in any kind of offensive activity. It was used as a deterrent force to stave off attacks while the Mormons left most of their possessions and temple and headed west in 1846 for Upper California and the Salt Lake Valley. 500 members of the Nauvoo Legion were conscripted into the U.S. Army as a unit during the Mexican War. They made the longest military march until that time from Council Bluffs, Iowa, to Leavenworth, Kansas and then to San Diego, California across the entire South West of the U.S in 1846-47. They never fired a shot in anger.

Muhammad faced the same dilemma. Would he begin aggressive raids against the Meccans and their commerce? The law of vengeance or "lex talionis" ("an eye for an eye"), denied by Christ, was in the *Korân* and might be construed to permit aggressive activity against the Meccans, who had persecuted, exiled and stolen their property. Badr (March 624 AD) might be justified. Even though many Jewish leaders were critical of Muhammad, this would not justify raids or outright war against all the Jewish tribes that were wealthy and held large amounts of oasis property around Medina. In addition, they had made peace agreements with Muhammad. By this time, he had already received permission to fight, but there was another matter. Muhammad married his daughter-in-law in May 625 and this was against all custom and was against the *Korân.*

"*Ye are forbidden to marry … and the wives of your sons who proceed out of your loins; and ye are also forbidden to take to wife two sisters; except what is already past: for GOD is gracious and merciful.*" (**4:23**)

There needed to be at least further clarification or a special exception given to Muhammad; and it came:

"*It is not fit for a true believer of either sex, when GOD and his apostle have decreed a thing, that they should have the liberty of choosing a different matter of their own: … But when Zeid* (Zaid – Muhammad's adopted son) *had determined the matter concerning her, and had resolved to divorce her, we joined her in marriage unto thee; lest a crime should be charged on the true believers, in marrying the wives of their adopted sons, Muhammad's adopted son when they have determined the matter concerning them: and the command of GOD is to be performed.*" (**33:36-7**)

Somehow all these inconsistencies regarding Muhammad's personal life and pending warfare against Infidels had to be resolved. The solution lay in a general law of abrogation which came early in the Medina period. Exactly when the doctrine of Abrogation was given is uncertain as Sūra **2** includes references to both the battle of Badr (March 624 **2:217**) and battle of Al-Tā'if (January 630 **2:278-279**).

"***Whatever verse we shall abrogate, or cause thee to forget, we will bring a better than it, or one like unto it. Dost thou not know that GOD is almighty?***" (**2:106**)

Further justification came in fighting and killing unbelievers in raids against Meccan commerce. It was really Allah who was doing the killing, not Muhammad and his followers: "*And ye slew not those who were slain at Bedr yourselves, but GOD slew them. Neither didst thou, O Muhammad, cast the gravel into their eyes, when thou didst seem to cast it* [It was customary for pagan pilgrims going around the Ka'ba to throw gravel in the face of the Devil.]*; but GOD cast it, that he might prove the true believers by a gracious trial from himself; for GOD heareth and knoweth. This was done that GOD might also weaken the crafty devices of the unbelievers.*" (**8:17-18**)

Is Allah also a murderer as well as a deceiver and plotter? The *Korân* says he is. (**4:142; 8:30**; 86:15) As the history of Islâm shows, these characteristics have remained unchanged since the 7th Century and bear no resemblance to the Judeo-Christian God worshiped today. None of this likely escaped Muhammad who was versed in the nature of both the Christian and Jewish gods. His revelation of a single supreme god was grafted onto the pagan Moon God of War.

A plot to deceive the enemy first with peaceful verses when forces are small and resources few, followed by bellicose verses when troops are many and means abound, would be permitted by these verses. This gave Muhammad the upper hand against those who believed in a non-contentious and unchanging god who loved mankind and mistakenly thought that Allah was the same as their god. This is a common mistake made by many Jews and Christians today who do not know their own scriptures or the *Korân.*

Permission to Fight

The first permission to fight is found in sūra **22:39**. [327] "***Permission is granted unto those who take arms against the unbelievers, for that they have been unjustly persecuted by them; (and GOD is certainly able to***

assist them); According to Dr. Rasheed S. Aazzam's chronology, this was given August 623 AD. This is consistent with the *Life of Muhammad*; [328] however, Sūra **22** also includes references to the Battle of Badr (March 624 **22:8-10**).

Although Muhammad had gathered a force of 73 armed fighting men sworn to do his bidding, this was not an army. It could be a very powerful intimidating force in a small town or a highly effective raiding party against small or moderate sized poorly guarded caravans. There followed shortly thereafter or almost coincidental with this permission, the following: "*And* ***fight*** *for the religion of GOD against those who fight against you, but transgress not by attacking them first, for GOD loveth not the transgressors.* ***And kill them wherever ye find them, and turn them out of that whereof they have dispossessed you; for temptation to idolatry is more grievous than slaughter: yet fight not against them in the holy temple, until they attack you therein; but if they attack you, slay them there. This shall be the reward of the infidels.*** *But if they desist, God is gracious and merciful.* ***Fight therefore against them, until there be no temptation to idolatry, and the religion be GOD'S: but if they desist, then let there be no hostility, except against the ungodly.*** *A sacred month for a sacred month, and the holy limits of Mecca, if they attack you therein, do ye also* ***attack them*** *therein in* ***retaliation****; and whoever transgresseth against you by so doing, do ye transgress* ***against him in like manner as he hath transgressed against you****, and fear GOD, and know that GOD is with those who fear him. Contribute out of your substance towards the defense of the religion of GOD, and throw not yourselves with your own hands into perdition; and do good, for GOD loveth those who do good.*" (**2:190-195**)

Note here the principle of the *Lex Talionis*, "an eye for an eye, etc." is restated. This is a declaration of all out religious war against non-believers or infidels. Muhammad now commanded his people to migrate to Medina.

Early Migrations to Medina

The Meccan Quraysh made attempts to block early migration by Muhammad's supporters to Medina. In the year before the pledge at al-Aqaba or AD 620 *The Life of Muhammad* recalls the trials of Abū Salama when he and his family attempted to go to Medina. [329] His in-laws pulled his son away so hard that they dislocated his arm. His wife was detained by her family. In about a year both were permitted to rejoin him. There followed occasional people, then little by little, more and more of Muhammad's followers made the trip to Medina until whole companies of migrants left. After 'Umar b. al-Khattāb and 'Ayyāsh b. Abū Rabī'a al-Makhzūmī left with their families many more followed in waves. This was not easy. It meant leaving one's home behind and a number apostatized. [330] These problems were said to have prompted (**39**:55): "*And follow the most excellent instructions which have been sent down unto you from your LORD, before the punishment come suddenly upon you, and ye perceive not the approach thereof;*"

In the meanwhile, Muhammad stayed behind in Mecca with Abū Bakr and Ali. There were a number of supporters who were restrained from migration including Muhammad. The Quraysh feared that Muhammad was gaining strength in Medina especially from other tribes. There is a story that the Devil visited the leaders of Quraysh in council. Some suggested they imprison Muhammad, but others said this would provoke his followers to attack. Another suggested they drive him out of town, but this was rejected because he was likely to settle with a Bedouin tribe and win them over with his talk. Then the idea of having a warrior from each of the tribes kill him with their swords was suggested. This would cause all the tribes to be responsible for the blood money. This was the preferred plan, but Gabriel warned Muhammad about it and he had Alī lie in his bed wrapped in his green mantle. When the assassins came, they were met by Muhammad at the door and he sprinkled dust on them so that they could not see and recited verses from sūra Ya-Sin 36:**1-9** Sūra **8:29-30** refers to this event and is cited above as demonstrating how Allah can plot. [331]

Following this incident, Muhammad fled Mecca with Abū Bakr and his family into the hills and hid in a cave in the mountains for 3 days. Alī was left behind in Mecca. 100 camels were offered as reward for Muhammad's capture and return to Mecca, but his hiding place was not found and after the excitement of his escape quieted down, they left Mecca. Alī eventually joined them. Most of the Ansār tribe of Medina joined Islâm. [332] According to Sunni chronology Sau'da and 'Ā'isha married Muhammad in 619; however, *The Life of Muhammad* does not mention either as being part of the party that left Mecca for Medina.

MEDINA
AD 622 - 632

"Remember, remember that it is not the work of God that is frustrated, but the work of men; For although a man may have many revelations, and have power to do many mighty works, yet if he boasts in his own strength, and sets at naught the counsels of God, and follows after the dictates of his own will and carnal desires, he must fall and incur the vengeance of a just God upon him." (D&C3:3-4)

Medina was blessed by several oases and wells. It lay on a high desert plateau about 2050 feet above sea level with the Hejaz mountains to the west dominated by Mt. Uhud, which rose more than 2,000 feet above the oasis. Medina was close enough to the major trails coming from the north, south and east towards Mecca to be in a strategic location. Along a trail that ran 100 miles to the south and west lay the Red Sea. About 70 miles from Medina on that trail lay the wells of Badr. Badr was on the overland route from Damascus to Mecca. Medina was initially settled by Jewish tribes and a few Arab tribes that were their vassals for many years. However, with the climatic catastrophe of AD 535 that eventually ruined the Mārib dam and brought the plague, many pagan Arabs migrated north. Several tribes settled in Medina and its environs. Arabs now outnumbered and dominated the Jews in the region and made them their vassals. (See the Map on page 118.)

One hundred eighty miles south (a 10 to 11-day camel caravan trip) and slightly west lay Mecca in a bowl of the Hejaz Mountains. It was about 910 feet above sea level. Its climate was hotter, 45° C or 113° F in summer and its mountains to the west rose only 1200 feet above the town. A 50-mile trail connected it to the Red Sea port city of Jeddah. This gave it many advantages over Medina as a trade center. Overland trails from the east, north, and south plus a short direct connection with the Red Sea intersected the city at about the half-way point between Damascus and Aden. Mecca was controlled by the powerful Quraysh clan and was the holy city for Arabia as it had the Ka'ba or temple of the Moon God, Allah, his consort Shams and their daughters, Allat, Al-'Uzzā, and Manāt plus his retinue of lesser gods. In all, the temple held 360 idols. It hosted the annual hajj, or religious pilgrimage to pay homage to the pagan gods. [333]

The *Hijra*

Muhammad arrived in Medina at noon on Monday the 12th of Rabi'u'l-awwal" in 622 AD. He was 53 years-old. It had been 13 years since God called him. His arrival is significant and is known as the Hijra or migration and marks the beginning of the Islâmic calendar.

Shortly after his arrival Muhammad drafted an agreement that all his followers would release their prisoners with justice and kindness befitting believers. *The Life of Muhammad* uses the phrase, "wrote a document" indicating that Muhammad was not illiterate. [334] This contradicts the *Korân.* (7:157, 158) This document laid out the conditions that were to exist between the Muslims and Medinans and their Jewish neighbors. It separated believers from unbelievers. Jews were to contribute to the cost of war of believers against unbelievers so long as they fought along the side of the believers. No separate peace was to be made. The Jews were required to bear their expenses as were the Muslims. The close friends of the Jews were "as themselves." None were to go to war without Muhammad's permission. Believers were not to go against other believers. They would not aid unbelievers against believers. Believers were to be friends to each other and exclude outsiders. As for the Jews and others, if they followed Muhammad, they were to be treated as equals and their enemies should not be assisted. Those believing in more than one god would not be permitted to take the property of a believer or those under Muhammad's protection. Jews would continue to contribute to the cost of war if they fought with the believers. The Jews of B 'Auf, B. al-Najjar, B. al- Hārith, B. Sa'ida, B. Jusham, B. alAus, B. Tha'laba, and the Jafna, a clan of the Tha'laba and the B. al-Shutayba were considered allies and could continue to practice their religion. The treaty was one of mutual defense as well. [335]

Muhammad developed a system of paired brothers or "helpers." Muhammad took 'Alī b. Abū Ṭālib as his brother. The helper pairs are listed in *The Life of Muhammad.* Abū Bakr was paired with Khārija b. Zuhayr; and 'Umar was paired with 'Itbān b. Mālik; these were at the top of the list. 'Uthmān b. 'Affān was teamed with Aus b. Thābit b. al-Mundhir towards the middle of the list. Those destined to become the first four caliphs of Islâm were Abū Bakr, 'Umar, 'Uthmān and Alī. [336]

Early on, a Mosque was built in Medina and Muhammad then instituted prayer. He first thought that a call to prayer should be by trumpet after the manner of the Jews. Then he decided on a clapper. However, one of his followers went to Muhammad and told him of a dream in which a call to prayer was a voice that said, "*Allah Akbar* (three times) followed by "*I bear witness that there is no God but Allah. I bear witness that Muhammad is the apostle of God. Come to prayer. Come to prayer. Come to divine service. Come to divine Service. Allah Akbar. Allah Akbar. There is no God but Allah.*" 'Umar also reported having the same vision. [337]

Although agreements had been made with the Arab tribes that had converted to Judaism, many of their rabbis did not agree that Muhammad was their prophet. They began questioning and confusing their people over what was allowed and forbidden. These tribes had Arabic not Hebrew names. The tribes with troublesome rabbis were the B. al-Nadīr, B. Tha'laba b. al-Fityaun, B Qaynuqā', the B. Qurayza, the B. Zurayq, B. Hāritha, B. 'Amr b. 'Auf, B. al-Najijār. [338]

There were two notable exceptions, 'Abdullah b. Salām and Mukhayrīq. Both were rabbis and both were well to do. Because of the activity of the questioning rabbis some hypocritical Arabs also joined in the questioning about Muhammad's sanity and possible lying. However, there was another problem, more personal, but serious. Muhammad was developing a need for women and enlarging his harem.

MUHAMMAD'S WIVES AND WOMEN

Introduction

In ancient societies men and women had relatively fixed roles. There is archaeological evidence that in the early Stone Age, men formed themselves into groups or tribes. A single man and woman with a family would find themselves defenseless against other men and the larger carnivorous animals. Hunting and gathering was safer as a group activity. Tribes can still be found operating much as they did in ancient times. These exist in some of the smaller more primitive islands of the Pacific, in the equatorial jungles, remote deserts, and tundra of the far north, and the high mountain areas of Asia. Within tribes, ancient man hunted and fought. Women gathered, raised the children and managed the household. The labor of each directly benefited the tribe. There was little specialization. Marriage customs varied depending on the tribe; however, fertility was valued and worshiped. Tribes varied in size from about 10 households to several hundred. Territories were guarded and warfare between tribes was common and often brutal. Life was not easy for either sex. The number of fighting men skilled with the use of weapons in a tribe was very important. As previously mentioned, the book of Numbers in the *Bible* includes an accounting of armed fighting men over 20 years-old apart from heads of household. (Num 1:2-3, 21)

With the advent of farming larger tribes congregated close to fertile land and major fresh water sources. Land became valuable territory with boundaries that could be defended. Surpluses and wealth developed as society became more specialized. This led to villages, cities, nations, governments, nobility, armies, and trade. With the end of the last great ice-age many of these collected in river valleys in the earth's temperate zone. By the time of Abraham (2000 BC) agriculturally sophisticated civilizations with domesticated animals, bronze age weaponry and tools, post and lentil architecture, and wheeled vehicles were found along the Tigris & Euphrates Rivers, the Indus valley, the Yellow and Yangtze Rivers in Asia and the Nile River (upper and delta regions) in Africa. Climate and geography favored sea lanes between these major civilizations. As the climate began to warm a land route, the Silk Road, also developed between China, the Indus Valley, Persia, Babylonia, Saba, and Egypt. Organized warfare with armies developed. Piratical activities threatened maritime and land commerce. Control of these regions and their trade routes meant control of commerce and greater wealth.

Despite these developments, marriage customs changed little. Monogamy, polygamy, and polyandry were practiced. Mankind knew well before the dawn of history that women had their monthly courses that could be predicted based on phases of the moon. They knew when a woman was fertile and how reproduction occurred. Fertility became associated with the lunar calendar and other gods used a solar calendar that worked best for predicting seasons for planting, harvesting, trading, and warfare. The mathematics necessary for travel and trade had already determined that we lived on a globe and not a flat surface. Scribes recorded religion, epics, entertainment, commerce and history on clay, stone, and other materials. Astronomy was studied and associated with various gods. There were two large visible heavenly bodies – sun and moon. There were other bright objects in the sky, some moved or wandered (planets) and others were relatively fixed (stars). The Bible mentions the "hosts of heaven." Navigation using them became known early in man's history.

By the time of Moses, about 1500 Bc, Israel, had been nurtured in Egypt in the fertile Nile Delta land of Goshen for 430 years (Exodus 12:40). It had increased in size to the point that nation building was possible so long as they found a land for themselves. The 12 tribes had the ability to swap women easily between them without the need for alliances and marriages between close relatives. According to Numbers, the total census that left Egypt included 600 men armed for war, "thousand," and 3550 households (Num 1:46). Assuming 5 members of each household this would be about 17,750 people with 600 warriors, not counting the Levites which included 580 heads of household, about 2320 total, and 8 fighting men (Num 4:48). This would be about the same number, 20,000, in Nauvoo before Brigham Young's migration west.

Childbirth was a great risk and many women died of it; however, many men often died in hunts, warfare, and the hazards of daily toil. Most first marriages were arranged and the women were purchased from their fathers with dowries or "the bride's price." Women were often betrothed before adolescence and married a few years after their menses began. Only the more mature men could afford a dowry and this meant a surplus of young women when compared with the numbers of mature men. Under such circumstances, polygamy was possible. Man is not monogamous by nature, but a monogamous family works best. Fertility rites were common and mostly for youth, but family law included divorce and serious penalties for adultery.

If a tribe lost a woman, it also meant a reduction in the domestic labor force. In smaller and even medium sized tribes only cousins were available for marriage. Chiefs in danger of assassination found marriage to a very close relative such as a sister safer. Marriage outside a tribe was usually reserved for chiefs who wished to make permanent alliances. It was tougher to attack your sister's or daughter's husband than a total stranger. In such cases, a swap was often arranged, since sending one woman to another tribe meant that if that woman was not replaced, the labor pool was reduced. Such customs continue in the tribal societies that exist in the world today.

By 1500 BC instructions to Moses as written in Leviticus 18 gave new laws that revolutionized marriage and were at least 1500 to 2000 years ahead of their time even among the more technologically advanced nations. Marriage between close family members, brothers, sisters, cousins, aunts, uncles, fathers or mothers was not allowed. In addition, various abominations such as sacrificing children, engaging in homosexual relations and bestiality were prohibited. Adultery, fornication and fertility practices were out. All of this was common in Egypt where Israel had come from (Lev 18:27) and in Canaan where they were headed (Exodus 34:10-16). It was such a scourge that when the Israelites waged war against 7 specific Canaanite tribes, they were to kill every man, woman, child and animal so that the young men of Israel could not marry anyone from these tribes or have any vestige of their culture remaining to contaminate them (Deut 7, 20). This was true "ethnic cleansing" and not uncommon at the time. However, Israel had other rules of warfare that were to be used when fighting anyone else (Deut 20).

Warfare meant slaves, including men women and children. These could be ransomed, sold, or kept. Only a limited number of the best could be kept; however, this also confronted the young unmarried soldier with the possibility of marriage to a captive. Again, Israel was constrained by rules that were ahead of their time. Outside of Israel a man could keep several for sex slaves or a larger number and operate a brothel for profit. The new rules for the Children of Israel banned these options for slave women and children. In Israel a man could marry a captive after permitting her to mourn for a month, but he could not enslave or "merchandise" her. If he decided he did not want her, he had to let her go free (Deut 21:10-14). By 622 Islâm was in the process of developing its own rules with regards to women.

Muhammad's Wives and Others

Many of Islâm today believe that Muhammad's wives after Khadija were simply married to protect them and were not true wives; evidence is otherwise. Their exact number is unknown. He had been married to only one woman from age 25 until she died when he was about age 50. Khadīja / Khadījah was his first wife and his first convert to Islâm. She supported his prophetic calling and may have rescued him from his initial deep depression over it. *Zina*, extramarital and premarital sexual relations, was common in the Arabian Peninsula during these years and before, but we have no indication that Muhammad engaged in it. After Khadījah's death in 620 AD, Muhammad developed a harem. *Korân* **33:50** allowed him to keep all the women he had possessed up to that time. He did not have to adhere to the old custom of spreading his affections evenly among them (**33:51**), but he was permitted no more wives after **33:52**. Some sources find him marrying others after that. A commentary on 13 wives can be found in Ibn Hishām's Notes in *The Life of Muhammad.*[339] Those for whom information is given in this source are marked with an asterisk (*) followed by (**Q** – Quraysh), (**A** – Arab) or (**J** – Jew). This source lists 13 marriages of which 6 were Quraysh (Khadīja, 'Ā'isha, Hafṣa, Umm Habība, Umm Salma and Sauda). There were 6 other Arab women (Zaynab d. Jahsh; Maymūna; Zaynab d. Khuzayma; Juwayriya; Asmā; and 'Amra. Ṣafīya d. Huyay was a Jewish captive. Most information comes from several on-line sources that are noted below. There are several lists.[340]

Rules Pertaining to Wives and "Gifts of the Right Hand"

Then and now a Muslim man may have up to four wives at a time, "*And if ye fear that ye shall not act with equity towards orphans of the female sex, take in marriage of such other women as please you, two, or three, or four, and not more. But if ye fear that ye cannot act equitably towards so many,* [This meant giving each their turn on a rotational basis.] *marry one only, or the slaves which ye shall have acquired. This will be easier, that ye swerve not from righteousness.*" (**4:2-3**)

However, Muslim men are to, "*keep themselves from carnal knowledge of any women* ***except their wives, or the captives which their right hands possess****; (for as to them they shall be blameless: …)*" (23:**5-6**) This assurance is repeated: "*and who abstain from the carnal knowledge of women other than their wives, or the slaves which their right hands possess (for as to them they shall be blameless; but whoever coveteth any woman besides these, they are transgressors):*" (70:29-31) Many Muslim men interpret this to mean they can have any non-believing woman they conquer for a night without counting against them. The "gift of the right hand" is a woman taken in battle as a slave. [A man can have as many "gifts of the right hand" as he can acquire. This included many not counted as battlefield brides.]

Muslim men are restricted in their choice of a marriage partner. "*Marry not women whom your fathers have had to wife (except what is already past)* [These rules did not apply to Arabs before the *Korân*.]: *for this is uncleanness, and an abomination, and an evil way. Ye are forbidden to marry your mothers, and your daughters, and your sisters, and your aunts both on the father's and on the mother's side, and your brother's daughters, and your sister's daughters, and your mothers who have given you suck, and your foster-sisters, and your wives' mothers, and your daughters-in-law which are under your tuition, born of your wives unto whom ye have gone in (but if ye have not gone in unto them it shall be no sin in you to marry them), and the wives of your sons who proceed out of your loins; and ye are also forbidden to take to wife two sisters; except what is already past: for GOD is gracious and merciful. Ye are also forbidden to take to wife free women who are married,* ***except those women whom your right hands shall possess [those taken in war]*** *as slaves. This is ordained you from GOD. Whatever is beside this, is allowed you; that ye may with your substance provide wives for yourselves, acting that which is right, and avoiding whoredom. And for the advantage which ye receive from them, give them their reward, according to what is ordained: but it shall be no crime in you to make any other agreement among yourselves, after the ordinance shall be complied with; for GOD is knowing and wise.*" (**4:22-25**) This is not unlike the marriage restrictions found in Leviticus 18. In the ancient world it was also customary for the victorious soldiers to rape the women in the loser's camp following a battle. **4:25** was inspired by events following the massacre of the Banu Qurayza, in May 627 AD. This was the last remaining Jewish Tribe in the Medina area. For details see the chapter on the Beginning of the 1300 Years' War, Battles and Raids, #19. The Raid on the Banu Qurayza, April 627 AD. This raid is also described in detail in *The Life of Muhammad.*[341]

However, when it came to Muhammad, there were exceptions to these rules. "*O prophet, we have allowed thee thy wives unto whom thou hast given their dower, and* ***also the slaves which thy right hand possesseth****, of the booty which GOD hath granted thee; and the daughters of thy uncle, and the daughters of thy aunts, both on thy father's side and on thy mother's side, who have fled with thee from Mecca, and any other believing women, if she give herself unto the prophet; in case the prophet desireth to take her to wife. This is a peculiar privilege granted unto thee, above the rest of the true believers.* **[This is an exception granted to Muhammad only. Other true believers were limited to 4 wives plus slave-girls received as the spoils of war.]** *We know what we have ordained them concerning their wives, and the slaves whom their right hands possess: lest it should be deemed a crime in thee to make use of the privilege granted thee; for GOD is gracious and merciful. Thou mayest postpone the turn of such of thy wives as thou shalt please, in being called to thy bed; and thou mayest take unto thee her whom thou shalt please, and her whom thou shalt desire of those whom thou shalt have before rejected:* **[This is another break in custom; married women were to have the privilege of their husband's attentions on a rotational basis. See 4:3.]** *and it shall be no crime in thee. This will be more easy, that they may be entirely content, and may not be grieved, but may be well pleased with what thou shalt give every of them: GOD knoweth whatever is in your hearts; and GOD is knowing and gracious. It shall not be lawful for thee to take other women to wife hereafter, nor to exchange any of thy wives for them, although their beauty please thee; except when thy right hand shall possess: and GOD observeth all things.*" **[Muhammad is not to take any more wives after this sūra.] (33:50-52**)

"Ā'isha remarked, "It seems to me that your Lord hastens to satisfy your desire." [*Sahih Muslim* vol.[2] book 8 no.3453-3454 p.748-749.] Some Muslim sources declare that every one of Muhammad's marriages were for humanitarian or alliance purposes or for the care of widows. 'Ā'isha and Hafsa were daughters of powerful chiefs, Abū Bakr and 'Uthmān. Muhammad needed their support. Both became Caliphs following Muhammad's death. Most of the widows were allegedly young and pretty. Then there are Safiyah and Zainab bint Jahsh about whom you will read. They do not seem to fall into these categories of benevolence. The sources used here are from *The Life of Muhammad*, the *Hadiths*, or the *Korân*.

Brief Biographical Sketches of Muhammad's Wives

The following list of Muhammad's wives is from the Muslim scholar, Alī Dashti. He probably based much of this on an earlier list in the History of al-Tabari vol.9 p.126-241. It should be mentioned that scholars and Hadiths are not entirely agreed on the wives of Muhammad. For example some hadiths (not *Bukhari* or *Sahih Muslim*) mention a couple of wives of Muhammad that he divorced, and these are not shown here. Nonetheless, Alī Dashti's list, while perhaps not entirely agreed upon as being comprehensive, shows many of the wives. Following this is the evidence from the hadiths, independent of Alī Dashti, for these relationships.

List of Wives

* Consummated; **Q**uarysh; **A**rab; **J**ewish; **C**hristian

1. Khadīja/Khadījah bint Khuwailid/Khywaylid–died first sometime about 618-9 AD, towards the end of the Meccan Period. ***Q**
2. Sawda/Sauda bint Zam'a (may have married Muhammad before the consummation with "Ā'isha took place) married 619 AD***Q**
3. 'Ā'isha or Aesha or Aishah–6 to 9 yrs old, 2nd wife by betrothal 619 AD; consummated 620-3.***Q**
4. Omm/'Umm Salama/Salamah***Q**
5. Hafsa/Hafşah***Q**
6. Zaynab/Zainab of Jahsh***A**
7. Jowayriya/Juwairiyya bint Hārith***A**
8. Omm Habība***Q**
9. Safiya/Safiyya bint Huyai/Huyayy bint Akhtab***J**
10. Maymūna/Maimuna of Hārith***A**
11. Fatima/Fatema/Fatimah
12. Hend/Hind
13. Asma of Saba***A**
14. Zaynab of Khozayma
15. Habla?
16. Asma of Noman / bint al-Nu'man

Concubines

17. Mary the Christian/Copt – a Concubine at first, may have become a wife * **C**
18. Rayhana/Raihana/Rayhanah bint Zayd/Zaid – a Concubine at first, may have become a wife ***J**

Uncertain Relationship

19. Omm Sharik ***A**
20. Maymūna/Maimuna (slave girl?)
21. Zaynab/Zainab the third?
22. Khawla / Khawlah

Alī Dashti missed at least nine possible other wives. Muhammad married 15 women and consummated his marriages with 13. (*al-Tabari* vol.9 p.126-127) *Bukhari* vol.1 Book 5 ch.25 no.282 p.172-173 said that [at one time] Muhammad had nine wives. Following is a short description of what the hadiths and early Muslim historians say about the wives of Muhammad.

1. Khadīja/Khadījah bint Khuwalid bin Asad bin 'Abdu'l-'Uzzā bin Qusayy (AD 550-619)*Q (Muhammad's 1st wife)

Pronounced **ka-DI-ja** bint Khuwailid/Khuwaylid was noted in Ibn Hisham's *The Apostle's Wives.*[342] Another source is *Sahih Muslim* vol.4 book 29 no.5971-5972 p.1297. Muhammad gave her 20 camels as a dowry. She died in 619 or 620 at the age of 65, three years before 'A'isha married Muhammad. She is mentioned in Bukhari vol.5 book 58 no.164, 165 p.103. Her full name was Khadījah, daughter of Khuwaylid bin Asad bin. 'Abd al-'Uzza bin Qusayy. [al-Tabari vol.39 pages 3 and 127] Khadījah was previously married to Abū Hāla b. Mālik. She bore him Hind b. Abū Hāla and Zaynab. She was also married previously to 'Utayyiq b. 'Ābid bl 'Abdullah b. 'Umar b. Makhzūm. She had 'Abdullah and Jāriya by her second husband.

According to most sources Muhammad was 25 when he married Khadījah. She was 40. 'Ā'isha says that Khadīja took Muhammad to a Christian who read the Gospels in Arabic. [Bukhari vol.4 book 55 ch.17 no.605 p.395] 'Ā'isha was jealous of Khadīja. "*On that, the Prophet remembered the way Khadīja used to ask permission, and that upset him. He said, 'O Allah! Hala!' So I ['Ā'isha] became jealous and said, 'What makes you remember an old woman amongst the old women of Quraysh an old woman (with a toothless mouth) of red gums who died long ago, and in whose place Allah has given you somebody better than her?*" [*Bukhari* vol.5 book 58 no.168 p.105]

Muhammad and Khadīja allegedly had 6 children, Qasim, Zaynab, Ruqaiyyah, Umm Kulthum, Fatimah, and Abdallah. Two boys, Qasim and

'Abdullah died in infancy. They brought up a cousin Alī b. Abū Ṭālib from age 4 and a freed slave Zayd b. Hārithah at age 14.

2. Sauda/Sawda bint Zam'a/Zam'ah bin Qays b. 'Abdu Shams b. 'Abdu Wudd b. Naṣr b. Mālik b. Hisl b. 'Āmir b. Lu'ayy. (AD 571-about 644) *Q (married previously to Abyssinian Christian)

References include [343] Sahih Muslim vol.2 book 8 no.3451 p.747; Bukhari vol.3 book 34 ch.4 no.269 p.154; vol.3 no.853 p.29; Sahih Muslim vol.2 book 7 no.2958 p.651; Sahih Muslim vol.2 footnote 1918 p.748 says that 'Ā'isha was probably married to Muhammad before Sauda when she was 6 or 7, but did not enter Muhammad's house until she was about 9 years old. There is disagreement about whether Muhammad consummated the marriage with Sauda or 'Ā'isha next. [al-Tabari vol.9 p.128-129 says it was Sauda]. She and her previous husband were early converts to Islâm and went into exile, but Sauda's ex-husband, al-Sakrān b. 'Amr b. 'Abdu Shams became a Christian in Abyssinia and died there [al-Tabari vol.9 p.128]. Her husband's brother Sheikh Suhayl of Amir agreed to take her if she gave up Islâm; she refused and Muhammad married her in 620. She became the foster-mother to Muhammad's daughters. 'Ā'isha called Sauda "a fat huge lady". [Bukhari vol.6 book 60 ch.241 no.318 p.300] Sauda was old and feared divorce, so she gave her turn to 'Ā'isha. Abū Dawud vol.2 no.2130 p.572 The Korân 4:128-130 possibly pertains to this. Sauda is mentioned in al-Tabari vol.39 p.169. Some believe she was little more than a housekeeper. Muhammad gave her 400 dirhams as a dowry. Although plump she had a jolly, kindly disposition. One source claims she lived until the end of Umar's reign as caliph. [344] Other sources claim she died in 633 AD. Some sources claim she had 6 children. [345]

3. 'Ā'isha bint Abū Bakr (613-678 AD)*Q

There are many sources about 'Ā'isha bint Abū Bakr. [346] 'Ā'isha was Abū Bakr's daughter. Her mother was named Umm Ruman according to *al-Tabari* vol.9 p.129. She married Muhammad in Mecca when she was 6 or 7 years old and went to his house when she was 9. Her father married her to Muhammad who gave her 400 dirhams as a dowry [1 dirham = 4g silver or 0.1411 oz. This is 56.44 oz. of silver or about $1693 at $30 per ounce]. [Bukhari vol.7 book 62 ch.60 no.88 p.65; Sahih Muslim vol.2 book 8 no. 3309, 3310, 3311 p.715, 716]. Abū Bakr, 3rd convert to Islâm, became Caliph when Muhammad died in 632 AD. 'Ā'isha is mentioned in many places, including *Sahih Mus*lim vol.1 book 4 no.1694 p.372; Abū Dawud vol.1 no.1176 p.305; vol.1 no.1268 p.335; vol.1 no.1330 p.350; Abū Dawud vol.1 no.1336 p.351; vol.1 no.1419 p.373; vol.2 no.2382 p.654. Muhammad came to know her thus, "You have been shown to me twice in my dream. I saw you pictured on a piece of silk and someone said (to me). 'This is your wife.' When I uncovered the picture, I saw that it was yours. I said, 'If *this is from Allah, it will be done.*'" [Hadith, Sahih Bukhari 5:58:235]

Most sources say 'Ā'isha was nine when her marriage was consummated. However, Muhammad practiced *mufa'khathat* or "thighing" with her according to several sources. It was also acceptable in Islâm then and now for Muslim men to marry pre-pubescent girls. [347] The *Korân* states: "*As to such of your wives as shall despair having their courses* **[no longer having menses]**, *by reason of their age; if ye be in doubt thereof, let their term be three months: and* ***let the same be the term of those who have not yet had their courses****. But as to those who are pregnant, their term shall be, until they be delivered of their burden* "(**65:4**). See **33:49** for rules involving annulments. Abū Bakr's daughter Umm Kulthum was born to his wife Habība bint Zaid Ansāri after his death and married 'Umar in 639 AD. 'Ā'isha's half sister would have been 5 years-old at the time of her marriage according to Shia sources. [348] More evidence for 'Ā'isha's youth include: 'Ā'isha played with dolls while Muhammad was present. [Sahih Muslim vol.4 book 29 no.5981 p.1299] 'Ā'isha was 6 (or 7) years old when she was married, and the marriage was consummated when she was nine years old. [al-Tabari vol.9 p.130, 131] 'Ā'isha was married when she was six years old, and nine when she went to Muhammad's house. [Ibn-i-Majah vol.3 no.1876 p.133] 'Ā'isha was seven years old when she married, nine years old when she lived with Muhammad, and 18 years old when he died. [Ibn-i-Majah vol.3 no.1877 p.134] A rationale for 'Ā'isha's marriage is given in Sahih Muslim vol.2 footnote 1859 p.715: as being an exceptional event. Another excuse was that Islâm did not define puberty since it varies from one country and race to another. They also mention support from the disreputable Kinsey report on *Sexual Behaviour in the Human Female*. Some sources claim that she was 17 when she married Muhammad. Her death date is also disputed by some – anywhere from 670 to 680 AD. [349]

Muhammad once deliberately struck 'Ā'isha "on the chest which caused me pain". [Sahih Muslim vol.2 book 4 ch.352 no.2127 p.462.] There was other discord. One incident, started by 'Ā'isha and Hafsa was so reprehensible that Muhammad did not visit his wives for 29 days. [Ibn-i-Majah vol.3 no.2060 p.241. Ibn-i-Majah vol.3 no.2063 p.243.] 'Ā'isha is mentioned as an important source to those later interested in the early history of Islâm. [350]

'Ā'isha's Slaves

'Ā'isha had at least one servant who cooked for her during the time of the delegation from Banu'l Muntafiq. [Abū Dawud vol.1 no.142 p.34] 'Ā'isha had a male Muslim slave she later freed named Abū Yunus. [Sunan Nasa'i vol.1 no.475 p.340] 'Ā'isha had a slave girl. [Abū Dawud vol.1 no.371 p.96] Barirah was a female slave of 'Ā'isha's, whom she later freed. [Abū Dawud vol.2 no.2223 and footnote 1548 p.601]. 'Ā'isha was quick-tempered. She struck the hand of a servant for breaking a bowl of food for Muhammad from another wife. [Abū Dawud vol.2 no.3560-3561 p.1011]. 'Ā'isha's voice was strong and loud. [al-Tabari vol.17 p.65]

'Ā'isha freed many slaves because of an allegedly broken unstated vow. "*He* [Ibn Az-Subair] *sent her* ['Aisha] *ten slaves whom she manumitted* [freed] *as an expiation for* (not keeping) *her vow.*" 'Ā'isha freed more slaves for the same purpose till she released forty. She said, '*I wish I had specified what I would have done in case of not fulfilling my vow when I made the vow, so that I might have done it easily.*'"(1) Footnote (1) says, "*'Ā'isha did not specify what she would do if she did not keep her promise, this is why she manumitted so many slaves so that she might feel at ease as to the adequacy of her expiation.*" [*Bukhari* vol.4 book 56 ch.2 no.708 p.465.]

The Hadiths do not tell us how many slaves 'Ā'isha had, or how much money she payed to buy forty slaves? Two clues are: 1) Muhammad's wives could command that tents be set up [Ibn-i-Majah vol.3 no.1771 p.67]. 2) One-fifth of the war booty sent to the treasury was Muhammad's to use as he saw fit. This included family purposes or for distribution to the poor [Sahih Muslim vol.2 no.2347,2348; vol.2 footnote 1463 p.519; Bukhari vol.4 book 51 ch.80 no.153 p.99; vol.6 book 60 ch.297 no.407 p.379].

4. 'Umm Salama (597-681AD)*Q (Widow of Abü Salma b Abdu'l-Asad)

'Umm Salama bint Abū Umayyah b. al-Mughīra bin al-Makhzūmīya also known as **Hind** is mentioned in many sources. [351] She discussed intimate things with the apostle [*Sahih Musli*m vol.2 no.2455 p.540]. Her full name is found in al-Tabari vol.9; p.133; vol.39 p.175. Her status as a wife is controversial according to a few, but not most. [Sahih Muslim vol.2 no.2992 p.656; vol.2 no.3445 p.746; wife Bukhari vol.4 book 53 ch.4 no.333 p.216; Bukhari vol.7 book 62 ch.34 no.56 p.40. Ibn-i-Majah vol.2 no.1634 p.473; *Abū Dawud* vol.1 no.383 p.99]. Muhammad was married to Umm Salama, widow of Abū Salama [*Al-Tabari* vol.39 p.175.]. Umm Salama died in 59 H. (AD 681) at the age of 84 [Sahih Muslim vol.2 footnote 1218 p.435]. Umm Salama was Muhammad's cousin. Her first husband, Abū Salama b. Abdu'l-Asad also known as Abdullah was also one of Muhammad's cousins. They were among the first to join Islâm and participated in the Abyssinian exile. When they returned, they sought refuge with Abū Ṭālib until he died. She and her son were captured and kept prisoner. When she and Abū Salama reached Quba they married. They had 4 children (Salma, 'Umar, Zaynab) and she was pregnant with Ruqayya when Abū Salama was killed at Uhud. Abū Bakr and 'Umar offered to marry her, but she wished to be with her husband in paradise, but Muhammad married her when she was 29 (March AD 626) just before her daughter Zainab bint Abū Salama was born [*Sahih Muslim* vol.2 no. 3539-3544 p.776-777]. Muhammad's dowry to her consisted of a bed stuffed with palm-leaves, a bowl, a dish and a hand mill. This may be the same woman as Zainab bint Umm Salama. This wife of Muhammad is mentioned in Abū Dawud vol.1 no.274 p.68; vol.3 no.4742 p.1332; vol.2 no.2382 p.654; Sunan Nasa'i vol.1 no.240 p.228; Ibn-i-Majah vol.3 no.1779 p.72; al-Tabari vol.17 p.207; al-Tabari vol.39 p.80. 'Umm Salamah had a son before she married Muhammad. Her son went with 'Ā'isha [al-Zubayr and Talhah. al-Tabari vol.17 p.42]. Clients of Umm Salamah were Nabhan (Abū Yahya) and Ma'in bin Ujayl (-Abū Qudamah) al-Tabari vol.39 p.320. Another source lists her death at age 84 in 683. The Wives of the Prophet by Sr. Ruqaiyyah Waris Maqsood is another source. [352]

5. Hafsa/Hafṣah (AD 607-668)*Q (Widow of Khunays b. Hudhäfa al-Sahmï)

Hafṣah bint 'Umar was the daughter of 'Umar bin Khaṭṭāb, 2nd Caliph. She is mentioned in many sources. [353] These include: *Sahih Muslim* vol.2 no.2642 p.576; vol.2 no.2833 p.625; vol.2 no.3497 p.761; Abū Dawud vol.2 no.2448 p.675; vol.3 no.5027 p.1402. She was the beautiful 18-year-old widow of Khunais ibn Hudhāfa Ibn Qays as-Sahmī Al Khaṭṭāb, killed at Uhud. Mohamed married her in 624-5 and gave her 400 dirhams as a dowry. She was born in 607, and died, depending on the source–either in 647/648, 661/662, or 665. She is also mentioned as a wife in Ibn-i-Majah vol.3 no.2086 p.258. After Hafṣa's husband died of his wounds, 'Umar wanted her to marry 'Uthmān or Abū Bakr, but they declined because Muhammad wanted her. They married in 3 A.H. AD 625 when she was 20. She was four years older than 'Ā'isha. [Sunan Nasa'i vol.1 #32 p.117.] Some say that Muhammad married most if not all his harem wives to take care of them, but in this case Hafsa had other options. She was said to be well educated and had a quick temper. 'Umar told his daughter Hafsa not to be misled by 'Ā'isha who is proud of her beauty and Muhammad's love for her [Bukhari vol.7 book 62 ch.106 no.145 p.108]. Hafsa said to 'Ā'isha "I have never received any good from you!" [Bukhari vol.9 book 92 ch.5 no.406 p.299-300]. 'Umar said Muhammad divorced Hafşah (revocable divorce) and then took her back [Abū Dawud vol.2 no.2276 p.619. & al-Tabari vol.9 footnote 884 p.131]. This probably refers to the incident with Mary the Copt. According to some sources Hafsa ordered one of her slave girls killed because she had used sorcery against her [Muwatta Malik 42.19.14]. Hafsa died when she was 60 years old [al-Tabari vol.39 p.174]. Other sources indicate she was 63 years old at death. Some say she died in 665. She was allegedly the final guardian of the *Korân* before its publication.

6. Zainab/Zaynab bint Jahsh (593- 641 AD)*A (previously married to Muhammad's adopted son)

Zaynab "Barrah" bint Jahsh married Muhammad February 627. [354] References include: Sahih Muslim vol.2 no.2347 p.519; vol.2 no.3330 p.723,724; vol.2 no.3332 p.725; vol.2 no.3494 p.760; Bukhari vol.3 book 33 ch.6 no.249 p.138; vol.3 no.829 p.512; vol.4 no.6883 p.1493. Her original name was "Barrah", but Muhammad changed it to Zainab [Bukhari vol.8 book 72 ch.108 no.212 p.137; Abū Dawud vol.3 no.4935 p.1377-1378]. Abū Dawud vol.1 no.1498 says Juwairyiha's name used to be Barrah. She was born in 588 or 593 depending on sources. She married Muhammad in 627 at the age of 30 or 35. [355]

Zainab was reputedly to have been very beautiful and the wife of his adopted son, Zayad. Despite this, Muhammad wished to marry her. Marriage to a son's wife was against the custom and morality of the region, but the *Korân* of the Medina changed this for Muhammad: "*It is not fit for a true believer of either sex, when GOD and his apostle have decreed a thing, that they should have the liberty of choosing a different matter of their own: and whoever is disobedient unto GOD and his apostle, surely erreth with a manifest error. And remember when thou sadist to him unto whom GOD had been gracious, and on whom thou also hadst conferred favours, Keep thy wife to thyself and fear GOD: and thou didst conceal that in thy mind which GOD had determined to discover, and didst fear men; whereas it was more just that thou shouldest fear GOD. But when Zeid (Zaid) had determined the matter concerning her, and had resolved to divorce her, we joined her in marriage unto thee; lest a crime should be charged on the true believers, in marrying the wives of their adopted sons, Muhammad's adopted son when they have determined the matter concerning them: and the command of GOD is to be performed. No crime is to be charged on the prophet, as to what GOD hath allowed him, conformable to the ordinance of GOD with regard to those who preceded him (for the command of GOD is a determinate decree), who brought the message of GOD, and feared him, and feared none besides GOD: and GOD is sufficient accountant"* (**33:36-39**). Her name is not mentioned. She is identified only as Zaid's wife.

The Hadiths provide further comment: Zainab bint Jahsh was married to Muhammad's adopted son, until Muhammad spoke the Sūra that she was to divorce his son and marry him. Zainab "*used to boast before the other wive*s of the Prophet and used to say, 'Allah married me (to the Prophet) in the Heavens'" [Bukhari vol.9 book 93 ch.22 no.517 p.382. Also vol.9 book 92 ch.22 no.516,518 p.381-383; al-Tabari vol.9 p.133].

Zainab of Jahsh had a brother who died before her [Abū Dawud vol.2 no.2292 p.624]. A statement that Zaid divorced his wife so that Muhammad might marry her is noted [al-Tabari vol.39 p.180-182]. Zainab bint Jahsh died at age of 53 [al-Tabari vol.39 p.182]. Zainab bint Jahsh should not be confused with Zainab who was Abū Sa'id al-Khudri's wife [Ibn-i-Majah vol.3 no.2031 p.223].

Zainab verbally abused 'Ā'ishah, so Muhammad told 'Ā'ishah to abuse her. "…The Apostle of Allah (may peace be upon him) came upon me ['Ā'ishah] while Zainab daughter of Jahsh was with us. He began to do something with his hand. I signaled to him until I made him understand about her. So he stopped. Zainab came on and began to abuse 'Ā'ishah. She prevented her, but she did not stop. So he (the Prophet) said to 'Ā'ishah: Abuse her. Then she abused her and dominated her. Zainab then went to 'Alī and said: 'Ā'ishah abused you and did (such and such). Then Fatimah came (to the Prophet) and he said to her: She is favorite of your father, by the Lord of the Ka'bah! She then returned and said to them: I said to him such and such, and he said to me such and such. Then 'Alī came to the Prophet (may peace be upon him) and spoke to him about that." [Abū Dawud vol.3 no.4880 p.1364-1365.] Following Muhammad's marriage to Zainab, the Korân forbade him to marry other wives, except those which he might take as slaves in battle, "I*t shall not be lawful for thee to take other women to wife hereafter, nor to exchange any of thy wives for them, although* *their beauty please thee; except when thy right hand shall possess: and GOD observeth all things.*" (**33:52**) Despite this, several more marriages took place as noted below.

7. Juwairiya/yya/yah (608 – 672)*A (Captive B. Muşţaliq of Khuzā'a)

Juwayriya bint al-Hārith b. Abū Dirār al-Khuza'iya was a captive taken during the raid against the B. Muşţaliq of Khuzā'a. There are many references to this marriage including *The Life of Muhammad.* [356] She was originally given by lot to Thābit b. Qays b. al-Shammās al-Anşārī, who wrote her a contract of redemption. She took this to Muhammad and asked him for help in the matter. He proposed, she agreed and they married in December 626 [Bukhari vol.3 book 46 ch.13 no.717 p.431-432]. Another source says that Muhammad attacked the Bani Muşţaliq tribe without any warning while they were heedlessly grazing their cattle. Juwairiya was a daughter of the chief [Sahih Muslim vol.2 no.2349 p.520; Sahih Muslim vol.3 no.4292 p.942; Abū Dawud vol.2 no.227 p.728; al-Tabari vol.39 p.182-183]. They also say Juwairiya/Juwairiyyah was captured in a raid on the Banu Muşţaliq tribe. She had been married to Musafi' bin Safwan, who was killed in battle. Muhammad's wife Juwairiya used to be named Barrah [Abū Dawud vol.1 no.1498 p.392]. Some sources say Zainab's name used to be Barrah. Juwayriyyah bint al-Hārith bin Abi Birar bin Habīb, great grandson of Jadhimah al-Muşţaliq of the Khuza'ah group. She became booty when Muslims raided the al-Muşţaliq tribe in AH 6 (AD 628). Her husband, Musafi' bin Safwan Dhu al-Shuir bin Abi Asrb bin Malik bin Jadhimah died in the battle. She agreed to marry Muhammad [Bukhari vol.8 book 72 ch.107 no.212 p.137; Abū Dawud vol.3 no.4935 p.1377-1378; al-Tabari vol.39 p.182-183; al-Tabari vol.9 p.133]. She was 20 years old [al-Tabari vol.39 p.184.] Because of this union, it was said that 100 families of the B. Muşţaliq accepted Islâm. [357]

It is said that her father came with a camel as ransom to release his daughter. Muhammad took the ransom, but asked why he had held out two others. Al-Hārith stated that there was no way anyone could have known this except a prophet. He then handed them over, gave permission for the marriage of his daughter to Muhammd, and immediately converted to Islâm. Muhammad gave her 400 dirhams as a dowry. She died in 670 or 676 at the age of 64. [358]

If the above information on marriage and age at marriage is correct, her death date would have been in 672 given an age of 64. This source states she was married in 628 to Muhammad either at age 16 or 22. All captives from her tribe were set free.

8. Omm/Umm Habība (594-673)*Q (Husband, Khalid b. Sa'id b. al-'Äs, converted to Christianity)

Umm Habība or **Ramlah bint Abu Sufyān** married Muhammad in April 628 by proxy and joined him after the battle of Khaybar. She died in 666 at 73.[359] She does not appear in Alī Dashti's list of wives. She was the daughter of Abū Sufyān ibn Harb and Hend/Hind Utbah**.** The Negus gave her 400 dirhams in behalf of Muhammad as a dowry. There are many references to this marriage.[360] [*al-Tabari* vol.9 p.133; Sahih Muslim vol.2 no.3413 p.739; vol.2 no.2963 p.652; Sahih Muslim vol.2 no.1581 p.352; vol.2 no.3539 p.776 Ibn-i-Majah vol.5 no.3974 p.302; al-Tabari vol.17 p.88]. Umm Habība was 23 years younger than Muhammad. [Sunan Nasa'i vol.1 #60 p.127.] She and her first husband 'Ubaydullah b. Jahsh al-Asadī were Muslims who went to Abyssinia; however, while they were there 'Ubaydullah converted to Christianity [al-Tabari vol.39 p.177]. Mention of Zainab bint Jahsh is noted [al-Tabari vol.39 p.180-182]. Umm Habība, wife of Muhammad, should not be confused with another woman who was also named Umm Habība. She was the daughter of Jahsh, wife of 'Abd al-Rahman and sister-in-law of Muhammad, since Zainab of Jahsh was his wife [Abū Dawud vol.1 no.288 p.73].

9. Safiya/Safiyya/Saffiya (611-673)*J (Slave-Girl Convert; Husband tortured to death; battle of Khaybar)

Safiyya d. Huyayy b. Akhtab was a Jewess taken as a "slave-girl" during the battle of Khaybar.[361] Some say she was born AD 610 and died in 670. She was 17 when she was captured. Despite her loyalty to Judaism, she converted to Islâm under pressure. Her father was Huyayy ibn Akhtab, the Banu Nadir chief in Medina. Her mother was Barra bint Samawal of the Banu Qurayza tribe. In 625 the Banu Nadir were expelled from Medina and went to the oasis of Khaybar near Medina. According to *The Life of Muhammad*[362] she was the favorite of her father and uncle Abū Yāsir. She is identified as a wife of Muhammad in *The Life of Muhammad.*[363] It is said that she heard an uncle ask her father what he thought of Muhammad and he replied that he would be an enemy as long as he lived.

When the Meccan and Desert Arab forces besieged Medina during the Battle of the Trench in 627 AD, her father and brother allied with them and were killed. The next year at age 17 she married Kināna ibn al-Rabī' b. Abd'l-Huqayq, the treasurer of the Banu Nadir. In May 629 Muhammad attacked Khaybar. Despite their resistance, lack of preparation and central command problems allowed Muhammad's forces to overcome their fortresses. The Jews negotiated surrender. The land would belong to the Muslims and the Jews would pay over half of their annual production as tribute. However; the agreement did not cover the Banu Nadir tribe. When Muhammad and his followers demanded an alleged secret treasure they believed the Banu Nadir had hidden, Safiya's husband was tortured. A fire was built on his chest and then he was killed. [364] Much of this story is included in the website reference below [Bukhari vol.2 book 14 ch.5 no.68 p.35; vol.4 book 52 ch.74 no.143 p.92; vol.4 book 52 ch.168 no.280 p.175 and al-Tabari vol.39 p.185]. A massacre occurred in which all the males of the Banu Nadir were killed, the town was pillaged and all the women taken as slaves and divided among the troops. Safiyya was captured with two of her cousins. She was raped first by Dihya ibn Khalifa, but Muhammad was smitten by her beauty, threw his mantle over her, chose her for himself, took her to his tent and raped her. Depending on the source, Muhammad gave Dihya the two cousins, or seven head of cattle, or seven female slaves for her. Muhammad suggested that she convert to Islâm. She did and became Muhammad's wife much to the consternation of the other harem wives who shunned her because she was a Jew. They did not believe the sincerity of her conversion. A number of sources validate this; however, Muhammad and 'Umar reaffirmed her conversion. Some sources suggest that Muhammad married her as part of a peace treaty or a gesture of goodwill. She did not have any children with Muhammad. A website reference includes a number of additional references. [365]

Random statements from various sources state: Safiyah's husband was Sallam bin Mishkam bin al-Hakam bin Hārithah bin al-Khazraj bin Ka'b bin Khazraj [al-Tabari vol.9 p.134-135]. Safiyyah was called Safi, "pure" for the first share of the booty, which went to Muhammad [Abū Dawud vol.2 no.2988 p.848; Abū Dawud vol.2 no.2985-2989 and footnote 2406 p.846-849]. Safiyya was purchased by Muhammad for seven slaves [Ibn-i-Majah vol.3 no.2272 p.357]. She was 17 when Muhammad married her [al-Tabari vol.39 p.184]. Muhammad felt kindness toward Safiyya. "If Safiyyah were not grieved, I would have left him [her husband whom Muhammad executed] until the birds and beasts of prey would have eaten him, and he would have been resurrected from their bellies" [Abū Dawud vol.2 no.3130-3131 p.893]. Safiyyah was short [Abū Dawud vol.3 no.4857 p.1359]. She was 17 when Muhammad married her and died at the age of 60 or 64 in 676 AD depending on sources.

There was discord between wives. Zainab did not want to lend a camel to Safiyya when Muhammad asked her to. Zainab called Safiyya a "Jewess" [Abū Dawud vol.3 no.4588 p.1293]. See 49:11. When Safiyya complained to Muhammad about the insult, he allegedly said, "Canst thou not say, Aaron is my father, and Moses is my uncle, and Mohammed is my husband?" – from Al Beidawi, see note #3-page 498 George Sale Translation.

Muhammad had nine wives at one time, including Safiyya bint Huyayy, and later he did not give her a "turn" [Sahih Muslim vol.2 no.3455-3456 p.749]. She is also mentioned in Sahih Muslim vol.2 no.3325; vol.2 no.2783 p.605; vol.2 no.3118 p.678; vol.2 no.3497 p.761; Bukhari vol.3 book 33 ch.8-13 no.251-255 p.139-143; vol.2 book 21 ch.22 no.255 p.143; Ibn-i-Majah vol.3 no.1779 p.72; Abū Dawud vol.2 no.2464 p.681; al-Tabari vol.39 p.169. Safiya bint Abi 'Ubaid Muhammad's wife in Bukhari vol.4 book 52 ch.136 no.244 p.151 is probably the same person. Despite her problems with many of the harem wives she became a close friend of 'Ā'isha. One source states that Safiya said she was the favorite child of her father and uncle, Abū Yasir. It was said that the two went to visit Muhammad and when they returned her father said he would be his enemy as long as he lived. Safiyya was also reputed to be studious and well educated.

After Muhammad died she was involved in the politics of Islâm and became wealthy. She sided with the third caliph 'Uthmān, an Umayyad. When he was besieged in his home, she brought him food and water by crossing a plank between their adjacent dwellings. She defended him to 'A'isha, Alī and al-Zubayr. However, her efforts were to no avail. When she died she left an estate of 100,000 dirhams in land and goods. One third went to her sister's son, a Jew. Her Medina home was bought for 180,000 dirhams by Muawiyya, the caliph who succeeded Ali and the founder of the Umayyad Dynasty. One might say that this wife of Muhammad was clever, patient, and had tremendous survival instincts. In the end she was close to the Umayyad side and against Muhammad and the Hashim. She did not forget her Jewish heritage.

10. Maimūna/Maymūna bint Hārith b. Hazn (595-675)*A (Divorced & Widowed)

Maymūna bint Hārith b. Hazn b. Bahīr b. Huzam b. Ruwayba b. 'Abdullah b. Hilāl b. 'Āmir b. Ṣa'ṣa'a is mentioned in *The Life of Muhammad.*[366] *Sahih Muslim* vol.1 no.1671,1674,1675 p.368-369; vol.2

no.1672 p.[369] gives further reference. Muhammad married Maymūna bint Al-Hārith in 7 A.H (March AD 629) while he was in a state of ritual purity during his pilgrimage to Mecca. [367] She received a dowry of 400 dirhams [*al-Taba*ri vol.8 p.136; al-Tabari vol.9 p.135]. Maymūna had been divorced once, and widowed before marrying Muhammad. One of her husbands was Abū Ruhm b. 'Abdu'l-'Uzzā b. Abu Qays b. 'Abdu Wudd b. Nasr b. Malik b. Hisl b. 'Amir b. Lu'ayy [al-Tabari vol.39 p.185]. Maymūna was 80/81 when she died [al-Tabari vol.39 p.186]. Maimuna was 36 years old and Muhamad was said to be 53 and the time of marriage and died 4 years later. [Sunan Nasa'i vol.1 #43 p.120]. This would make Muhammad 57 when he died, not the reputed 62 years of age that most sources state. Maymūna "screened" Muhammad [Bukhari vol.1 book 5 ch.22 no.279 p.170-171]. People were screened when they bathed or went to the bathroom; this was appropriate for a wife. This wife of Muhammad is also mentioned in: Ibn-i-Majah vol.3 no.2408 p.435; Sunan Nasa'i vol.1 no.809 p.492; vol.2 no.1124 p.108; Abū Dawud vol.1 no.1351 p.356; vol.1 no.1359, 1360, 1362 p.357; Sunan Nasa'i vol.1 no.243 p.229. She was allegedly his last wife to die. One source states she was born in 594 and died 674. [368] Her marriage is mentioned in *The Life of Muhammad.* [369] She was part of a group known as "the Sisters." She was the sister of Umm Fadl, wife of Abbas, the second woman to be converted to Islâm after Khadījah. She married Muhammad after his pilgrimage to Mecca in AD 629 at the age of 28. She died either in AD 671 or AD 681 at the age of 70 or 80. [370] Her marriage to Muhammad prompted **33:50** that gave exceptions to Muhammad about the number of women he could marry. However, he was to marry no more after her. (**33:52**)

11. Fāţima/Fatema/Fatimah

Muhammad married **Fatimah bint al-Dahhak bin Sufyān** (also called al-Kilabiyyah) ['Alī Dashti. *al-Taba*ri vol.9 p.39]. Muhammad also married Fatimah bint Shurayh/Sara'[al-Tabari vol.9 p.139]. It is unclear if Shuray and al-Dahhak were two different people or if they had alternate names for the same father. A woman named Fatimah bin al-Dahhabi, Aliya bint Zahyah, Sana bint Sufyān is mentioned in another source [al-Tabari vol.39 p.186]. Muhammad consummated his marriage with "the Kilabiyyah". This would be Fatimah bint al-Dahhak bin Sufyān or 'Aliyah bint Zabyan bin 'Amr bin 'Awf or Sana bint Sufyān bin 'Awf [al-Tabari vol.39 p.187].

Fāṭima, Muhammad's daughter is different

The following could be Muhammad's wife, but was probably his daughter. In the year of the conquest of Mecca, Fatima screened Muhammad [Ibn-i-Majah vol.1 no.465 p.255 and Sunan Nasa'i vol.1 no.228 p.224; vol.1 no.417 p.307]. A Fatima screened Muhammad while he was bathing [Bukhari vol.1 book 5 ch.22 no.278 p.170-171]. However, Muhammad was taking a bath and was screened by his daughter Fatima [Bukhari vol.4 book 53 ch.29 no.396 p.263]. Fatima was Muhammad's daughter and the wife of 'Alī [Bukhari vol.3 book 34 chg.29 no.302 p.171; Bukhari vol.4 book 53 ch.1 no.325 p.208]. Muhammad did not want 'Alī to marry anyone else besides his daughter Fatima [Ibn-i-Majah vol.3 no.1998-1999 p.202-204]. However, 'Alī later had a captive slave girl, the daughter of Rab'iah, who bore him a daughter named Umm Ruqayyah [al-Tabari vol.11 p.66]. While Muhammad gave many slaves to 'Ā'isha, Fatima thought she got a bad deal. Fatima complained to Muhammad about her having to use a grinding stone and asked for a slave (prisoner of war). Muhammad did not give her one, but he said he gave her something better. He told her to say, "Glory be to Allah" 33 times, "Praise be to Allah" 34 times, and "Allah is most great" 34 times [*Abū Dawud* vol.[3] no.5044-5045 p.1405].

12. Hend/Hind Utbah (formerly married to Abū Sufyān ibn Harb)

Hend/Hind Utbah was married to Abū Sufyān, whom she said was a "very stingy man" [*Sahih Muslim* vol.3 no.4251-4254 p.928-929].[371] Controversy surrounds her being a "wife." or companion (*sahaba*) of Muhammad. Although appearing in Ali Dashti's list of Muhammad's wives, common sources about her make no such claim.[372] She was the mother of Muawiyah I, 5th Caliph and founder of the Umayyad dynasty and Ramlah bint Abū Sufyān, Muhammad's 8th wife. She is mentioned as having mutilated the bodies of Muslim soldiers on the field of Uhud by cutting off "*their ears and noses and*" making them "*into anklets and collars.*" These she gave to Wahshi, the slave of Jubayr b. Mut'im, who had killed Hamza with a javelin. She also attempted to eat the liver of Hamza at Uhud after his death. Some have accused her of adultery with several men, but she eventually found favor with Muhammad when she converted to Islâm with her husband. She is listed in the Index of Proper Names in the *Life of Muhammad* numerous times, but is not listed there as a wife of Muhammad.[373]

13. Sana bint Asma' / al-Nashat*A (marriage for alliance, not consummated)

Muhammad married **al-Nashat bint Rifa'ah** of the Banu Kilab bin Rabi'ah, allies of the Qurayzah. Some called her **Sana bint Asma' bin al-Salt al-Sulamiyyah**; while others say Sana bint Asma' bin al-Salt of the Banu Harm. She died before the Prophet consummated the marriage. She was also called Sana. Al-Tabari vol.9 p.135-136 and al-Tabari vol.39 p.166 say the same thing about Sana bint al-Salt.

14. Zainab/Zaynab bint Khozayma/Khuzaima (595–626)*A (divorced then widowed, died before Muhammad)

Zaynab bint Khuzayma b. al-Hārith b. 'Abdullah b. 'Amr b. 'Abdu Manāf b. Hilāl b. 'Āmir b. Sa'sa'a belonged to the tribe of Banu Hilal and was known as "Mother of the Poor" because of her kindness and concern for them. She was about 16 when she married Muhammad's cousin, Tufayl b. Hārith, but he divorced her. She then married another of Muhammad's cousins Ubaydah b. Hārith b. Muṭṭālib b. 'Abdu Manāf when he was 48 and she was still 16. He died at Badr and in 625 Muhammad married her when she was 33. She was born AD 595 and died in AD 626 at 31. See al-Tabari vol.7 p.150 footnotes 215,216 and al-Tabari vol.39 p.163-164 for more information. Al-Tabari vol.9 p.138 also says she died while Muhammad was alive [Sunan Nasa'i vol.1 #64 p.129]. There is some dispute about her birth date being 592 or 595 AD.

15. Habla?

Habla is on Alī Dashti's list and is listed in a number of on-line lists of Muhammad's wives; however, I cannot verify this marriage from another source.

16. Annulled Asmā' bint Nu'mān*A (married; not consummated)

Asmā bint al Nu'mān bin Abi Al-Jawn, of the Kindite tribe, was married to Muhammad, but the marriage was never consummated and she was returned to her people with a gift. See al-Tabari vol.10 p.185 and footnote 1131 p.185. Internet sources give other information such as she may have had leprosy [al-Tabari vol.9 p.137 &Bukhari vol.7 book 63 no.181 p.131, 132]. Al-Nu'man al-Jawn offered his daughter to Muhammad, but he declined her. This may mean a divorce before consummation [al-Tabari vol.10 p.190; al-Tabari vol.39 p.187].[374]

17. Mary/Māriya the Copt/Christian (–632) *C (sent as gift from Egypt with her sister)

Mary the Copt was a concubine of Muhammad's according to *al-Tabari* vol.9 p.141, 193, 194; *Sahih M*uslim vol.4 footnote 2835. P.135. She was not quartered in Muhammad's harem, but lived elsewhere in Medina. She gave birth to Muhammad's son Ibrahim [al-Tabari vol.9 p.39]. He died when he was two years old. In 628 AD Hatib ibn Abi Balta'ah, a eunuch emissary, returned from Egypt after delivering a letter inviting Al-Muqawqis, ruler in Alexandria, to become a Muslim. He was not persuaded, but honored the letter by sending back two young women, Maria al-Qibtiyya, known by Islâm as Māriya or Mary the Copt, her sister Sirin, garments, and a mule for Muhammad to ride. Hatib invited the sisters to become Muslims; they did [according to Tabari]. Mariyah was beautiful; Muha**mmad kept her and sent her sister Sirin to Hassan b. Thabit, his court poet. Sirin and Hassan were the parents of 'Abd al-Rahman ibn Hassan [al-Tabari vol.8 p.66, 131]. Although Mary was said to have accepted Islâm, Muhammad kept her as a slave-girl or concubine and ordered her to veil. As a slave-girl she was an extra with whom he could bed when he wanted. She died in 637-8 [al-Tabari vol.39 p.**22].[375] Some indicate that Mary had affairs with other men in Medina and that Ibrahim may not have been Muhammad's child. Sura **66:1-3, 5** describes an incident in which Muhammad was caught by Hafsa making love to Mary in the Harem in her bed. Hafsa created uproar in the Harem by reporting this to other wives. Muhammad threatened to divorce Hafsa for gossiping. He punished all his wives by moving in with Mary for a month.

18. Raihāna/Raihāna/Rayhanah bint Zaid/Zayd (aft 613–632) *J (Slave Girl of Banu Qurayza)

Raihāna bint Zaid was a Jewish captive from the raid on the Quraiza tribe in AD 627. She was probably a teenager and reputedly very beautiful. Muhammad offered to make her a wife instead of a slave, but she declined and remained Jewish [al-Tabari vol.8 p.39; al-Tabari vol.9 p.137,141]. Thus she was either a concubine or "slave-girl." However, the source says

Muhammad set her free and then married her [al-Tabari vol.39 p.164-165]. Muhammad had two concubines: Māriya bint Sham'un the Copt, and Rayhanah bint Zayd al-Quraziyyah of the Banu al-Nadir. She died before Muhammad in AD 632.

19. Omm/Umm Sharik / Ghaziyyah bint Jabir*A

Omm/Umm Sharik is the same person as Ghaziyyah bint Jabir. She was also called "Umm Sharik" because she was the mother of a son named Sharik by a previous marriage. [376] [*al-Tabari* vol.9 p.139, &] "When the Prophet found she was an old woman, he divorced her" [al-Tabari vol.9 p.139]. However footnote 922 says Ibn Sa'd in *Tabaqat*, 8 p.110-112 " lists her among the women to whom the Prophet proposed but "postponed" marriage.

20. Maymūna / Maimuna

Maimuna offered herself to Muhammad according to *Sahih Muslim* vol.2 footnote 1919. It could be the same Maimuna as #10, or a different one. She came to Muhammad in 7 AH or AD 629. An unnamed woman said she gave herself to Muhammad as a wife. Muhammad did not accept her, but gave her to a poor Muslim. The only thing the poor Muslim could give as a dowry is his memorization of a sūra of the *Korân*. [*Muwatta' Malik* 28.3.8].

21. Zainab the Third?

Alī Dashti lists this wife, but there is little independent evidence for this marriage.

22. Khawla / Khawlah bint al-Hudayl

Khawlah bint al-Hudayl is said to have married Muhammad [al-Tabari vol.9 p.139]. She was a wife of Muhammad's according to al-Tabari vol.39 p.166. There is little other information.

23. Divorced Mulaykah bint Dawud

Mulaykah bint Dawud al-Laythiyyah was married to Muhammad, but when she was told that Muhammad was the one who had her father killed, she took refuge in Allah from Muhammad, who separated from her [*al-Tabari* vol.8] p.189]. The same thing is said of Mulaykah bint Ka'b (They may be the same person.) in *al-Taba*ri vol.39 p.165. Mulaykah bint Ka'b was married very briefly to Muhammad. 'Ā'isha asked her if she wanted to marry the man who killed her husband. She "took refuge in God" from Muhammad, so Muhammad divorced her [al-Tabari vol.39 p.165].

24. Divorced al-Shanba' bint 'Amr

Al-Shanba' bint 'Amr al-Ghifariyyah married Muhammad. Her people were allies of the banu Qurayza. When Ibrahim died, she said that if he were a true prophet his son would not have died. Muhammad divorced her before consummating the marriage [*al-Tabari* vol.9 p.136].

25. Divorced al-'Aliyyah

'Aliyyah bint Zabyan bin 'Amr bin 'Awf bin Ka'b, stayed for a while with Muhammad before he divorced her [*al-Taba*ri vol.39 p.188]. Muhammad married al-'Aliyyah, but then divorced her. She died while Muhammad was still alive [al-Tabari vol.9 p.138].

26. Divorced 'Amrah bint Yazīd*A (divorced possibly because of leprosy)

'Amra bint Yazīd a Kilab According to *The Life of Muhammad* page 794 she came saying, "I seek God's protection against you," and was immediately returned to her people. No marriage likely occurred [al-Tabari vol.39 p.188]. Other sources claim that Muhammad married 'Amrah bint Yazīd, but there is no mention of divorce [al-Tabari vol.9 p.139]. Others state she was divorced by him [Ibn-i-Majah vol.3 no.2054 p.233 vol.3 no.2030 p.226 (daif [weak], not Sahih)]. Muhammad divorced a woman because she had leprosy [al-Tabari vol.39 p.187].

27. Divorced an Unnamed Woman

Muhammad divorced an unnamed woman because she would peek at those leaving the mosque [al-Tabari vol.39 p.187].

28. Qutaylah bint Qays (Died before consummation)

Qutaylah bint Qays was married by Muhammad but she died before they consummated the marriage. Curiously, it also states she and her brother apostatized form Islâm. So she may have apostatized after the marriage and before her death [al-Tabari vol.9 p.138-139].

29. Sana bint Sufyān

Sana bint Sufyān was briefly married to Muhammad [*al-Tab*ari vol.39 p.188].

30. Sharaf bint Khalifah

Sharaf bint Khalifah, sister of Dihyah bin Lhalifah al-Kalbi was married briefly to Muhammad, but she died while Muhammad was still alive [al-Tabari vol.9 p.138].

31. Women of Muhammad's Right Hand

"*... and who keep themselves from carnal knowledge, except with those joined to them in the marriage bond, or (the captives) whom their right hands possess–for (in their case) they are free from blame,*" Sūra 23:**5-6**. *Ye are also forbidden to take to wife free women who are married, except those women whom your right hands shall possess* ***[those taken in war]*** *as slaves. This is ordained you from GO*D. Whatever is beside this, is allowed you; that ye may with your substance provide wives for yourselves, acting that which is right, and avoiding whoredom. 4:24. "He [Muhammad] replied, 'Conceal your private parts except from your wife and from whom your right hands possess (slave-girls)'" [Abū Dawud vol.3 no.4006 p.1123]; Abū Dawud vol.3 no.4443-4445 p.1244] states that having sex with a slave-girl a man owns is permitted, but a man will be flogged for having sex with his wife's slave-girl unless permitted by his wife. Marriage to a slave girl is unnecessary [Ibn-i-Majah vol.4 no.2551 p.12].

As was typical of wealthy Arab men, Muhammad apparently had need of a few slave girls in addition to the legal limit allowed him according to Bukhari vol.7 book 64 ch.6 no.274 p.210. Severl are mentioned. Salmāh was a maid-servant of Muhammad [Abū Dawud vol.3 no.3849 p.1084]. Maimuna was a freed slave-girl of Muhammad [Ibn-i-Majah vol.3 no.2531 p.514; Abū Dawud vol.1 no.457 p.118]. Muhammad briefly had a "very beautiful" captive before he gave her to Mahmiyah b. Jaz' al-Zubaydi[al-Tabari vol.8 p.151]. It is also said that another slave-girl belonging to Muhammad's house committed fornication with someone else. It is the "someone else" part that was a problem [Abū Dawud vol.3 no.4458 p.1249]. Muhammad reportedly called a black slave-girl to come and conceal Abū Dharr behind a curtain while he was taking a bath [Abū Dawud vol.1 no.332 p.87]. Al-Tabari vol 39 p. 287 mentions Umm Ayman (=Barakah), a slave with whom Muhammad could spend the night. Muhammad was reported to have a good sense of humor. One evening the Prophet got up and urinated an earthenware chamber pot. Later the same evening Umm Ayman became thirsty, got up, and drank from the same vessel. The following morning Muhammad told her, 'O Umm Ayman, take that earthenware vessel and pour away its content.' She replied,'By God, I drank what was in it.' The Prophet laughed until his molar teeth showed, then said 'After this you will never have a bellyache'" [al-Tabari vol.39 p.199].

Rape of captured women following a battle was mentioned following raids against the Banu Nadir, Banū'l-Muşţaliq of Khuzā'a, and Banu Qurayza. Safiya, Muhammad's 9th wife was first subjected to rape by one of his officers and then by Muhammad before he married her. Numerous incidents of this nature are found in this on-line reference. [377] Sources listed are from the Hadith.

Muhammad Did Not Marry Everyone!

'Ā'isha felt jealous of the women who offered themselves to Muhammad as wives [Sahih Muslim vol.2 no.3453 p.748]. It was permitted for a woman to offer herself to Muhammad [Ibn-i-Majah vol.3 no.2000-2001 p.304-305]. Some thought Muhammad married al-Ash'ath, but al-Tabari says this was not true according to al-Tabari vol.39 p.190i. Overall, al-Tabari did a masterful job of trying to keep up with all of Muhammad's women.

Marriage Proposals Declined

Muhammad asked to marry Ghaziyyah on account of her beauty, but she declined. Tabari claims she was in a state of infidelity but provides no evidence [al-Tabari vol.9 p.136]. There is no evidence she was unfaithful and Muhammad was lax in not punishing her, or that she was and Muhammad punished her. Layla clapped Muhammad's shoulder from behind and asked him to marry her. Muhammad accepted. Layla's people said, "'What a bad thing you have done! You are a self-respecting woman, but the Prophet is a womanizer. Seek an annulment from him.' She returned to the Prophet and asked him to revoke the marriage and he did" [al-Tabari vol.9 p.139].

From to al-Tabari vol.9 p.140-141, Muhammad proposed marriage to, but did not marry:

1) Umm Hani' bin Abi Tālib [Hind] because she said she was with child. It is unknown whether Umm Hani' became a Muslim before or after Muhammad asked her to marry him [al-Tabari vol.39 p.197 and footnote 857 p.197].
2) **Duba'ah bint 'Āmir**; she was too old
3) Reportedly he proposed to **Saffiyah bint Bashshamah**, a captive. She was allowed to choose between Muhammad and her husband, and she chose her husband.
4) **Umm Habīb bint al-'Abbas** Since al-'Abbas was his foster brother, it would have been unlawful so Muhammad backed out. This reasoning did not prevent him from marrying **Zaynab bint Jahsh**, his foster son's wife.
5) **Jamrah bint Al-Hārith**. Her father claimed she was suffering from an illness. When he returned, he found that she was afflicted with leprosy.

For pure fortitude, I have to admire several of these remarkable women. **Khadīja**, Muhammad's first wife stuck to him and encouraged him to the point that Muhammad was able to get through his depression and begin his work as a prophet. She continued her support in the face of criticism from members of her own tribe. **'Ā'isha** ruled the roost in a harem full of tough, determined older women. She, became a credible military commander leading an army of 10,000 men at the Battle of the Camel in Basra. The litter atop her camel was bristling with arrows, yet she survived without a scratch. She is the only woman mentioned in the *Korân* besides Mary, mother of Jesus. **Safiya**, the 17-year-old Jewish widow, raped on the battlefield amidst the butchering of her entire family and torture-murder of her husband, came up like a cat standing on its feet after being tossed from a window. She gained the respect and friendship of 'Ā'isha, handled the prejudice of the other harem wives with patience and managed to engage in the politics of Islâm despite her Jewish background. She put her life on the line attempting to support 'Uthmān, the 3rd Caliph when he was under siege by assassins, yet ended up with a sizeable fortune by the time of her death without the support of a husband. She got the last laugh when 1/3 of her estate went to her Jewish nephew. She is also memorialized in the *Korân*, but not specifically by name.

On-line references used in the section on wives and other women are included in the end notes. [378]

BEGINNING OF THE 1300 YEARS' WAR

We have learned by sad experience that it is the nature and disposition of almost all men, as soon as they get a little authority, as they suppose, they will immediately begin to exercise unrighteous dominion. Hence many are called, but few are chosen. (D&C 121:39-40)

Battles and Raids

A major characteristic of warfare until the 18th Century was the "baggage train" with its camp followers. Most Phase I armies moved no more than 10 to 15 miles per day. Infantry marched with heavy packs always prepared to fight. Officers rode on horses, mules, or camels. Cavalry moved faster, but usually screened an army on the move. The baggage train carried the commissary, pay for the soldiers, tentage, heavy weapons and other accouterments. In addition, they carried the loot and often a large contingency of camp followers. Camp followers often included the wives of officers and some common soldiers plus a cortege of single women to perform services such as washing, cooking and other comforts for the men. Faster moving Phase III cavalry armies, often capable of 60 miles per day, had much smaller more rapid baggage trains that included heavier weapons and little else. Camp followers, if any, were temporary and from the local populations. It was also common practice to fight only when weather conditions were right. There was a season for campaigning as noted below. Settled Arabs from places where water was available were more likely to use Phase I tactics while those from places with less water had to move fast and far. These used mostly cavalry and Phase III tactics.

It was customary for the victors of Asiatic armies to rape and sodomize the loser's wives and children in the baggage train. We know from the Hadiths and the *Korân* that by the time of Khadīja's death, Muhammad had developed an unusually strong libido. This accounted for his large harem of mostly pretty young women. The doctrine of abrogation, and exceptions he was granted for marriage in the *Korân* made this possible. After battles in which he won Muhammad encouraged his troops in such practices and was an active participant. Ransoming the well-to-do officers of the losing side, killing all the rest of the enemy's soldiers and enslaving all the women and children after keeping the "better ones" was common practice.

Twelve months after arriving in Medina, Muhammad began active war against unbelievers; it has continued for more than 1300 years with few breaks. *The Life of Muhammad* pg. 659-60 lists 27 battles. However, this same source indicates that Muhammad personally attended only 10 of them indicated by *. He rarely participated in the active fighting unless his observation post was overrun. This happened twice. *** He had a body guard close to him. The index for *The Life of Muhammad* is poor. Page numbers following **(TLM)** within the text will are for easier reference. Other references will be in the endnotes.

1. Waddān (*The Life of Muhammad (TLM* page 281) August 623

The raid of al-Abwa was aimed against a Quraysh Caravan. 60 to 80 riders, under Ubayda b. al-Hārith went as far as the water in Hijaz. The Quraysh had greater numbers; no fighting took place. One arrow was fired and was the alleged first shot in the jihād against the Meccans. A non-aggression treaty made in September AD 623 with a Bedouin tribe that had deserted the Meccans helped in later raids. Another raiding party under Hamza b. 'Abdu'l-MutTālib went to Juhayna with 30 riders. It is said that Hamza carried with him the first flag commissioned by Muhammad. On the seashore they met 300 riders from Mecca. No fighting took place.

2. Buwat near Radwa (*TLM* page 285), Oct 623 AD.

Muhammad took a party of 200 men to a point on the caravan route where they hoped to ambush a Meccan / Quraysh caravan with 1500 – 2500 camels. The caravan was protected by 100 men; there was no battle or booty.

3. Al-'Ushayra (*TLM* page 285)

In November 623 Muhammad received word from Mecca that a rich caravan was on its way to Syria. He took 150 to 250 riders to ambush it and waited for 1 month, but discovered that the caravan had already passed by their spot. When the caravan returned, it became the object of the raid leading to the Battle of Badr. Muhammad also sent a raiding party of 8 men under Sa'd b. Abū Waqqas to Hijaz, but no fighting took place.

4. Badr I in pursuit of Kurz b. Jabir (*TLM* page 286). December 623

Spies were active on both sides. The Quraysh knew of all these attempted raids against their caravans and sent their own raiding party towards Medina under Kurz b. Jabir al-Fihri to raid the pasturing camels near Medina. Muhammad took his own men in search of Kurz but did not find him.

5. Battle of Badr (*TLM* page 289) March 17, 624AD*.

Following the unsuccessful pursuit of Kurz, Muhammad sent 'Abdullah b. Jahsh b. Ri'ab al-Asadi with 8 men towards Mecca. He carried sealed instructions to be read two days later. These told him to go to Nakhla, a valley ½ way between Mecca and Al-Taif; lie in wait for the Quraysh; and find out what the Meccans were doing. [379] As they were observing the trail, the caravan that eluded them at Buwat, returned. It had only 4 guards, since it was the "sacred month" when no attacks were permitted. One of 'Abdullah's men shaved his head to appear as a pilgrim. This fooled the caravan guards into believing that 'Abdullah's men were on the lesser hajj. The caravan carried raisins, dates, leather and other merchandise. Despite the sacred month 'Abdullah and his men attacked. While the four guards were preparing their meal, 'Abdullah's men killed the leader, took two prisoners and the fourth escaped. They brought the caravan back to Medina.

The apostle took 1/5 of the booty and the rest was split up by the other raiders. Muhammad kept the prisoners and eventually ransomed them for 1600 Dirhams or 160 Dinar each. One Dinar was 4.235 g. of gold, equivalent to the U.S. 2 ½ dollar gold piece of the 19th Century (4.18 g or 0.12094 oz. pure gold each or $30,960 at $1600 per ounce.) [380] Then intelligence reached Muhammad that Abū Sufyān b. Harb was bringing a caravan from Syria that contained more Quraysh property. Muhammad requested that the Damdam Bedouins send spies towards Mecca.

They reported a richer caravan headed for Mecca down the main trail with only 30 to 40 guards. Muhammad assembled about 300 men to take this caravan. The Battle of Badr (23.44°N, 38.46°E) that resulted on March 17, 624 AD, was probably the most significant battle ordered by Muhammad.

The Life of Muhammad gives a detailed report from pg. 289 to 314. When Muhammad began gathering his forces to ambush the caravan at the Badr wells, Meccan spies sent word of the pending ambush at Badr on the main caravan trail. The Meccans assembled a force of between 900 and 1000 men to meet Muhammad and his Medina followers and defend the caravan. However, Abū Sufyān had also learned from his own scouts of the ambush and changed the caravan's route to the coast of the Red Sea at Yanbu to follow the alternative route that avoided Badr. Neither side knew about the caravan's diversion, but both were spoiling for a fight.

Muhammad's forces reached Badr first, created a cistern where they stored water and capped the wells. This denied water to the Medina forces.[381] They arranged themselves in a defensive posture in front of the wells and cistern facing Mecca. Sa'd b. Mu'adh urged Muhammad to remain in a booth that they constructed for him and observe with Abū Bakr acting as a body guard. If the battle went against them, he could escape on his camel.[382]

The Meccans were divided into two groups, one with arms and the other without. Muhammad would have preferred to face the unarmed group first, but the *Korân* described the situation. See **8:7**. Many of Muhammad's troops were Ansārs who were recent converts and had pledged only to defend Muhammad in Medina. Nonetheless, these men participated during the battle and honored themselves in the victory.

The day before the battle Abū Sufyān came personally to the Meccan force to tell them that he had slipped the trap and his caravan was behind them on the coast road to Mecca. A fight was senseless and all should go home. This caused consternation in the Meccan army and two tribes, the Banu Zuhrah, Banu Adi, and a contingent from the Banu Hāshim (Muhammad's clansmen) returned home, thus weakening the Meccan forces. The *Korân* states that the odds were 2:1. (Sūra **3:13**)

The following day (March 17), the Quraysh approached Badr and sent a scout to determine the strength of Muhammad's army. He reported that the army was small, without reserves, and without nearby reinforcements. However, Muhammad held the high ground and the water. The attack would be difficult and might fail. This created doubt in the ranks, but their leader, Amr ibn Hishām, squelched it. As was common three champions from each side came out to fight. The Muslims, Ali, Ubaydah and Hamza, prevailed, but Ubaydah was mortally wounded. Arrows came from both sides and Muhammad gave the signal to charge the enemy by picking up a handfull of pebbles and throwing them at the Quraysh. This was like the ritual throwing of pebbles at Satan when walking around the Ka'ba. The Meccans were routed.

[See *Korân* **3:13**, **3:123-125** and **8:65-75**). The Hadiths and *The Life of Muhammad* tell the rest. At the time most Arabs were illiterate and oral traditions carried the details until they could be written many decades later. The *Life of Muhammad* quotes a great deal of poetry later written about the battle (pages 340-360).]

It was said that God slew many chiefs of the Quraysh. Prisoners were taken. Muhammad felt that Sa'd b. Mu'adh who was one of Muhammad's guards seemed displeased and when asked why, stated that they should be slaughtering the prisoners, not taking them captive. Muhammad ordered the sparing of several who had been his supporters in Mecca. [383] Booty, mostly weapons, livestock and prisoners were then taken back to Medina. *The Life of Muhammad* gives complete lists all those Muslims who participated (pages 327-336) and the 14 martyrs (pages 336-7). He also lists the 50 Meccan dead (pages 337-8) and 43 Meccan captured (pages 338-9). The number of wounded is unknown. Sad and 'Umar wanted to kill the prisoners, but Abū Bakr and Muhammad wanted clemency. [1 Samuel 15:1-26 is often cited as a similar situation. However, it is not. In this case Saul had been ordered to utterly destroy the Amalekites, one of the seven Canaanite tribes ear-marked for total destruction. Saul kept some animals for sacrifice and for disobedience to God's command, lost the kingship of Israel.] Amir ibn Hisham and Umayyah ibn Khalaf ibn Safwan were executed along with two others who had dumped sheep excrement on Muhammad's head in Mecca. 20 of the Quraysh dead were thrown into the Badr well polluting it.

Because of the beating they suffered following the Battle of Badr, the Quyrash of Mecca thirsted for vengeance. Because of the victory, Muhammad and the Muslims suddenly became a threat to the political stability of Medina and its surrounding region. His power and influence were felt in murderous terms. Those critical of him were silenced. **Abū Afk**, a poet who wrote verse critical of Muhammad and Muslims, attempted to stir up his tribesmen of the Banu Amr ibn Awf against them. He was assassinated in his sleep at his own home. **Asma bint Marwan** of the Banu Umayyah ibn Zayd also was a propagandist against Muhammad and Muslims. She was attacked in her bedroom and killed by Umayr ibn Awf while she was nursing a child. The assassination of **Ka'b B. Al-Ashraf**, a famous poet, [384] occurred in September of AD 624. Following Badr, he was distressed by the Muslim victory, went to Mecca and stirred up the Quyrash with his poetry, and then returned to Medina. According to Hadith from

Sahih Bukhari Vol. 5, Bk 59, N. 369 Muhammad asked, "Who is willing to kill Ka'b bin Al-Ashraf who has hurt Allah and His Apostle?" Muhammad bin Maslamaa then volunteered, but after waiting 3 days was unable to do it and said that he and his henchmen would have to tell lies to accomplish the mission. He was ordered to do what he needed. Ka'b was tricked into friendship with his assassins and then suddenly murdered. Following the killing of Ka'b Muhammad issued an extermination order against all Jews. "**Kill any Jew that falls into your power**" (**TLM** pg. 369). This led to the killing and beheading of **Ibn Sunayna**, a Jewish merchant friendly with Muslims, by Muhayyish b. Masud. [385]

Following Badr in April 624 AD an unfortunate incident occurred between Muslims and the Qaynuqā. A desert woman came to the Jewish quarter to repair jewelry. She was asked repeatedly to remove her veil, which she refused to do. One of the Jews tacked her robe to a wall and when she stood, she was completely disrobed. The Jews laughed at her nakedness and a Muslim passerby jumped the store keeper and killed him; whereupon he was killed by the Jewish crowd. This led to a street riot between Muslims and Jews. Muhammad went to the B. Qaynuqā and appealed to them to honor their agreement and become Muslims. They refused claiming that the Quraysh knew nothing of war, but if Muhammad fought them, he would find out that they were "real men." [386] This brought about a verse from the *Korân* (**3:12-13**). This tribe was the first to break their agreement with the Muslims. They were besieged in their quarter for 15 days until they surrendered unconditionally. When 'Abdullah b. Ubayy b. Salūl pleaded with Muhammad to deal kindly with them he put him off repeatedly. In contrast 'Ubāda b. al-Sāmit who had previously had an alliance with the B. Qaynuqā', renounced them. The *Korân* **5:51-56** is said to refer to this incident. Badr also led to a series of aggressive forays by the Muslims against opposition in the region of Medina.

The victory over the Quraysh established Muhammad and the Muslims forces as a significant power in the region. The prestige of defeating the Quraysh, the predominant clan of the Arabs, was huge. It strengthened Muhammad's position in Medina and in Mid-Arabia and allowed him to banish the Banu Qaynuqā'Jews as noted below. Abd-Allah ibn Ubayy, Muhammad's chief opponent in Mecca, was weakened. Many Quraysh nobles were killed. This strengthened Abū Sufyān who became the chief. Abū Bakr, Umar and Ali, future caliphs, all participated at Badr. 'Uthmān of the Umayya clan was home tending a sick wife. However, the most important effect of the battle was the threat to Mecca's economy. Medina was located in a strategic position to cut off all trade between Mecca and

Damascus, the Mediterranean and Baghdad. The Red Sea lane was still open as was trade from Saba, but the principle sources of commerce and the life blood of Mecca via land routes were threatened.

6. Sulaym until he reached al-Kudr (*TLM* page 360) March 624

Kudr was a raid later in March 624 that resulted in no battle or booty. Ransom for most of the prisoners from Badr was paid at that time.

7. Siege of the Banu Qaynuqā' April 624 (TLM page 260 & 363-4)

This battle was not listed as an official battle fought by Muhammad's troops. According to *the Life of Muhammad* plus other sources the Qaynuqā', one of 3 tribes of Arab Jews that lived around Medina, had a number of craftsmen who worked gold. They had not agreed to be allied with Muhammad, but had agreed not to get in his way or oppose him. Following the Battle of Badr, Muhammad's forces laid siege to the town. After 15 days they surrendered. He plundered the town, took many of their pretty women as slaves and rounded up the men threatening to kill them. These were saved at the insistence of Ibn Ubayy, but they were weakened by the raid.

8. Al-Sawīq in pursuit of Abū Sufyān b. Harb (*TLM* page 361) May 624

Following the ransoming of prisoners, Abū Sufyān_led a party of 200 horsemen to raid Medina's outlying settlements. He burned some property and killed a few people. Muhammad sent out a pursuit party, but they could not find him.

9. Ghatafān, The Raid of Dhu Amarr (*TLM* page 362) September 624

Spies sent word that Ghatafān tribesmen were gathering with an intent to raid the Muslims. Muhammad ordered 450 horsemen out in pursuit. The Ghatafān were fortified at the top of a mountain. One was captured and converted to Islâm, but no fighting took place. [387]

10. Bahrān, a mine in the Hijaz (*TLM* page 362) October 624.

After the B. Qaynuqā expulsion from Medina, spies brought word of a gathering of the Banu Sulaym tribesmen from Buhran in al-Qudr. They were planning a raid on Medina. Muhammad sent about 300 to attack them. The enemy had dispersed and no fighting or booty resulted.[388] See the reference to Islâm-watch immediately preceding this one.

11. Raid of Zayd B. Hāritha to al-Qarada (*TLM* page 365) November 624

Of all the post Badr military actions, this was the most successful. A Quraysh trading caravan under the leadership of Abū Sufyān b. Harb made its way towards Syria via the Baghdad route so as to avoid Badr. They stopped at the Najd springs. The Najd is a region of desert east of Medina in the middle of the Arabian Peninsula. Zayd with 170 riders attacked the caravan and took a great deal of silver plus other merchandise. Most of the Quraysh escaped, but according to Ibn Sad, Tabaqat 8/23, they took a number of prisoners, but Abū Sufyān escaped.[389]

12. Battle of Uhûd (*TLM* pages 370-426) March 23, 625***.

Following Badr and the raid at al-Qarada, Abū Sufyān b. Harb encouraged the Meccans to raise an army of about 3000 men and 200 horse to go to Medina and punish the Muslims. When word of the pending attack reached Medina, Abdullah b. Ubayy b. Salūl 390 advised remaining behind Medina's protective fortifications. Others felt this showed cowardice. When the Meccans arrived, they camped outside Medina and began destroying crops. Most inside Medina were convinced that they would have to leave the city and fight. 'Abdullah continued to recommend staying behind the walls. However, Muhammad put on his armor and declared that he and 700 plus 50 archers 391 would go out to fight on Friday after prayers. They managed to get behind the Meccans without detection and set a defensive position across the mouth of a small valley on mount Uhûd. Behind them were stationed archers under 'Abdullah b. Jubayr to protect their rear and left flank. Their mission was to remain on the hill and fire at the Meccan cavalry to keep them away. *The Life of Muhammad* recounts that Muhammad gave his sword to Abū Dujāna Simāk b. Kharasha.

The battle began with the usual duel of champions.[392] It ended six to none with the Muslims taking round one. The initial charge by the

Meccans was driven back. Abū Dujāna advanced into the enemy lines using Muhammad's sword to kill everyone he confronted until he came to the woman, Hind. He spared her. Hamza killed one of the Meccan standard bearers, then killed Abū Niyār, but while Hamza was engaged with Sība, Wahshī, a slave of Jubayr b. Mut'im threw his javelin at Hamza. It penetrated his lower abdomen and came out between his legs. Hamza died shortly thereafter.[393] After the fall of Mecca several years later, Wahshi, who had been freed following Uhud, became a Muslim.

Despite orders, the archers left their positions to become part of the Muslim pursuit of the Meccan infantry. This permitted the Meccan cavalry under Khālid ibn al-Walīd to get behind the Muslims and attack their left flank from the rear. Khalid was destined to become one of the most famous generals in military history following his later conversion to Islâm. Many were scattered and fled towards Medina. A mele swirled around Muhammad's outpost, but Abū Dujāna shielded the prophet from arrows while Sa'd b. Abū Waqqas defended him with his bow while Muhammad handed him arrows. Muhammad also shot his bow until it broke.[394] Mus'ab b. 'Umayr was defending the Prophet. He was killed by al-Laythī Ibm Qami'a who mistakenly thought he had killed Muhammad. False reports that Muhammad had been killed began circulating on the battlefield. One group of Muslims who had advanced too far into the fleeing Meccans were cut off from the main body. Most were killed trying to get back to Medina. As the Muslim forces began to re-establish their original lines at the base of mount Uhûd, they found Muhammad, although wounded, very much alive. The Meccans believed they had avenged themselves of their defeat at Badr and withdrew from the field after their women had mutilated the bodies of the Muslim dead. After the battle, Muhammad ordered the slain to be buried where they had fallen. The following day he sent out a party to pursue the Meccans. Sixty-five Muslims and 22 Meccan polytheists were killed in action.[395]

Although some claim a tactical victory for the Meccan forces, they lost the battle from a strategic standpoint. They failed to follow up and annihilate the rest of the Muslims and take Medina when they had a chance. They left behind many Jewish communities that had sided with them. Muhammad and his forces systematically slaughtered and despoiled these former Jewish allies. This resulted in more spoil, gave the Muslims the ability to stamp out all opposition in the region, caused many to convert to Islam, and allowed Muhammad to increase his power, prestige, and army. Uhûd was a classic example of failure to follow through after initial military success. Despite the greater number of casualties, the Islâmic forces held the field and were capable of mounting a counter attack. Muhammad had displayed courage under fire although armed only with bow and arrow. He had wounds to prove it.

13. Hamra'u'l-Asad / The Day of Al-Rajī' *TLM* pages 426-29) 24 March 625.

This battle was the counter attack pursuit phase of the Battle of Uhûd. There was no fighting, casualties or booty. Six Islâmic missionaries were sent to teach the 'Adal and al-Qara at **al-Rajī**. When they reached a watering hole of the Hudhayl they were set upon and 3 were killed. The others were taken to Mecca where they were killed. See *The Life of Muhammad* pages 426-429. 4 months after the Battle of Uhud an incident known by some as the **Raid of Ma'unah** occurred. Abū Bara came to Muhammad stating that if he would send some of his people to the Najd, many might convert to Islâm. [396] Muhammad hesitated, but sent 40 men. When they reached a well at **Bi'r Ma'una**, they sent a messenger with a letter from Muhammad to Amir b. Tufayl, but the messenger was immediately killed. Then Amir b. Tufayl gathered men of the tribes of B Sulaym of Usayya, Ri'l, and Khakwan and surrounded the 40 missionaries and killed all but two who were outside the camp. When these saw vultures circling their camp they investigated. One was killed immediately, but "Amr b. Umayya al-Damri was let go.

14. Banu Nadir *TLM* page 437) AH 4, May / June 625.

The Banu Nadir, Banu Qurayza, and Bunu Qaynuqā' were three Jewish tribes that first settled in and around Medina. The Nadir had settled in a fortress a half days march to the south of Medina. They possessed some of the better lands in the Medina area and were wealthy from their agriculture and weapon making ability. In 617 a war broke out between two Arab tribes, the Aus and the Khazraj. The B Nadir and B. Qurayza allied with the Aus and the Qaynuqā sided with the Khazraj. Following Muhammad's arrival in Medina in September 622 he attempted to broker a peace between the Jews and the Ansār, the indigenous Arabs of Medina. In the process he banished the Qaynuqā and established a Constitution that called for all parties to live in peace and cooperate in defending each other if Medina were attacked. Following the Battle of Badr, Ka'b ibn al-Ashraf, one of the leaders of the B. Nadir went to Mecca and wrote poetry critical of the Muslims. Muhammad ordered his assassination that was carried out by deception. There followed the extermination order against all Jews as previously noted.

Following Uhud the B. Nadir challenged Muhammad's leadership. Muhammad banished them and gave them 10 days to depart. At first, they decided to go, then supporters in Medina urged them to stay and offered support, but when Muhammad laid siege to their fortress and began cutting down and burning their palm trees (**59:5**), they gave up. Muhammad's terms stated they could take only what they could carry. This turned out to be most everything they had because of their 600 camels. The B. Nadir left with the great pomp of a huge caravan and moved to the Jewish settlement of Khaybar. Muhammad then divided the land among his followers and took a large piece for himself, which made him wealthy. See *Korân,* sūra **59**, Exile, which is about this incident.

15. Hatu'l-Riqa of Nakhl or the Raid of Dhātu'l-Riqā' (*TLM* page 445) October 625

This raid was against a large Arab conglomerate of tribes (Banu Abs, Banu Notair) north of Medina. At Dhātu'l-Riqā' they met a large contingent of the Ghatāfan and the Muhārib; no one dared attack the other and all went home without a fight. At this time **4:102**, the prayer of fear, was given. It was said that when facing the enemy, prayers could be shortened. Muhammad ordered half his men to face the enemy while the other half, behind him, faced backward. Only a minor skirmish with bow shots occurred.[397] When one of the Ghatāfan approached to kill Muhammad, Muhammad let him have his sword, which he brandished menacingly. He asked Muhammad if he was afraid. Muhammad replied, "No, God will protect me from you." The man returned Muhammad's sword. Muhammad then quoted the *Korân*, "*O true believers, remember GOD'S favour towards you, when certain men designed to stretch forth their hands against you, but he restrained their hands from hurting you; therefore fear GOD, and in GOD let the faithful trust*" (**5:11**).

16. Last battle of Badr (*TLM* page 447) AH 4 or 626.

This was not a true battle. Muhammad traveled to Badr to meet Abū Sufyān and a delegation from Mecca, however, before arriving at Badr, Abū Sufyān allegedly went back to Mecca without meeting Muhammad.

17. Dūmatu'l-Jandal (*TLM* page 449) AH5 or 627

Muhammad sent a raiding party to Dūmatu'l-Jandal, but the place could not be found and the expedition returned home without any contact.

18. Battle of Al-Khandaq or Al-Ahzab or the Trench (*TLM* page 450-60)*.

In early 627 the Jews of B. Nadir who moved to Khaybar close to the Ghatafān Arab tribe approached the Quraysh of Mecca about an alliance and campaign against the Muslims in Medina. The Nadir managed to put together an alliance of Confederates including the Ghatafān from Khaybar plus several tribes from the Najd. This brought a combined total of 10,000 to 12,000 Meccans and Confederates to attack Medina under the leadership of Abu Sufyan. Muhammad was warned and he and his chieftains decided on a Persian style defense by building a ditch along the northern approaches of the city. This would nullify horse and make defense easier against foot. Coincident with the digging, they harvested all their crops to deny the enemy of any nearby food. Despite the attitude of the *Hypocrites* (**24:63-64**) the trench was completed within hours of the Quraysh and Confederates arrival on March 31 (**33:9-27**). An initial effort to force the trenches with cavalry failed and for the next 2 weeks the two armies faced each other hurling insults and arrows at each other with minimal effect. Muhammad had assembled his army of 3000 at the Sala, a hill north of Medina, where it was in good position to counterattack any breakthroughs. After two weeks there was little progress. The weather was wet, cold and windy and food was in short supply on both sides. The morale of the Quraysh and confederates was dimming.

A group under the leadership of 'Amr ibn ' Abd Wudd, said to be worth 1000 men in combat, managed to break through the trench line into a swampy area. Muhammad sent Ali out to challenge him; Ali dispatched him in a few minutes. The confederates retreated. More attempts were made to break through, but all failed. Psych warfare now began. The B Qurayza, a Jewish village to the south of Medina had a shaky non-aggression pact with the Muslims and at first appeared to be sitting out the fight. The B. Nadir sent agents to the B Qurayza in an effort to recruit them to attack the Muslims from the rear, but they were not allowed entry. Eventually, Huyayy ibn Akhtab of the Nadir got in and convinced them that a coordinated attack from front and rear would succeed. Rumors of repudiation of the treaty reached Muhammad who sent in three leaders to determine the facts. They found the B. Qurayza siding with the B Nadir despite warnings about what had happened to Jewish tribes who had gone against Muhammad. Rumors leaked out to the Muslims who were rapidly becoming disheartened (**33:10**). Counter negotiations between Muslims and Ghatafāns ensued and they began wavering in their support of the Quraysh. This sent chills through the Quraysh Camp. The weather was nasty and there had been no progress made in the siege. When a storm blew down the tents in the Quraysh camp, Abu Sufyan addressed his troops, "*O Quraysh, we are not in a permanent camp; the horses and camels are dying; the B. Qurayza have broken their word to us and we have heard disquieting reports of them. You can see the violence of the wind which leaves us neither cooking-pots, nor fire, nor tents to count on. Be off, for I am going!.*" [398] He mounted his camel and left leaving the Qurayza to contend with the Muslims (**33:9-27**). Events described for this battle are covered in Suras **4**, **24**, and **33**.

19. The Raid on the Banu Qurayza (pages *TLM* 461-82) April 627*

After the Battle of the Ditch or Trench, Muhammad decided to stop fighting at least for a while. However, Gabriel came about noon and asked Muhammad if he was through fighting. He said he was, but Gabriel said that he and the angels had not put down their arms and were headed for the B Qurayza.[399] Muhammad immediately ordered a pursuit of the Qurayza. They surrounded the town and lay siege to it for 25 nights. Muhammad sent them three alternatives: 1) accept Muhammad as prophet and accept Islâm and all would be saved. They replied that they would never abandon the laws of the Torah and never change it for another. 2) They could kill all their wives and children and go out against them so as not to be encumbered by family. They replied, "What would be the good of life if their families were dead?" 3) They could attempt a night surprise attack on the Sabbath against Muhammad's encampment. However, they refused to go against God and the Sabbath. The following morning, they surrendered placing their lives in Muhammad's hands. The men were taken to Medina and confined in the quarter of d. all-Hārith. Muhammad had trenches dug in the market. As the prisoners were brought to him in batches, he struck off their heads. There were 600 or 700 in all, though some put the figure as high as 800 or 900. ... This went on until the apostle made an end of them." [400] One woman was also beheaded. The booty including women and children were divided with Muhammad getting 1/5th and lots were cast for the rest. Each horseman got 3 shares – one for each horse and one for himself. Each soldier got 1 share. From this group Muhammad chose Rayhana d. 'Amr b. Khunafa of the B 'Amr b. Qurayza for himself. She never accepted Islâm, but remained in Muhammad's power until her death.

Following the disposition of spoils of the Trench and the Qurayza there was the matter of Sallām ibn Abū'l –Huqayq also called Abū Rāfi' who had helped put the alliance of Jews together to oppose Muhammad.[401] Among the tribes of the Ansār there were two that competed with each other to see how well they could serve Muhammad. These were the Aus and the Khazraj. The Aus had assassinated Ka'b b. al-Ashraf and now the Khazraj wanted the honor of killing Sallām. They went to Muhammad who told them to do it, but to avoid killing women and children. 5 assassins from the Khazraj went to Khaybar (25.45° N, 39.17° E), 85 miles north, sought out Sallām's home, tricked his wife into letting them in, stabbed him multiple times as he lay in his bed and then left him to die amidst the shrieks of his wife and the general commotion within the community. When they reported to Muhammad, he determined that 'Abdullah b. Unays sword had killed him because there were traces of food on it.

20. Banu Lihyān of Hudhayl (Page *TLM* 485-6) July 627

As stated earlier six missionaries were sent to teach the 'Adal and al-Qara in March 625. All were eventually murdered and revenge was now sought against the B. Lihyān. A surprise attack was planned and despite taking a circuitous route, when they reached their objective, they found their intended victims had been warned and were in defensive positions on the tops of mountains. The surprise attack was foiled and Muslims returned home.

21. Dhū Qarad (Page *TLM* 486-90) August 627

Hudhayfa b. Badr al-Fazārī and cavalry from the Ghatafān raided Muhammad's milch-camels, killed their shepherd and took his wife, Salama b.'Amr b. al-Akwa' al Aslamī. A slave came upon the Ghatafān raiders at the al-Wadā pass and began stalking them and taking pot shots at them with bow and arrow. He also sent for aid. When Muhammad received word, he rallied his cavalry and went to al-Akwa's assistance. The cavalry killed several of the raiders and recovered the stolen woman and some of the camels, but did not pursue further than the mountain of Dhū Qarad.

22. The Raid on Banu'l Muşţaliq of Khuzā'a (Page *TLM* 490-93) Dec 626 or Oct 627*

The date of this raid is uncertain because of conflicting chronologies of when Juwayriya and Muhammad married vs. the actual date of the raid.[402] When Muhammad heard that the B. al-Muşţaliq were gathering to attack him under al-Hārith b. Abū Dirār, Juwayriya's father, he took a ADstrong force to al-Muraysī, a watering hole, met them, killed some, put the rest to flight, took booty and enslaved their wives and children.

The troops were reluctant to rape the married women, but Muhammad who was apparently eager for the orgy to begin, shouted to his troops "Verily you do it" three times and they immediately raped the captives. (Sahih Muslim Book 8 # 3373). The Korân sanctions this behavior **4:24**. Among the captives was Juwayriya who had been given by lot to Thābit b. Qays b. al-Shammas. It was said that she was very beautiful. She was the daughter of al-Hārith b. Abū Dirār. She appealed to Muhammad who married her. When the B. Muşţaliq found that they were Muhammad's relatives by marriage, many of their families accepted Islâm. During this campaign 'A'isha was accused of adultery with Safwān b. al-Mu'attal al-Sulamī. This was later determined to be a lie. "O true believers if a wicked man come unto you with a tale, inquire strictly into the truth thereof; lest ye hurt people through ignorance, and afterwards repent of what ye have done:" (**49:6**) This incident was also referred to in **24:11** and **12**:18.[403] The citation in **12**:18 a Meccan sura, is internal evidence within the *Korân* of a later addition.

Analysis of First 3 Years of Battles

From March 624 until March 627 the Muslims fought 3 major battles, Badr (March 624), 'Uhud (March 625), and the Trench (March 627). At Badr the Muslims brought 83 men and 170 Helpers to the field. They lost 8. We do not know the exact number of Meccans that fought at Badr; they began with about 1000 men; however, there were desertions and discouragement before the battle began. The Meccans lost 50 killed and 43 captured and ransomed, including Abū Sufyān. The Badr wells were contaminated with dead bodies by the Muslims making the overland trade route less usable, which may have weakened the Meccan economy. The Raid of Zayd B. Hāritha to al-Qarada (November 624) was against a wealthy Meccan caravan lead by Abū Sufyān. Considerable booty resulted in increasing the war chest and prestige of the Muslims.

At 'Uhud the Muslims were able to field about 700 infantry and 50 archers, while the Meccans brought 3000 infantry and 200 horse. The Muslims lost 65 killed and the Meccans lost 22. But the Muslims held the field and were able to counter attack. Immediately after 'Uhud they had chased out the B Nadir (Meccan allies) and took their profitable oasis lands. Muhammad's action as a soldier and his wounds increased his prestige. At the close of the battle a curious incident occurred. Following his wounds Muhammad was carried to a small canyon in the mountain for protection. Abū Sufyān with a troop of horsemen rode up to the mouth of the canyon where Muhammad was being sheltered and treated. He shouted out to his enemies. "*You have done a fine work; victory in war goes by turns. Today in exchange for the day (T. of Badr). Show your superiority, Hubal,' i.e. vindicate your religion.*

The apostle told 'Umar to get up and answer him and say, 'God is most high and most glorious. We are not equal. Our dead are in paradise; your dead in hell.' At this answer Abū Sufyān said, 'I adjure thee by God, 'Umar, have we killed Muhammad?' 'By God, you have not, he is listening to what you are saying now,' he replied. He said, 'I regard you as more truthful and reliable than ibn Qami'a,' referring to the latter's claim that he had killed Muhammad. Then Abū Sufyān called out, "There are some mutilated bodies among your dead. By God, it gives me no satisfaction, and no anger. I neither prohibited nor ordered mutilation.' When Abū Sufyān and his companions went away he called out, 'Your meeting place is Badr next year.' The apostle told one of his companions to say, 'Yes, it is an appointment between us.'" [404] It is clear from this incident that Abū Sufyān could have brought his forces up and easily killed Muhammad, but he did not. In fact, a meeting at Badr was arranged for the following year. The only activity between Mecca and Medina in 625 was the attempted meeting at Badr that allegedly failed.

The rationale for Abū Sufyān's leaving the field at Uhud and at the Battle of the Trench is puzzling. However, it should be noted that virtually nothing military happened in the Arab world in 626 according to *The Life of Muhammad* except an abortive attempt to meet with the Meccan chief, Abū Sufyān. He was no fool and was highly connected with the political structure in Mecca. Was this to be a planning meeting? Did it occur at other times through emissaries or was it really aborted? More will be said later.

In 627 at the Battle of the Trench, there was little fighting and over all casualties are not noted in *The Life of Muhammad*. The effect was to show a steady growth in the number of fighting men available to Muhammad and his generals along with an increase in wealth. Muhammad had 3000, but the Meccans mustered 12,000, yet Abū Sufyān left the field before any major action took place despite his favorable 4:1 odds. The Battle of the trench left the road open to attack the Jewish settlements that had betrayed the Muslims in their attempted alliance with the Meccans. It was as though the Meccans had drawn in the Jews, then abandoned them to face Muhammad alone, be conquered and further increased his wealth and power.

The conquest of the B Nadir showed how impotent the Jewish communities were and how much booty could be gained by eliminating them. Immediately following the Battle of the Trench, Muhammad's forces moved against the Banu Qurayza, laid siege to their forts and forced them to surrender. The men were taken prisoner, beheaded and their women and children enslaved and sold.

Muhammad's next major conquest came in the raid against an Arabic tribe, the Banu'l Muşţaliq of Khuzā'a, that was allegedly organizing an attack against him. Muhammad arranged a pre-emptive strike that caught them completely unprepared in either Dec 626 or Oct 627. The dates are uncertain. The outcome was the same as with the Banu Qurayza.

Meanwhile, the international situation was changing. Byzantium under Heraclius was becoming a power to be dealt with. The Persian Empire was on the verge of collapse. In 626 Heraclius fought the Persians at the eastern end of the Black Sea in Lazica and won. At the same time, the Slavs, Avars and Bulgars were attacking Constantinople from the west by sea. The Byzantine naval forces won a decisive naval battle against this advance. The Persians were defeated and Heraclius' army routed the Avar land army.

The Byzantine juggernaut had chased the Persians out of Byzantine territories in Asia Minor, defeated the Avars in the north, and was on the verge of invading Persia. This would take place with the Battle of Nineveh in December 627 and the subsequent capture of Ctesiphon (33.05°N,44.35°E) the Persian capitol in 628. Ctesiphon is on the east bank of the Tigris River about 35 k south of Baghdad. These events were known in both Medina and Mecca.

Abū Sufyān's behavior may have signaled that the Umayyad Meccan conspirators were ready to join Muhammad's cause and take over. It was probably no secret that Muhammad was ill. Let Muhammad take all the booty he could, wipe out the Jews, possibly die and leave the field open to them. A strong Umayyad presence was already in Medina. 'Uthman was Umayyad. Harem politics were probably leaking secrets like a sieve. Abū Sufyān was acting like an ally more than an enemy. Mecca would fall without a whimper in January 630 and the city would be delivered to Muhammad by none other than Abū Sufyān. He would convert to Islâm, turn from "bitter enemy" to staunch supporter and become a general in the Islâmic army. His his son would be the 5th Caliph. The Jews were doomed. They had gambled and lost on alliances with the Meccan polytheists. The Meccan cabal would profit. There would be no further warfare with Mecca, only the surrounding Arab and Jewish settlements would suffer.

THE END GAME

23. Treaty of Hudaybiyyah (Page *TLM* 499-510) March 628AD

Muhammad determined to go on a pilgrimage to Mecca in 628 AD. He prepared the sacrificial animals for the trip and left with about 700 of his followers for Mecca. The Quraysh did not trust them and came out to Dhū Tuwa with a blocking force to stop the pilgrimage despite Muslim protestations that they had not come to make war. Muhammad brought his group as far as the pass of al-Murār where his camel refused to go further. He asked 'Umar to continue to Mecca and deliver the message. 'Umar feared for his life. 'Uthmān the Umayyad went instead, but allegedly was taken prisoner. Rumors first indicated that 'Uthmān had been killed. This prompted Muhammad to change to a war mission, but further information indicated he was alive and had arranged an armistice with the Quraysh. When the Meccans spotted Muhammad's entourage approaching, they sent several to confirm its peaceful intentions. One of these was al-Hulays b. 'Alqama or Ibn Zabbān of the B. al-Hārith, chief of the "black troops." He saw the sacrificial camels and reported that Muhammad was on a peaceful mission. Nevertheless, the Quraysh refused to believe him and said, "*Sit down! You are only a Bedouin, utterly ignorant.*" [405] Al-Hulays then threatened to take his "black troops" home. Muhammad had the sacrificial camels killed, shaved his head and his men did the same. Muhammad then took his group and headed for home without entering Mecca.

The *sūra al-Fath*, **48**, was given at this time. George Sale's notes identify it with the conquest of Mecca, but others believe it has to do with Muhammad's attempt to make a pilgrimage to Mecca, his patience with the Quraysh, and the armistice. [406] For this, his sins will be forgiven and he will attain his ultimate victory later. "*Verily We have granted thee a manifest victory: that GOD may forgive thee thy preceding and thy subsequent sin,* *and may complete his favour on thee, and direct thee in the right way:* [Sale identifies these "sins" as marrying Zainab/Zaynab bint Jahsh, wife of his adopted son, Zaid and his affair with Mariya The Copt.] *and that GOD may assist thee with a glorious assistance.*" (**48:1-3**)

Later in the sūra is found an important doctrinal belief that those who swear alliance to Muhammad swear alliance to Allah. "*Verily they who swear fealty unto thee, swear fealty unto GOD: the hand of GOD is over their hands.*" (**48:10**)

The Bedouin chief, al-Hulays b. 'Alqama or Ibn Zabbān of the B. al-Hārith, who refused to fight is memorialized, "*The Arabs of the desert who were left behind will say unto thee, Our substance and our families employed us, so that we went not forth with thee to war; wherefore ask pardon for us.*" (**48:11**)

Next are predictions of victory to come, possibly Khaybar and Mecca according to Sale's interpretation. "*Now GOD was well pleased with the true believers, when they swear fidelity unto thee under the tree; ... wherefore he sent down on them tranquility of mind, and rewarded them with a speedy victory and many spoils which they took, ... GOD promised you many spoils which ye should take; but he gave you these by way of earnest; and he restrained the hands of men from you: and the same may be a sign unto the true believers; and that he may guide you into the right way. And he also promiseth you other spoils, which ye have not yet been able to take; but now hath GOD encompassed them for you; ... .*" (**48:18-21**)

The interpretation in *The Life of Muhammad* is further verified as the sūra continues. Note that these events occur in the valley of Mecca, not in Mecca, itself. *"It was he who restrained their hands from you, and your hands from them, in the valley of Mecca; after that he had given you the victory over them: ... These are they who believed not, and hindered you from visiting the holy temple, and also hindered the offering ... that it should not arrive at the place where it ought to be sacrificed. Had it not been that ye might have trampled on divers true believers, both men and women, whom ye knew not, being promiscuously assembled with the infidels, and that a crime might therefore have lighted on you on their account, without your knowledge, he had not restrained your hands from them: but this was done, that GOD might lead whom he pleaseth into his mercy."* (**48:24-26**)

Muhammad's attempt to make a peaceful pilgrimage to Mecca had other unforeseen consequences. A number of Muslims that were confined inside Mecca were released, whereupon 70 men joined Abū Basīr and began raiding the Quraysh caravans on the road to Syria near the coast near Dhū'l-Marwa. The Quraysh then appealed to Muhammad to take them into Medina and he did. Also, a number of women came from Mecca to convert to Islâm. This prompted the following: "*O true believers, when believing women come unto you as refugees, try them: GOD well knoweth their faith. And if ye know them to be true believers, send them not back to the infidels: they are not lawful for the unbelievers to have in marriage; neither are the unbelievers lawful for them.*" (**60:10**)

Despite pleas from the Quraysh, these women were not returned, but he permitted the men to do what they pleased – return or stay. The women's dowries had to be returned to the Quraysh.

24. Battle of Khaybar (*TLM* Page 510-18) June 628 *

When Muhammad returned from the thwarted pilgrimage to Mecca, he turned his attention to Khaybar (25.42°N, 39.17°E) and the wealthy Jewish settlements of the Banu al-Nadīr who had escaped with 600 camels loaded with treasure after 'Uhud and who had opposed them at "the Trench.". Their defenses included a series of forts. Muhammad moved his troops into a wadi at Rajī between the Ghatafān and Khaybar thus splitting the two potential allies. The Ghatafān came out, but fearing an attack against their settlement, retreated home after only one day leaving the Khaybar forts undefended. Even though superior in total numbers, the Jews remained behind their walls. This allowed the inferior Muslim troops to defeat them in detail by attacking one small fort after another. In the process they also gained much loot.

The fort of Nā'im was the first to fall followed by al-Qamūs of B. Abū'l-Huqayq. The first to die was the Khaybar champion, Muhammad b. Ibrāhīm b. al-Hārith. An Islâmic movie about Khaybar indicates that Ali took al-Hārith's sword and killed him. After defeating the forts one by one only forts al-Watih and al-Sulalim were left. According to the same film Ali allegedly dispatched Ibrāhīm's brother, Marhab. [407] According to the *Life of Muhammad* it was Muhammad b. Maslama that delivered the fatal blow. [408] Among the captives was Safiya d. Huyayy b. Akhtab, the wife of Kināna b. al-Rabī b. Abū'll-Huqayq and her two cousins. [See the story of Safiya in the wives of Muhammad above.] The two cousins were given to Dihya b. Khalifa al-Kalbī in exchange for Safiya and the rest of the women were distributed among the troops. Muhammad ordered that there would be no carnal knowledge of pregnant women, eating the flesh of domestic donkeys, eating any carnivorous animals and selling booty before it had been allotted.

The fort of al-Sa'b b. Mu'ādh fell and had the richest food in Khaybar. He next besieged the forts of al-Watīh and al-Sulā-lim for ten nights and these also fell. They also attacked the Maghrib and took one of their towns, Jirba. When the people of Fadak found out what happened they asked Muhammad to spare them and they would leave all their property. He agreed and they left. Those men captured alive at Khaybar and at Fadak agreed to work for half share of their produce and Muhammad accepted their offer with the understanding that they could be expelled if Muhammad so decided. Khaybar became the spoil for the Muslims and Fadak became Muhammad's personal property. It was at this time that an attempt to poison Muhammad by Zaynab d. al-Hārith wife of Sallām b. Mishkam took place. One of Muhammad's companions ate the poisoned lamb and died. When she told the truth under direct questioning, Muhammad forgave her.

Ali's involvement in the Khaybar campaign is mentioned. Abu Bakr was sent against one of the forts of Khaybar. After suffering losses, he returned having failed. Muhammad next sent'Umar and he too failed. So Ali, suffering from an eye disorder was sent with the flag and the fort finally fell. [409]

The Life of Muhammad makes it clear that Muhammad instituted the custom of morning attacks. "*One whom I do not suspect told me from Anas b. Malik: When the apostle raided a people he waited until the morning. If he heard a call to prayer he held back; if he did not hear it he attacked. We came to Khaybar by night, and the apostle passed the night there; and when morning came he did not hear the call to prayer, so he rode and we rode with him, and I rode behind Abū Ṭalha with my foot touching the apostle's foot. We met the workers of Khaybar coming out in the morning with their spades and baskets. When they saw the apostle and the army they cried, 'Muhammad with his force,' and turned tail and fled. The apostle said, 'Allah akbar! Khaybar is destroyed. When we arrive in a people's square it is a bad morning for those who have been warned.*'" [410]

The first reference to Muhammad's final illness is stated in *The Life of Muhammad* in association with the Khaybar campaign. [411] "The apostle had said when Umm Bishr d. al-Bara' came to visit him, 'O Umm Bishr, this is the time in which I feel a deadly pain from what I ate with your brother at Khaybar." For reasons to be reviewed later, abdominal pain was not part of Muhammad's final illness. When the campaign at Khaybar was finished, Muhammad moved on to Wādi'l-Qurā. He besieged them and returned to Medina. 14 men are listed as having died in the Khaybar campaign as martyrs. [412] Following Khaybar the remainder of the exiles in Abyssinia returned. [413]

25. Last pilgrimage (Page *TLM* 530-1) March 629

Upon returning from Khaybar, Muhammad stayed several months sending out raiding parties. One year after he had been turned away from Mecca by the Quraysh he returned with many followers and the Meccans left them alone. Rumors in Mecca were that Muslims were poverty stricken and starving. Muhammad kissed the southern corner and black stone. He then made three circuits around the Ka'ba. Muhammad stayed in Mecca for 3 days. Although supposedly in a state of ritual purity, he invited the Quraysh to a wedding feast for himself and Maymūna bint Hārith b. Hazn. The Meccans refused. They didn't need his food and his time was up. He should get out of town. This time oxen were sacrificed because camels were difficult to find and he consummated his marriage with Maymūna in Mecca before returning to Medina.

26. The Raid on Mu'ta (page *TLM* 531-540) August 629

By now many of the Arab tribes in the south and in Saba had converted to Islâm thus swelling Muhammad's ranks. The Treaty of Hudaybiyyah between the Muslims and the Quraysh allowed Muhammad to concentrate his efforts around Medina and wipe out and despoil not only Jewish communities, but also on the recalcitrant northern Arab tribes. Under the command of Zayd b. Hāritha a force of 3000 was sent north to Mu'ta in Jumāda'l-Ūlā, east of the Jordan River to raid these tribes. Second in command was Ja'far b. Abū Ṭālib. As they were about to leave, Muhammad read from the *Korân* 19:**71-2**, "*There shall be none of you but shall approach near the same: this is an established decree with thy LORD. Afterwards we will deliver those who shall have been pious, but we will leave the ungodly therein on their knees.*" They started on their way into Syria to punish the Arab tribes east of the Jordan River. When they reached Ma'ān, they learned that Heraclius had taken a 200,000-man army of the Eastern Roman Empire to Ma'āb in the Balqā. They quickly sent word to Muhammad about the Byzantine army operating in the region and waited temporarily for further orders and possible reinforcements. However, their third in command, 'Abdullah b. Rawāha, reminded them that they had come for either victory or martyrdom so it mattered little which. So, they continued on without waiting for a reply. The Muslims skirmished with the Byzantine forces in their camp near a village called Mashārif and withdrew to Mu'ta where a pitched battle ensued. This is allegedly located east of the Jordan River. All three chiefs died. The army asked Thābit b. Aqram to take the standard, but he deferred to Khālid b. al-Walīd who took it and began to ward off the enemy. The fighting became so hot that Khālid broke nine swords.

In what would eventually prove to be a winning tactic, Al-Walīd broke off contact with the main Byzantine force and began engaging them in skirmishes. Following one night his rear-guard appeared with new banners that made the enemy believe that reinforcements had arrived. To further convince them, Al- Walīd had his cavalry retreat behind a hill and create a huge cloud of dust. The enemy believed a large force was arriving and broke off all contact. This permitted al-Walīd to get his troops away. When the army returned to Medina, the populace called them "Runaways;" however, Muhammad did not. Seven martyrs were named. [414] The Muslims had made their presence felt on the frontier with the Eastern Roman Empire for the first time. Byzantine sources tell a different tale. The Eastern Roman army learned of the planned attack. They mobilized, met the Muslims at Mu'ta, killed three chiefs, and the Muslims fled. [415]

27. The Conquest of Mecca (page *TLM* 540-566) January 630*

The Battle of Mecca (21,25°N, 39.49°E) began over a tribal feud. Mālik b. 'Abbad of the al-Hadramī was killed and robbed when he attempted to trade with the Khuzā'a, which were allied with the Muslims. The Bakr clan, allied with the Quraysh of Mecca, retaliated by killing a Khuzā'a man. The Hadramī were allies of al-Aswad b. Razn. The Khuzā'a killed the sons of al-Aswad b. Razn al-Dīlī, Salmā, Kulthūm, and Dhu'ayb, powerful chiefs of the B. Kināna. Since the Bakr were allied to the Quraysh of Mecca and the Khuzā'a were allied with the Muslims, it meant that a state of war now existed between the forces of Medina (Muslims) and the forces of Mecca (Quraysh). More attacks by the Bakr clan further aggravated the situation. Muhammad now considered the truce of Hudaybiya broken and decided to attack Mecca. Abū Sufyān of the Quraysh came to Medina to put the truce back together, but failed to gain an audience with Muhammad or his principal advisors, Abū Bakr, 'Umar or Ali. To make matters worse a woman spy attempted to carry a letter in her hair or waistband (depending on the source), to the Quraysh warning them of the impending attack, but she was intercepted and returned to Medina.

Muhammad now gathered his troops, at least 10,000 strong and marched towards Mecca. By the time he reached Marr al-Zahrān, Abū Sufyān, after seeing this huge host, again tried to reach Muhammad's camp. He knew that without a truce Mecca was lost. Abū Sufyān accepted Islâm and carried a message back to the city that those who sought protection in his home, those who went to their own homes or those who went to the Ka'ba would be safe. Others would be killed. A few resisted, but most did as advised and were spared.

In the aftermath of the taking of Mecca, Muhammad sent Khālid b. al-Walīd to go into the surrounding country and invite the Arab tribes as a missionary to accept Islâm; however, he also sent the tribes of Sulaym b. Mansūr and Mudij b. Murra with him who acted as "persuaders." The Jadhīma accepted Islâm only after some were killed. Some resisted, but gave in to the wishes of the majority, but some of those who complied were beheaded anyway by Khālid's cavalry. Muhammad later compensated the families. In other cases property and money was stolen, but Muhammad also compensated the families for these losses. Khālid then proceeded to Nakhla where the temple of al-'Uzzā was located. He destroyed her statue. Muhammad tarried in Mecca for 15 nights.

28. Battle of Hunayn (22.97°N, 38.82°E) (*TLM* Pages 566-587) January 630***

When the Hawāzin discovered that a huge Muslim army was headed for Mecca they gathered together the Thaqīf, Nasr, Jusham, Sa'd b. Bakr and a few from the B. Hilāl. Intelligence on both sides rendered surprise impossible. The Thaqīf had two principal commanders, Qārib b. al-Aswad b. Mas'ūd b. Mu'attib commanded the Ahlāf. Dhu'l-Kimār Subay' b. al-Hārith b. Malik and his brother Ahmar commanded the B. Mālik. The overall commander was Mālik b. 'Auf al-Nasrī. Mālik had ordered the men to bring their wives, children and their herds with them to make them desirous of fighting to the death in defense of them. With the Jusham came Durayd b. al-Simma who was old but had a great deal of knowledge of war. The troops were assembled in the wadi Autās, which Durayd said was a fine place for cavalry because of its lack of dust. However, the presence of so many camp followers and animals disturbed him. He said that nothing would stop a man from running if he took a mind to it and added, "*If all goes well nothing will help you but sword and lance; if it goes ill you will be disgraced with your family and property.*" [416] He wondered why Ka'b and Kilab were absent and said that "*bravery and force are not here; were it a day of lofty deeds, Ka'b and Kilab would not have stayed away.*" His advice was to send the main force onto the high ground an inaccessible part of the land and meet the Muslim army "*on horseback. If all goes well those behind can join you, and if the battle goes against you, you will have saved your families and stock.*" [417]

The Life of Muhammad is deficient in describing the initial phases of the battle. At first the confederates planned to attack the Muslim army while they besieged Mecca; however, there was no siege since most of the Meccans did not fight and the city fell easily. The Confederates held their position in the mountains and waited for several weeks. Then Muhammad ordered his army to hunt down the confederates. When the Muslim army reached the road to Al-Tā'if where it enters the mountain gorge about 3 miles from Mecca, the confederate cavalry ambushed them. Other accounts claim archers launched hundreds of arrows at them. This threw the army into a panic and an organized retreat turned into a rout. Muhammad was isolated with only a few body guards and as at Uhud, was in danger of death or capture. However, he held his position and the confederates were unable to take full advantage of the battle because of the narrow front that favored defense. Those that stayed and protected Muhammad are named in *The Life of Muhammad.* These were Abū Bakr, 'Umar, 'Alī, al-'Abbās, Abū Sufyān b. al-Hārith and his son, al-Fadl b. 'Abbas, Rabī'a b. al-Hārith, Usāma b. Zayd, and Ayman b Umm Ayman b. 'Ubayd, who was killed. [418] Eventually the Muslim army gained the advantage and surged past Muhammad's position. The Bedouin confederates parted into two groups with one heading for Tā'if and the other for Autas. All abandoned their families and cattle. The spoils left behind included 6000 women and children and 24,000 camels. Initially the troops were reluctant to rape the captured Arab married women, but when Muhammad shouted to them, "*Ye are also forbidden to take to wife free women who are married, except those women whom your right hands shall possess as slaves. This is ordained you from GOD.*" (**4:24**) the men began raping all the married women. (Sunan Abū Dawud, Book V, Chapter 711, Number 2150)

Little is known of the battle of Autos except that a part of the Muslim army secured the road through the pass and part of it pursued the main body of Confederates that went to Autos where they were defeated with great slaughter and loot. Another branch of the army under Muhammad headed for Tā'if and a siege. The battle is mentioned by name in the *Korân* which gives a good summary of events. See **9:25-27**

29. Siege of Tā'if (*TLM* Pages 587-592) January 630*

When elements of the Confederate army arrived at Tā'if (21.16°N, 40.25°E), they shut the gates and prepared for a siege. Initially the Muslim camp was too close to the wall and arrow fire killed several until the camp was moved. The gate could not be breached and a siege of 25 days began.

Finally, the town surrendered and most of the confederates and people in the town accepted Islâm. When the spoil of the battle was about to be given out, the Hawazin captives who had accepted Islâm came to Muhammad and begged for mercy. They reminded him that their tribe had included his foster parents who suckled him when he was a child and begged kindness. He asked what they would rather have back and they said their wives and children. Muhammad promised that what he possessed and what 'Abdu'l-MutTālib had would be given back and that he would ask for the others to be given back by the Muslims who now possessed them. Captives were repatriated at the price of 6 camels each. After the transaction, Muhammad then gave back many camels as well.

30. The Raid on Tabūk (*TLM* Pages 602-624) October 630*

In the early fall of AD 630 (AH 9) the heat was oppressive and there was a drought. By this time many Arab tribes around the Arabian Peninsula had converted to Islâm. The Arabs of the Central Arabian Peninsula were subdued and Mecca was under the command of 'Attāb b. Asīd. [419] In Medina Muhammad felt strong enough to challenge parts of the Byzantine army and ordered a raid on the Byzantine outpost at Tabūk (28.23°N 36.35°E). It was a little more than 400 miles up the trail towards Petra (Thamûd) and Damascus and about 100 miles south of the modern-day Jordanian border. Traveling would be long, hard and hot. Logistics from just water alone would be a challenge. Fighting Byzantine army regulars would likely be fierce and not nearly as easy as against the Arab tribes or Jewish oasis farmers. Many did not want to go, but Muhammad managed to put together a very large force that included 500 cavalry. The faithful none the less began to prepare.

Muhammad ordered the men of means to provide money and mounts. Bedouins arrived and as usual, apologized for not going. Then Muhammad set off with Abū Bakr as second in command. There was a lot of straggling, noise and dust. When Muhammad reached Tabūk he found that the Byzantine troops had abandoned the city and he set about lining up various tribes in the region to join Islâm. His army was impressive and Yuhanna b Ru'ba, governor of Ayla came and made a treaty with him and paid him the poll tax. The people of Jarba and Adhruh also came and paid the poll tax. Muhammad gave them documents promising them "safe passage" for their trade caravans and ships. There was no fighting described and Muhammad stayed in Tabūk for 10 nights and then returned to Medina.

Muhammad's Participation in Battle

According to known records Muhammad fought in ten engagements including Badr, Uhud, al-Khandaq (Trench), Qurayza, al-Muşţaliq, Khaybar, Mecca, Hunayn, and al-Tā'if.[420] These are designated by an "*" after the date of the battle. He participated in the others through orders to his generals. Muhammad also attended a number of raids during which there was no fighting such as Tabūk. In every engagement in which he was an active participant, he appears to have been protected by a squad of skilled body guards; however, this did not mean he was not in danger. He was exposed to direct enemy action at Hunayn and at Uhud, where he was wounded. However, his body guard always stayed. He is not described as killing enemy in hand-to-hand combat in any of these engagements, but he did shoot arrows. Following the raid on the Banu Qurayza Muhammad allegedly personally supervised th beheading 600 or more captives.

Muhammad's Campaigns of 622-630 AD

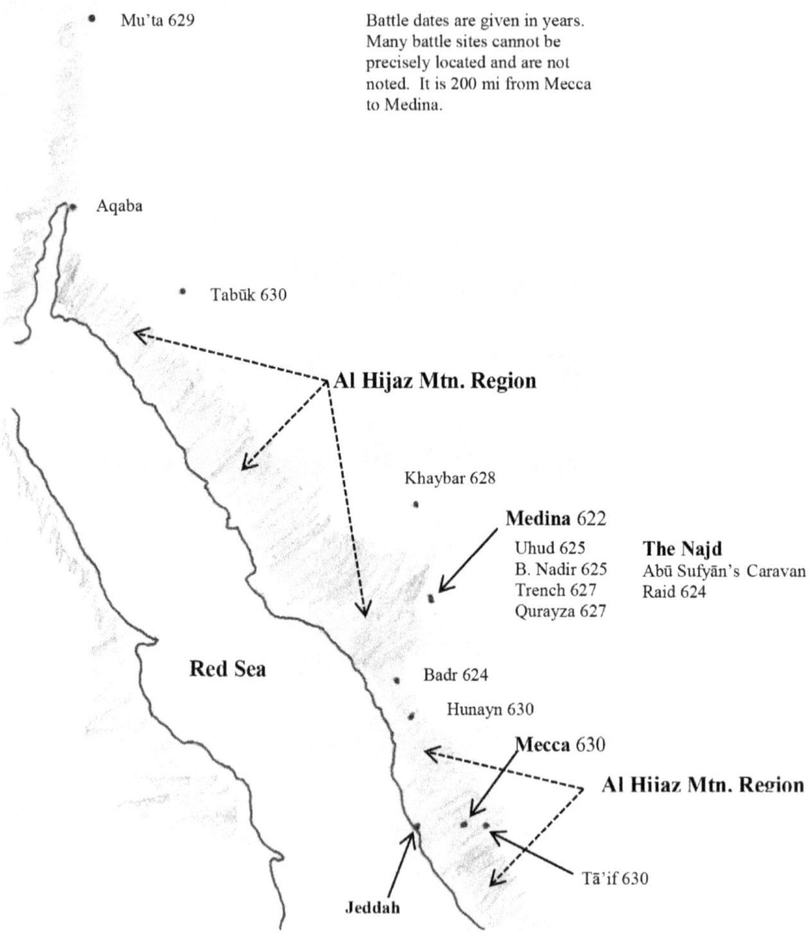

EVENTS PRECEDING MUHAMMAD'S DEATH 632 AD

Unfinished Business

A few well-placed assassinations could control the "press" or shift the balance of power in the ancient world. With the collapse of the resistance in Mecca and the rest of the Central Arabian Peninsula there would be some "unfinished business." Following Muhammad's return to Medina after al-Tā'if, Bujayr b. Zuharyr b. Abū Sulmā wrote his brother, Ka'b, informing him that Muhammad had killed writers in Mecca who had satirized and insulted him. Other poets had fled in all directions. He advised Ka'b to go quickly to Muhammad, confess and repent. Muhammad usually forgave under those circumstances. If he couldn't do that, he would have to go into hiding. [421] Ka'b was already distressed over some in Mecca who were spreading false rumors about him. He followed his brother's advice, wrote a complimentary poem and went to see Muhammad immediately, who, as predicted, pardoned him. However, this did not appease the Ansār of Medina whom he had called *"short black men."* However, K'ab immediately began writing poems in praise of the Ansār.

While Muhammad was preparing for Tabūk, leaders of an "opposition mosque" near Medina came and asked him to pray with them in their mosque as it was devoted to the sick, needy, and nights of bad weather. Muhammad told them he would do it after his upcoming campaign "if God wills it." This is an expression that usually means "no" in the Arab World. A short time later he called Malik b. al-Dukhshum and his brothers and told them to destroy the mosque with fire. This is memorialized in the *Korân*, *"There are some who have built a temple to hurt the faithful and to propagate infidelity, and to foment division among the true believers, and for a lurking-place for him who hath [fought against GOD and his apostle in time past; and they swear, saying, Verily we intended no other than to do for the best: but GOD is witness that they do certainly lie."* (**9:107**) [422]

Three men (Ka'b b. Mālik, Murāra b. al-Rabī, and Hilāl b. Umayya) who did not go to Tabūk were shunned on orders from Muhammad. [423] The shunning was temporary. It was mentioned in the *Korân*, *"And he is also reconciled unto the three who were left behind, so that the earth became too strait for them, notwithstanding its spaciousness, and their souls became straitened within them, and they considered that there was no refuge from GOD, otherwise than by having recourse unto him. Then was he turned unto them, that they might repent; for GOD is easy to be reconciled and merciful. O true believers, fear GOD, and be with the sincere. There was no reason why the inhabitants of Medina and the Arabs of the desert who dwell around them, should stay behind the apostle of GOD, or should prefer themselves before him. This is unreasonable: because they are not distressed either by thirst, or labour, or hunger, for the defense of GOD'S true religion; neither do they stir a step, which may irritate the unbelievers; neither do they receive from the enemy any damage, but a good work is written down unto them for the same; for GOD suffereth not the reward of the righteous to perish."* (**9:118-20**)

As a harbinger of things to come, Abū Bakr was selected to lead the *hajj* of AD 631. Muhammad may have had considerable trouble with his illness at this time and could not physically attend the *hajj*. Another possible reason for Muhammad's inability to attend was the large number of deputations coming to Mecca to see Muhammad and accept Islâm.

Many Tribes Accept Islâm

This website includes useful chronology about the months and dates that specific tribes accepted Islâm. [424] In May 628 Muhammad sent invitations to the chiefs of a number of tribes to accept Islâm. Skepticism caused many Arab tribes to wait and see how successful Muhammad and the Muslims were before signing up. After Mecca, Tā'if, and Tabūk deputations began arriving in droves. *The Life of Muhammad* even calls AH 9 AD 631, "The Year of the Deputations." It must be remembered that so long as the Quraysh opposed Muhammad, the rest of Arabia was not of a mind to accept Islâm. However, after their subjugation and acceptance of Islâm by Mecca and the Quraysh, the rest came quickly.

The **Hawazan** accepted Islâm in February 630; the **Ghadra** in May 630; the **Balli** in June 630; the **Ghuttan** in Ramadān 631; and the **Nakha'** in April 632 *The Life of Muhammad* also includes such information:

Envoys of the **Thaqīf** arrived in Ramadān 631 immediately after the Tabūk campaign. This conflicts with the October 630 date for Tabūk. However, a delay may have occurred since 'Urwa b. Mas'ūd al-Thaqafī asked to go back as a Muslim to attempt to convince his clan to become Muslim. Muhammad advised against it for fear he might be killed. He did it anyway and was killed by an arrow shot from his own people. Later a deputation requested permission to keep their statue of Al-Lāt for three years to get the women used to the idea of Islâm, but again Muhammad refused and instead sent Abū Sufyān b. Harb and al-Mughīra b. Shu'ba to destroy it. When all had been finalized, Muhammad appointed 'Uthmān b. Abū'l-'Ās as their chief. [425] The **B. Tamīm** came next. They were mentioned in the *Korân, "As to those who call unto thee from without the inner apartments; the greater part of them do not understand the respect due to thee."* (**49:4**)

The **B. 'Āmir** followed, but they had no intention of accepting Islâm. They were led by 'Āmir b. al-Tufayl, Arbad b. Qays b. Jaz' b. Khālid b. Ja'far, and Jabbār b. Salmā b. Mālik b. Ja'far. 'Āmir was a sworn enemy of Muhammad and had great difficulty accepting any kind of leadership from the Quraysh. When he arrived with his retainers, his intent was to kill Muhammad by treachery; however, the plan for 'Āmir to distract Muhammad while Arbad killed him with a sword could not be carried out. On his way back to the tribe 'Āmir was struck with the bubonic plague in his neck and died. When Arbad was asked by his tribesmen, he said nothing about Islâm or Muhammad and continued to be recalcitrant. In fact he told others that if Muhammad were there, he would kill him with an arrow. A couple of days later he and his camel were killed by a bolt of lightning. [426]

The **'Abdu'l-Qays** and **B. Hanīfa** accepted Islâm, but the latter brought with them Musaylima b. Habīb al-Hanafi, "the arch liar." [427] They left Musaylima to tend the baggage and shortly after they left Medina, he apostatized and claimed he was the co-equal of Muhammad.

The **B. Tayyi'** next accepted Islâm and were good converts. [428] A number of specific noblemen are also mentioned: a deputation of **Kinda**, 429 the kings of **Himyar**, 430 and the **B. L-Hārith**. [431]

One of Muhammad's great conversions was that of the **Negus, or King of Abyssinia**, a Christian. This may be further evidence that early Islâm was a Christian heresy as claimed by Saint John of Damascus (670-753 AD) in his work *On Heresies* he claimed that the Ishmaelites were Umayyad Christians. Despite Nicea in AD 325 and the Council of Constantinople in 381 the nature of God was still in dispute. Was Jesus the divine Son of God or not? Was the tripartite God of Christianity of one monotheistic substance as claimed in the Nicene Creed or was each member of the Godhead distinct or of "similar" separate substances? Inscriptions in the Dome of the Rock in Syro-Aramaic calligraphy of about 690 A.D. indicated that the Syrian and Hellenistic Christians were still arguing over the divinity of Christ. The letters between Muhammad and the Negus support the Syrian Christian side favoring Jesus' lack of divinity. Muhammad's letter of congratulation to the Negus over his conversion to Islâm includes this statement, "*I bear witness that Jesus son of Mary is the spirit of God and His word which He cast to Mary the Virgin, the good, the pure, so that she conceived Jesus. God created him from His spirit and His breathing as He created Adam by His hand and His breathing. I call you to God the Unique without partner and to His obedience, and to follow me and to believe in that which came to me, for I am the apostle of God.*" The Negus concurred in his letter to Muhammad, "*Peace upon you, O prophet of Allah, and mercy and blessing from Allah beside Whom there is no God, who has guided me to Islâm. I have received your letter in which you mention the matter of Jesus and by the Lord of heaven and earth he is not one scrap more than what you say.*" The full text of these letters is given in *The Life of Muhammad.* [432]

The Life of Muhammad describes a series of 19 raids or missions. Note how the author entitles many as raids and some include the killing of a specific person. Dates are lacking. [433]

1. Ghālib's raid on the B. Al-Mulawwah;
2. Raid of Zayd B. Häritha against Judhām;
3. Zayd B Hāritha's raid on B Fazāra and the Death of Umm Qirfa;

4 'Abdullah B. Rawāha's Raid to Kill al-Yusayr B. Rizām;

5. 'Abdullah B Unays's Raid to Kill Khālid B Sufyān B. Nubayh;
6. Raid of 'Uyayna B Hisn on B. al-'Anbar of B. Tamīm;
7. Ghālib B. Abdullah's Raid on the Land of B. Murra;
8. 'Amr B. al-'Ās raids Dhātu'l-Salāsil;
9. Raid on Ibn Abū Hadrad on the Valley of Idam and the Killing of 'Āmir B. Al-Adbat al-Ashja'ī;
10. Raid of Ibn Abū Hadrad al-Aslamī on al-Ghāba to kill Rifā'a B. Qays al-Jushamī; 11.'Abdu'l-Rahmān B. 'Auf's raid on Dūmatu'l-Jandal;
12. Abū 'Ubayda B. al-Jarrāh's raid to the coast;
13. Sālim B 'Umayr's Expedition to Kill Abū 'Afak;
14. 'Umayr B. 'Adīy's Journey to Kill 'Asmā' D. Marwān;
15. Capture of Thumāma B. Athāl al-Hanafī;
16. Expedition of 'Alqama B. Mujazziz;

17. Kurz B Jābir's Expedition to Kill the Bajīlīs Who had Killed Yasār;
18. 'Ali's raid on the Yaman (twice);
19. Usāma B Zayd's Mission to Palestine.

Muhammad's Death

According to a chronology of Muhammad's life, he fell ill on 25 May 632. He was suffering a severe headache. [434] He is next described with "dragging feet" and a cloth bound head. His illness worsened with more pain. He asked for 7 skins of water to be poured over him. His head continued to require binding and the pain was now described as severe. Pain and exhaustion were described and his friends forced him to take medicine which seemed to relieve him somewhat. He asked why they had given him medicine and his uncle told him they were afraid he might get pleurisy. This did not satisfy Muhammad and he forced his wife, Maymūna to take the medicine as a punishment. [435] He commented that pleurisy was a disease from the Devil and God would not let him get it. As his illness progressed, he was "unable to speak." His last words were, "Nay, rather the Exalted Companion of paradise." Muhammad died on 7 June 632 and was buried 2 days later. The severe headache and foot dragging suggest a neurological condition with increased intracranial pressure to be the primary cause of Muhammad's death.

Towards the end, Abū Bakr was the one selected by Muhammad to lead the prayers, but he allegedly appointed no successor. The final symptoms were rapidly progressive and fatal. Before burial arrangements had been made, a meeting of the Medina Arabs and the Ansār, took place in the Hall of B. Sā'ida. Here they swore fealty to Abū Bakr, who now became the first caliph. Muhammad's alleged last injunction was "*Let not two religions be left in the Arabian Peninsula.*" [436] However, 'Ā'isha allegedly said, "*When the apostle died the Arabs apostatized and Christianity and Judaism raised their heads and disaffection appeared. The Muslims became as sheep exposed to rain on a winter's night through the loss of their prophet until God united them under Abu Bakr'.*" [437] Abū Bakr was her father.

DID MUHAMMAD HAVE A CHRONIC DEBILITATING DISEASE?

Psychiatric History

Much of the motivation behind Islam after 622 seemed to evolve around power, women, and booty. Despite the commonly held belief of Muhammad as a peaceful, God-fearing prophet, who lived a life of poverty, profane history, the *Korân,* the *Hadith*, *The Life of Muhammad* and many non-Muslim sources do not give this picture. His childhood was not easy. He lost his father before his birth. He was cared for by a Bedouin nursemaid of the B.Sa'd b. Bakr. At age 5 he was sent home after an incident that may have been a seizure [See *Korân* 94:1), but apparently had no further problems with this until possibly age 35. Following his return home, Muhammad and his mother went on a trip and she became ill and died while he was 5. His grandfather, 'Abdu'l-Muṭṭalib had Muhammad care for live-stock outside Mecca for the next 3 years until he died at the age of 80. By his 8th birthday he had been orphaned twice. An uncle, Abū Ṭālib now cared for him. At first Muhammad continued his work as a shepherd to help support the family. At the age of 12 his uncle took him on a business trip into Syria. Here he came in contact with both Judaism and Christianity. Some sources indicate that he spent much of his time as a teen outside Mecca in the countryside. Whether he learned to read and write is disputed. Eventually he went to work for a large caravan company owned by Khadija, *a merchant woman of dignity and wealth.* [438] She ran caravans between Yemen and Damascus, a distance of about 1800 miles. This required many pack animals, outfitters, armed men and much equipment, supplies, and possibly retail outlets. Such a trip usually took 120 days or more. At the suggestion of his uncle, Khadīja asked Muhammad to act as one of her agents on a caravan headed north. He did better than expected.

She then proposed marriage. She was allegedly 40 and he was 25. For the next 15 years he earned a reputation for fair and honest business dealing, piety, and devotion to the old religion. Whether or not he had any children with Khadīja is controversial.

He may have had his first adult seizure at age 35 while working on the Ka'ba (temple) in Mecca. There are allusions to the possibility of seizures in the term "wrapped up" or "enwrapped" found as a chapter heading of Sūra 73 and alluded to in 74. [439] At age 40 he began to report having religious visions. It was at the same time that serious personality changes became noticeable.

It is customary for Arabs to wrap themselves in clothing that cover most of their body. How long this has been practiced no one can know for certain, but pictures back to antiquity show that it was likely present then. Such a custom would shield the body from receiving adequate amounts of ultraviolet light essential in the conversion of D vitamin precursors to its active form, D3, (1-25dihydroxy cholecalciferol). Modern studies show low blood levels of D3 among people, including the Arabs who wear "modest clothing." [440]

The active form of vitamin D, D3, is responsible for the modulation of cell growth. Its deficiency is linked to solid tissue cancers such as breast, prostate, colon and lymphomas. Besides bone and joint ailments, some autoimmunity and wheezing disorders, its deficiency is also linked to disorders of the mind such as depression and schizophrenia. [441]

Personality Changes: Sex & Violence

His first vision in 610 was followed by more at lengthy intervals and allegedly came with serious depression to the point of suicidal ideations. (See *Korân* 90:11 – "*he attempteh not the cliff.*") His wife supported him and believed that he was to be a prophet of Allah. For several years visions were short, peaceful, poetic, and tolerant of other religious views. His public ministry did not start until about AD 613. He was even told by God late in his Meccan ministry, "*But as to those who take other gods for their patrons, besides him, GOD observeth their actions: for thou art not a steward over them. Thus have we revealed unto thee an Arabic Korân, that thou mayest warn the metropolis of Mecca, and the Arabs who dwell round about it; and mayest threaten them with the day of the general assembly, of which there is no doubt: one part shall then be placed in paradise, and another part in hell.*" (**42**:6-7) Sūra **42** was thought to be #83 in order of revelation and occurred late in the Meccan ministry (about AD 617) according to Nöldeke. However, conversions were few and Muhammad's frustrations must have been great. Meccans ridiculed him and his few converts to the point that exile was their only escape. Several early sūras (before AD 616) promised an X-rated heaven that included flowing fountains of water, wine, food and sexual pleasures with dark eyed *houris*, virgins for those who achieved paradise. (See sūras 37, 44, 52, 55, 56, 76, and 78) The foremost martyrs got better couches, more jewels, the dark-eyed *houris*, plus pederasty (Suras 52, 56, and 76). The *Korân* describes numerous accusations against Muhammad by the Quraysh claiming he was out of his head, distracted, etc. These have been listed above. In 37:**102** the *Korân* explains that it didn't matter whether or not Abraham had his revelation about sacrificing Isaac in a dream or whether he was wide awake. Both ways would be valid. This could be an explanation to those who had seen Muhammad receive his revelations in a trance or spell. In the Hadiths trances or spells are described coincident with revelations. This would require more than Vitamin D3 deficiency and suggests the atypical seizures of temporal lobe epilepsy.

The year 619 was a terrible year for Muhammad. He had just turned 50. His faithful, supportive wife, Khadīja, aged 65, and his uncle, Abū Ṭālib, 80-year-old, who had been his mentor, father, and protector died within either a few months or days of each other. He spent the next 2-3 years exiled from Mecca, but was able to find more converts from Medina and some of the Arab tribes. He was now given the permission to fight against the Infidels and he turned to raiding Meccan caravans. With his move to Medina in 622 his slowly developing verbal aggression changed radically to overt brutality. The sūras lengthened becoming more disjointed, paranoid, violent and self-serving. This may have resulted from extensive editing that occurred when the *Korân* was finally published in its "official" form 30 years after Muhammad's death. It also could have happened due to a shift in his personality or the possibility that his close associates began to take control of the organization and influence it towards their own personal goals through conquest. This latter possibility is supported by the fact that two of his most supportive retainers, Abū Bakr and 'Umar (Omar) gave Muhammad their daughters for harem wives. 'Ā'isha (A'isha) from Abū Bakr was probably age 7 at betrothal, age 9 at marriage and consummation in 623 AD. Hafṣah (Hafsa) from 'Umar was age 18 at the time of her marriage (AD 625). Following Muhammad's death in AD 632, Abū Bakr and 'Umar became the 1st and 2nd caliphs. Muhammad might have had other women during his first marriage, but all indications are that he remained loyal to Khadīja. However, his personality was changing to one of overt hyper sexuality and violence.

After about a year of failure, one small caravan was taken that was followed by a major victory against Meccan forces at the Battle of Badr. He led a number of raids, but managed to avoid direct conflict most of the time during the fighting. During the battle of Uhud outside of Medina, he was wounded and almost killed when the battle raged over his observation post. Body guards protected him.

He ordered the assassination of a number of enemies that were carried out by his retainers. He then began the conquest of wealthy Jewish settlements in and about Medina probably in reprisal for their participation with the Meccans, but also for their loot and women. His army grew with brutality and booty. The beheading incident occurred in 627 during the raid on the Qurayza.

"*Then the apostle went out to the market of Medina and dug trenches in it. Then he sent for them and struck off their heads in those trenches as they were brought out to him in batches. ... There were 600 or 700 in all, though some put the figure as high as 800 or 900. As they were being taken out in batches to the apostle, they asked Ka'b what he thought would be done with them. He replied, 'Will you never understand? Don't you see that the summoner never stops and those who are taken away do not return? By Allah it is death!' This went on until the apostle made an end of them.*"[442]

Shortly after his first wife's death both the *Korân* and the *Hadīth* note that he had a harem and a voracious sexual appetite. Three quotes from the Hadith state that he had sexual power equal to that of forty men.[443] This is unusual for men over 50 who usually lose their libido coincident with reduction in testosterone levels. Increasing libido to this degree must be considered a symptom of an underlying brain disorder. The *Korân* even documents this: "*O wives of the prophet, ye are not as other women; if ye fear GOD, be not too complaisant in speech, lest he should covet, in whose heart is a disease of incontinence.*" (**33:32**). His betrothal to a 7-year-old child, 'Ā'isha, and consummation of the marriage at age 9 was unusual in Arab society, but not unheard of. Muhammad was also accused of being a womanizer by the family of a young woman who intended to give herself to Muhammad. [See "Marriage Proposal Declined page 206. This marriage never came about. (*al-Tabari* vol.9 p.139.)] In several early sūras he disputed accusations of "madness". Despite sexual activity with his young wives, he was unable to successfully father a child with the exception of Mary the Copt; this child died in infancy and its father is in question. To some this suggests gonadotropin difficulties with infertility and adds to the possibility of acromegaly with a pituitary tumor. However, this complication of acromegaly is extraordinarily rare.

Apart from the paradise where male believers could have an unlimited sexual feast, an effort was made to reward them here on earth. The faithful could have 4 wives except for the Muhammad who was given special permission in the *Korân* to have more. In addition to 4 wives, the *Korân* allowed all men to have as many captive women, "gifts of the right hand" as they were given. *"Now are the true believers happy: who humble themselves in their prayer, and who eschew all vain discourse, and who are doers of alms-deeds; and who keep themselves from carnal knowledge of any women except their wives, or the captives which their right hands possess; (for as to them they shall be blameless: but who whoever coveteth any woman beyond these, they are transgressors: and who acquit themselves faithfully of their trust, and justly perform their covenant; and who observe their appointed times of prayer:) these shall be the heirs, who shall inherit paradise; they shall continue therein forever"* (23:**1-11**). This statement appears almost exactly the same in "The Ladders" 70:22-35.

A note in Prohibition **66:1-3** in the Sale Translation and in Hadiths, tells us that Hafşah found Muhammad in her bed with Mary, the Coptic Christian slave-girl. Muhammad promised Hafşah that if she didn't tell anyone else, he would not see Mary again. However, Hafşah told 'Ā'isha and word spread through the harem. Muhammad was furious, threatened Hafşah with divorce and refused to visit anyone in the harem for a month. During that time, he moved in with Mary, who was housed in separate quarters across town. This sūra provides justification for the prophet to continue his sexual relationship with the Coptic girl, an Infidel or unbeliever. – "*GOD hath allowed you the dissolution of your oaths: and GOD is your master; and he is knowing and wise.*"(**66:2**)

In the Medina period obsession with sex and violence seemed to afflict Muhammad. The sūras' style change from a well-organized flowing thought to one of disjointed thought. Instead of a live and let live with infidels and allow God to take care of them in the hereafter, the frequency of verbal attacks against infidels increased. The *Korân's* pages are full of "us vs. them." Believers are superior to Infidels or unbelievers. When conquered by believers, infidels have three choices – 1) convert to Islâm; 2) accept Islâmic rule and demi-status, pay a huge tax and serve their Islâmic masters; or 3) be killed. Such choices were not uncommon during the spread of Christianity throughout Europe and later in the Americas. However, in those times Christianity was a state sponsored religion. Modern Christianity has decried these methods, but Islâm persists. They appear in their holy book as the verse of the sword (**9.5**) prescription for morning attacks, an invention of Muhammad [444] (**3:121**; 7:98; **11**:81; 15:**66, 83**; 37:**177**;

54:**38**; 68:17-28; 100:3) along with throat cutting, beheading (**8:12; 47:4**) fire (**3:131; 8:14; 9:68**; **13**:35; **33:64; 48:13**; 76:4), and crucifixion or cutting off hands and feet on opposite sides (**5:33**; 7:124; 26:**49**). The loss of a lower limb and opposite arm as has been reported in the Sudan. It often causes the victim to get around only by groveling on the ground. These are prescribed methods for dealing with infidels and are frequently found during an Islâmic attack even today.

Muslim Clerics around the world, including those in our own country, have yet to condemn "terrorists," who have perpetrated violence in many countries and against many peoples. They remain silent and will probably continue to do so. Censure of their fellow Muslims would be criticism of the *Korân* and would likely endanger their lives. The cities of Basra and Koresh known as hot beds of rebellion during the establishment of Islâm continue with this reputation today. Sunnis and Shiites (formed before the *Korân* publication) still have blood feuds. The *Korân* is also filled with statements that promote the worship of God, protection of the less fortunate, and kindness towards all men and women. However, the law of abrogation (cancellation of verses written earlier in the *Korân*) is noted: "***Whatever verse we shall abrogate, or cause thee to forget, we will bring a better than it, or one like unto it. Dost thou not know that GOD is almighty?***" (**2:106**) and all the tolerance previously given, is taken away in sūra **9**.

The later sūras also define women as decidedly inferior to men. Women were made for the sexual pleasure of men (**2:224**). Men are superior (**4:34**) and women are of less value (**4:171-2**). Women can be divorced by the say so of their husbands (**24:6-8**). They must be covered to keep lust under control (**24:31; 33:33**). They are subject to "honor killings" for disobedience. They and their children constitute an enemy to men (**64:14**). Two sūras are named Women (sūra **4**) and Divorce (sūra **65**). Special permissions regarding women are given in two sūras (sūra **66**) and (sūra **33**). Note that all of these sūras are from the Medina period. Given the doctrine of abrogation in The Cow (**2:106**) and the fact that Nöldeke, Grimme, Muir and Sale believe Sūra **2** to be either the first or second sūra from Medina allows all the other Medina period suras to take precedent over those of the Meccan period. The progressive changes in personality after age of 40 have caused speculation of a possible central nervous system disease. His visions and associated symptoms and signs noted in the Hadiths confirm temporal lobe epilepsy.

Evidence for Muhammad's Epilepsy

From the beginning, Muslims recognized that the prophet received revelations only "*when in a state of trance.*" [445] Since the mid-nineteenth century, a number of scholars have speculated that Muhammad suffered from epilepsy. One of the first to recognize this was David S Margoliouth (1858-1940), Professor of Arabic at Oxford University. He observed that Muhammad's revelations were "*attended by a fit of unconsciousness, accompanied (or preceded) at times by the sound of bells in the ears or the belief that someone was present: by a sense of fright, such as to make the patient burst out into perspiration: by the turning of the head to one side: by foaming at the mouth: by the reddening or whitening of the face: by a sense of headache.*" [446]

In 1973 FR Freemon published an article in the medical literature: "*A differential diagnosis of the inspirational spell of Muhammad the Prophet of Islâm,*" [447] He postulated that Muhammad's visions occurred during spells probably the result of psychomotor, partial seizures of temporal lobe epilepsy. Other physicians believe his visions and hyper sexuality resulted from temporal lobe epilepsy. A few have postulated progressive acromegaly, but the symptoms described would be most unusual for acromegaly.

In 2006 Abbas Sadeghian published a book, *Sword and Seizure.*[448] In it he quotes from early sources and the *Hadith* that describe these spells. He cites many of these sources in their original Arabic along with an English translation. At first Muhammad was noted to go to the hills around Mecca and spend time meditating in caves. Afterwards he performed religious rituals while walking around the Ka'ba. He reported that while meditating in a cave, the Angel Gabriel visited and nearly squeezed the life out of him. Sūra 96 resulted. Sadeghian's research indicates that it took Muhammad about 3 years to finally accept the fact that God was trying to speak through him as a prophet. Khadīja supported and encouraged him in this belief. Then came a period when there were no visions, but this was broken probably by sūra 93. Sadeghian then sites evidence that his first two converts were Ali, his 10-year-old cousin and his wife, Khadīja. Despite his apparent illiteracy, the *Korân* is considered by many to be one of the best pieces of Arabic literature. [449] Sadeghian goes on with his analysis. Many in Mecca called him "mad" or crazy. However, he did not have the disorganized thought and lack of focus of the typical schizophrenic. Also, he was never observed to have a grand-mal seizure. The Meccans became furious with their former "favorite son" and forced him into exile and prevented those with him from trading or finding wives from among them. What was likely is that he suffered from psychomotor or partial epilepsy of the temporal lobe. Sadeghian catalogs a number of his symptoms and the evidence for them. He had olfactory hallucinations otherwise known as "uncinate fits." [450] These can be quite bothersome to the sufferer. Muhammad took to using perfumes such as musk and ambergris (*Korân* 83:26). He was even reputed to have said in response to a question about what pleasures he enjoyed; it was "women and perfume." It was said by many that they could always smell Muhammad coming because of his perfume. He also did not like onions and garlic.

Other symptoms documented by Dr. Sadeghian had to do with a feeling of nausea and bitter taste that could be relieved by frequent teeth brushing with *siwak* (soft branches of palms) and sweets such as halva (honey, spices, rose water). His tooth brushing was noted to be compulsive. He did not fast as prescribed sometimes because of his gastric distress. [451] Excessive perspiration is commonly associated with temporal lobe epilepsy even when temperatures are cold. [452] 'Ā'isha and others observed this and came to recognize excessive perspiration was a sign he was receiving revelations. See Appendix II.

The most tell-tale signs of temporal lobe epilepsy are auditory and visual hallucinations. [453] Dr. Sadeghian documents these from the observations of others that have been written in the Hadith and other sources. Such seizures are often preceded by the sound of a bell or other object. [454] This too was documented by others. Occasionally patients with temporal lobe epilepsy are subject to falls. These were not commonly reported, but there was such an incident documented when he was 35 years old. [455] Facial grimacing and lip smacking are also symptoms associated with temporal lobe epilepsy. [456] In fact, temporal lobe epilepsy is an easy diagnosis for physicians who know this type of seizure because of all the associated findings such as those cited above. Typically, partial seizures are manifested by "dreamy" states in which the patient is apparently unconscious to his surroundings and may stare at the sky and be unresponsive, yet remain seated or standing as in a trance. During partial seizures the victim may have auditory and / or visual hallucinations.

Dr. Sadeghian gives evidence that even points to the source of the seizure as being in the left temporal lobe. [457] Because it is so precise in its description, it is quoted here: "Hāshim Ignu Alqaasim reported … 'Abdullah Ibnu Abbas said, *"As the Apostle of Allah (PBUH) was sitting in the courtyard of his home in Mecca, Othman Ibnu Madhuun passed by and smiled at him. The Apostle of Allah (PBUH) said, 'Will you have a seat with me?' 'Certainly,' said Othman and sat facing him. As they were conversing,* ***the Apostle of Allah*** *(PBUH)* ***stared at the sky for a long time and slowly***

moved his eyes to a spot on the ground on his right-hand and, turning his back on Othman, he started nodding his head as if he understood something said to him. Then he kept staring once more at the sky as if he was following something until it vanished. *He, then, resumed the conversation with Othman. Othman said, 'Oh Muhammad, as we were conversing a while ago, I saw you do something that I have never seen you do before.' He said, 'And what did you see me do?' Othman replied:* ***'I saw you stare at the sky and, then, move your eyes slowly to the ground on your right-hand, turn your back on me, and leave me on my own.'*** *He said, 'Did you realize all that?' Othman answered, 'Indeed.' The apostle of Allah (PBUH) said, 'As you were sitting, a messenger of Allah came to me.' I said, 'A messenger of Allah?' He said, 'Yes.' I said, 'What did he say to you?' He replied, 'Allah commands justice, the doing of good, and liberality to kith and kin, and He forbids all shameful deeds, and injustice and rebellion: He instructs you, that ye may receive admonition.' Othman concluded, 'It was at that very moment that faith settled in my heart and I loved Muhammad'* (Ibn Saad 1990, 1:.138)." Persons with fixed lesions such as strokes who develop complex seizures have a tendency to look to the side of the lesion. Lesions such as those that might cause inflammation or pressure have a tendency to cause the victim to look away from the lesion. [458]

Sexual addiction is noted when the neurotransmitter, dopamine is increased. This hormone is produced in the substantia nigra, ventral tegmental area (VTA) and hypothalamus. These are all deep midline structures. The substantia nigra is located in the midbrain between the red nuclei and the pyramidal tracts at about the level of cranial nerve III. It is affected in Parkinsonism and Schizophrenia and plays a role in addictions. [459] The VTA is located near the midline in the floor of the midbrain and is tied to the nucleus accumbens, the center associated with reward, pleasure, laughter, addiction, aggression, fear, and placebo effect. Addictions can include nicotine and various drugs, but can also include behavioral addictions such as the need for salt, sex, pornography, gambling, and food. The nucleus accumbens is a bilateral structure close to the midline. It and the olfactory tubercle form the ventral striatum, part of the basal ganglia. [460] Addictions are associated with Delta Fos B that stimulates dendritic branching, part of neuroplasticity. With increasing stimulation, the control centers of the frontal lobes tend to be reduced thus unleashing cravings that feed on themselves making it more difficult for the person to control them. A brain tumor in the midline region near this area can potentially stimulate these nuclei rich in dopaminergic cells and stimulate this part of the brain that causes increased sexual urges as well as "blood lust." Paul spoke to

Timothy about breaking such a cycle occurring from willed behavior (Tim 2:22-26). A person suffering such a lesion will likely be out of control.

Muhammad sought treatment by bloodletting to protect him against mental problems. [461] In Chapter 5 of his book, Dr. Sadeghian notes the personality changes previously mentioned. As much as we know about his wives has been discussed. This conclusion is worth noting, "The hypersexuality that overtook him also took over a large portion of his life. Sex became such a major part of his thinking that it became a part of the *Korân*." In the account of the raid against the Banu'l Muşţaliq of Khuzā'a, he was apparently eager to begin the orgy as soon as the fighting was over. His troops hesitated in raping the captive women in front of their husbands on the battlefield, but he ordered them to begin immediately. His periodic vicious aggressive behavior and the torture of captives is further evidence of his changed personality that came later in life. It too can be accounted for by a brain tumor that can affect neurons in the nucleus accumbens. What is important is that it was written into the *Korân* as part of the jihadist doctrine of death and violence that has been the hallmark of Islâm.

The *Night Journey* described in *The Life of Muhammad* [462] is a classic case of **depersonalization disorder**, currently described as a dissociative disorder characterized by altered perception or experience of the self. It is not to be confused with out-of-body experiences in which one views his body from afar. According to *The Life of Muhammad*, 'Ā'isha said, "The apostle's body remained where it was but God removed his spirit by night." [463] Descriptions of the night journey as told to others describe Muhammad as a participant, not an observer. Depersonalization is rare and there is no known etiology, but it is associated with anxiety and depression. The Night Journey occurred several months after the deaths of Khadīja and Abū Ţālib, about the time of his expulsion from Mecca and a year before the flight to Medina in 622.

Increased Intracranial Pressure

Towards the end of his life, Muhammad suffered further signs and symptoms of a brain tumor causing increased intracranial pressure. Dr. Sadeghian demonstrates that many witnessed these events recorded in the Hadiths. Some of these observations were by 'Ā'isha. Headaches began suddenly and were very severe. [464] Almost simultaneously he began dragging his feet. [465]. The interval between the onset of headaches and foot dragging and his death on 8 June 632 are unclear, but records available to us suggest they took place over a 6-week period. Dr. Sadeghian ends his book with this statement, "*Muhammad's accomplishments make him one of the most influential men in human history. However, his claim of being a messenger of God is simply a byproduct of his seizure disorder – nothing more and nothing less.*" [466] As a physician I, too, believe that the evidence is overwhelming in regards to temporal lobe epilepsy. I do not believe that Muhammad deliberately set out to deceive anyone about what he thought were revelations, nor do I believe that his supporters knew the true nature of his clinical situation. Until the Middle Ages those of both East and West (with the exception of Hippocrates) understood cognition, perception and soul to be located in the heart, not the brain. In retrospect, his behavior as it changed and evolved was that of a man with serious brain illness. With the exception of Moses and possibly Abraham, Muhammad's life did not follow those of the typical prophets described in the *Bible*. His calling did not occur at a young age. His history included trade, politics, warfare, plunder and a harem of young women. His condition after the age of 40 was one that could have been easily manipulated by those around him.

A Possible Diagnosis

What then was Muhammad's likely diagnosis? Merritt's *Textbook of Neurology* offers some possibilities. [467] Although this text was written a number of years ago, it is still thought to be one of the best because of its precise description of various neurological diseases. There was no autopsy. Clinical descriptions must be used to determine the likely cause of death. The prophet's illness probably began about age of 35. He died at age 62 – a 27-year course. This is very long for most brain disorders. Chronic infections (viral, bacterial, fungal and parasitic) usually kill their victims in a few years once symptoms are noted not decades later. Vascular abnormalities can grow and cause difficulty but symptoms usually begin earlier than age 35 and kill within months or a few years. However, brain tumors, especially the more benign ones can fit this picture. According to *A Textbook of Neurology* seizures accompany: Hemangioma – 69%; Cysts – 60%; Astrocytoma – 55%; Abscess – 50%; Meningiomas – 41%. [468] Hemangiomas (vascular tumors), Cysts (usually parasitic), Astrocytoma (malignant brain tumor) and Abscess (usually bacterial, tubercular, or spirochetal) would all take less time to kill. Meningiomas are usually round or globular and eventually cause pressure on various parts of the brain. There are several types that kill when the tumor enlarges sufficiently to cause increased intracranial pressure. This can take many years. Most nowadays are recognized earlier and are surgically removed resulting in cure. The following table from the above source shows the age of onset of meningiomas.

Note that 55% of meningiomas manifest themselves between ages 31 and 50. Muhammad may have had his first fall from his tumor at age 35. His first visions occurred at age 40. His possible seizure early in childhood may have been the result of any one of a number of childhood illnesses associated with fever. There were apparently none recorded between then and age 35.

This fits the picture of meningiomas as does the following description:

Table VII Meningioma Age At Onset [469]

Age	No of Cases	Per Cent
1-10	2	3
11-20	4	6
21-30	12	16
31-40	**25**	**33**
41-50	**17**	**22**
51-60	11	14
61-70	4	6
Total	75	100

"*The average duration of symptoms before operation ... was eight years, but* ***cases have been reported in which local bony swelling or focal convulsive seizures indicating the presence of a meningioma have extended over a period of from twenty to thirty years.***" [470]

Meningiomas are tumors that arise from the brain covering and not from neurological tissue. This can include the lining of ventricles filled with spinal fluid. They rarely invade the brain, but apply steady pressure against it, which can compress veins, arteries, ventricular channels within the brain and irritate brain tissue. Blockage of ventricular channels can lead to increased intracranial pressure with resulting headache. Pressure against the vital centers of the brain stem can lead to death. The location of the tumor and its growth determines its manifestations. 24% of meningiomas apply pressure to the Temporal lobes; 30% to the frontal lobes; 24% the precentral; 10% the parietal lobes; and 12% the occipital. [471] A temporal / frontal pressure syndrome would be most likely.

"*Meningiomas of the outer third of the greater wing of the sphenoid bone – are subdivided into two types. ... The second sub-type ... is the large round or globoid tumor which grows into the Sylvian fissure. The symptoms and signs of this tumor are those due to intracranial pressure – usually headache – and convulsive seizures, which are more frequently generalized than jacksonian in nature. Olfactory [smell] and gustatory [taste] hallucinations as well as visual hallucinations are common.* ***The latter are apt to be so vivid that the patient can describe in detail the people and objects in his hallucinations.***" [472]

Merritt's *A Textbook of Neurology* continues: "*Seizures preceded by or consisting mainly of olfactory or gustatory hallucinations (uncinate fits) localize the lesion in the temporal lobe, but do not indicate the side of the lesion. Visual phenomena preceding or accompanying a convulsive seizure localize the lesion to either the temporal or occipital lobe, but usually these symptoms have no lateralizing value. As a rule,* ***hallucinations of formed images with or without an auditory accompaniment occur with lesions in the temporal lobe*** *and unformed images (flashes of lights) with lesions in the occipital lobe. Psychomotor seizures may occur with tumors in any portion of the cerebrum but they are more commonly associated with lesions in the temporal lobe.*" [473] This fits the descriptions attributed to Muhammad's condition.

One of the more vivid descriptions quoted by Dr. Sadeghian possibly localizes the lesion to the left temporal lobe. Merritt's text continues, "*The minor attacks of* ***psychomotor epilepsy*** *are similar to those of petit mal epilepsy in that they are brief and the* ***patient does not fall*** *to the ground in coma. They differ, however, in several clinical characteristics. First, the* ***duration of the attack*** *is greater, usually lasting from* ***thirty seconds to two minutes***. *Second, the* ***range of muscular movements is greater***. *There may be twisting or writhing movements of the extremities or trunk, smacking movements of the lips, incoherent speech, the* ***involuntary performance of apparently purposeful activities****, or resistance to any attempt to aid them during the attack.*" [474] Temporal lobe epilepsy is also associated with hyperreligiosity. [475]

Muhammad's apparent development of hypersexuality after age 40 can also be caused by brain pathology. Cases of hypersexuality have been reported as the result of lesions of the basal frontal region. Four such cases involving lesions (aneurism, meningioma, right hypothalamic infarction following subarachnoid hemorrhage, and post encephalitic lesion of the R temporal lobe) are described. References by others cite lesions that cause hypersexuality. [476]

The fact that Muhammad might have had hallucinations from a seizure disorder would not diminish God's ability to use his illness to give true revelations. However, alterations added to these by conspiring men would make a great difference on how we might interpret the *Korân* as a work of God. The final *Korân* was not put together until 20 or more years after Muhammad's death. From all that we know there were many opportunities to alter the text.

Were Sūras the Result of Hallucinations?

George Sale's translation is ideal for calculating the time of recitation in English. Since the human brain operates at the same speed regardless of language, it should take approximately the same time to express an idea in any language. Sale's translation is not set up in verses that leave gaps in the text; rather it is in the form of a continuous narrative in the same font in single column format of the same width on each page. Notes are separated from the text at the bottom of each page. Measurement with a metric rule along the left margin of the text permits an accurate method of determining the time of recitation for each sūra.

Table VIII shows the length of sūras based on the space it occupies on a printed page and the length of time it takes to read the revelation or express the idea. These lengths are given in the "length" column in centimeters. One column notes the sūra followed by the initials "em" for early Meccan, "m" for mid-Meccan, "lm" for late Meccan and "M" for Medina. Verses are of varying length and their number cannot be used to gauge the length of time it takes to recite the entire sūra. Those sūras in **bold face** take 3 minutes or less to recite – the maximum time for a temporal lobe seizure. This table shows that only 35 sūras can be recited in 2 minutes or less (left margin 12.0 cm or less). The typical time for a complex seizure is 2 minutes or less. Sūras taking 2 minutes or less to recite are: 1, 80, 81, 82 and 84 to 114. An additional 11 sūras between 61 and 83 those in (black) that are less than 18.0 cm can be recited in 3 minutes or less. All the rest exceed the usual length of a temporal lobe hallucination by 1 or more minutes. It is important to note that in this group there are only two sūras from the Medina period and only one from the mid-Meccan period. All the rest are from the early Meccan period. The remainder of the 67 sūras cannot have occurred completely in a single trance. They either include a combination of several hallucinatory revelations or other types of additions.

In conclusion there is overwhelming evidence that Muhammad suffered from temporal lobe epilepsy and that his visions were the result of his illness. It is likely that his seizures were the result of a meningioma emanating from the left basal area of the brain with pressure effects on the hypothalamus, the dopamine rich paranigral nucleus and / or the parabrachial pigmented area, the temporal and frontal lobe. Death came from increased intracranial pressure with blockage of the ventricular system. The delay in publication of the *Korân* made it possible for others to change the text for a variety of reasons. The destruction of original source material ordered by those after Muhammad's death adds to this suspicion. A careful stylistic study of the *Korân* would be helpful to determine the author(s) of various parts of the *Korân*.

Possible Location Of Muhammad' Brain Tumor

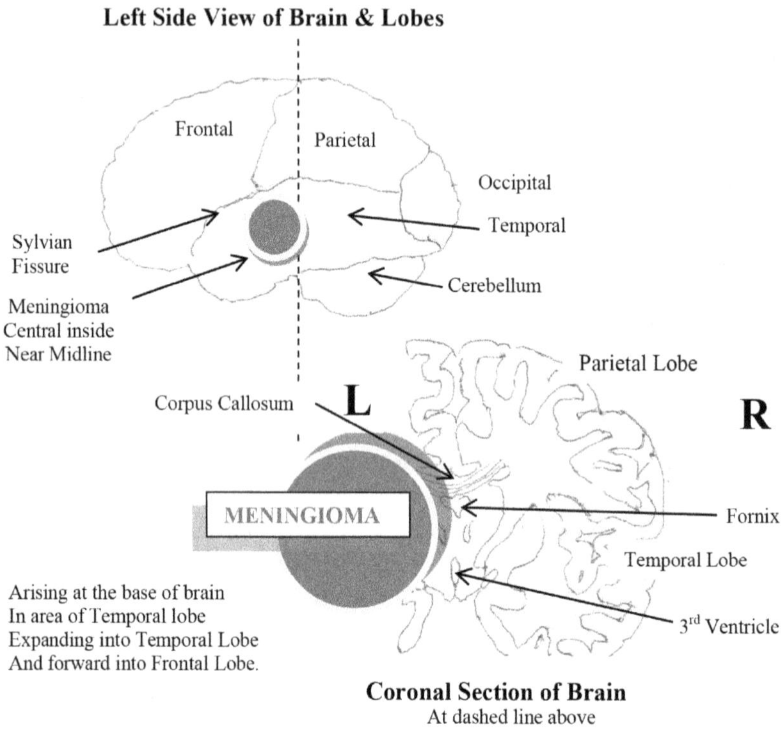

Table VIII Sūra Length: 2.9 cm = 30 sec 5.7 cm = 55 sec 6.0 cm = 60 sec

	Verses	Length	Sūra	V's	Lgth	Sūra	V's	Lgth	Sūra	V's	Lgth
1 em	7	**2.0**	30lm	60	60.1	59M	24	34.3	**88em**	26	**7.4**
2 M	286	$446.^{9}$	31lm	34	36.3	60M	13	$24.^{8}$	**89em**	30	**10.8**
3 M	200	245.5	32lm	30	27.1	**61M**	14	**(16.2)**	**90em**	20	**6.0**
4 M	176	252.6	33M	73	$90.^{7}$	**62M**	11	**(13.0)**	**91em**	15	**5.4**
5 M	120	196.7	34lm	54	65.1	**63M**	11	**(13.1)**	**92em**	21	**6.4**
6 lm	165	$224.^{7}$	35lm	45	$54.^{7}$	64M	18	21.8	**93em**	11	**3.8**
7 lm	206	252.3	36m	83	53.8	65M	12	20.2	**94em**	8	**2.5**
8 M	75	93.5	37m	182	65.7	66M	12	21.7	**95em**	8	**3.0**
9 M	129	181.3	38m	88	56.9	67m	30	25.8	**96em**	19	**5.7**
10lm	109	$99.^{7}$	39lm	75	86.4	68em	52	$25.^{3}$	**97em**	5	**2.2**
11lm	123	136.6	40lm	85	89.0	69em	52	19.2	**98M**	8	**6.8**
12lm	111	131.3	41lm	54	58.9	**70em**	44	**(17.1)**	**99em**	8	**2.9**
13lm	43	62.5	42lm	53	62.9	**71m**	28	**(15.9)**	**100em**	11	**2.9**

14lm	52	58.6	43m	89	64.8	72m	28	19.4	**101em**	11	**2.9**
15m	99	49.3	44m	59	25.3	**73em**	20	**(15.4)**	**102em**	8	**2.5**
16lm	128	134.^{0}	45lm	37	35.8	74em	56	19.1	**103em**	3	**0.9**
17m	111	119.5	46lm	35	49.1	**75em**	40	**(14.7)**	**104em**	9	**2.9**
18m	110	119.^{5}	47M	38	40.7	76m	31	18.9	**105em**	5	**2.1**
19m	98	76.^{4}	48M	29	40.9	**77em**	50	**(15.9)**	**106em**	4	**1.8**
20m	135	104.^{8}	49M	18	25.0	**78em**	40	**(14.3)**	**107em**	7	**1.8**
21m	112	94.^{7}	50m	45	30.2	**79em**	46	**(14.4)**	**108em**	3	**0.6**
22M	78	92.1	51em	60	28.7	**80em**	42	**11.3**	**109em**	6	**1.4**
23m	118	75.^{4}	52em	49	25.6	**81em**	29	**7.4**	**110M**	3	**0.9**
24M	64	91	53em	62	26.2	**82em**	19	**6.8**	**111em**	5	**1.3**
25m	77	66.5	54m	55	30.6	**83em**	36	**(13.3)**	**112em**	4	**0.5**
26m	227	100.4	55em	78	31.8	**84em**	25	**8.3**	**113em**	5	**1.7**
27m	93	88.5	56em	96	29.5	**85em**	22	**7.7**	**114em**	6	**0.9**
28lm	88	106.3	57M	29	43.2	**86em**	17	**6.0**			
29lm	69	73.3	58M	22	33.0	**87em**	19	**6.4**			

Muhammad's World 619-641 AD

Flavius Heraclius Augustus (575-641), the Byzantine Emperor lived during most of Muhammad's life time. On 5 October 610 his blood-stained hands took the reins of power when Muhammad had his first visions. At the time of his coronation he married Fabia. They had a daughter Eudocia and a son Heraclius Constantine. His wife Fabia died of epilepsy in 612. Heraclius Constantine, their son, was declared co-emperor in 613. Heraclius now married his niece, Martina. The Church in Rome and his people opposed it.

Heraclius' rule from 610 to 620 was dangerous and risky. His treasury was bankrupt, his borders invaded by the Persians, and most of his empire's valuable territory had been sacked by the Slavs and Avars. Many innocent Christians left behind paid with their lives for the policy of appeasement and troop withdrawals of previous emperors. Heraclius instituted two major policy changes designed to re-build his treasury. He decentralized the government by giving local governors more freedom to rule as they saw fit. He stopped the "gold for peace" program. In the meanwhile, he reorganized his army, strengthening it. However, his enemies did not wait. See *Korân* sūra **30**, "Greeks."

Avars and Slavs were pouring into the once rich Dalmatian Coast (Croatia). Slavs were pressing south out of the Danube basin into Macedonia and central Greece. The Persians took Damascus in 613 and Jerusalem in 614 where they destroyed the Church of the Holy Sepulcher and captured the "holy cross." They invaded Egypt in 619 (**30**:2). However, by 621 Heraclius was ready to take the field. Since Theodosius I (347-395), he was the first Emperor to lead troops in battle. In 622 Heraclius reformed his army making the cavalry more prominent. Later that year he invaded Armenia and defeated the Persians and pushed into their homeland. However, the main force of the Persian army was advancing east towards Constantinople while the Avars and Slavs, threatened from the West. Heraclius bought off the Avars and concentrated on the Persians, which he failed to defeat. Nonetheless he continued improving his military.

In 626 the tide turned. At Lazica at the eastern end of the Black Sea Heraclius and his army defeated the Persian Army that was attacking Constantinople from the east. A decisive naval battle defeated the invasion fleet of Slavs, Avars, and Bulgars who were attacking from the West. Next Heraclius routed the Avar land army. This freed him to turn against Persian forces that had retreated into Syria. In 627 (the same year as the Battle of the Trench) Heraclius took Nineveh and destroyed most of the Persian army in the process. (**30**:3-5) When the Persian emperor, Chosroes, refused peace offers, Heraclius advanced on the Persian capitol. The Persian nobility rose up and deposed Chosroes. His son, Kavadh-Siroe, became emperor. Heraclius now negotiated a peace treaty which returned to Byzantium all the previously lost territories. After proclaiming Heraclius to be his son's guardian, Chosroes II fell ill and died. A series of coups and weak monarchs further weakened the Persian government. It never recovered until after the Muslim conquests. In 630 Heraclius restored Jerusalem and the Church of the Holy Sepulcher and returned the true cross to it. He was now master of the Eastern Mediterranean Coast. Both the defeat and victory of Byzantium was predicted in Sura **30** of the *Korân*.

Shortly after his victories Heraclius became too ill to lead his army. His generals could not keep up with his standards. Muslims first challenged Byzantium in 629 (Mu'ta) and 630 (Tabūk) and took Syria and Palestine in 634. Heraclius' forces were decisively defeated at the Battle of Yarmuk in 636. By the time of his death in 641 most of Egypt was in Muslim hands. Despite this, his reformed government eliminated much government corruption that had gone before and his armies were able to keep the Muslims out of Turkey and away from Carthage for the next 60 years. Flavius Heraclius Augustus along with Justinian I and Maurice rank as the greatest of the Byzantine Emperors.

With the Persian Empire now defenseless, the Arab armies under the Caliphs, Abu Bakr and Umar swept into Persia, conquering it and seizing its vast treasury. This removed the Persian buffer between Arabia and Byzantium and brought the now powerful armies of Islâm into direct contact with Byzantium. In 634, after the deaths of Muhammad and Abu Bakr, Islâmic armies invaded Syria. Heraclius raised an army in 636 to retake the region, but was defeated. This now quickly led to the loss of

Armenia, Mesopotamia, Syria and Egypt. In 641 as Heraclius was dying, he left Byzantium in a confused rulership to two sons. Heraclius Constantine from his first wife Fabia and Heraclonas by his second wife Martina were to rule with Martina as Empress. By this time Europe was beginning to emerge from the Dark Age.

Saint Patrick's Legacy & the Irish

Despite the Dark Ages, there was an outpost in Europe where chaos did not penetrate – Ireland. It began in AD 401 when a 16-year-old lad named Patricius of lesser nobility was kidnapped in Britain by Irish tribal raiders and taken to Ireland as a slave to tend sheep. Six years later after concentrated prayer he had a vivid dream telling him to head towards the coast where a boat awaited him. He walked 200 miles to the seacoast near Wexford, where there was a boat that left within hours for the Continent. He returned to Britain where he had another dream calling him to return to Ireland. To prepare himself he went to Gaul to receive a theological education and ordination. In AD 432 he returned to Ireland as the second missionary bishop of Christianity; Paul was the first. Saint Patrick spent the rest of his life Christianizing Ireland until his death in AD 461. His Christianity was mostly free of Greco-Roman influence and adapted to the native Irish including some of their pagan customs. Confession of sins was a private matter. There was no public penance. Among his major accomplishments was the establishment of monasteries. These were rural walled enclosures with a small church in the middle surrounded by huts, each housing a monk. The monks began as quasi hermits, but were soon looking to the fellowship of others. Students came to learn at their feet. The monasteries gradually became centers of learning where students from other lands came. Some carried scrolls and codices, which the monks began copying. It didn't matter whether the material was religious or secular; they copied everything without censorship they could lay their hands on. Word traveled throughout Europe that a safe haven existed in Ireland, free of blood thirsty barbarians. What was a trickle at first became a flood of men carrying all the written material they could find. From these texts, the monks learned Latin, Greek, and Hebrew.

With Patrick's death, others continued the work. Columcille (521-597) / Saint Columba, spread the monastery system into Iona, an island off the Scottish coast and began the conversion of the fearsome Scottish Picts and their druid pagan priests. He was allegedly responsible for personally copying 300 books. With the success of Columcille, the way was now prepared for the Irish monks to begin to spread monastic Christianity with its emphasis on learning and scribal tradition back into Europe. Saint Columbanus (540-615), a contemporary of Muhammad, was Irish born. He received part of his monastic training at Bangor where he lived until the age of 40. While there he heard the voice of God urging him to preach in foreign lands and at the age of 50 headed for Gaul with 12 companions. He set up monasteries in Annegray, Fontaines, and Luxeul. Most of his opposition came from the Roman Christian Clergy, but neither they nor the Pope could stop him. He established 60 to 100 monasteries in France, Germany, Switzerland, and Italy. By 612 he arrived in Lombardy in northern Italy where he opened another monastery at Bobbio. The work begun by Saint Patrick led to the preservation of part of ancient knowledge and its re-implantation into Europe. The Dark Age was fading and the early Medieval Age beginning. An on-line list of 172 Irish saints that includes many from this era is available. [477] [478]

China

After 400 years of disunity China was united into one country under Yang Jian, founder of the Sui Dynasty (581-618 AD). Buddhism was a unifying force. The building of the Grand Canal became the basis of urban spread and commerce in later years. At the end of the Sui period the population had reached approximately 80 million. This was followed by the Tang / T'ang Dynasty (AD 618-906). Its capital was Chang'an (modern Xi'an), then the largest city in the world. It was a period of great commercial expansion along with expansion of the borders to include much of modern China and beyond. Block-printing, clock works, other mechanical devices, gunpowder, and banknotes began during this period. There was greater development during the continuation of commercial expansion in the Song Dynasty (960-1279). The Tang Code issued between 624-637 included laws protecting private property ownership and invention which Hernando de Soto considers to be the key to commercial development of a market economy. [479] The Tang code can be found on-line. [480]

In 1276 The Emperor Kublai Khan picked the famous Chinese mathematician and astronomer, Guo Shou Jing to develop a unified calendar and correct the errors of previous calendars. More will be said about this later.

Although the climate was back to normal and plague outbreaks less serious, the population and productivity of the old Roman Empire and the rest of Europe would take several more centuries to begin recovery.

Both Persia and Byzantium were financially and physically ruined. Persia was destined for conquest in a few years. Byzantium would hang on for another 800 plus years. A list of Byzantine Emperors with short biographical sketches can be found on line. [481] The only bright light in the world was China, but they were too far away. Their trade routes were tightly controlled. Several major mountain ranges separated them from Europe. The new kid on the block was Islâm. Their traders would have exclusive rights to both the sea lanes via the Red Sea and Persian Gulf to the Indian Ocean and the land routes via the Silk Road into China. Here they would be able to borrow much science, medicine, mathematics, astronomy and navigational abilities.

THE MEDINAN CALIPHATE 632 - 661

In the 30 years following Muhammad's death there were four *khalifa* or *caliphs*, successors. All were leaders in Muhammad's army, two had given him wives and two had married into his family. This was a time of consolidation, expansion and conquest. It was also a time when the rift between Sunni and Shia developed over the legitimacy of the first three caliphs. Who would control – Hāshim or Umayya? Muhammad of the Hāshim had left no specific instructions about how his successor should be chosen. Shiites favored Alī because he had married Fatima, Muhammad's daughter and had born two sons, Hassan and Husayn. Sunnis maintained that this would have opposed Arab democratic custom and that a council would decide. This is allegedly how Abū Bakr was selected; most Muslims agreed with the selection.

Abū Bakr 1st Caliph

Abū Bakr, (573- August 23, 634) 'Ā'ishah's father, early male convert to Islâm and supporter of Muhammad was of the Banu Taim of the Quraysh Tribe. As a Taim clansman, he had no blood connection with Muhammad. He was Caliph from 632 to 634. Sunnis accept him as legitimate successor to Muhammad; Shias say he violated Muhammad's orders and gained power in a *coup d'état*. His major accomplishment was suppression of tribal revolts and consolidation of all the gains made by Muhammad. He did not have to wait long. Musaylimah ibn Habīd al-Hanifi, also known as "the Liar, was one of several who claimed to be a prophet. He controlled the forces of the Banu Hanifi in Eastern Arabia, the region of Yamamah which included more territory than that of Muhammad's. [482] Abu Bakr sent one of his lesser commanders, Ikrimah with a force to tie down Musaylimah's large force at home while his best general, Khalid ibn al-Walid was engaged elsewhere. However, Ikrimah blundered into a battle with Musaylimah's force and was defeated in 632 AD. Another lesser commander, Shurahbil seeking glory attacked Musaylimah and met the same fate. Musaylimah's forces now numbered 40,000 and were eager for a scrap. In the Battle of Yamamah that followed, Khalid's troops slaughtered Musaylimah's army and killed him. The man that killed him was Wahshy ibn Harb who struck him down with the same javelin that he had used to kill Hamza at Uhud. [483] Casualties included many who had memorized the *Korân.*

Khālid ibn al-Walīd (592-642AD) was one of *Islâm's* greatest generals. Initially Khālid opposed Muhammad and was responsible for the Quraysh victory at Uhud. His brother Walīd ibn Walīd had accepted Islâm after the Battle of Badr and in 628 AD. Khālid ibn al-Walīd also accepted the Faith. In 629 Muhammad sent an envoy to the Ghassanids asking them to accept *Islâm.* The envoy was killed, whereupon Muhammad sent an army with specific instructions about the leader and command structure. During the Battle of Mu'ta all three designated leaders were killed and in accordance with Muhammad's instructions, the men chose Khālid. He held his 3000 against 20,000 at Mu'tah and broke 9 swords during the conflict. In recognition of his accomplishment he received the title, *Sword of Allah.* In the conquest of Mecca, Khālid commanded one of the 4 Muslim armies. During the Battle of Hunayn, he was made commander of cavalry. During the Tabûk campaign he was sent to Daumat-ul-jandal where he took the Prince prisoner and forced them to submit.

'Umar 2nd Caliph

'Umar ibin al-Khāttab al-Khāttab (584-644), father of Hafsa/Hafṣah, Muhammad's 5th wife and staunch companion of Muhammad was born in Mecca. He was of the Banu Adi clan of the Quraysh Tribe and had no direct blood ties to Muhammad. He was 2nd caliph 634-644AD. At first he opposed Islâm and considered killing Muhammad, but found his sister reading the *Korân*, hit her, but then read Ta Ha, sūra 20, and immediately converted. He is sometimes referred to by Sunnis as 'Umar al-Farūq ('Umar the Distinguisher between Truth and Falsehood). During his caliphate he organized the financial, military and legal systems of Islâm and pushed attacks against Byzantium in the north and Persia in the east. Shortly after the death of Abū Bakr, 'Umar decided to conquer Syria. When a Byzantine force of 50,000 headed into northern Syria, Khālid's Muslim forces of 25,000 fell back from Damascus, concentrated their forces and maneuvered to cut the Byzantine communication and supply lines. On 20 August 636 the Muslims annihilated the Byzantine army. The native Syrians hated Byzantine rule and the populace regarded the Muslim troops as liberators and assisted Khālid. In 635 a local Persian chieftain helped Muslim troops defeat a Persian army at Buwaib, south of Kufa (32.02°N, 44.24°E). In June 637 the Persian army, although superior in numbers, was routed by Sad ibn Wakkas. The King of Persia fled into the Iranian mountains. Finally, all of the Tigris and Euphrates system was in Muslim hands. Before his death he had a group select his successor, 'Uthmān. His murderer was a Persian slave taken in war who stabbed him 6 times as he led dawn prayers in the Medina mosque.

Battle of Kadisiyah & Conquest of Persia [484]

Abu Bakr died August 23, 634. During his short caliphate he had fought against various Arab tribes to consolidate all the gains made by Muhammad. 'Umar, who succeeded him, had talent as an administrator and Khalid ibn al-Walid, his chief of military operations was a superb general. Khalid developed the tactics of skirmishing into a strategic principle. This allowed him to attack and defeat forces of equal or greater size and led to one of the greatest conquests of all time – Persia. The Arabs had several things going for them. The King of Kings in Persia had a difficult job. His local leaders possessed almost absolute power over their own bailiwicks to the point that the King was chairman of a committee. There were also the religious leaders of Magi, the Mazdean priests. They defined heresy which could include incorrect conduct. This was always a threat to the man or woman in the street.

The King of Kings had to be a member of the royal house. The question was "which member" and "which house." This led to intrigues and *coups*, both during and at the end of a successful reign. The nobility knew only one thing – war. They studied it, practiced it and did it. It was all heavy cavalry with mastery of an array of weapons–spear, bow, mace, hand ax and lasso. Infantry was strictly limited and lightly armed. The knights used metal armor and shields. They had to be great horsemen capable of moving and fighting in tight formation. In addition, they used armored elephants and were capable of sieges. All this required a great deal of logistical support. The problem with a single effective military technique and equipment is that it may work well in one set of geophysical circumstances, but not in another.

Khalid adopted his techniques with patience. His battles included lightning raids and skirmishes, especially against supply lines. His logistics were simple – water and dates and his light cavalry was highly mobile. His battles could last days instead of the usual "set piece" single great confrontation which he avoided like the plague until he had worn out his enemy. He was a Phase III warrior in a Phase I world. As we learned in Desert Storm and as practiced by Genghis Khan, a smaller army using Phase III tactics easily defeats a Phase I or II opponent.

Before and during Muhammad's time, the Arabs had two economic problems. One was over population and out migration into Syria, Palestine and Egypt. This markedly increased the Arab peoples in these lands which were already populated by peoples who used the same or very similar languages. This increased the blood and clan connections with those of the Arabian Desert. The second was the increase in sea transport of goods when compared with caravan transport along the Red Sea. This brought unemployment to Arabian Desert lands. As Muhammad's precepts of Islam spread it included polygamy and law against infanticide. This increased the number of children. Fighting and plunder had become religious acts especially when used against unbelievers and it spread the idea of a pan-Arabic cohesion.

The Persians had another problem – Heraclius. Despite Byzantium's disastrous economic loss of their most productive lands to Avar/Slavic interests, Heraclius managed to put together a credible force that drove the Slavs and Avars out of much of their conquered territory and then the Persians out of his southern and eastern border areas. This led to a serious bloodletting of both Byzantium and Persia. Just before Muhammad's death, Heraclius' forces had taken Palestine and Syria from Persia. Persian religious leaders sent into the country turned to persecution rather than persuasion and riled up the entire population, now heavily ethnic Arabs. They were looking for a "liberator." Heraclius was too sick to lead the two Byzantine armies sent in to stabilize Syria and Palestine; both were destroyed by Kalid. Everything south of the Ionian Peninsula all the way to the Egyptian border was now Muslim. The field was open to Islâm. As it is now, Islam was a clannish movement that favored Arabs. Christian and Jews had to pay the head tax, but this was less than the payments usually required by Byzantium.

The Campaign before al-Qādisiyyah (November 636) did not begin well for the Arabs. In the north and east at about the latitude of Alexandria, Abu Abaid had been encouraged by victories in minor skirmishes against the Persians. Against his advisor's council he engaged his 9000 troops against Muthanna and his 10,000 Persians near Hira on the Euphrates at the Battle of the Bridge (November 26, 634 AD) near Kufa. The Persians (30K men) led an assault against the Arabs (number unknown) with elephants and killed 4000 as well as Abu Abaid. The Arabs retreated from the field. Persia lost about 600. However, following the battle, Muthanna was called back to the Persian capitol, now in revolt and could not take advantage of his victory.

The Persian Sassanid Empire had accumulated wealth for 300 years. Its people were not Semitic and its religion, Zoroastrianism, was unlike Christianity and Islâm. As one of the principle super powers of the Middle East and neighbor of Rome, they had fought many border wars with the Romans and had what was considered a modern army, based mostly on heavy horse cavalry and elephants. 'Umar and Rustam, the Persian King, were not interested in bothering each other. 'Umar had sent a small force to help Muthanna and it had been decisively defeated at the Battle of the Bridge in 634 AD. Only two years later the strategic situation had changed. Byzantine armies had been forced out of Jerusalem, Antioch, and Damascus by the Muslims.

Rustam, commander in chief of the Persian forces, needed to rid himself of this Arab nuisance. Word reached 'Umar of a Persian mobilization and he sent Sa'ad ibn Abu Wakkas to the Northeast to take command of Islâmic units and reconnoiter south of Baghdad. In May or June 637 Rustam's Persian hosts crossed the Euphrates and camped at al-Qādisiyyah or Kadisiyah (about 100 miles south of Baghdad – 31.35°N, 44.30°E) where they received Arab envoys demanding a "head-tax" or adoption of Islâm, "*The prince speaks truly. Whatever you have said regarding the former condition of the Arabs is true. Their food was green lizards; they buried their infant daughters alive. But God in His Mercy has sent us a holy Prophet, a holy volume which teaches us the true faith. Now the Arabs have sent us to ask you either to adopt our religion or fight with us.*" [485] [Note reference to a written *Korân.*] The demand was unacceptable. The Persian prince, Yezdigerd threatened to behead them as imposters and gave them sacks of dirt as "the tax."

Sa'ad did not wish to fight then because of his numerical disadvantage, but skirmishing attacks and "man to man" combat challenges by the Persians under Rustam forced the issue. When the Persian elephants arrived, the Arabs scattered and retreated for the night. Syrian reinforcements began arriving. Khalid now sent in his light cavalry to skirmish and caused significant casualties, 5:1, among the Persians. That night Syrian allies arrived in force. Sa'ad, who suffered from boils, could not continue as commander and appointed the Syrian chief, Kakaa ibn Amru, to lead the following day in his stead. On the Persian side Rustam was frustrated with the skirmishing tactics that made little sense to him. There was no Arab camp to attack and no lines of communications to cut and he couldn't get the Arabs to hold still long enough in one spot for a knockout punch. That night he received a resupply of elephants and decided that he would use these the following day to scatter the Arabs. The Syrians who had fought against elephants before as Byzantine soldiers were familiar with anti-elephant methods. As the elephants came at them, they attacked with bowshots, spears, swords, pikes and turned them around to stampede back through the tightly packed Persian troops creating panic and massive casualties. In an effort to rally his troops, Rustam left his battlefield throne and rallied his troops near a canal. Fighting continued throughout the night, Rustam retreated to his baggage train and then tried to escape in the canal, but was caught and beheaded by Hillal ibn Alkama, who rushed with Rustam's head to the official throne, captured by the Muslims. The Persian army panicked and tried to escape across the canal. Hundreds drowned in their heavy armor and thousands were mowed down by Arab archers on the banks. It was total annihilation and included the loss of their sacred banner and battle throne. There had been no interest in "quarter." The booty was so immense that when it arrived in Medina, 'Umar decided that a campaign against the Persians would be profitable. Arab armies now went on the offensive.

Al-Hira (31.53°N, 44.27°E) fell as did a number of forts on the Tigris and Euphrates rivers. Yezdigerd III offered to accept the line of the Tigris, but this was not acceptable. Why should "Umar accept peace when he was winning the war? "*Faint not, therefore, neither invite your enemies to peace, while ye are the superior: for GOD is with you, and will not defraud you of merit of your works.*" (**47:35**)

Yezdigerd III attempted to hold Ctesiphon, the Persian capital city in Babylon (33.05°N, 44.35°E). Muslim armies of about 15000 placed the city under siege between January and March 637 and forced the city's evacuation. By 638 the Tigris and Euphrates River basin was under Muslim control. Further campaigning led to the conquest of western Persia by 644, much of the rest of Persia fell by 651 except for Persian territory in the Caucasus and Transoxiana, land east of the Oxus river. The immense treasury of the Persian Empire now funded the rest of the Islamic campaigns in the West and into Central Asia and India. The Battle of Kadisiyah meant the end of the Persian Empire; it never recovered. Zoroastrianism went into decline. However, as Persians slowly converted to Islâm, the conquered became the rulers of the Abbasid Dynasty of Baghdad & Sammara (750 – 1258).

‘Uthmān 3rd Caliph

‘Uthmān ibn ‘Affān (644 to 656), was born in 574 and was an early convert to Islâm. He gave much of his wealth to charity and was a great supporter of Muhammad serving him as his secretary. Although married to Ruqayyah and Umm Kulthum, Muhammad’s daughters, he was of the Banu Umayyad of the Quraysh Tribe without any direct blood lines to Muhammad. He promised to continue the policies of Abū Bakr and ‘Umar while Alī did not. He appointed many of his own Umayyad kinsmen of the Quraysh Tribe to positions of power probably because he could trust them not to kill him. Many accused him of nepotism, corruption, and ruling like a king. The main problem appears to have been disagreements over the redistribution of taxes favored by Muhammad’s widow and son-in-law, ‘Ā’ishah and Alī. Muhammad ibn Abū Bakr ‘Ā’ishah’s brother besieged his home and killed him. He is considered the first of the Umayyad Caliphs. During his reign, Muslim armies took control of the Persian Gulf in 652 AD. About the same time Egypt fell to the Muslims and the Coptic faith was banned. There were efforts to build naval superiority in the Mediterranean from 644 to 656. In 645 Abdullah bin Sa’ad bin Abi’l Sarh was made Governor of Egypt and recognized the need for a Muslim navy. In 646 the infant Muslim navy repulsed the Byzantine fleet in its efforts to retake Alexandria. At the battle of the Masts (36.28°N, 30.26°E) in 655 the Muslim fleet beat the Byzantine fleet and gained naval superiority in the Mediterranean. ‘Uthmān of the Umayyad was assassinated in 656 and major conflict ensued within Islâm leading to a war between the clans – Umayyad v. Hashim. The Battle of the Camel occurred at this time and Alī of the Hashim lasted five years, before he, too, met the assassin’s blade. With the treasury of Persia in their hands and the building of huge military power for purposes of expansion of Islâm, conflict erupted between Sunni and Shia.

‘Ā’isha and the Battle of the Camel [486]

‘Ā’isha accused ‘Uthmān of disbelief and supported those who killed him. She claimed ‘Uthmān was a disbeliever despite his publication of the *Korân*. However, after ‘Uthmān’s murder she wanted to avenge his death. In an ironic twist ‘Ā’isha’s brother, Muhammad bin Abū Bakr, was executed by Mu’awiyah in 38 A.H. for murdering ‘Uthmān. He put Muhammad’s, body into the carcass of a donkey, and burned it. ‘Ā’isha mourned her half-brother greatly and made extra prayers for him. [*al-Tabari* vol.17 p.158]

In 656 forces allied to Alī, the 4th Caliph and those allied to 'Ā'isha fought a major battle near the city of Basra, Iraq (30.30°N, 47.49°E). It began when 'Uthmān ibn Affan, the 3rd Caliph, was besieged in his home and eventually murdered. Many felt that Alī's first priority should be the capture and execution of 'Uthmān's assassins. Following the hajj, 'A'isha went to Mecca where she met with her two brothers-in-law, Talha and Zubayr ibn Awwam, Abd-Allah Ibn Umayr al-Hadrami, Marwa Ibn al Hakam and other members of the Banu Umayya. 'Ā'isha engineered an alliance among all these individuals and received financial support from Yala, the ex-governor of Saba who provided her with 600 camels and 60,000 dinars. One of the camels, designated for 'Ā'isha's personal use was named al-Askar. He was huge and worth 200 gold pieces. She attempted to get Umm Salmā, Muhammad's 4th wife to side with them, but she would not go along with the plan. One of her brother's-in-law, Zubayr was also cool on the idea, but his son convinced 'Ā'isha to go ahead with the plans. She had also convinced Hafṣa bint 'Umar, Muhammad's 5th wife, to go along, but her brother Ibn 'Umar persuaded her otherwise. Nonetheless, 'Ā'isha gathered a 1000-man army, mounted her camel with Talha and Zubayr at her side and left Mecca. The other widows of Muhammad residing in Mecca went a little way with them, but then departed on the "Day of Tears." As 'Ā'isha's force continued 2000 more joined the ranks. The soldiers worried about who would become caliph in event of 'Ā'isha's victory and it was decided that this would be left up to the men of Medina.

Meanwhile Alī refused to move against the rebels so long as there was no overt act of conquest, but when he heard they were headed for Basra, Alī took 900 troops on their way to Syria and led them towards Basra. When 'Ā'isha's column arrived outside of Basra a message was sent to the governor, 'Uthmān ibn Hanif and his chief, Alī ibn Abi Taleb. It demanded justice for the murder of 'Uthmān. The people of Basra rallied to Alī's side. In addition, they accused Talha and Zubayr of violating their loyalty oath to Alī. Talha and Zubayr protested that the oath had been forced upon them and fighting broke out.

The following day both sides agreed to send an envoy to Alī to mediate the problem, but not receiving a satisfactory answer, the rebels ordered 'Uthmān ibn Hanif to abandon Basra. He refused. That night the rebels moved to the mosque and overpowered the guards thus capturing part of Basra and the governor, himself. Conflict broke out.

Basra and its treasury were taken. Talha and Zubayr ordered that anyone having to do with 'Uthmān's assassination be brought out. 400 were produced and summarily executed. The governor was shaved, but unhurt.

In the meanwhile, Alī sent a message to Abū Musa, the governor of Kuffa to send troops, but the city was so divided that there was no response. A personal appeal by Alī deposed Abū Musa. 10,000 troops were raised making a sufficient number to move on Basra. By this time 'Ā'isha's forces had increased to equal Ali's, but Alī was not in favor of fighting. He preferred a negotiated settlement. The mood of the rebels, however, was fixed on vengeance. Alī now sent a message to Talha and Zubayr stating that they had already killed 600; how many more would they need?

Ali's army included a significant number of those that had besieged 'Uthmān's home and these now met in secret conclave. They determined that their only hope was to precipitate a battle by throwing themselves into the fray at a critical time. When Ali's forces reached Basra, negotiations began again with Alī telling Zubayr and Talha that he was just as interested as they in seeing that justice was done. With this promise serious negotiations began while the armies rested within sight of each other. However, while it was still dark, 'Uthmān's assassins began an attack against 'Ā'isha's forces. This started a full-scale battle. Alī tried to stop it, but it had become its own animal. Zubair tried to leave the battle, but was followed by Amr ibn Jarmouz who killed him while at prayer. Marwan ibn al-Hakam shot his own general, Talha, fatally wounding him. In the meanwhile, 'Ā'isha mounted on her camel in a well-protected litter shouted to her forces to kill the murderers. The conflict now raged about the camel. [70] perished while holding its bridle. Finally, a warrior from Ali's army hamstrung the camel and it fell crashing to the ground. 'Ā'isha's litter was bristling with arrows. The rebel insurgents now retired into Basra. 'Ā'isha's brother Muhammad ibn Abū Bakr was the one that Alī asked to pull the curtains of the litter and he convinced 'A'isha, who was miraculously unhurt to enter Ali's tent. The field of battle was covered with 10,000 bodies. Losses were equal on both sides. Alī was generous. He raided the treasury of Basra and split the loot evenly with the remaining troops of both sides. The Banu Umayyad fled the city. 'Ā'isha agreed to surrender and return to Mecca.

Alī 4th Caliph and the First Fitna

Alī bin Abū Ṭālib (656-661) of the Banu Hāshim of the Quraysh (Muhammad's clan and tribe) married Fāṭimah Zahra (614-632), Muhammad's daughter, and became his son-in-law while being a natural cousin. Some also consider him to be the first male to convert to Islâm, and the father to the prophet of Islâm's only bloodline. Because of this Shias consider him to be the first legitimate Caliph, Imam or "guide." Sunnis consider him the 4th rightful Caliph and foremost authority on the Quran and Sharia Law. The period of his Caliphate (656 to 661AD) was marked by social upheavals and tribal warfare. Ali believed strongly in Islam and was a fundamentalist. The period is known as *Al-Fitna Al-Kubra,* or First Fitna. The Battle of the Camel noted above was part of this controversy sparked by the murder of 'Uthmān of the Banu Umayyah.

In 657 Ali led his troops into Syria to confront Mu'āwiyah, one of 'Uthmān's relatives. The Battle of Siffin (657 AD) near Ar-Raqqah in north-central Syria (35.57°N, 39.01°E) was inconclusive, but began Ali's undoing. Mu'āwiyah was governor of Syria. He held Alī responsible for 'Uthmān's murder. At first Ali's forces got the better of Mu'awiyah's troops, but Mu'awiyah had his troops attach verses from the *Korân* to their lances and refuse to fight. Alī's troops then refused to fight and wished to resolve the issue by negotiation. Fighting ceased, arbitrations were concluded and Ali began his march back to Kufa. However, 12,000 of Ali's troops, the Kharijites, believed that the results were incompatible with the *Korân* and refused to accept it. They mutinied and gathered at Nahrawan. Although Ali attempted to appeal to them by admitting his mistake they would not accept it. Ali, was on his way back to Syria to finish his war against Mu'āwiyah, but fearing an attack by the Kharijites against Kufa, changed course to subdue them. The Battle of Nahrawan (34.52°N, 43.78°E) was a total victory for Ali's army. Only nine of the Kharijites survived and fled to Basra. Ali's troops then returned to Kufa. Mu'āwiyah's forces took advantage of the situation by quickly turning on Egypt and most of the Arabian Peninsula including the Tigris and Euphrates river area. Ali was left with only Kufa. This caused distress among his supporters and ultimately led directly to his assassination in 661. In 659 Mu'āwiyah made peace with Byzantium and became the founder of the Umayyad Caliphs. Ali was fatally wounded by a poisoned sword cut while praying in his mosque. He died 2 days later. Mu'āwiyah I (AD 602 – 680) seized the Caliphate.

Table IX First 4 Caliphs, Clans, Tribes, Acceptance

Caliph	*Name & Reign*	*Clan*	*Tribe*	*Acceptance*	
1	***Abū Bakr***	***(632-636)***	***Taim***	*Quraish*	*Sunni*
2	***'Umar ibn al-Khāttab***	***(634-644)***	***Adi***	***Quraish***	***Sunni***
3	***'Uthmān ibn 'Affān***	***(644-656)***	***Umayyad***	***Quraish***	***Sunni***
4	***Alī bin Abī Ṭālib***	***(656-661)***	*Hāshim*	*Quraish*	*Sunni & Shia*

Significance of the Medina Caliphs – 632-661

The 30-year period of the Medina Caliphs included the conquest of Persia and Egypt. The capture of the Persian treasury funded a huge army and made further conquest possible. The *Korân* was first published as a whole work, but "all" sources were destroyed. The conquest of Egypt and Persia secured both sea and land trade routes to China with all the benefits of that trade. The capture of these trade routes denied Christian Europe access to the advances of Chinese Civilization in mathematics, technology, astronomy, navigation, weaponry, paper, block printing and sophisticated water clocks. The luxury of Chinese silk, African gold and Far Eastern spice goods was denied them except at very high prices. Meanwhile Islâm enjoyed exclusive access to the China trade and its advances which it claimed for itself. It still takes credit for the information that many in the West continue to believe came from Islâm. Also, as a consequence of taking Egypt, the Alexandria Library, the repository of most of the ancient world's wisdom and scientific knowledge went up in flames. By 713 the entire North African Mediterranean coast and the Iberian Peninsula was in Umayyad hands. Christian Europe, still reeling from the Black Death and starvation period of the climatic catastrophe of 535, was plunged into what we call the Dark Ages. Religious superstitions continued to extend into the Medieval Period. It would not begin to lift until after the Mongolian conquests and exploration of Marco Polo of the 13th Century, and the Renaissance beginning in the 15th Century. Trade with China became possible with the gradual economic and military weakening of the Ottoman Empire during the 16th and 17th Centuries. Finally, a major religious schism developed between the Banu Hāshim and Banu Umayyad over the caliphate succession. It continues to this day.

Significance of the Fall of Persia and Conquest of Egypt

As stated above, the conquest of Egypt by Islamic armies had great significance that was to last for nearly 800 years. Cairo (30.03°N, 31.13°E) was the seaward gateway to the Far East and its lucrative trade. For nearly 1500 years a connection between the Nile and the Red Sea's Gulf of Suez had been functional. Canals had been dug connecting the delta region of the Nile with the Red Sea. These permitted ships to pass from the Indian Ocean trade through this route to the Mediterranean. From time to time the canal would silt in. This required dredging. Both the Greek and Roman Empires had recognized the importance of this territory, conquered it and controlled the trade that flowed through it bringing untold wealth to the merchants that operated first in Alexandria (31.20°N, 29.92°E) and later Cairo, the Islâmic base.

The conquest of Egypt by the Muslims was due to the bold general, Amr ibn al Aas. Following Yarmouk (636) it was Umar's intention to concentrate his efforts against Persia. However, Yarmouk (32.81°N, 35.95°E) ended in the annihilation of the Byzantine army and ended its influence in the Levant (Syria and the northern Fertile Crescent). Losses had been so terrible in men and territory that there was little will left in Byzantium to strengthen the relatively weak scattered garrisons in Egypt. Amr then the governor of Palestine finally convinced Umar that an attempt should be made to take Egypt. Amr gathered a force of about 4000 men and headed for Egypt in 639. Umar had second thoughts about the project and sent a currier with a letter to Amr to turn back if he had not crossed into Egypt. However, it gave Amr the option to continue if he was already in Egypt. The day the currier arrived Amr was about to cross the border and refused to open the message until that evening after he had crossed into Egypt. Then he opened it and sent this message back to Umar, "*We have received your letter when we have reached Egypt. Therefore in the fulfillment of destiny we proceed seeking Allah's blessing.*" [487]

The campaign in 640 began and ended with the successful reduction of one garrison after another. Following Amr's first victory Bedouins, like sharks smelling blood in the water, came out of the Sinai Peninsula to join in the share of certain riches. This strengthened Amr's forces. Later when Byzantine resistance stiffened in the besieged town of Babylon (near Cairo), Umar sent a small relief force of another 4000 men. Babylon was abandoned after an unsuccessful sally, and the Byzantine commander in Alexandria surrendered and agreed to pay protection to stop the war in December 640.

With Islâm in control of Egypt (Nile, Red Sea) and Persia (642-644), they kept all Christians away from the trade routes to China.

Between 700 and 900 China underwent a great age of invention. Much of their information must have filtered west along the trade routes now dominated by Islâm. This information included accurate water clocks, mathematics, and more precise astronomical observations and methods.

By 190 BC the Silk Road existed between Europe and Chang' An. Luxury goods from the Far East such as silk were greatly desired by the patricians of Greece and Rome. This overland trade route continued to operate until the Islâmic conquest of Persia and the Central Asiatic States. Before then there had been commerce and knowledge flow between east and west. Afterwards, there was a near total blackout of the advances occurring in China. However, this information was readily available to the Arab and eventually Persian dynasties that controlled Islâm. Some of the more notable inventions now attributed to the Arabs in time keeping, medicine and mathematics were possible adaptations of Chinese knowledge. It was during this time that a golden age in science and gadgetry flourished until the Ming Dynasty. According to Gaven Menzies [488] this wealth of knowledge was unknown in Europe until 1434.

The west had received word through the efforts of the Polo family of Venice when young Marco (1254-1324) returned from his trip to the court of Kublai Khan (1271-1295). He had traveled overland into China, but returned home by sea (Indian Ocean and Persian Gulf). At the time the Great Khan had known of the Pope and had asked that information from the West be brought to him. This was the original purpose of the Polo's second trip to China, when Marco accompanied them. When Marco returned, most thought his stories astounding fiction.

For their part, the Chinese had a colony of Muslims involved mostly as ship captains and sailors located in Canton (Guangzhou). Until 1500 and the Renaissance that began in the Italian city states, they owned the exclusive rights to trade with the Orient. The explorations by Vasco de Gama around the tip of Africa and those of Columbus, Vespucci, and Magellan across the Atlantic and into the Pacific were efforts to break this monopoly by routes other than through Muslim lands. Gavin Menzies in his book, *1434,* has compiled evidence backing the title of his book. From it we learn of the advanced mathematics, astronomy and navigational science that came out of China dating back to the time of the Early Roman Empire. Islâm with her open connection to China no doubt derived tremendous knowledge from this source much of which is attributed to them by most Western historians, but may be plagiarized from the Chinese. To demonstrate this point let us digress for a moment forward in time.

Leon Battista Alberti and the Night Sky

Located in the little dome above the altar in the Old Sacristy of San Lorenzo Church in Florence, Italy (43.47°N, 11.15°E) a fresco depicts what appears to be a night sky. However, the painting includes sun and moon plus a celestial meridian and a graduated band of the ecliptic marked off in measured degrees.

Stars relative to sun and earth change daily over a 1461-day cycle. The painting was begun in April 1433, but halted during the exile of the Medici. It was begun again in1435 and completed by Leon Battista Alberti possibly assisted by Paolo Toscanelli in the period between January and September 1440. [489] As well as being artists Alberti and Toscanelli were the leading mathematicians and astronomers of their day in Florence. Alberti served as Pope Eugenius IV's notary and if Gavin Menzies is correct, had met a Chinese delegation and obtained a copy of the astronomical calendar and star maps presented by the Chinese to the pope in 1434. The star map was the likely source of the information used to position the sun, moon and stars in the dome. Until recently the significance of this painting was unknown. It was just a "night sky" or was it? Computer technology used in most modern planetariums was applied to the painting and it was found to show the position of the sun, moon and stars for 6 July 1439 at *noon!* No one at that time knew where the stars were at noon. To paint this picture with this degree of accuracy required precise knowledge of the solar system and how it worked. The painting can be seen in Google images. [490]

What did the Chinese know and when did they know it? In 1276 (either shortly before or shortly after Marco Polo's arrival) Kublai Khan ordered the production of a new calendar and assigned the task to a Chinese astronomer named Guo Shou Jing. [491] In this task Guo made careful observations using precise instruments from various locations in China and examined nearly 900 years of astronomical observations. From these he was able to calculate the earth's year at 365.2425 days. He was off by only 10 seconds. It is of some interest that in 1252 Spanish King Alfonso's astronomers calculated the year to be 365 days, 5 hours, 49 minutes, and 16 seconds or very close to Guo's calculations. [492] Guo calculated the lunar month to be 29.530593 days. Guo knew that the ellipse traveled by the earth around the sun changes. He also had to know that the earth and moon do not travel at the same speed. As the earth approaches the sun, it speeds up, as it retreats from it, it slows down. Likewise, the rotation of the moon around the earth also changes depending on its distance from the sun – the closer it is to the sun, the more rapid is its rotation around the earth. He also knew that the earth was not a perfect sphere, that it was flattened at the poles and that it wobbled. He knew from previous astronomers that the period of Polaris (the "pole star") was about 26,000 years. The Chinese had held an accurate view of the solar system since AD 85 when they also knew about the planetary movements around the sun – Mercury (115 days), Venus (584 days), Mars (779 days), Jupiter (398 days) and Saturn (378 days). [493] These were correct to within a few hours. Much of this information may have been known to the Roman geographer, Claudius Ptolemy (AD 90-168) whose geography takes great pains to demonstrate how to map locations on a spherical world and who illustrates an armillary sphere. [494]

Guo constructed star maps for each of the 1461 days (365x4+1) in a complete earth cycle. Guo also had to know that the stars were at what amounted to an infinite distance from the earth and that their positions were relatively fixed, while the earth was closer to the sun, so the sun's position relative to the earth was changing. To do this Guo had to know the difference between sidereal time (star time – 24 hrs.) and solar time (sun time – 23 hrs. 56 min). This so-called "slip time" amounts to 4 minutes per day and accounts for the difference that we make up every 4 years by adding a day ("leap year"). It means that each day the stars will have changed their position relative to Polaris by 4 minutes precisely at midnight – thus the need for 1461 different star maps. These became the guides for Chinese navigators of that era. These navigators were often Muslims from the Middle East and Mongolia. It also permitted the Chinese navigators to calculate longitude and thus make maps with greater accuracy. [495] Only with a star map could Alberti know precisely where the stars were at mid-day on 6 July 1439, the moment when a mass celebrating the agreement signed by Pope Eugenius IV and the Eastern Orthodox Church had sealed a union between the two the previous day. The decree issued at that time began with the words, "Let the heavens rejoice." Despite this information the old Julian calendar (365 day 6 hr. year) was not abandoned until Pope Gregory XIII's (1502-1585) bull of 1582. Even then Protestant Europe took another 100 years to adopt the change from "old time" to "new time."

SUNNI'S MAINTAIN CONTROL UMAYYAD CALIPHS – DAMASCUS (AD 661– 750) 496

5th Caliph

Mu'āwiyah I ibn Abū Sufyān of the Banu Umayyad (602-680) was founder of the Umayyad dynasty and first Umayyad Caliph. Banu Umayyad was one of the most powerful clans in Mecca. Initially they opposed Muhammad, but Mu'āwiyah's father, Abū Sufyān b. Harb, had negotiated the surrender of Mecca to Muhammad when it could not be avoided. He was part of a possible conspiracy to take over Muhammad's work after his death. It will be discussed later in "Success of the Umayyad Sunni Conspiracy.

Umar of the Banu Adi, 2nd Caliph had military success seizing parts of Persia and Egypt. Uthman of the Banu Umayyad, 3rd Caliph conquered more of Persia. As noted both were assassinated. Following Ali's assassination the Shia hoped that Ali's son Hassan would succeed him, but Mu'āwiyah was able to stop clan warfare by getting Hassan to ally with him. Mu'āwiyah continued expanding Islam's influence by extending conquests along the North African coast from Libya to Algeria and further into Transoxiana Persia and beyond into Pakistan and the Punjab. In 668 Mu'āwiyah attempted to gain naval superiority and managed for a time to control the Bosporus (41.07°N, 29.04°E) from 672 to 677, but the Byzantium naval forces defeated his fleet and a storm destroyed the rest of it. This forced Mu'āwiyah to make peace with Byzantium. He realized that religion was an integral part of his rule and had himself proclaimed "Caliph of God" (*Khalifat Allah*). He made no pretense of being a prophet – only "protector of the faith." In an effort to avoid further clan feuds he established a hereditary dynasty. He named his son, Yazīd, as his successor. This broke with traditional succession practices in which brothers of the leader, rather than sons, succeed to the position of family patriarch. This provoked another rebellion or Fitna. [497]

6th Caliph and the Second Fitna

Yazīd I ibn Mu'āwiyah (645-683) succeded to Caliph in 680. His caliphate lost ground with defeat by Berbers in North Africa and by Byzantium to the north. His legitimacy was challenged by Husayn ibn Abi Talib (626-680), 3rd legitimate Imam, Lord of the Martyrs and one of the Masters of the Youth of Paradise, grandson of Muhammad and son of Ali ibn Abi Talib (4th Caliph) over the question of dynastic succession. He was encouraged in this effort by Ibn al-Zubayr (*Banu Adi*), 'Ā'isha's nephew. The Shi'a faction considered Yazid I immoral and hoped that Husayn would become caliph. However, he and many men of the Banu Hashim (70-150) were hunted down by Yazid's army of 4-5000 and massacred at the Battle of Karbala. The women were taken as prisoners. Some were released and went to Demascus. This cemented the Shi'a Sunni rift that has persisted to this day. It began the Sunni idea that any Caliph who succeeded in battle against another was legitimate because he had God's help. He had to belong to Muhammad's blood lines (*Quraish*), be expert in religious matters, and be able to lead in political matters. The Shiites maintained that the caliph must be a direct descendant of Alī and Fatimah (*Hashim*). Only these could be *Imams* and can carry the title of *Mahdi* ("the guided one"). However, the Fitna didn't end.

7th Caliph

Mu'āwiyah II or Muawiyya ibn Yazīd (661-684) was the 3rd Umayyad caliph for 4 months. However, 'Abd Allah ibn al-Zubayr (624-692) noted above, lived in Mecca. He refused to support the Umayyads because of the murder of Husayn at Karbala and gained popular support among the Arabian and Syrian Arabs. He also had the support of the aforementioned Kharijite survivors. He claimed the caliphate on moral grounds and was recognized as such for a time. [498]

8th Caliph

Marwan I ibn Hakam (623-685) was the 4th Umayyad Caliph **(684-685)** after Muawiva II abdicated in 684, but died in May 685. [499] This caused a shift in lineage from descendants of Abū Sufyān to Hakam, both of the Banu Umayyad. He was the first cousin of 'Uthmān ibn Affan (3rd Caliph) and had been exiled for killing his General Talha during the Battle of the Camel for his participation in Uthman's murder. The exile was lifted later and Marwan and become the governor of Medina. Upon his death, his son, Abd al-Malik ibn Marwan (685-705) became the Caliph and a capable ruler, but now had another challenger, al-Zubayr. The Battle of Karbala (32°37N 44°02'E) obliterated all other potential Imams. [500] Shiites give the title of Imam to twelve descendants of Muhammad, but the last died at age 8. They believe he simply disappeared and will come again as the Mahdi. The 12 Shiite Imams are noted above.

Table X the Twelve Shiite Imams

Name	*Known for*	*Life Span*
Alī Abū al-Hassan Ibn Abi Tālib Amir al-Mu'minin (Commander of Faithful	*The first Imam, the most significant person after Muhammad*	*600-661 AD*
al-Hassan Abū Muhamma Ibn Alī ibn Alī Tālib Al Muitaba (leader of wisdom)	*Signing peace treaty for Islâm, Master of the Youth of Paradise*	*625-669 AD*
al-Hussayn Abū Abdillah Ibn Alī ibn Abi Tālib Sayyid ash-Shuhada	*Lord of the Martyrs and Master of Youth of Paradise Died at Karbala*	*626-680 AD*
Alī Abū Muhamma Ibn all-Hussayn Zayn al-Abidin (Jewel of the worshipers)	*Wept continually 40 years for the Martyrs of Karbala*	*658-713 AD*
Muhammad Abū Jafar Ibn Alī Al Baqir	*Wore clean clothes; had good character; least oppressed*	*676-743 AD*
Jafar Abū Abdillah Ibn Muhammad As-Sadiq	*High Scholar respected by Sunni & Shia*	*703-765 AD*
Musa Abū Ibrahim Ibn Jafar Al-Kazim	*Grew up in prison to be weak & thin*	*745-799 AD*
Alī Abū al-Hassan Ibn Musa Ar-Rida	*Only Imam buried in Iran*	*765-818 AD*
Muhammad Abū Jafar Ibn Alī Al-Jawad	*Defeated people in debates at age 8*	*810-835 AD*
Alī Abū al-Hassan Ibn Muhammad Al-Hadi ad-Naqi	*To be added later*	*827-868 AD*
Al-Hassan Abū Muhammad Ibn Alī Al-Askari	*Lived life under house arrest, yet preached to people*	*846-874 AD*
Muhammad Abū Qasim Ibn al-Hassan Al-Mahdi	*Current Imam; the Mehdi or savior; will come again*	*868–present*

9th Caliph End of the Second Fitna

Abd al-Malik ibn Marwan (646-705), (the 5th Umayyad Caliph) ruled from 685-705. By 685 the Byzantine Empire had reached its nadir of power. It had been plundered and depopulated by the Eastern European Slavs and Bulgars along with recurrences of the plague. It had been hit by Saracens from Asia Minor. Its army and navy were in constant mutiny and its government had been in almost total anarchy for 20 years. Constantinople and the Byzantine Empire appeared doomed.

Considered to be one of the greatest Caliphs, Abd al-Malik consolidated gains towards the Persian Gulf and expanded Islâmic rule at the expense of Byzantium into north Africa as far west as Carthage (Tunis). He dispatched armies under Al-Hajjaj bin Yousef to reassert Umayyad control over the Islâmic Empire. Hajjaj defeated the governor of Basra, and then went to Hejaz where he killed Ibn Zubayr, ending his claim to the Caliphate. Abd al-Malik had made Al-Hajjaj bin Yousef governor of Iraq and allowed him to increase the size of the empire. Hajjaj Arab armies squashed a revolt by Abd al-Rahman ibn Muhammad ibn al-Ashath between 699 and 701. He also took control of Turkestan.

Abd al-Malik made Arabic the official language across the entire empire, built a mint that produced a uniform coinage, and expanded a postal service. He repaired the Kaaba, allegedly built the Dome of the Rock in Jerusalem, and put down a revolt in that city. He ordered that all records be in Arabic and minted a unifying Islâmic currency based on gold. He was credited with completing the Dome of the Rock in Jerusalem. [501] It was between 700 and 715 that Muhammad became well known as the prophet of Islâm, and that prayers were said facing Mecca. Many mosques were rebuilt to unify this religious practice. Ibn Ishaq first published *The Life of Muhammad.* The coinage of the region that had reflected its Christian roots until this time changed to depict Islâmic roots. Was the *Korân* also changed and re-issued?

10th Caliph

Al-Walīd ibn Abd al-Malik (668-715) ruled as the 6th Umayyad caliph from **705-715**. He was an effective ruler and continued Islâmic expansion to its greatest extent thus far including the Atlantic coast and Iberian Peninsula (Spain / Portugal), the entire North African Coast, all of the Eastern Mediterranean including Syria, Assyria to the Black Sea and East including all of the Tigris and Euphrates valleys, Persia and modern-day Armenia, Afghanistan and Pakistan. He allowed Al-Hajjaj bin Yousef a free rein. He picked the generals and allowed them to use whatever means it took to conquer. In addition, he built hospitals, started educational institutions and began a welfare system. Al-Walīd was a lover of architecture. He demolished the Christian basilica in Damascus and built the Great Mosque of Damascus known as the Umayyad Mosque in its place. His reign is considered to be the apex of Islâmic power during this period of history.[502] He was succeeded by his brother, Suleiman. In the West Musa ibn Nusair, the governor of North Africa first raided the Iberian Peninsula with 400 men. This success prompted him to send a larger force of 7000 men into Spain in 711 under Tarik ibn Ziyad. In July he routed the Visigoth army under Roderic and pushed on to Toledo (39.51°N, 4.01°W), the capital. In 712 Musa arrived with a larger force and took all of Spain by being lenient to those who became Muslims and harsh to those who did not. In 712 the invasion of France began in Aquitaine. The objective was to invade France, head into Germany and then sweep down on Constantinople from the North thus taking the entire Mediterranean Sea coast. However, the Muslims stalled here for about 5 years during efforts to take Constantinople in the East.

The 7th Century had been a phenomenal success for Islâm. Its armies raged along the Mediterranean coasts pushing its borders further and further to the West and East. The eastern, southern and western borders of the Mediterranean were theirs. Their territory extended into Pakistan and northward into central Asia to what is now Uzbekistan. However, Constantinople and Rome, the seats of Christian power were still intact. Constantinople although severely weakened by wars with the Avars and Slavs to the north was still standing and a repeated thorn in the Muslim's side. Recent conquest of the Iberian Peninsula encouraged their armies to move further north into the territory of the Franks. Success there could isolate Rome and Italy which might then fall. In the East Constantinople still held out, but had to be eliminated. What would the 8th Century bring?

11th Caliph

Suleiman ibn Abd al-Malik (674-717) ruled from 715 to 717 as the 7th Umayyad Caliph. Instead of moving to Damascus, Suleiman remained in Palestine. Expansion continued into the mountainous parts of Iran. During his short tenure wells were built in Mecca for pilgrims and there was organized enforcement of prayers. However, he executed two generals in the army and this did not enhance his reputation.

Umayyad Eastern Expansion 7th & 8th Centuries

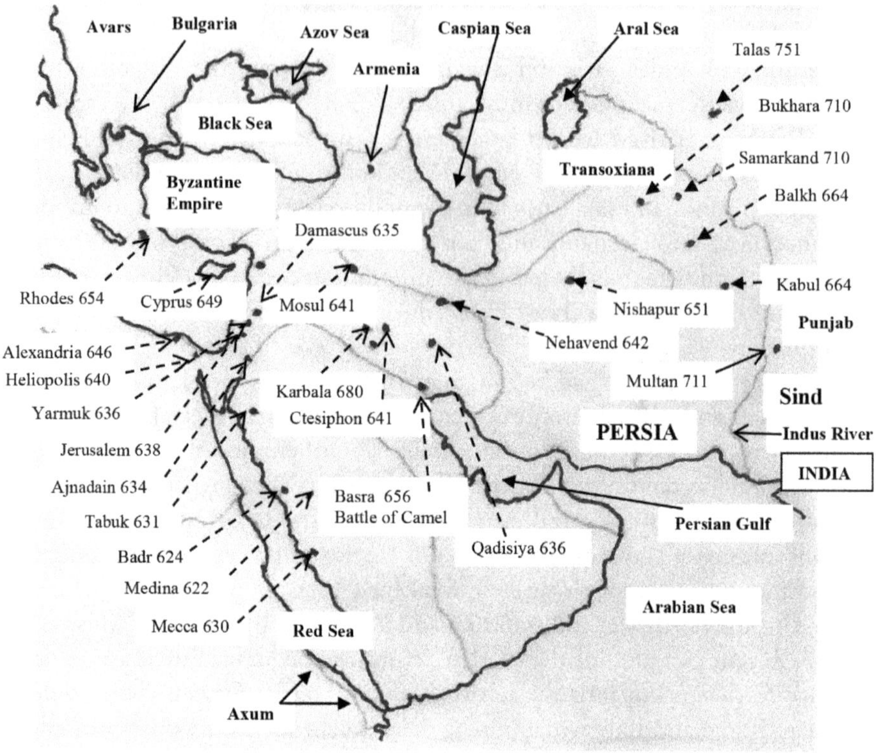

Suleiman sent two armies into Romania and threatened all of Central Europe. A giant pincer movement between there and the Umayyad forces in Spain advancing into southern France might take the entire European Continent. Then in 717 Leo the Isaurian or Konon / Leo III (685-741) rose to power almost out of nowhere. He not only evaded capture, but stopped the Romanian incursion. He went south and further embarrassed the Umayyad's advance by taking control of the southern Turkish mountains. His alliance with local Christians, eager to throw out the Saracens in the region, permitted his forces to advance all the way south through Syria and Lebanon to the Golan in Palestine. Suleiman counterattacked. He struck Constantinople in August 717 and lost most of his 80,000-man army and his navy to Greek fire.

Umayyad Western Expansion 7th & 8th Century AD

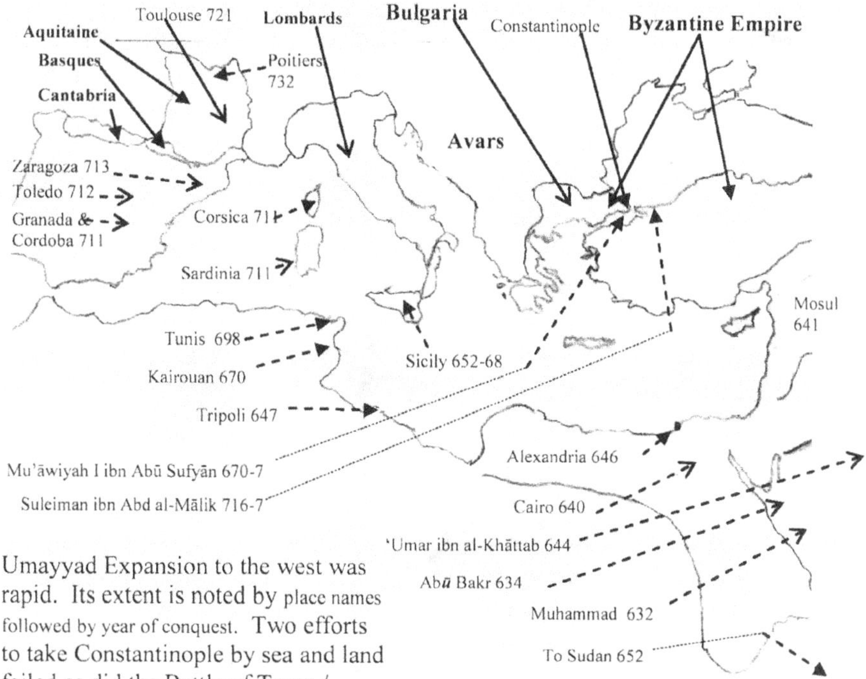

Umayyad Expansion to the west was rapid. Its extent is noted by place names followed by year of conquest. Two efforts to take Constantinople by sea and land failed as did the Battle of Tours / Potiers. **Bold face indicates countries and peoples.**

12th Caliph

'Umar ibn Abd al-Aziz (682-720) was the 8th Umayyad Caliph. He ruled from 717-720. 'Umar was an appointed Umayyad Caliph rather than a hereditary one, but he was a son of Abd all-Malik's younger brother Abd al-Aziz. He was a fundamentalist who attempted to bring the empire into greater conformity to the precepts of Muhammad and made religious reforms. He shunned wealth and fine things and preferred to live in a tent. Some considered him a religious bigot and no soldier. He stopped the cursing of the fourth Caliph at the end of Friday sermons and had the following verse from the *Korân* substituted: *"Surely God enjoins justice, doing of good and giving to kinsfolk."* He enforced Sharia putting an end to drinking and mixed bath houses. He expanded the welfare programs with special programs for orphans and the destitute. He abolished the Jizya tax for converts to Islâm. He ordered the first collection of Hadith material and ordered its compilation. [503] His armies repelled attacks from Azerbaijan and he put down rebellions led by his cousin, Maslama. He inherited a siege of Constantinople, but suffered fearsome losses of his soldiers. This stronghold would await the arrival of gunpowder before its walls and moats could be breached. As noted the crafty Leo III of Isaurian outwitted this Caliph and the Muslim defeat gave Constantinople another 700 years of life and prevented further extension of Muslims into central Europe. With total failure in Constantinople, efforts in the West resumed. In 719 Narbonne fell, but the Muslim invasion failed at Toulouse in 721. In the meanwhile, Frankish power was coming back in France. In 714 Charles Martel was in prison for the murder of Pepin II's legitimate son, Grimoald. When anarchy swept Gaul in 718, Charles escaped. He took over Austrasia in 719 and then moved south. When he had taken territory in the south, he turned north against the Germans.

13th Caliph

Yazīd bin Abd al-Malik or Yazīd II (687-724) was 9th Umayyad Caliph from 720 to 724. Internal strife and civil war spread through Africa and Spain. He destroyed Christian icons. This led to anti-Umayyad cells bent on bringing down the Dynasty. He died of tuberculosis. [504]

14th Caliph

Hisham ibn Abd al-Malik (691-743) was the 10th Umayyad Caliph from 723 until 743. He inherited many problems but the Umayyad Dynasty continued under his direction. He instituted fundamentalist reforms originated by 'Umar bin Abd al-Aziz and encouraged art and architecture. He built more schools and caused the translation of scientific and literary masterpieces into Arabic. He promoted stricter enforcement of Sharia Law. His armies enjoyed limited success by ending the Hindu rebellion in Sindh allowing the Umayyads to regain control in parts of India. He ended the internal conflicts in Spain. He sent a large army into France, but this was turned back by Charles Martel and the Burgundians at the Battle of Tours. More attacks against Byzantium were unsuccessful. Along with these setbacks the Persian Abbasids continued to rebel and gain power especially in Mesopotamia (Iraq). [505]

The Battle of Tours / Poitiers AD 732

During the 6th Century, most of the Frankish region was Christianized and ruled by Merovingian kings of Liege in Belgium. Pippin II (of Herstal) defeated them and his line took over rule of the Franks after the Battle of Tertry in 687. On his death in 714, his popular, but illegitimate son, Charles Martel, a competent military man, fought his two legitimate brothers for 3 years of civil war and won. In 717 Muslims invaded and held the Languedoc after capturing Toulouse in 721.

In 725 Charles Martel was in the Rhone River Valley attempting to conquer all of Gaul. Internal strife had temporarily halted further Muslim advances out of their holdings north of the Pyrenees Mountains, south of Gascony. Aquitaine to the north was ruled by an alliance of local rulers, principally Eudo, a Frankish barbarian. Abdul Rahman Al Ghafiqi, the Muslim general assembled his army of light cavalry and decided to move north against Aquitaine, the province between Gascony and Armorica (Brittany). His army headed for Bordeaux where he defeated Eudo, pillaged the countryside and then began to move towards Poitiers in central Aquitaine where there were rumors of a wealthy abbey. Upon his arrival the city gates were closed, so he laid siege with part of his army and began advancing northward to Tours on the Loire River. In 731 Charles Martel completed his Saxon and Danubean campaign and returned to France from the East. He crossed the Loire River northeast of Tours at Orleans. Abdul Rahman's army was loaded with loot and began to fall back toward Poitiers. His light unarmored cavalry was armed with lance and sword, but not bow and arrow. Neither was up to the standards of former Byzantine armies. There was little thought of commissary; both armies lived off the land. Both were undisciplined and stayed together only so long as there was food and plenty of plunder.

Charles Martel understood his enemy. He wrote to Eudo, "*If you follow my advice you will not interrupt their march nor precipitate your attack. They are like a torrent, which it is dangerous to stem in its career. The thirst of riches and the consciousness of success, redouble their valour, and valour is of more avail than arm or numbers. Be patient till they have loaded themselves with the encumbrance of wealth. The possession of wealth will divide their counsels and assure your victory.*" [506] When Martel's army approached, Abdul Rahman sent most of his loot south and then fell back towards Poitiers to cover it. The two armies faced each other for 7 days without fighting. The exact battle site and date are unknown except that it was fought in late October 732. Rahman had little defensive power. He had to rely on attack. Martel knew it and drew up his forces in a solid phalanx on good defensive ground tempting Abdul Rahman to attack him. When Rahman took the bait, he charged Martel repeatedly with his cavalry as was his custom, but his lines held. In the evening Eudo's Aquitanians attacked Rahman's flank and surged into Rahman's camp where the loot was. The Muslims fell back and discovered Rahman had been killed and fled south in terror. Night stopped the battle. Next morning, Martel reformed his army to meet an attack. Scouts were sent out, but found only the loot in an empty camp. He did not pursue. He collected the booty and moved north.

Martel's victory was said to have been great with "350,000 Muslims killed" to his losses of 1500. Most authorities believe these figures to be an extreme exaggeration since the logistics of the day were insufficient to keep any army of that size concentrated at one point in the field. Removing a couple of zeros from Muslim losses may be more realistic. Martel, nonetheless, acquired the nickname of "The Hammer." Many have said that this victory saved France from Islam; however, Abdul Rahman Al Ghafiqi had left little reserve power in the Iberian Peninsula to follow up a victory and the Franks would not have been an easy conversion. [507] In addition, the Umayyad Dynasty would collapse in 750 only 18 years hence. There would be no further efforts at expansion.

The significance of Tours was regional. It permitted Charles Martel to establish the Frankish Empire. Eudo died in 735 and Martel took Aquitaine and harried the Muslims until they abandoned the Languedoc and retreated south behind the Pyrenees. Charles Martel died in 741. His son, Pepin "The Short," became king; his grandson was Charles the Great – Charlemagne.

In the meanwhile, Leo III was busy in Constantinople re-establishing the Byzantine Empire through reorganization of the army, the police and judiciary, the encouragement of trade, elimination of governmental corruption, and iconoclastic religious reforms. The latter had the effect of increasing the distance between Eastern Orthodoxy and Roman Catholicism. On the diplomatic front he decided to let Italy go. By so doing, the Lombards moved south into the country.

His religious reforms at home included banning the worship of icons and relics which reduced the power, influence and income of the Eastern Church and freed the people for more productive secular pursuits. The complimentary victories of Leo at Constantinople and Charles "the hammer" at Poitiers / Tours, 1500 miles distant, strengthened both Western and Eastern Europe that was to have a lasting effect for nearly 700 years.

Battle Of Poitiers / Tours 732 AD

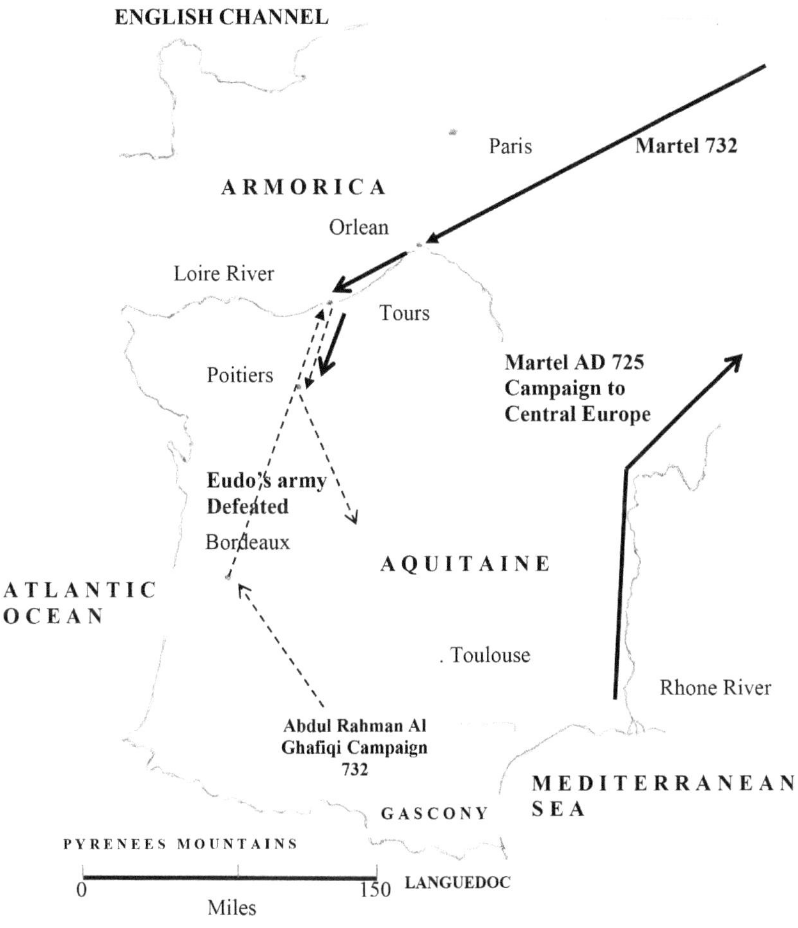

Charlemagne "The Father of Europe"
The Holy Roman Empire

The exact year of **Charles the Great**'s birth is not known but he ruled much of Western Europe between 768 and 814. He was the legitimate son of Pepin the Short (714-768) and initially ruled jointly with his brother Carloman. After Carloman's death (December 771), he acquired all his territory. He was a large man, nearly 6'3" (190 cm) in an age when most men were short. He considered himself a devout Roman Catholic and defender of the papacy against military insurgency and against the Muslim Saracens who controlled the Iberian Peninsula and the Mediterranean. He was literate (very unusual for his time) and a good administrator. He established a currency based on silver; gold was in short supply. He set up rules of accounting, promoted scholarship, art and architecture and insisted his children be well educated. He established his headquarters at Aachen. However, he spent most of his life at war and put together a huge territory comprising most of Western Europe that included everything south of the Elbe River and included all Western Europe, except for Brittany (Armorica) and the Bretons. This included most of modern Germany, France, a strip of northern Spain including Barcelona (Catalan), Bohemia (Czech R) Bavaria (Austria, as far east as Vienna and south to Trieste) and all of the Italian peninsula north of Naples plus the Islands of Corsica and Sardinia. He is rightfully known as the father of Europe. He was crowned king of the Roman Empire by the Pope Leo III in 800. This was later known as the Holy Roman Empire, which was neither holy, Roman, nor an empire. This further divided Christendom. At the time there was no emperor in Byzantium; it was ruled by a queen. So, the Pope took the opportunity to name one and thus establish a tradition for the popes of Rome. Charlemagne used force to convert Saxons and other conquered peoples to Christianity. In 782 he had 4,500 Saxon noblemen beheaded for practicing their old paganism at the Massacre of Virden. He never permitted his daughters to marry, but rather put them out as concubines. He was of no mind to share power or wealth with anyone. He considered the Franks as God's elect. This was later proclaimed in the 19th Century throughout much of Lutheran Germany, later to form much of Hitler's thinking about the "master race." Christianity became a tool of these kings to suppress and control populations with the power of the priests as their political supporters and propagandists. This led to wickedness and injustice in Christianity that poisoned the minds of many and ultimately led to the Reformation. With the death of two of his sons in 810 and 811, he crowned his son Louis to be co-ruler in 813. He reigned as Louis I ("the Pius") from 814 to 840.[508]

Europe 800 AD

BREAK UP OF THE UMAYYAD DYNASTY

15th Caliph

Al-Walīd II ibn Yazīd II (707-744) ruled as 11th Umayyad Caliph from 743-744. Unlike the 7th Century, the 8th Century was unkind to Islâm. In the West their armies had broken themselves in France. In the East Constantinople continued to hold out bleeding Islâm's armies. Even worse, there were signs of internal rebellion. The Muslim Persians were unhappy. The Shiites and other non-Arab Muslim were "outsiders" and wanted respect and "in." Walid's ascension was opposed by much of the Umayyad court because of his reputation for immorality. He reacted by purging those who opposed him. This further made the Umayyads unpopular. He lasted only a year and was killed in civil conflict against Sulayman ibn Hisham, son of the previous caliph. His cousin, Yazīd III, succeeded him. [509]

16th Caliph

Yazīd ibn Al-Walīd ibn Abd al-Malik or Yazīd III (701-744) 12th Umayyad Caliph lasted even less time. Although well-educated he was not interested in politics. Known as Yazīd "The Deficient," he refused to raise the pay of the army promised by Walid II. He was succeeded by his brother, the **17th Caliph Ibrahim ibn al-Walīd** who fled and went into hiding after only a few months out of fear of his political opponents.

18th Caliph

Marwan II ibn Muhammad (688-750) ruled as 13th Umayyad Caliph from Harran between 744-750 until his death following the Battle of Zab.

Marwan had been governor in Azerbaijan. He had won a pyrrhic victory over Khazar Khanate. The empire was falling apart and anti-Umayyad feelings were running high in both Persia (Iran) and Mesopotamia (Iraq). The Abbasids had gained strength in these areas. During this period Ibrahim the Imam had considerable success in a revolt, but was captured in 747 and died in prison probably by assassination. This prompted his brother, Abdulla or Abū Al-Abbas as-Saffah to raise an army of disaffected non-Arab Persian Muslims, Shiites and others. They met Marwan's forces on the banks of the Great Zab River. The Great Zab rises in Turkey and courses through Iraq in that part held by Kurds until it empties into the Tigris. Abdulla lined his troops in a solid phalanx and had them point their spears forward facing the enemy to form a spear barrier. Marwan thought he could break it and charged his cavalry against it. They were slaughtered and this started a retreat of the Umayyad forces and Marwan fled the scene. He was caught in the Nile Delta region 2 months later and killed. [510] Allegedly, the 300 plus members of the Umayyad royal family were invited to banquet by Abdulah who had them all clubbed to death before the first course. [511]

Abü Al-Abbas as-Saffah (721-754), "The Slaughterer," becomes the **first Abbasid caliph**. One of the Umayyad royalty, Abd ar- Rahman, escaped and fled to Spain where he reestablished the Umayyad line and became Caliph in 756. [512] Abü Al-Abbas as-Saffah ruled only briefly until 754, but in that time reformed the army by allowing non-Muslims and non-Arab Muslims to serve in it. He selected a good General for his army and saw to the construction of the first paper mill in the land. However, he did not carry out his promises to the Shiites that would give them significant influence in an Abbasid regime. Second class citizenship of Shiites and non-Arab Muslims plus importation of non-Muslim Turks into the army eventually broke up the Abbasid Empire.

The Umayyad Dynasty (661-750) that came in roaring like a lion finally lost steam and suffered corruption and was eventually stopped at Poitiers in the West and Constantinople in the East. However, it managed to hold all of the Middle East to the borders of India on the East, Uzbekistan in the North and the Iberian Peninsula in the West. It was unable to give up its internal infighting, but it still controlled the China trade.

THE VIKINGS

Men constantly yearn for peace. The reign of Charlemagne and Offa of Mercia created peace and prosperity in Western Europe not seen since the fall of Rome. It was a true "golden age." However, there is always someone or group ready to take advantage of "golden ages" by swooping down and seizing the gold. This is what happened beginning about 789 when a pagan group of fierce raiders broke out of their Scandinavian villages in long boats and began raiding every coast line they could reach. As pagans they had none of the Christian scruples that protect people and property. [513] Their reach included the European Atlantic seaboard, the coastlines of the Baltic, Mediterranean, Black, and Caspian Seas, Iceland, Greenland, and eventually the North American coastline. Also known as the Rus, they colonized and settled Russia. One of the most concise sources about the Vikings is John Haywood's *The Penguin Historical Atlas of the Vikings* noted in the references.

Some believe that Vikings began using a loadstone (compass) to navigate. [514] The Vikings, "men of the creeks," were the ancestors of the modern Danes, Norwegians and Swedes. There is evidence that a century or two before the raids began, they had built their society from local chiefdoms, to princedoms and finally kingdoms. They constructed a fortress, the "Danevirke," (726) [515] across the southern neck of the Jutland Peninsula and began raiding the European Atlantic Coast. This brought them into contact with Catholic Europe, Orthodox Byzantium, and Islâm. Although Haywood does not mention contact with China or Mongolia, Genghis Kahn's red hair and green eyes had to come from somewhere.

The eastern coast of Scotland at Lindisfarne's monastery (55.67°N, 1.80°W) was sacked in 793 with a raid the following year at Jarrow (54.97°N, 1.48°W). The Irish coasts were hit between 812 and 839 and Viking chieftains ruled in Dublin from 852 to 1114. In Ireland the Vikings had limited success except in the seacoast regions around Dublin, Waterford and Wexford. Scotland was dominated between 800 and 1014. [516]

The first raid against England was said to have occurred in 789 on the southern coast. [517] York was ruled by Norsemen from 867 to 954, Orkney from 870 to 1103, and Normandy from 911 to 1087. The name, "Normandy," itself comes from Norman or north men.

They controlled Brittany from 836-939. Besides York, Northumbria and East Anglia many others were under Norse domination for many years. From 865-79 a Danish army occupied most of England. Wales was the only region not taken. William the Conqueror (1066) was the last Viking King of Normandy. English is the only language that adopted prepositions from a foreign tongue, Danish. After 1066 French was the language of the English court from which our "fancy words" derive. The commoner lives in a house, eats cow, and stores his clothes in a chest; the rich man lives in a mansion (*maison*), eats beef (*boeuf*) and stores his clothes in a bureau (no translation needed).

In France, raids extended along the Seine to Paris where the Vikings routed the Frankish army in 866. Paris was occupied until 892. [518]

The Baltic Sea had a great deal of Viking activity. They became the Princes of Kiev and Rus (Novgorod) from 862 to 1271. Viking raiders reached the Black Sea by 838 and the Caspian by 912 where the Rus defeated the Muslim fleet. Trade treaties were made in Constantinople in 907 and the Roman Emperor employed the Rus as a royal bodyguard called the Varangians (Men of the Oath). Harald Hardrada (1015-1066), *The Thunderbolt of the North*, made extensive raids from 1030-66 in the Mediterranean Sea. The inhabitants of Finland along the Baltic Sea coasts responded to the threat by abandoning the sea coast and moving their settlements many miles inland, however, they also had to build fortifications and band their communities together for defense. [519]

Colonies ranged from the Faeroes (825-1100), Iceland (860s to 1263), to Greenland (900 to 1490). Much of their language persists in Iceland. Irish monks were said to have been navigators for the Norse in their trans-Atlantic explorations. From Greenland the North American continent was visited by Bjarni Herjoffsson (Markland 985) and **Leif Ericson** (Vinland 1000), but no permanent colonies were established. Ericson may have spent the winter of 1000 at Lanse aux Meadows in Newfoundland. Our climates today suggest this is too far north to be Vinland, but a warm period in earth's history existed between 1000 and 1500. [520]

Early in their careers, the Vikings from the regions near Stockholm discovered that trading was at least as lucrative as raiding and about half as dangerous. They began a systematic colonization of the lake and river routes to the Middle and Far East. They also discovered the importance of religion. Many in the West felt the influence of Europe and became Roman Catholics, while those in the East, became Russian Orthodox.

THE UMAYYADS OF CORDOVA 711 TO 1492

During the invasion of 711 under Tarik ibn Ziyad the Moors conquered most of the Iberian Peninsula (Portugal and Spain). With the breakup of the Umayyad Dynasty in 750, the only member of the royal house to escape was Abd al-Rahman (731-788), his brother, Yahiya and a servant Bedr. After a harrowing escape in which his brother was caught and beheaded, he found his way to Tunisia where he remained until 755 when it was unsafe for him to stay. In 756 he reached Cordoba where he organized an army and fought entrenched rulers before becoming Emir. With the establishment of a safe haven for remnants of the Umayyad line he and his successors established themselves in Cordoba and eventually began a "cooperative" relationship with the Abbasids. By 761 they had built their first paper mill. In 778 Charlemagne invaded northeastern Spain, but was thrown back. In 785 the Great Mosque was built in Cordoba. In 801 Louis I, son of Charlemagne, took Barcelona and a line of territory in Southern France up to the Pyrenees mountain range and slightly south into what is now Spain – Aragonia and Catalonia. In 822 Abd al Rahman II became the Emir and began construction of the Alcazar of Sevilla. In 912 Abd Rahman III abandoned all pretense of association with Abbasids by declaring Spain's independence. In 961 Al-Hakam II al Mustansir, the Caliph of Spain, fostered scientific and philosophical studies, but in 976 Hisham II al Muayyad became caliph and ordered the destruction of books on astronomy and logic as being heretic. From 1008 until 1031 there was considerable confusion in leadership, which changed hands 13 times. [521]

In the first half of the 11th Century the Umayyads broke up into small kingdoms permitting Christian principalities in the north to begin the reconquest of Iberia. A group of Gothic nobles fled into the far northwest corner of the land, where they continued to live and plot the reconquest of their territories in stages. The territory between the Minho and Douro

Rivers was retaken in 868. Ties with Galacia were finally broken in 1095 when a Burgundian Knight named Henry became the Count of Portugal. His territories were mostly mountains, moors and forests from the Minho in the north to the Mondego in the south. Henry's son Alfonso Henriques following the Battle of Sao Mamede in 1128 proclaimed himself first Prince of Portugal and later declared King by the Pope. Further conquest was delayed by two other Muslim dynasties, the Berber Almoravids and later the Almohabs from southern Morocco.

The Battle of Las Navas de Tolosa

In 1195 Alfonso VIII of Castile was defeated by a Muslim Almohab army in the Disaster of Alarcos. The Iberian Christians lost Trujillo, Plasencia, Talaver, Cuenca and Uclés. This marked the apex of Medieval Muslim power in Iberia and may have encouraged Muhammad al-Nasir. In 1211 he arrived with a large Islamic force from Mauritania, Morocco, Algeria, Tunisia and Senegal. They crossed the Straits of Gibraltar, landed on the southern Iberian coast and moved on Salvatierra. He was victorious and all the Christian holdings on the peninsula were endangered. This motivated Pope Innocent III to call for a European Crusade to repel the invaders. Afonso II of Portugal, Sancho VII of Navarre and Peter II of Aragon joined Alfonso VIII of Castile and answered the call. On July 16, 1212 Alfonso VIII crossed a mountain range through Despeñaperos Pass and caught the Moorish army completely by surprise. In the Battle of Las Navas de Tolosa, the Christian alliance allegedly slaughtered more than 100,000 Muslims to 2000 Christian deaths. This routed the Almohab Berber Army with the Caliph Muhammad al Nasir fleeing to Marrakesh where he died. This was the beginning of the end of Islâm on the Iberian Peninsula. [522]

From 1249 to 1250 a series of battles pushed the Moors out of Portugal and the capital was finally established in Lisbon in 1255. The country was now officially Catholic, headed by The Order of Christ, a Templar institution. The most famous of the Grand Masters was Henry the Navigator (1394-1460) who may have been the king who acquired Chinese maps from the Pope showing parts of America. With further help from the Pope the remainder of the Iberian Peninsula that is now known as Spain was liberated. The Inquisition's *reconquista* forced conversion to Christianity and Muslims fled to Granada in southern Spain. Finally King Ferdinand forced all remaining Muslims back across the Straits of Gibraltar into North Africa in 1492. At the same time approximately 250,000 Jews were given one month to leave Spain. About 100,000 found their way to

Portugal; many went to the Berber Kingdoms of North Africa and to other Islamic countries where they were not treated well. A group that went to Naples was welcomed, but those who went to Genoa were persecuted.

Abbasid Dynasty of Baghdad & Samara (AD 750 – 1258)

The Abbasids claimed their rights to the caliphate from their Hashemite blood lines through Abbas ibn Abd al-MutTālib (566 – 652), a paternal uncle of Muhammad. The Umayyads could claim no direct blood lines as they were of the clan of Umayya. This was one factor favoring the Abbasids. Shiites and non-Arab Muslins were too secular and demi class according to the Umayyads. As such the Umayyads could continue to tax them as non-Muslim. Once the Sunnis were firmly in control of the Abbasid Dynasty, the Shia and non-Arab Muslims, *mawali*, faced the same discrimination and second class citizenship they had under the Umayyads. Despite the fact that both these groups had provided personal treasure and blood to establish the Abbasid Dynasty, it did them little good. This planed a seed of rebellion that plagued the Abbasids until they fell.

Battle of Talas

In July 751 one of **Abul `Abbas al-Saffah's** (721-750-754) first acts was to send 200,000 Abbasid troops north to fend off a Tang Chinese attempt to expand their borders beyond the Talas River in Central Asia (Kyrgyzstan). [523] They faced a small army of 10,000 Tang Chinese troops backed by 20,000 Karluck mercenaries. Despite the odds, the Chinese cavalry got the best of the Abbasid cavalry. However, 5 days into the battle the Karluck mercenaries went over to the Muslims. They attacked the Chinese from the rear while the Muslims attacked from the front. The Chinese general, Gao Xianzhi, escaped with only 2000 men. As the Muslims pursued what was left of the Tang forces, they were mauled by a Chinese rearguard action. In 755 all fighting in the region came to a halt when a rebellion in China broke out and all Chinese troops were withdrawn to crush the rebellion. None of this was significant from a military point of view except for further expansion of Muslim territory into the wastes of Central Asia. If this had been the only result, this battle would not have been significant. However, among the Chinese prisoners were a few craftsmen that knew how to make paper. Within a few years a paper mill had been established in Muslim territory.

The Abbasids & China

Chinese Tang Dynasty (687 – 907) records note the presence of Tazi or Ta shi / Da shi in China. The Tazi were Persians or Arab peoples. Records of 731 also note the arrival of a Da Shi ambassador. In 756, the year after Chinese troops were recalled to put down an internal revolt, Persia sent troops to help the Emperor, Su-Tsung, quell the rebellion. Within 50 years an alliance between the Abbasids and China had been formed to help put down Tibetan attacks in Central Asia. Records also show that a large Muslim settlement in Guangzhou (Canton) erupted in violence in 758 and sacked and burned the city. It was not re-opened to foreign trade until 792. Persian immigrants also brought their knowledge of medicine and the game polo to China. By the time of the Song Dynasty (960-1279) Muslims went to China as traders and eventually as navigators for the Chinese Navy, then the largest navy in the world.

During the Tang, there were great advances in technology which included the development of accurate water clocks and cog-wheel water driven machines useful in saw mills, stone cutting, and milling. Astronomy, already far advanced continued to be studied along with advanced mathematics necessary to acquire this knowledge. Highly accurate water clocks were necessary in the study of astronomy. This information probably found its way back to Persia and the Abbasids. There must have been much give and take between the two. How much of the great advances attributed to the Islâm and China during these years must await careful studies of the time lines for each advance. Until then it is anyone's guess as to who was primary.

Both governments Abbasid and Chinese encouraged personal freedom and even private property in the case of China. Laws protecting private property ownership correlates well with patent law, invention and technology besides agriculture, trade and mining advances. During this period there were efforts to keep Christians / Europeans away from all Chinese trade by prohibiting their use of the Silk Road and entry into the Indian Ocean via the Red Sea. The Abbasids apparently understood that technology equaled wealth and military prowess, not natural resources and were unwilling to let their Christian enemies share it.

Cultural & Scientific Development

Although Europe was blocked from trade and cultural exchanges with the Far East, Islam was not. Many inventions and concepts attributed to the Middle East during this period, may have had their roots in China. There are records from the Abbasids that give us accurate time lines of certain developments. In 825 Caliph Al-Mamun promoted the translation of Greek classics into Arabic and founded the first madrasa or "house of wisdom" in Baghdad. This was the first of a number of schools for basic and advanced learning developed by Abbasid Caliphs. The same year the Arab mathematician Al Khwarizmi of Baghdad wrote a book on Hindu numerals that spread the use of "Arabic" numerals. Although it is claimed that the Muslims invented "zero" the concept was well known to the Chinese as early as 400 BC with development of the abacus – the first computer. The Muslims used a written symbol for it eventually copied in the West. In 850 the Persian mathematician Khwarazmi founded Algebra and invented Arabic numerals. However, higher mathematics had to be known in China by AD 85 for them to have worked out the elliptical travel and period of observed planets around the sun.

In 830 Ahmad ibn Hanbal promoted strict fundamentalist obedience to the doctrines found in the *Korân* and Hadiths. In 840 Kindi began Islamic philosophy. In the same year Sibovayh, a Persian scholar, codified Arabic grammar and wrote the first Arabic dictionary. In 850 Hunayn ibn Ishaq translated Greek Classics. In 900 the sufist Junayd preached the ecstasy of enlightenment. In 922 the sufist Hallaj was executed in Baghdad for heresy.

On the religious front in 849 Caliph al-Mutawakkii deposed the patriarch of the Eastern Christian Church and began active persecution of Christians. In 870 Bukhari collected and classified the "Hadiths." In 874, the Twelfth Imam disappeared.

Abbasid Government

"*That government is best which governs least,*" is from an essay entitled *Resistance to Civil Government* by Henry David Thoreau. [524] He apparently adopted it from the motto of *The United States Magazine and Democratic Review* which read, "The best government is that which governs less." In many respects this fit the old Persian style of government which left much of the governing of sections, states or provinces to appointed officials and did not try to dictate all from the top. Very shortly after the Abbasids took over, they began to develop this style of government by appointing Viziers who appointed local governors. By this they gained the Persian non-Arab Muslim support. However, with time the viziers took most of the power causing the caliphs to assume a more ceremonial role. Over time the Arab aristocracy that had been so prominent in the old Umayyad Dynasty and the new Abbasid Dynasty was replaced by Persian bureaucrats. This caused a serious division between the Persian *Malawi* and the Arabs. With Sunnis in control, Shia beliefs were discarded.

Black, White, and Checkered Flags

A bit of trivia is of interest. The flag of the Abbasids (mostly Sunni) was a solid black flag and the Sunni wore black robes. The Shia, however, wore solid white robes. Eventually a checkered black and white flag in a maroon red field was used as the flag of the Almoravid Dynasty. This Dynasty which was more religiously tolerant controlled Mauritania, Morocco and Cordoba and lasted from 1040 to 1147.

THE EARLY ABBASID DYNASTY AD 750 TO 946

The Abbasid Dynasty lasted from 750 to 1258. [526] There were a total of 37 caliphs. In 762 under **Al Mansur**'s (714-754-775) direction, the Abbasids moved the caliphate from Damascus to Baghdad. Baghdad would become the largest city in the world outside of China with upwards of 400,000 inhabitants. It required much treasure to build. Al Mansur's reign was like his brother's. He had a weakness for food and an obsession for power. He eliminated personal rivals and "enemies." Unlike his Umayyad predecessors he encouraged conversion to Islam. This meant fewer taxes on non-Muslims. He established a stable currency based on the gold Dinar. He also was a proponent of Persian literature. His son **al Mahdi** (744-775-785) was his successor. Although he was ruthless when it came to eliminating enemies, he had other talents. He loved music and erotic poetry. He was poisoned by one of his concubines. During his reign the bureaucracy and Viziers gained more power. **Al Hadi's** (764-785-786) reign of one year was characterized by rebellion and palace intrigue. From 750 to 800 Byzantium fought the Abbasids for control of Syria and Anatolia (Western Turkey from the Bosporus to the Aegean).

Harun al-Rashid (763-6-786-809) ruled as Caliph during the height of the Abbasid power and wealth. [527] Government was more centralized and a quasi-golden age occurred. He had two top officials, viziers, Yahya al-Barmaki and his son Fadl. Al-Rashid was a sponsor of literature and new academies and universities. He sponsored mathematical sciences and the translation of Greek and Sanskrit works. Medicine advanced with accurate description of diseases such as measles and small pox. Some have estimated that at the time of Harun's death, the treasury contained 100 million gold dinars. As general wealth increases, borrowing comes with it, but this requires charging interest. Money lending for usury is not permitted according to the *Korân* (**2:275**). Jews are not permitted to lend with usury to a "brother" or the "poor," but they may to a "stranger." (Exodus 22:25; Deut 23:19-20) so Jews took over this function. Among Christians usury is expected (Matt[25]:27; Luke 19:23). Loans make money a commodity and a price for its use must be paid or it will not be available. Without it there can be little new industry or wealth. Low or no interest rates discourage loans and growth. However, when lent for consumption, loans become destructive to the borrower.

Al-Rashid's government concentrated on improving communications and keeping order throughout the empire. This proved difficult. At the time of his assumption of power in 786, Shiite partisans fomented a bloody revolt in Mecca during the Haij. It ended in their defeat. Many Shia fled west of the Nile into the Maghreb, place of the setting sun – Libya, Tunisia, Algeria, the Atlas Mountains, Morocco and Mauritania. Within a few years Abbasid power no longer extended into this region with the formation of three separate emirates: Idrisids, Aghlabid, and Tulunid.

Idrisids

In 790 Idris ibn Abdallah (788-791), a descendant of Ali ibn Abi Talib and Fatimah, daughter of Muhammad, conquered what is now Mauritania and Morocco and formed the Idrisid Dynasty and ruled an area known as Idrisid. His son, Idriss II (791-828) developed Fez as the royal capital and extended his borders to the Atlas Mountains (Mt.Toubkal – 13,671'in elevation (31.03°N 07'54°W). His son, Muhammad (828-836) divided the territory among his 8 brothers and this ultimately led to internal struggles, attacks by the Fatimids, and finally collapse with the Cordoba Caliphate taking over in 985. [528] This was to become the Almoravid Dynasty from 1054 to 1147 which included Fez (Morocco), Mauritania and Cordoba.

Aghlabid

In 800 Harun al-Rashid replaced the governors of an area occupied by Algeria, Tunisia and Tripolitania with Ibrahim I ibn al-Aghlab and made him a hereditary Emir. His dynasty recognized the Abbasid Caliphate as supreme. In 824 there was a revolt of Arab troops who objected to unequal treatment between them and the Muslim Berbers. The Berbers helped quell the rebellion. In an effort to quiet down the Arabs, they were sent to Sicily in 827 to conquer the Byzantine island. This took many years, but was finally successful in 902. Attacks by the Byzantines and revolts by the Berbers brought an end to the dynasty as the Shiite Egyptian Fatimids took control in 909. [529]

Tulunid

In 833 the Abbasids imported Mamluk Turks as a private army loyal only to them. It was not long before the Mamluks and Abbasid Caliphs began having their differences. In 868 a Turkic officer, Ahmad ibn Tulun was sent by Caliph al-Muʿtazz to be military governor of Egypt. Tulun did not recognize the Baghdad Caliph as supreme, made it an independent state, and kept the taxes. This part of the world was strategic since it controlled all sea trade between the Mediterranean and China and the Far East. He made himself more popular by aligning himself with the merchants. With the wealth he established a navy, irrigation projects, and an army. His son and heir, Khumaramayh, was a capable administrator. In 878 he invaded Palestine and Syria and added these territories to his growing empire. It now added the major land routes from Aden to Damascus to the sea lanes. His son, K͟hu̱mārawayh repelled an Abbasid invasion of Syria, then defeated them and pushed his borders further east into northern Iraq and Tarsus. These efforts exhausted his treasury and destabilized the government. Political infighting and incompetent leadership brought an end to the dynasty in 905 at the hands of the Abbasid army. However, they too would fall to the Fatimids by 909. [530]

Back to Baghdad

As previously stated, most "golden ages" lead to trouble. The period from 809-946 was tumultuous with erosion of the Caliph's power. [531] During this period there were 17 who held the title of Caliph.

1. **al-Amin** (787-809-813) faced internal rebellions and foreign wars. He was killed during the siege of Baghdad.
2. **al- Ma'mun** (786-813-833) took over after executing his brother. His reign was distinguished for advances in astronomy and alchemy. He may have died of poison and was replaced by his half-brother.
3. **al-Mu'tasim** (794-833-842) faced internal rebellions, but was noted for his kindness and agreeable nature.
4. His son, **al-Wathiq** (?-842-847) became caliph. As a fundamentalist he faced several internal rebellions.
5. **al-Mutawakkil** (821-847-861) succeeded his brother and put an end to an Islamic brand of inquisition that had begun under al-Wathiq. He was murdered by one of his Turkish soldiers.

6. His brother, **al-Muntasir** (?-861-862) became Caliph but died of unknown causes in 6 months.
7. **al-Musta'in** (?-862-866) was selected by the Turkish council. He fought a "holy war" against Christians and lost. He then faced internal rebellion. Following his abdication, he was put to death.
8. **al Mu'tazz** (?-866-869) was put in power by the Turkish party. He assassinated two of his brothers and faced intrigues. At age 24 he was beaten, imprisoned in a hot room and allowed to dehydrate to death.
9. **al-Muhtadi** (?-869-870) was first selected and then assassinated by Turks.
10. **al-Mu'tamid** (?-870-892) was mostly a figure-head. The country prospered during his time, but he drank himself to death at age 50.
11. **alMu'tadid** (857-892-902) had a relatively peaceful reign, but had secret prisons. He was tolerant towards the Shia, but not towards the Umayyad, whom he had cursed in prayers.
12. **al-Muktafi** (?-902-908) was relatively popular especially for getting rid of the secret prisons.
13. **al-Muqtadir** (895-908-932) was weak and easily manipulated by sex with the court women; thirteen Viziers came and went during his reign. He was dethroned twice and finally killed.
14. **al-Qahir** (899-932-934) was cruel to his friends; when he refused to step down, he was blinded, imprisoned and released after 11 years as a beggar.
15. **Ar-Radi** (907-934-940) – had no real authority, but was a tool of his cruel chief minister; he died at age 33.
16. **al-Muttaqi** (?-940-944) was non-functional. He was blinded & deposed by Turkish general, Tuzun.
17. **al-Mustakfi** (?-944-946) – suffered a similar fate – blinded & deposed by the Buwayhid Sultan, Muiz ud-Daula.

Cultural battles between Persians and Arabs boiled over and the caliphate lost most of its power. As previously noted, this prompted the caliphate under al-Mamun (813-833) and al-Mu'tasim (833-842) to form an army of Turks called the Mamluks. These were Turkic slave-soldiers from the Caucasus and Georgia along with a mix of Slavs and Berbers. The Malmuks became a military caste and at first helped keep the peace, but over time became a threat to the caliphate. In 836 the Mamluks provoked riots in Baghdad causing al-Mu'tasim to move the capital to Sammara, a town about 100 miles north and east from Baghdad on the Tigris. Here Shias eventually built the Al-Askan Mosque, burial place for the 10th and 11th Shia Imams. It also housed the shrine of Muhammad al-Mhadi, the Hidden Imam, to be the 12th and final Imam who disappeared at a young age in 844. The net effect was to further remove the caliphate from those it was supposed to rule. By 950, the once great empire of 850 was broken into 12 different sections each ruled by its own dynasty. Three of these are mentioned above; 9 are briefly described below. Aghlabid also eventually included the islands of Sicily, Sardinia, Corsica and the heel and toe of the Italian boot.

The others included:

1. **Abbasid** controlled territory squeezed into the Arabian desert region
2. **Qarmatians** / Carmathians (Bahrain)–a Shia Ismali group centered in eastern Arabia, which established a republic in 899. They are famous for their revolt against the Abbasid Caliphate. During the Haij of 930, their sect leader, Tahir Sulaymanm, attacked Sunni pilgrims in Mecca, stole the Black Stone from the Kaba and dumped Muslim corpses into the Well of Zamzam polluting it. [532]
3. **Sajid** (modern Azerbaijan) – From 901 until 928 this land was outside Baghdad's control under the rule of Yusuf ibn Abi'l Saj. [533]
4. **Samanid** is a part of Transoxiana [across the Oxus River – lies between the rivers Amu Darya and Syr Darya. Part of the area belonged to the old Persian Empire where it was known as the satrapy of Sogdiana]. It was the northeastern part of the Persian Empire that included northern Afghanistan and Uzbekistan. Between 819 and 999 this part of the Persian Empire became independent under the leadership of Saman Khuda who converted to Sunni Islam from Zoroastrianism. By 873 its capital was in Bukhara. In 899 it extended its rule over the Saffarids. By 942 it had extended its control northward into much of central Asia. By 962 it controlled all of Afghanistan. In 985 Turkic-speaking Seljuks (led by Seljuk) invaded Transoxiana and converted the region to Sunnite Islam. [534]
5. **Saffarid**, southern part of Transoxiana became independent of Persia in 867. It includes most of Afghanistan and most of Pakistan. In 879 the ruler united most of Persia under his control, but was soon defeated by the Samanid. [535]

6. **Albi** is an area covering the Alborz Mountain Range in northern Iran just to the south of the Caspian Sea. The Buyid Dynasty was a Shia Persian dynasty that originated from this region founded a confederation originally led by 'Ali ibn Būyah and his brothers, al-Hassan and Ahmad. In 934 this confederation was able to take control of what was left of the Abbasid Caliphate from the Turks and ruled until 1055. Then it began to fracture into smaller autonomous authorities. [536]

7-9. **The Fatimids, Ayyubids and Zengids** will be mentioned below

The Abbasid capital was returned to Baghdad in 892. During the reign of al-Radi (934-941) the Mamluks caused most of his power to be transferred over to Mahommed bin Raik. It was at this time that a confederation by Buwayhids (Shia / Persian) took over control in Baghdad and ruled in central Iraq for more than a century. [537] From 1000 to1500 the earth warmed bringing greater agricultural yields and a marked increase in the population. It was also the period of Viking threat and expansion.

TURMOIL

The 10th to the 13th Centuries was a period of political turmoil in the Middle East. The Abbasids (946-1258) were weak and inept. This invited attack. The Fatamids (909-1171) pushed east out of the southern shores of the Mediterranean into Egypt. The Ayyubids (1095-1291) was a middle-eastern Kurdish empire that eventually controlled the region until the Mongul invasion. The Seljuk Turks (1016 – 1153) came out of Central Asia from the East and later dominated as the Ottoman Empire. Their blockage of Christian pilgrimages into the Holy Land brought appeals from dying Byzantium that prompted Roman Catholic popes to dislodge them with the Crusades (1095-1291) and brought about war with the Ayyubids. All were victims to the brief Mongol invasions of the 1260s.

The Late Abbasid Caliphs 946 to 1258

Between 946 and 1258 there were 15 Caliphs in Baghdad. **Al-Muti** (?-946-974) was a religious figurehead. When the Buwayhids (Shia Persians from the mountainous regions south of the Caspian) arrived in Baghdad in 946, the Caliph Al-Muti came out of hiding as a fundamentalist Shia religious leader. However, he had no political power. He could not even help name a vizier. [538] **At-Ta'i** (932-974-991); was eventually deposed and despoiled. [539] **Al-Qadir** (?-991-1031) championed Sunni fundamentalism over Shia and outlawed rational philosophical interpretations of the *Korân*. This put an end to various schools of philosophy. [540] During the first half of **Al-Qa'im's** (?-1031-1075) reign Baghdad was in chaos as the Buwayhid rule collapsed. Toghrul (990-1063), of the Seljuk Turk Dynasty took the city in 1055 and brought order. He had previously overrun Syria and Armenia. The Caliph accepted his Sultanship. [541] His son, **Al-Muqtadi** (?-1075-1094) was honored by the Sultan who gave his daughter to him in marriage. The purpose was to combine sultan and caliph, but after the daughter bore a son, she left him and fled to the court of Malik Shah I, a far more powerful ruler in Isfaham a large cultural center in Persia. This ended the dream of combination. He died before being deposed. [542] **Al-Mustazhir** (1078-1094-1118) was another irrelevant Caliph who ruled during the height of the first Crusade. Despite desecration of Islâmic sites after the capture of Jerusalem in 1099, no army was sent west. [543] **Al-Mustarshid** (1092-1118-1135) was able to exercise some power when the Seljuks left Baghdad, but there was upheaval in much of Iraq. The Crusaders were now at the height of their power. Muslim forces from the East under **Imad ad-Din Zengi,** founder of the **Zengid Dynasty** in 1127, could not dislodge them from Damascus in 1130. Al-Mustarshid attacked in 1134 with his army and was taken prisoner. While under Zangi's "protection" he was murdered. [544] His son, **Ar Rashid** (1109-1135-1136) planned an intrigue with Zangi, who was no fan of the Sultans. The Sultan was able to have him deposed. He fled to the court of Isfaham where he was assassinated. [545] The continued infighting of Seljuk Turk leadership permitted **Al-Muqtafi** (?-1136-1160) to extend his power outside the environs of Baghdad into Iraq. He successfully defended Baghdad against attacks and even joined with the Turkish Sultan in efforts to dislodge the Crusaders, but he was unsuccessful. Nevertheless, he has received praise from a number of Muslim historians for his efforts. [546] His son, **Al Mustanjid** (1160-1170) continued to maintain some independence and had a small force with which he could conduct some local campaigns. [547] His son, **Al Mustadi** (1142-1170-1180) held power similar to his father. He did little, but reigned as Caliph at the time when Saladin ended the Fatimid Dynasty and formed an alliance with him. [548] **Al-Nasir** (1158-1180-1225) is considered the last great Abbasid Caliph. He restored the power of the Caliph. He defended his capital and extended his territories throughout Iraq and into Persia by crushing a Seljuk Turk invasion. During his reign there was also a cultural resurgence. [549] **Az-Zahir** (1176-1225-1226) reigned for only 9 months and died of natural causes at the age of 50. He lowered taxes and strengthened the army. [550] His son was **Al-Mustansir** (1192-1226-1242). His greatest accomplishment was the establishment of the Mustansiriya Madrasah, a great center of learning. It featured an accurate water clock built in 1235 that could announce the times of prayer both day and night. [551] **Al-Musta'sim** (1213-1242-1258) was the last of the Caliphs. His kingdom comprised what is now Iraq and Syria. In 1258 as the Golden Horde under Hulagu Khan approached, he did nothing. Although he had enough money, he did not raise an army or any kind of defense other than to send insulting messages to Hulagu. Baghdad was sacked on 10 February; the Caliph's family was enslaved and most of the citizens massacred. *The Travels* *of Marco Polo* state that before he died, he was sent into his treasury without food and water and told, "*eat of thy treasure as much as thou wilt, since thou art so fond of it.*" Other accounts state that he was rolled up in a rug and trampled to death by horses. [552] Mamluk sultans appointed Abbasid Caliphs to be ceremonial figureheads in Cairo, but they had little power. There were 18 of them from 1261 to 1517. [553]

Cairo & The Fatimids AD 909 – 1171

The Fatimid Dynasty of the green banner was founded in 909 by **'Abdullah al-Mahdi Billah** in the area of Tunisia. He claimed legitimacy through Ali's line that included Fatimah, thus the name Fatimid. He quickly controlled all of Morocco, Tunisia, and Libya and built a capitol, Mahdia in Tunisia. With the conquest of Egypt (920) and the Ikhshidid Dynasty in 972 the capital was moved to Cairo. By this time Cairo was prospering from the Far East trade. Conquest continued until all of Palestine, Syria and southern Italy with Sicily were under their control. This was one of the most tolerant of all the Muslim dynasties. Coptic Christians, Jews, Sunni and Shia could worship as they pleased and serve as bureaucrats and other government officials by merit and not heredity. The Fatimids began to fall apart in 1040 when the governors of North Africa declared independence and started a civil war. The First Crusade beginning in 1096-1099 was highly successful. It took Jerusalem and set up an occupying force. A second Crusade 1147-1149 reinforced the first. This weakened the Fatimids. [554] It was all over by 1169 when **Salah Al-Din Al-Ayyubi** (known as **Saladin** 1137-1193) conquered Egypt in 1171 and formed the Sunni Ayyubid Dynasty.

Ayyubid Dynasty (1171 – 1250)

Saladin's Sunni, Kurdish Ayyubid dynasty ruled over Egypt, Syria and Western Arabia. He attacked the Crusader occupied Mediterranean coast, crushed their army at the Battle of Hattin, and besieged Jerusalem in 1189. When Christians attempted to negotiate an armistice, he quoted the *Korân*, "*Faint not, therefore, neither invite your enemies to peace, while ye are the superior: for GOD is with you, and will not defraud you of merit of your works.*" (**47:35**) Negotiations with **Richard I** of England in 1192

permitted the Christians to ransom themselves, but eventually all, including those who could not pay the ransom were permitted to leave. Those who remained behind were enslaved. Those that left managed to take out about 200,000 dinars worth of treasure from the city. This prompted the Third Crusade (1189-1192) that ended in disaster when Saladin's forces expelled the Crusaders from the Middle East. However, Byzantium still held in Ionia (Turkey). When the Ayyubid Dynasty was threatened by the Mongol Golden Horde in the 13th Century, they obtained Mamluks ("the owned") slave troops from the Caucasus. [555]

In 1244 the Mongol forces set their sights on Mesopotamia, Syria and the Nile area. In 1250 An-Nasir Yusuf of the Ayyubids sent an ambassador all the way to Karakorum in Mongolia to negotiate. The understanding reached did not last. Mongke, the Great Khan, sent an order to his brother Hulegu, commander of the Mongol army, to begin the conquest of Mesopotamia. In 1258 his army of 120,000 sacked Baghdad and killed most of its inhabitants including the Abbasid caliph and most of his family. Al-Musta'sim's death is mentioned above. His son and daughter were sent to Mongolia as sex slaves. The Mongols now moved on Syria. An-Nasir Yusuf had failed to send a relief army to help Baghdad and his protestations were empty and disregarded.

Mongols & Mamluks

In 1260 the Horde moved west to Syria and took Aleppo. The Great Mosque went up in flames, the citadel was destroyed and the inhabitants were either slaughtered or enslaved in typical Mongolian style. This created panic in Muslim Syria. Several local princes surrendered or formed alliances with the Mongols and were permitted to remain in power while the Horde moved on Damascus where An-Nasir Yusuf had fled. Anticipating his next move, Hulegu sent a message to the Sultan in Cairo: "*To Qutuz the Mamluk, who fled to escape our swords. You should think of what happened to other countries and submit to us. You have heard how we have conquered a vast empire and have purified the earth of the disorders that tainted it. We have conquered vast areas, massacring all the people. You cannot escape from the terror of our armies. Where can you flee? What road will you use to escape us? Our horses are swift, our arrows sharp, our swords like thunderbolts, our hearts as hard as the mountains, our soldiers as numerous as the sand. Fortresses will not detain us, nor arms stop us. Your prayers to God will not avail against us. We are not moved by tears nor touched by lamentations. Only those who beg our protection will be safe. Hasten your reply before the fire of war is kindled. Resist and you will suffer the most terrible catastrophes. We will shatter your mosques and reveal the weakness of your God and then we will kill your children and your old men together. At present you are the only enemy against whom we have to march."* The Mamluk was not amused. He killed the Mongol envoys and displayed their heads over a Cairo gate. [556]

At this point the Great Khan died and Hulegu left for Karakorum with the majority of his force. He turned the rest of his command 10-20,000 men over to Kitbuka Noyan, a Nestorian Christian to continue the conquest. Damascus fell under artillery fire. The Mongols, no longer a horde, moved into Samaria and killed the Ayyubid garrison in Nablus, then rolled unopposed into Gaza as fighting would lead to horrible consequences for those who resisted. All of Syria and Palastine were in Mongolian hands; Cairo, the Nile, and riches beckoned.

After obtaining transit and camping rights from the Christian Crusaders near Acre, Qutuz lead his Mamluk army out of Cairo and headed for Acre. On September 3, 1260 he entered the infamous Jezreel Valley, Armageddon, or "the battle-field of empires" and started up the 1100-foot 12-mile incline to the top. Here the two forces would meet in the Battle of Ain Jalut.

The Jezreel Valley had been the site of many famous battles. Deborah and Barak defeated the Canaanites (Judges 4-5). Gideon and his 300 defeated the Midianites (Judges 6). Saul and Jonathan died here (about 1000 BC) fighting the Philistines (1 Sam 31), and Josiah the king of Judah died (609 BC) fighting the Egyptians (2 Kings 23:29-30; 2 Chron. 35:20-24). Within a month the Mamluks had taken back most of Syria. An-Nasir Yusuf, now in Mongol hands was killed and the Emirs who had surrendered or cooperated with the Horde were discredited. Those Abbasid rulers who sided with the Mamluks and supported them continued to rule, but these and their families were retired or gone by 1299 when the Mamluks took direct control of the region.

The Battle of Ain Jalut

Mamluk tactics were brilliant. Qutuz hid most of his force in the forests and hills on the ridge top of the Jezreel Valley. Halfway down the eastern slope, a smaller force tempted the Mongols to battle with hit, run and retreat tactics on the field. They backed steadily up the hill. The Mongols took the bait and surged after them time and again towards the highlands. As they moved upward the Mongols became tired. Once near the top the Mamluk main body poured out of the forests and from the surrounding hills and attacked them on all sides. Mamluk archers showered them with arrows while cavalry harassed them with hit and run skirmishes. The Mongols began retreating down the eastern valley and threatened to break out of the encirclement. Qutuz threw off his helmet and led his reserve legion to plug the gap. It was a rare humiliation of the Golden Horde in close combat.

It was also the first battle in which gunpowder with "hand held cannons" was used in the West. Now it was employed against the Mongols of the East to frighten their horses and cause confusion in their ranks. These weapons were made in China. Qutuz was rewarded for his victory upon return to Cairo by assassination. The Battle of Ain Jalut marked the high point of the Mongol Invasion. From here it was downhill; they could only look back. The Mamluks had routed a Mongol army and halted the Westward movement of the Golden Horde.

Later Battles and Skirmishes

Despite their defeat the Mongols continued to hold most of Mesopotamia and Persia. In December of 1260, a small force of 6000 Mongols from Persia invaded Syria in an effort to reclaim it. They were met by Ayyubid princes with a force of 1500. Without the help of the the Mamluks from Cairo, the Mongols were again beaten at the First Battle of Homs. [557] In October 1271 10,000 Mongols and Seljuk auxiliaries moved on Aleppo, Syria but were forced back beyond the Euphrates when the Mamluk leader, Baibars came after them from Egypt. Another battle at Albistan proved the superiority of the Mamluks in 1277. A Stronger effort to take Syria occurred at the Second Battle of Homs in October 1281. 50,000 Mongols with 30,000 auxiliaries engaged a Mamluk army. The Mamluks left flank was turned, but the Mongol center was destroyed and they retreated from the field. There was no pursuit. [558] From 1299 to 1303 a full-fledged war (Mamluk-Ilkhanid War) broke out over Mongol efforts to retake Syria. They first sent an army of 60,000 Mongols with 40,000 auxiliaries and beat a force of 20-30,000 Mamluks. In 1303 they returned to Syria to extend their conquests and reached Damascus unopposed, but there they were soundly defeated by the Mamluks at the Battle of Marj al-Saffar (April 1303). It was the last Mongol attempt to take Syria. [559] A peace treaty at Aleppo was signed and the Mongols ceased their efforts in the region. How did a Mongolian army come out of nowhere, get all the way to the Middle East and crush the Abbasid Dynasty?

Battle of Ain Jalut

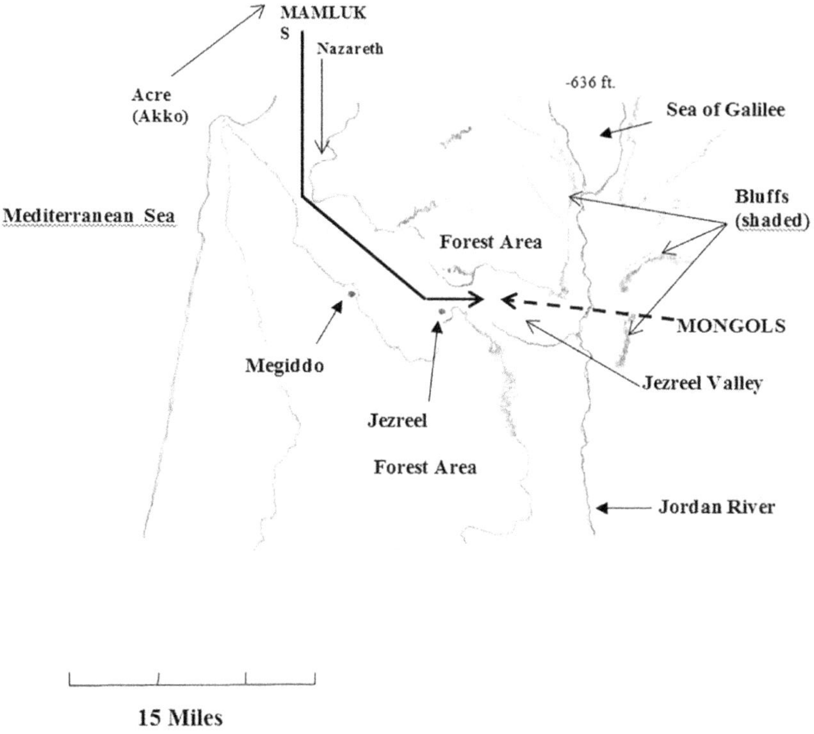

The Jezreel Valley is triangular and slopes upward for about 12 miles from its Jordan River base to the town of Jezreel 1100 feet higher at its apex. It is bordered by forests north and south and by the high bluffs of Mount Gilboa on the south. It forms a choke point at Jezreel. A small creek runs through it. As Kitbuka Noyan moved his Mongol Army up the Valley from the east, Qutuz hid his main force in the forested hills at the top on both sides of the valley. A smaller force tempted the Mongols to battle with hit, run and retreat tactics on the field. Finally the Mongols rushed upward against Qutuz's detachment at the choke point. The Mamluks ambushed them from the surrounding forests and high ground and annihilated the Mongols.

THE GOLDEN HORDE 1207-1480

Temüjin (1162-1227) founded the Mongolian Empire by uniting the Mongolian tribes. He brought them together by conquest that expanded their borders to include much of Eurasia. His early life is unknown except that he was the third son born to a minor chief near modern day Ulaanbaatar. He was tall with red hair and green eyes. His father died when he was young and he and his brothers, sisters and mother had to fend for themselves. Life involved hunting, arranged marriages, and feuds. By 1206 Temüjin united the major tribes of the Mongolian Plain – Keraits, Merkits, Mongols, Naimans, Tartars, and Uyghurs with a number of tribal wars, betrayals and conspiracies. Good military intelligence was the cornerstone of his success. He knew the characteristics of his enemies' leaders, their country, and their army's strength and placement. He adopted good methods from others. At a council of chiefs, the consolidated tribes Temüjin was elected Khan and given the name **Genghis**.

Genghis Khan's campaigns of expansion began in 1207 against the Western Xia. From 1209 to 1215 he made vassals of the northern Chinese and the Jin Dynasty. In 1218 Korea was added. From 1211 to 1218 a campaign to the West extended through Samarkand and northern Afghanistan. In 1221 this line of attack was carried further west into Uzbekistan. In 1222 and 1223 his troops went around the Caspian Sea through Georgia and northward in a huge circular route around the environs of modern Moscow. In 1226 he found it necessary to revisit the Western Xia for attempting to form an alliance against him. While he was engaged against the Tanguts, he was thrown from his horse, developed fever and died.

His policy of conquest was simple. If a city or region surrendered without a fight, they remained intact as a vassal state or region, but had a strong alliance with the Great Khan. This included expansion of the Mongolian Empire's trade base, tribute, soldiers for Mongolian Empire, but also a share in the booty of further conquest. If they stood and fought and lost, which they usually did, they were massacred and all was taken as booty. A few were spared, especially young women, for the pleasure of his troops and other slaves as needed. The organization of his army was described earlier.

It operated on the principles of Phase 3 warfare. All were mounted cavalry or soldiers. He chose men by talent, not family ties, except that his family was boosted into multiple leadership positions by the time of his death in 1227. All the great Khans from this point on would feel his influence as they knew him personally as a father or grandfather. [560] Genghis Khan was buried in Mongolia in an unmarked and unknown grave. Besides being a military genius, he promoted writing and religious toleration. His son, Ögedei (1186-1241) became the next Khan.

Őgedei Khan (1186 – 1241), Genghis Khan's third son, fought his first campaigns against Persia and western Afghanistan. He occupied Persia in 1230, but bypassed the Albi in the mountains south of the Caspian. The campaigns of 1233 and 1234 brought an end to the Jin and Western Xia's Dynasties. In 1235 the Song Dynasty area was invaded and campaigns penetrated south to the mountains bordering modern Tibet. He re-opened the Silk Road for trade.

He next turned his attention to Central Asia where campaigns were conducted from 1232 to 1240 resulting in the conquest of Georgia, Azerbaijan and Armenia. He moved east again in 1231 against Korea after one of his envoys was killed and the Koreans stopped paying tribute. By 1241 he had re-established his authority in Korea. The Indus Valley was invaded in 1241. Ogedei was in the midst of a campaign to take all of Europe when he died. His armies had succeeded in taking Russia, Poland, Hungary and Transylvania and were at the gates of Vienna. His other efforts included establishing his capital at Karakorum, building post roads, and taxes devoted to care for the poor. He was described as a good-hearted jovial man who had lots of charisma and ability in keeping his alliances together. [561] However, he was a binge drinker and died following one of them. [562] Alcoholism afflicted all Genghis' sons and grandsons who occasionally got into violent quarrels; this was to be their undoing.

Guyuk (1206-1248) was the first son of Ogedei and grandson of Genghis Khan. He succeeded his father, but only because of his mother who was regent for 5 years. He was a loud angry alcoholic and created problem within the family. He was the third great khan, but ruled only 2 years. After receiving a letter from the Pope begging him to avoid Europe, Guyuk decided to turn the full power of the Mongol armies against Europe, but other family members wanted to concentrate on the rest of China. A family squabble ensued and Guyuk died mysteriously. Europe was spared. [563]**Möngke Khan** (1208–1259), grandson of Genghis, son of Tolui ruled from 1251 to 1259. He began his military career at age 22 against the Jin Dynasty. In 1235 he campaigned against the Russians and Bulgars where he engaged in hand to hand combat. He next campaigned in the Caucasus and in 1240 in Kiev. He was called home and witnessed the unsuccessful effort of **Temüge** (1168–1246), Genghis Khan's youngest brother, to seize the throne. He was partial to both Buddhism and Shite Muslims. He had women auxiliaries attached to his armies who on occasion were called on to fight. In military matters he humbled Korea and took Yunnan, Vietnam and Tibet so that he could more easily attack southern China and the Song Dynasty. He died during this campaign after becoming ill. [564] His successor was his brother, **Kublai Khan** (1215-1294), **founder of the Chinese Yuan Dynasty.** He ruled from 1246 to 1294. One of his chief envoys who served about a quarter of century was a young man from the West, Marco Polo (1254-1324). [565] Kublai's military exploits against Japan, Mesopotamia and Vietnam were mostly frustrated.

THE SELJUK TURKS

The rise of the Ottoman Empire is as difficult to explain as the geometric patterns of a Turkish rug. It was put together primarily by Turkish Central Asiatic peoples whose names are nearly impossible for westerners to pronounce. Their family structures were divided into clans and tribes, much like the Arabs. The Central Asian environment consists of mountains and steppes.

In an elegant book based on Y chromosome data, Spencer Wells (*The Journey of Man A Genetic Odyssey*) outlined the spread of mankind across the globe.[566] Central Asiatics are thought to be the genetic forebears of both the European and Asiatic peoples. A current theory is that Homo Sapiens originated in the African Rift Valley 59,000 years ago (Y-chromosomal data) or about 1-200,000 years ago (mitochondrial chromosomal data). About 50,000 years ago some migrated into Australia. About 45,000 years ago another migration occurred north to the headwaters of the Tigris and Euphrates rivers. A group pushed across Persia into South Central Asia about 40,000 BC. From there a group went north and west about 35,000 BC into the Eastern Urals and another, the Aurignacien, pushed into south-western Europe in 32,000 BC. One group migrated from there east towards Southeast Asia and into China about 30,000 BC. About 30,000 BC South Central Asiatics migrated south and east into the Indian sub-continent. A group from North Central Asia went west into Central Europe about the same time. About 20,000 years ago a group moved towards Siberia from North Central Asia. This corresponded to the retreating continental ice sheet towards the end of the last ice age. A group from eastern Europe migrated back into the Caspian and Aral Sea regions about 10,000 years ago and a group from the headwaters of the Tigris and Euphrates migrated into the Ionian Peninsula (Turkey), Greece and the Balkans along the Adriatic about 10,000 BC. The populating of the Americas is currently under intense archaeological and DNA re-evaluation and indicates probable Asiatic,

Polynesian, European and possibly Middle Eastern origins of peoples as far back as 20,000 to 10,000 years ago. Potential migration routes include the Alaskan land bridge, north Atlantic ice sheets and both Atlantic and Pacific Ocean currents.

Climate partly depends on the changing axis tilt of the earth that follows a 41,000 year cycle between 22.1° and 24.5°. The Persian astronomer, Abu-Mahmud Khojandi (940-1000) is credited to have discovered this. The last maximum tilt was 8700 BC. Its last mean value was in 1550. [567] Following the retreat of the northern ice sheet, the climate became wetter and the areas of the Sahara and Arabian deserts were fertile and lush. About 4000 BC the Sahara became arid. [568] There is evidence of migration of people to the Nile and Tigris-Euphrates river systems beginning civilizations in those locations. The climate of the past several thousand years has been harsh, cold and generally dry. Climate also depends on the sun's heat production and the amount of volcanic activity – the more ash in the atmosphere, the cooler the climate.

The main industry in Central Asia was herding sheep, goats, cattle, and horses. Periodically the people in this region responded to invasions from the east by moving west. Such migrations included the **European Hun Empire** of 375 to 469 that included land from the Ural Mountains to eastern France. Attila the Hun was its most infamous leader. The **Gokturk Empire** (552-745) stretched between the Pacific Ocean and the Black Sea across the steppes of Asia and Central Asia. Their rulers were known as Kagans that became "king" in English. Being king was dangerous; few lasted more than 10 years. The **Avars** were forced west and formed their own empire from 565 to 835. Their boundaries ran from the Volga River into Hungary, Southern Russia and eventually, with its Slav clients, threatened Byzantium from the north through the Balkans and Greece. Like most invaders from the east their methods were brutal. Many Turks that associated with Persians in the Khwarizmi (Uzbekistan, Afghanistan, and Caucasus, Georgia) converted to Islâm in the 8th and 9th Centuries. Other Turkish peoples formed a number of empires [569] during this period including the:

1. **Khazar Caspian Empire** (651-983) between Crimea, Caucasia, Dnieper, Don and Volga areas;
2. **Uygur State** (745 – 1368) Central Asia and northern Mongolia;
3. **Karahanli State** (940–1040) between Aral lake to Mongolia;
4. **Gazneli Sultanate** (962–1183) stretching between Maveraunnehir (S. Anatolia) to Ganja (Azerbaijan), and from

Caspian shores to Pamir highlands (Tajikistan) approximately 4.7 million sq. kilometers. This brings us to the Seljuks.

The Greater Seljuk Empire (1040 – 1157) [570] extended from Lake Balkash (central Kazakhstan) on the east to the Aegean and Mediterranean Seas in the west. It is bounded by the Aral and Caspian Seas and Caucasus in the north and the Amman Sea to the south. It included much of Persia and the Arabian Peninsula. Its approximate area was 10 million square kilometers. Because of the tendency of Abbasid viziers to grant client tribal chiefs the right to control their autonomous regions, the Seljuk prospered.

The Seljuks were Central Asiatic Turkish people who arose from the **Great Hun Empire** (204 BC to AD 216) whose borders were almost the size of the great Mongolian Empire under Genghis Khan of the 13th Century. Their governmental structure was patriarchal and tribal with a hereditary monarchy. They were organized much as the Arabs into clans and tribes. The principle economy was herding, sheep, cattle and horses. Their war methods were brutal, fierce, and cavalry based. They were much like the Mongolians, but they were smaller and less well organized.

During the 10th Century Turkish migrations primarily from Central Asia by the Kayi Tribe of the Oguz Turks occurred. The Seljuks migrated into Persia and then began to press into Anatolia (eastern Turkey) in the 11th Century. [571] As they crossed the Euphrates River, their leader Suleiman Shah drowned. He was buried in Syria. This brought them into contact with Greeks of Byzantium. Following victory in 1071 over the Byzantine army at the Battle of Manzikert [572] they established the **Anatolian Seljuk Sultanate** [573] under the leadership of Ertugrul, Suleiman's son. His system of government offered protection to the local Beyliks (Turkish Osmanoglu). Ertugrul established alliances with the people of the region, many of whom were Christians. However, the Sultanate was soon crushed by the **Golden Horde** and the Mongol invasions of 1236. The Mongols selected vassals from among the Anatolian Turkish Beyliks and they rose to power. The name Ottoman comes from **Osman I (1258-1324)**, Ertugrul's son. [574] Osman translates into 'Uthmān in Arabic. Osman I became the first Bey of the Ottoman State in 1299. Osman I continued to push his territories closer and closer to Constantinople to the edge of Byzantium and the Ottoman capital was moved to Bursa (40°11'N, 29°04'E), southeast coast of the Sea of Marmara. Osman I formalized the government into a non-military bureaucracy and set up a system whereby various religious bodies and ethnic minorities were tolerated throughout the territory and permitted to set up their own laws to govern themselves. However, this did not mean the end of the army. Following Osman I's death, it further expanded the territory to include much of the Balkans. The Battle of Kosovo [575] and the annihilation of the Christian army marked the end of Serbian power. Now the objective was the conquest of Constantinople and Byzantium itself, but this had to wait because, Timur Lenk (Tamerlane 1336-1405) invaded in 1401 and took Sultan Beyezid II prisoner.

THE EARLY OTTOMAN EMPIRE

The invasion of Central Asia and Russia by The Golden Horde began in 1220. In 1258 Hulagu Khan entered the city of Baghdad and ended the Abbasid Empire. Most of the invaders converted to Islâm. However, they were unable to take Egypt under the Mamluks and destroyed so much of the infrastructure, libraries and the like, that Islâm of the Arabian Peninsula was plunged into a dark age from this time on. The Mongols also deported or killed many scholars. About 1300 Ghazan Khan Mahmud adopted Islâm as the official religion for the region. The Mongols began to repair the damage and built schools and mosques.

The Ottoman Turks

The Ottoman Turks appeared in Asia Minor in 1227.[576] They were nomads from the steppes, relatives of the Seljuk Turks. The Seljuks gave them territory around Ankara (39°52'N, 32°52'E) as reward for military service. Tribal tendencies seemed to make the Seljuks inept at political organization. However, the Ottomans had a line of ten leaders of tremendous ability. They were energetic, cruel, adventurous, just, intelligent and picked good advisors. Conquest was their goal. Ala ed-Din, the oldest son of Othman, 'Osmân I, the first Amir, was a philosopher, theoretician who left ruling to his younger brother so that he could work on military and administrative systems. Their primary method of fighting was horse cavalry. Conquered territories were divided into fiefs, each to supply one horseman. These were part of districts that were part of a larger authority, "beylerbey." Family meant little; each man had to prove himself by valor and service. Osman's son was Orkhân (1288-1362). This family began a dynasty of Sultans that held both religious and temporal power through the rule of Suleiman I "the Magnificent" (1494 -1566).[577] It came to an end because of a woman.[578]

Wars & Battles of the Ottoman Empire

By 1683 the Ottoman Empire had reached its greatest size. It controlled the southern Mediterranean coast line from Gibraltar to Egypt. It controlled the Arabian Peninsula and the lands to the west and south of the borders of the Caspian Sea. This included the lands of ancient Mesopotamia, and the entire Fertile Crescent plus Anatolia (Turkey) and lands between the Black Sea and Caspian. It extended into Europe including the modern states of Greece, the Balkans (Albania, Serbia, Bosnia, Herzegovina, and Croatia), Bulgaria, Romania, Moldova, much of the Ukraine & parts of Russia (Black and Sea of Azov regions), Hungary, Slovakia, and southern Poland. It threated to invade Austria and take Vienna.

Below is a tabular summary of the Sultans and various battles of the Ottoman Empire in wars with its neighbors. This account of Ottoman wars is intended to show how frequently and persistent Muslims were about conquest when they have the funds and opportunity. It also shows that they are not always successful and how often internal and external conflicts interrupt their plans. It should be noted that the Muslim Brotherhood came about in 1928. Its purpose was to re-establish Muslim power following the collapse of the Ottoman Empire. It predated the State of Israel by a quarter of a century. Our great grandfathers who lived in the late 19th Century were familiar with this history. Since 1830 we have lived without this threat. This has dulled our memories of the fearsome reputation of the Ottomans, Berbers, Umayyads, Abbasids and Fatimids. *The Thirteen Hundred Years' War* is no exaggeration. It should persuade us that Korânic Islâm is not a religion of peace by our definition. It will also show us that at times of privation, Islâm lives peacefully with its neighbors. Once the Persian Empire had been conquered and converted, Islâm's spread into the East seemed to meet little opposition. The East and African civilizations had a fatalistic approach to religion and were prepared to go through the motions, be more flexible and profit from the protection and exclusivity offered. Christians had firm beliefs and were not prepared to compromise. In short, this is the story of a religious war on how men and women perceive God and whether or not they accept the redemptive power of Jesus Christ. On this there is no compromise. Islâm says no; true Christian belief says yes.

The history of the Ottoman Empire can be divided into several phases:

1. From 1289, until 1402 the Ottoman Empire was born, but was interrupted by the Timurid invasion of 1402.

2. 1402 to 1421following Tamerlane's death was a period of temporary chaos
3. 1421 to 1683 was a period of growth and conquest.
4. 1683 to 1827 was a period of stagnation, decadence, and the Valide Sultans.
5. 1827 to 1922 was marked by decline and collapse. The modern era can be divided into 3 phases in the rise of Islâm.
6. 1922 to 1960 was a period of inner struggle and resource discovery
7. 1960 to 1996-8 was a period of great economic renewal fueled by the Organization of Petroleum Exporting Countries (OPEC). It included mass migrations of Muslims into Europe and North America and the spread of Wahhabis mosques into these regions. At the same time the Christian west had abandoned the development of petroleum-based economy and its religious ideals and relied on inflation, the printing money, to maintain its standard of living.
8. 1996 to the present marked the declaration of jihad. In 1998 Osama bin Laden defined it thus: "***with God's orders to kill the Americans and plunder their money wherever and whenever they find it.***" And "***to kill Americans and their allies – civilians and military – is an individual duty for every Muslim who can do it in any country in which it is possible to do it.***" With it has come the outbreak of hostilities worldwide (see appendix I).[579]

On September 11, 2001, the anniversary of the high watermark of the Ottoman Empire when she was forced back from the gates of Vienna in 1683, the United States suffered a brutal attack against New York and its general economy. Since the declaration of jihad, skirmishing Phase IV warfare attacks by Militant Islâm against its enemies have been common throughout the world. The U.S. has made some half-hearted responses with her mostly reluctant allies against it.

The Birth of the Ottoman Empire

The principal opposition to the Ottoman's expansion to the north and west came from **Louis the Great of Hungary** (1326-1342-1382). He held his power by virtue of a limited written constitution, statecraft, and inheritance. He was the son of Charles I of Hungary and Elizabeth of Poland and had distant connections with the royal houses of Sicily and Naples. He was a Roman

Catholic. Although he had a parliament, he called it only twice. His main military effort was against Venice and Naples with mixed results. He had success against Lithuania and the Golden Horde in the north. In 1344 Moldova and Wallachia became Vassal States of Hungary. In 1349 and 1354 his army of 80,000 repelled Serbian invaders. Peace was made in 1355. Later campaigns starting in 1366 encouraged the Serbs, Wallachians, Bosnians and Bulgarians to become Roman Catholic and present a united front against the Muslim Turks. This goal failed. Despite the ongoing collapse of Byzantium these regions remained loyal to Orthodoxy. Louis created a vassal state of Moldova in 1352 and Vidin in 1365. The Serbs and Wallachians turned out to be unreliable allies against the Turks. Louis defeated the Turkish army in Wallachia in 1374. Lands under the control of Hungary at the height of its power in the 1370s included modern Hungary, Poland, parts of the Ukraine, Moldova, all of modern Romania (Wallachia, Transylvania, and Vidin), Bulgaria, and parts of Belarus. [580]

Osman I (1258 – 1324) arose from a Turkish region to the southeast of Constantinople. His reign began in 1281. He expanded his holdings west, taking Nicaea in 1302 and later Ephesus on the Aegean Sea in 1304. He spread eastward in Anatolia taking territory on the Black Sea. His army in western Anatolia took the city of Bursa (on the southern shores of the Sea of Marmara) two years after his death in 1326. It became the first Ottoman Capital. [581]

Orhan I, son of Osman I (1281-1361) suggested that his brother share power with him, but his brother, Alaeddin, refused. He was made Vizier (bearer of burdens) and established a standing professional regularly paid army. Janissaries came later. Orhan's principle objective was further expansion in Anatolia. He was obliged to retake the city of Nicaea in 1331. In 1337 Nicomedia the first Capital of the Eastern Roman Empire until the founding of Constantinople (modern Izmit 40.26° N 29.43°E) was conquered. In 1329 he defeated the Byzantine Army attempting to recapture the cities of Nicomedia and Niceae in the Battle of Pelekanon. The Byzantine army never again challenged the Ottomans capture of more lands in Anatolia. Most of northwestern Anatolia was in Ottoman hands and Byzantium's Asiatic holdings were being compressed. He next went after Karesi, a Muslim Turkish territory. This gave him even more of Western Anatolia. Orhan I spent the next 20 years strengthening the government. In 1346 Orhan married the Emperor of Byzantium's daughter, Theodora, to help cement relations between the two powers.

Janissaries 582 were the elite corps of Ottoman armies. It is a Europeanized name from *yeniçheri*, "slave-soldiers" or "new soldiers."

They were first organized by the caliphs of Egypt and known as Mamluks. Originally, they had been Turkish prisoners taken by the Mongols and sold in Egypt. Ala ed-Din, 'Osmân I took his tribute in the form of male children instead of a head tax. These were brought up in *Islâm*, often castrated or forbidden to marry and engage in trade. They were held under strict discipline and confined to camp after age 25. These were infantry. This corps was a celibate military community devoted to the Sultan and to Islâm and trained from childhood in the business of war. The lords of feudal districts had no such resource. Thus, the Sultan had a standing army with an elite infantry and a competent cavalry with relatively weak nobility unable to challenge him. There was nothing comparable in the West.

The Fall of Gallipoli 1352-4 From 1352 to 1354 a civil war was fought in Byzantium. Turkish mercenary troops pillaged much of Thrace (southeastern Bulgaria). In 1352 they occupied a small fortress near Gallipoli (40.22°N, 26.27°E), a town on a peninsula at the west end of the Sea of Mar Mara on the European side. In March 1354 an earthquake hit the region destroying most structures in Gallipoli. Greek inhabitants left whereupon Suleiman brought in 3000 troops plus all the Turkish families he could find and re-occupied the town. He built a fort on this strategic site – it controlled the Dardanelles, entry to the Sea of Mar Mara. Emperor John VI Kantakouzenos of Byzantium attempted to buy it back, but Suleiman stated he could not give up something granted him by Allah. Those in Constantinople feared an invasion by the Turks and overthrew John VI that same November. Gallipoli became a stepping stone in the conquest of Greece and Thrace which fell in the next 10 years. [583] By 1355 Byzantium had been all but wiped out.

The Battle of Ihtiman in 1355 between Ottomans and Bulgarians occurred in Thrace. Raiding parties of Ottoman Turks took their first fortress in 1352. Little is known of this battle except that the Ottoman forces won and began more serious campaigns against countries in the Balkans especially Bulgaria. [584] In 1361 Murâd I crossed the straits and took Adrianople (41°40'N 26°34'E), making it his capital and began a methodical conquest of the Balkans. With each conquest came more fiefs and Janissaries. Even the Mongol Invasion of the 14th Century didn't stop the progress for long. By the middle of the 15th Century all of the Balkans and Greece were in the Ottoman hands.

Murad I (1326 – 1389) was the First Sultan of the Ottoman Empire. He ruled from 1361 to 1389 when he died at the Battle of Kosovo (42.6°N 20.85°E). He was responsible for establishing the Ottoman Empire by conquering the Bulgarians and Serbs. [585]

Battle of Maritsa September 1371, named after the river, took place in Greece's northeast corner on the Maritsa River near the present town of Ormenio (41°43N, 26°13E). About 70,000 Turks and a Serbian force of unknown size fought. Casualties are not known. It was the first battle in which Christians fought the Turkish Janissaries. As a result parts of Greece and Macedonia fell under Ottoman control. The Serbian Empire was broken up into a number of principalities. [586]

The Battles of Sofia 1382 and **Tarnovgrad 1393** about which little is known was part of the conquest of northern Greece and modern Bulgaria. [587]

In 1385 the Ottoman **Turks invaded Albania** and fought Serb troops at Savra (20.16°N *41.15°E). Serbian and Albanian Lords became Ottoman vassals. A second battle fought on the* same site in 1480 known as the Battle of Savra or **Battle of the Saurian Field** was fought in 1480 in Southern Albania. [588] At the **B**attle of Pločnik in 1386 Serbian forces turned back the Ottomans near Prokuplje (43.24 N, 21.59 E). 589 The conquest of Bosnia began in 1388. The Battle of Bileca near the village of Rudine (43.47 N 19.40 E) ended in defeat for Ottoman forces. When Serbia fell in 1389 a second offensive began against Bosnia. [590]

The Battle of Kosovo was fought in June **1389.** The forces of Sultan Murad I numbering 27-40,000 fought those of Prince Lazar Hrebeljanović of Serbia – 12-30,000. Casualties on both sides were horrible and included both Murad I and Prince Lazar. The Ottomans won a pyrrhic victory. Its significance was that Serbia had no more fighting men, but the Ottoman Turks could raise another army. This might have led to the first conquest of Serbia except that Bayzed I laid a siege of Constantinople lasting 7 years. The Timurids under Tamerlane arrived in Anatolia and conquered the Turks. Tamerlane died and a civil was ensued over succession of the Sultanate. This allowed a pocket of resistance to develop in Albania that held out for 25 years while the Ottoman Empire was otherwise engaged. [591]

Bayezid I (1360-1403) was Sultan from 1389-1402. His father was Murad I. Immediately following the battle of Kosovo, Serbia became a vassal state. Bayezid solidified his status with Serbia by marriage with Prince Lazar's daughter. He also had his younger brother strangled to avoid a fight over succession. From 1389 to 1395 he conquered Bulgaria and northern Greece. He fought two important battles. [592]

The Battles of Karanovasa and/or Rovine (October 1394 / May 1395) were fought in Romania against the Wallachian forces of 10,000 men and resulted in a strategic victory for Wallachia. From a tactical view it was another pyrrhic victory for Ottoman forces of 40,000 men. The site of the battle is unknown except that the Ottoman troops had to cross the

Danube and it was near the Arges River that flows from the Carpathian Mountains into the Danube in southern Romania. This battle may be confused with another allegedly fought in 1394, the **Battle of Karanovasa** in the same region in which the Wallachian forces won and Ottoman troops were forced to withdraw. [593]

In 1394 Bayezid besieged Constantinople. This led to an alliance of Christian Crusaders from France, Hospitaller Knights, and troops from the Kingdoms of Wallachia, Hungary, Bulgaria and the Republic of Venice who came to the aid of their Byzantine cousins. Numbers are disputed, but best estimates are 7.5-16,000 troops. These met the Ottoman Turks with 12-15,000 men at the Battle of Nicopolis on the north bank of the Danube, 4 k downstream from the junction of the Osam River (43.42 N 24.^{51} E) in 1396. The Christian alliance was destroyed, the 2nd Bulgarian Empire extinguished, and 3000 Christian prisoners were executed. This ended Crusader activity until the 15th Century. Ottoman losses were unknown, but the siege against Constantinople continued until 1401. [594]

In 1400 Tamerlane's Timurid forces invaded Anatolia from the east and persuaded other Muslim Turkic vassals to join him in throwing off the yoke of the Ottomans. They did and the invasion continued. This caused Bayezid to break off the siege of Constantinople and direct his attention further east. Bayezid's forces were defeated at the **Battle of Ankara July 1402.** The size of the armies is unknown, but casualties were estimated as 15-25,000 for the Timurids and 15-40,000 killed or wounded for the Ottomans. The Timurids fought much as did the Golden Horde with a cavalry army. Their sizes have been estimated as high as 800,000–400,000 to a more realistic 140,000 Timurids to 80,000 Ottomans. It is said that the Ottomans attacked first, but met the arrows of the Timurid horse archers. The Timurids diverted the water supply away from the Ottomans and there were many Ottoman desertions especially from other ethnic allies. The Timurids were victorious on the final day. Although Bayezid escaped with some of his horsemen into a mountainous region, Tamerlane's forces surrounded the area and captured him. He was a prisoner until his death in 1403 under uncertain circumstances. Bayezid's four sons were not captured. Following the death of Tamerlane in 1404, the Timurid hosts evaporated and the four sons began a civil war of succession. [595]

Tamerlane & Temporary Chaos of the Ottoman Empire

Tamerlane (Timur or Teymur-e Lang–1336-1405) of the Timurid Dynasty temporarily interrupted the progress of the Ottoman Turks. He was from Kesh / Shahrisabz (39.03°N, 66.50°E) 50 miles south of Samarkand in modern Uzbekistan. It was part of what was then known as Transoxiana. He was born a Muslim of unknown persuasion. By age 24 he was known as a military genius and leader. He lacked political abilities. He never styled himself as a king, but only an amir. After the death of Tughlugh Timur of Kashgar, a descendant of Genghis Khan and the defeat of his rivals, he became ruler in Samarkand. Following the death of Abu Sa'id of the Ilkhanid Persian Dynasty in 1335 a power vacuum existed in Persia. This gave Timur a chance to invade Persia in 1385 and by 1387 he had completed its conquest. In 1385 the khan of the Golden Horde, Tokhtamysh invaded Azerbaijan. This began the Tokhtamysh-Timur War. Timur attacked him at the Kondurcha River in 1391 and beat him, but part of Tokhtamysh's army escaped. Timur now invaded Muscovy north of Tokhtamysh's territory. On his way to Moscow, Timur found that Tokhtamysh had begun to follow him. Timur had gone 700 miles north and 1000 miles west with a 100,000-man host. Lack of food on the Steppes forced him to spread out and hunt then return to his base. In 1393 he invaded Anjudan and despoiled it. Further campaigning destroyed Sarai and much of the Astrakhan region, home base of the Golden Horde. At the Battle of the Terek River, April 1395, he defeated Tokhtamysh. He had caused so much havoc in the region that the power base and Silk Road trade that had kept the economy of the Golden Horde alive was gone. The Golden Horde ceased to exist as a power. Before his death Tamerlane said, "*Who ever opens my tomb, shall unleash an invader more terrible than I.*" In 1941 exhumation began. Two days later Hitler began Operation Bararosa against the Soviet Union.

Tamerlane was succeeded by his son Shah Rukh. At the time of his death his empire included: southeastern Turkey, Syria, Iraq, Kuwait, Iran, Kazakhstan, Afghanistan, Armenia, Azerbaijan, Georgia, Turkmenistan, Uzbekistan, Kyryzstan, Pakistan, northwestern India and as far as Kashgar in China, but most of this other than the Central Asiatic and Indian parts would be lost. His most famous descendant was Babur (1483 -1531) whose descendants expanded the Mughal Empire (1526-1858) to include most of the Indian Subcontinent. It introduced Islam into this entire region.[596]

In the meanwhile, the Ottoman Sultan Bayzed I had besieged Constantinople beginning in 1394. This lasted until 1401, but ceased when Tamerlane convinced a number of local Turkish leaders to oppose him. This led to the **Battle of Ankara in July 1402,** the death of Bayzed I, and the resulting civil war between his sons. Following this the Timur Empire went into decline awaiting resurrection by his descendants as noted above. The Ottoman Empire survived and recovered. [597]

The Interregnum was a period of chaos and civil strife from 1404 to 1413. Each of Bayzed I sons wanted the Sultanship. **Suleiman,** 1st son, had his capital at Adrianople (41°40'N, 26°34'E). He ruled northern Greece, Thrace and Bulgaria. **Mehmed**, 3rd son, ruled in Amasya (40.39°, 35.50°E), in a mountainous region in north central Turkey on the Black Sea. **Isa Celebi**, 2nd son, ruled at Bursa (40.11°N, 29.04°E), but was killed by Mehmed's partisans in 1406 at a public bath. Suleiman invaded Anatolia and took Bursa and Ankara in 1404. **Prince Musa**, 4th son, allied with Mehmed suggested an attack against Suleyman in Thrace and Mehmed encouraged him. This succeeded in getting Suleiman back to his own territories. Eventually Suleiman's army defected to Musa and Suleiman was executed at Edirne (Adrianople) in 1411. Musa became master of Thrace. This brought him in opposition to his ally, Emperor Manuel II Palaiologos of Byzantium. Musa attacked towards Constantinople and Manuel II asked his ally, Mehmed to come to his aid. Mehmed moved his troops into Thrace, obtained an alliance with the Serbs and finally faced battle against Musa in the southeastern part of Serbia near Sophia. Musa died and Mehmed became Sultan. [598]

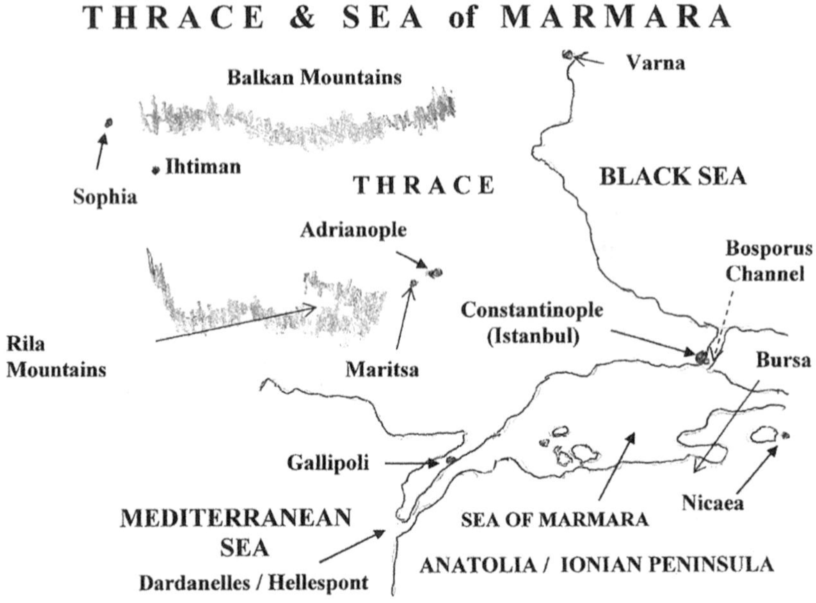

Mehmed I (1382-1421) In 1413 Mehmed was Sultan and for the rest of his reign put things in order. He moved the capital from Bursa to Edirne (Adrianople) and spent his time establishing his Anatolian base. [599] A map below shows areas of early Ottoman Empire Conquests.

The Growth of the Ottoman Empire

Battle of Ceuta August 1415. Two hundred Portuguese ships carrying 45,000 men led by King John I of Portugal landed at Ceuta, caught the small garrison by surprise and annihilated it in 12 hours. Casualties included 8 Christians and several thousand Muslims. Ceuta is located on a point of land at the Straits of Gibraltar on the African side. [600]

Murad II (1404 – 1451) who ruled from 1421 to 1451 was in almost constant warfare against Christendom. In 1421 he besieged Constantinople, but had to abandon it in 1422 to chase down and execute his 13-year-old brother. Once again in July-August of 1424 he besieged Constantinople and forced the Byzantine Emperor, Manuel II to begin an annual tribute to the Ottomans starting in 1425. What little the perennial cash-cow had would be milked away until the end. Later in 1424 he organized campaigns against Wallachia, the Greek Peloponnese and Serbia. [601]

The Siege and Capture of Thessalonica 1422 – 1430. The Byzantine royalty owned the city. As a hotbed of rebellion, it was a thorn in the side of the Ottomans and Murad determined to punish it. He laid siege to the city. However, governor Andronikos Palaiologos sold it to Venice, which then became responsible for its defense. This brought Murad into conflict with Venice. Thessalonica (40.6 N, 22.9 E) held out despite several famines until 1430 when it fell.[602] In 1446 – 47 Murad II turned the throne over to his son and as general began a campaign against Venetian held Athens. It would not be successful until its fall in 1458 to the forces of his son, Mehmed II. In 1448 he reclaimed the hrone and held it until his death in 1451.[603]

The **Tsardom of Vidin** included land that encompassed Bulgarian territory south of the Danube in the Danubian plain from Vidin (43.59 N, 22.52 E) in its northwest corner, south to the Balkans thence east to the Black Sea plus that part of Romania encompassing the Danube River as it flows north to its delta. It was part of the Bulgarian empire, but fell to the Ottomans in **1422** under Murad II.[604]

Murad now turned his attention against the Karamanid Emirate in the south-central portion of Anatolia, the Republic of Venice and Serbia. As Murad began his campaign against Thessalonica, the Mamluk Egyptians invaded Cyprus in 1426 with a fleet of 180 vessels carrying 5000 men plus cavalry. Murad was not distracted. In 1427 he besieged Thessalonica in Greece; it fell in 1430 and Venice quit in 1432. He defeats the Karamanids (Muslim Turks) in 1428. The Serbs came next. His campaign against them began in 1430 against Transylvania and Serbia. By 1439 he had taken Serbia. Christian concerns in Western Europe had reached a point that the Holy Roman Empire formed a coalition with Poland and Albania to join with the Hungarians and Serbian partisans against Murad II. Ottoman problems at home caused a lull in the fighting, but this resumed in 1444 with the Battle of Varna.[605]

The Reconquest of Serbia Following Prince Lazar's death at the first Battle of Kosovo in 1389, his son, Stefan Lazarevic, a minor, succeeded him. Serbia became a vassal state of the Ottomans. Stefan's mother, Princess Milica, became regent. To further protect the country Milica arranged a marriage of her daughter, Olivera, to Sultan Bayezid I, but he was dead by 1403 and the fledgling Ottoman Empire was thrown into the Interregnum, a decade of civil strife. This gave conquered territories such as Serbia a reprieve. By 1421 Serbia had regained all its territories that it had lost in the first Battle of Kosovo. Stephan was able to keep both the Ottomans and Hungarians at bay. The economy also improved through rich silver mines. In 1427 Stephan died and his nephew, Đurađ Branković, succeeded him and Serbia rejoined the Hungarian Empire. A peace treaty signed in 1428 promised to keep Hungary and the Ottomans out of war following the death of King Sigismund. Đurađ constructed a fortress from 1428-30 in Smederevo (44.40°N, 20.56°E) on the Danube near the Hungarian border. By 1437 Murad II was again on the march. This time he invaded Transylvania. In 1438 Murad II invaded and sacked most of Serbia. In May 1439 Đurađ fled to Hungary. The Ottomans besieged Smederevo which fell after 3 months in August 1439. [606]

Count Dracula

Not all was smooth sailing for the Sultans and their conquests in Central Europe. One of the most fearsome characters of all time periodically held power in Wallachia (Romania) and struck terror into the sight and minds of the Turks – a very difficult feat. It was Vlad III otherwise known as Vlad "the impaler" or Vlad Dracula (1431-1476 AD). [607] Count Dracula was one of the cruelest men that ever lived, but times were brutal. His prisoners of war, criminals, political and personal rivals were impaled on stakes. The Mongolian invaders had used this method of intimidation 150 years earlier.

Wallachia (Romania) was a battle ground between the Turks and the Hungarians during the first phase of expansion by the Ottoman Turks into Central Europe and harsh measures were called for. Vlad II had sent his son as a hostage to the Sultan, where he developed a life-long hatred for the Turks. "Dracula" originated from a title that both Vlad II and his son held, "The order of the Dragon" (from the Legend of St. George and the Dragon). [608]

It was a Christian order developed by King Sigismund (1368 – 1437), King of Hungary, Croatia, Bohemia and Holy Roman Emperor, to prevent expansion of the Ottoman Empire into Central Europe. Its founding members included a number of Kings and Princes of many royal households in Europe. In 1431 membership was expanded to lesser nobility and princes of other countries; Vlad II was inducted. Following Vlad II, his father's death in 1456, Vlad III became prince of Wallachia and maintained his rulership until his scalping by the Turks in 1476.

As a boy hostage Vlad III was whipped frequently and developed hatred towards Mehmed, later to become Sultan. His older brother had his eyes put out with hot irons by political enemies. Between 1447 and 1451

Vlad III was chosen as the puppet ruler of Wallachia by the Sultan, but when Vlad's uncle was assassinated, he fled to Moldova. In 1456 Hungary retook Serbia and Vlad III led a small army into Wallachia and retook this territory from the Turks. He reigned there until 1462. In 1459 he stopped paying tribute to the Sultan, formed an alliance with Hungary, and took a small army into an area between Serbia and the Baltic killing 20,000.

When Mehmed II came after him with an army of 90,000, he found 20,000 Turkish prisoners all impaled on a forest of stakes along the main road. Vlad III did not have the force to resist openly and resorted to this form of effective psychological warfare and partisan attacks against the Turks. He was imprisoned by the Hungarians later that year and was held until he was reinstated as ruler of Wallachia in 1474. This did not last long as the Sultan brought in another army to remove him. Vlad III was killed under unknown circumstances in 1476.

Hunyadi & the Hungarians

In 1441 **John Hunyadi** (1407-1456), "the white knight of Wallachia," counterattacked the Ottoman garrison at Smederevo (44.40°N, 20.56°E) and defeated it. Murad sent one of his commanders in Transylvania after Hunyadi. Mesid Bey with 17,000 met with another Ottoman contingency of about the same size and fought a skirmish with a detachment of Hunyadi's force consisting of 2000 men at Sântimbru (46°21'N, 25°51'E) in March of 1442.

The Hungarians retreated, but Mesid failed to pursue. Hunyadi reformed his force of about 10-15,000 at Sibiu, near the Danube Gorge or the "Iron Gates" (44.40°N, 22.31°E). Hunyadi ordered part of his army to make a frontal attack against Mesid's forces of 80,000 while he hit the Ottoman flank. It was a massacre with the Ottomans losing 15-20,000 killed while the Hungarians lost only 3-4,000. Mesid was killed. [609]

From July 1443 to January 1444 John Hunyadi conducted what has been called "the Long Campaign." He led a force of 35,000 men to the south of Belgrade taking the cities of Krusevac (43.35°N 21.19°E), Niš (43.3°N 21.9°E), and Sophia (42.42°N, 23.20°E). He then combined with the Hungarian army and defeated Murad II at Snaim (Kustinitza). Murad II was forced to leave the field for a season and Serbia, Romania and much of Bulgaria were cleared of Ottoman troops for the time being. [610] Murad II turned over the throne to his son in 1444, but later that year he was back with his troops at Varna (43.13°N 27.55°E).

"**The Battle of Varna November 1444** was fought between the Ottoman forces of Murad II numbering 50,000 and a Crusader coalition army (Poland, Hungary, Wallachia, Moldavia, Lithuania, Papal States, Croatia, and the Teutonic Knights) under the command of, the 20 year-old Władysław III, King of Poland and Hungary, and Janos Hunyadi with 20,000 near Varna in Bulgaria. Coalition forces faced west with their left flank on Lake Varna with the town and Black Sea behind them. The Ottomans approached from the West. Their initial attack came from their left. It was repulsed. However it tended to separate the Coalition's right flank from its center. An attack from the Coalitions left against the Ottoman's right was partly successful with the Ottoman right falling back. Hunyadi advised Wladyshaw to hold his position, but he impetuously charged the center of the Ottoman force into the face of the professional Janissaries. In the process he lost his cavalry and his life. This weakened the Coalition center and wth his own right giving way, there was nothing else for Hunyadi to do but break off, retreat from a potential catastrophe, and leave the field to the Ottomans. In the end 12,000 Coalition troops were lost while the Ottomans lost 20,000. Although the Ottomans held the field and the advantage, Hunyadi returned to Buda with his army and entered the city in triumph. [611] The Ottomans had no opposition to their movement and would shortly take advantage of it. [612]

Hunyadi considered the possibility of Turk-proofing Hungary's southern borders. He moved his troops to Smederevo, the Serbian capital. When Albanian troops came to join the Hungarians, Durad Branković, an Ottoman Serbian vassal attacked him and ravaged his lands. In September Hunyadi moved his camp across the Danube to Kovin (44.45°N 20.58°E) near Smederevo where he awaited reinforcements from German Crusaders, Bohemians and Wallachians. Then the uncertain Branković brought his 20,000 Serbian troops to camp to negotiate the possibility of joining Hunyadi's forces. However, he was unwilling to place his troops under Hunyadi's command. The attempted negotiations ended in personal hatred. When the German Crusaders arrived, they began burning and pillaging their way through Serbian lands, Branković returned to the Ottoman side. He had a plan to defeat the German Crusaders.

Second Battle of Kosovo October 1448 was a follow up of the battle of Varna four years earlier. The Crusaders were first to arrive on the field and were immediately flanked by the superior Ottoman force of 60,000. They retreated back to Hunyadi's main force. Once again the Ottoman attacked both flanks while Hunyadi threw his troops at the Ottoman center. Although he broke through the Janissaries, they did not retreat and continued to fight where they were. The Wallachians held the right flank and were said to have behaved treacherously. Once again Hunyadi was forced to retreat, but in the process the Ottomans killed most of the Hungarian Nobles. Hunyadi was captured later that day and later ransomed. The Coalition lost 17,000 men. Ottoman casualties were unknown. The way north was once again opened for Murad II. [613]

With the Serbian front stabilized Murad went south in 1449 to defeat the Timurids at Karaman (37°11'N, 33°13'E) in the south-central part of the Ionian Peninsula bordering the Mediterranean and Syria. He also invaded Corum-Amasya in central Anatolia south of Bursa. His final campaign in 1450 was unsuccessful against the fortress of Krujë (41.31°N 19.48°E) in central Albania. He died February 1451. At the end of his reign, the Ottoman Turks held most of Anatolia and most of Bulgaria east and south of the Carpathians. He had made serious incursions into northern Greece and was pressing Albania and southern Serbia.

Mehmed II "The Conqueror"

Mehmed II "the Conqueror" 1432-1481 reigned from 1451 until his death in 1481. His first battle was the Second Battle of Kosovo (42.6°N 20.85°E) and he never turned back. At the age of 11 he was sent to rule Amasya. In 1444 he abdicated in favor of his father, Mehmed I. His tutors taught him devotion to Sharia Law. Initially he did not seem interested in the ways of fighting men and in 1444 ordered his father as general to lead the Ottoman armies at the Battle of Varna. The grand Vizier at the time did not like Mehmed II and insisted that his father return to the throne. Later Mehmed I had the Vizier executed. On his father's death in 1451 he once again became Sultan and began strengthening the Ottoman navy. One of his first tasks was casting guns that could throw 25" diameter stone balls at castle walls. By the use of gunpowder and large siege guns (Bombards), the walls of Constantinople that had resisted so many invasions for 1000 years would be breached. Constantinople fell in 1453 and became Istanbul. [614]

The following map shows battle sites in the Central European corridor from Serbia to Slovakia bordering the Adriatic during the period of Ottoman growth 1338 to 1683. There are many others fought off the map, especially to the south and east.

Bayezid had built the fortress Anadoluhisari on the Asian side of the Bosporus. Mehemed II began building an even stronger one on the European side to give him command of the channel. He now levied a tax on all ships going through the strait. When a Venetian vessel refused to stop, he sunk it and beheaded all the sailors. [615]

The War against Venice of 1463 consisted mostly of naval campaigns with land skirmishes. A peace treaty in 1479 ceded Kefalonia (38.15°N, 20.30°E) to the Ottomans. This also lessened raids against the Venetian trading fleet. However, wr resumed in 1499. [616]

EASTERN EUROPE 1460

Numerous land wars between **Croatia and the Ottoman Empire** occurred between 1403 and 1606. Between the pitched battles there was so much countryside resistance that ruling the entire land was impossible. The period is called **The Hundred Years' Croatian-Ottoman War** and began with the **Battle of Krbava Field** in September 1493, near Udbina (44°53'N, 15°76'E). Ottoman cavalry pushed its way into Croatia. A small Croatian army of 8000 infantry and 2-3000 heavy cavalry came against a numerically superior Ottoman army which lost 8-10,000 killed and 1500 captured. Many Croatians migrated into Austria and Italy, but those that stayed fought many battles along the eastern border. They lost most of them, but continued fierce partisan resistance. This situation gained much notoriety in Catholic Europe. Typical of the resistance was fortress **Klis** near Split (43°30' N, 16° 26' E) on the Adriatic coast that held out for about 25 years. The south-central regions were unprotected. However, resistance persisted among fortified border towns. The war against **Croatia lasted nearly 200 years** but ended in failure for the Ottomans at Petrinja (45°26'N, 16°17'E) in 1595.[617]

Capture of Algiers in 1510 by the Spaniards was a rare victory. Spain had chased the Muslims out in 1492 and seized the opportunity to control the Straits of Gibraltar. Spanish forces landed at the city of Algiers (36°42'N, 3°13'E) and took it from the Muslim Kabylians. Selim-bin-Teumi was forced to pay tribute and accept Spanish domination. [6] years later, the Amir invited two infamous corsairs, Khair ad-Din Barbarossa and his brother, Aruj to get rid of the Spaniards and their puppet ruler. With the help of Ottoman troops, they seized Algiers and killed Salim. The Spanish tried to retake the town in 1516 and 1519, but failed. Algiers was back in the hands of the Ottoman Empire.[618]

The Siege of Constantinople 1453 was fought between the Ottoman army of about 80,000 of Mehmed II and 7,000 plus 26 ships of the Byzantine Empire under Constantine XI. Casualties are unknown on the Ottoman side, but 4000 were killed on Byzantine side along with their Emperor. The majority of troops on the Ottoman side were Christian allies from Serbia and elsewhere while Janissaries numbered only about 10,000. For many years the Byzantine Empire, squeezed into a small strip of land to the West of Constantinople on the Sea of Marmara and its Greek holdings had attempted to form a union with the Roman Catholics.

As noted previously this had been accomplished in July 1439 as memorialized by Alberti and possibly Toscanelli in the painting of the "Night Sky" in the Old Sacristy of the San Lorenzo Church in Florence, Italy. Now another understanding was confirmed in late 1452. However, the Pope had little influence with the rest of Europe to mount a Crusade to help Constantinople. There had been many such small crusades, mostly in concert with a coalition of countries. Most had failed.

The total population of Constantinople at the time was only 50,000; it was no longer a city of hundreds of thousands. There were only 7,000 troops of which 2000 were foreign. Mehmed II was not thought to be too dangerous at the age of 21. However, for two years he had been busy building a fort on the European side to the North of the city. Siege guns cast in Hungary by Orban including a monster capable of hurling a 600 lb. stone one mile arrived and were now deployed. Constantinople had been offered these weapons earlier, but refused to pay the price for them and they were then sold to the Sultan. The city had 20 k of walls, but only enough defenders to man the outer perimeter. Even so, most inhabitants felt confident. No one had breached these walls for 1000 years.

Mehmed II reduced the outlying fortresses first. Cannon fire against the wall was ineffective at first. It took as much time to reload and fire as it did to repair the damage. The Ottoman fleet could not enter the Golden Horn due to a chain on buoys across its entrance. Even so a path of greased logs allowed the Ottomans to slide several of their ships into the Golden Horn. This forced defenders to guard the harbor and weaken the wall defenses. Initial attacks against the walls by the Janissaries failed with heavy casualties. Mining under the walls also failed with many Ottoman miners killed in counter mining operations. After torturing several captives, the Ottomans were able to get knowledge of all the countermining efforts. An all-out attack against the North wall began on 29 May. This part of the wall was newer, less well constructed and had sustained more damage from the bombardment. Several waves of troops followed by the elite Janissaries managed to breach the wall and enter the city. The gates were opened and the Muslim army poured in. For 3 days the city was plundered and those found raped or massacred. Then on the 3rd day Mehmed ordered the looting and reprisals to cease and promised those in hiding they would suffer no more. Life could go on as before. The Catholic Pope called for a crusade to retake the city, but no European monarch responded. [619]

In 1456 Athens fell without resistance. The Parthenon was converted to a Mosque. Greek occupation continued until 1821. Venice attempted to retake Athens in 1464 and 1687. They successfully landed, but remained only 2 years. Ottoman troops held the top of the Acropolis and other strong points. [620]

With the fall of Constantinople Mehmed II looked north to get rid of the Hungarian menace. The fortress capital Nandorfehevar (Belgrade) stood in his way. This was the gateway to the Hungarian plain. Hunyadi also saw the same possibility and sought to strengthen the fortress with more supplies and weapons. He left his brother-in-law and eldest son in charge of the garrison. He also organized a fleet of 200 ships in the Adriatic and called for allies to assist in the land war that was sure to follow. In July 1456 his fleet destroyed the Ottoman fleet. When Belgrade (44°49; N, 20°27'E) was attacked later that year, Hunyadi repulsed the Muslim force and pursued it. Mehmed retreated to Constantinople. This insured relative peace for 70 years, but 3 weeks later in August plague broke out in the camp and many including Hunyadi died. Even Mehmet II said of him, "*Although he was my enemy I feel grief over his death, because the world has never such a man.*" [621]

The **Wallachian Moldavian Wars** were fought from 1456 to 1475. Matthias Corvinus Hunyadi (John Hunyadi's son), Matthias I of Hungary (1443 – 1458–1490) was a capable military commander. He was crowned at the age of 15 in Buda in 1458. Between 1458 and 1490 he re-established a Serbian alliance. The Turks took Herzegovina in 1467. After pillaging Transylvania, a homeward bound Turkish army of 6-20,000 was caught and annihilated at Orastie in the **Battle of Breadfield** (45.57 N, 23.20 E) in 1479 by the Hungarians numbering 10-16,000. The Hungarians lost 3000 and Ottomans 10-16,000. Estimates vary. Matthias I recaptured **Jajce** (44°20'N 17°15'E) and drove the Ottomans out of northern Serbia and Bosnia with his **Black Army**. The Black Army (from the color of their armor) of Hungary was one of the first well-paid full-time mercenary armies of Europe. [622]

Also prominent during this period was the influence of one of the world's most infamous partisans, Vlad III Dracula who led an internal revolt in Wallachia (Romania) and Moldavia from 1462 to 1476. Eventually guerilla warfare and plague defeated the Ottoman army of Mehmed II. However, Islâm is patient. Moldova would be attacked again in 1538. [623]

Venice engaged the Ottoman Empire's forces periodically with skirmishes starting in 1463. A peace treaty ceded **Kefalonia** in 1479 to Ottoman rule. This lessened raids against the Venetian trading fleet; however, war resumed in 1499. [624] Between 1463 and 1527 the Ottomans returned and attempted the reconquest of **Bosnia / Herzegovinia**. Bosnia fell first in 1463 with the execution of their king and the taking of the Castle of Jajce (44.20°N, 17.15°E). The Ottomans took the country quickly, but the occupying troops were withdrawn leaving only 80 men in the fort at Zvecaj (near Zenica – 44.12°N, 17.56°E). As soon as the conquerors moved out, the Hungarians returned and liberated the northern territories of Bosnia. In 1482 tax breaks for the converts to Islâm temporarily helped the Ottomans retake most of the country. The Turks returned and began whittling away at the liberated territories and finally secured it by 1527. During this period some estimate that 100,000 people were taken into captivity and 30,000 youth were pressed into Janissary service. Its nobility was killed, but the Provence maintained its identity as a semi-autonomous part of the Ottoman Empire until 1878. A census from 1520 to 1530 found that 38.7% were Muslims. By the 16th and 17th centuries it was up to 75%. By the end of the 19th century the religious census was much where it had been for years: 42% Greek Orthodox, 38% Suni Muslim and 18-19% Roman Catholic. Religious preferences were generally not disturbed by the Ottomans. [625]

In 1476 the Turks returned to **Moldova** won the battle, but could not subject the populace. They disappeared into the hills and forests and behaved like modern partisans. When the Hungarians offered assistance, the Turks moved out and Matthias I retook the territory.

In April 1480 a botched Turkish attack against the Island of Rhodes (36.10°N, 28.00°E) failed. The Janissaries denied spoils refused to fight. In August 1480 Mehmed II sent a fleet of 128 ships to Southern Italy. They took Otranto (40°28'N 17°14'E) and beheaded 800 civilians and some clerics when they refused to become Muslims; this is disputed. Coasts were raided and a garrison of 800 infantry and 500 horse were left behind to guard Otranto. Ferdinand I of Naples raised an army of relief in 1481. It besieged the city in May and negotiations brought about its return to Naples the same year. [626]

Italy might have been retaken easily, but on May 3, 1481 **Mehmed** died and his sons squabbled for control instead of continuing the conquest of Italy. The French seized the opportunity, invaded in 1494-95 and took it. By the end of 1490 Hungary was back in control of Wallachia, Serbia, and Croatia. The Ottoman Empire held territories south of this line. The seaport of Otranto was once again part of the Kingdom of Naples. [627]

Bayezed II "the Just"

Bayezed II (1481-1512) "the just" ruled from 1481 to 1512. His first concern was **civil war** with his brother, Cem, who sought Egyptian Mamluks help. Cem fled to Rhodes seeking the protection of the Knights of St. John. Since the West had an idea of placing a pro-western Sultan in power, Bayezed did little to provoke Christian Europe until his brother died in 1492. One of his main objectives was the conquest of Morea, the Peloponnese peninsula of southern Greece. He felt that holding this for the Ottoman fleet would give him control of the Eastern Mediterranean. He spent much of his time putting down rebellions in Persia. He sent his

Navy to southern Spain in 1492 to save Arabs and Jews from the Spanish Inquisition. His last years were spent in another civil war with his sons. [628]

The Conquest of Greece 1371–1500 took place in stages. Northeastern Greece was already in Ottoman hands by 1371 after Maritsa. Following the fall of Constantinople in 1453 Greece was whittled away bit by bit. Athens fell in 1458. Most of the Peloponnese was vanquished by 1460. Cyprus fell in 1571. Many Greek Islands held by the Genoese and Venetians along with most of the mainland had fallen into Ottoman hands by 1500. The Venetians held Crete until 1670. The Ottoman Navy was instrumental in this conquest. Many intellectuals fled to the West, especially Italy and many common people went into the mountainous regions where they could escape Ottoman interference. In this part of the Empire there were restrictions placed on those who were not Muslim. A feudal system overseen by Muslim nobles, usually cavalrymen ruled the country. Non-Muslims were forbidden to carry arms or even ride a horse. A Child tax was imposed on Christians – one male child out of every 5 was recruited for Janissary service. Unlike Bosnia-Herzegovina where there was freedom and an improving economy, the economy of Greece declined. The Patriarch was held responsible to the Sultan for the good behavior of the Greek Orthodox Christians. The suppression of Christians, the child tax and heavy general taxation against Christians led to much corruption, underground resistance and eventually Greek Nationalism. [629]

Montenegro, a small fiercely independent principality, lies between Bosnia, Serbia and Albania with a port city on the Adriatic. It was finally taken into the Ottoman Empire in 1499, but shortly after developed a form of autonomy from Ottoman rule. Greek Orthodoxy is its primary religion. [630]

From 1403 through 1606 Croatia was a battleground for the Ottoman Empire. Despite their losses the Croatians would not give up. **The Hundred Years' Croatian-Ottoman War** began with the **Battle of Krbava Field** in September 1493, near Udbina (44.53°N, 15.17°E). Ottoman cavalry invaded Croatia, but the locals with 8000 infantry and 2-3000 heavy cavalry came against 8000 Ottoman infantry, which lost 8-10,000 killed and 1500 captured. As the continuous partisan activity continued, many Croatians migrated into Austria and Italy, but those that stayed fought many battles along the eastern border. Most were lost, but resistance continued. Much of the conflict was reported throughout Europe. [631]

In 1510 the Spaniards temporarily captured the city of Algiers, but as noted earlier it was retaken 6 years later by Khair ad-Din Barbarossa and his brother, Aruj. Efforts by the Spanish to re-take the city were unsuccessful in 1516 and 1519. [632]

THE OTTOMAN EMPIRE'S YEARS OF EXPANSION

The rule of Selim I was marked by a change in direction of conquests. He first had to eliminate competition for the throne from his brothers supported by the Safavids. The Safavids controlled Persia, much of Anatolia and the Arabian Peninsula including Tigris and Euphrates Rivers. Persia was Shia and Selim was Sunni. When he had firmly established himself as ruler of the Ottoman Empire he invaded Persia and in August 1514 fought against the **Safavids at the battle of Chaldiran** (39°05'N 44°19'E) in a bleak mountain valley. Exact numerical strength is unknown but the Ottoman's had 60-100,000 while the Shah had only about 40,000. The major difference between the two was that the Shah had ignored modern firearms and artillery. The Ottomans won with 2000 casualties while the Shah suffered 5000. The Shah was deposed and the Ottomans took over, but it would take another century or so before the entire region was subdued. [633]

From here Selim moved against the **Egyptian Mamluk Sultanate**. The Mamluks held Egypt, Syria and the Holy Land. By 1516 both sides were prepared for war and approached each other in August 1516 at Marj Dabiq, Syria. The Ottoman side included 65,000 men and 50 cannons. The Mamluks had 80,000 and no cannon. Mamluk losses were staggering 72,000 to 13,000 for the Ottomans. The Ottomans now moved on Damascus, which gave up without a fight. [634]

The **Battle of Ridaniya** (31.07°N, 31.27°E) was fought on 22 January 1517 in the Nile delta. Exact army strengths are unknown, but casualties were said to be 6000 for the Ottomans and 7000 for the Mamluks. Following their victory, the Ottomans entered Cairo and beheaded the Mamluk sultan thus ending Mamluk rule. Selim also extended his rule to all of Syria, Palestine and Egypt. He placed Al-Mutawakkil III, the last of the Abbasid caliphs as nominal ruler over the old Mamluk Sultanate.

Mutawakkil would not receive the Caliph's mantle or sword of Muhammad. His next project was to resume the Hungarian campaign, but he died of uncertain cause at age 55 and his son took over. [635] The end of the official Croatian war came with the Peace of Zsitvatorok between the Ottomans and Austrians. [636]

In the preceding 100 years the Ottoman Empire gradually expanded to include most of Central Europe. This included the Balkans, Bulgaria, Romania, Hungary, parts of the Ukraine, Southern Russia, and the North African Coast. In the far west, the armies of Ferdinand and Isabella of Spain extinguished the last vestiges of Umayyad Islâmic rule in the Iberian Peninsula in 1492, the year that Columbus set sail for America. [637] For 5 years inhabitants were permitted to remain and practice their religious beliefs, but when conversions remained few, the Spanish took a more proactive policy and expelled non-Catholics. The Iberian Peninsula was now firmly Catholic.

Suleiman "the Magnificent"

Suleiman the Magnificent (1494–1520–1566) continued Selim I's goals. He too realized the importance of Belgrade, which lies at the junction of two great rivers, the Sava originating from the Southern Alps and the Danube, from the Northern Alps. It is the site of one of the oldest settlements of Europe dating back to the 6th millennium BC.

In July–August 1521 Suleiman laid siege to the city with an alleged 40-50,000 troops; estimates vary. Defenders included only 700 Hungarians. The City surrendered and all Christians were taken as slaves to Istanbul. By 1540 Serbia was totally occupied. [638]

The Island of Rhodes was taken by the Crusader Knights of Saint John (Hospitallers) after their expulsion from Acre in 1291. Rhodes lies just off the Coast of Anatolia and was in a position to harass Ottoman commerce from the Levant of northern Syria at the north end of the Fertile Crescent. Taking it would strengthen Ottoman Sea Power in the Eastern Mediterranean. An attack against the Island had been repulsed in 1480. The knights maintained several fortresses and a fleet that defended the harbor. Their strength included only 7,500 men 700 knights and 500 archers. Suleiman's army numbering 100,000 in 400 ships arrived in June 1522. At first direct assaults and mining the fortress walls failed, but by

December the Knights had run out of food and calls for reinforcements and more supplies fell on deaf ears. Casualties included 20,000 Ottomans and 2,000 of the Rhodes army. Rather than be killed if the city had to be taken by storm, the Knights surrendered. Suleiman offered them generous terms that included allowing the Knights to go to Malta. [639]

Suleiman the Magnificent (1520-1566) built on Selîm's Persian and Egyptian successes by moving into the Balkans. He captured Belgrade in 1521 and Hungary at the Battle of Mohács in 1526. The road for the Ottoman Turks would be rocky and uncertain from here on. In 1529 he laid siege to Vienna, but was defeated by a markedly inferior force largely due to the rainy weather. This is discussed below under the Battle of Vienna. Transylvania, Wallachia, and Moldavia became tributary states. Baghdad (Iraq) was taken from Persia in 1535 which gave the Ottoman Empire control of Mesopotamia and the Persian Gulf. Three years later Ottoman sea power prevailed at the Battle of Preveza (1538) when Barbarossa Hayreddin Pasha destroyed the fleet of Charles V commanded by Andrea Doria (1456-1650). Barbarossa went on to control the Mediterranean and took Tunis and Algeria from Spain. He transported the Jews and Muslims from Spain and settled them in Salonika, Cyprus, and Istanbul. In 1543 Nice (43°42'N, 7°15'E – SE corner of France) was taken from the Holy Roman Empire and the Pasha engineered an alliance between the French and Ottomans against Hapsburg Austria to keep them away from their South-Central Europe conquests. This was an alliance that would last into the 20th Century. In return France received tax free trading rights within the Ottoman Empire. The Ottoman Empire also entered into an alliance with England, France and Holland against Habsburg Spain, Italy and Austria. However, none of this complex diplomacy opened the sea lanes to the Far East. This began the great age of exploration to find another route to the Far East. The voyages of the 15th and 16th centuries by Vasco de Gama (around Africa), Columbus (the Caribbean), Magellan (around the world), and Cabot (North America) were part of this effort. These voyages led to a huge influx of wealth for Spain and Portugal in gold looted from the Incas and Aztecs. Gold fever spread to the rest of Europe in their explorations and colonization of the Americas. The Tables below list the rulers of the Ottoman Empire in chronological sequence and gives principle occurrences during each rule. [640]

After the death of Mathias I Corvinus, King of Hungary (1443-1490), Vladislaus II (1456-1490-1516) of Bohemia (Western Czech R) was selected. He was weak and did not believe in spending money to maintain a credible army. He dissolved the famous mercenary **Black Army.**

Although he crushed a peasant revolt in 1514, his parliament squabbled over defense spending. In 1521 they paid no attention to their new king, Louis II (1506-1526). Then only age 15, he warned them of their strategic danger. Sulieman had just taken Belgrade, gateway to Hungary. Lack of military strength forced Louis II of Hungary and Bohemia to rely on an Alliance (never a good plan) to defend his country. [641]

Behind the scenes was a dispute between Francis I of France and Charles V Habsburg of Austria. Charles had defeated Francis at the Battle of Pavia (north western Italy 45°11'N, 9° 09'E) in 1525. Francis sought an alliance with any prince that might be a threat to Austria and with whom he could promise a two-front war against Austria. Although illogical from a religious standpoint, an alliance with Suleiman made perfect sense even if a reconciliation between the two faiths could not be reached. This is what he did. It has lasted to this day with current disastrous results for Christian France. Francis asked Suleiman to make war against his own faith, the Holy Roman Empire. Suleiman was more than obliging. [642]

Suleiman did not rest for long. In 1526 he took an army of 45,000 regular troops supported by 10,000 irregulars and 160 stone throwing cannons to the region of Mohács (southern Hungary on the east bank of the Danube (45°99'N,18°67'E) and met the forces of Louis II of Hungary in August 1526. Louis, still unsupported by his parliament had an inferior force of allies (Croatia, Holy Roman Empire, Baaria, Poland and Papal States) consisting of 26,000 troops with 53 cannons. His own flesh and blood Bohemian allies with 32 cannons failed to show up. The Ottoman troops won a decisive victory killing 14-20,000 Hungarians including their young King Louis II while losing only 1500. Hungary ceased to exist. It was occupied by the Ottomans and Austrians until 1920. [643] Neglecting one's defense is poor policy.

Although the southwestern part of Hungary along with Transylvania (north western Romania Carpathian region) was taken following the Battle of Mohács the Balkans were not fully subdued. Rugged mountainous terrain, heavy forests and brutal winters favored pockets of partisans that continued resistance. Nonetheless, Suleiman was master of Central Europe.

The Western powers did not wait long. With the return of Suleiman to Istanbul to refit his forces Ferdinand I, Archduke of Austria, led a coalition army from Bohemia, Croatia, Papal States and expat Serbs back into Hungary in 1527-8 and took the city of Budapest. The size of the belligerents and their losses are unknown. [644]

In January 1529 Suleiman declared war against Ferdinand I of Austria. At the same time, he decided to extend his rule into north western

Africa and sent financial and military (2000 Janissaries and artillery) support to Barbarossa who had assisted the empire in the reconquest of Algiers a decade earlier. Barbarossa first bribed the Sheiks to support the Ottomans instead of the Spanish. After entering the city of Algiers, he besieged the remaining Spanish fortress in the harbor and it surrendered in May 1529. He killed the garrison and used Christian slaves to build a seawall. Barbarossa then subdued the entire Barbary Coast and brought it under the Ottomans. Suleiman named Barbarossa High Admiral of the Ottoman Empire in 1535. [645]

Challenges from the West

During the 16th Century Portuguese sea power challenged the Ottomans successfully in the Persian Gulf, Indian Ocean, and the Spice Islands while the Ottoman Empire was preoccupied with land battles in Austria and what remained of Persia. Logistics was a defining problem. [646] Supply lines to the east and west were beyond what even the Ottomans could hope to control. As the century progressed, Christian European powers made efforts to weaken the Ottoman Empire's control of all trade routes. The huge influx of silver and gold from the New World created "hard" currency in the West while Ottoman currency inflated rapidly and became relatively worthless.

Although the southwestern part of Hungary along with Transylvania (north western Romania Carpathian region) was taken following the Battle of Mohács the Balkans were not fully subdued. Rugged mountainous terrain, heavy forests and brutal winters favored pockets of partisans that continued resistance. Nonetheless, Suleiman was master of Central Europe.

The Western powers did not wait long. With the return of Suleiman to Istanbul to refit his forces Ferdinand I, Archduke of Austria, led a coalition army from Bohemia, Croatia, Papal States and expat Serbs back into Hungary in 1527-8 and took the city of Budapest. The size of the belligerents and their losses are unknown. [647]

In January 1529 Suleiman declared war against Ferdinand I of Austria. At the same time, he decided to extend his rule into north western Africa and sent financial and military (2000 Janissaries and artillery) support to Barbarossa who had assisted the empire in the reconquest of Algiers a decade earlier. Barbarossa first bribed the Sheiks to support the Ottomans instead of the Spanish. After entering the city of Algiers, he besieged the remaining Spanish fortress in the harbor and it surrendered in May 1529. He killed the garrison and used Christian slaves to build a seawall. Barbarossa then subdued the entire Barbary Coast and brought it under the Ottomans. Suleiman named Barbarossa High Admiral of the Ottoman Empire in 1535.[648]

OTTOMAN EMPIRE BATTLES 1338–1666

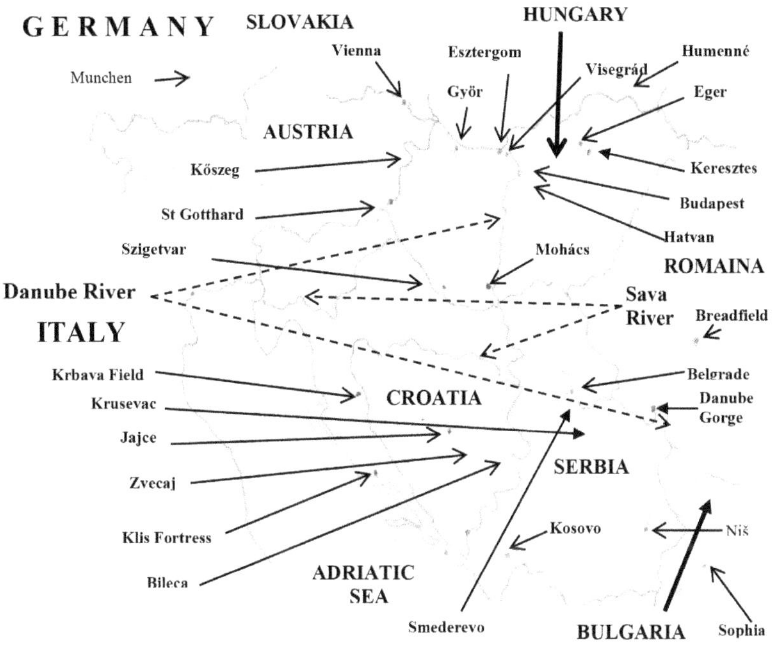

Battles With the West

Bileca 1338
Kosovo 1389, 1448
Smederevo 1441
Danube Gorge 1442
Belgrade – 1456, 1521
Zvecaj 1463
Jajce 1463-64, 1527
Breadfield – 1479
Krbava Field 1493
Klis Fortress 1493
Mohács 1526
Budapest 1527-8, 1541, 1686
Vienna 1529
Kőszeg 1532
Szigetvar 1556
Györ 1595
Esztergom 1595
Keresztes/Mezőkeresztes 1596
Visegrád 1595
Hatvan 1596
Eger 1596
Humenné 1619
St Gotthard 1664

Table XI Ottoman Empire Rulers AD 1290 – 1566 Period of Growth

Dates	Ruler	Events
1290–1326	Osmân I (Amir)	Romans defeated – Nicomedia 1302 Seljuks overthrown – 1307 Bursa taken 1326
1326-1359	Orkhân (Amir)	Defeats Andronicus III – 1329 near Nicaea – taken 1331 Nicomedia taken 1337 Gelibolu & Ankara taken 1354
1359 – 1389	Murâd I (Sultân)	Adrianople (1369) Konya (1387), Thessalonica (1387) Serbs defeated at Kosovo / Murâd I killed (1389)
1389 – 1402	Bâyezîd I (Sultân) "the thunderbolt"	Siege of Constantinople 1394-1402 Batle of Nicopolis – Sigismund of Hungary defeated (1396) Battle of Ankara, Sultân defeated, captured by Tamerlane (1402)
1402 – 1421	Meh.med I (Sultân)	Civil War 1402 – 1421 Meh.med vs. Süleymân & Mûsâ Thessalonica ceded to Romania 1403
1421 – 1451	Murâd II (Sultân)	Siege of Constantinople 1422 Thessalonica taken from Venice (1430)
1451 – 1481	Meh.med II Fâtih "The Conqueror"	Constantinople taken (1453) Bosnia taken (1463) Khanate of Crimea becomes vassal (1475) Siege of Rhodes repulsed (1480)
1481 – 1512	Bâyezîd II (Sultân)	"the just" Consolodated the Ottoman Empire – kept peace at home – built naval power
1512 – 1520	Selîm I Yavuz "the Grim"	Conquest of Syria and Egypt (1516-1517)
1520 – 1566	Süleimân I "the Magnificent	Fall of Rhodes (1523), Battle of Mohács, Conquest of Hungary death of Louis II of Hungary & Bohemia (1526); first siege of Vienna 1529; Conquest of Mesopotamia 1534; Siege of Malta 1565; influence of **Roxelana** Sultan's Ukranian wife.

Challenges from the West

During the 16th Century Portuguese sea power challenged the Ottomans successfully in the Persian Gulf, Indian Ocean, and the Spice Islands while the Ottoman Empire was preoccupied with land battles in Austria and what remained of Persia. Logistics was a defining problem. [649] Supply lines to the east and west were beyond what even the Ottomans could hope to control. As the century progressed, Christian European powers made efforts to weaken the Ottoman Empire's control of all trade routes. The huge influx of silver and gold from the New World created "hard" currency in the West while Ottoman currency inflated rapidly and became relatively worthless.

THE OTTOMAN EMPIRE TO 1566

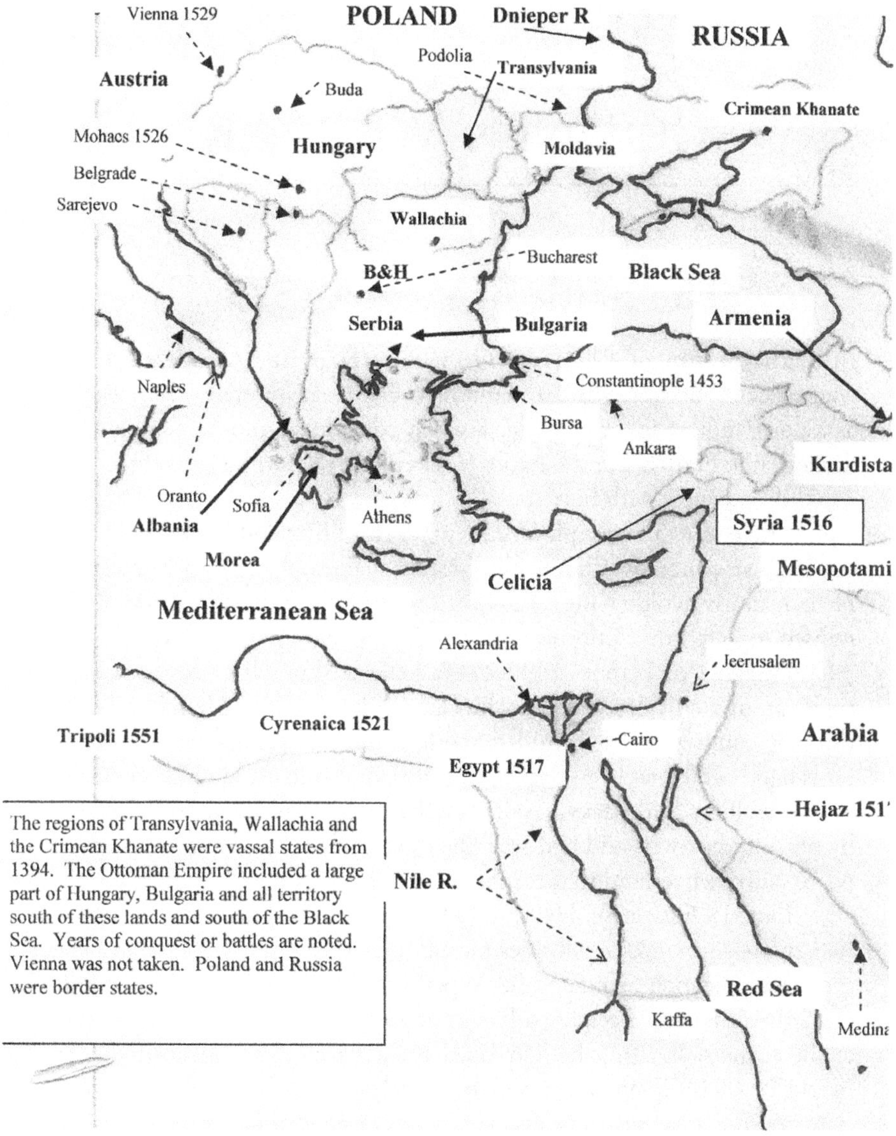

The regions of Transylvania, Wallachia and the Crimean Khanate were vassal states from 1394. The Ottoman Empire included a large part of Hungary, Bulgaria and all territory south of these lands and south of the Black Sea. Years of conquest or battles are noted. Vienna was not taken. Poland and Russia were border states.

THE TRANSITION FROM EARLY TO MODERN WARFARE

The Battle of Vienna 1529 [650]

In 1520 the son of Selîm the Grim, Suleiman "the Lawgiver" or "the Magnificent" became the 10th Sultan. [651] European interests regarded him as a positive new force in *Islâm*. He was considered another "enlightened despot" like Francis I and Charles V. Everyone in Europe agreed that they could do business with him.

There were 5 major players: Henry VIII of England (1491-1547) who had his own concerns at home plus his personal problems with "succession." He constantly avoided any complications on the European Continent and refused to help other European kings.

Francis I of France (1494-1547) believed himself to be born in the tradition of a chivalrous knight, but acted like a bandit. He had inherited the first country to be a unified modern state in Europe. All the feudal lords had been brought to heel except the Burgundians. He had an army of mostly artillery and heavy cavalry. He had taken on the conquest of Italy by beating the Swiss and had won the duchy of Milan. He made perpetual peace with Switzerland that turned out to be "perpetual."

In 1519 Charles V, Habsburg (1500- 1558) had inherited dominions that encircled France on all sides plus an inherent hostility to France. Then there was gold-rich Spain and her superior military methods. This included the Spanish square–disciplined blocks of armored pikemen with musketeers at the corners. In 1525 he had faced Francis I at Pavia, in northern Italy (45.11°N, 09.09°E) and destroyed the French army and took Francis prisoner. Italy became a Spanish possession for several generations and the Spanish military system was so overwhelming within Europe that warfare degenerated into the siege of towns and villages that offered the mercenary troops more plunder at less risk. No one wanted to meet Spain on the field of battle.

The fourth member of the club was Pope Clement VII (1478-1534). Before he was Pope, he had been Giulio de' Medici, of the ruling house of Florence (43.47°N, 11.15°E). Although his Holy Roman Emperor was Charles V, he opposed Charles and refused to help him in any way especially with the fifth member of the group, the religious leader, Martin Luther (1483-1546) who's Protestantism was beginning to take on a nationalistic "look" in the southern German Principalities.

What none understood (like today) was that rulers in Islâm, specifically Suleiman, "the Magnificent", combined Pope, Prime minister, and Commander in Chief into one person, and was rooted in the *Korân* and the recently codified Muslim, Sharia Law. This meant spreading the religion by conquest. Suleiman's interest in the West was conquering it. He began by demanding tribute from King Lajos of Hungary. The Sultan's ambassadors were killed. Suleiman sent his army to Belgrade and Fortress Szabacs. Both fell. He next attacked the Knights of St John of Rhodes who surrendered. The Europeans now fell into a familiar trap. Francis I of France sent a letter to Suleiman encouraging him to take the rest of Hungary while he kept Charles V of Spain and Holy Roman Emperor busy in a two-front war. Suleiman was happy to oblige. Hungary was in a state of discontent. The peasantry paid huge taxes to support degenerate nobility. Upon his arrival in Belgrade, Suleiman had an army of 100,000 while King Lajos could muster only 30,000. The people far preferred to pay the Sultan rather than their nobility and king. The Turks and Huns met at Mohács on August 28, 1526. The King, two archbishops, 5 bishops and 24,000 men were all killed. Buda was plundered and Hungary ceased to exist. [652] The loot was impressive, but Suleiman had better things to do in Persia and abandoned Hungary leaving it in a state of chaos; he could come back later and fix it. By 1528 he had whipped the heretic Persian Shi'ites and returned to Hungary to set up another fief system. Vienna would be his next victim in 1529 and he planed to conquer Germany the following year. Suleiman had discovered that Christian nations were individually opportunistic. Despite a common religion they had no loyalty to one another.

On April 10, 1529 the Sultan left Istanbul with 200,000 men. His Janissaries and light siege guns were sent up the Danube in boats. King John Zápolya was to join with a contingent in Hungary. King Ferdinand I of the Habsburgs (1503-1564) held the title of King of Hungary, Archduke of Austria, King of Bohemia, and King of practically everything else in Central Europe. However, he had little more than weak police power and was only

26. Despite the Diet of the Empire's intention to send every 10th man to Vienna to fight the Ottoman menace, they could not enforce it. Bohemia voted to send every man, but sent only 2,000. When the Diet of the Holy Roman Empire met in Speyer, it voted to send 12,000 soldiers and 2,000 horse, IF an investigative deputation found that the Sultan was really coming. Pope Clement VII was interested in re-establishing the Medici dukedom of Florence and couldn't be bothered. Charles V in Italy was concerned only with what the French were doing. Those in Vienna knew they were in mortal danger. Suleiman was on the march and headed towards them.

Fortunately, Vienna had two good German military leaders. One was a 70- year-old professional soldier with combat experience, Graf Nikolaus zu Salm-Reiffercheidt and Duke Friedrich of the Palatinate (Rhineland region) sent by the Diet at Speyer. Graf Nikolaus arrived in Vienna in early September. Pest in Hungary had fallen to Suleiman and every male slaughtered by the Janissaries. Vienna's defenses were in shambles; nothing had been done. There was one weak 6' high wall. The citadel was an old brick and timber building roofed with shingles. There were no magazines for powder or reserve food supplies. The city was filled with women, children and weak non-combatants ready to consume all the food in sight.

Graf Nikolaus sent out foragers and destroyed all the houses immediately outside the wall to deprive the enemy of cover. Earthwork bastions were built. Defenses along the Danube River were reinforced. Paving stones were pulled up to prevent cannon balls from ricocheting in the city after they hit; these were used to reinforce the earthworks. He conducted a census and sent as many women, children and infirm out of the city as he could. On 21 September word came that the Ottoman's were approaching. Just in the nick of time a 700-man contingent of well-trained Spaniards and 1000 Germans arrived on September 23. On the same day Turkish skirmishers engaged the defenders in a fire-fight. Seven prisoners were taken and roasted to death on Turkish campfires. At Vienna the Sultan mustered 120,000 troops; however, 1/3 were cavalry and useless in this siege since there was little left to forage.

The Sultan sent his terms – surrender and only his administrators would enter the city and all would be spared. Resist and all would die a terrible death. Facing the Turks were 22,000 foot and 2,000 horse, 72 guns of different calibers and makes. However, Vienna had one major ally – rain. It had rained nearly all summer making most roads impassable. The heavy siege guns that had to be dragged over the roads by teams of horses were mired down and could not be brought to the city.

Battle of Vienna 1529

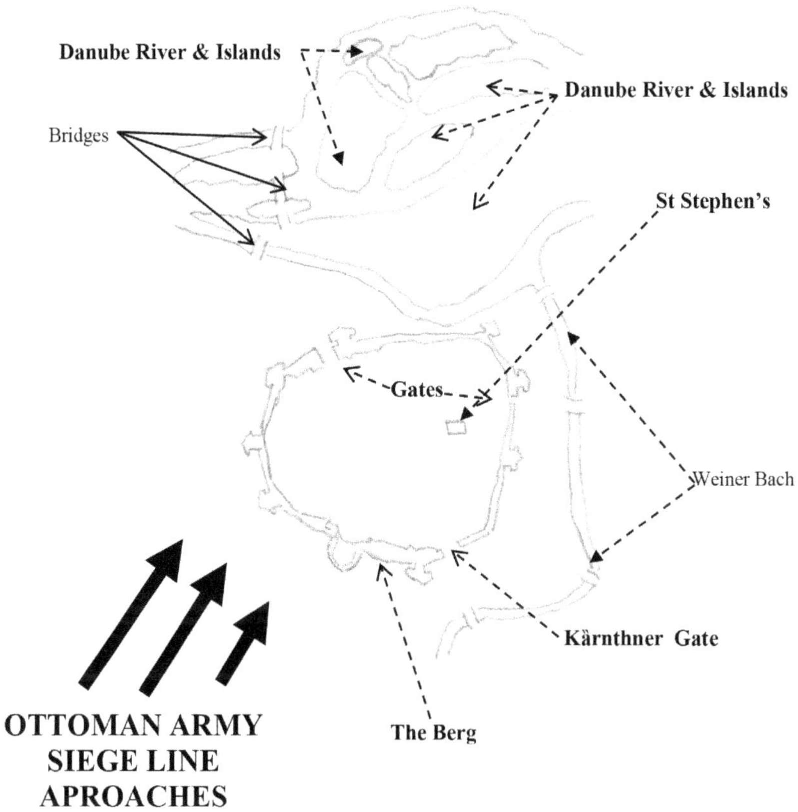

Adapted from: Pratt F.*Battles that Changed History*, Doubleday Co. & Inc. pg 143

Supplies could only come by boat. However, there were 20,000 cavalry that were already raiding the countryside and foraging. They had found 5000 non-combatants in a group and slaughtered all of them. In addition, the Sultan's barges bringing in food supply were vulnerable to attack. Suleiman was not concerned; he planned to use his gunpowder to mine the walls.

Light artillery on both sides opened the siege. Accuracy was bad and the earthwork walls, softened to mud by the rain, absorbed the shot which only added to its bulk. However, as time passed, the Viennese artillery was moved back to higher positions and their accuracy began to take its toll. The Ottoman light artillery continued to have little effect on the earthworks and walls other than adding shot to its bulk. Mining was attempted, but countermining served to capture large amounts of powder from the enemy. Nevertheless, many mines were blown, but the breaches in the line were well defended and the attackers lost many men attempting to take the city. The Janissaries were offered a huge reward for the first man to get inside Vienna, but with each failed attack their morale sank, then finally collapsed. The Spanish armed with matchlock and wheel lock muskets poured withering fire into their ranks and the German *Landsknechts* with long swords and huge halberds cut them to pieces. [653]

To make matters worse, provisions were not arriving fast enough to feed the Sultan's army. Casualties rose daily up to 20,000 and were mostly among the Janissaries and nobility horsemen. By October 12, the situation had reached the breaking point. The vizier advised that the law of the *Korân* had been satisfied, but Suleiman was not satisfied and decided to attempt another assault by mining the city walls. The mine at the main gate blew a 130' wide breach in the wall, but the defenders could see Turkish officers driving their men with sabers and whips forward into the slaughter pit. For the first time the Janissaries refused to advance. Gun fire mowed them down and halberds chopped the wounded to bits. That night the Janissaries burned their camp, threw their prisoners into the fires and left. When the victors rummaged through the camp, they found strange black beans that cooked into a tasty drink. Europe experienced its first cup of coffee. Suleiman's retreat was harassed by partisan attacks and more were killed.

The results of Vienna were profound and lasting. Suleiman was discouraged, but he would recover. The Janissaries had been broken; they were no longer trusted. Eventually they developed into a hereditary unit with power to make or break Sultans. Europe was saved.

Between 1532 and 1555 Suleiman was also engaged in putting down the Shia Safavids of Persia. Although his father, Selim I had been victorious in battle of Chaldiran, the victory was hard to maintain. Efforts to subdue the Safavids failed. Shah Tahmasp constantly retreated while using hit and run plus scorched earth tactics. He refused to come to a pitched battle. Baghdad had to be re-taken after the Shah, loyal to Suleiman was killed. [654]

Barbarossa, Venice and Other Wars

In 1537 **Barbarossa Hayreddin Pasha** [655] began a series of naval attacks against The Republic of Venice. He took eight Aegaen islands belonging to the Duchy of Naxos and annexed them to the Ottoman Empire. He then turned his wrath against Venetian forts on the island of Corfu (39.40°N, 19.45°E) in the Adriatic off the northern Greek coast, and Spanish held territories in southern Italy. Pope Paul III countered by raising a fleet from the Knights of Malta, Genoa and the Republic of Venice to be led by Charles V's admiral, Andrea Doria. This included 122 galleys, 50 galleons and 140 barques and 60,000 soldiers. The fleet gathered at the Island of Corfu. Initial attempts failed to take the fortress of **Preveza** (38.57°N, 20.44°E), a town in northwestern Greece on northern peninsula guarding the Ambracian Gulf. When Barbarossa arrived with his fleet of 122 Galleys and 12,000 soldiers, he seized **Actium** (38.95°N, 20.77°E) on the southern peninsula guarding the entrance to the gulf. This provided valuable artillery support against the Alliance's fleet during the **Battle of Preveza**, September 1538. The Alliance lost 13 galleys sunk, 36 captured and 3000 prisoners. [656]

In 1541 **Buda and Pest** (47°28'N, 19°03'E) fell to the Ottoman troops. Ferdinand I was forced into a treaty with Suleiman. Ferdinand I renounced his claim to Hungary and a substitute ruler of Suleiman's preference was selected. By 1543 the western half of Hungary was in Ottoman hands. In 1547 Suleiman concluded a peace with the Habsburgs allowing Charles to take a breather. It was soon disregarded by the Austrians. [657]

Following Charles V's humiliation at Buda in 1541, he planned revenge in another sector; it would be **Algeria**. Once again he formed a coalition: Spain, the Holy Roman Empire (Germany), Knights of Malta, Republic of Genoa, Papal States, Kingdom of Naples, Kingdom of Sicily, and Italian troops. Land operations would be commanded by Charles V. His troops numbered 24,000 soldiers and 700 knights. The naval force would be commanded by Charles' admiral, Andrea Doria with 80 galleys plus up to 500 other ships, and 12,000 sailors. They faced Hassan Agha and 800 Ottoman soldiers and 5,000 Moors. Coalitions, as mentioned, are always a problem unless dominated by one strong partner. Problems in Germany delayed the fleets embarkation until late in September. Their troops landed on 23 October,1541 near **Algiers**. The following day a storm blew up and wrecked 15 galleys. Other galleys were dispersed and as more troops were landing in the foul weather, the Ottomans began slaughtering them as they landed. Charles V was saved by some Knights of Malta. Andrea Doria re-established his fleet 5 miles east of the city and persuaded Charles to join him. The weather hampered further operations and the campaign was abandoned. Storms from then to January 1542 caused more casualties. Total losses included 17 galleys 130 smaller vessels, many soldiers and sailors. With Spain thus weakened and defeated the Spanish town of Oran (35°41'N,0°37'W) was lost in July 1542. [658]

Meanwhile Suleiman's turned his attention to the **Indian Ocean** and the **Far East**. In 1535 the Portuguese (Christians) obtained the right to trade at **Macau** in China; port facilities were set up after 1552-3. Trading colonies were set up without permission in India and Pakistan from which to base overseas trade. Between 1538 and 1548 Suleiman conducted a successful naval campaign against them. He took **Aden** (12°48'N, 45°02'E) in 1548 and the rest of Yemen and the Arabian Peninsula. Aden provided him with a naval base from which he could control the west end of the Indian Ocean.[659]

In 1551 Suleiman returned to the Mediterranean. Ottoman Corsairs began raiding Spanish Christian commerce. In 1551 they laid siege to **Tripoli** and forced the Maltese Knights out. Raids by Ottoman Corsairs continued threatening Mediterranean Spanish Christian Commerce. A Christian fleet of 54 galleys and 66 other vessels landed supporting troops on the Island of **Djerba** (33°47'N, 10°53'E) off the Tunisian coast in 1551. They built a fort in March and took refuge. In May they were surprised by an Ottoman fleet of 86 galleys. Christian forces lost 30 galleys, 9000 dead and 5000 captured. The Mediterranean was open to Ottoman intimidation. [660]

In 1552 Ottoman armies were once again in central Europe. A successful Ottoman campaign took the Eastern half of **Hungary**. In 1556 **Transylvania** (Romania's Mountainous region) fell. From 5 August to 8 September 1556 another advance on Vienna began well with the siege of **Szigetvar Fortress** near Barcs (46.03N, 17.47E) close to the present Croatian-Hungarian border. Losses were heavy on both sides with both commanders killed, but it was too late in the season to continue on to

Vienna. Cardinal Richelieu was reputed to have said this was "*the battle that saved civilization.*" [661]

Operations in the Mediterranean continued. In 1565 an Ottoman army with allegedly 22-48,000 attacked the **Maltese** (35°53'N, 48°14'E) garrison of 6100-8500 defenders south of Sicily and failed. The Empire suffered 10,000 casualties while the knights lost 2,500 troops, but the Ottomans also killed 7000 non-combatants and took 500 slaves. This had the effect of stopping the westward expansion of the Ottoman Empire in the Western Mediterranean. Voltaire was quoted as saying, "*Nothing is more well-known than the siege of Malta.*" [662] Despite the "*well-known siege of Malta*" and "*the battle that saved civilization,*" **Cyprus** was successfully invaded in 1570 and the siege of **Famagusta** (35°7'N, 33°57'E) was successful. **Nicosia** fell in September. 20,000 Greeks were massacred and all public buildings and churches were looted. The island was secured by August 1571. The **Battle of Lepanto** (October 1571- 38.12°N, 21.18°E) came too late to help the Island which remained under Ottoman rule for 3 centuries. Today Cyprus is ½ Christian. [663] Shortly thereafter Suleiman died at the age of 71. This ended any further campaigns that year.

Suleiman was succeeded by his son to Roxelana, **Selim II** "the sot" or drunkard "or "the blond" (1524-1574). He ruled from 1566 to 1574. He was more interested in drunken orgies and affairs of harem than affairs of state. He turned over most problems to his Grand Vizier, Mehmed Sokollu, a Bosnian. [664] Who was this Roxelana, where did she come from? What kind of influence was she to have on the Ottoman Empire and how did her son, Selim II, become sultan instead of Suleiman's first legitimate son, Şehzade Mustafa?

VALIDE SULTANATE – ON A SLIPPERY SLOPE

Roxelana

Suleiman's first-born son, the heir apparent, was Şehzade Mustafa, but Suleiman preferred his younger brother, Mehmet. When Mehmet died, the way appeared open to Mustafa. When Suleiman returned home from his humiliation at Vienna, he found in his harem a new slave-girl, a 23-year-old Ukrainian beauty, **Roxelana** or **Alexandra Lisowska** [665] (known as Hürrem or "Cheerful one" and Karima "noble one" – 1506-1558). She was kidnapped by Crimean Tartars and sold in Constantinople, a fate of many beautiful Ukrainian girls. Jealousy flared in the harem. Roxelana was injured in a fight with Suleiman's wife, "Flower of Spring," and mother of his two sons. Suleiman banished Flower and freed "The Cheerful." He married her making her his only legal wife. She bore him 5 children including a son, Bayezid, whom she wished to become Sultan. According to legend, Roxelana conspired with Rüstem Pasha, her son-in-law, to send a rumor to Suleiman that his troops, including the now hated Janissaries, thought it was time for him to abdicate in favor of Mustafa. Suleiman took the bait and had his son strangled. Roxelana's son, known as **Selîm II** "the Sot" or "the blond" became Sultan from 1566 to 1574. This began a period in the history of the Ottoman Empire when the Sultan "Moms" ruled. The harem played a decisive role in state affairs, and a period of decay set in. As previously noted, Selim II was disinterested. He turned most problems over to his Grand Vizier, Mehmed Sokollu. [666] With Suleiman gone, Christian Europe had a chance.

The Battle of Lepanto 1571

The Battle of Lepanto (7 October 1571) is one of the most important sea battles in the history of naval warfare. It began the era of sail driven, cannon armed fighting ships. At issue was the defense of Mediterranean commerce against Muslim domination. It took place in the Southern Adriatic in the Gulf of Patras off the coast of Greece and was the last one in which oar powered galleys were used extensively in the West. The Chinese navy of the early 15th century already had huge, 12-masted sail driven, cannon toting battleships. These dwarfed western ships-of-the-line until the age of 20th Century iron-clads. [667] On the European Christian side, the Triple Alliance, Austria, Spain and the Republic of Venice had 206 galleys under the command of Don John of Austria. Venice contributed, their new secret weapon, 6 cannon armed galleasses with sail; they also provided 109 galleys. The galleasses were to spell the difference between victory and defeat for the Triple Aliance. Spain provided 80 galleys; the Order of Saint Stephen gave 12; Genoa, Knights of Malta and Duchy of Savoy gave 3 each. Fighting infantry aboard ship came from Spain, Germany, Croatia and Venice. Facing him were the galleys of the combined Turkish fleet, 216 in all, under the command of Alī Pasha. This kind of sea fight was like a land battle on floating platforms. Formations were rigid, commands were military and the tactics were based on 1st generation warfare–line, close and engage. Casualties were often heavy on both sides. Don John ordered all the rams removed from his ships to given them greater maneuverability. He also ordered his men not to fire their weapons until they could be splashed by the blood of their enemies. This conserved ammunition and made fire more effective than that of the Turks. The Spanish armor was heavy enough to withstand the Pasha's bullets.

Commanding the Genoese right wing of the European fleet was Giovanni Andrea Doria (1539-1606) great nephew of Admiral Andrea Doria. Opposite him were Uluch Alī and the left wing of the Turkish fleet. Don John commanded the center. The center of the Turkish fleet was commanded by Alī Pasha. The Venetians on the Christian left was under Barbarigo. He maneuvered his wing as close to the Greek shore as possible. His Turkish opposite was Mahomet Sirocco.

The six Venetian galleasses armed with cannon had oars, but were primarily sail driven. These led the 3 European wings into battle. The galleasses' guns were heavier than anything in the Turkish fleet. Initially the Turks mistook them for supply ships and attacked them immediately. The guns on the galleasses took out several galleys at long range. None of the Turkish galleys could close with them without being blasted out of the water. This led to an initial heavy loss of Turkish galleys in the center and separated the Turkish left and right wings. These now made efforts to lank the Christian Allies.

Battle of Lepanto October 1571

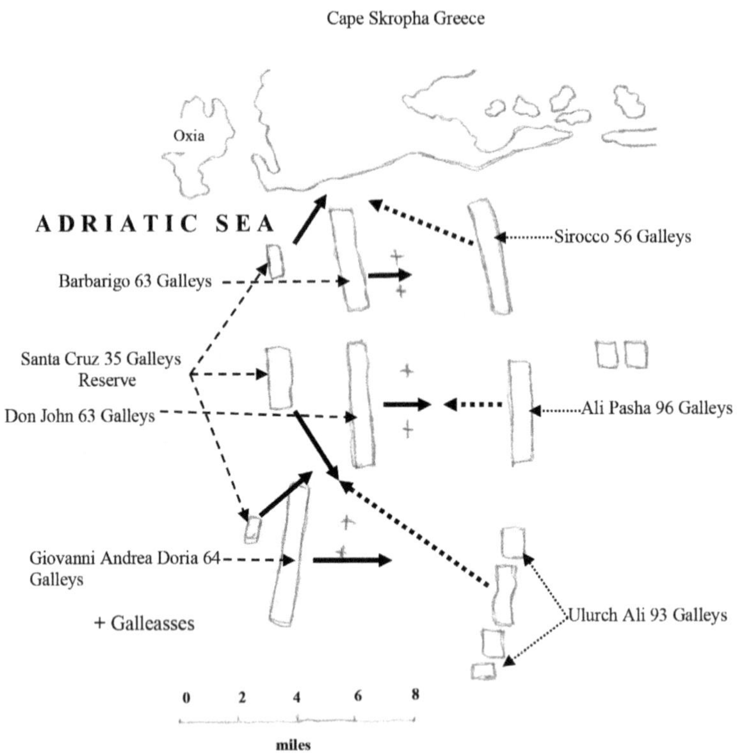

The battle began with a Muslim attack against the Galleasses that were mistaken for supply ships. These ships carried heavy cannon that almost immediately sank 70 Muslin Galleys as the attack surged past their positions. Although Sirroco was able to flank Barbargio a fierce fight caused him heavy casualties. Ulrich Ali started moving forward, but Giannandrea Doria started moving to his right leaving a hole in the Alliance's line. The reserves were instrumental in stopping Ulrich Ali's flanking movement against Don John's center force.

Mahomet Sirocco maneuvered his galleys closer to the shore than Barbarigo and succeeded in flanking him. Both Barbarigo and Sirocco lost their lives in the fierce melee that followed. On the Christian right, Uluch Alī was unable to outflank Doria, but found space between Don Juan's center and Doria's squadron and pushed through to attack Don Juan from the rear. Santa Cruz who had a small contingency of ships in reserve behind Don Juan's center attacked, plugged the hole, and drove Ali's ships back. The decision was settled in the center where Don John's ships were lower in the water allowing their guns to shoot easily into the Turks. The Turks being taller could not lower the aim of their guns to effect. Don John riddled the center of the Turkish fleet's galleys below the water line with his guns. Spanish armor allowed Don John's men to successfully fire often at close range into the Turks. Alī Pasha's galley was boarded, he was beheaded, and the Turkish flagship taken. Fear swept the Turkish fleet when they saw Ali's head mounted on a pike overlooking his ship. The sacred Ottoman standard with Allah's name inscribed 29,000 times was lowered and captured. It had never been lost before. Santa Cruz attack against Uluch Ali's squadron succeeded and forced him to retreat.

In the end 8,000 Spanish and Italian soldiers perished. The Turks lost 24,000. 12,000 Christian slaves were rescued from the oar benches of the Turkish fleet. The victory was decided by the better weapons and greater maneuverability of the Christian Allies, not the bravery of the troops. From the standpoint of European naval battles, it proved the superiority of sailing ships that could maneuver easily and carry cannon. This ushered in the age of sail for Western navies, which was to have its first major test 17 years later in the English Channel in 1588 with the defeat of the Spanish Armada. Never again was the Ottoman Empire able to mount a large-scale fleet action. Lepanto was the first major battle that began the Ottoman Empires' slippery slope into oblivion.

The Valide Sultans Continue

Murad III (1546 – 1595) began his rule in 1574, succeeding his father whose rule was undistinguished, by having his 5 younger brothers strangled. [668] The Grand Vizier Mehmed Sokollu who had been the administrator under Selim II continued in power until his assassination in 1579. From that time on his mother, Nurbanu and his favorite wife, Sofia Baffo, also a Venetian known as Safyie Sultan, made most of the major decisions. During this period, Elizabeth I of England corresponded with Murad III and believed that Anglican England and the Ottomans had more in common than they did with Catholic Europe. This has been a common error of diplomats and chiefs of governments before and since. England exported tin and lead to help them in cannon casting. Economic decline and corruption continued along with wars between the Ottoman Empire Austria and Iran / Persia. [669] During his reign Murad III purchased 1200 slave girls for his amusement in the Seraglio (harem). He was said to have sired 103 children. His sale of public offices and high taxes led to political and economic instability. [670]

Ottoman–Safavid War (1578–1590) was between the Ottoman Empire and the Safavid Persians. The Ottoman's objective was conquering Azerbaijan and the Caucasus (territory between the Black and Caspian Seas). Georgia became a vassal state of the Ottoman Empire by 1585. This ended Shiite beliefs there. Its principal effect was to distract the Ottoman Empire from attempts to take European lands. A peace treaty in 1590 confirmed the Ottoman conquests. [671]

In 1595 Murad III died and was succeeded by **Mehmed III (1566 – 1603)**. True to the tradition of his father he had 19 of his brothers and half-brothers plus 20 of his sisters strangled to death. He had little interest in statecraft and his mother, Safiye Sultan, ruled from 1595 until his death in 1603. [672]

"The Long War" or 15 Year War – 1593–1606

From 1593 to 1606 the Ottoman Empire fought for 13-15 years with a large Coalition of Christian countries (Austria, Hungary, Croatia, plus others including The Holy Roman Empire, Bohemia, Transylvania, Wallachia, Zaporozhian Host (Ukrainians), Spain, Serbian Rebels, Papal States, Venice, Saxony, Tuscany, Persia, Knights of St. Stephen, and more). It is sometimes called "The Long War" or "15 Year War." There were several principal commanders including Rudolf II, Holy Roman Emperor and Sigismund Báthory of Transylvania for the Christian Alliance. This time period covered the reigns of Murad III, Mehmed III, and Ahmed I for the Ottoman Empire. They were generally disinterested rulers. Some of this war is covered in the Chapter, "Adventurer, Soldier of Fortune & Publicist." The alliance put together 95,000 men from time to time and the Ottomans fielded 160-180,000. Casualties were heavy on both sides, but unknown. [673]

The principal objective of the Ottomans was the capture of Vienna while the Hungarians wanted to free much of their southern territories in the Balkans. Most of the war was fought in Slovakia, Hungary and along the Danube River south from Buda-Pest to Belgrade. In 1595 the Alliance took a string of 3 forts on the northern Border of Hungary near the Danube

[Győr (47°41'N, 17°38'E), Esztergom (47°47'N, 18°44'E) and Visegrád (47°78'N, 18°97'E), but did not besiege Buda. In 1596 the Ottomans took Eger (47.89N, 20.37E).

In Eastern Romania, Michael the Brave of Wallachia engaged the Turks in 1594 and took several castles in the Romanian lower Danube – Giurgiu (43°54'N, 25°58'E), Bräila (45°16'N, 27°57'E) in Romania, and Hârşova (44°41'N, 27°57'E) and Silistra (44°7'N, 27°16'E) in Bulgaria. The Moldavians also took Iași (47°9'N, 27°35'E) plus other areas. Michael continued to press south taking Nicopolis (39°0'N, 20°44'E), Ribnic (45°44'N, 14°43'E), Chilia (45°25'N, 29°17'E), and went as far as Adrianople. His forces came within 24 k of Constantinople. Michael finally fought a major battle at Călugăreni (44°18'N, 26°0'E) on August 13, 1595. It was estimated that there were 30-40,000 Ottomans and only 10,000 allies with 5000 mercenaries. Although he killed 10-15,000 Muslims while losing only 1000, he was compelled to withdraw northward leaving behind Bucharest and Târgovişte because he knew the total Ottoman force numbered about 100,000. The Ottomans occupied both cities leaving behind garrisons of 10,000 and 1,500 troops. Sigismund arrived from Bohemia with reinforcements (7,500 cavalry and 1,500 foot) and retook both cities plus Giurgiu (43°54'N, 25°58'E) by the end of October 1595.[674]

Poor logistics hampered the Allied effort. The following year (1596) another major battle occurred in northeastern Hungary – the Battle of Mezökeresztes (47°82'N, 20°68'E) also called Keresztes (October 1596). It was fought 22 miles south of Miskolc (48°06'N, 20°47'E) in Northern Hungary. This time the Ottomans were able to get 100,000 on the battlefield to confront 40-50,000 Allies with 30 cannon. Preliminary action occurred when Austrians besieged Eger in Hungary. They reduced another castle, Hatvan (47.40 N, 19.40 E), and in the process killed all Ottomans including women and children. The Ottomans besieged Eger (47°89'N, 20°37'E), but despite capitulation, the Ottomans retaliated by killing all the occupants. The two armies finally met at Haçova. Turkish casualties were 20-30,000 troops to 12,000 of Allies, but the Ottomans prevailed. The Christians won the battle of plunder by stealing all their gold in the baggage train, but the Ottoman's returned to Constantinople declaring victory.[675]

Ahmed I (1590 – 1617) came to power in 1603 when his father died. He was an Islamic fundamentalist. His mother was Handan, Sultan, a woman of Greek extraction. Instead of killing his younger brother he sent him to live with his grandmother, Safyie Sultan. His favorite concubine was Kösem, a Greek beauty. He was well educated and good at fencing, but his wars with Persia and Hungary ended in failure. In 1606 the Empire was humiliated by the Treaty of Zsitvatorok that ended the Long War. This ended Austria's annual tribute obligation. Humiliation for the Ottomans didn't stop there.[676]

A second **Ottoman–Safavid War** was fought from 1603 to 1618. Following the humiliation of Persia in the war of 1578 to 1590, the weak Shah Mohammad was overthrown by a coup in 1587 and his 16 year-old son Abbas I (1571-1629), "the Great" was placed on the throne. He quickly took power and immediately modernized his army along English lines. Within the first year of the war Abbas erased the gains made by the Ottomans up to 1590. Georgia and Azerbaijan were back in Persian hands; but Abbas didn't stop. In 1605 he seized Basra (30°30'N, 47°49'E) and extended his territory beyond the Euphrates to include Baghdad. The Shah's army continued to pile on victory after victory as they added Shirvan (eastern Caucasus) and Kurdistan to their conquests by 1611. The final Battle of Soltaniyeh (36°26'N, 48°47'E) in 1618 resulted in terms favorable to Persia. When the Ottomans resumed the war in 1623, Baghdad was subdued again and by the time of Abbas I's death in 1629, his empire reached from the Tigris to the Indus Rivers.[677]

Ahmed I was known as a scholar and pious man spending money to support these efforts and enforce Sharia Law including restrictions on alcohol and forced payment of alms. He was responsible for the building of the Blue Mosque in Istanbul. The tribute paid by Austria ended. He spent a great deal supporting religion and scholars. His marriage to Valide Sultan Mahfiruze Hatice (Maria, a Greek) produced Osman II. His marriage to Valide Sultan Kadinefendi (Kösem Sultan, also a Greek) produced Murad IV and Ibrahim I. He died of Typhus.[678]

With the death of Amhed I in 1617 **Mustafa I (1591-1639)**, brother of Ahmed I was installed as Sultan. He was considered mentally deficient and possibly neurotic, but clearly incapable of ruling.

Osman II (1604 – 1622) ruled from 1618-1622. He was well educated and knew 5 foreign languages. He was considered a poet. Although only 14 when he assumed the role of sultan, he was determined to succeed in war and politics. He secured the eastern borders of his empire by treaty and then attacked northward into the Polish-Lithuanian Commonwealth. With the encouragement of Frederick V of the Simmernline, Elector of Palatine, he brought the Ottoman Empire into alliance with the Protestant Union in 1620 and attacked the Poles who were sympathetic with the Catholic Habsburgs. (See 30 Years' War below.) In the **Battle of Cecora or Ţuţora** in Moldavia near the Prut River (September-October 1620) Osman II was victorious. His army of 13-22,000 annihilated a Polish army of about 10,000. However in the second, the **Battle of Khotyn** (48°30'N, 26°30'E), Ukraine / Moldavia (1621), despite numerical superiority, Osman II's forces were forced to retire without victory because of the lateness of the season (9 October). He blamed the cowardice of the Janissaries for the defeat. The Janissaries paid him back in 1622 with strangulation. [679]

Following the assassination of Osman II by the Janissaries a series of revolts began in Anatolia (modern Turkey) known as the Abaza revolts. Clans that had been part of building the empire found themselves the victims of corrupt government with increasing inflation, increasing taxation on agricultural products, and discrimination against joining the army in favor of the Sultan's palace guards or janissaries.

All this was part of the "Sultanate of Women," [680] which began with Roxelana's son, Selim II in 1566 and lasted about 130 years. The *Valide* Sultan, *Bas Kadin* or "Chief Lady," the mothers of the reigning Sultan occasionally exercised so much power that they controlled state affairs. Moms ruled in their son's name and brought down several governments. The size of the harem or Seraglio increased upwards of 1000 women and took much treasure to maintain. This was another factor in the ruin of the Ottoman Empires economy. [681]

Mustafa I returned to the throne from 1622 to 1623. His mother was Handan Sultan, a Greek named Helena. He ruled briefly, had the assassins of Osman II executed, but then went about trying to find his nephew and had to be replaced by Murad IV [682]

Murad IV

Murad IV (1612-1640) came to power at the age of 11 by virtue of palace intrigue in 1623. [683] He was the son of Amehd I and Valide Sultan Kadinefendi (Kösem Sultan). Kösem was the actual ruler, but was unable to stop the anarchy that followed. At the age of 19 Murad IV began exercising his power by enforcing strict religious rules against alcohol and tobacco. Personally, he paid no attention to the alcohol restrictions and was frequently drunk. He did part of the police work by killing offenders on the spot with a mace. He was very large and strong and took pleasure in hand to hand combat in the streets and on the field of battle. He wielded a huge 50 k broad sword with one hand while swinging a 60-k mace with the other. His war against Persia was successful in the recapture of Baghdad in 1638 and the rest of Mesopotamia. Although he was able to suppress various revolts, this further weakened the Empire. He was the last sultan to personally lead troops in battle. He died of cirrhosis of the liver at age 27. Before his death he ordered the execution of his brother Ibrahim, but this order was ignored. As the Sultans became weak, the bureaucracy became more intrusive.

Ibrahim I "the mad"

Ibrahim I (1615-1648) also known as "the mad" was emotionally unstable and incapable of rule; he allegedly ordered the drowning of 280 in his harem; at least two escaped. He came to power in 1640 with the death of his brother, Murad IV, and ruled until 1648. In 1646 his forces lost the **Island of Tenedos** (39°49'N, 26°03'E) to a Venetian naval force. [684] It was an island strategically located near the opening of the Dardanelles and had been taken by Ottoman forces in 1464. His mother Kösem was the de facto sultan; she ruled ineffectively. He was strangled to death. Ibrahim I sired three future sultans by 3 of his harem wives, Mehmed IV, Suleiman II and Ahmed II. [685]

Table XII Rulers of the Ottoman Empire Period of Valide Sultans & Stagnation (1566 – 1648)

1566 – 1574	Selîm II "the Sot" "**Sultanate of women**" Begins	Peace of Adrianople; tribute from Austria (1568); Conquest of Cyprus 1571; Battle of Lepanto (1571) Sultâns no longer kill brothers. Succession passes to brothers & cousins before next generation; Queen Mothers begin influence; "Sultanate of Women" Begins and ends about 1700. **Nurbanu** was his harem favorite
1574 – 1595	Murâd III (Sultân)	Inconclusive war with Austria 1593 – 1603. Authority undermined by his mother, **Nurbanu**, and numerous other women.
1595 – 1603	Meh.med III	The Seraglio contained 100 to 1000 women. **Safyie**, Valide Sultan.
1603 – 1617	Ah.med I	**Kösem** favorite concubine, Greek beauty. War and rebellion weaken Sultans
1617 – 1618	Mustafâ I	**Kösem**, Valide Sultan
1618 – 1622	'Osmân II	Killed by Janissaries at age 18 following defeats at Cecora and Khotyn by Polish, Lithuanian and Cossack armies
1622 – 1623	Ah.med I (restored)	Construction of the Blue Mosque in Istanbul
1623 – 1640	Murâd IV	Conqueror of Baghdad
1640 – 1648	Ibrâhîm	**Kösem**, continues as Valide Sultan till assassination in 1651

(Endnotes)

[1]REFERENCES

1 [Fatalities included 246 on four planes, 2602 in New York (including 343 NYC fire-fighters, 23 NYC police officers and 37 Port Authority Police), 125 at the Pentagon.]

2 http://www.pbs.org/newshour/terrorism/international/fatwa_1996.html

3 http://en.wikipedia.org/wiki/sociobiology

4 Schwartz JM et al. *Quantum physics in neuroscience and psychology: a neurophysical model of mind-brain interaction.* Phil. Trans. R. Soc. B. doi:10,1098/rstb,2004, 1598. Published online.

5 http://en.wikipedia.org/wiki/Midbrain

6 http://en.wikipedia.org/wiki/Limbic_system

7 http://en.wikipedia.org/wiki/Neuroplasticity

8 http://en.wikipedia.org/wiki/Fetal_alcohol_syndrome

9 http://en.wikipedia.org/wiki/Amblyopia

10 http://en.wikipedia.org/wiki/Amygdala

11 http://www.loni.ucla.edu/~thompson/DEVEL/PR.html

12 Marcus Aurelius, *Meditations*, New York E.P. Dutton & Co Inc., 1961 pg. 1 axiom 4

13 Marx & Engles *Communist Manifesto* Part II, Proletarians and Communists

14 http://en.wikipedia.org/wiki/Vocabulary_development

15 ***Diagnostic and Statistical Manual of Mental Disorders 4*th *Ed.* Pub American Psychiatric Association**

16 **Benson ET. *An Enemy Hath Done This.* Parliament Pub., Salt Lake City. 1968. Pg. vi.**

17 Tzu, Sun. *The Art of War*, Translated by Samuel B Griffith. Oxford University Press, New York, 1963 Pg. 73

18 Tzu, Sun *The Art of War*: Complete Texts and Commentaries. Translated by Cleary. Shambhala Pub Inc. Boston, 2000. Pg 22.

19 http://en.wikipedia.org/wiki/History_of_money

20 http://inventors.about.com/od/pstartinventions/a/papermaking.htm

21 **Yeoman RS. *The Official Red Book: a Guide Book of United States Coins 61*st *Ed.* Whitman Pub. LLC 2008 pgs. 87, 135, 237,** 249
22 http://en.wikipedia.org/wiki/Banknote
23 **Levin MR. Ameritopia: The Unmaking of America. Threshold Editions. New York. 2012. Pg 202**.
24 Pilzer,PZ. *God Wants You To Be Rich: The Theology of Economics*, Simon & Schuster, New York, 1995, Pgs. 241-243
25 http://en.wikipedia.org/wiki/Letter_of_marque
26 **Fleming, T. *Benjamin Franklin; A Biography in His own Words.* Newsweek, New York, 1972. Pg 398.**
27 Marx, Karl *Manifesto of the Communist Party* (Part II) 1848
28 Johnson,Paul. *Intellectuals*, Harper Perennial, 1988, pages 1-27
29 *Ibid* pgs.52-81
30 See *Animal Farm* by George Orwell
31 De Soto, Hernando *The Mystery of Capitalism*
32 Op cit.Johnson, P. pages 1-27
33 http://www.scaruffi.com/politics/massacre.html
34 *Ibid* pgs.52-81
35 http://marxmyths.org/terrell-carver/article.htm
36 http://www.forbes.com/2003/02/14/cx_da_0214pres.html
37 http://www.forbes.com/sites/afontevecchia/2010/11/17/millionaire-congress-half-of-our-lawmakers-top-1m-in-net-worth/
38 *Declaration of Independance*
39 Lewis, Bernard. *Notes on a Century; Reflections of a Middle East Historian.* Viking 2012. Pgs. 146-150.
40 http://entomology.montana.edu/historybug/napoleon/typhus_russia.htm
41 http://en.wikipedia.org/wiki/List_of_United_States_presidential_assassination_attempts_and_plots
42 Keys, David. *Catastrophe*,(Ballantine Books, New York, 1999
43 Wells, Spencer. *The Journey of Man: A Genetic Odyssey.* Princeton University Press, 2002; pgs. 182-3
44 http://en.wikipedia.org/wiki/Toba_catastrophe_theory
45 Sadeghian, Abbas. *Sword and Seizure: Muhammad's Epilepsy & Creation of Islam* Annotation Press, 2006
46 http://www.pbs.org/wgbh/pages/frontline/shows/binladen/who/edicts.html
47 http://www.pbs.org/wgbh/pages/frontline/shows/binladen/who/edicts.html

THE CHANGING FACE OF WARFARE

[48] Patai, Raphael. *The Arab Mind*, Revised Edition, Charles Scribner's Sons, New York, 1983, page 213)
[49] *Ibid* pg. 215
[50] http://www.d-n-i.net/fcs/4th_gen_war_gazette.htm
[51] http://en.wikipedia.org/wiki/Fire_and_Movement
[52] Eisenhower DD *Crusade in Europe,* Doubleday & Co. Inc 1948. pg. 4
[53] www.generalpatton.com/quotes.html
[54] Blumenson, M. The *Patton Papers 1940-1945*, Houghton Mifflin Co. Boston 1974
[55] General James M. Gavin. *On To Berlin.* Bantam Books, New York. 1978
[56] Omar N Bradley. *A Soldier's Story.* Henry Holt & Co., New York, 1951 pgs. 355-56, 402-3

THE CHANGING FACE OF WARFARE (CONTINUED)

[57] Personal participation, *Operation Deepwater NATO Exercise.* Galipoli, Turkey & Thrace. USMC deployed 3-6-2. August 1957.
[58] Tzu, Sun, *The Art of War,* translated by Samuel B. Griffith, Oxford University Press, New York, 1963, p. 73.
[59] http://www.carpenoctem.tv/military/khan.html
[60] http://www.ccc.nps.navy.mil/si/aug02/homeland.asp
[61] Von Clausewitz, Carl, *On War*, translation by M. Howard and P. Paret, Princeton University Press, Princeton NJ 1976 p 119
[62] http://www.snopes.com/rumors/pershing.htm
[63] **http://www.military-quotes.com/william-sherman.htm** http://www.brainyquote.com/quotes/authors/w/william_tecumseh_sherman.html
[64] Blumenson, Martin. *The Patton Papers 1885-1940*, Houghton Mifflin Co. Boston 1972 pgs. 15-16
[65] Blumenson Ibid pgs. 7-8
[66] General Merrill B Twining, *No Bended Knee, the Battle for Guadalcanal.* Presidio Press, Novato CA, pg. viii. General Lucius A Paulus 229-160 BC – Rome
[67] http://en.wikipedia.org/wiki/William_Tecumseh_Sherman
[68] http://www.civilwarhome.com/casualties.htm
[69] Ghaemi, N. A First-Rate Madness: Uncovering the Links Between Leadership and Mental Illness. Penguin Books 2012, Pgs 23-39.

ISLAM & WAR

70 Fallaci, Oriana. *La Forza della Ragione.* Rizzoli International, New York, 2004, page 146

71 Huntington, Samuel P. *The Clash of Civilizations and the Remaking of World Order*, Simon & Schuster, New York, 1996 (paperback 2003), Chapter 10 "From Transition Wars to Fault Line Wars"

72 *Ibid* pg. 254

73 *Ibid* pg. 258

74 http://www.dw-world.de/dw/article/0,5655554,00.html

75 Huntington op cit. pg. 264-5

76 *Webster's New Universal Unabridged Dictionary*, Simon & Schuster 2nd Edition, New York, 1979, pg. 1317

WHAT ARE ARAB, ISLÂM, & THE *KORÂN*? WHO WAS MUHAMMAD?

77 Patai, Raphael. *The Arab Mind* (Charles Scribner's Sons, New York 1983 pg. 44

78 *Ibid* pg. 13

79 *Ibid* pg. 14

80 *Ibid* pg. 15

81 ***The Ecclesiastical History of Eusebius Pamphilus*, Baker Book House, Grand Rapids, 1984, pages 44-45**

82 http://www.corkscrew-balloon.com/02/03/1bkk/04b.html

83 http://debate.org.uk/topics/books/origins-koran.html

84 Nibley, HW *Teachings of The Book of Mormon Semester 3*, FARMS, 1988-1990 Brigham Young University, pg.60

85 Josephus, Flavius. *The Antiquities of the Jews*, 93-94AD, 18.3.3

86 http://www.newadvent.org/cathen/08375a.htm

87 http://www.israeltoday.co.il/default.aspx?tabid=182&view=item&idx =1149

88 http://isaalmasih.net/archaeology-isa/quran-archaeology.html

89 Johnson, Paul *A History of the Jews*. Harper Perennial, 1988, pgs.166-8

90 *Encyclopaedia Britannica* 11th Ed, 1910-11, Vol. XVII pages 423-24

91 Kufa (32.02°N, 44.24°E); Jerusalem (31.47°N, 35.13°E); Mecca (21.25°N, 39.49°E)

92 http://travel.state.gov/travel/tips/regional/regional_1175.html

EVIL

93 **Richard R Hopkins, *How Greek Philosophy Corrupted the Christian Concept of God.* Horizon Publishers, 1998 pg.** 54

94 http://rosemck1.tripod.com/bible.html

95 http://ichthys.com/mail-Bible%20chrono.htm

ISLAMIC DOCTRINE

96 http://www.usc.edu/dept/MSA/reference/searchhadith.html

97 http://www.usc.edu/dept/MSA/fundamentals/hadithsunnah/bukhari/052.sbt.html

98 http://www.usc.edu/dept/MSA/fundamentals/hadithsunnah/bukhari/059.sbt.html

99 http://www.frontpagemag.com/Articles/ReadArticle.asp?ID=13371

100 http://www.frontpagemag.com/Articles/ReadArticle.asp?ID=25185

101 **Hopkins RR. *How Greek Philosophy Corrupted the Christian Concept of God*, Horizon Publishers, Bountiful, 1998 page 103, 115.**

102 http://www.answering-islam.org/Authors/Arlandson/dead_poets.htm

103 http://www.primechoice.com/philosophy/shelp/muhammad.htm

104 http://www.flex.com/~jai/satyamevajayate/heaven.html

105 http://www.hti.umich.edu/k/Korân/

106 http://etext.lib.virginia.edu/Korân.html

107 http://quod.lib.umich.edu/k/Korân/

108 http://www.religionfacts.com/homosexuality/islam.htm

109 http://www.guardian.co.uk/commentisfree/2010/apr/25/middle-east-child-abuse-pederasty

110 http://www.faithfreedom.org/Articles/SStephan/slavegirls.htm

MODERN CONCEPTS

111 http://en.wikipedia.org/wiki/Salafihttp://en.wikipedia.org/wiki/Wahhabi

112 http://en.wikipedia.org/wiki/Muhammad_ibn_Abd_al-Wahhab

113 http://en.wikipedia.org/wiki/Ibn_Saud_of_Saudi_Arabia http://en.wikipedia.org/wiki/Saudi_Aramco

114 http://en.wikipedia.org/wiki/OPEC

115 http://www.indexmundi.com/g/r.aspx?c=us&v=88

116 http://en.wikipedia.org/wiki/Saddam_Hussein

117 http://www.fas.org/irp/world/para/mb.htm

HISTORY OF ISLÂM

118 Benson ET. *An Enemy Hath Done This.* Parliament Pub. Salt Lake City. 1968 pg. 3.

119 Jens O. Parsson. *Dying of Money.* Wellspring Press, Boston, 1974 page 103

120 Letter:Thomas Jefferson to John Wayles Eppes, 1813. ME 13:430

121 Letter:Thomas Jefferson to Edward Carrington, 1788. ME 7:36

122 http://en.wikipedia.org/wiki/Winston_Churchill#Rejoining_the_Conservative_Party.E2.80.94Chancellor_of_the_Exchequer

123 http://www.roman-empire.net/army/army.html

124 Nibley H. *The Ancient State: the Rulers and the Ruled.* Deseret Book Co., Salt Lake City. FARMS, 1991 pgs. 198-99

125 Medieval Sourcebook: Priscus at the court of Attila (http://www.fordham.edu/halsall/source/priscus1.html)

126 Phillips & Keatman, *King Arthur: The True Story*, Century, London, 1992

127 Cahill,Thomas. *How the Irish Saved Civilization: The Untold Story of Ireland's Heroic Role from the Fall of Rome to the Rise of Medieval Europe.* Bantam, Doubleday, Dell, New York, 1995

128 http://www.avesta.org/zfaq.html

129 http://www.answering-Islâm.org/Books/Tisdall/Sources/chapt5.htm

130 http://www.answering-Islâm.org/Books/Tisdall/Sources/chapt5.htm

131 Keys, David. *Catastrophe: An Investigation into the Origins of the Modern World.* Ballantine Books, 1999, pgs. 183-235.

132 Ibid pg. 189-90

133 Ibid pg. 192

134 Ibid pgs. 194-197

135 http://womenshistory.about.com/library/bio/blbio_theodora.htm

136 Wellman, Paul I. *The Female*, Doubleday & Co. Inc, Garden City, New York, 1953, a fascinating historical novel.

137 Pratt, Fletcher. *The Battles that Changed History*, Dover Publication Inc., Mineola, NY, 2000, pgs. 57-73

138 Ibid pg. 70

139 Keys, David. *Catastrophe: An Investigation into the Origins of the Modern World.* Ballantine Books, 1999, pg. 281

140 Ibid pgs. 281-282

141 Ibid pg. 251

142 Ibid pgs. 5 & 239

143 Ibid pg. 253

144 Ibid pgs. 254-55

145 Ibid pg. 9
146 Ibid pg. 10
147 Ibid pg. 10
148 Ibid pg. 10
149 Ibid pg. 11 (all quotes to this point)
150 Ibid, "*The Winepress of the Wrath of God*," pgs. 9-16
151 Ibid pgs. 29-30.
152 Ibid pgs. 31-33
153 Ibid pg. 35-38
154 http://en.wikipedia.org/wiki/United_States_Bullion_Depository
155 Yeoman, *The Official Red Book:a Guide Book of United States Coins 2008*. Whitman Pub Atlanta. Pg 229
156 Ibid pg. 13
157 Ibid pgs. 54-56
158 http://www.biblebelievers.org.au/moongod.htm
159 Chandler, *The Military Maxims of Napoleon*, Macmillan Publishing Co., New York, 1988, pg. 55
160 Keys, David. *Catastrophe: An Investigation into the Origins of the Modern World.* Ballantine Books, 1999, pgs. 59-61
161 Ibid pg. 60
162 *The Life of Muhammad*: A translation of Ishāq's Sīrat Rasūl Allāh. Introduction and notes by A. Guillaume, Oxford University Press, Oxford New York, Twentieth Impression 2006 pgs. 693-699, and the notes of Ibn Hishām and "How 'Āmr B. 'Āmir left the Yaman
163 Keys, *Catastrophe* pg. 63
164 *The Life of Muhammad pgs.* 24-30
165 Ibid pg. 27
166 Ibid pg. 62
167 Ibid pgs. 66-68

JUDAISM & CHRISTIANITY, BACKGROUND OF ISLAM

168 Patton GS. *War As I Knew It.* p.49) http://en.wikipedia.org/wiki/George_S._Patton
169 http://www.freemars.org/jeff/2exp100/answer.htm
170 http://en.wikipedia.org/wiki/Septuagint
171 *The Interlinear Bible: Hebrew-Greek-English.* Jay P. Green, Sr., general editor and translator. Hendrickson Publishers. Peabody, Massachusetts, 1986, pg. 2
172 Ibid pg. 2

JUDAISM & CHRISTIANITY, BACKGROUND OF ISLAM

173 http://www.jesus-is-lord.com/transtoc.htm is an article "Who Were the King James Version Translators?" It notes that 54 of some of the "world's best scholars" were selected to do the work. These were divided into companies and that either 47 or 51 actually participated. Their first work was published in 1611. They relied on original sources and not on previous translations by Wiclif 1380, Tyndale 1534, Cranmer 1539, or the Geneva Bible 1557. See also "The Rules for Translating" in this article.

174**Judaism & Christianity, background of islam (Continued)**
The Interlinear Bible pg. 11

175 Ibid pg. 117

176 Ibid pg. 2

177 https://biblehub.com/lexicon/genesis/2-18.htm

178 Marks & Engels. *Manifesto of the Communist Party.* International Publishers. New York 1948. Pgs. 26-7

179 https://en.wikipedia.org/wiki/List_of_American_Utopian_communities

180 https://en.wikipedia.org/wiki/Population_decline

181 http://www.margaretbarker.com/Papers/TheHolyAnointingOil.pdf

182 http://www.joehunt.org/joseph-smith-margaret-barker-talk.html

183 http://www.joehunt.org/joseph-smith-margaret-barker-talk.html

184 Hopkins, Richard R. *How Greek Philosophy Corrupted the Christian Concept of God*, Horizon Publishers, Bountiful Utah, 1998

185 Talmage, James E. *The Great Apostasy*, Deseret Book, Salt Lake City, 1981 Chapters 3-6

186 *Eusebius' Ecclesiastical History.* Baker Book House, Grand Rapids, 12th printing, June 1984, pgs. 479-480

187 http://essenes.net/index.php?option=com_content&task=view&id=458&Itemid=961 on Constantine's Bible

188*Eusebius' Ecclesiastical History* Chapter XXVII pg. 302

189 http://en.wikipedia.org/wiki/Battle_of_the_Milvian_Bridge

190 http://en.wikipedia.org/wiki/Arch_of_Constantine

191 http://en.wikipedia.org/wiki/Mithraic_mysteries

192 http://en.wikipedia.org/wiki/Sator_Square

193 http://www.thunderministries.com/history/Nicea.html

194 Can be found on various on-line references. Search quotes.

195 *Eusebius' Ecclesiastical History: A Historical View of The Council of Nice Council of Nice*, with a Translation of Documents by Rev. Isaac Boyle, J.B. Lippincott & Co, Philadelphia 1879, pg. 13

196 Ibid pgs16-17
197 http://www.apostolics.net/Nicea.html
198 http://www.apostolics.net/Nicea.html
199 http://www.apostolics.net/Nicea.html
200 http://www.stopthereligiousright.org/theodosius.htm
201 http://www.stopthereligiousright.org/theodosius.htm
202 http://en.wikipedia.org/wiki/English_versions_of_the_Nicene_Creed_in_current_use
203 http://www.stopthereligiousright.org/theodosius.htm
204 **http://www.frmichel.najim.net/antiochandsyriacchristianity.pdf**
205 *The Life of Muhammad*: A translation of Ishāq's Sīrat Rasül Allāh. Introduction and notes by A. Guillaume, Oxford University Press, Oxford New York, Twentieth Impression 2006 (See Index of Subjects)
206 *The Life of Muhammad* pgs. 179-180
207 http://www.newadvent.org/cathen/08459b.htm
208 http://en.wikipedia.org/wiki/Family_life_and_children_of_Vladimir_I
209 http://en.wikipedia.org/wiki/Vladimir_I_of_Kiev\

Judaism & Christianity, background of islam (continued)

210 *The Library of Alexandria: Centre of Learning in the Ancient World*, Edited by Roy Mac Leod paperback edition, I B Tauris & Co. Ltd., London, New York. 2005 pg. 74 – found on line

MUHAMMAD'S BIRTH AND ADULT LIFE 570 – 610 AD

211 http://www.Islâm.com/chronology.htm
212 *The Life of Muhammad*: A translation of Ishāq's Sīrat Rasül Allāh. Introduction and notes by A. Guillaume, Oxford University Press, Oxford New York, Twentieth Impression 2006, pg. 69
213 *The Life of Muhammad* page 70
214 *Ibid* pg. 72
215 *Ibid* pg. 79
216 *Ibid* pgs. 79-81
217 *Ibid* pg. 81 footnote #1
218 *Ibid* pg. 81 footnote #2
219 http://s155239215.onlinehome.us/Turkic/70_Dateline/avardatelineEn.htm
220 http://www.kutriguri.com/culture_timeline_body.html
221 Keys, David. *Catastrophe: An Investigation into the Origins of the Modern World.* Ballantine Books, 1999, pgs. 31-38
222 *Catastrophe* pgs. 33-34
223 *Ibid* pg. 35

224 Phillips & Keatman, *King Arthur: The True Story*, Century, London, 1992
225 http://en.wikipedia.org/wiki/Battle_of_Deorham
226 http://en.wikipedia.org/wiki/Rudder#Ancient_Egypt
227 http://en.wikipedia.org/wiki/Armillary_sphere
228 Menzies G, *1434: The Year a Magnificent Chinese Fleet Sailed to Italy and Ignited the Renaissance.* Harper Collins, 2008, New York, pg. 85
229 http://en.wikipedia.org/wiki/Chinese_currency#Early_history
230 *Castastrophy* pg. 36
231 *The Life of Muhammad* pgs. 90-95
232 *The Life of Muhammad* pg. 104 (quotation from Syriac Bible (John 15:23-16:1)
233 *Ibid* pg. 82
234 *Ibid* pg. 82
235 http://www.al-Islâm.org/masoom/bios/Khadīja.htm
236 *Ibid* pg. 82
237 http://lexicorient.com/e.o/Khadīja.htm
238 *The Life of Muhammad* pg. 73
239 *Ibid* pg. 83
240 *Ibid* pg. 99
241 *Ibid* pg. 103, 107
242 *Ibid* pg. 144
243 http://www.momineen.com/Client/SubPage/Page.aspx?PID=701&ID=399
244 Eastman NJ & Hellman LM. *Williams Obstetrics* 12th Edition, Appleton-Century-Crofts, New York, 1961, pgs. 54, 223-4
245 http://www.al-Islâm.org/gracious/7.htm
246 *The Life of Muhammad* pg. 83
247 Sadeghian A. *Sword and Seizure: Muhammad's Epilepsy & Creation of Islâm*, Annotation Press 2006, pg. 49
248 *The Life of Muhammad* pgs. 84-87
249 *Sword and Seizure* pg. 81 (quotes the *Hadith* by Al-Bukhari M. *The Translation of the Meaning of Sahib*, 1988 vol. 1-9 5:108)
250 *The Life of Muhammad* pg. 81 Note #2
251 *Ibid* pg. 87

MECCA: THE BIRTH OF ISLÂM IN MECCA: 610 – 619

252 *The Life of Muhammad*: A translation of Ishāq's Sīrat Rasūl Allāh. Introduction and notes by A. Guillaume, Oxford University Press, Oxford New York, Twentieth Impression 2006, pg. 111

253 Sahih (authentic) Hadith (traditions) of Bukhari, [2], Volume 9, number 111
254 http://answering-Islâm.org/Silas/suicide.htm
255 Tabari, volume 6 page 76 Bukhari, volume 9, #111
256 Pickthall M. *The Meaning of the Glorious Qur'an Text and Explanatory Translation.* Jajarmi Publications, Tehran, Iran ISBN 964-6766-01-3. Pg 5.
257 *The Life of Muhammad* pg. 111
258 *Ibid* pg. 114
259 *Ibid* pg. 115
260 *Ibid* pgs. 115-117
261 *Ibid* pg. 117
262 *Ibid* pgs. 121-122
263 Patai, R. *The Arab Mind*, Charles Scribner's Sons, New York, 1983, pg. 213
264 *The Life of Muhammad* pgs. 130,131
265 *Ibid pg.* 143
266 *Encyclopaedia Brittannica*, 1911 edition, Vol. XVII pp 403
267 *The Life of Muhammad* pg. 143
268 *Ibid* pg. 136
269 *Ibid* pg. 308.
270 http://www.answering-islam.org/Muhammad/Enemies/nadr.html
271 *The Life of Muhammad* pg. 676
272 *Ibid* pg. 675
273 *Ibid* pgs. 367-368
274 *Ibid* pg. 369
275 *Ibid* pgs. 674-5
276 *Ibid* pg. 550
277 *Ibid* pg. 551
278 *Ibid* pg. 131
279 *Ibid* pg. 132
280 *Ibid* pg. 134
281 *Ibid* pg. 132
282 *Ibid* pg. 133
283 *Ibid* pg. 136
284 *Ibid* pg. 136-7
285 *Ibid* pg. 141-2
286 *Ibid* pgs. in 146-8
287 *Encyclopaedia of Britannica*, 1911 Edition, Vol. XVII pg. 403
288 *The Life of Muhammad* pg. 152
289 *Ibid* pgs. 159 to 161 and 172-175

290 http://www.Islâm.com/chronology.htm
291 http://en.wikipedia.org/wiki/Meccan_boycott_of_the_Hashemites
292 *The Life of Muhammad* pg. 160
293 http://www.geocities.com/Athens/Stage/8217/15/1rst_believer.htm
294 http://en.wikipedia.org/wiki/First_migration_to_Abyssinia
295 *The Life of Muhammad* pg. 162
296 *Ibid* pg. 162
297 *Ibid* pg. 164
298 *Ibid* pg. 164
299 *Ibid* pg. 165
300 *Ibid* pg. 165 Note #3
301 *Ibid* pgs. 165-66 and footnote #3
302 *Ibid* pg. 166 note #1
303 *Ibid* pg. 165
304 *The Life of Muhammad* pgs. 168-9
305 *Ibid* pgs. 155-7
306 *Ibid* pg. 167
307 *Ibid* pgs. 168-9
308 *Ibid* pg. 187
309 *Ibid* pg. 187
310 Sale, George. *The Korân: Translated into English from the Original Arabic*, with Introduction y Sir Edward Denison Ross, Frederick Warne & Co. Ltd., London, 1734, pg. 256, Sura XVI Note #1
311 *The Life of Muhammad* pgs. 172-3 and footnotes
312 *Ibid* pg. 175
313 *Ibid* pgs. 176-7
314 *Ibid* pg. 180
315 (http://www.blessedcause.org/complaint/Mary%20Habeck.htm
316 www.themiddleages.net/people/heraclius.html

BETWIXT & BETWEEN 619 TO 621 AD

317 *The Life of Muhammad* pg. 191
318 *Ibid* pg. 191
319 *Ibid* pgs. 191-2
320 *Ibid* pgs. 181–187
321 *Ibid* pg. 183
322 *Ibid* pg. 195
323 *Ibid* pgs. 194-7
324 *Ibid* pg. 199
325 *Ibid* pgs. 201-5

326 *Ibid* pgs. 208-12
327 *Ibid* pg. 213
328 *Ibid* pg. 212-213
329 Ibid pg. 213-4
330 *Ibid* pgs. 213-4
331 *Ibid* pg. 223
332 *Ibid* pgs. 224-31

MEDINA 622–632 AD

333 *Ibid The Life of Muhammad* pg. 281
334 *Ibid* pg. 231
335 *Ibid* pgs. 231-3
336 *Ibid* pg. 234
337 *Ibid* pg. 236
338 *Ibid* pgs. 239-40

MUHAMMAD'S WIVES AND WOMEN

339 *The Life of Muhammad* pgs. 792 – 798
340 http://www.muslimhope.com/WhyDidMuhammadGetSoManyWives.htm
341 *The Life of Muhammad* pgs. 461-482
342 *Ibid* The Apostle's Wives pg. 792
343 *Ibid* The Apostle's Wives pg. 792
344 http://www.myIslâmweb.com/forum/archive/index.php/t-7871.html
345 http://www.ruqaiyyah.karoo.net/articles/wives.htm
346 *The Life of Muahammad* pg. 792
347 http://www.sout-al-hage.com/pal/musical/mofakhaza.ram cited by http://Islâmreview.blogspot.com/2006/01/aisha-ayesha-child-wife-of-muhammad.html
348 http://www.answering-Islâm.de/Main/Shamoun/prepubescent3.htm
349 http://www.ruqaiyyah.karoo.net/articles/wives.htm
350 *The Life of Muhammad*, pgs. xiv, xv
351 *Ibid* pgs792-3
352 http://www.ruqaiyyah.karoo.net/articles/wives.htm
353 *The Life of Muhammad* pg. 792
354 *Ibid* pg. 792
355 http://en.wikipedia.org/wiki/Zaynab_bint_Jahsh http://www.a2youth.com/Islâm/articles/wives/wives07.html http://www.ruqaiyyah.karoo.net/articles/wives.htm
356 *The Life of Muhammad* pg. 793

357 *Ibid* pg. 493
358 http://www.ruqaiyyah.karoo.net/articles/wives.htm
359 http://www.ruqaiyyah.karoo.net/articles/wives.htm
360 *The Life of Muhammad* pg. 793
361 *Ibid* pgs. 514-15
362 *Ibid* pg. 241
363 *Ibid* pgs. 793 – 794
364 *Ibid* pg. 515
365 http://en.wikipedia.org/wiki/Safiyya_bint_Huyayy
366 *The Life of Muhammad* pg. 793-4
367 *Ibid* pg. 531
368 http://en.wikipedia.org/wiki/Maymūna_bint_al-Hārith
369 *The Life of Muhammad* pg. 531
370 http://www.ruqaiyyah.karoo.net/articles/wives.htm
371 http://www.muslimhope.com/WhyDidMohammedGetSoManyWives.htm#Hend
372 http://en.wikipedia.org/wiki/Hind_bint_Utbah
373 *The Life of Muhammad* pg. 385
374 *Ibid* pg. 794
375 *Ibid* pg. 711 Note # 129
376 *Ibid* pg. 794
377 http://religionresearchinstitute.org/index_articles/ahnaf.htm
378 www.muslimhope.com/WhyDidMuhammadGetSoManyWives.htm http://www.ndtvblogs.com/views/viewcomments.asp?gl_guid=&blogname=Wiki&q_blogid=10477 http://en.wikipedia.org/wiki/Aisha; http://www.answering-Islâm.de/Main/Shamoun/sauda.htm http://www.Islâm-watch.org/AbulKasem/MdViolatedKorân .htm http://www.myIslâmweb.com/forum/archive/index.php/t-7871.html http://answering-Islâm.org.uk/Responses/Osama/umar_mary2.htm http://en.wikipedia.org/wiki/Zaynab_bint_Jahsh; http://www.ruqaiyyah.karoo.net/articles/wives.htm http://www.a2youth.com/Islâm/articles/wives/wives07.html; http://en.wikipedia.org/wiki/Maymūna_bint_al-Hārith; http://en.wikipedia.org/wiki/Safiyya_bint_Huyayy

BEGINNING OF THE 1300 YEARS' WAR

379 *The Life of Muhammad* pg. 287
380 *Op. Cit Yeoman RS Red Book Pg* 233
381 *Ibid* pg. 297
382 *Ibid* pg. 289
383 *Ibid* pg. 301

384 *The Life of Muhammad* pages 364-9
385 *Ibid* pg. 369
386 *Ibid* pg. 363
387 *Ibid* pg. 362; http://www.Islâm-watch.org/AbulKasem/RootsTerrorism/RootsTerrorism5.htm
388 *The Life of Muhammad* pg. 362-364
389 *Ibid* pg. 364
390 *Ibid* pg. 371
391 *Ibid* pg. 373
392 http://www.witness-pioneer.org/vil/Articles/companion/13_ali_bin_Tālib .htm
393 *The Life of Muhammad* pg. 375
394 *Ibid* pg. 381
395 *Ibid* pg. 401-403
396 *Ibid* pgs. 433-436
397 *Ibid* pgs. 447
398 *Ibid* pg. 460
399 *Ibid* pg. 461
400 *Ibid* pg. 464
401 *Ibid* pg. 482-84
402 http://abdulmateen.com/chronology.htm
403 *The Life of Muhammad* pgs. 493-97
404 *Ibin* pg. 386

THE END GAME

405 *Ibin* pg. 502
406 *Ibid* pgs. 505-507
407 *The Battle of Khaybar – the Victory of Ali* http://www.youtube.com/watch?v=tXScDocR_ME&NR=1
408 *The Life of Muhammad* pg. 513
409 *Ibid* pg. 514.
410 *Ibid* pg. 511
411 *Ibid* pg. 516
412 *Ibid* pg. 518
413 *Ibid* pg. 526-30
414 *Ibid* pg. 540
415 **http://en.wikipedia.org/wiki/Battle_of_Mu'tah#The_battle**
416 *The Life of Muhammad* pg. 566
417 *Ibid* pg. 567

418 *Ibid* pg. 569
419 *Ibid* pg. 597
420 *Ibid* pgs. 660-661

EVENTS LEADING TO MUHAMMAD'S DEATH 632 AD

421 *The Life of Muhammad* pg. 597
422 *Ibid* pg. 609

EVENTS LEADING TO MUHAMMAD'S DEATH 632 AD (CONTINUED)

423 *Ibid* pg. 610
424 http://abdulmateen.com/chronology.htm
425 *The Life of Muhammad* pgs. 615-6
426 *Ibid* pg. 632
427 *Ibid* pg. 635-6
428 *Ibid* pg. 637
429 *Ibid* pg. 641
430 *Ibid* pgs. 642-4
431 *Ibid* pgs. 645-8
432 *Ibid* pg. 657
433 *Ibid* pgs. 660 – 678
434 *The Life of Muhammad* page 678-9
435 *Ibid* pg. 680
436 *Ibid* pg. 689
437 *Ibid* pg. 689

DID MUHAMMAD HAVE A CHRONIC DEBILITATING DISEASE?

438 *The Life of Muhammad* pg. 82.
439 . See also *The Life of Muhammad* page 718 #177.
440 Holick, MF. Vitamin D Deficiency. *New Eng J Med*; 357:266-281. Jul 19, 2007
441 www.uvadvantage.org/portals/0/pdf/NEJournalofMedicine.pdf
442 *The Life of Muhammad* page 464
443 **Ibn Sad's "Kitab al-Tabaqat al-Kabir"**9**, volume 1, pages 438, 439. (Book of the Major Classes), translated by S. Moinul Haq, Pakistan Historical Society**. http://answering-islam.org/Silas/mo_sex.htm
444 *Ibid* pg. 511

445 **Pickthall M. *The Meaning of the Glorioius Qur'an Text and Explanatory Translation.* Jajarmi Pub. Tehran, Iran ISBN 964-6766-01-3 pg. 5.**
446 http://www.answering-islam.org/Books/Jeffery/historical_mhd.htm http://en.wikipedia.org/wiki/David_Samuel_Margoliouth Margoliouth, *Mohammed*, GP Putnam's Sons, London, England, 1905 p. 46
447 *Epilepsia*, 1976 Dec 17 (4): 423-7. And http://www.ncbi.nlm.nih.gov/sites/entrez
448 Sadeghian, Abbas. *Sword and Seizure, Muhammad's Epilepsy & Creation of Islâm,* Annotated Press, Enumclaw, Washington, 2006
449 *Sword & Seizure* pg. 53
450 *Ibid* pg. 73
451 *Ibid* pgs. 75-78
452 *Ibid* pg. 78
453 *Ibid* pgs. 79-80
454 *Ibid* pgs. 80-1
455 *Ibid* pg. 81
456 *Ibid* pg. 82
457 *Ibid* pg. 83-4
458 Brazis, Masdeu, Biller. *Localization in Clinical Neurology*. Lippincott Williams & Wilkins, 2011. pg. 223
459 http://en.wikipedia.org/wiki/Substantia_nigra
460 http://en.wikipedia.org/wiki/Nucleus_accumbens
461 *Ibid* pg. 86
462 *The Life of Muhammad* pgs. 181-187
463 *Ibid* pg. 183
464 *Ibid* pgs. 678-9
465 *Sword & Seizure* pg. 150
466 *Ibid* pg. 151
467 Merritt, H Houston. *A Textbook of Neurology*, 2nd Edition Revised, Lea & Febiger, Philadelphia, 1959
468 Merritt, *A Textbook of Neurology* pg. 217
469 *A Textbook of Neurology* pg. 234
470 *Ibid* pg. 234
471 *Ibid* pg. 235
472 *Ibid* pg. 236
473 *Ibid* pg. 216-17
474 *Ibid* pg. 682
475 http://en.wikipedia.org/wiki/Temporal_lobe_epilepsy

476 B L Miller, J L Cummings, H McIntyre, G Ebers, and M Grode. Hypersexuality or altered sexual preference following brain injury. *J Neurol Neurosurg Psychiatry*. 1986 August; 49(8): 867–873. http://www.ncbi.nlm.nih.gov/pmc/articles/PMC1028946/

477 http://en.wikipedia.org/wiki/Category:Irish_saints

478 Cahill T. *How the Irish Saved Civilization: the Untold Story of Ireland's Heroic Role from the Fall of Rome to the Rise of Medieval Europe.* Doubleday, NewYork, 1995

479 de Soto, Hernando. *The Mystery of Capital: Why Capitalism Triumphs in the West and Fails Everywhere Else.* Basic Books, New York, 2000. Pages 105-152

480 http://209.85.173.104/search?q=cache:12yeQ9CNclwJ:www.jurist.org.cn/doc/uclaw200507/uclaw20050703.pdf+Tang+code&hl=en&ct=clnk&cd=3&gl=us

481 http://en.wikipedia.org/wiki/Byzantine_emperor#Valentinian-Theodosian_dynasty_.28364-457.29

THE MEDINAN CALIPHATE 632 – 661 AD

482 http://en.wikipedia.org/wiki/Musaylimah

483 http://en.wikipedia.org/wiki/Battle_of_Yamama

484 Pratt, Fletcher. *The Battles that Changed History*, Dover Publication Inc., Mineola, NY, 2000, pgs. 74-91

485 *Ibid* pg. 86

486 http://www.newworldencyclopedia.org/entry/Battle_of_the_Camel

SUNNI'S MAINTAIN CONTROL

487 http://en.wikipedia.org/wiki/Muslim_conquest_of_Egypt

488 Menzies, Gavin. *1434: the Year a Magnificent Chinese Fleet Sailed to Italy and Ignited the Renaissance*. Harper Collins, 2008

489 Menzies *1434* pgs. 89-93

490 http://www.google.com/images?hl=en&biw=1021&bih=471&gbv=2&tbs=isch%3A1&sa=1&q=%22The+night+sky%22+San+Lorenzo+Florence&btnG=Search&aq=f&aqi=&aql=&oq=

491 Menzies, *1434* pgs. 23-28

492 **Duncan D.E, *Calendar* (New York: Avignon Books, 1998), pg. 202.**

493 *Menzies, 1434* pg. 27

494 *Claudius Ptolemy Geography*. Trans. by Stevenson, EL Dover Publications, Inc. New York,1991, pg. 22, 42-46.

495 *Menzies, 1434* pgs. 29-38

496 http://en.wikipedia.org/wiki/Umayyad_Caliphate

497 https://sites.google.com/site/historicdynasties/caliphate/umayyad/umayyad-2

498 http://www.search.com/reference/Muawiya_II

499 http://en.wikipedia.org/wiki/Marwan_I

500 https://sites.google.com/site/historicdynasties/caliphate/umayyad/umayyad-2

501 http://radioislam.orgza.info/a/index.php?option=com_content&task=view&id=16077&Itemid=47

502 http://en.wikipedia.org/wiki/Al-Walid_I

503 http://tajamfikir.blogspot.com/2005/04/umar-ibn-abd-al-aziz.html

504 http://translate.google.com/translate?hl=en&sl=es&u=http://www.esacademic.com/dic.nsf/eswiki/1235131&ei=QDJGTYOZLJCcsQP6vaXZCg&sa=X&oi=translate&ct=result&resnum=2&ved=0CCEQ7gEwAQ&prev=/search%3Fq%3DYaz%25C4%25ABd%2Bbin%2BAbd%2Bal-Malik%2Bor%2BYaz%25C4%25ABd%2BII%2B(687-724)%2Btuberculosis%26hl%3Den%26site%3Dwebhp%26prmd%3Divns

505 http://www.wordiq.com/definition/Hisham

506 Fuller, J.F.C. *A Military History of the Western World Vol. I*, Da Capo Paperback, New York, 1987, pg. 344-45

507 Pratt, F. The Battles that Changed History. Dover Publications, Inc. Mineola, NY 1956, Dover 2000 pg. 92.

508 http://en.wikipedia.org/wiki/Charlemagne#Charles_and_his_children

BREAK UP OF THE UMAYYAD DYNASTY

509 https://sites.google.com/site/historicdynasties/caliphate/umayyad/umayyad-5

510 http://en.wikipedia.org/wiki/Marwan_II

511 http://www.fsmitha.com/h3/islam12.htm

512 http://en.wikipedia.org/wiki/Abd_ar-Rahman_I

THE VIKINGS

513 Haywood, John. *The Penguin Historical Atlas of the Vikings*. Penguin Books, London, 1995, pg. 8

514 http://www.loadstone.co.uk/

515 Haywood. *The Penguin Historical Atlas of the Vikings* pg. 20.

516 *Ibid* pgs. 72-77

517 *Ibid* pg. 55, 63, 66-71

518 *Ibid* pg. 57, 61, 65

519 *Ibid* pgs. 104-9, 124-5

520 *Ibid* pgs. 86-99

THE UMAYYADS OF CORDOVA 711 TO 1492

[521] http://en.wikipedia.org/wiki/Caliphate_of_C%C3%B3rdoba

[522] Pratt, Fletcher. *The Battles that Changed History*, Dover Publication Inc., Mineola, NY, 2000, pgs. 92-110

ABBASID DYNASTY OF BAGHDAD & SAMMARA (750 – 1258 AD)

[523] http://en.wikipedia.org/wiki/Battle_of_Talas

[524] http://en.wikipedia.org/wiki/Civil_Disobedience_(Thoreau)

[525] http://www.crwflags.com/fotw/flags/ma_hist.html

THE EARLY ABBASID DYNASTY 750-1258 AD

[526] http://en.wikipedia.org/wiki/Abbasid_Caliphate

[527] http://www.answering-islam.org/Authors/Stenhouse/harun_al_rashid.htm%20-%20Cached

[528] http://en.wikipedia.org/wiki/Idrisid_dynasty

[529] http://en.wikipedia.org/wiki/Aghlabids

[530] http://en.wikipedia.org/wiki/Tulunids

[531] http://en.wikipedia.org/wiki/Abbasid_Caliphate See separate notes for each Caliph.

[532] http://en.wikipedia.org/wiki/Qarmatians

[533] http://en.wikipedia.org/wiki/Yusuf_Ibn_Abi'l-Saj

[534] http://en.wikipedia.org/wiki/Samanids

[535] http://en.wikipedia.org/wiki/Saffarid_Dynasty

[536] http://www.forumbiodiversity.com/showthread.php?t=1425&page=2

[537] http://answers.yahoo.com/question/index?qid=20101221191934AAK6F5y

TURMOIL

[538] http://en.wikipedia.org/wiki/Al-Muti

[539] http://en.wikipedia.org/wiki/At-Ta%27i

[540] http://en.wikipedia.org/wiki/Al-Qadir

541

http://en.wikipedia.org/wiki/Al-Qa%27im_(caliph)

[542] http://en.wikipedia.org/wiki/Al-Muqtadi

[543] http://en.wikipedia.org/wiki/Al-Mustazhir

[544] http://en.wikipedia.org/wiki/Al-Mustarshid

[545] http://en.wikipedia.org/wiki/Harun_al-Rashid_(1135)

Turmoil (Continued)

546 http://en.wikipedia.org/wiki/Al-Muqtafi_(Abbasid_Caliph)
547 http://en.wikipedia.org/wiki/Al-Mustanjid
548 http://en.wikipedia.org/wiki/Al-Mustadi
549 http://en.wikipedia.org/wiki/An-Nasir
550 http://en.wikipedia.org/wiki/Az-Zahir_(caliph)
551 http://en.wikipedia.org/wiki/Al-Mustansir
552 http://en.wikipedia.org/wiki/Al-Musta%27sim
553 http://en.wikipedia.org/wiki/Abbasid_Caliphate
554 http://en.wikipedia.org/wiki/Fatimid_Caliphate
555 http://en.wikipedia.org/wiki/Ayyubid_dynasty
556 http://en.wikipedia.org/wiki/Battle_of_Ain_Jalut
557 http://en.wikipedia.org/wiki/First_Battle_of_Homs
558 http://en.wikipedia.org/wiki/Second_Battle_of_Homs
559 http://en.wikipedia.org/wiki/Battle_of_Marj_al-Saffar

THE GOLDEN HORDE

560 http://en.wikipedia.org/wiki/Genghis_Khan
561 http://en.wikipedia.org/wiki/%C3%96gedei_Khan
562 http://www.fsmitha.com/h3/mongols03.htm
563 http://www.fsmitha.com/h3/mongols03.htm
564 http://en.wikipedia.org/wiki/M%C3%B6ngke_Khan
565 http://en.wikipedia.org/wiki/Kublai_Khan

THE SELJUK TURKS

566 Wells, Spencer. *The Journey of Man A Genetic Odyssey*, Princeton University Press. Princeton & Oxford, 2002, pg. 182
567 **en.wkipedia.org/wiki/Axial_tilt**
568 www.livescience.com/4180-sahara-desert-lush-populated.html
569 http://www.allaboutturkey.com/states.htm
570 http://turkmeniya.tripod.com/id8.html
571 http://en.wikipedia.org/wiki/Seljuq_dynasty
572 http://en.wikipedia.org/wiki/Battle_of_Manzikert
573 http://en.wikipedia.org/wiki/Sultanate_of_R%C3%BBm
574 http://en.wikipedia.org/wiki/Osman_I
575 http://en.wikipedia.org/wiki/Battle_of_Kosovo

THE EARLY OTTOMAN EMPIRE

576 http://en.wikipedia.org/wiki/Ottoman_Empire
577 http://en.wikipedia.org/wiki/Suleiman_the_Magnificent

578 http://en.wikipedia.org/wiki/Ottoman_family_tree_(simplified) [An excellent general reference]
579 http://www.pbs.org/wgbh/pages/frontline/shows/binladen/who/edicts.html
580 http://en.wikipedia.org/wiki/Louis_I_of_Hungary http://en.wikipedia.org/wiki/Ottoman%E2%80%93Hungarian_Wars#Mehmed_II_.281451_-1481.29_and_fall_of_Constantinople
581 http://en.wikipedia.org/wiki/Osman_I
582 http://en.wikipedia.org/wiki/Janissary
583 http://en.wikipedia.org/wiki/Fall_of_Gallipoli
584 http://en.wikipedia.org/wiki/Battle_of_Ihtiman
585 http://en.wikipedia.org/wiki/Murad_I
586 http://en.wikipedia.org/wiki/Battle_of_Maritsa
587 http://atheism.about.com/library/FAQs/christian/blchron_xian_crusades12.htm
588 http://en.wikipedia.org/wiki/Battle_of_Savra
589 http://en.wikipedia.org/wiki/Battle_of_Plo%C4%8Dnik
590 http://en.wikipedia.org/wiki/Battle_of_Bile%C4%87a
591 http://en.wikipedia.org/wiki/Battle_of_Kosovo
592 http://en.wikipedia.org/wiki/Bayezid
593 http://en.wikipedia.org/wiki/Battle_of_Rovine http://en.wikipedia.org/wiki/Battle_of_Karanovasa
594 http://en.wikipedia.org/wiki/Battle_of_Nicopolis
595 http://en.wikipedia.org/wiki/Battle_of_Ankara
596 http://en.wikipedia.org/wiki/Timur
597 http://ottomanmilitary.devhub.com/blog/623555-the-first-challenge-bayezid-is-siege-of-constantinople-13941402-i/ http://en.wikipedia.org/wiki/Battle_of_Ankara
598 http://en.wikipedia.org/wiki/Ottoman_Interregnum
599 http://en.wikipedia.org/wiki/Mehmed_I
600 http://en.wikipedia.org/wiki/Battle_of_Ceuta
601 http://en.wikipedia.org/wiki/Murad_II
602 http://en.wikipedia.org/wiki/Siege_of_Thessalonica_(1422%E2%80%931430)
603 http://en.wikipedia.org/wiki/Murad_II
604 http://en.wikipedia.org/wiki/Tsardom_of_Vidin
605 http://en.wikipedia.org/wiki/Murad_II
606 http://en.wikipedia.org/wiki/Serbian_Despotate
607 http://en.wikipedia.org/wiki/Vlad_III_the_Impaler

608 http://en.wikipedia.org/wiki/Fall_of_Gallipoli http://webcache.googleusercontent.com/search?q=cache:4kA6qWC_1akJ:en.wikipedia.org/wiki/Order_of_the_Dragon+the+order+of+the+dragon&cd=1&hl=en&ct=clnk&gl=us&source=www.google.com

609 http://www.newworldencyclopedia.org/entry/John_Hunyadi

610 http://en.wikipedia.org/wiki/Long_campaign

611 http://en.wikipedia.org/wiki/Ottoman%E2%80%93Hungarian_Wars#Mehmed_II_.281451_-_1481.29_and_fall_of_Constantinople

612 http://www.medievaltimes.info/medieval-battles/battle-of-varna.html

613 http://en.wikipedia.org/wiki/Battle_of_Kosovo_(1448)

614 http://en.wikipedia.org/wiki/Fall_of_Constantinople

615 http://en.wikipedia.org/wiki/Mehmed_II

616 http://en.wikipedia.org/wiki/Ottoman%E2%80%93Venetian_War_(1463%E2%80%931479)

617 http://en.wikipedia.org/wiki/Battle_of_Krbava_field

618 http://en.wikipedia.org/wiki/Capture_of_Algiers_(1529)

619 http://en.wikipedia.org/wiki/Fall_of_Constantinople

620 http://www.greekhotel.com/sterea/attica/athens/history/ottoman-domination.htm

621 http://en.wikipedia.org/wiki/Ottoman%E2%80%93Hungarian_Wars

622 http://en.wikipedia.org/wiki/Black_Army_of_Hungary http://en.wikipedia.org/wiki/Battle_of_Breadfield

623 http://en.wikipedia.org/wiki/Vlad_III_the_Impaler

624 http://en.wikipedia.org/wiki/Ottoman%E2%80%93Venetian_War_(1463%E2%80%931479)

625 http://www.bosniafacts.info/web/Bosnia_and_Ottomans.php http://en.wikipedia.org/wiki/Jajce http://en.wikipedia.org/wiki/History_of_Bosnia_and_Herzegovina#Ottoman_Era_.281463.E2.80.931878.29 http://en.wikipedia.org/wiki/Demographic_history_of_Bosnia_and_Herzegovina

626 http://en.wikipedia.org/wiki/Ottoman_invasion_of_Otranto

627 http://en.wikipedia.org/wiki/Ottoman%E2%80%93Hungarian_Wars

628 http://en.wikipedia.org/wiki/Bayezid_II

629 http://en.wikipedia.org/wiki/Ottoman_Greece

630 http://en.wikipedia.org/wiki/Montenegro#Ottoman_rule_and_Metropolitanate

631 http://en.wikipedia.org/wiki/Hundred_Years'_Croatian%E2%80%93Ottoman_War

632 http://en.wikipedia.org/wiki/Capture_of_Algiers_(1529)

THE OTTOMANEMPIRE'S YEARS OF EXPANSION

633 http://en.wikipedia.org/wiki/Battle_of_Chaldiran
634 http://en.wikipedia.org/wiki/Selim_I
635 http://en.wikipedia.org/wiki/Battle_of_Ridaniya
636 http://en.wikipedia.org/wiki/Peace_of_Zsitvatorok
637 http://en.wikipedia.org/wiki/Granada
638 http://en.wikipedia.org/wiki/Suleiman_the_Magnificent
639 http://en.wikipedia.org/wiki/Siege_of_Rhodes_(1522)
640 http://en.wikipedia.org/wiki/Timeline_of_the_Ottoman_Empire
641 http://en.wikipedia.org/wiki/Black_Army_of_Hungary
642 http://en.wikipedia.org/wiki/Francis_I_of_France
643 http://en.wikipedia.org/wiki/Battle_of_Moh%C3%A1cs#Decline_of_Hungary_.281490-1526.29
644 http://en.wikipedia.org/wiki/Hungarian_campaign_of_1527%E2%80%931528
645 http://en.wikipedia.org/wiki/Capture_of_Algiers_(1529) http://en.wikipedia.org/wiki/Ferdinand_I,_Holy_Roman_Emperor
646 http://en.wikipedia.org/wiki/Persian_Gulf

GUN POWDER: THE BEGINNINGS OF MODERN WARFARE

647 http://en.wikipedia.org/wiki/Hungarian_campaign_of_1527%E2%80%931528
648 http://en.wikipedia.org/wiki/Capture_of_Algiers_(1529) http://en.wikipedia.org/wiki/Ferdinand_I,_Holy_Roman_Emperor
649 http://en.wikipedia.org/wiki/Persian_Gulf
650 **Pratt, F. *The Battles that Changed History, "7 Vienna and the Failure to Complete the Crescent."* Doubleday & Co. Inc. 1956. Pgs 131-150**
651 Pratt, Fletcher. *The Battles that Changed History*, Dover Publication Inc., Mineola, NY, 2000, pgs. 131 – 150
652 http://en.wikipedia.org/wiki/Battle_of_Moh%C3%A1cs
653 http://en.wikipedia.org/wiki/Siege_of_Vienna
654 http://en.wikipedia.org/wiki/Ottoman%E2%80%93Safavid_War_(1532%E2%80%931555)
655 http://en.wikipedia.org/wiki/Hayreddin_Barbarossa
656 http://en.wikipedia.org/wiki/Battle_of_Preveza_(1538)
657 http://en.wikipedia.org/wiki/Siege_of_Buda_(1541)
658 http://en.wikipedia.org/wiki/Algiers_expedition_(1541)

659 http://en.wikipedia.org/wiki/Macau#History http://en.wikipedia.org/wiki/Capture_of_Aden_(1548)
660 http://en.wikipedia.org/wiki/Battle_of_Djerba
661 http://en.wikipedia.org/wiki/Siege_of_Szigetv%C3%A1r
662 http://en.wikipedia.org/wiki/Siege_of_Malta_(1565)
663 http://en.wikipedia.org/wiki/Famagusta
664 http://en.wikipedia.org/wiki/Selim_II
665 http://www.worldlingo.com/ma/enwiki/en/Roxelana
666 http://en.wikipedia.org/wiki/Selim_II
667 Menzies, G. *1434*, Harper Collins, New York, 2008, Pgs. 41, 45-6.
668 http://en.wikipedia.org/wiki/Murad_III
669 Ibid
670 http://ottomanempire.info/decline.htm
671 http://en.wikipedia.org/wiki/Ottoman%E2%80%93Safavid_War_(1578%E2%80%931590)
672 http://en.wikipedia.org/wiki/Mehmed_III
673 http://en.wikipedia.org/wiki/Long_War_(Ottoman_wars)
674 http://en.wikipedia.org/wiki/Battle_of_C%C4%83lug%C4%83reni

VALIDE SULTANATE – ON A SLIPPERY SLOPE

675 http://en.wikipedia.org/wiki/Battle_of_Keresztes
676 http://en.wikipedia.org/wiki/Ahmed_I
677 http://en.wikipedia.org/wiki/Ottoman%E2%80%93Safavid_War_(1603%E2%80%931618)
http://en.wikipedia.org/wiki/Abbas_I_of_Persia
678 http://en.wikipedia.org/wiki/Ahmed_I
679 http://en.wikipedia.org/wiki/Osman_II
680 http://en.wikipedia.org/wiki/Valide_Sultan
681 http://www.allaboutturkey.com/harem.htm
Valide sultanate – on a slippery slope (Continued)
682 http://education.yahoo.com/reference/encyclopedia/entry/Mustafa1
683 http://www.xs4all.nl/~monarchs/madmonarchs/murad4/murad4_bio.htm
684 http://en.wikipedia.org/wiki/Tenedos
685 http://en.wikipedia.org/wiki/Ibrahim_I

THE 30-YEARS' WAR

IT NEVER RAINS

Murder and kidnap in the heart of England

TONY BASSETT

THE BOOK FOLKS

Published by The Book Folks

London, 2024

This book is a work of fiction. Names, characters, businesses, organizations, places and events are either the product of the author's imagination or are used fictitiously. Any resemblance to actual persons, living or dead, events or locales is entirely coincidental.

ISBN 978-1-80462-246-9

www.thebookfolks.com

IT NEVER RAINS is the sixth standalone mystery in the Detectives Roy and Roscoe crime fiction series by Tony Bassett.

The full list of books is as follows:

MURDER ON OXFORD LANE
THE CROSSBOW STALKER
MURDER OF A DOCTOR
OUT FOR REVENGE
HEIR TO MURDER
IT NEVER RAINS

Details about these books can be found at the back of this one.

Chapter 1

Marilyn Willis was fretting about the meal planned for that evening. While she scurried round the manor house kitchen, collecting plates from the dishwasher and placing them in the wall cupboard, she was aware she still needed to make a good impression upon her new employer, the Frenchman Jean-Jacques Beauvais, and his family. Now in her early forties, the gardener's wife had only been in charge of the catering for three weeks.

'The French are so particular about their food,' she muttered to herself.

When interviewed for the post two months earlier, she'd explained her skills stretched to international cuisine. But her boss had already taken her to task over one of the meals she cooked. Marilyn didn't want another argument.

Tonight, she would be serving a mixed vegetable starter, French onion soup, salad and cheese, chicken casserole, yoghurt and fruit.

She glanced at her watch. It had turned four o'clock. Time to make a start.

But as she began preparing vegetables on the chopping board, the housekeeper happened to glance through the window. Her eyes widened in horror on catching sight of three men in masks standing on the patio.

They had propped a ladder up against the side of the building and were brazenly peering at her through the glass.

She knew at once they were intent on breaking in – and she was alone in the eight-bedroom house.

How she wished her husband, David, was with her. He would have set the dog on them, but he had taken their pet for a walk and would no doubt be gone for at least another hour. She was alone.

In a panic, she rushed into the vaulted hallway and hurried into the staff quarters.

'Where's my mobile?' she wailed as she cast her eyes around. She eventually found it on the sofa, beside a newspaper.

But the moment she grabbed it, she heard footsteps on the wooden floor and felt a presence behind her. In an instant, a rough hand gripped her round the face and she felt a sharp object prodding her back.

'No, you don't!' a male voice insisted.

Her heart was pounding and her breath came in short bursts. She was shaking.

'Please don't hurt me,' she begged as the stranger snatched the phone from her hand and hurled her onto the sofa.

Who was this brute of a man who'd burst into their private space and attacked her so forcibly? she wondered. Was he going to hurt her? And how did he get in?

She knew he could not have entered through her kitchen door. She'd locked it after her husband left with the dog.

She tried to sit up but the stranger warned her, 'Don't move a muscle or I'll kill you.'

Despite the overwhelming sense of fear coursing through her, Marilyn forced herself to glance round. She found a man in light-blue jeans and a white balaclava standing over her. He was holding a Beretta pistol in his right hand.

She could not take her eyes off the gun. Was this how her life would end?

After sliding her handset into the pocket of his jeans, the stranger plucked his own phone from his jacket and dialled a number, which was promptly answered.

'All right, mate?' he asked. 'I've found the woman. What do you want me to do with her? Shall I kill her?'

Marilyn cowered on the sofa as she heard the reply. 'Don't kill her. Not for the moment. Just tie her and gag her. Any issues with the electrics?'

'No, it's all taken care of. I slashed the cables to four cameras and cut the landline, so that screwed the alarm. I've also blocked the motion sensors for the main house.'

The frightened housekeeper saw there was no point in struggling. She allowed herself to be tied to a chair and tape was wound round her mouth. The man was rather rough with her. The rope made her wrists sore and the gag round her mouth made it hard to breathe.

While he was doing this, she could hear voices from upstairs talking about Nikon and Canon cameras and fifty-pound notes.

'Looks like we've uncovered Aladdin's bleeding cave,' she heard one of the gang shout before the man finished tying her and left.

Ten minutes later, she heard a car engine and wondered if the men were loading a vehicle with the family's belongings.

'One last trawl, boys, before we go,' one of the gang yelled.

Then Marilyn was relieved to hear the hum of a car engine coming up the drive. She convinced herself it was the sound of a car she recognised – a silver Bentley Continental owned by the family.

She heard a man with a Birmingham accent yelling, 'We've got company, lads.'

'Oh, thank God,' she said to herself. 'Danny must be back. I just hope he realises one of them has got a gun.'

Chapter 2

Perched uneasily on his stepladder, Detective Chief Inspector Gavin Roscoe was attempting to drill holes into the wall above a bedroom window. As a tall, stout man, this required concentration. Then the doorbell rang.

He swore beneath his breath. He always hated being interrupted when tackling a demanding task, and putting up a new curtain rail in the spare bedroom was challenging his limited DIY skills. He reluctantly climbed down, put his electric drill on the floor and peered out of the window.

His son George was standing on the front lawn, waving up at him.

Roscoe hurried down the stairs, wiping his hands on his paint-stained overalls, and threw open the door.

'George! This is an unexpected surprise,' said Roscoe. 'Come on in. How's married life?'

'Pretty good, Dad. Pretty good,' said George with a broad smile. 'I see you've been working. I'm not interrupting an important job, am I?'

'No, only fixing a curtain rail. It can wait. Your mother has a plan to revamp your old room,' Roscoe replied. 'She's been on at me since you moved out that we ought to turn it into a proper guest room.'

He led his twenty-six-year-old son into the living room.

'Can I get you some tea or coffee?' he asked George.

'Tea would be great, Dad. Thanks.'

While the kettle was boiling in the kitchen, George explained he had left his new wife, Amanda, shopping in the nearby town of Queensbridge. Then he had called in at the family's business, where his mother and sister worked.

'I saw Mum and Mel at the tearooms, but they were rushed off their feet,' he said.

'They'll both be back in a minute. They'll be so pleased to see you,' said Roscoe.

'How's life at headquarters, Dad?'

'I've had a really tiring week. Two of our team are on holiday and we've had two suspicious deaths. We arrested a guy supplying drugs and had a harassment case to deal with.'

After his father had fetched two china mugs of steaming tea, George told his father about the new flat in Warwick that he and Amanda had moved into.

'It's great to have our own place, Dad,' said George as he sipped his tea. His legs were jiggling as if he was nervous. 'We've got great neighbours. I had a problem with a curtain rail myself but the guy from next door is a carpenter and he came round and screwed it in for me.'

'Can you send him round to me?' Roscoe asked as he strode across the room and glanced through the patio doors into the garden. 'And how are you getting on with your grumpy old sergeant?'

'Oh, he's not so bad, Dad. He's giving me some time off next week because I've put in a lot of extra hours.'

A faint smile crept across his face.

'Listen, Dad, I've got some news. I was going to wait until Mum and Mel got here, but I just can't hold on any longer. Amanda's pregnant.'

'That's wonderful news, George!' said Roscoe. He placed his mug down on a side table and stepped over to the brown leather settee, where his son was sitting. George stood up and the pair hugged.

'When's the happy event?' asked Roscoe.

'The baby's due in April, Dad. Amanda will be here in a minute and she can tell you all about it.'

'There won't be much more for her to say at this stage,' said his father with a grin, 'although I expect your mother will find plenty of questions. I don't suppose you know…'

'The sex of the baby? No, not yet,' said George, resuming his seat.

'This is a good time for me to open my new bottle of whisky,' said Roscoe, making his way to a cocktail cabinet in the corner.

'I'll have a small one with you, Dad,' said George as his father selected two glasses. 'That's not my only news. I'm joining Stratford CID as a trainee detective.'

'I suppose it had to happen one day,' said Roscoe. 'You used to talk about being a detective as a child. Neat or on the rocks?'

'Just a little tap water with mine. Thanks, Dad. Yes, the way I'm thinking, maybe I could have a year there and then join your team.'

'We'll have to see about that, George,' his father replied. 'I mean, two Roscoes in the same CID department? Would that work?'

Roscoe stepped into the kitchen and added chilled water to both drinks before returning and handing one glass to his son.

'By the way, is DS Roy leaving?' asked George.

His father nearly spilled his drink on hearing the question.

'What do you mean?' he asked.

'Well, it's just that, as you know, we don't live far from her flat. The other day we noticed a "For Sale" sign outside.'

'I haven't heard anything,' his father admitted as he sat down at the dining table. 'I'd be devastated to lose her from CID.'

'I know you think a lot of her. That's why I was surprised to see the sale board. But then I remembered that West Midlands Police have been advertising for detectives and I wondered if she'd been tempted to apply.'

'I sincerely hope not,' said Roscoe. 'You've got me concerned now.'

'Well, maybe she's just climbing up the property ladder or moving closer to work,' George suggested.

'That's possible. I'm just surprised she hasn't mentioned anything to me. I see her in the office nearly every day.'

'You told me before that your sergeant can be a very private person.'

Roscoe nodded. 'She's that all right, and she can be very stubborn and headstrong. But I'd have thought she'd have mentioned it if she was moving home.'

He got up and clinked his glass with George's.

'Here's to the new baby,' said Roscoe.

'Yes, cheers,' said George as he smiled and sipped his drink.

'You haven't annoyed your sergeant, have you, Dad?' he asked.

'Not that I can think of.'

'Mum told me a few months ago you were against her taking a trip abroad, but the chief super overruled you and the trip helped solve one of your cases.'

'I was only concerned about the budget,' his father explained. 'We have to watch our expenditure, you know, but you're right with the facts. I was against the idea of her leaving the country. But she made the trip and went on to crack the case. I hope she didn't hold that against me.'

Roscoe sat back on his chair. The more he thought about it, the more he convinced himself there was some simple explanation as to why his sergeant had not mentioned she was selling her flat. It was pointless worrying about the matter. But, on the other hand, if she was leaving, her departure would prove a huge loss to CID.

'Ah, that sounds like your mother now,' he told George.

Roscoe gazed through the front window as a blue Fiesta came roaring down the lane outside and advanced

onto the drive. As he stepped into the hall, his mobile phone rang.

'Roscoe,' he announced to the caller while opening the door to his wife.

He found himself speaking to the duty inspector at his force control room.

'We're getting early reports of a break-in at a country house in Norton Prior,' said the caller.

Chapter 3

The driver of the brand-new Bentley knew as soon as he arrived at the country house that all was not well. The electric gates were wide open. So, as he travelled up the drive towards the back of the main building, bodyguard Danny Jukes was mentally preparing himself.

After passing the swimming pool complex and the garage block, he turned left and saw a tall, muscular man in a mask beside a car. Realising a crime was under way, he stopped the Bentley at the corner of the house and made a phone call.

'Ken, I'll make this quick,' he said as his boss answered. 'Just got back to Upper Norton Manor. There's a guy in a balaclava robbing the place, loading gear into a Range Rover.'

Jukes, who was six feet four inches tall, shaven-headed and wearing a blue suit, peered over the top of his dark glasses and recited the vehicle's registration before adding, 'Can you call the cops and alert the family? I'm going in.'

He hung up and slipped the phone into his pocket. His employer's teenage son was in the back seat, so Jukes ordered him to lie on the floor, then flung a blanket over him.

'Stay there and don't move,' he said.

After hurling his glasses onto the passenger seat, he leaped from the silver car.

The masked man came towards him, brandishing a knife, but Jukes grabbed the burglar's arm with his left hand and chopped his wrist with his right. He tried to grab the knife.

'You bastard!' cried the robber as Jukes managed to wrench the knife from his grasp, letting it fall to the block paving.

Jukes thrust him back against the side of the Range Rover and tried to grab him round the throat. But the robber managed to duck away and the pair then grappled together beside the car.

Jukes's opponent seized him by the throat, but, in return, Jukes grasped the robber's wrist with his left hand, jerking himself free of his grip, and struck him on the jaw with his right fist. He kneed him hard in the groin and punched him again in the face and stomach. The muscular man tumbled onto the paving badly winded, which allowed Jukes a chance to regain his breath.

While gasping for air, Jukes noticed his opponent stretching out his hand for the fallen blade. He stamped hard on the man's outreached hand, causing him to cry out. Then he used his foot to crush his neck against the ground.

'Wayne!' screamed the robber, a blond, muscular man in his thirties called Kyle O'Shane. 'Where the hell are you? This is the guy we were told about.'

Jukes was puzzled by the robber's words and glanced around. A first-floor window opened above the front door and a man in a white balaclava leaned out. A gun appeared and two shots were fired.

Jukes cried out in agony before toppling onto the ground like a skittle struck by a bowling ball.

* * *

From the back of the Bentley, Marcel Dubois had listened in terror to the sound of shouting and the gunshots. Even with minimal English, the teenager knew enough to be terrified.

A few minutes passed. Then Marcel heard the car door open and a man leaped behind the steering wheel. As he peered out from beneath the blanket, the man removed his mask. This was a young man with spiky short hair and a beard.

Marcel heard his new driver engage reverse gear with a clunk. The car sprang backwards and stalled. The driver tried again. This time he was more successful and the car lurched slowly forward.

Marcel pulled the door handle and jumped out of the car while it was moving. He sprinted off towards the tennis courts at the far side of the house.

Within seconds, he realised the bearded man had stopped the Bentley and was pursuing him, along with a second, taller man who was masked.

'Come on,' he told himself. 'You can get away from these older men.'

But he hadn't noticed the pebbles and tripped over, grazing his leg.

'*Laissez-moi partir. Je n'ai rien fait*,' the boy screamed at the men as they caught up with him.

Then the bearded man spoke. 'Who the hell is this?' he demanded.

'Search me,' said the other man. 'But we'll have to take him with us.'

The pair grabbed the boy's arms and hauled him to his feet before marching him back to the Bentley.

The sandy-haired lad, with two gold medallions round his neck and a small ring in his nose, wriggled in vain.

'He'll have to stay with us while we decide what to do,' said O'Shane.

'So we might have to kill him?' asked the bearded man, Lewis Tigworth who was nicknamed Tiggs.

‘Maybe,’ came the reply. ‘But it ain’t down to us.’

The two men searched the teenager’s pockets and discovered a mobile phone in a black case, which they threw into some bushes.

‘He sounds French,’ said Tigworth.

‘Don’t worry about that now,’ said his companion. ‘We’ll tie his hands and stick the hood on him. Then we’ve really got to get the hell out of here.’

Marcel was thrust into the back of the Bentley. A grimy brown hood was forced over his head and tied round his neck. Then they set off down the drive.

Within fifteen minutes, the gang reached a place on the town’s outskirts, where the car came to a halt.

One of the men forced the teenager out of the car and led him inside, his head still covered.

‘Take him straight upstairs,’ said a voice. ‘We’ll lock him in the back bedroom while we decide what to do. Make sure the window’s locked.’

Marcel was frogmarched upstairs and the hood was removed.

He found himself in a small room containing only a single bed, a single wardrobe and a bedside table. There was a small multicoloured rug on the floor beside the bed. Faded green wallpaper was peeling from the walls and there were damp stains on the ceiling, suggesting rainwater was seeping in.

The man who had caught him, whom he had decided to call ‘*L’Homme Barbu*’ – the bearded man – pushed him onto the bed.

‘You’re the footballer’s stepson, aren’t you?’ he asked Marcel.

‘*Quoi?*’ replied the boy.

‘It’s all right. We know about you. We’ve been talking to our boss and we’ve decided to keep you here for a while. It won’t be too bad, mate. We’ll get you food and everything, and the bed’s all right.’

‘*Laissez-moi partir!*’ Marcel shouted.

Marcel leaped up and tried to force his way out through the door but the man barred his way and thrust him back onto the bed.

The boy stared at his abductor, wide-eyed and terrified.

'*Vous ne pouvez pas me traiter comme ça*,' he said while hearing footsteps outside.

A ginger-haired man peered round the door.

'What's he saying?' asked the newcomer, their electronics expert Wayne Jordan.

'I think he's saying we can't treat him like this,' said Tigworth, 'but the fact is we can't let him go for the moment.'

'That's right,' said his associate. 'He's far too valuable.'

Chapter 4

They seemed to Detective Sergeant Sunita Roy to be an oddly matched couple. He was an educated man in his late thirties who peered over his glasses like a university professor. She was much younger with dyed green hair and an impish smile.

'The kitchen is far too small for us,' the man concluded. 'How on earth do you manage? And we'd have to rip those cupboards out and start again.'

'I like the main room,' said the woman, 'although I'd have to make drastic changes to the colour scheme.'

Sunita, who was slim, with silky, black hair and dark eyes, stood in the centre of her living room, gritting her teeth and attempting to smile. After five happy years at her one-bed flat in Crompton Gardens, Warwick, she had decided to sell. It was the first property she had ever owned and, although compact, she held it in great affection.

'Thank you for showing us round, Miss Roy,' said the man, apparently unaware of how much their visit had irritated the sergeant.

Sunita returned upstairs after seeing the couple out. Her friend, Rupa Chakrabarty, whom she'd known since university, had been watching the entire homebuyers' visit in quiet amusement while sitting on the beige settee and sensed her friend was annoyed.

'What a cheek some people have got,' said Sunita. 'They had the gall to ask about a large price reduction before they drove off.'

'I don't know how you put up with it,' said her friend. 'Wouldn't it be better to let the agent show people round? Isn't that what you pay them for?'

'They were too busy today and I didn't want to lose the chance of a sale,' replied Sunita.

'I'm sure there must be a breed of people who just spend their spare time snooping around other people's homes, collecting design ideas without any intention of buying.'

Rupa smiled. 'Never mind. I'm sure you'll sell the flat soon and move to pastures new. You're very lucky, Sunita. I'm still renting with no chance of owning my own place for a while. Anyway, I'll have to think about going soon.'

Sunita took a seat beside her.

'It's been so good to catch up,' said Sunita. 'Do you really have to go?'

'Yes. I've got marking and ironing to do tomorrow,' replied Rupa, a teacher at a Stoke-on-Trent school. 'But I've really enjoyed it. I loved the market and seeing Anne Hathaway's Cottage was the highlight of the day.'

The pair had spent three hours that morning exploring the charming, thatched farmhouse and gardens near Stratford-upon-Avon where William Shakespeare's wife lived as a child and where the Bard had wooed her.

When Sunita's phone rang, it took her by surprise. She glanced at the screen.

'It's my boss,' she told Rupa before answering.

'Everything all right, sir?' she asked breezily.

'So sorry to trouble you on a Saturday afternoon,' said the chief inspector. 'Do you know Upper Norton Manor?'

She thought for a moment. 'Wasn't that where the businessman Dominic Carlton used to live, on the outskirts of Norton Prior?'

'That's right. Carlton died three years ago. It's currently being rented by the Aston Villa footballer Jean-Jacques Beauvais and his family. Well, during today's game, Beauvais's bodyguard and stepson turned up to find a gang of burglars had broken in. Now both are missing. How soon do you think you can get over there?'

'Well, I'm with a friend right now, sir. But I can leave in a few minutes and should be there at around five thirty.'

'Good,' he replied. 'I'll see you there.'

After ending the call, Sunita turned to her friend and sighed.

'I'm sorry, Rupa. Crime never takes a day off.'

Rupa stood up. 'Oh, don't worry. I'm used to you by now after all those years we shared that flat in Hall Green. I'll get my coat.'

'I can drop you at the station,' said Sunita, rushing into her bedroom to change her clothes. 'But after that I've got to head off.'

* * *

It had turned half past five by the time Sunita approached Norton Prior and it took her a few more minutes to reach Ploughman's Lane, where the three-million-pound Upper Norton Manor was located.

After travelling for some distance along the lane, she had to pull over to allow an ambulance to pass.

Although it was now becoming dark, she quickly found the entrance to the mansion without difficulty. A constable in uniform had been posted to stand by the open, wrought-iron gates.

'DS Roy,' she announced as a police helicopter with a searchlight could be seen soaring across the sky in the fading light.

'Just head straight up the drive. You'll find your colleagues round the back,' he told her.

She followed the illuminated driveway past ornamental shrubs until she reached the paved area behind the house, which had been taped off.

In the brightly lit garage area to her right, she noticed the chief inspector's navy-blue BMW and a white Kia Sportage belonging to senior forensic scientist Dr Alice Ling.

As she parked her white Peugeot 208 next to the BMW and climbed out, an amiable uniformed constable approached.

'All right, Sarge?' asked PC Derek Underhill. 'You've missed a bit of excitement.'

'How do you mean?'

'They've just taken the housekeeper away in an ambulance.'

'I saw an ambulance travelling down the lane.'

'That was her,' he said. 'They're taking her to Queensbridge General.'

'What happened?'

'The poor woman was in the house on her own when she spotted three men in ski masks. One of them threatened her with a gun and tied her up.'

Sunita was concerned. 'Is she all right?'

'I think so. They just roughed her up a bit.'

Sunita shook her head. 'Must have been a hell of an ordeal for her.'

'Yes, poor soul,' said Underhill. "They've taken her away for a check-up. Her husband's here, but he didn't see anything. He was out at the time, walking the dog.'

Sunita found the chief inspector talking to Dr Ling beside the main doorway to the house. A police photographer was taking pictures of a pool of blood on

the block-paved forecourt. Three forensic staff in white coats were examining the entrance area. A fourth was inspecting possible tyre marks left among leaves, still damp following that morning's light rain. Rubber anti-contamination plates had been placed at certain points along the ground so that detectives and forensic staff could walk around without the risk of damaging potential evidence. The scene was bathed in the white glow of arc lights.

Sunita stepped across carefully to join her boss.

'Ah, Sergeant,' said Roscoe sternly, 'I'm glad you're here. I don't know how much you know, but around four o'clock a gang of burglars appear to have disabled the alarm, cut the landline and disconnected the CCTV. Then they got in through the first-floor bathroom window on the other side of the house using a ladder and stole valuables and designer goods.'

'Do we have any idea how many were in the gang?' asked Sunita.

'Not at the moment,' he said. 'The housekeeper, Mrs Willis, believes there were three, but there may have been more.'

'What happened to Mrs Willis, sir?'

'She was tied up and threatened with a gun.'

'You've managed to speak to her, sir?'

'Yes, I just grabbed a few words. She's still in a state, of course. Underhill and another constable from Queensbridge were the first here and called an ambulance. She's not badly hurt – just bruised wrists. It's more the shock than anything else. Anyway, about ten minutes later, she heard a bit of conversation, a car engine and soon after that, two gunshots. Bear in mind she was strapped to a chair with her hands and feet tied and her mouth gagged.'

Sunita frowned. 'Terrible, sir.'

'After that, she heard what sounded like two cars driving away. Roughly twenty minutes later, our officers

from Queensbridge arrived and untied her. The husband came back half an hour later.'

'Where's the husband now?' she asked.

'In their staff quarters just behind us. Police were alerted by a firm called Top Rank Protection in Wiltshire. One of their operatives, a guy called Danny Jukes, has been hired by the family as a bodyguard. He called the company's boss, Ken Woodman, at around ten minutes past four. He'd been given charge of the footballer's sixteen-year-old stepson, Marcel, for the afternoon. Jukes told his boss they'd arrived at the house to find a guy with a balaclava loading gear into a Range Rover.'

'Have we got the registration?' Sunita asked.

'Yes, but you know what these people are like,' said Roscoe. 'Chances are they were false plates and may have been replaced by now in any case. Anyway, Danny Jukes's last words to Ken were, "Can you call the cops and alert the family? I'm going in." And since then, he and the boy have vanished off the face of the earth.'

Sunita shook her head and stared across at the bloodstains on the ground and at the hedge beyond.

'We know two shots were fired by someone,' her boss continued. 'As you can see, there are traces of blood on the forecourt here, but we don't know what the outcome of that was – although someone was obviously harmed.'

Sunita cast her eyes towards the hedge and trees on the far side of the forecourt.

'What about the family, sir?' she asked.

'Jean-Jacques and his wife Camille are on their way back from watching the team play in Newcastle and should be here in a few hours,' he said. 'We obviously need to speak to them. In the meantime, I suggest you have a chat with the gardener, David Willis, and see if he can add anything to what we know.'

He handed her a scrap of paper with a phone number scribbled on it.

'Maybe you could also have a word with Woodman. Here's his number. Whatever you do, don't go into the house right now. The forensic team are up to their eyes.'

'Sir, do we have any idea at all what might have happened to Danny Jukes and Marcel?' she said.

The chief inspector shook his head. 'No. But it's not beyond the realms of possibility that they've both fallen victim to foul play.'

Chapter 5

The man she wished to see was pacing around his living room, continually glancing at his watch when Sunita approached the open door of the staff quarters. His dog, who was sitting on a mat in front of a blazing gas fire, leaped up and began to bark.

'It's all right, Rocky. Be quiet,' David Willis said before turning to the sergeant. 'Don't worry. He won't hurt you.'

'I'm Detective Sergeant Roy,' Sunita said, eyeing the dog warily. 'I promise I won't take up much of your time.'

'I've already given PC Underhill my statement,' said David, who appeared to be in his forties. 'Have I got to go through it all again?'

'Just a few more questions, sir,' she assured him.

'Good, because I need to get over to the hospital and see how my wife is getting on,' he replied.

She took a seat on the sofa in the small, dark room. A spiral staircase in the corner led, she assumed, to the Willises' bedroom. A door facing her gave access to the couple's small kitchen.

'I was shocked to hear what happened to your wife, Marilyn,' Sunita began. 'It's dreadful to be confronted by a stranger in your own home and then tied up.'

'Those men were brutes, Sergeant, who wanted money and valuables and weren't prepared to let anything stand in their way. I've never seen my wife so traumatised in twenty years of marriage.'

He sat down on an armchair before leaning forward and stroking his pet.

'Mr Willis, I've been told you'd gone for a walk with the dog while all this happened. Is that right?'

'Yes. I left the house with Rocky here at about twenty to four. I always try and take him on a two-mile walk over to the village and back.'

'And what time did you return?' she asked, as she took out her notebook and pen.

'Must have been about twenty past five. I got the shock of my life. There were loads of police here. I had to explain I lived here and they let me through the cordon to see Marilyn. I was only able to speak to her briefly before the ambulance crew whisked her away.'

'And did she manage to tell you much, sir?'

'She just said she was shocked to find a man in a ski mask in here. He threatened her with a gun. Then he struck her and was very rough with her.'

'I don't suppose she was able to give much of a description of what the man looked like?'

'She said he'd got a white balaclava on. He was slightly overweight and spoke with a southern accent. He trussed her up with rope and fixed a cloth round her mouth. She was shaking while telling me all this.'

'Did she say anything else before the paramedics took her?'

'Only that she'd heard two gunshots near the kitchen. That really spooked her. I only had a couple of minutes with her before they put her in the ambulance. My God, I really wish we'd been here. Rocky would have seen them off, wouldn't you, Rocky?'

Sunita shook her head. 'I think perhaps it was just as well in a way that you and Rocky *weren't* here, sir. They tied

up your wife. They might not have been so easy-going towards you and the dog. Have you seen anyone in the lane outside acting suspiciously over the past few weeks or have there been any unusual incidents?'

He shook his head. 'Nothing I can recall. But this lane isn't a quiet haven of peace and tranquillity all the time, despite appearances. Anglers are constantly driving up and down here on their way to the River Avon. We also get dog walkers and teenage couples around here from time to time.'

After she'd finished speaking to David Willis, Sunita returned to the main house and, for a while, stood near the front door, watching a scenes-of-crime officer at work. The woman, who was wearing white overalls, was examining tyre tracks among some damp leaves. Sunita assumed the chief inspector and other members of their team had switched their attention to the other side of the building or were examining places inside the house where the burglars had been.

She removed the piece of paper Roscoe had handed her earlier from the pocket of her brown quilted jacket and dialled the number for Top Rank Protection. Then, while waiting for the firm to reply, she stared across the forecourt towards the brown hornbeam hedge as she had done earlier. Was that something white on the ground that she could see among the dark twigs? Some litter carried there by the autumn wind? Some white fungus among the soil?

Ken Woodman answered almost immediately. 'Top Rank. How can I help?' he asked.

'This is DS Roy from Heart of England CID,' Sunita explained. 'Is that Mr Woodman?'

'Yes. Any news?' he asked.

'I'm afraid not,' she said. 'I've just been assigned to the case and I'm at Upper Norton Manor right now. I gather Mr Jukes phoned you as soon as he arrived here this afternoon.'

‘That’s right. He said he could see a guy in a balaclava loading stolen gear into a Range Rover.’

‘What time was this?’

‘Exactly twelve minutes past four. Since then I’ve texted him and heard nothing.’

‘I’m afraid we’ve had a report of two gunshots being heard but there’s absolutely no sign of your employee,’ she said. ‘As far as you’re aware, Mr Jukes declared he was going to tackle the man in the balaclava?’

‘Yes. He was with the army in southern Helmand before he got into security work. He’s the type of guy who’s never been worried about having a go. Since then I haven’t had a word from him, so I’m obviously fearing the worst. Especially since I’ve now heard a gun was fired. I’m worried not only for Danny, who’s one of our best and most reliable operatives, but also for the lad he was caring for, Marcel Dubois.’

‘Where was he speaking from when he vowed to tackle the man?’

‘He was sitting in the driver’s seat of the Bentley belonging to the Beauvais family. He wasn’t far from the entrance to the house.’

‘Mr Woodman, would you do me a favour?’ Sunita asked. ‘As we speak, I’m near the main door myself. As I stand here, there’s a large forecourt with a set of garages to the right and tennis courts to the left. Directly in front – about ten metres away – is a clump of bushes and some trees. I want to make sure nothing’s been overlooked here. Would you mind calling Mr Jukes’s phone again?’

‘Not at all. I’ll remain on the office phone with you while I use my mobile to make the call.’

A few seconds passed. Then Sunita heard a phone ringing from the hedge that bordered the forecourt.

Chapter 6

After telling Danny Jukes's boss that she would call him back, Sunita Roy walked round the forecourt and stepped through the clump of bushes that lay behind the hedge. She had only walked a short distance when she stopped in her tracks.

Lying on his back in a pool of blood beneath one of the bushes was the body of a burly man in a suit.

The sergeant was gradually becoming accustomed to such gruesome sights after serving eight years with the police – including the past six spent with CID – but she was nonetheless distressed to find the man she suspected to be Danny Jukes had been killed in an act of brutality.

She took a step back in shock at her discovery and sought a moment to compose herself. Then she retraced her steps to the building's entrance and shouted for the chief inspector.

When he failed to respond, she guessed he was at the other side of the house and set off to find him. She hurried past the tennis courts and found Roscoe watching a team of forensic investigators hard at work inspecting the patio. The metal ladder used by the thieves was still resting against the first-floor balcony.

'Sir, I've found a body,' she said.

He took a step back in surprise before glancing at her.

'Have you? Well done. Let's go and take a look,' he said.

Dr Ling, overhearing their conversation, followed a few paces behind as Sunita led them to the spot behind the hedge, explaining how she got Ken Woodman to call Jukes's phone.

Dr Ling rushed forward and examined the corpse.

'Well done, Sergeant. Using your initiative again,' Roscoe remarked. Then, in a lower voice so that Dr Ling could not hear, he added, 'What a shame some of our colleagues who got here earlier missed this.'

The detectives watched from a few metres away while Dr Ling used her phone to alert the police photographer and then carried on making her initial appraisal of the bloodstained body.

'He's been shot from behind,' Ling remarked as she continued her examination.

Sunita outlined to her boss what Woodman had told her about the bodyguard.

'Poor guy,' Roscoe remarked. 'He arrives and finds a masked man loading loot into a car. If the initial information from Mr Woodman is correct, he realises his employer's home's being robbed and, with little thought for his own safety, decides to tackle the thief.'

Sunita shook her head. 'Maybe he should have realised there would be more than one robber involved. Maybe he should have held back and protected his charge.'

'I hear what you're saying, Sergeant, but, in my book, he's to be commended for having the bravery to confront the guy. He wasn't to know there was more than one person engaged in the robbery. If there were more men like him in the country, we might not be in the mess we're in at the moment.'

'These men were incredibly ruthless, sir. I mean, to shoot someone from behind in cold blood like that.'

At that moment, Dr Ling removed a mobile phone from the man's jacket and held it up for the pair to see.

After acknowledging that they had seen it, Roscoe turned his attention back to Sunita.

'I totally agree, Sergeant. We're now on the hunt for a group of really callous individuals.'

* * *

An hour later, as reporters and photographers began to gather outside the gates of Upper Norton Manor, a green Land Rover Discovery roared up the dark country lane and turned into the drive.

Its occupant was the portly, middle-aged Home Office pathologist Dr Silas Reynolds, who parked next to the swimming pool complex. He changed beside the car into his white overalls and collected from the boot his brown leather 'murder bag' containing a thermometer, syringes, a handsaw, sterile swabs, a small torch and a camera.

'You're lucky I've made it today,' he said as he bustled towards the detectives in his white overshoes. 'The Scots are about to face the Aussies at Murrayfield. I'd been looking forward to it all week.'

'Never mind, Silas,' said Roscoe. 'You'll be able to watch the game on catch-up.'

'It's not the same, old fruit,' Reynolds moaned. 'Now what have we got?'

The chief inspector and his sergeant moved a short distance away to allow the pathologist space. Reynolds began by taking several photographs of the body on the damp grass behind the hedge. Then, assisted by scenes-of-crime officers, the operation began to move the body onto the block paving so it could be fully examined under the lights. This proved more difficult than they first expected because of the man's size and weight but, within a few minutes, they managed to lift him onto some plastic sheeting on the ground.

As Reynolds stooped down and began his examination, Roscoe smiled towards his sergeant.

'By the way,' he said quietly, 'George saw a "For Sale" board up outside your flat. Are you moving on somewhere?'

'Yes, sir. I've been in Crompton Gardens for five years now,' she said.

'Is it as long as that?'

‘Yes. I feel it’s time I got out of my poky flat and looked for a house.’

‘Whereabouts are you looking?

‘I really like Warwick, but I don’t really mind what area.’

‘Oh, so you’re not moving on work-wise?’

‘Oh no. Of course not, sir. I want to stay at Heart of England.’

‘That’s good news.’

As they spoke, Reynolds carefully turned the corpse over and studied the back of the victim’s head. He glanced across at the two detectives.

‘Any idea who the poor fellow is?’ he asked.

‘He’s believed to be Danny Jukes,’ said Roscoe. ‘He’s a bodyguard hired by the family who live here.’

‘He’s got the right physique,’ Reynolds muttered as he studied a bullet hole in the victim’s back. ‘He’s been shot twice. I’ll get a scan done when we get him to the mortuary at Queensbridge, but it’s quite clear he’s suffered a catastrophic gunshot injury to the back of the head with no sign of an exit wound. He’d have lost consciousness immediately and death would have followed extremely quickly. A second shot penetrated the back of the right shoulder, again without an exit wound. There’s no sign of singeing, gunpowder residue or stippling at the site of either wound, indicating the gun wasn’t close by when it was fired.

‘This fellow also has abrasions to his face and scratches on his neck which indicate he’d been engaged in a fight with someone ante-mortem. Lastly, he has a facial injury consistent with him falling forward onto the ground after the shots were fired. It’s not usually possible to determine the sequence in which such injuries are inflicted. But in this case, it seems likely the shot in the head came first.’

‘What about the time of death, Silas?’ asked Roscoe.

‘Judging by the temperature of the body, I’d say it happened two or three hours ago,’ he replied.

'That fits with what we know,' Roscoe said with a nod.

'Dr Reynolds,' said Sunita, 'I know it's early days, but do we have any idea where the gunman would have been positioned and how close to the victim he'd have been?'

'From the angle of the wounds, I'd hazard a guess that the shots may well have been fired from an upstairs window.'

'Could the shots have been fired from that window above the front door?' asked Roscoe.

'Is it a bedroom?'

'No. It's halfway up the stairs.'

'The shots could have come from there,' said Reynolds. 'Death from the bullet in the head would have been instantaneous – occurring within seconds rather than minutes,' the pathologist continued. 'That shot on its own would have caused extensive brain injuries and he'd have died quickly. It would have done massive damage to the cerebral cortex and was unsurvivable, in my opinion.'

Chapter 7

Clutching a partly eaten bacon sandwich, Lewis Tigworth strolled up the stairs of the dilapidated house and unlocked the door to the back bedroom.

Marcel Dubois had been lying on the bed, staring at the ceiling. Now he stirred in the dim light and turned his eyes towards his visitor, standing in the doorway.

'Where's Danny?' he asked.

'Back at the house,' said the man with spiky hair, taking a bite out of his sandwich. 'You don't need to worry about him. I'm sure he's OK.'

'*Sommes-nous dans le Warwickshire?*' the boy asked.

'Eh?' said the visitor. 'Speak English.'

'This is hard for me,' said Marcel. 'Are we in Warwickshire?'

The man laughed. 'Yes, mate. We're in Warwickshire. Before we go any further, write your name.'

'You're speaking too fast,' said the boy. 'More slowly.'

'Write… your… name,' said the man, repeating the phrase one word at a time.

He pulled an old bus ticket from his pocket and handed it to Marcel along with a pencil. The boy carefully wrote out his full name and passed the paper back.

'Marcel Doo-boys,' recited the visitor, who vaguely remembered from reading news reports online that the footballer Jean-Jacques Beauvais had married Marcel's mother, an ex-model. The lad had to be the player's stepson.

The visitor stepped slowly into the room. 'We've got some clothes for you – two pairs of trousers, four shirts and some underwear. We'll put them in the wardrobe for you later.'

'*Je suis fatigué*,' said the boy, sitting up in bed. 'I am so tired. You drug me?'

'Never mind about that. It was just something to make you sleep.'

'I want more sleep.'

'I'll be back downstairs in a minute. You can sleep as long as you like then,' said Tigworth.

'What is happening at the house? I am hearing a gun.'

'A gun was fired in warning,' said Tigworth.

'I'm not seeing what happened,' Marcel continued. 'I am in the car. Please, I can go home?'

'Sorry, mate, we can't do that for the moment,' came the reply.

'How long?'

'We don't know yet. Maybe a few days.'

'I know there are other men here,' said Marcel. 'Please help me.'

Tigworth shrugged his shoulders and ate the rest of his sandwich.

'It's not down to me. I don't take the decisions. Time will soon pass, you'll see. Why didn't you go to Newcastle with your folk?'

'No Newcastle,' Marcel explained. 'I'm going to the cinema instead.'

'Your dad hasn't played a game for the Villa yet, has he?' said Tigworth.

'He is playing soon.'

'I've heard he earns more than three hundred thousand a week in wages. Is that right?'

'Sorry?' asked Marcel.

'It says so on *Birmingham Live*,' the visitor continued, 'which ain't bad for a bloke who's not scored a goal since March. So do you think your folks will cough up a nice sum of money to get you back?'

Marcel shook his head and gestured with his hands.

'I do not understand,' he replied.

'All right, mate. Don't worry about that. Look, I tell you what. Do you do a bit of gaming?

'*Quoi?*'

'Nintendo.'

'Oh, Nintendo. Yes.'

'I've got my games console here and you can have a go with it,' said Tigworth.

For the first time, the boy's face lit up.

'That is the very nice idea,' said Marcel.

'My mate downstairs has got a small telly for you back at his gaff and we'll bring that as well.'

The boy looked puzzled but said nothing.

'Let's have a look at what you brought with you.'

Tigworth stepped across to a chair in the corner of the room where the boy had placed his checked shirt, green pullover and black jeans. He searched the trouser pockets and found a five-pound note, some coins, a comb, chewing gum and a penknife.

'I'll be keeping this,' said Tigworth, slipping the penknife into his own trouser pocket. He put the other items back in the jeans. 'How are you for food and drink? You had half a pizza a few hours ago, and you've still got your bottle of Coke, yeah?'

Marcel nodded. 'The Coke, it is fine,' he said.

'All right. I'm going to look for my Nintendo,' said the man.

He left, turning the key in the lock behind him, and returned to the front room downstairs.

Although exhausted, Marcel crept to the door and pressed his ear against it. At first, he could hear nothing. Then voices became louder and he guessed Tigworth and another man were speaking near the stairs. Marcel only understood part of the heated conversation.

He began to tremble as he heard one of them saying, 'Listen, if we've got to kill him, count me out. I don't want any more killing.'

'Don't worry, mate,' his companion insisted. 'If there's any of that involved, it'll be like this time – down to me and Wayne.'

'I'm really pissed off about us using the shooter,' said Tigworth. 'There was no need.'

'There was every need, mate,' came the reply. 'That guy was getting the upper hand and nearly bloody strangled me, the bastard. Look, if that guy hadn't been shot, it would have been me lying out cold on the bloody driveway. Anyway, it's done now. That guy just shouldn't have interfered. Listen. The boss wants you to be the person who deals with the boy.'

'I bloody hope we don't have to keep him for long,' Tigworth continued. 'That would be a real pain in the ass. When I agreed to help you today, I didn't sign up for taking bleeding hostages. Anyway, how come the boss wants *me* to deal with him?'

'You've got younger brothers and sisters, haven't you? You're used to dealing with kids. You can probably relate

to the boy better than me and Wayne. Find out what you can from him.'

For a short time, the men's conversation was out of earshot. Then Marcel heard footsteps on the stairs and the ginger-haired man burst through the door with a syringe followed by Tigworth.

'I'll just give him a shot of sleepy-juice to calm him down,' said one of the men. Marcel was forced onto the bed and injected in the arm.

'That was the boss just then,' the ginger-haired man announced. 'It's on. We're going to ask the family for two million quid for the boy's safe return.'

Chapter 8

Ploughman's Lane was in darkness when Detective Constable Omar Khalid arrived there at half past six, more than two hours after the break-in.

He'd come to the end of his daytime shift, so he'd been surprised when the chief inspector had phoned and asked him to carry out house-to-house inquiries regarding the burglary.

The conscientious detective parked on a grass verge beneath a clump of trees and ran a comb through his black, curly hair. It was warm for October. He left his coat in the car as he passed through the open gates and walked up the short drive that led to Old Larks' Cottage. This quaint house with a thatched roof occupied the land next door to Upper Norton Manor.

He presented his warrant card to a woman in her early fifties who came to the door.

‘DC Khalid from Heart of England CID,’ he explained. ‘We’re just calling on neighbours in case you witnessed anything this afternoon.’

The blonde-haired woman drew a quick breath.

‘Oh, you mean the break-in?’ she replied. ‘No, I wasn’t aware of it until I saw it on the news a moment ago. I feel sorry for the people who’ve just moved in.’

‘You didn’t hear gunshots, then?’ he asked.

‘Well, yes, I did. But you get shooting in the country. I just thought someone had bagged a couple of pheasants.’

‘Were you here all afternoon, Mrs…’

‘Morris is the name – Angela Morris,’ she said. ‘I went shopping in Worcester between two and four, but I’m sorry, I didn’t see anything strange either beforehand or when I got back. You could ask Irene Meadows at The Lodge. She might know something.’

Khalid followed her suggestion and made Irene Meadows’ house his next port of call, but she was unable to assist him at all. In fact, none of the neighbours proved very helpful.

He was about to return to his car and head home when he remembered seeing four brick-and-flint terraced farm cottages a short distance away, lower down the lane. As he approached, he saw a sign above the terrace saying ‘Woodside Villas’.

The detective noticed a light on in the front room of the first cottage he came to, number four, and he strode up the red-brick path. Within minutes of him knocking, a man with short, grey hair and a moustache drew back the door.

‘Heart of England Police,’ explained Khalid, showing his warrant card. ‘I’m DC Khalid and I’m making inquiries about the break-in up the road.’

‘Oh, I know,’ said the man with a nod. ‘My mate was just telling me on the phone about it. The buggers waited till the French football fella was away at a match and then robbed his place. I don’t know if the guy is worth all the

money paid for him. Twenty million, wasn't it? But it must be awful for him and his folk. Someone was killed, weren't they?'

Khalid nodded. 'Yes. That's right,' he said. 'Not much information about that at the moment. Did you see or hear anything this afternoon?'

'I heard some shooting, but you get that round here all the time with the gamekeepers and the shooting parties,' the man replied.

'Anything else unusual happened round here?' asked the detective.

'I tell you what I've noticed and it's a bit strange. You see, I'm out at the side of my house tinkering with my old car on Saturdays. Provided I'm not underneath it, I get to see who comes up and down this lane. Well, last Saturday and the Saturday before, I saw this black Range Rover travelling up and down, past my house.'

'What sort of time would this have been?' asked Khalid.

'I'd say it was about a quarter to four in the afternoon. It was going in the Norton Prior direction and then it must have come back about two hours later.'

'How can you be so sure about the times?' said the detective.

'Well, I tell you what – David Willis, the gardener up at the big house, always takes his dog out for a walk on Saturdays round about the same time. He comes past here with Rocky at about twenty to four, regular as clockwork, he does. He often stops for a quick chat.'

'So Mr Willis stopped to talk to you both Saturday afternoons?'

'Yes, at about the same time. And soon afterwards this black Range Rover would come down the lane really slowly as though they were looking for something.'

Khalid smiled. 'They might have been lost or looking for somewhere to park,' he suggested.

'Maybe.'

'I don't suppose you took the registration?'

'No.'

'Pity. Anyway, that's useful information.'

'Hey, I hope David's missus is OK. I heard they tied her up. Is that right?'

'She discovered the thieves after they broke in. She's been taken to Queensbridge General. It's only for a check-up. Listen, can I take a note of your name?'

'Yes, of course,' said the householder. 'It's Dennis. Dennis Walker.'

The detective wrote his name in his notebook.

'It sounds to me as if the man in the car might have been following Mr Willis to check on his movements,' said Khalid.

Walker nodded. 'Oh, I see what you mean. They swotted up on his times and wanted to make sure he'd gone out before they went in?'

'It's just one possible theory,' said Khalid. 'Tell me more about this car. It was black, you say?'

'Yes, with darkened windows.'

'So it stood out a bit and you remembered it?'

'Look, all the toffs round here have got big luxury cars with blackened windows, so I didn't remember it for that reason.'

'So why did you remember it?' asked Khalid.

'It had a dented wing where it had probably been in a crash. I'm into motors. I remember things like that. You see, a fault like that stands out in these parts. They just send the chauffeur down to the nearest garage and get it fixed straight away, the folk who live round here. They don't always wait for insurance companies.'

'Did you by any chance get a look at the driver as the car flashed past?'

'Yeah. Big, muscular bloke with short, blond hair,' said Walker.

'Did you see this same car today?'

'No, I didn't. I decided to jet-wash the patio round the back of the house at about half past three, so I wasn't in my usual place.'

'That's a pity. If you'd been working on your car like the previous Saturdays, you'd almost certainly have seen the robbers arriving and departing from the manor.'

Chapter 9

The scenes-of-crime staff were still at work when, just before ten o'clock the same evening, a black Audi RS 7 Sportback swept past the crowd of journalists beside the gate and glided up the drive at Upper Norton Manor. By then, the chief inspector and his sergeant had been banished to the staff quarters – the only part of the site where forensic work had been completed.

Roscoe stepped outside the building and greeted the weary footballer behind the wheel as he parked his car next to the garages.

'Monsieur Beauvais,' he said as the footballer got out. 'I'm DCI Roscoe from Heart of England Police.'

The tall, olive-skinned midfielder with short, dark hair shook the detective's outstretched hand.

'Pleased to meet you, Chief Inspector. I'm Jean-Jacques Beauvais. Any news of Marcel and Monsieur Jukes?'

Roscoe shook his head.

'I'm very sorry to tell you that your son is missing,' he replied.

Two women, both looking exhausted, stepped out of the car.

'Monsieur Roscoe,' said the footballer as a dusky-skinned blonde woman hurried towards them. 'This is my wife, Camille.'

'What is this you are saying about Marcel? He is still missing?' said Camille.

'We believe Mr Jukes arrived here in your Bentley with Marcel at ten minutes past four,' Roscoe explained. 'We believe Marcel was then abducted by the burglars and your Bentley stolen.'

'*Oh, mon Dieu*,' said Camille as her husband quickly put his arm round her. '*Mon petit garçon*. Please. You must find him quickly.'

She stared in shock at the chief inspector.

'All forces in the Midlands have been alerted about the break-in and the disappearance of your son,' Roscoe continued. 'Traffic patrols have been notified to look out for your Bentley and a full-scale operation will launch in the morning.'

Camille burst into tears. Her husband led her a few steps away and did his best to console her. Camille's more reserved companion, a slim woman with light-brown hair, joined them.

'Chief Inspector, I'm Katrina Drake, PA to Monsieur Beauvais,' the woman explained. 'I'm pleased to meet you, although this is such a terrible time.'

She confidently shook the detective's hand.

'So why are you here exactly?' Drake asked. 'Shouldn't you be out right now searching for Marcel?'

'*Exactement*,' said Camille as she and her husband rejoined them.

'We're still in the process of gathering information about what precisely happened,' Roscoe replied.

'But I do not understand. Where is Monsieur Jukes?' asked Jean-Jacques.

'I'm sorry to have to tell you that Mr Jukes is dead, sir,' said Roscoe. 'He acted very bravely in confronting the thieves. Mrs Jukes is on her way to the mortuary to identify the body. I also have to mention that Mrs Willis was slightly injured after being tied up. She is being checked in hospital.'

'*C'est terrible, monsieur*,' said Jean-Jacques. 'I'm so sorry. This has been such a terrible day for us. Chief Inspector, what have the thieves taken? I only received a brief phone call about the burglary from your local police.'

'We're not sure what's been taken,' said Roscoe. 'They broke in through the bathroom window on the first floor.'

'*Mon Dieu!*' shouted Camille.

She ran through the open doorway and raced up the stairs. A few moments later, she was back and reeling off in her mother tongue a long list of missing items which a forensic officer upstairs had allowed her to search for.

'*Monsieur le Chief Inspector*,' said Jean-Jacques, 'I'm afraid these criminals have taken clothing, handbags and my wife's precious jewellery and a pair of my watches.'

'If it's any consolation,' Roscoe continued, 'it doesn't appear that your son was deliberately targeted. It seems likely the gang were unaware that your son was in the car at the time they decided to steal it.'

'So where is Marcel? Why haven't they let him go?' Camille wailed.

'We don't know at this stage, I'm afraid,' said Roscoe. 'It's too early to say. Perhaps he's escaped their clutches as we speak and is in a place of safety. Or perhaps they're considering using him to barter.'

'To barter – what does this mean?' Camille asked.

'They may wish to do a deal,' said Roscoe, 'but it all depends on the situation. The gang members may not even be aware your boy, Marcel, is in the car. I mean, if he's hidden himself away, when night comes, he might be in a position to escape. But this is all conjecture.'

The chief inspector glanced over his shoulder as Sunita emerged from the Willises' quarters and approached them.

'This is Detective Sergeant Roy. In a minute, I'm going to go down to the gate and have a word with the waiting press. While I'm doing that, DS Roy here can take statements from you all and, most importantly right now,

we need a photograph and description of Marcel. Then we can move forward.'

'Very good, Chief Inspector,' said Jean-Jacques. 'Our greatest concern is for our son, Marcel, isn't it, Camille?'

He threw his arms round his wife, who was weeping.

'The jewellery and watches can be replaced,' he went on. 'Marcel can never be replaced, so please focus your investigation on him, if you please.'

'Yes, Chief Inspector, do your best to find Marcel,' said Camille as tears trickled down her face.

Roscoe nodded before walking away.

The Beauvais couple followed Sunita into the Willises' living room, where they sat down on the sofa. Katrina Drake murmured something about making tea and strolled off into the kitchen.

'Let's begin by sorting out a photograph,' said Sunita.

'I have several on my phone. Here,' said Camille, leaning forward and showing the photo gallery on her handset.

'Could you email me the third and fourth images?' Sunita asked, writing down her email address for her on a scrap of paper.

'I'll do that now,' said Camille.

The footballer explained that Marcel had sandy-coloured hair.

'He's aged sixteen,' he said. 'He will be seventeen on 15 January. He's a hundred and seventy-five centimetres tall. His hair is not short and it's not long. His hair has the parting in the middle.'

Sunita wrote that down in her small notebook.

'What was he wearing?'

'As far as I know,' Jean-Jacques replied, 'he had a green pullover and black jeans.'

'*Mademoiselle*,' Camille said, 'he has *les deux colliers* – how do you say in English?'

'Two medallions,' explained Jean-Jacques.

‘Any other distinguishing marks? Any tattoos, moles on his skin or scars?’

‘No. That’s all,’ said the footballer.

‘I understand Marcel is your stepson, Monsieur Beauvais. Is that right?’ Sunita asked.

Camille answered for him. ‘Marcel is from my first marriage, to Monsieur Dubois,’ she explained.

‘Has he been informed of the abduction?’

‘I will see to it but–’

‘I’m afraid there is bad feeling between Monsieur Dubois and our family, Sergeant Roy,’ Jean-Jacques said.

‘Well, he will still have to be informed,’ Sunita insisted.

‘Look, we’re very tired,’ he continued. ‘Is there any chance we could bring this to an end? We haven’t eaten and we want to see what has been taken.’

‘I don’t expect the chief inspector had a chance to explain,’ said Sunita, ‘but unfortunately you won’t be able to access the main part of the house tonight.’

‘Why is that?’ asked Jean-Jacques.

‘I’m really sorry but we have to carefully collect evidence – even the slightest trace – left behind by the criminals. This can be vital both in terms of finding them and getting your son back as soon as possible.’

‘*Mon Dieu*,’ said Camille. ‘*Quelle catastrophe absolue!*’

Jean-Jacques patted her on the arm. ‘It’s all right, *ma chérie*. We will take a room at that hotel in Worcester where I stayed twice before. Sergeant Roy, do you know when the police work will be completed?’

‘I’d think by tomorrow or Monday at the latest,’ Sunita replied. ‘When you’ve got a moment, sir, it would be helpful if you could give us a list of everything that’s been stolen.’

The pair nodded.

‘You can understand that there has been a lot for us to think about,’ said the footballer. ‘But, as I told your boss, getting Marcel back is our priority.’

'*Mademoiselle*,' Camille added, 'Marcel suffers from the epilepsy.'

'He's an epileptic?' said Sunita.

'*Oui*,' she said. 'He suffers with the convulsions.'

'I see,' replied Sunita, who knew very little about the medical condition.

'So it's even more vital that we find him quickly,' Sunita said.

'*Oui*,' said Camille. 'I don't think Marcel has got his medicine and that's very dangerous for him.'

Chapter 10

With a heavy heart, Sunita Roy set off the next morning to visit the newly bereaved wife of the murdered bodyguard. She knew Natalie Jukes deserved time to grieve, but, by the same token, all information about the murdered man – no matter how apparently trivial at first glance – needed to be collected and assessed. So, despite her misgivings, she knew she had to encourage the woman to talk to her.

The couple's modern mid-terraced house lay on a private residential housing estate on the southern side of the picturesque riverside town of Evesham. A small grey Ford Fiesta was parked in the drive of 43 Primrose Way as the sergeant parked her car and hurried through a light shower of rain.

The widow opened the door promptly. She was around the same age as Sunita with medium-length, black-dyed hair and blue eyes. Dressed casually in a T-shirt and jeans, she appeared athletic and tanned, but her mascara was running as though she had been crying.

'DS Roy, Heart of England Police,' Sunita explained, producing her warrant card. 'So sorry about your loss.'

'You'd better come in,' said Natalie, holding the door wide open. 'I've got two of the neighbours here.'

She led the sergeant through a gloomy hallway and into a bright, modern living room at the back where a middle-aged couple were holding a quiet conversation.

'Doug and Carol, the police are here,' she said loudly in her Yorkshire accent before peering across at the detective.

'We're just leaving,' said Doug, a stocky, balding man who immediately rose from his seat on the blue settee.

'Don't leave on my account,' said Sunita.

'We're only next door and can easily come back later,' his wife added as they headed for the hallway.

'Any time you need us, just give us a knock,' the woman told Natalie, giving her a hug.

'Thanks so much, both of you,' Natalie said as she showed them out.

Sunita glanced around the room. A photograph of Natalie and Danny on their wedding day took pride of place on the mantelpiece. Another photograph, on a bookshelf, showed Danny as a sapper in army fatigues. In pencil beneath, someone had written, 'Daniel Jukes. 32 Engineer Regiment Group, Catterick, September 2013'.

'That was taken when we were based in Yorkshire,' said Natalie as she returned.

Sunita picked up a photograph and turned it over. There was an article from a local newspaper, the *Halifax Courier*, which was stuck to the reverse of the photograph. It stated, 'Danny Jukes, aged twenty-four, has been mentioned in dispatches for his brave leadership while searching for homemade bombs in Helmand Province, Afghanistan. He also led a team of engineers in building an observation post in hazardous terrain. Although under constant sniper fire from the enemy at one point, he managed to rescue a wounded soldier from a rooftop.'

Sunita put the photograph back.

'My boss wanted to thank you for visiting the mortuary last night and identifying Danny,' she told Natalie while settling down on the settee.

'This has been an absolute nightmare,' said Natalie. 'Yesterday morning, I kissed him goodbye. He was driving the smartest car I've ever seen – a Bentley Continental. He was going to pick up Marcel, the Beauvais couple's boy, and take him to the cinema before going to the manor. Both he and the boy were really looking forward to their day out. My last words to him were, "Have a good time and I'll see you later." I kissed him on the cheek and he was gone.'

Sunita took her notebook out of her jacket pocket.

'What film did they see?' the detective asked.

'*See How They Run*,' Natalie replied. 'It's a light-hearted whodunnit. They went to the Odeon in Queensbridge. They were originally going to see *All Quiet on the Western Front* but the boy's mother said it was too violent.'

'Did they do anything else while in town?' Sunita asked. 'I mean, did they have lunch there?'

'Yes. Mr Beauvais paid for the pair of them to have lunch in the town. Danny phoned me at about three o'clock to say that Marcel was having his hair cut.'

'How long had you been married?' Sunita asked.

'Seven years,' said Natalie. 'Do you want a drink? Tea?'

Sunita shook her head. 'Thanks, but I'm fine.'

'We knew each other from school in Yorkshire. Then, when I was twenty-two, I ran into him while out shopping. We had a long chat and he asked me out. We were married a year later. When he came out of the army, he got this job with the security firm and we moved down here.'

She sat down in an armchair and bent forward with her head in her hands. When she looked up, Sunita could see she was crying.

'I don't know what I'm going to do,' she said, between sobs. 'That man was my life.'

'One of your officers broke the news to you yesterday, did they?' Sunita asked.

'That's right – PC Underhill. He was very kind and had a quiet word with Doug and Carol. Asked them to keep an eye on me, but I'm all right. He later came back and took me over to Queensbridge General so I could identify the body.'

'You've had an awful shock,' said Sunita.

'While he was out in Helmand, I got used to being on my own and there was always the thought that something might happen to him over there. Unlike many of his comrades, he came back in one piece – only to be shot and killed by some bastard thief.'

She broke down and sobbed.

'Can I get you a tissue from somewhere?' asked Sunita. 'I'm afraid I don't have one.'

Natalie glanced up. 'They're on the sideboard by my black handbag,' she replied.

Sunita stepped across to the low-level sideboard where a black handbag was lying beside a gold clutch bag bearing the initials NJ. She found the box of tissues and handed it to Natalie, who wiped her eyes.

'How long had Danny been working for Jean-Jacques?' Sunita asked.

'About three months. Since he signed with Aston Villa. Jean-Jacques chose Danny because he could speak French. Danny lived in France for a year when he was younger.'

'Have you got a job, Natalie?' Sunita asked.

'Yes. I work for an accountancy firm in Evesham.'

'You haven't got any children?'

'No. We were trying for children together, but hadn't been lucky. Now it'll never happen.' She paused. 'I really don't know what I'm going to do now. My mother wants me to move back to Halifax. But it's too early for a decision like that.'

‘Natalie, this could be important,’ said the detective with an earnest expression. ‘How long had the cinema trip been planned?’

‘It was a long-standing idea of Marcel’s,’ she replied. ‘He’d told his parents he didn’t fancy going all the way to St James’ Park to watch the game. Jean-Jacques has always tried to encourage Marcel to take an interest in football, but it never appealed to him and the prospect of a long car journey to Newcastle filled him with dread.’

Sunita nodded as she wrote this in her notebook. ‘What would Marcel have been doing yesterday if they hadn’t gone to the Odeon?’

Natalie shrugged. ‘The lad would have been at the house and probably under the care of the housekeeper.’

‘And Danny?’

‘He’d have been washing one of the cars or checking the grounds, if he hadn’t gone to the match.’

‘Did Danny ever stay over at the house?’

‘Sometimes. He said it was a terrific place. He loved using the swimming pool when the family weren’t around. A week ago, Jean-Jacques said he didn’t mind if Danny missed out on going to Newcastle and the cinema trip was arranged.’

Sunita stared across at Natalie.

‘Did anyone else know about this plan, Natalie?’ she asked.

‘Probably a lot of people. Jean-Jacques discussed a lot of things with his teammates, with the Willises, and with people at Top Rank.’

‘I just wondered,’ Sunita continued, ‘if someone got to hear that the housekeeper would be on her own. I was wondering if someone could have obtained advanced knowledge that the whole family and their bodyguard, together with the gardener, would be absent. It might be a factor behind the gang’s decision to break in yesterday.’

Natalie stared back at her.

'Oh, God. I see what you mean,' she said. 'But I'm sorry. I don't know the answer.'

After a pause, Natalie said, 'Can you tell me something – exactly how did Danny die?'

'We don't know much at this stage,' Sunita said, deciding to choose her words carefully. 'We believe he interrupted the robbers. Without a thought for his personal safety, we understand he tackled at least one of the men. But another of them shot Danny twice from behind.'

Natalie scowled. 'What bastards,' she said in a low voice.

'He wouldn't have known much about it,' Sunita added. 'He'd have gone instantly. My boss, DCI Roscoe, says Danny should be commended for his bravery.'

Natalie shrugged. 'It would be nice if something like that happened. Danny was praised a few years ago for his courage in Helmand. But, at the end of the day, no bravery award is going to bring my Danny back to me. But what about Marcel? Is he all right?'

'Well, no,' said Sunita. 'Haven't you heard? He's missing.'

'Oh, my God.'

'We think he may have been abducted by the burglars.'

'That's awful. His poor mother must be in pieces. Danny told me the boy has fits.'

'Yes,' said Sunita. 'We need to find him and get him back as quickly as possible.'

Chapter 11

Sunita Roy and DC Brett Dawson were pinning photographs of cars to a whiteboard when the chief inspector arrived in the CID office on Monday. They both greeted him with a cheerful 'Good morning, sir' before continuing with their task.

Roscoe unlocked his door and began reading through that day's national newspapers. One of the tabloids had devoted two inside pages to the raid at Upper Norton Manor under the headline, 'Bodyguard killed in gems heist'. One of the up-market rivals reported on the break-in under the headline, 'Murder at football star's mansion'.

A few minutes later, Sunita tapped on the door of his room, which was partitioned off from the rest of the CID department. She smiled at him as she stepped inside.

'I suppose you've seen these papers, have you?' he asked her.

'Some of them, sir. No mention of the boy,' said Sunita. 'I feel so sorry for him. He must be terrified at being kept captive by strangers.'

'Yes, we've asked for a news blackout for the moment,' he said. 'I had a chat with our media team over the weekend. The grounds are that the life of a sixteen-year-old boy may be at risk. The clampdown may not be for long, but, if it were lifted, we'd be inundated with the press from the UK, France and all over the world. Our lives would become extremely difficult, Sergeant. I had to get approval from the assistant chief constable.'

'Omar's told me we're carrying out house-to-house on the Troutbeck Estate, sir.'

He nodded. 'Yes, and officers from Queensbridge are checking all vehicles entering and leaving the estate. They've got leaflets showing the boy's photograph. Anyway, I think it's time we called everyone together, don't you?'

Over the next few minutes, DC Khalid took a seat near Sunita's desk. He was joined shortly afterwards by DC Wendy Hopkirk; PC Pam Listers, the family liaison officer; Dr Alice Ling from forensics; digital forensic analyst John Hepworth; and PC Underhill from Queensbridge police.

He clapped his hands to attract attention.

‘Good morning, everyone,’ he declared. ‘I wanted to bring you all up to date on the Norton Prior murder and abduction. We’re looking for at least three men. There’s the man that the bodyguard Danny Jukes went to tackle while loading the Range Rover. We’ll call him Suspect One.’

He glanced at the board where his sergeant had written ‘Suspect One’ beneath the silhouetted figure of a man. She stood up and began writing a description beneath the picture.

‘DC Khalid found a witness in Ploughman’s Lane who reported seeing a blond-haired, muscular man behaving suspiciously, driving up and down the lane,’ he continued. ‘We’ve reason to believe that was also Suspect One.’

He turned his attention to Dawson, who was patting his spiky blond hair while sitting close to the whiteboard.

‘Dawson, you spoke to Mrs Willis when she came out of hospital yesterday, didn’t you?’

The constable nodded.

‘As I understand it, she claims the man that attacked her and tied her up was of short to average height. Is that right?’

‘Yes, sir,’ said the constable. ‘She reckoned he’d have been five feet four or five feet five inches tall.’

‘She also described him as having a southern accent,’ Roscoe went on.

‘Yes, sir. A southern or London accent. She said he was in his late twenties. In fact, she reckoned from the sound of the men’s voices they were all about the same age.’

‘So, we’ll call this fellow Suspect Two,’ said Roscoe, glancing at the second picture on the board. ‘Mrs Willis believes there was a third man present because she heard at least one other Midlands accent. So this last man becomes Suspect Three.’

He glanced again at the board, where his sergeant had added a third silhouette.

‘If I can turn now to what we found on the cameras. DC Dawson’s found footage of a black Range Rover

turning into Windermere Drive on the Troutbeck housing estate in Queensbridge at 4.35 p.m. on Saturday.'

'That's right,' said Dawson.

'And a few minutes later it was followed by a silver Bentley, recognised as the one owned by the Beauvais family and which Danny Jukes had earlier been driving. A short while later, the Bentley was caught on camera leaving the Troutbeck Estate and heading along the main road towards Worcester.'

Derek Underhill interrupted. 'Sir, as you know, it's a huge housing estate with many exit roads. DC Dawson and I have had a thorough look round the entire area, but we've so far failed, unfortunately, to find any trace of a black Range Rover. We're still looking.'

'Thank you,' said Roscoe. 'That's fine. Keep at it. Now the Bentley was also picked up by a camera on the outskirts of Worcester at about seven o'clock on Saturday night, but since then it's gone off the radar.'

Dr Ling waved to catch the chief inspector's attention.

'I thought you might be interested to know, sir, that we found a shoeprint in some soil at the edge of the forecourt,' she said. 'It was right opposite the front door of the manor. So, if you make any arrests, it'll be interesting to see if there's any match to footwear. We also found a print from an index finger on the window where Dr Reynolds decided the gunman must have been standing.'

'Really? That could prove extremely helpful,' said Roscoe.

Sunita, who had been standing behind the chief inspector, interrupted him. 'Sorry, sir, is this a suitable moment to mention the timing of the raid?' she asked.

'Of course. What did you want to say?' said Roscoe.

'Well, DC Khalid found that really helpful witness who saw the guy in the Rover apparently carrying out reconnaissance.'

Dawson laughed. 'It's what they used to call "casing the joint",' he said.

'Thank you, Dawson,' said the chief inspector, glaring at the young constable. 'Yes,' he continued, 'the gang clearly gathered information in advance. We're not dealing with amateurs. They knew what they were doing. They obviously kept watch on the house and its occupants. As DS Roy discovered, they may even have known that Danny Jukes and the boy, Marcel, were going to be away from the house for several hours. On the other hand, it might simply have been a matter of fate that brought Danny Jukes to the house shortly after four.'

'Blimey,' chipped in Dawson. 'If I'd been left with a luxury car like that, I wouldn't have been in any hurry to rush back.'

'That's enough, Dawson,' said Roscoe. He turned back to the team. 'So, we know we're dealing with cunning individuals who've the nous to collect intelligence before they strike. They're also ruthless individuals who are happy to use guns if someone gets in their way. Now, lastly, we come to the missing boy. Getting him safely returned to his family must take precedence. Pam Listers, our family liaison officer, spent most of yesterday with the family. Pam, how did it go?'

All eyes turned towards the woman sitting in the centre of the team of officers.

'Mr and Mrs Beauvais are extremely upset, obviously, about their missing son,' said PC Listers. 'Mrs Beauvais spent most of the day in bed while her husband was watching television on his own. Luckily, I found he was happy enough to speak with me. I think he found it helped to talk to a total stranger about his stepson and I believe I've struck up a good working relationship with him.'

'Good,' said Roscoe.

'As you suggested, sir, I asked him if there'd been any unusual incidents over the past month – you know, strange phone calls, strange visitors, anyone behaving suspiciously.

He said no. He asked a lot about police procedure in the UK and what steps we were taking to find Marcel. I told him as much as I thought would be helpful and as much as I thought would be safe to tell him.'

'Very good,' said Roscoe as she broke into a smile. 'Keep up the Listers charm offensive and let us know of anything significant coming from the family.'

'I'm going to be visiting the family every day for the next week or so,' she assured him.

He glanced at Underhill, who was sitting directly in front of him.

'Incidentally, Derek, I gather one of your colleagues from Queensbridge found some bricks dislodged from a garden wall at the manor. Is that right?'

Underhill nodded. 'We couldn't tell if they'd been removed from the wall by something falling, such as a tree, if it had been done by vandals or if they'd been removed by the gang, sir. But we'll be giving the owners of the house security advice.'

Underhill's phone bleeped. He glanced at its screen.

'Sir, a call's just come into the control room,' he said. 'A black Range Rover has been sighted leaving the Troutbeck Estate.'

'That's great. Let's see if one of the patrol cars can pick them up.'

Chapter 12

Marcel Dubois woke from his drug-induced slumber at the house in Juniper Lane and shivered. He must have slept for hours and hours inside his makeshift prison cell. Yet he still felt exhausted. That must be because of that drug the men gave me, he told himself.

He remained still in his bed and listened. He could hear an argument downstairs. Two voices were involved, but he couldn't hear what the disagreement was about.

He climbed out from beneath the white duvet and stepped across the floor in his bare feet.

He examined the double-glazed window which consisted of one fixed pane and one opening window. He had a view of trees and open fields. Considering it was nearly November, it was a mild, sunny day, although he had no idea what time it was. Sometime in the morning, he assumed. He tried the handle on the window. It wouldn't budge. It was probably locked.

What a contrast from his room at the manor house. There he had enjoyed a huge bedroom with fitted wardrobes stacked with designer clothes. He had a wide-screen television and a desk for his computer games. *Vive la différence!*

He studied the window. If he still had his knife, he might have been able to prise out the rubber and remove the glass. But he had no knife or any other tool that could dig out the moulding. Moreover, he could see by looking through the pane that the white plastic beading was on the outside and the glass was certain to remain fixed – even if he removed the internal rubber. Of course, he could use the bedside cabinet to try to smash the window, but the men would quickly come running.

He wondered if he could try to make a hole in the ceiling while standing on the wardrobe. Maybe he could climb out through the hole, get into the loft and try for access to the roof, but he had nothing to make a hole with. In any case, he had no head for heights and had no idea how he would get down to the ground if he succeeded in reaching the roof.

All this meant his only means of escape was through the door.

Marcel had no idea how many men had been involved with his abduction. He guessed three or possibly four. His

solitary visitor was the skinny man with spiky hair and a beard which poked out from beneath his facemask. He had refused to give a name, but Marcel thought he was called Tiggs as he had heard the men downstairs calling him that. He brought Marcel meals and escorted him to the bathroom next door.

This visitor fascinated Marcel. He was confident and seemed to have his wits about him. Whenever he arrived, he peered at Marcel like an owl watching a vole. He ordered him to stay by the window whenever he brought his food and plastic cutlery and always made sure the door was securely locked when he left. He also watched him carefully whenever he escorted him to the bathroom. So Marcel knew that, if he were to escape, it would involve distracting this man in some way.

If he could elude him, Marcel thought, he would then flee downstairs and the rest would be easy. He could be gone from the house in a matter of moments. But tricking the man would prove a challenge. He would have to spend some time planning how to do it.

Marcel had been frightened when he and Monsieur Danny had first arrived at Upper Norton Manor two days earlier. He had heard gunshots but had remained still on the floor of the car. It was only after hearing the men's voices that he had decided to peer out from under the blanket and see what was going on. He was then shocked to discover the new driver behind the wheel. This was his very first encounter with the bearded man, Tiggs, and he was suddenly struck by the full horror of his situation. He was being abducted.

How he wished events had taken a different course. How he wished he was back at the house with his mother and stepfather. He closed his eyes for a moment and imagined he was safe in his bedroom, listening to his favourite tracks on iTunes. Or maybe he was in the skateboard park in Paris, trying out some new techniques

with his friend, Gabriel. Or walking through Le Jardin des Tuileries with his real father, Philippe.

For a moment, he was close to tears. Then he remembered something Philippe used to say, back in the good old days, before the quarrels started and his parents' marriage ended. *À vaillant cœur rien d'impossible* – to a valiant heart, nothing is impossible.

Marcel's father believed in that. Marcel believed in that too. He had to steel himself. Surely it would not be long before he was rescued. Maybe his parents would pay money to the men so that he could be freed. That's what usually happened, wasn't it? Or maybe the British police would come. Or maybe he would take charge of events himself and escape.

Meanwhile, he would have to make the best of it. So far, the men had treated him fairly well, apart from giving him the injection that made him sleep. Tiggs had been friendly when he'd come to see him. He would probably be arriving soon with his first meal of the day. The food had been all right. He'd loved the pizza.

Tiggs, *mon nouvel ami*. He could never be a proper friend, of course. He and the other men, who had brought him to this hellhole, had robbed his parents' home. They must now be getting rid of the family's possessions. They may have taken his PlayStation. But, if they had, he was sure Jean-Jacques would buy him another one when all this was over. He always seemed to have plenty of money.

Tiggs seemed to know about gaming and the pair had exchanged views on the subject. He agreed with Marcel that *Call of Duty: Modern Warfare II* was 'the best game ever' and they shared an appreciation of the new underwater gunplay.

He wondered if his father, Philippe, had been told about him being taken away. He thought his father might travel to Britain from Paris and join the search. He was sure his father would help. Oh, how he missed him.

The night before, Marcel had been handed a plate of beans on toast. He had asked questions about Monsieur Danny again and the reply came back that there was no information.

Marcel had become absorbed with thoughts about Jean-Jacques and his mother. He wondered what they were doing. Knowing his mother, she would be very worried about him. He expected the police would be out looking for him.

Any moment the police may burst through the door and find me, he told himself.

And where was Danny now? Why hadn't he come to his rescue? Tiggs always became quiet whenever he asked about Danny.

'I hope Monsieur Danny is OK,' he said quietly to himself.

Unexpectedly, he heard a sound in the hallway below followed by the rush of heavy footsteps on the stairs. Someone began unlocking his door.

Tiggs came in carrying some rope and some black gaffer tape.

'Sorry, mate,' he said. 'We're going to have to tie you up for a short time. We're going into the movie business.'

Chapter 13

Sunita Roy was queuing in the canteen for tea and a sandwich on the morning of Tuesday, 1 November when a voice in a Black Country accent asked, 'Didn't you have time for breakfast this morning?'

She turned round to be greeted by her former boyfriend, DI Tom Vickers. Tall and smartly dressed, Vickers had short brown hair and a wide smile.

'Tom, how great to see you,' she said as she collected her steaming hot drink from the assistant behind the counter. 'You're right. I was a bit rushed this morning.'

'I thought it was you when I came through the door just then,' said her friend. 'Got time for a chat?'

'I don't think the boss will miss me for a few minutes,' she said as she paid the cashier. 'I'll go and grab a table.'

A few minutes later, the pair were happily sitting in a corner of the canteen at St James Street police headquarters, catching up with recent events in their lives.

'Did you do anything for Halloween?' she asked.

'No, just stayed in,' replied Vickers. 'I don't get invited to parties these days.'

He took a sip from his mug of coffee.

'I've just been in to see Niggler,' he explained, using the nickname officers used for their pernickety chief superintendent, Nicola Norris. 'I might be heading back here.'

'Have you had enough of being your own boss?' she asked. For the past three years Vickers had been in charge of a CID team in North Warwickshire.

'No, it's just that she wants me to run a special unit to do with undercover work and it'll mean some extra money,' said Vickers, sipping from his cup of black coffee.

'That sounds very much like the old job you had here,' she said, sounding surprised.

'Not exactly. It's all hush-hush at the moment, so I'd better watch what I say. To be honest, Sunita, I never really settled in Summerstoke. What are you doing with yourself now?'

'Did you know I've split up with Samir? I'm managing quite nicely on my own. I've decorated the flat and I'm currently house-hunting.'

'Are you staying in Warwick?'

'I haven't really decided. I've looked at a four-bedroom detached house in Warwick and tonight I'm going to see a

five-bedroom place in Shawley Green,' she explained with a smile.

'You *are* going up in the world,' he said. 'Actually, I'd already heard you were moving.'

Her smile faded. 'Who told you that?' she demanded.

'I can't remember now. I thought it was common knowledge.'

'Well, you know my uncle Ramit died and left my sister and me some money.'

'Of course. You were nearly drawn into a disastrous Ponzi scheme, weren't you?'

'Yes. I'm glad I was suspicious and took your advice. Well, in the end, I decided to follow the example of my uncle, who made his money by investing in bricks and mortar.'

'Are you going to rent out your current flat, Sunita?'

'I'm not planning to become a landlord like my uncle. I just see property as a safe haven for some of the money I was left in his will. I'm also going to buy a new car. I've nearly run my poor old Peugeot into the ground. The DCI found out at the weekend there was a "For Sale" board outside my flat. He buttonholed me over it.'

'Oh, his son George only lives round the corner, doesn't he?'

'Yes, George mentioned something about it to him and the DCI seemed to think I might be taking a job with West Midlands.'

'You're not, are you?'

'Of course not. I'm happy here. Right now, I'm heavily involved in the Beauvais case.'

'Oh, the missing boy? How's that going?'

She shrugged her shoulders. 'Not as well as we'd like. A camera picked up a black Range Rover – like the one the gang had been using – leaving the Troutbeck Estate. Patrol cars were notified but we lost it. It's a damn nuisance. I went to see the bodyguard's widow on Sunday. She's devastated, of course.'

'Those guys have been behaving like animals. I hope they're caught quickly.'

'So do I.'

'So, tell me more about the car,' he said.

'Well, they used a black Range Rover with a particular number plate when they entered the estate but the car leaving had a different number. We're fairly certain it was the same car, so they'd obviously swapped plates.'

'I expect it'll turn up in a day or two.'

'Yes,' she said. 'Probably burnt out in some remote spot. Anyway, we're going into overdrive today. We're checking garages, empty buildings, bins, the lot for any evidence relating to the gang.'

'I expect the boss is in his element,' said Vickers.

'Coming up with fresh ideas all the time and keeping us on our toes,' she said with a smile.

Vickers sipped more of his coffee before leaning back in his chair.

'Listen, Sunita, I was just wondering if you fancied going out for a meal sometime or maybe a drink.'

'I– I– I'd like that,' she stuttered. 'A meal would be great.'

'Any thoughts on where we might go?'

'I've always loved The Wheatsheaf near Redditch with its dark oak beams and roaring log fire,' she said.

'Yes, we used to go there a lot, back in the day. It would be great to have a meal there. When are you free?'

'That's the big question. I suppose this Friday would be good.'

'Shall I come and pick you up?'

'Oh, Tom,' she said, 'my place is right out of your way. I tell you what, I'll meet you there.'

'I haven't been to The Wheatsheaf since I took you three or four years ago,' he said. 'Listen, I'll give them a call and, if they're still operating as before, I'll book a table.'

She was about to remark that they shouldn't sit too close to the fire when her phone rang.

'It's the boss,' she said as she answered the call.

'Sergeant, where are you?' asked the chief inspector. 'Jean-Jacques has received a text message from a number he didn't recognise. It looks as though it's from the gang that abducted their son.'

Chapter 14

Clutching a wad of leaflets about the missing boy, PC Nina Kaur stood talking patiently to a householder outside their front door. Then she walked back down the garden path, shaking her head.

'No,' the constable told PC Derek Underhill, who was waiting for her on the pavement. 'Another resident who doesn't remember seeing a black Range Rover over the past few days. That must be the tenth blank face this morning.'

Her colleague shrugged. 'Never mind, Nina. I'll do the next one,' he said.

They were one of several teams of uniformed officers who had been asked to visit householders on the Troutbeck Estate in Queensbridge on Tuesday morning. The area comprised more than thirty roads, crescents, avenues, lanes, drives and closes.

Underhill, who was carrying an umbrella since rain was forecast, opened the gate at 27 Grasmere Road. He followed a concrete path beside a lawn strewn with children's toys and rang the bell. At once, a barking poodle appeared in the front window.

'Hello, mate. Is your owner around?' asked the constable, which only seemed to spur the pet into barking even more.

A tubby woman in her thirties in a blue top and jeans came to the door, yelling, 'Stop that noise, Daisy.'

'Police. We're searching for a missing boy,' he explained to the anxious householder, passing her a leaflet.

'No one's mentioned anything to me,' she replied. 'I'll just have a word with my husband. I'll have to shut the door because of the dog.'

A balding man in a T-shirt and jeans appeared and Underhill had to repeat the details.

The man said nothing for a few seconds. Perhaps he was contemplating whether he should assist the police, Underhill thought.

Then he took his visitor by surprise.

'Yes. I've seen a black Range Rover,' said the man.

'Have you? When?' asked the constable.

'I was on my way to the shops in Windermere Drive yesterday morning to get cigarettes. I crossed the road and it came hurtling round the corner. Nearly knocked me over.'

Underhill took out a small, black notebook.

'What time would this have been, sir?'

'Let me think. It must have been about ten thirty. So how old is the kid that's missing?'

'He's sixteen, sir. What sort of speed would he have been travelling at?'

'Must have been doing well over forty. It's a wonder I'm here.'

'You didn't take the car number?'

He shook his head. 'I was too shocked. It took my breath away.'

Underhill paused as he wrote the details down. Then he asked, 'How many people were in the car?'

'No idea. I didn't get a look at them.'

'Did you see what direction it came from?'

'Yeah. He came from the Coniston Road area.'

Underhill, who knew the area well, nodded. 'So, he came from the southern side of the estate?'

'Yes. I guess so,' said the man.

'You've been very helpful,' said Underhill. 'We'll probably come and take a fuller statement from you later. Could I take your name, sir?'

'Merton,' said the man as he retreated inside his house. 'Pat Merton. Hope you find the boy.'

PC Kaur was waiting impatiently for her colleague by the wooden garden gate. When Underhill returned, he quickly explained what he had just been told.

'I suggest we give up here and start calling on houses on the southern part of the estate,' he said. 'I'll send a message to our colleagues as well. This could save us all a lot of time.'

After lunch, Kaur and Underhill spent an hour calling without success at doors along leafy Rydal Avenue as well as checking garages and bin areas. They were close to the edge of the estate and there was only one more street left to try, tranquil Juniper Lane – a motley series of older detached and semi-detached red-brick houses, which had rear gardens overlooking open fields.

Many residents were out or were unable to help. The pair eventually reached number thirty-three and, after moving aside two plastic barriers at the entrance, they made their way up the driveway past a Mercedes.

The red-brick, semi-detached house was being renovated. A side extension to the left was half-built and covered in blue tarpaulin. A thriving blackthorn tree at the bottom of the drive and a thick hedge by the lawn partly screened the property from prying eyes.

'Place looks empty, like next door,' Underhill remarked as he rapped on the partly boarded-up front door.

'They could do with getting the garden sorted out,' Kaur remarked.

As they waited, the faded grey curtains twitched before the face of an overweight, ginger-haired man in his late twenties appeared at the window.

'Hold on,' he shouted.

The officers had to wait several minutes. Then the ginger-haired man, looking slightly flustered, returned to the window. He opened it and leaned out.

'Is there a problem?' he asked in a croaky voice.

'Police. We're looking for a missing boy,' said Underhill, overlooking the man's apparent reluctance to come to the door. He handed him a leaflet. 'You haven't seen someone with a black Range Rover, have you, by any chance?'

The man shook his head.

'Haven't been here long,' he mumbled. 'But haven't seen a Range Rover round here. Tell you what. I'll keep my eyes open. If one turns up, I'll give you a call.'

'That would be great, if you could,' said PC Kaur. 'The number's on the leaflet.'

The two officers left and continued knocking on doors further up the lane.

Chapter 15

Chief Superintendent Nicola Norris peered over her reading glasses as the chief inspector arrived at the door to her spacious second-floor office.

'Gavin, come in,' she said. 'Terrible business at this footballer's place. The assistant chief constable's been calling me non-stop about it. That text you sent to my phone a few minutes ago – is that the entire message received from the gang?'

‘Morning, ma’am!’ Roscoe remarked as he stepped across the beige carpet towards her large oak desk. He drew up a chair. ‘Yes, that’s the entire message.’

Roscoe’s eyes unconsciously dwelt on the photographs of police award ceremonies on the wall behind Norris.

‘If it’s genuine,’ Norris said, ‘and there’s no reason to suspect otherwise, the gang are confirming they have the French boy and will make further contact soon. Is that correct?’

‘Yes, ma’am. The message was received on Mr Beauvais’s phone early this morning. I gather the Kidnap Unit at the National Crime Agency are now becoming involved.’

‘Yes, one of their senior investigators is coming over from their Birmingham office. I trust you’ll afford him every courtesy?’

Roscoe nodded. ‘Of course, ma’am,’ he replied.

‘Kidnappings and ransom demands are extremely challenging for a force like ours and the extra resources they bring can be invaluable.’

Norris, who had neatly combed, mid-length grey hair, moved closer to her desk in her wheelchair, to which she had been confined since being seriously injured in a riding accident seven years earlier.

‘The investigator they’re sending is DI Joseph Parkes. I’ve already spoken to him, and he seems to be fairly up to speed with our operation. He should be arriving here in the next hour or so. Have there been any other developments in the case?’

Roscoe shook his head. ‘Not as yet, ma’am. We’re trying all avenues. There’s a good chance they’re hiding out in the Queensbridge area, but we’ve drawn a blank so far. We’ve been setting up roadblocks.’

‘Good. Well, keep up the good work.’

‘With one person gunned down and one person taken hostage, we know we’re dealing with a ruthless gang who may not have operated on our patch before. DS Roy’s

been going through records, looking at potential suspects. She's had no luck so far. We're trying various approaches.'

'All right, Gavin. Meet up with DI Parkes and see if you and the sergeant can form a good working relationship with him. And please keep me informed of your progress.'

* * *

'Come straight in, Sergeant,' the chief inspector shouted as soon as he returned from his visit to the second floor.

'Have a look at this,' he told Sunita. 'It was sent to the footballer from a mobile phone. I expect they used a burner phone. Underhill called round to see him and obtained a copy for me.'

She carefully studied a text message which Roscoe had converted into a paper document.

> *Mr Beauvais, we've got your boy, Marcel. He is being cared for and he hasn't been harmed. But you must do exactly what we tell you.*
> *Stop dealing with DCI Roscoe and the National Crime Agency if you want to see Marcel alive again. We are watching you and will know at once if this demand is ignored. We will contact you again in the next few days with fresh instructions. We will later today be sending you some proof of Marcel's safekeeping. Remember: We will be watching you. The Matchday Boys.*

When Sunita had finished reading, she glanced across at Roscoe, who was leaning back in his executive chair.

'Who are the Matchday Boys?' she asked.

'Possibly the name or code name for the gang?' Roscoe suggested.

'So what do you think they mean by sending proof of the boy's safekeeping?' she asked.

'I'm not sure,' said Roscoe. 'Perhaps they're going to be sending over a photograph or a video. That would be my guess. Obviously, the family are ignoring the demand not

to involve police. We're already heavily involved. It's important we go over to the manor in a few minutes. They're going to be increasingly worried about their son. We need to reassure them of our full support and that they can have faith in us.'

Sunita stroked her chin. 'That warning that the gang are watching the family is almost certainly an empty threat,' she said, 'but we've got to bear it in mind. For all we know, they may have some way of keeping tabs on the family.'

She handed the text message back to him.

'John Hepworth is in touch with the phone companies,' Roscoe continued. 'I expect they'll do some cell site analysis in a bid to trace the location the message was sent from. You never know. They may even be able to get some results through geo-mapping.'

He stood up and stepped away from his desk.

'Listen, Sergeant. We're about to be joined by a fellow from the NCA's Kidnap Unit, a DI Parkes.' Roscoe peered through the window.

'There's a guy in a white Vauxhall Insignia taking a space in the car park right now and that's probably him. Apparently, he's an expert in the field of child abduction, so we'll no doubt be seeing a lot of him over the next few days.'

Sunita nodded. 'I'll help him in any way I can, sir,' she replied. 'My father always used to warn that one and one can sometimes make eleven.'

'Your father's a wise man,' said Roscoe as he opened his door and peered out across the open-plan office. 'We'll have to hope this new guy fits in well with us.'

Five minutes later, a tall, confident man with receding dark-grey hair came striding past the desks in CID. Over the top of his grey shirt and jeans, he was wearing a black cotton gilet with the letters 'NCA' on the back.

He smiled as he approached. 'You must be DCI Roscoe,' he said with a gravelly voice as he reached Roscoe's open doorway. 'DI Parkes.'

‘Pleased to meet you,’ said the chief inspector, shaking his hand.

Parkes stood and stared at Sunita for a few seconds until Roscoe belatedly introduced them.

‘Sorry. This is my sergeant, DS Roy, a valuable member of my team,’ he said as Parkes awkwardly shook her hand.

Sunita received the impression that Parkes had expected to speak to the chief inspector in private, but, grudgingly, he came inside the room and took a seat beside her.

‘I’ve got a copy of the text,’ said the senior investigator. ‘It all seems fairly straightforward. I take it Mr Beauvais hasn’t sent back any sort of reply yet?’

Roscoe shook his head.

‘Good,’ said Parkes. ‘I suggest we get over there as soon as possible and meet the family. I don’t think there’s any need for you to come with us, Sergeant. The DCI and I will manage just fine.’

‘No,’ insisted Roscoe. ‘DS Roy’s been playing a crucial role in this investigation. She must come with us.’

‘Very well, sir if that’s the way you feel. I’m not sure she is needed. Anyway, shall we make a move? Once we get there, we can arrange for Mr Beauvais to send a reply, confirming he’s seen the message and is prepared to cooperate with the sender. This is the first contact the gang have made and the couple will obviously be extremely upset about it. We need to help them compose their response. It’s all right, I can suggest the appropriate wording.’

The rather overbearing officer paused to gather his breath before adding, ‘On the way over there, perhaps you’d be kind enough to refresh my memory, Chief Inspector, on what actions and tactics you’ve employed so far.’

While they travelled in her boss’s car, Sunita sat quietly in the back and let the two men discuss the words Jean-Jacques Beauvais should use in his reply.

She had a puzzle of her own to resolve. How did the gang leader know so promptly that the National Crime Agency had become involved?

Chapter 16

Trying to put his stepson's disappearance to the back of his mind, Jean-Jacques Beauvais was stretched out on one of three cream-coloured settees in his sumptuous living room. He was making an effort to watch recorded highlights of a football match. Camille was sitting in a nearby armchair, flicking through the pages of a fashion magazine.

'I wish the police would hurry,' she said. 'We've got to reply to that message.'

'*Tout va bien*,' he said. 'They will be here very soon.'

'Are you sure we've done the right thing in telling the police?' she continued. 'Katrina says we need to follow any instructions to the letter.'

Jean-Jacques shook his head. 'It's too late. They're on their way. In any case, the people holding Marcel can't know if we are talking to the police or not talking to the police.'

'I think we should consider calling in a private detective – maybe someone from France.'

Jean-Jacques shrugged his shoulders.

'We have to trust the British police,' he replied. 'I like that chief inspector. He seems to know what he's doing, and Sergeant Roy too. We should let them get on with the job.'

'No,' said Camille. 'Katrina is right, *mon chéri*. We need to get Marcel back as quickly as possible, and I'm always hearing that the British police – they do not always do things the right way. We must hire someone today.'

'I can't agree. We must wait and see what progress the British police are making,' he insisted.

‘Oh, you’re impossible sometimes,’ she yelled, storming out of the room.

He heard her footsteps clattering up the stairs. It was a sound he had become used to since Marcel went missing three days earlier.

The footballer’s mobile beeped. He slipped the slim handset from his pocket and glanced down. A video had arrived from the same phone number as before.

* * *

The chief inspector’s BMW drew up outside the ornamental gates to Upper Norton Manor and he pressed the intercom button. The gates opened and his car glided up the drive.

The family’s timid housekeeper, who was wearing a smart blue tunic, opened the door to the three visitors.

‘Ah, Mrs Willis,’ said Roscoe with a smile.

‘Yes, sir,’ she replied.

‘I hope you’re a lot better now than when I last spoke to you.’

‘Yes, thank you, sir,’ she said, returning his smile. ‘I received good care at the hospital. The family are expecting you. I’ll just take you through to the living room.’

They found Jean-Jacques Beauvais in a bright room which contained a modern gas flame fire and bi-folding patio doors offering spectacular views across the landscaped gardens.

‘Chief Inspector,’ said the footballer, giving a gentle smile as he rose from his seat. ‘Good of you to come.’

‘You know my sergeant, DS Roy, don’t you?’ said Roscoe. ‘And I’d like to introduce DI Parkes from the National Crime Agency, who has great experience of dealing with these situations.’

‘The DCI is very kind,’ said Parkes, shaking hands with Jean-Jacques. He was carrying a small laptop.

‘No Madame Beauvais?’ asked Roscoe.

'I expect she'll be down in a minute,' the footballer replied. 'She's been resting.'

Roscoe and Roy took seats on one of the settees while their colleague placed his laptop on a dining table and sat beside it.

'We've just received a video from the same phone number as before, Chief Inspector,' explained Jean-Jacques. He seemed stoic and focused, trying to keep his emotions in check.

'Oh, would you allow me?' asked Parkes, holding out his hand towards the footballer. After being handed the phone, Parkes switched on his laptop, connected a USB cable and, while Jean-Jacques expressed his growing concerns about Marcel to Roscoe and his sergeant, Parkes downloaded the video.

'We believe the men who took Marcel are only a few miles away,' the chief inspector was saying. 'We've drafted in extra officers and we're optimistic that his release won't take very long–'

Parkes interrupted him. 'Chief Inspector, I'm ready to play the video.'

All four watched intently as the poorly made recording played.

The silent, one-minute clip showed a boy bound with rope, lying on a bed inside a modest bedroom. Two strips of black gaffer tape were wound round his mouth and the back of his head, but there was no mistaking the same distinctive sandy-coloured hair and the slightly tanned face that the detectives had seen in the photographs obtained from Camille. Two medallions could be seen round his neck and a nose ring in his right nostril. His brown eyes betrayed an anxious look.

The hand of an unseen figure appeared, ripping the tape from the boy's mouth. Marcel faced the camera and mouthed the words '*Aidez-moi*' before the screen went blank.

Jean-Jacques had watched the clip in stunned silence. Now the footballer put his hand to his face.

'I must call my wife,' he muttered, dashing from the room. He could then be heard calling, 'Camille! Camille!' from the hallway.

The detectives overheard a brief shouted conversation between the couple before the footballer returned, accompanied by his tearful wife. Camille shook hands with the visitors in turn, but Roscoe was uncertain how much attention she was paying to the introductions. The absence of her son was clearly taking its toll on her. Her face was etched with worry and, when she spoke, there was a tremor in her voice.

'We're very sorry this has happened and will do all we can to return your son to you quickly and safely,' Roscoe assured her.

'That's right,' said Parkes as he unclipped Jean-Jacques's phone and handed the handset back to the footballer. 'Mr Beauvais, you received the text message at 9.05 a.m. today and the video at 12.20 p.m. Is that correct?'

Jean-Jacques nodded. 'That's right,' he said.

'I take it you haven't replied?' said Sunita.

'No. I was waiting to hear from you about what we should do,' said the footballer.

'I think you should reply simply by acknowledging you received their text and video,' said Parkes.

'What is this – acknowledging?' asked Camille, wiping her eyes with a tissue.

'Just confirming you received the message,' Parkes quickly explained.

'*D'accord*,' said Camille, running her fingers absent-mindedly through her long, blonde hair. She strode across the room to the dining table.

'Is this the video?' she asked, pointing to the laptop. 'May I?'

Parkes nodded. 'Sure. Go ahead,' he assured her, handing her the device.

She began watching it while sitting on the settee and could be heard sobbing at seeing her son's plight.

Roscoe was meanwhile concerned about drafting a proper response to the text message.

'Shall we sort out a reply now?' he asked.

'Yes,' said Jean-Jacques. 'What do you suggest?'

'Just keep it simple,' said Parkes. 'I suggest you say, "Thank you for your message and for keeping Marcel safe. We await further instructions."'

'All right,' said the footballer. 'I will send that now.'

Parkes stepped across the room and took the phone from the Frenchman.

'Allow me,' Parkes insisted as he typed out the words. He handed it to Roscoe for his assent.

The chief inspector nodded his approval and Parkes pressed the 'Send' key.

They did not have to wait long. Jean-Jacques received a text back saying, 'Message not delivered'.

'What does this mean, Chief Inspector?' he asked.

'Well, it could mean a number of things,' Roscoe replied. 'It could mean the phone's been turned off, in which case the message will be received when it's next switched on. Or it could mean they've ditched the phone.'

'Ditched? What is this?' asked Jean-Jacques.

'Discarded,' said Roscoe.

Parkes interrupted. 'They may be using what's called a burner phone,' he explained. 'Such a phone can be thrown away after use by criminals to evade detection by police.'

The footballer nodded.

'Don't worry about this,' said Roscoe. 'The people who have your son will almost certainly be contacting you again soon and next time, just as certainly, they'll be demanding money. Have you got the funds available?'

'Yes, of course,' replied Jean-Jacques.

Sunita had been listening quietly throughout the conversation.

'Mr and Mrs Beauvais,' she said. 'I was wondering how you both feel about the video?'

'Very upsetting,' Jean-Jacques admitted. 'Excuse me. I need to speak to my wife in private for a moment.'

The French couple stepped out of the room and could be heard holding a heated conversation in the hallway.

'Clearly the video was taken in a bedroom somewhere,' Parkes told the chief inspector, glancing out of the window at the stone steps and the lawn beyond. 'But there's little in the way of clues. He's dressed in a blue shirt. You can see part of a white sheet. These things don't tell us very much.'

'Yes. It could have been taken anywhere,' Sunita agreed. 'We know the room has a modern double-glazed window with the very latest kind of handle, and it has a blue, striped window blind like those sold at the Mondales department store in Queensbridge.'

'Very well observed, Sergeant,' said the chief inspector. 'Anything else?'

'Only the pizza box,' she replied.

'What pizza box?' asked Parkes.

'Just at the bottom of the video we can see a corner of a cardboard pizza box decorated with pink spots. The only shop in that corner of Warwickshire that serves pizzas in that kind of box is the Pink Palace Pizza Company, which is close to the Troutbeck Estate.'

Sunita glanced round at everyone in the room. The chief inspector was full of admiration for her keen perception, but Parkes was unimpressed.

'Don't know how important any of that is,' he said dismissively. 'People have to eat.'

As the couple resumed their seats, Parkes turned to Jean-Jacques. 'I suggest you wait for an hour or two and then send your message again to the gang. Let us know later if you're still having problems.'

'*Certainement.* But I must mention something, if you please,' said the footballer.

'Of course,' said Parkes.

'We are so desperate in finding our son that we are looking to hire a private detective from France,' he said.

'I wouldn't recommend that,' said Parkes. 'That could only make the investigation more complicated.'

'Added to that,' said Roscoe, 'a French investigator who's unfamiliar with the Midlands, together with our language, culture and legal procedures, would find it a struggle. Please leave it to us. We know the kind of men we're dealing with. We know the territory where they're operating. We're confident that it won't be long before your son is safely back with you again.'

Jean-Jacques leaned back on the settee.

'You say this,' he said, 'but it is now three days since Marcel was taken. Apart from this phone message and video, nothing's changed. You think Marcel may be in Queensbridge, but you don't know that for certain. In France, we would have had a big meeting with the press. Our boy would have been seen on television and in the newspapers.'

Parkes nodded. 'We hear what you're saying, but a decision's been taken at senior level to maintain a news blackout for now. This means details of Marcel's abduction won't be reported in the national newspapers or on TV until such time that we consider it appropriate. News reports can make the situation more complicated. The ransom demanded can be driven up. Victims' families can face extra pressure. Certain comments in the media could cause the abductors to act irrationally.'

'The inspector's right,' added Roscoe. 'We've publicised Marcel's disappearance only in the local area, where we firmly believe him to be. The police locally have issued leaflets bearing Marcel's photograph and posters have been put up. Our incident room at headquarters is receiving calls all the time.'

While this conversation had been going on, Sunita had been watching Camille's behaviour. She had been shaking

her head and muttering some words in French repeatedly since viewing the video.

Sunita detected the words, '*Ce n'est pas mon fils.*'

The chief inspector tapped her on the arm. 'What's she saying?' he asked his sergeant.

'She's saying the boy in the video isn't her son,' Sunita replied.

Chapter 17

Someone was unlocking the door and calling his name. Marcel Dubois opened his eyes and stared across the cold, comfortless room. For a brief moment, he wondered if the police had finally come to rescue him. Then he heard Tigworth's voice, which brought him down to earth.

'Get dressed,' his visitor demanded. 'We're moving.'

The boy placed his arm on his forehead and tried to focus his eyes.

'*Quoi?* Moving where?' he asked.

'Never you mind,' came the reply. 'Get dressed. We're going in ten minutes.'

As Marcel put on a fresh check shirt and jeans the gang had found for him, he could hear the men bustling about downstairs. Every now and then, he would hear one of them shout, 'Get a move on,' or 'Can you hurry up?'

After a few minutes, Tigworth returned.

'Can I eat?' asked Marcel.

'You'll have to wait. We're in a hurry,' the man explained. 'I'll get you something when we get to the new place.'

Marcel noticed his visitor had the brown hood in his hand that had been used to cover his head before, along with some rope.

‘Sorry, mate,’ said Tigworth. ‘Got to do this to you again.’

Shortly afterwards, with his left arm gripped tightly, Marcel felt himself being led to the top of the stairs and escorted down. After walking forward a few feet, he felt a cold breeze and, for the first time in days, he stepped out into the fresh air. He was then pushed through the open rear door of a car which he knew was a Mercedes. The string around his hood had loosened and he caught a glimpse of the car firm’s logo on the wheel.

Within minutes, they were off, at first bumping along an uneven track and then speeding up as the road surface improved. As they travelled, Marcel listened to the men. He knew now there were three – Tigworth, who spoke with a soft voice; a man always moaning who had a slightly croaky, raspy way of speaking; and a man who appeared to be in charge. This third person had a deeper voice, which suggested he might be a well-built man.

‘How did you find this place?’ he overheard Tigworth asking.

‘I didn’t. The boss found it,’ said the man in charge. ‘I don’t want to say more in case the kid’s listening.’

After three quarters of an hour and what seemed like a distance of more than thirty kilometres, Marcel felt the vehicle draw to a halt.

‘This is the place,’ he heard the man in charge announce.

‘It’ll be much safer here,’ said one of the others. ‘This is the bloody middle of nowhere.’

‘I know. It’s ideal, ain’t it?’ the man in charge admitted. ‘I’ll go and open the gates.’

Marcel heard someone get out of the car and return shortly afterwards.

‘Here we are, mate,’ Tigworth shouted. ‘This is your new gaff. You’ll like it here.’

‘Where are we?’ asked the boy.

‘Don’t you worry. Somewhere safe,’ came the reply.

‘Shut up,’ snapped the man in charge. ‘You’re getting too friendly with the boy. I’ve warned you about that.’

The car moved off again – this time at a slower rate. It rocked from side to side on uneven ground before stopping for a second time moments later. The driver cut the engine and the doors opened.

‘Here you are, mate,’ one of the men told Marcel. He felt two of them hauling him out of the vehicle by the arms and helping him gain his footing on the ground.

He could see his feet. He was standing on a muddy, brick-paved yard. A slight smell of manure told him it might be a farmyard. This was confirmed when he pulled the hood up a little and realised he was surrounded by agricultural buildings.

At once, he feared he was to be locked up in a cowshed or barn, but instead he was led over a stone step and through the door of what appeared to be a farmhouse kitchen. After being guided along a corridor and escorted upstairs, his escort pulled off the hood. Marcel had to blink while his eyes gradually became accustomed to the brightness of the winter’s day.

He found himself in a dingy, first-floor bedroom not dissimilar in size to the one in Juniper Lane. He stepped across the shabby green carpet and glanced around. It had magnolia-coloured walls which needed decorating and contained a bed, a wardrobe and a chest of drawers. The wooden-framed window overlooked fields. The Nintendo and television were on the carpet, waiting to be set up.

‘All right, mate?’ said Tigworth from behind his facemask. ‘I’ll go and get you something to drink now.’

* * *

A few minutes passed and Tigworth returned with a fizzy drink for Marcel and unlocked the bedroom door. But he was shocked to find Marcel moving in a bizarre manner in the centre of the room. He appeared to be under hypnosis and spun round several times in a circle

like a whirling dervish. The man was mystified and frightened. He had never witnessed anything like this before. Within seconds, Marcel had slumped onto the multi-coloured carpet and his whole body was shaking uncontrollably. Blood was seeping from his mouth.

Tigworth ran in panic from the bedroom.

'Oh my God!' he cried. 'Come quick! Something's happening to the boy.'

His tall, muscular companion sprinted along the corridor towards him.

'What's going on?' O'Shane demanded after attaching a mask to his lower face.

'I don't know. Look at him.'

They both peered into the room.

'Don't worry. He's having a seizure,' said O'Shane. 'The main thing is to make sure he's comfortable and put part of a cloth or handkerchief between his teeth to stop him biting his tongue.'

'I think it might be too late for that, mate,' said Tigworth. 'There's already some blood.'

'Leave him. He'll be fine,' the second man insisted.

Tigworth remained highly agitated. 'But what is it the boy's got?' he asked. 'What's wrong with him?'

'It's an epileptic fit, mate,' his companion explained. 'Haven't you seen one before?'

He shook his head.

'He'll come round in a minute and won't remember a bloody thing.'

'I don't like this,' Tigworth remarked as Marcel's convulsions continued. 'I wish I'd never been involved in this now. You told me we'd be robbing an empty house. But this job's turning into a nightmare.'

'Pull yourself together,' said the second man. 'The lad will be all right. He should have told us he was an epileptic. We'd have been better prepared for it. Don't worry. My sister-in-law's always having fits.'

‘It’s like the devil’s got in him,’ said Tigworth. ‘I wish I’d never got involved.’

‘Stop going on about it,’ his companion demanded as Marcel’s convulsions became less erratic. ‘Look. The boy’s coming round now.’

While they watched, the twitching came to a stop. Marcel glanced over to the doorway, where the pair were standing. Then, slowly, he tried to haul himself to his feet. The pair gently lifted him by the arms and sat him on the bed.

‘Are you all right?’ asked Tigworth, staring into the French boy’s eyes.

‘Yes. I think so,’ Marcel replied. ‘What happened?’

‘You had a fit, mate,’ O’Shane explained.

‘Yeah, you didn’t half get me worried,’ said Tigworth. ‘You were dancing round the floor like you was in a trance and then you fell down.’

‘*Mon Dieu*,’ said Marcel. ‘*J’ai eu une crise d’épilepsie*.’

The second man stood back and folded his arms.

‘You’re an epileptic, ain’t you, mate? Where’s your medicine for it?’ he asked.

Marcel nodded. ‘I stopped the medicine. I thought I was better.’

‘When did you last have a seizure?’

‘What is this word – seizure?’

‘A fit.’

‘Three years ago I had a fit,’ said Marcel.

‘All right, mate,’ the boy was told. ‘Take it easy for a while. Just lie on your bed.’

He turned to his accomplice. ‘Cheer up, Tiggs. He’s going to be all right now. Let’s go and get the boy some food. He must be starving.’

Chapter 18

Sunita Roy looked up as she heard DC Brett Dawson arrive in the CID office, breathless and flustered.

'Morning, Sarge,' he said, slipping off his coat and searching for a hanger. 'I've been over to the pizza shop, as you asked, and collected the disks from the CCTV.'

She turned round in her chair. 'Good. What dates are they for?'

'Last three days of October.'

'Great,' she said. 'That's exactly what we want. You make a start and I'll come and join you in a minute. Remember, we're interested in men in their late twenties.'

Dawson sat down at a nearby desk where there was a large monitor and began scanning the footage.

'By the way, Sarge,' he said after a few minutes, 'how did you know the pizza box in the video came from Pink Palace?'

'Do you remember earlier this year we had to interview a suspect in Queensbridge called Logan Price? The pizza shop is close to where he lived. Afterwards I called in for a pizza and I've been back a few times since. One of their boxes with pink spots was in the video.'

'I'd call that well-spotted, Sarge,' he said.

'Your jokes don't get any better,' she remarked.

'Sarge, I heard a strange rumour yesterday that the kidnappers might have taken the wrong boy.'

'Where did you hear that?'

'Someone was talking about it in the canteen.'

'Do you remember who?'

'I don't want to get anyone into trouble, Sarge.'

Sunita stood up and stepped towards him. ‘All that happened was that the boy’s mother was shocked when she saw the video sent by the kidnappers. While Marcel was in town on Saturday with Danny Jukes, he had his hair cut really short. He had cat scratches shaved on each side of his head.’

‘Oh, that’s a bit of a craze among kids,’ said Dawson. ‘My nephew wants them done but my sister’s said no.’

‘Camille Beauvais said no as well. But that didn’t stop the lad,’ she said with a smile. ‘Marcel was on his first outing in England without his parents and obviously convinced Danny Jukes, the bodyguard, to let him go and have his hair cut before they went to the cinema. He also went to a shop and had his nose pierced and a ring inserted.’

‘So even his own mother didn’t recognise him?’ said Dawson with a laugh.

‘Exactly. You can imagine how the boss and I reacted when she started mumbling, “It’s not my son. It’s not my son.” She went onto say – in French – that their son must be dead and that the gang must have murdered him. She became hysterical and this upset her husband as well. It took a few minutes for me to calm them both down. Then we studied the video with them again and she realised it was her son after all.’

‘She must have been really distraught at seeing the boy on film,’ said Dawson. ‘People who are in an emotional turmoil tend not to think straight.’

Sunita nodded.

‘We’re now planning to use video stills so our publicity pictures are more accurate,’ she said.

‘Has this lad enrolled at a school round here?’ asked Dawson.

‘Yes. He’s just started at a private one, Biddington Hall School,’ said Sunita.

‘They may not take to him having a nose ring and a dodgy haircut,’ said Dawson. Then he drew a quick breath.

‘Hey, Sarge. How about this guy?’ he asked. ‘He’s leaving the shop around seven.’

Sunita leaned over his shoulder and peered at the black-and-white image of a stocky man in jeans strolling from the doorway clutching a pizza box. He weaved his way through a group of people before heading in the direction of the Troutbeck Estate.

‘He looks a likely candidate,’ she said. ‘Print off a few images which best show his face and we’ll see if we can identify him. Carry on searching. You might find others.’

But as the day went on, Dawson failed to find any other men in their late twenties that matched the sketchy details they had for the three suspects.

Sunita studied the series of blown-up photographs taken from the shop’s camera.

‘We’re lucky,’ she said. ‘These pictures are fairly clear. We’ll try a facial search on the database and see if we can pick this guy out.’

Half an hour later, she excitedly tapped on the door of the chief inspector’s room. ‘Sir, I’ve made some progress,’ she announced excitedly.

‘You’d better come in and tell me about it,’ he said.

She dropped four photographs of the pizza customer onto his desk.

Roscoe leaned forward in his executive chair and studied them closely.

‘Doesn’t look familiar,’ he muttered.

‘We found this guy on CCTV outside the pizza shop in Worcester Road,’ she explained. ‘He left the shop at around ten past seven on Saturday evening and he’s come up on the database as Wayne Francis Jordan. Date of birth: 10 May 1994. No fixed abode. He’s got a long list of antecedents stretching back to his juvenile years. His most recent offences have included burglary, aggravated burglary, possession of a firearm and a serious assault on an ex-girlfriend.’

‘Good work, Sergeant,’ Roscoe replied. ‘So there’s no address for him?’

‘No, sir, but I’ve found his mother’s details – Amy Barton, 45 Forester’s Close, Droitwich. I’ve sent Dawson round there.’

‘Good. We now need to go through the files, check co-defendants and any associates. I’ll have a word with Pat Clancy and see if he can make some inquiries among his underworld contacts.’

* * *

The chief inspector was feeling tired by the time he had made his twenty-five-mile journey through the south Birmingham suburbs and reached his home on the outskirts of Queensbridge.

It had been an arduous four days since Marcel Dubois was abducted. He knew the force faced even greater challenges in the coming days until the kidnapping was resolved, one way or the other.

He finally drove down the narrow, tree-lined lane that led to his home, The Willows, and parked in his garage. As he walked past the leaded-light windows, he noticed his wife, Helen, standing by the open front door.

‘Hello, darling,’ he said, kissing her on the cheek as the aroma of roasted chicken wafted from the kitchen.

‘You look absolutely whacked,’ she said as they stepped into the hallway.

‘I am,’ he admitted. He entered the dual-aspect living room and slumped down on their leather settee.

At that moment, he heard their landline phone ringing.

‘It’s all right. I’ll get it,’ said Helen, hurrying into the hall.

‘I’ll just get him,’ she said after a brief conversation.

‘Joseph Parkes,’ she announced from the doorway before making her way into the kitchen.

Roscoe picked up the handset from the hall table.

Parkes spoke in a calm, crisp voice. 'Have you heard about the ransom demand, sir?' he asked.

'No, I haven't,' he replied.

'The gang have asked the couple for two million pounds to be paid in cryptocurrency,' he said. 'The text message was signed as being from the Matchday Boys, as before. I've gone to the house to talk to them about it. I thought I'd inform you.'

'Very good of you,' said Roscoe. 'I'm afraid I'm not very familiar with the world of cryptocurrency.'

'That's why I thought you'd want me to handle this, sir. I'm quite used to dealing with these sorts of demands. They want the payment made through Monero.'

'What's that exactly?' Roscoe asked.

'It's a currency like Bitcoin, but some individuals prefer using it because it obscures the source and the destination of payments. Of course, Beauvais is willing to pay the money. The trouble is, even if the payment's made, there's no guarantee the boy will be released alive.'

Chapter 19

A burly man in a white Ford Transit van found a parking space close to Queensbridge police station in the town's High Street late on Friday afternoon. He climbed the stone steps and pushed open the door of the red-brick building. He was already in a bad temper and was further irritated by having to wait while the constable at the counter dealt with a motorist accused of a minor traffic offence.

Finally, the motorist left and the young constable beckoned him forward.

'How can I help you, sir?' the constable asked.

'I've come to report a break-in,' the visitor explained.

'Whereabouts?' said the fair-haired constable.

'At a place I'm doing up on the Troutbeck Estate,' he replied. 'Looks like I've had squatters in. It's looking like a tip.'

The constable frowned. 'I'll just get someone to come and speak to you,' he said, reaching for the phone on his desk. 'What's your name, sir?'

'Ridley,' said the man. 'Jeff Ridley.'

A few minutes later, Derek Underhill emerged from a side door.

'Mr Ridley? Would you come with me?' asked the officer.

He led Ridley into a brightly lit interview room and invited him to take a seat while he shut the door.

'I'm PC Underhill. How can I help?' he asked, sitting down on the opposite side of a small table.

'I bought a house at auction and I've been waiting for the funds to do it up,' Ridley explained.

'You're a builder?' asked Underhill.

'That's right,' said Ridley. 'I've been on a roofing job but I finished earlier than expected, so I thought I'd go and check on my house. But some bastard's broken in and there are signs that a load of people have been staying there.'

'Where is this place?'

'In Queensbridge. They've been using electricity and water and, knowing my luck, the companies are going to be chasing me for payment.'

Underhill shrugged his shoulders. 'Are the squatters still on the premises?'

'No.'

'Do you know where they are now?'

'Haven't got a clue. I've no idea who they are either.'

'I'm afraid I don't think there's much I'm going to be able to do to help you,' said the constable. 'If they were still there now and trespassing, maybe we could go and arrest them. But if they've been and gone…'

'So you can't do anything to help me. Is that what you're saying?' said Ridley. 'Typical of the police these days.'

Underhill was determined to maintain his composure.

'We always do the best we can, sir,' he insisted. 'Our aim is to serve the public, but in this case, unfortunately, our hands are tied. If they come back, let us know and we'll see if there's anything we can do then.'

Underhill stood up with a faint smile and moved towards the door. 'Out of interest, where exactly is your house?' he asked.

'It's on the Troutbeck Estate,' said Ridley.

Underhill's smile quickly vanished.

'Troutbeck?' he said. 'What street?'

'Juniper Lane,' replied Ridley. 'My house is number thirty-three.'

Underhill resumed his seat and gestured for Ridley to do the same.

'That puts a different complexion on it,' said the constable.

'How do you mean?' asked the builder.

'Well, because of our ongoing investigation involving the missing boy.' He took a small notebook and pen from his trouser pocket.

Ridley stroked his chin. 'I've heard something about a missing French boy. Is that what you mean? You lot were checking vehicles.'

'Yes. That's right,' said Underhill. 'One possibility we've been looking at is that he may have been held at a house or flat on the Troutbeck. So your report that some strangers have been staying in your house is of obvious interest. Number thirty-three Juniper Lane, you say?'

Ridley nodded as Underhill jotted down the address.

'So you visited your house today,' the constable continued. 'Was that for the first time in a while?'

'That's right,' said Ridley. 'It's been empty since August. I've just been getting some money together. See?'

‘Hold on a minute,’ said Underhill, gazing out of the window at traffic travelling along the High Street. ‘I know Juniper Lane fairly well. Does your house have plastic safety barriers blocking the entrance?’

‘Yes. You’ve got it.’

‘Grey curtains and an overgrown garden.’

‘Yeah, well, as I say…’

‘You’ve been waiting for the money,’ said Underhill.

‘How do you know my house?’

‘Officers, including myself, have been going door-to-door round the estate. I remember this house. There was a black Mercedes parked by the front door.’

Ridley shrugged his shoulders. ‘Nothing to do with me, if there was,’ he said.

‘What time did you go round there today?’

‘Just now,’ replied the builder. ‘About four thirty.’

‘You just walked in and looked around?’

‘No. I had to force the door. The cheeky bastards had changed the locks.’

‘It’s definitely your house?’

‘Yes. Of course. I can bring you the solicitor’s letters if you like. I know they broke in. There was a smashed window in the kitchen and the sods had left an electric fire on. Looks like they bypassed the meter. There were a couple of mattresses on the floor as well.’

‘You’ve put your own lock on now?’

‘Not yet, but I’ve made it secure.’

‘Well, Mr Ridley, I don’t quite know how to tell you this,’ Underhill said with a broad smile, ‘but please don’t go inside the place for the moment. There’s a chance your house may have been used as a hideout for the gang who kidnapped the boy. They may well have kept the boy prisoner there, so we wouldn’t want you to go inside. You might accidentally destroy evidence. I’m going to have to call headquarters and report what’s happened. I imagine they’ll send a SOCO team round there.’

‘A SOCO team?’

Underhill leaped up and nodded excitedly. 'Yes. Scenes-of-crime officers. A search of your house could lead to the vital evidence we need to find the boy.'

* * *

DI Tom Vickers gave Sunita Roy a peck on the cheek after stepping out of his car and greeting her beside her vehicle outside the roadside pub near Redditch. She reached up and kissed him back before grasping his hand.

'The place doesn't seem to have changed at all since we were last here,' she said with a smile as they entered The Wheatsheaf Inn.

The interior was just as Sunita had remembered it. There were flagstone floors, low ceilings with dark oak beams and wood panelling. At the heart of the gastropub stood a roaring log fire.

A barman in a white shirt and tie showed them to a quiet corner and fetched menus. He lit a candle in the middle of their table.

'Shall we have a bottle of chardonnay like before?' he asked when they had taken their seats.

'Fancy you remembering that,' she said with a shy smile. 'Yes. Let's.'

Once the wine had been served, she ordered grilled salmon while he opted for roast chicken. Vickers, who was six years older than her and wearing a smart suit, gazed at her affectionately.

'How's the house-hunting?' he asked.

'I looked over a five-bedroom place on Tuesday night. It had huge rooms and a massive garden but I wondered if it was just too big for me.'

'Maybe. Any news on the missing teenager?' he asked.

'We've got a steer on one of the kidnappers, Wayne Jordan,' she replied. 'Dawson's trying to see the mother, although she hasn't been around for a day or two. I've also just had a call from the DCI to say we might have a lead on the gang's hideout.'

'That's great,' he said.

'I feel we're getting nearer to finding the boy now. I just feel so sorry for the whole Beauvais family. They've only been in the UK for a few weeks and this happens.'

'The money these footballers earn is obviously the big attraction,' Vickers remarked. 'On top of that, they never get to lead quiet lives, keeping under the radar. The location of their homes is often featured on social media and everyone knows they're away most Saturdays.'

After their meal, they ordered coffees.

'I'm glad I asked you out,' he confessed, reaching across the table and patting her hand. 'I've missed you, you know.'

He gazed into her dark eyes and she smiled.

'I've missed you too,' she said. 'And if you hadn't remained so close to your ex-wife, our lives could have been so different.'

He frowned. 'As I told you four years ago, we were going through a divorce. I merely let her stay at my house for a few days after her boyfriend threw her out. I was just doing the decent thing, giving her a roof over her head until she could move in with her sister.'

'I lost my trust in you at that point, Tom,' Sunita said. 'You still seemed to be tied to her.'

Vickers sighed. 'I wish you'd had more patience. I was completely over my wife and only wanted to be with you.'

She shook her head. 'Tom, you have to try and see it from my position. You were seen by one of our colleagues helping your wife into a doctor's surgery.'

He grimaced. 'She'd sprained her ankle. She needed treatment and she couldn't very well walk in unaided. We know all this. I don't know why you're bringing it up again. You'd think after four years you'd have let it go.'

Sunita took a sip of her coffee. 'I was very upset at the time, Tom,' she said. Her hurt pride showed in her eyes.

'I know,' he said in an exasperated tone. 'Look, I'm really sorry about what happened. I was never going to get

back with my wife. That part of my life was well and truly over. I wanted to make a fresh start and thought that maybe we could have made a go of things.'

'I was so upset when I heard you'd been helping her into the surgery.'

Vickers, who had not touched his coffee, stood up. 'I've had enough,' he said. 'I'm going to the bar to pay the bill and then I'm leaving.'

'Why, Tom?' she asked, looking startled.

'Because it's quite obvious you're never going to give me a chance to show how much you mean to me. I've always loved you, Sunita, from the moment we first met and that will never change. That year we spent together was the greatest time of my life. I'd hoped we might be able to start again. But I can see that's not going to be possible.'

He stormed off.

Chapter 20

While dark clouds drifted ominously overhead, Sunita drove onto the Troutbeck Estate just before nine o'clock on Saturday morning. Juniper Lane was too narrow for vehicles to be able to park in the street, so she found a place to leave her car in nearby Coniston Road. As a light rain began to fall, she retrieved her small umbrella from the back seat and locked the vehicle.

She had only taken a few steps towards the lane when the chief inspector arrived and parked directly behind her.

'Bit of luck that builder coming forward, Sergeant,' he said as he opened his own umbrella and accompanied her along the street.

'Yes, sir,' she replied. 'Just a shame we couldn't have caught them in time before they moved on. Underhill said it looks like they flew into a panic, judging by the state they left the house in. With any luck this morning, we'll find the room where the video was filmed.'

'You look tired this morning,' he said as they entered Juniper Lane.

'Didn't get much sleep last night, sir,' she admitted.

She was pleased when he didn't probe her any further about the reason behind her lost sleep. She had been extremely upset at the way the conversation in the pub between her and Tom Vickers had culminated in an argument. But she was determined, for the moment, to try to forget about him and focus on the job.

By the time they reached the entrance to number thirty-three, the rain had stopped. They found the front door was open and a small team of police staff were scurrying around in white suits, overshoes, masks and gloves.

Roscoe asked one of them if Dr Ling was available. Seconds later, the senior forensic officer emerged in the doorway, peering at them over a pair of wire-framed glasses.

'Good morning, sir,' she said. 'Morning, Sergeant. Unfortunately, it looks like one of the gang's been around wiping finger-marks off doors, the TV screen, plates and dishes and all smooth surfaces. But we've had some luck. We've got a fingerprint off the mirror in one of the bedrooms. We've also found a discarded beer can, which may give us a trace of DNA.'

'Excellent,' said Roscoe. 'My sergeant and I are eager to look at the bedrooms.'

'Come right in,' she said. 'We've been here since late yesterday and we're nearly finished.'

Roscoe stepped into the house cautiously, recognising some of the floorboards were rotten and some missing. There was a threadbare carpet in the front room but only bare floorboards in the hall. Curtains, where they existed,

were worn and faded. Old clothes, litter, builders' rubble, empty pizza boxes and items of mail were strewn across the floor.

The pair climbed the uncarpeted stairs and began inspecting the bedrooms. They soon found themselves in the back bedroom, where a forensic expert in white overalls was examining the single wardrobe and realised at once that the filming had been carried out there.

They recognised the window, the blue striped blind and the edge of the cream-coloured mattress. The pizza box that had led to them identifying Wayne Jordan was no longer there.

'I've nearly finished,' remarked the female technician while running a brush over the wardrobe's internal mirror.

Sunita glanced across the room towards her.

'I think you might have overlooked something,' she said.

'How do you mean?' asked the woman.

Sunita had crouched down and was inspecting the rug beside the bed.

'What've you found, Sergeant?' asked Roscoe, who was standing in the doorway.

It was clear to her there was something under the mat causing an almost imperceptible bulge. She lifted the corner of the floor covering and exposed a folded sheet of paper. 'I think it's a letter,' she said.

'I don't know how that was missed,' the technician muttered. 'A colleague was meant to be overseeing that part of the room.'

The sergeant unfolded the paper and then placed it on the window ledge, where she carefully studied it.

'It looks like a torn scrap of fish-and-chip paper,' Roscoe observed, joining her by the window as the technician left.

'Yes. It's a letter in French from Marcel. He's written it in pencil to his mother. I'll have a go at translating it.'

She spent a minute studying the words, trying to recall her classroom French, before translating it out loud.

My dearest, darling mother. I appreciate this is a worrying time for you and Papa Jean-Jacques. Don't be anxious about me, if you please. I am in good health. The men are looking after me correctly. I have enough food and drink and I have a Nintendo and television.

I am in a house somewhere. I'm not sure where, but it took between twenty minutes and half an hour approximately for us to travel here from our house. So I'm guessing I'm not far away. They put something over my head, so I could not see where we were going.

My room is upstairs at the back of the house. I can see fields from my window. I sometimes see sheep. Some nights I'm watching fireworks.

I'm thinking there are three men altogether. Only one of them visits me, the man with the beard. He is called Tiggs. He is older than me but he is a gamer like me.

I can hear the voices of the men rising up from downstairs but I haven't seen them. I heard the men downstairs saying they have obtained another car, a Mercedes.

I guess the men want money. So please say yes to whatever they ask. Your most devoted child is desperate to see you again. With much affection, Your adoring son, Marcel.

She turned to the chief inspector. 'What do you think, sir?'

'Clever boy,' said Roscoe. 'Thoughtful boy. He knows his parents will be worried. He wanted to reassure them he's all right. So he's written a letter and hidden it, hoping it'll be found and passed on.'

'You're right, sir. He's also very brave,' she said. 'Reading between the lines, he's desperate to get away from his captors and get home, but he doesn't want to let his mother see that. He wants to ease her fears. I think I should take a copy of this letter round to the Beauvais couple.'

'Good idea,' said Roscoe, 'but unfortunately none of this really helps us to locate him.'

Sunita nodded. 'We at least know the name of one of the men now, sir. It's Tiggs.'

'Sounds like a nickname,' muttered Roscoe.

'This could have been written at any time over the past few days,' said Sunita. 'He wrote it and concealed it here – knowing, if he'd left it in a prominent place, the men would have found it.'

Roscoe smiled. 'He's mentioned the gang have got a Mercedes. That's of some help. Derek Underhill remembers a black Mercedes outside this house when they were doing the house-to-house. A car like that was caught on camera leaving the estate at just before ten o'clock on Wednesday morning. It was heading in the Worcester direction.'

'They might have switched cars again since then,' said Sunita.

'The gang don't seem to have any shortage of addresses they can go to,' Roscoe remarked.

Chapter 21

Despite feeling unwell after attending a fireworks party with his girlfriend the night before, DC Brett Dawson managed to haul himself out of bed just after half past eight on Saturday morning. He showered and dressed and enjoyed a light breakfast before taking some painkillers for his nagging headache.

A few minutes after nine, he clambered into his red Ford Focus and set off from Birmingham for the Worcestershire spa town of Droitwich. Forester's Close consisted of a row of three-storey townhouses that lay

among a maze of streets on the northern side of the town. He had called round twice before and profoundly hoped Wayne Jordan's mother would now be at home.

The detective locked his car outside the woman's address and dashed through a haze of rain to the front door.

Number forty-five appeared to be the most neglected house in the quiet cul-de-sac. An old van was parked on the driveway beside a narrow, poorly tended lawn.

Shivering beneath a porch canopy, Dawson pressed the doorbell and waited. A dog began to bark before a woman drew back the door.

'Mrs Barton?' he asked, producing his warrant card. 'Heart of England Police. DC Dawson.'

The plump woman in her mid-fifties had grey, untidy hair and eyed him suspiciously. 'What's this about?'

'You're the mother of Wayne Jordan, we believe.'

As soon as the words passed his lips, a man in a string vest and dark trousers appeared behind her in the hallway, coughing and spluttering.

'He doesn't live here no more,' he shouted. 'He's nothing to do with us. Close the door, Amy.'

Amy looked uncertain. She glanced over her shoulder at the man behind her.

'It's police, Steve,' she explained. Turning to Dawson, she whispered, 'My husband.'

'I won't take up much of your time,' Dawson assured them, leaning with his hand on the doorpost. 'Just need to find out a little bit about Wayne's current life.'

'You won't take up none of our time,' Steve retorted. 'We don't know nothing about his current life, so I suggest you leave.'

'He's right. We don't have no information,' said Amy in a low voice.

'What's the little toerag done now anyway?' asked Steve.

'We believe he might have been involved in a crime that we're currently investigating,' Dawson said. 'I'm sorry if this is a bad time or if it's upsetting for you to talk,' he added.

Amy glanced at her husband again.

'Steve, if it's only a few questions, I think we should invite him in.'

Dawson, sensing her attitude was softening, said, 'It's really only a few questions and it might help solve a crime that's affecting a good number of people.'

'All right. Let him in,' snapped Steve. Then, staring into the visitor's face, he added, 'So long as you realise her wayward son ain't nothing to do with us no more.'

Dawson noticed a smell of damp laundry as he followed the couple through their narrow hallway. He was invited to sit on a settee in the living room, where clothes were airing on racks.

A German shepherd barked as soon as it saw him. The dog climbed down from the settee and sniffed the visitor's clothes.

'Is your dog all right?' asked Dawson, looking cautiously at the pet.

'You're not scared of dogs, are you?' asked Steve, a tall, balding man with a stern expression. 'Don't worry about Teddy. He won't hurt you.'

'He doesn't know me, you see,' said Dawson.

The dog growled and watched as the newcomer sat down.

'His bark's worse than his bite,' said Amy.

'But not by much,' said her husband before bursting into peals of laughter, followed by more coughing. The dog continued growling until finally Amy locked her pet in another room.

Dawson felt more comfortable as he took out his notebook and asked, 'When did you last see Wayne, Mrs Barton?'

'I can honestly say I haven't seen him in three years,' she said, settling down in a nearby armchair.

'The blighter's been nothing but trouble to his mother all her life,' said her husband, clutching the end of a clothes rack.

'That's going a little far, Steve,' Amy insisted. 'He used to be a good lad before we moved from Basingstoke but, up here, he fell in with the wrong crowd.'

'I suppose you know about all his previous, do you?' asked Steve. 'Burglary, aggravated burglary…'

'You don't need to go on, Steve,' said his wife.

'You know what the aggravated burglary involved, do you?' he continued, ignoring his wife's entreaties. 'He and a couple of mates broke into an old man's house while he was at home. They beat him up, tied him up and stabbed his cat to death in front of his eyes. Then they stole all his life savings and war medals.'

Dawson shook his head. 'That's absolutely terrible,' he said, jotting a few words in his book.

'So what's this crime you're investigating then?' asked Amy leaning forward in her chair.

'The burglary last weekend in Norton Prior in which a man was shot dead,' Dawson replied.

'Oh, my God. I hope Wayne wasn't involved with that,' she said.

'Have you spoken to him recently?' asked Dawson.

'No. There's been no contact whatsoever,' she said.

'I've barred him from the house,' her husband explained. 'We don't want nothing more to do with him. He just brings trouble wherever he goes and we don't want it brought here. So, if you've finished asking your questions, young man…'

Dawson glanced down at his notebook and then looked at Amy.

'Just a few more questions. Do you know where he's living now?' he asked.

'Not for certain, I'm afraid,' she replied. 'But I've picked up from gossip that he may be in Queensbridge or somewhere around there. Sometime last year he also spent some time staying with friends in Cheshire.'

'And who are his associates?' asked Dawson. 'Any idea?'

'That changes all the time,' she said.

Her husband interrupted. 'He's spent some time staying over in Bromsgrove. He's got a lot of pals round there. If it helps, I remember one guy he used to hang around with had a beard and was called Lewis. I got the impression they might be close mates.'

'Any idea where…' asked Dawson.

'Where Lewis might be? No. Somewhere in Worcestershire, I'd guess.'

'Did you ever meet him?'

'No. You see, we don't keep up with Wayne and his activities. We're trying to get away from all that. His mother's suffered a lot in the past with all the court cases and prison sentences. We've had enough of it, to be honest with you. We just want to forget about Wayne and all the problems he's caused. We just want to get on with our lives.'

Chapter 22

His mind clouded with thoughts, Jean-Jacques Beauvais stepped into the living room at Upper Norton Manor.

'Darling, have you seen Katrina this morning?' he asked his wife, who was sitting on one of the settees, gazing out of the windows.

'Yes,' she replied with a stern expression. 'She's gone into Queensbridge to buy some printing ink and

envelopes. She should be back in a minute. Oh, this waiting is getting me down, *mon chéri*.'

'I know,' he replied. 'Monsieur Parkes and our insurance man arranged the transfer of money, but I called Parkes five minutes ago and he still has no confirmation the payment's been received and there's still no news about Marcel.'

He joined her on the settee and they remained sitting there together in silence.

The peace of the morning was broken by the sound of a car drawing up outside the main door.

'Maybe that's Katrina now,' said Camille.

A few moments later, their personal assistant came bustling into the room, her arms laden with shopping. 'Any news?' she asked.

Jean-Jacques shook his head.

'I heard in town police have uncovered the gang's hideout,' Drake continued.

'What is this?' Camille asked.

'*La cachette*,' Drake explained.

Camille nodded in response.

'So where's Marcel? Can they be holding him in another building somewhere?' said Drake.

'We mustn't allow ourselves to become too disheartened,' Jean-Jacques remarked. 'Perhaps this is a sign the men are getting ready to liberate Marcel.'

'Perhaps,' Drake said, although she looked doubtful.

'What happened about the private detectives you spoke to?' he asked.

Drake shrugged. 'No one was able to help us at short notice,' she said. 'If they were to become involved, they said they'd have to leave their current work immediately and come to Queensbridge. Then it would take a long time for them to get up to speed with the investigation and the boy would probably be found as soon as they became familiar with the case. They said we should leave it to Heart of England Police.'

Camille glanced down at the carpet. 'We are trapped in a private hell and there is no passage out,' she said.

The housekeeper, Marilyn Willis, poked her head round the door.

'The lady from the police is here,' she said. 'Detective Sergeant Roy.'

'Ask her to come in,' said Jean-Jacques.

Sunita Roy smiled as she entered, shaking hands with Drake, who was standing in the middle of the room.

'Sorry to call round uninvited,' said the sergeant, plucking a photocopy of Marcel's letter from her coat pocket, 'but I thought you'd want to see this, Mrs Beauvais.'

She stepped across and handed over the crumpled paper.

'*Mon Dieu*. What is this?' asked Camille. As she began to read the letter, tears rolled down her cheeks.

'Oh Marcel, *mon chéri*,' she said repeatedly.

She held a brief conversation in French with her husband, explaining excitedly it was a letter from their son. He read it over her shoulder. When the footballer reached the end of the letter, he turned to the sergeant.

'Thank you so much for bringing this to us,' he said. 'It means so much. Where did you find it?'

'Marcel had hidden it close to the bed where he'd been sleeping,' Sunita explained.

'Marcel is talking about a house. Where was this house and what was it like?' he asked.

'It was on the western side of Queensbridge.'

'So was it a good house?' he said.

Sunita shrugged. She recognised that she had to choose her words carefully for fear of upsetting the couple further.

'The conditions weren't too bad,' she said.

'Can we go there?'

'I'm sorry. That won't be possible,' she said. 'Police are still examining the house. I think it would be good if the family could share this letter with your ex-husband, Madame Beauvais.'

She shook her head vigorously.

'I'm sorry, DS Roy, but I'm not in regular contact with that man. How do you say in English? He is a waste of space.'

'I see,' said Sunita.

'What about this man, Tiggs?' asked Camille. 'Do you know how to catch him?'

'All our focus is on finding your son and bringing him back to you. Rest assured we're doing everything we can,' she said.

* * *

When Sunita returned to CID, the chief inspector had just launched into a briefing for all the staff.

'Ah, Sergeant,' he said. 'You haven't missed a lot. I was just telling everyone about the ransom.'

She made herself comfortable on top of one of the desks as Roscoe, who was holding a document in his hand, continued addressing the team from his position in front of the whiteboard.

'So the ransom's been received?' she asked as other members of the team craned their necks to look her way.

'Yes,' he said. 'Joseph Parkes confirmed it to me this morning. But so far no response from the gang about the boy. So the wait goes on.'

'The parents are so grateful we showed them the letter from their son that we found in Juniper Lane,' she said. 'It's proved very comforting for them.'

'That's good to hear,' said Roscoe. 'Now the chief superintendent called me this morning. Marcel's biological father, Philippe Dubois, has arrived in the UK from Paris.'

He glanced at DC Khalid. 'Omar, on top of your work trying to locate the gun, I'd like you to call him at his hotel in Worcester and get a statement from him. I doubt whether he'll be able to add much to what we already know, but it's worth making contact with him and seeing what he's got to say.'

Khalid, who was sitting in a chair beside his boss, nodded.

'No problem, sir,' he said. 'I'm afraid it's bad news regarding the Mercedes. We can't identify any car number. Maybe they've used a Fresnel lens or some reflective cover on the plate.'

Roscoe nodded. 'Quite possibly,' he said. 'Now, Dawson, you've just been to see Wayne Jordan's mother. Can you update us?'

Dawson stood up and stepped towards the whiteboard. He pointed to a photograph captioned 'Suspect Two.'

'Wayne Jordan spent his early life in Hampshire,' said the constable, 'and he was a good lad, according to his mother. But when his parents' marriage fell apart and the family moved to the Midlands, she says he began mixing with a bad bunch of people.'

'Someone showed me his Facebook page,' said Roscoe. 'It mainly shows photographs of guns. He hasn't been in contact with the parents. Is that right?'

Dawson nodded.

'But you've at least come up with a possible first name for Suspect Three, haven't you?'

'Yes, sir. Wayne is meant to be best mates with a bearded guy called Lewis, who hails from Worcestershire. Unfortunately, the parents don't know any more and the neighbours didn't have anything to add.'

'We know from the hostage's letter to his mother that there's a character with the nickname Tiggs who has a beard and is clearly not the guy giving orders,' said Roscoe. 'So it's reasonable to assume that this guy might be Suspect Two and that his first name could be Lewis. We'll have to check through records and see if anything comes up.'

As Dawson returned to his seat, Roscoe added, 'Dawson, you're into video games, aren't you? See if you can find out about him through the gaming community.'

Sunita took a step towards him.

‘Sir, is there any news from the post-mortem?’ she asked.

‘Yes. Mr Jukes’s cause of death was a gunshot wound to the head. Not a great surprise there.’

‘Do we know what happened to the bullets that were fired?’ she asked.

The chief inspector referred to the piece of paper he was holding.

‘Silas managed to retrieve them both – one from the victim’s chest and one from his head,’ he said. ‘He discovered the gun used was a Beretta 9000S, firing .40 Smith & Wesson rounds. He carried out an experiment which, he says, firmly suggests the two bullets were fired into the victim’s body from the stairwell window – a distance of approximately fifteen feet.’

* * *

After the meeting broke up, Sunita joined the chief inspector in his room.

‘How come Joseph Parkes wasn’t at the briefing this morning?’ she asked, taking a seat near the door.

‘After arranging the payment, he had a meeting in Birmingham to attend with one of his superiors,’ Roscoe explained as his desk phone began to ring.

‘Ah, here he is now,’ he said with a glance at the phone’s screen.

‘Roscoe,’ he announced as he pressed the handset’s answer key.

‘DI Parkes here,’ said the caller. ‘And I’ve got a complaint to make about your sergeant.’

‘You want to complain about DS Roy?’ said the chief inspector, adopting a quizzical expression and shaking his head in exasperation. He switched the call to speakerphone so Sunita could overhear the conversation.

‘Yes, sir,’ said Parkes. ‘I’ve just been round to visit the Beauvais family and your sergeant has caused the family some unnecessary anguish.’

‘How did she do that, then?’ asked Roscoe.

‘She’s taken them a copy of a letter purported to have been written by Marcel Dubois which was allegedly found at the house in Queensbridge where the gang were staying. I’m meant to be in charge of this operation to support the family and bring their son home. First of all, your sergeant should have informed me about this letter and, secondly, I’m afraid it’s done nothing but cause upset.’

‘Listen,’ said Roscoe, ‘I was with DS Roy when she found the letter and I authorised her to take a copy to the family.’

‘Did you, sir?’ Parkes spluttered. ‘Did you really?’

‘Yes, I did, and very pleased they were at the time she showed it to them.’

‘Well, sir, with respect,’ said Parkes, ‘when I visited the couple just now, they were crying about their son. I’m not sure this has helped matters at all.’

‘I’m in overall charge of this case, Inspector,’ Roscoe insisted. ‘In my judgement, presenting them with the letter – instead of withholding it from them, as you seem to be suggesting – can only have helped cement the relationship between them and the police.’

After ending the call, Sunita glanced across the room.

‘I’m not sure I can continue working with him,’ she remarked.

Chapter 23

‘I remember you,’ said the man behind the desk as Sunita Roy stepped inside the estate agents. ‘It’s Miss Roy, isn’t it? We showed you round a house in Old School Lane last week.’

'Yes,' she replied. 'I've been thinking long and hard about it, Mr Hussain. I've decided I'd like to make an offer.'

'Well, that's splendid. Would you like to take a seat?'

The smartly dressed negotiator in his early thirties with receding dark hair, glasses and a small moustache began tapping on his computer keyboard.

'Here we are. Number five, Old School Lane, currently priced at £695,000. And what offer would you like to put forward?'

Sunita thought for a moment. 'I think I'd like to start at £680,000. There's a fair bit of work I'd like to do to bring it up to standard.'

Hussain frowned. 'That's quite a bit under the asking price. Still, I'm happy to have a go,' he said.

Sunita studied the details of other properties displayed on the walls while Hussain held a quiet conversation with the seller. After a few minutes, he replaced the receiver.

'Well, I've spoken to the owner and, as I thought it would be, the offer you've made has been rejected. He says he and his wife wouldn't be able to afford the house they're moving to if they accepted that figure.'

Sunita shrugged her shoulders. 'All right. I'll leave the offer on the table for now while I've a think about whether I want to make a fresh offer. There are a few other places I'm interested in.'

'Please let us know if we can show you round any other houses,' said Hussain. 'But I think you'll find the house in Old School Lane offers an awful lot for the money. It's in a very sought-after area and the landscaped gardens are stunning.'

Sunita resumed her seat by his desk while he tapped on his keyboard and stared at his screen.

'I think we've got all your details, Miss Roy,' he said without looking up. 'You've worked for Heart of England Police for six years and, before that, you served for a while with West Midlands Police. Your current home is a one-

bed flat in Warwick. Could I ask whether you need any help with a mortgage? We at Royal County Properties have our own exclusive mortgage advisor and we can sort out the best deal for you.'

'Thank you but I won't be needing any finance,' said Sunita.

While they were talking, a slim, grey-haired man in a dark suit emerged from a back office.

Hussain turned on hearing footsteps. 'Ah, Mr Biddle,' he said. 'Miss Roy here is interested in buying the property we have in Old School Lane. I was just explaining about the wonderful range of mortgages that are available.'

The newcomer, in his late forties, approached Hussain's desk and leaned over his colleague's shoulder to view the screen. Then he smiled across the desk at Sunita.

'I'm James Biddle, one of the directors of Royal County,' he explained.

'Pleased to meet you,' she said, rising and shaking his hand.

'So, Tahir's been talking to you about mortgages, has he?'

'Yes, he has,' said Sunita. 'But I've got the funds in place already.'

'You have a mortgage arranged?' asked Hussain.

'No,' she said. 'Look, it's very good of you both to mention the deals you've got on offer, but I don't need a mortgage. I'm a cash buyer.'

Mr Biddle looked as shocked as if he had been mown down by his own car.

'Well, you're in a very fortunate position, then,' he said, striving to regain his composure. 'There aren't many people in this day and age who can turn down the offer of a mortgage because they have the funds already set up. Can I ask how this is possible? Do you have a wealthy benefactor?'

'I'd rather not discuss it, but my solicitor can vouch for the funds being there.'

Sunita wondered if she should explain that she benefitted from an inheritance left by a wealthy, eccentric uncle, but decided not to expound on it. It wasn't this stranger's business how she could afford the purchase.

A heavy silence hung in the air before Hussain told his colleague, 'Miss Roy's with the police.'

'Oh, really?' said Biddle with a grin. 'You're not traffic police, are you? I'll get the sidelight fixed tomorrow, I promise.' He roared with laughter.

She ignored the remark. 'No, I work in CID,' she explained.

'Wasn't it terrible that murder in Norton Prior at the footballer's house?' he continued. 'We were marketing that place over the summer.'

'Were you?' said Sunita. 'So you dealt with the Beauvais family?'

He shook his head. 'I never got to meet the footballer personally,' he said. 'We were one of three agents in the running and, in the end, the family rented it through rivals. Magnificent house, of course. But what a terrible thing to happen. I read an interview in the local press with the bodyguard's widow. Her life's been ruined.'

'I can't comment on the case, obviously,' Sunita said.

'Obviously,' he agreed.

'But you're right. It's devastating for her,' said Sunita, as she stood up and headed for the door.

'I'll let you know if anything changes regarding the house because there are other parties interested,' said Hussain. 'But, Miss Roy, I can assure you you'd be very happy there. It's a quiet street and, apart from the huge rooms, there's a double garage and off-street parking for several cars.'

* * *

Sunita's phone rang while she was walking back to the town's main supermarket, where she had left her car. It was her friend, Rupa.

'How did your date with Tom go the other night?' she asked.

'I'm afraid we argued and he walked out,' Sunita admitted.

'Oh dear,' said Rupa. 'What caused the argument?'

'It was probably my fault. I raised the issue of his ex-wife and he took exception to it.'

'Maybe you shouldn't have done that,' said Rupa.

'The trouble is that, just before he stormed off, he poured his heart out to me,' said Sunita. 'He said he'd loved me since the first moment we met and will always love me. He's never been so frank about his feelings before.'

'Oh God,' said Rupa. 'So now you realise what a mistake you've made?'

'Yes.'

'I suppose some men need a moment of high emotion to express the way they feel.'

Sunita was close to tears. 'Oh, Rupa,' she said. 'Since Friday night, I've been trying to talk to him. When he told me those things, they definitely came from the heart and it's left me devastated. I know now that Tom and I should be together. But he's been blocking all my calls. I just hope I can get to talk to him before it's too late.'

Chapter 24

Lewis Tigworth knocked on the bedroom door early on Wednesday afternoon. 'Marcel, I've got your lunch here,' he announced.

A feeble voice from within called out, 'I'm sick.'

The visitor unlocked the door and panicked. It looked as though the boy was still in bed, underneath his duvet. He rushed across the room.

'Marcel, are you all right?' he asked anxiously, hoping the boy had not succumbed to some illness – perhaps associated with his epilepsy.

When Tigworth lifted the duvet, he was shocked to see it had been stuffed with Marcel's spare pillow and clothes.

He was unaware that Marcel had been hiding behind the door. Now he crept out of the room unnoticed and hurried down the stairs. He slipped behind the door in the kitchen and listened.

Tigworth quickly realised he had been duped and raised the alarm, calling to O'Shane, 'The boy's got out.'

O'Shane came running along the first-floor landing.

'What do you mean? What's happened?' he demanded.

'He's tricked us,' said Tigworth. 'He slipped out of his room after pretending he was ill.'

'Well, let's get after him!' hollered O'Shane.

'Are you sure he's not still in the house?'

'No idea.'

'You're a useless prat,' muttered O'Shane. 'Get out onto the road and give me a shout if you see him. I'll search the house. You're a bloody idiot. You were meant to be looking after him, but the truth is I couldn't trust you to peel a bloody grape.'

* * *

Desperate to flee the gang, Marcel had darted into the yard and crossed the road. He had nimbly clambered over a five-bar gate that led into the muddy field opposite. Then he had crouched down beside the hawthorn hedge and witnessed the two men quarrelling.

The main farmhouse was larger than Marcel had expected. In front of it was a yard surrounded by several outbuildings. A black Mercedes was parked by the open farm gate, which bore a sign saying, 'Meadow Brook Farm'.

He gazed around at the wider location. He was dismayed to find he was in a remote area of rolling countryside. All he could see, for miles around, were fields

speckled, here and there, by bushes or small clumps of trees. Apart from the angry voices of the men, the only sounds he could hear were birds singing in the trees and sheep bleating.

Marcel watched the two men. Within minutes, they ended their argument. The tall, muscular man slipped a mobile phone from his pocket and made a call – perhaps to alert his other companion – before leaping into the Mercedes and speeding off down the narrow lane to the right. His regular visitor, Tiggs, set off on foot in the opposite direction.

For a moment, the teenager remained concealed by the hedge, wondering what to do. He could try to stop a passing vehicle and beg a lift. At least that would whisk him right away from the gang's orbit. But he had been there for around ten minutes already and there had been no passing traffic.

It would be dark in a few hours. The climate was too cold and the ground too damp for him to spend the night outside. Could he sneak into a deserted farm building to pass the night? Or could he walk to a village and find shelter? The problem was he didn't know how far it was to the nearest village.

He decided he would go to the nearest house and plead for help there in contacting his mother or the police. But, instead of travelling along the lane in open view, he decided to trek through the field while following the line of the hedge. That would at least provide him with some cover.

After a few minutes of squelching his way through the mud, his spirits were enlivened by the roar of a vehicle travelling along the lane behind him. The clattering sound drew closer. He could see it was a tractor being driven by a middle-aged man with a peaked cap. Marcel hurried to another farm gate, a few metres ahead, vaulted over it and ran into the centre of the lane. He raised both his hands in a desperate effort to bring the tractor to a halt.

To his amazement, the driver hooted his horn and gestured with a wave for the teenager to move out of the road.

'Stop!' shouted Marcel. '*Aidez-moi!*'

But the driver ignored him and Marcel was forced to leap aside and let the tractor speed by.

Perhaps the man had taken a dislike to his sandy, uncombed hair and unshaven look? Or his olive skin? Or his crumpled green pullover?

He would never know the reason. But the gravity of his situation struck home with him even more. If his luck didn't change soon, he might be forced to spend the night struggling to sleep beneath the stars. Or he might be recaptured by the men. Neither of these seemed an attractive proposition.

As he returned over the gate to the field, he heard the throb of a car engine in the distance. It was another vehicle heading towards him. He was concerned it might be a Mercedes. Sure enough, a black car was approaching at speed.

Marcel crouched down and remained motionless behind the hedge. He watched as the saloon car, with O'Shane behind the wheel, swept past.

With an uneasy heart, Marcel resumed his walk beside the hedge, hoping that, at any moment, he would see a house where he could seek help.

Twenty minutes later, darkness was beginning to fall and as he noticed a sign for the nearby hamlet of Monkswood, Marcel was overjoyed to find he was approaching a house.

On closer inspection, he realised the dark shape of the building, on the other side of the lane, was a traditional stone farmhouse surrounded by several barns, outbuildings and landscaped gardens. The main house was separated from an adjoining barn conversion with screen fencing and well-stocked borders with trees and shrubs providing

privacy. A blue Porsche Panamera sports car was parked on the red-brick forecourt outside the front door.

Marcel opened one of two wrought-iron gates, beside a sign saying 'Pinetree Farm' and hurried along the short gravel drive to the front door. He rang the bell in the fading light. He wasn't confident he would find anyone at home. All the lights were off.

He peered through a window into a sitting room with exposed beams, flagstone floor and an open-brick fireplace. Then he stepped back onto the forecourt and stared up at the first-floor windows.

As Marcel stood outside Pinetree Farm wondering what to do, a figure peered through the upstairs blinds, unseen by the frantic teenager.

They had heard the doorbell but had decided to ignore it. They were not really meant to be there. However, they recognised the boy from his appearance. It took them a few seconds to dial a number on their mobile phone.

When the call was answered, the figure in the window announced, 'I think I've found the missing boy.'

Chapter 25

Marcel Dubois flew into a panic the moment he saw the Mercedes draw up outside Pinetree Farm. He could see two men inside.

How had they discovered he was there?

The teenager ran into the back garden and cast his eyes around. There was no time to think. He simply had to get away.

There was a wooden shed to the rear of the garden, an overgrown vegetable patch and a clump of bare trees at the far side. In the corner, by a wire fence, there was a

wooden gate leading to a farmyard and a range of agricultural buildings.

He raced across the garden, through the gate, and sprinted along an uneven roadway, caked in mud and straw. He finally reached a barn and began desperately searching for a place to hide among the bales of hay.

* * *

Kyle O'Shane and Lewis Tigworth had spotted the teenager's bid for freedom and raced after him across the garden. O'Shane was so annoyed that the boy had managed to escape that he was determined to catch him. He approached the open barn and paced around it like a wild animal stalking its prey.

'You go the other way round, Lewis,' he ordered his companion.

Then he raised his voice.

'Come out, Marcel. We know you're in there,' he shouted.

The boy was hiding in an alley formed between piles of bales. He was keeping as quiet as he could, hoping and praying he could somehow evade them.

But O'Shane was on a personal mission now. He hurried round the outside of the barn, peering at the bales as he passed.

'Don't be a fool,' O'Shane yelled. 'It's too cold to be outside. Give yourself up.'

Finally, he spotted Marcel and ran along the passageway towards him.

Marcel pulled out a loose bale in an effort to delay his pursuer, but O'Shane simply leaped over it. He then made a failed attempt to grab Marcel's arm.

The boy ran from the barn and darted off across the fields with the two men in pursuit. But, unlike his stepfather, Marcel was no athlete and he was slightly overweight. Within seconds, O'Shane had caught up with

him. He and Tigworth each grabbed an arm and the pair led him across to the Mercedes.

'You're very stupid,' O'Shane told the snivelling boy. 'How did you expect to get away? It's like the back of beyond here.'

In the car, O'Shane clamped a set of handcuffs on Marcel. He placed the hood back on his head, tightened the string and fastened it round Marcel's neck. The two men then drove him back to Meadow Brook Farm.

On arrival at the farmhouse, they frogmarched Marcel back to his room, where O'Shane pushed him inside.

'You ain't getting no more food for the rest of the day as a punishment,' he told the teenager.

'Can you free my hands?' asked Marcel.

'No,' came the curt reply.

O'Shane closed the bedroom door and locked it.

'You've got to be more bloody careful, mate,' said O'Shane as he followed Tigworth along the corridor towards the stairs. 'He's only a kid but he bloody tricked you, didn't he?'

Tigworth became annoyed. 'He got me worried, saying he was sick,' he shouted back.

'Well, we've got to be bloody careful now. This can't be allowed to happen again. If it weren't for the boss, who was viewing a farm up the road and spotted him, the lad could be miles away by now.'

'Look,' said Tigworth as they reached the downstairs hallway, 'you seem to be blaming me for the kid getting out. If you'd been the one bringing him his meals, it would have been you he tricked.'

He stood in front of his associate and prodded him in the chest. 'Don't keep putting the blame on me,' he continued angrily. 'If it had been down to me, we wouldn't have taken the kid in the first place.'

'Don't you poke me,' yelled O'Shane. 'Your job was to get to know the kid, bring him his meals and let him out for washing and toilet breaks. You've fallen down on the

job, mate, and you've got to make sure that don't happen again. I'm going off now for a couple of hours. That should give you time to have a good hard think about what I just told you.'

O'Shane stormed out of the building, slamming the door behind him.

* * *

A fine rain fell from an overcast sky as Sunita Roy arrived in CID later that afternoon. She was in a rather despondent mood, in keeping with the weather. She had heard nothing more from the estate agents about the house in Old School Lane and suspected she had lost the property to another buyer.

'Oh well,' she told herself, 'if it wasn't to be, it wasn't to be.'

She was also perturbed that she had been unable to reach Tom Vickers. His phone was continually going to voicemail. How she wished she hadn't raised the thorny topic of his ex-wife. How she wished she could apologise for upsetting a man who had been so kind to her, so loyal.

When she reached her desk, she noticed Brett Dawson studying images of a black Mercedes on a monitor.

'What've you got there, Brett?" she asked.

'It's CCTV from a shop along the Worcester Road in Norton Prior, Sarge,' he said. 'Unfortunately, it's too dark for the camera to pick up the number plate.'

Sunita stood up and stepped across to his desk.

'Let me see,' she insisted.

Dawson stood up and let his sergeant take his seat. He watched while she peered at the image showing the front of a black Mercedes and a tall, muscular man behind the driving seat.

'You've done well here, Brett,' she said after studying the clip carefully. 'This seems to be a clear image of Suspect One. Tall, burly and with short, blond hair.'

She continued staring at the image.

‘There’s something else, Brett. There’s a sticker showing a company logo in the corner of the windscreen.’

He leaned over her shoulder and peered into the monitor.

‘I see what you mean, Sarge, but it’s too small to read.’

‘Hold on,’ she said. ‘Let’s see if we can zoom in on it with the region of interest filter.’

She pressed some buttons to enhance the image and the logo – three capital letters inside an oval-shape – filled the centre of the screen.

‘It looks like WAM,’ Dawson remarked.

She nodded. ‘That’s what I reckon. Do you remember Ricky Stanton, who featured in a murder case five years ago?’

‘Oh yes,’ he replied. ‘He worked for a car firm in Queensbridge, didn’t he?’

‘Yes,’ she said. ‘West Avon Motors. I’m wondering if that’s their logo.’

‘Makes sense,’ said Dawson. ‘Hang on. I’ll just have a look at their website.’

After locating the firm on his mobile phone, he confirmed it was a logo used by the Queensbridge car firm.

‘Good. I’m going to take a trip down there and see what they remember about this car. Perhaps you could see if we can use facial recognition to try and identify Suspect One?’

* * *

An hour later, Sunita drove into Marina Gardens, Queensbridge and parked outside West Avon Motors. Two dark-green Land Rovers, a silver Mercedes and a blue Toyota were parked on the forecourt. A young, smartly dressed salesman whose face was wreathed in smiles strolled over as she stepped from her car.

‘Looking for something in particular?’ he asked. ‘I could give you a good price for your Peugeot.’

Sunita laughed. 'I may be looking for a new car in a few weeks,' she said. 'But I'm here today about a rather serious matter. I'm from Heart of England Police. Is your boss still Jett Lumley?'

Sunita, who was clutching a large brown envelope, showed the salesman her warrant card.

'No,' he said. 'Mr Lumley's retired. The boss is Mr Swinford. He's with a client at the moment, but he won't be too long. I'm Michael, by the way. Would you like a tea or coffee?'

She nodded. 'A tea without milk would go down well,' she said.

A few minutes later, she was sitting in a corner of the large showroom by the vending machine, sipping a hot tea. She watched while the new general manager, Matt Swinford, chatted to a young woman in a trouser suit.

By the time she had drunk her tea, the woman had left and Swinford, a tall, bearded man in a grey suit, strode across to speak to her.

'Matt Swinford,' he announced with a stern face, stretching out his hand.

Sunita rose to shake it. 'Pleased to meet you,' she said, showing him her warrant card. 'DS Roy from Heart of England CID. I gather Mr Lumley's retired.'

'He left here a year ago,' Swinford explained. 'I've taken over the management.'

She took three black-and-white photographs out of the envelope she was carrying.

'Good,' she said. 'Well, you might just be able to help. This is a car we're trying to trace and we've found your company logo fixed to the windscreen.'

'So you've finally decided to do something about it, have you?' he asked.

'Sorry?' she said.

'You've come to investigate the theft from outside our showroom, have you?'

'Not exactly,' said Sunita. 'This vehicle's featured in a high-profile case and I needed to ask you questions about it. I wasn't aware it had been stolen from you.'

'Oh, that's bloody typical of the police these days. I wait ten days for someone to come round and talk to me about the car being nicked and when someone does finally turn up, they don't even know we'd reported it.'

'I'm very sorry, Mr Swinford. I don't know who you've been dealing with over your car, but it's just cropped up in a kidnap case and, with your help, we might be able to track down not only your car but the kidnappers as well.'

He shrugged. 'All right. At least you've bothered to show up. So what do you need to know?'

'When was it taken?'

'Sometime around the end of October. When Michael opened up the premises on the Monday morning, it was gone.'

'Nothing on your cameras?' she asked.

'Bit embarrassing. There was no camera in the corner of the forecourt where the Mercedes had been parked.'

'No alarm?'

'They managed to bypass it somehow.' He took another look at the photographs. 'It definitely looks like our stolen Merc. There's a slight dent in the offside wing but someone's put different plates on it. And I don't recognise the driver either, in case you were going to ask.'

'Looks like we've hit a dead end,' Sunita murmured to herself, shaking her head and glancing down at the varnished wooden floor.

'God knows how they managed to nick it,' said Swinford, 'but some of these crooks are bloody clever people, as you probably know. So, this kidnapping case – is that the French boy from Norton Prior?'

'Yes.'

'That's a terrible business,' he said. 'I know it says in the papers he's sixteen and I suppose he's nearly an adult. But still it's very scary for the kid, isn't it?'

'Yes. Very much,' she said. 'Mr Swinford, do you think the thief could have been watching these premises for a few days before taking the car? Were there any unusual incidents? Any customers behaving oddly?'

'Nothing springs to mind. I think it was just a chance thing. Someone passing needed a nice big car and thought, I'll have that. That's what I think happened.'

Sunita frowned as she took the photographs back and returned them to their envelope. She took out a small notebook.

'Could you give me the car's actual registration?'

'Of course. It skips my mind. I'll get Michael to dig out all the details for you. I've got to go now. Good to have met you,' he said before marching off to greet a customer he recognised.

Ten minutes later, Michael hurried across to her with a slip of paper in his hand.

'Here's the information – and good luck,' he said.

While travelling back to St James Street, Sunita received a call from the chief inspector. After switching the call to hands-free, she began updating him on the information she had gathered about the Mercedes.

But he interrupted her.

'Don't worry about that now,' said Roscoe. 'The gang have been in touch with the family again and they're refusing to let the boy go. They're demanding more money.'

Chapter 26

Brett Dawson spun round at his desk as his sergeant stepped into the CID office the following morning.

'I've had some luck, Sarge,' he announced. 'Our technology expert, John Hepworth, has come up trumps

after analysing those images of the Mercedes driver. The guy's called Kyle O'Shane.'

'This is Suspect One?'

'That's right, Sarge. He's thirty-two, comes from West Bromwich and he's got a police record stretching all the way to the moon and back.'

The sergeant hung her jacket on the coat stand before taking her seat at her desk.

'What sort of offences are we talking about, Brett?' she asked.

'Assault, burglary, criminal damage, theft of a motor vehicle – you name it. He's also got an infamous uncle. Do you remember a guy running a huge drugs factory in Acocks Green three years ago?'

'Was it in an abandoned church?'

'Yes. That was him – Rory O'Shane his name is. He's the brother of Kyle's dad. He got twenty months in jail for that. He was also a suspect in the Handsworth torture case – you know, that incident four years ago in which a man was branded with a hot iron in an attempt to make him reveal his pin numbers. But police could never prove it was him.'

'Nice family,' she observed.

'Yeah,' said Dawson. 'Rory's only recently come out of jail.'

'Do you know which one?'

'Ashwood Vale.'

'Do we know what the relationship's like between Kyle O'Shane and his uncle? I mean, is it possible the uncle played a part in the kidnapping.'

'The only problem is Kyle O'Shane's down as having no fixed abode.'

'Well, keep looking for an address,' she said.

* * *

Two hours later, Sunita Roy hoisted her umbrella in the air and pushed open the exit door at St James Street police

headquarters. She scurried across the rain-lashed car park until she reached the chief inspector's vehicle.

'I thought the forecast was just for a little light rain, sir,' she said as she opened the front passenger door and leaped inside.

'You can never trust these forecasts,' Roscoe remarked. He started the car and they set off down the street.

'So, we're off to see Philippe Dubois?' she said, placing her rolled-up umbrella in the footwell.

'Yes. I don't suppose he'll have much information for us. It's more of a goodwill mission, I suppose,' he said. 'He's the boy's natural father and he has the right to know how the investigation's going. Perhaps we can set his mind at rest about certain aspects of the case.'

'You never know, sir,' said Sunita. 'He might mention something about his son that no one else has brought up. When did Mr Dubois first arrive in the UK?'

'My information is that he arrived a couple of days ago,' said Roscoe. 'Parkes has been over to see him and says Philippe is a very excitable guy. He was ranting and raving about his ex-wife and the footballer, blaming them for the kidnap.'

'So, there's no love lost there,' she remarked.

'That's right,' he said as they joined the M42 motorway.

'Parkes isn't going to be at the hotel with us this morning?' she said.

'No. He seems to have struck up a good relationship with the Beauvais couple, so I agreed with him last night that he could go round on his own to see them this morning. He's going to give me a call and let me know about this new message the family are meant to have received from the gang. Ah, this might be him.'

The chief inspector's phone was ringing. He switched to hands-free.

'Morning, Parkes. What do you know?' asked Roscoe.

'Morning, sir,' said Parkes. 'I've just left the family. They're absolutely devastated that Marcel hasn't been

released, despite them making the payment that was requested.'

'What did the gang's new message say exactly?'

'I've got a copy of it here, sir,' Parkes said. He read the note aloud.

> *Mr Beauvais, thank you for the payment you made, but we have been looking closely at your finances. You are a very wealthy man and we are sure your boy is worth a lot more to you.*
>
> *We need to be fair to ourselves as well as to you. So we are going to ask you for a further payment.*
>
> *Don't worry about Marcel. He is being cared for very well and he hasn't been harmed in any way. But, as before, you must do exactly what we tell you.*
>
> *Despite our warnings, we have discovered to our intense disappointment that you spoke to the police on the morning of Tuesday, 1 November, the day we made our first demand. I must impress upon you that you must cease cooperating with them if you want to stand any chance of seeing Marcel alive again. You will receive new instructions shortly.*
>
> *The Matchday Boys.*

The chief inspector stroked his chin. 'Was the message sent from the same mobile phone as before?' he asked.

'No. They used a different phone, sir.'

'Parkes, can you send me over a copy of that note for my files?'

'Certainly, sir. No problem,' replied Parkes.

'How do the couple feel about releasing more money?'

'Well, we don't know yet how much the new ransom demand will be for, sir, but they're so desperate to get Marcel back that I don't think there's going to be any issue about sending more money.'

'If the family do make a second payment, they need to send a clear message that this will be the final amount and they won't be paying out any further sums,' said Roscoe as his car joined the M5 motorway.

'I'd already thought of that, sir. I've drafted a reply. This is what I'm proposing we say: *Thank you for your message and for saying that Marcel is being cared for. We are disappointed that, despite our paying the fee you demanded, you have still not released our son. Contrary to reports in the British press and on social media, our family are not extremely wealthy and any further outlay would hit our family finances hard.*

'*We await to hear from you about your fresh intentions. However, we must insist that, if we make any further payment, this would be the final sum and we would not be prepared to pay any more. We would also expect our son to be released immediately, once we have met this second request.*'

'That does the trick,' said Roscoe.

'I want to make sure the family are happy with this statement before we send it to the gang, sir.'

'All right,' said Roscoe. 'But we don't have to respond straight away, do we? I'll see you in the office later, Parkes, and we can discuss it again. We're off to Worcester right now to see Philippe Dubois.'

'Oh, are you?' said Parkes. 'I wouldn't have thought there was any need for you to do that. As you know, I've already spoken to him.'

Roscoe shrugged. 'Well, as the senior officer, I feel out of respect that I should give the guy a few minutes of my time. He is the boy's biological father, after all, and he deserves to be kept in the loop.'

'Very well. If that's how you feel, sir. I'll see you later.'

After travelling for a total of forty-five minutes, the chief inspector and his sergeant arrived on the outskirts of the cathedral city, lapped by the waters of the Severn.

'There's one aspect of the whole case I've been meaning to raise with you, sir,' said Sunita.

'Go on,' said Roscoe, as they made their way through the city's eastern suburbs.

'Well, assuming we find Marcel alive and arrest members of the gang for Jukes's murder and the abduction, there will still be some unfinished business,' she said.

'How do you mean?'

'Well, something tells me these guys haven't acted on their own. They seem to have resources – including properties they can access at a moment's notice. And someone has the wherewithal to negotiate and arrange cyber payments. I find it hard to believe that someone like Wayne from Droitwich and his pals would have the means to do that.'

'That's a fair point,' said Roscoe, 'and one that's crossed my mind several times. You think there could be a Mr Big behind the whole operation?'

'Yes, sir. It stands to reason. But how do we even make a start on tracking that person down?'

Chapter 27

The missing boy's father scowled as he met the two detectives in the foyer of Worcester's King's Arms Hotel.

'I thought you were coming an hour ago,' said Philippe Dubois as he led them to a seated area.

'I'm sorry. We got delayed at the office,' said Roscoe.

The Frenchman resembled his son. He had the same distinctive sandy-coloured hair, although there were signs some of it was turning grey. He had similar facial features with brown eyes and tanned skin. He even had a gold medallion like Marcel.

Dubois, a property developer, settled himself down in a dark-brown leather armchair while his two visitors made themselves comfortable on a nearby settee.

'How long have you been in the UK, sir?' asked Roscoe.

'I flew over on Monday,' he replied. He spoke in a heavy French accent.

'That's several days after your son's abduction,' Roscoe pointed out.

'*Exactement.* I wasn't informed immediately that my son was kidnapped. That was probably because my selfish ex-wife and her new husband, the arrogant, two-faced footballer, felt guilty after their lack of care towards Marcel. Anyway, now I'm here, I'm looking forward to the police acting with speed and efficiency.'

'All my officers are working hard to find Marcel,' said Roscoe.

'He is a member of the "Scoutisme Français" – the scouts,' said Dubois. 'He is in good physical shape, but he is only sixteen. He is in a strange country and he must be feeling nervous. So I am extremely anxious about how he is coping.'

'We understand that, sir,' Roscoe agreed. 'Have you been to the UK before?'

'Many years past. *Monsieur le Chief Inspector*, what I want to know is what you are doing to find my son. I mean, do you have any idea at all where he might be?'

Roscoe glanced at his sergeant.

'I can assure you we're doing our best to find Marcel,' he replied. 'We believe he's still in the Midlands.'

'We know it's a worrying time for you,' said Sunita.

'You've really no idea,' said Dubois. 'That boy means the world to me. He's all I've got since– since that obnoxious footballer used tricks to seduce my empty-headed wife and stole her away from me. So do you have an idea where he is and do you have any information about the men that have captured him?'

'We've identified the main suspects, sir,' Roscoe explained. 'And we're working hard to establish their current whereabouts.'

'*Eh bien.* But you don't have a clue where Marcel is, do you?'

'We traced the gang to a house in the town of Queensbridge, which is about eighteen miles from here,'

said Roscoe, 'but they disappeared before we got there. We know what car they're using, so it's only a matter of time now. I believe you received a visit yesterday from one of our colleagues, Inspector Parkes?'

'Yes, and the man is – how do you say, Chief Inspector?' he replied. '*Très pompeux*.'

'Are you saying he's pompous?' asked Roscoe.

'*Oui. C'est ça.* Pompous. All words and no substance. That's why I was very grateful when I heard you planned to come over to Worcester to give me a personal visit.'

'You didn't find Inspector Parkes helpful?' asked Sunita. Her interest had been piqued by the Frenchman's disparaging remarks about their colleague.

'No. He was saying how he's been involved in countless cases of kidnap. He came up with this weird phrase. Can I bring it to mind? He said he's "a master of the dynamics of forcible human abductions." I thought, what a pompous fool. So thank you so much for coming and for trying to put my mind at rest.'

'It's the least we can do,' said Roscoe.

'I am worried in particular because my son has epilepsy,' said Dubois. 'All the stress caused by being abducted in this way can make the condition worse.'

'Rest assured we're doing our utmost to bring the boy back as quickly as possible,' said Sunita.

'That's good. But I have to tell you that, once he is back, that will not be the end of the matter. The way my ex-wife, Camille, and her new husband have behaved is outrageous. It is a scandal. They should have taken Marcel to the football match where they could keep an eye on him – not let him go out on the town with a bodyguard they hardly knew.'

* * *

A gangly man with short, spiky, dark hair cycled along Queensbridge High Street just before 5 p.m. and stopped outside the police station. He glanced up and down in case

he was being watched. When he was sure he was safe from prying eyes, he leaned the rusty old bicycle beside the wall, climbed the stone steps and pushed open the door. A young constable was sitting behind a screen at the wooden counter. He beckoned the visitor forward.

'Too late for doubts now,' the man told himself. 'I'm crossing the line. There's no going back.'

'Can I help you?' asked the constable.

'I want to talk to somebody,' said the visitor.

'And what's it about?'

'Burglary and kidnap. I've come to give myself up.'

Chapter 28

The fair-haired constable was surprised at the visitor's admissions about burglary and kidnap. But he maintained his composure.

'Wait there just a moment,' he said, picking up his desk phone. After a garbled conversation with another officer, he replaced the handset.

'Can I take a note of your name, sir?'

'Lewis,' the visitor replied. 'Lewis Tigworth.'

'If you'd like to take a seat over in the corner, sir, someone will be down in a minute to talk to you.'

Within a few minutes, PC Derek Underhill hurried into the reception area through a side door.

'Mr Tigworth?' he said. 'Would you like to come this way? My name's Underhill. You're lucky to find me here. I was due off at five.'

He led his visitor into the bright interview room.

'I understand you've got some information about some crimes that have been committed. Is that right?' asked the

constable as the pair sat down opposite each other at the table.

'Yeah,' said Tigworth.

'So, you've witnessed something, have you? The desk constable said it was to do with burglary and kidnap.'

'Yes,' said Tigworth. 'You know the men who did the burglary at Norton Prior when the guy got shot? I was one of them. I can tell you everything.'

'Good God,' said Underhill. 'Have you come straight from the place where the boy is?'

'No. I've been round my parents' place. They live in Queensbridge.'

'All right,' said the constable. 'You'd better start from the beginning.'

Over the next five minutes, Tigworth gave the genial constable a brief outline of his involvement in the events that began with the burglary at Upper Norton Manor. Underhill took notes and then put his pen down.

'Why have you come in to tell us all this?' he asked the visitor. 'Have you fallen out with your friends?'

'You could say that,' Tigworth concurred.

'All right,' said Underhill. 'I know some people who are going to be very interested in talking to you. If you wait there, I'll go and make a quick phone call.'

* * *

The nervous young man was chewing one of his fingernails an hour later as he waited in the interview room at St James Street. Derek Underhill had driven him to the headquarters building after alerting the CID. Lewis Tigworth had already held a brief discussion with solicitor Roger Sims, but since then, for more than twenty minutes, senior officers had kept him waiting in this cold, unwelcoming room.

He had become increasingly worried over the previous week about how the gang's activities were proceeding. A simple burglary had turned into murder and kidnap. Their

hostage had a frightening illness. Events had reached a turning point and he had taken the crucial decision to hand himself in. But the longer he waited in the room, the more he began having second thoughts.

Of all the gang members, he had spent the most time with the French boy. If the police had caught them with the teenager, he suspected this would have gone heavily against him. Marcel would have clearly identified him as one of the gang. Furthermore, he no longer trusted O'Shane and Jordan, and believed they would have grassed him up if they were caught.

The murder of the bodyguard had appalled him. He had played no role in it. But the fact he was part of the gang meant he would still be in the frame – and he feared the other two men might even accuse *him* of pulling the trigger. He came to realise earlier, while cycling into Queensbridge, that, if he gave himself up and helped police, he could perhaps get a lighter sentence.

However, after his conversation with the lawyer, doubts had crept into his mind. Perhaps he should have remained with O'Shane at Meadow Brook Farm and seen the whole job through. The pay had been good. He had been promised a bonus. There was a good chance they would have evaded the law. And now he would be branded a grass who couldn't be trusted.

The door opened and two men in plain clothes came in.

'Mr Tigworth?' said the amiable, older man. 'I'm DCI Roscoe. This is my colleague, DI Parkes. We obviously need to ask you a few questions.'

'That's fair enough,' said Tigworth, glancing up.

Roscoe sat on the opposite side of the table while grim-faced Parkes, settled into a chair beside him.

After a few minutes, Tigworth's bespectacled lawyer entered the room and took a seat beside his client.

'As you're aware from when we spoke briefly earlier, you're under arrest on suspicion of aggravated burglary at

Upper Norton Manor with other possible charges likely,' said Roscoe.

Roscoe stared across the table at the prisoner while reciting the police caution.

'Before we go any further, Mr Tigworth,' he said, 'can you give us the address of the place where Marcel Dubois is being held captive?'

'If I cooperate with you on this, it'll work in my favour, won't it?' said Tigworth.

'We can't make promises, but the judge in your trial may look on you more favourably,' Roscoe agreed.

'All right. It's Meadow Brook Farm in a place called Monkswood.'

'I know it,' said Roscoe, tearing a piece of paper from the back of his notebook and jotting it down. 'It's a small hamlet, just outside Pershore. Hold on there, all of you, just one moment.'

The chief inspector stepped out of the room and the three men inside could hear a muffled conversation in which a custody officer was asked to take the address to DS Roy as a matter of urgency.

On his return, Roscoe was smiling and apologetic.

'Now, Mr Tigworth,' he said as he resumed his seat, 'perhaps you could tell us about the break-in.'

The two detectives spent a few minutes listening to Tigworth's account of the raid on Upper Norton Manor. He told them how the gang had earlier been holed up at the house in Juniper Lane and how they then moved to Meadow Brook Farm. He gave his accomplices' first names and surnames.

'So, what made you come into see us today?' asked Parkes.

'To be honest,' said Tigworth, 'I thought that the way they were running things was all wrong. I mean, to start with, they killed that bloke at the big house. Shooting that guy, as far as I knew, was never part of the original plan. I wasn't involved in that at all.

'Then I never agreed about taking the boy. He was ill. He had some kind of fit the other day, which shook me up. I've never seen anything like it. It's obviously wrong they took him. He should be at home with his mum and dad.'

'We're grateful to you for coming in,' said Roscoe. 'I know this can't have been easy for you.'

'No, it hasn't,' said Tigworth. 'But I thought I'd make a clean breast of things. The two guys I was with aren't very bright and, the longer they held onto the boy, the more chance I thought the cops would have of catching us. I know I'm in a lot of trouble and may get locked up for a while. But I thought, if I help you, then maybe, in return, I'll have the chance of a lighter sentence.'

'We don't do deals,' sneered Parkes. 'You'll take your chance like all the other villains–'

Roscoe interrupted. 'What the inspector says has an element of truth,' he told Tigworth. 'But the way you've decided to give yourself up and assist us won't go unnoted. I'm sure your lawyers will make a good deal of this in any forthcoming court case and the judge will be inclined to look rather more favourably upon you than upon your associates.'

'The point is,' Parkes continued sternly, 'you and your mates turned up at the mansion with a loaded gun. The housekeeper was terrified when she was threatened with that nasty weapon and tied up. Then a security guard was viciously shot. It doesn't matter who pulled the trigger. You went along with things.'

Tigworth nodded. 'I know,' he said. 'But, as I say, that was never part of the plan – like it was never part of the plan to take the boy. Look, the bodyguard fellow turned up just before we were about to leave. He turned on our driver.'

'That's Kyle O'Shane?' said Roscoe.

'Yes,' said Tigworth.

'So what happened?' asked Roscoe.

'Our mate, Wayne–'

'That's Wayne Jordan?' asked Roscoe.

'That's right. He saw what was happening through the window and shot the bloke.'

Roscoe frowned. 'In cold blood,' he said.

'Well, yeah,' said Tigworth.

'Whose gun was it?'

'Well, not mine. I don't know. Wayne got it from somewhere.'

'And where were you at the time of the shooting?' asked Parkes.

'I was in an upstairs bedroom,' Tigworth admitted.

'Nicking as many valuables as you could lay your filthy bloody hands on,' Parkes shouted.

Sims frowned. 'Chief Inspector, your colleague's line of questioning is quite uncalled for,' he said.

Roscoe nodded and glared at his colleague. 'Yes, please calm down, Inspector,' he said.

Tigworth was staring across the table at the two detectives.

'I've already fessed up, haven't I?' he said. 'I know I've done wrong. I'm here to help – not be shouted at.'

'And what about the boy, Marcel?' said the chief inspector. 'What's happened to him?'

Tigworth folded his arms. 'I ain't telling you no more. I don't like being shouted at when all I've done is put my neck on the line by coming in to talk to you. I know what I've done is wrong and I'm prepared to go to jail for it. But you guys have got to play fair with me.'

Parkes was determined to continue trying to extract information from the young man.

'How come you greedy bastards took two million pounds in crypto money and then decided it wasn't enough? Have you any idea of the misery you've put the boy's family through?'

'No comment,' said Tigworth stubbornly.

'So who was the major player in all this?' asked Parkes. 'Who's been pulling the strings?'

Roscoe leaned back in his chair, shaking his head.

'You'll get nothing more out of me,' Tigworth insisted.

'Come on,' said Roscoe. 'The lad's had enough. I'm suspending this interview at twenty minutes past seven. You'll be remaining in custody, Mr Tigworth, and we'll speak to you again in the morning.'

Chapter 29

Gavin Roscoe was fuming after the interview with Lewis Tigworth ended and two constables had escorted their prisoner back to the custody suite. Inspector Parkes mumbled a comment about needing to go away and make a phone call, but the chief inspector insisted he should accompany him back to CID.

No words were spoken while Roscoe led the way through the busy department on the first floor. Once they were inside his room, the chief inspector slammed the door and installed himself behind his desk.

Parkes leaned against the partition wall.

'Sit down, if you like,' Roscoe suggested.

'I'm all right, sir,' Parkes replied. 'I've been sitting down all afternoon.'

'Why the hell did you adopt that tough questioning style with Tigworth?' Roscoe demanded.

'I'm sorry if you're annoyed with me, sir,' he replied.

'Not much,' said Roscoe. 'It was my intention to keep the interview low key in order to find out as much information as we could about the gang's location and activities. We'd a clear agreement before we began the interview that we'd adopt a softly-softly approach, and you suddenly went off at a tangent with all guns blazing.'

'I've spent hours and hours with the Beauvais family,' Parkes replied. 'They're so devastated at the abduction of their son and I've started to share their anguish. It's been nearly two weeks and they're no nearer being reconciled with him. This piece of scum, Tigworth, has come in here, pleading for leniency in return for us being fed a tissue of lies. He's bleated that he never agreed to the bodyguard being shot and he never agreed to take the boy. I'm sure it's all hogwash.'

Roscoe gazed up at the ceiling in exasperation.

'I know all that,' he said. 'But this is about tactics in the interview room. Our gentler approach seemed to be working. He was sharing all kinds of information with us. Then you go and lose your temper, accusing him of wanting to nick as much as he could lay his filthy hands on and calling him greedy. Your bulldozing tactics caused him to completely shut down.'

'With respect, sir, I felt the laid-back approach we adopted at the start simply wasn't working. I felt we had to make the lad uneasy, hoping he'd blurt out some information that he'd been holding back on.'

Roscoe tutted. 'Well, you saw what happened. He totally clammed up. I want you to assure me, Inspector, that you won't adopt that line of questioning in interviews again on this case. If there's a need for more of a heavy-handed approach, it'll come from me. Is that understood?'

'Yes, sir. Sorry, sir,' said Parkes. He opened the door and stepped out of the room.

* * *

It was dark by the time Sunita Roy, accompanied by DC Omar Khalid, a firearms team and scenes-of-crime officers, arrived in the hamlet of Monkswood. Meadow Brook Farm was located at a sharp bend on a narrow country lane.

'This place is the land that time forgot,' she moaned as she stopped her car several metres away from the main building.

She stepped into the rain-soaked lane and had words with the chief firearms officer, whose vehicle, decked in Heart of England blue and yellow livery, had drawn up behind her.

Moments later, four burly officers in full body armour, wielding Heckler and Koch rifles and ballistic shields, slipped out of a police carrier and began moving slowly towards the open gate that led to the farmyard. They disappeared round the corner, leaving Sunita, Khalid and the SOCO team waiting outside in anticipation.

Within minutes, the squad members were back, shaking their heads.

'The birds have flown,' the firearms chief informed Sunita. 'Place is like the grave.'

'Did they leave the place unlocked?' she asked.

'They left a window open,' he explained.

Sunita paced up and down in the road, shaking her head.

'How do they always manage to keep one step ahead of us?' she demanded.

'It's only a matter of time, Sarge,' replied Khalid. 'If we keep plugging away, we'll catch up with them eventually.'

'Yes, but how much time have we got? The boy hasn't got his medicine with him and there's no knowing what could happen. He might fall and injure himself during a fit.'

After the firearms team had left, Sunita and Khalid stepped into the farmyard and watched as the scenes-of-crime team set to work, photographing and videoing the rooms in the main building.

The two detectives were barred from entering the first-floor bedroom where Marcel had been held, but they were allowed to walk along part of the corridor outside and peer

into the room from the doorway. A female SOCO was examining a wardrobe.

'Omar, tell me again. What's the name of the farm's registered owner?' Sunita asked her colleague.

'A guy called Brian Tyler, who died six months ago, aged eighty-six. No fresh name's been added to the title deeds yet.'

'OK. The whole place desperately needs decorating, particularly this bedroom. I suppose when you reach your eighties, you're not such a dab hand with a paintbrush.'

She gazed down at the room's patterned green carpet.

'Looks like blood,' she said, pointing to a red stain.

'It's all right,' said the forensics officer. 'We're aware of that.'

As the pair stepped onto the landing, Sunita turned towards the tall, dark-haired crime scene manager, who was standing at the top of the stairs. 'Any luck so far?' she asked.

'Nothing's jumped out yet,' the manager replied. 'There may be a few dabs but looks like they've had a good clean-up. Oh, we did find a man's grey sock in the next bedroom, so that might prove useful.'

Sunita phoned the chief inspector once they had returned to her car.

'Sir, the whole place down here is deserted,' she told him.

'What a damn nuisance,' said Roscoe. 'I may as well mention I've had Dawson carrying out checks on the Mercedes and it's been found dumped in woods near the town of Pershore.'

'So they've switched cars again?' said Sunita.

'Looks like it,' he replied. 'We're stymied at every turn.'

* * *

Sunita was leaving the headquarters building after finishing work for the day when she spotted Tom Vickers

wiping the windscreen of his Audi in the car park. She walked towards him.

As soon as he saw her, he opened the driver's door and was about to climb in.

'Why haven't you replied to my messages?' she demanded.

'You know why,' he said.

'Look, would it make any difference if I told you how sorry I am?'

'What about?'

'You know, about the silly argument we had the other evening. I was out of order. I'm sorry.'

Vickers stepped back from the car and put his hands on his hips. There was a pause. Sunita was crestfallen.

'All right,' he said with a shrug. 'I accept your apology.'

'I shouldn't have brought up the question of your ex-wife,' Sunita continued. 'It's water under the bridge really. Do you think we could put that behind us and try and move on?'

'I'd be happy to do that,' he said, breaking into a smile. 'What do you suggest?'

'Why don't you come over to Crompton Gardens one evening and I'll cook you a meal?' she suggested.

'I'd like that,' he said. 'The only thing is it won't be for a few days. I'm tied up on an undercover job and it involves a lot of nights.'

'When do you think you might be free?'

'How about Friday of next week?'

'Sounds good to me. It'll probably be one of my stir-fries.'

'My mouth's watering already,' he said with a grin.

Chapter 30

Marcel stirred from his drug-induced sleep and gazed at his surroundings. Fleetingly, he wondered if he was waking up in his bed at his father's duplex apartment in Paris. Would their pet Belgian shepherd wander in at any moment? Would his father call him for coffee and a croissant? Or perhaps they were at their holiday home in the Dordogne?

Then the grisly truth crept into his head like a detested interloper. Instead of being safely home, he was still incarcerated in this dank dungeon of a cellar, where he had so far spent five nights, shackled like a dog. A manacle was clamped round his right wrist, which was attached to a two-metre long, rusty chain. This, in turn, was fixed to the bottom of the exposed brick wall, beside the narrow bed. Nearby stood a wooden table and chair where he had eaten his meals ever since his arrival there. The only other objects in the room were a lamp on the floor, three barrels in the corner and some metal shelves stacked with wine bottles. The room imparted a damp, musty smell together with a hint of varnished, antique wood. It was also extremely cold. When he'd moaned about it, the men had simply provided him with a small electric fire which emitted hardly any heat.

Marcel had no idea where he was. His captors had left the farm in a panic and, after a journey of around half an hour – during which the gang had changed cars – they had arrived at the old building where he was now being held.

By day, he could hear traffic noise and, occasionally, church bells, so he surmised that he was in a large village or town.

He had a vague recollection of being injected several times over the previous days with the same drug he'd been given for weeks.

'Quel cauchemar!' he said out loud, using the French word for nightmare. He so resented the men who were keeping him there and he so longed to see his mother and father again.

There were no computer games. No conversations. One of the men had called at a second-hand bookshop while out shopping and had bought two books in French for him. One was *Les Voitures Françaises* about French cars manufactured between 1970 and 1979. The second concerned the history of the town of Caen in Normandy. It was hard to imagine two more obscure books to be invited to read, he thought, but he had made a start on both of them.

The only light streamed in through two clerestory windows, more than two metres above his head. If he stood on the bed, he could make out the tyres of the cars and vans that constantly roared past the building. On the far side of the road, he could see a grey, low-level wall, the lower part of a red lifebuoy on a post, and an overcast sky. A light rain was falling.

His spirits were now at their lowest ebb since he had first been seized by the gang. He stroked his stubbly skin. Although he showered frequently – when the men let him – he desperately needed a shave. He felt he was becoming scruffy, and this added to his feelings of despair.

As the morning sun slowly passed over the building, he began to wonder if something had happened to Tiggs. He had not seen him for several days. The tall, well-built man with blond hair was now bringing him meals and escorting him up the stone steps which led to the bathroom on the floor above.

Marcel got up and sat on the bed with his head in his hands. Then he heard the black door opening at the top of

the steps. The tall man was clambering down, holding a plate of hot bacon, eggs and buttered toast.

'Here you are, mate,' said the visitor, from behind a white facemask. 'Get this down you.' He placed it down on the table.

'Where's Tiggs?' Marcel asked.

'Don't ask daft questions.'

'Is he here?'

'You heard what I said,' O'Shane insisted, shaking his head. He pushed the boy hard, causing his head to strike the wall. 'Stop asking questions. Come on, your food's getting cold.'

Marcel winced in pain. 'Where are we right now?' he asked while rubbing the back of his head. 'It must be a town.'

'Never you mind about that. Just you focus on staying fit and healthy. I've got a feeling it ain't going to be long before you're back with your mum and dad.'

'*Quoi?*'

'I've just got a feeling that your folks are going to be helpful and cooperate so we can take you home. But no promises.'

Marcel pulled at the shackle on his wrist. 'Please, can you take this?'

O'Shane shook his head.

'Sorry, mate,' he said. 'I can't do that.'

'Why not? It's beginning to hurt my hand.'

'We were kind to you before and look where it got us. Instead of trusting us, you ran away over the fields. So now we can't take no chances. We've got to keep you fixed to the wall.'

Marcel rose from the bed and took a few paces across the stone floor to the table.

'I don't understand,' he said.

'You let us down, mate,' O'Shane continued. 'We can't trust you no more. Our boss, who found us this little place, says you've got to be chained up. See it from our

point of view. We're in talks with your folks. If they do what they're told, you could be handed over straight away. How does it make us look if you're not here? They'd think we were prize dicks and wonder who they're dealing with. We don't want that, do we?'

Marcel shook his head and picked up a slice of bacon with his fingers. He bit off half of the rasher and chewed it thoughtfully.

'*Non*,' he replied, although he was unsure what point his captor was making.

'Anyway, Marcel, you'll find this place is much more secure than the last one. You'll find it bloody hard to escape from here.'

* * *

After locking the cellar door behind him, Kyle O'Shane returned to the kitchen of the derelict pub and began reading messages on his phone. There was a knock on the side door.

He stepped along the corridor and asked who it was.

'It's only me,' said Wayne Jordan.

O'Shane drew the door back and his associate strode in, laden with bags of shopping.

'We've had some news about Tigworth,' said O'Shane, helping to unpack the groceries on the kitchen table.

'Yeah? He's grassed us up, has he?' asked Jordan.

'Yeah. I didn't think he'd be so stupid. I thought he'd just gone to see his parents. But the boss has just found out he's gone to the Old Bill.'

'What a bastard. Just as well we scarpered from the farm when we did. Just as we thought, he must have taken that old bicycle that was out in the yard.'

'Yeah, he must have done,' said O'Shane.

'Maybe you shouldn't have got him involved in the first place.'

'Don't have a go at me,' shouted O'Shane. 'He's never let us down before.'

'Maybe you shouldn't have let him get matey with the boy.'

'Well, *you* didn't step forward and say *you* wanted to deal with the kid,' said O'Shane. 'So you can shut up about that.'

'What's the betting he's tried to lay all the blame on us for what's happened?' said Jordan while putting bread, butter and some beer on a worktop beside the old Belfast sink.

'That scumbag will be a guest of His Majesty for a long time to come,' O'Shane continued. 'They probably won't give him an easy ride just because he came in and told them all about it, like a good little boy. But anyway, don't worry about Tigworth. The boss has got a plan.'

Chapter 31

The doorbell to her Warwick flat rang on Friday evening while Sunita Roy was cooking noodles in the kitchen. A whole week had passed since Lewis Tigworth handed himself into the police and she discovered the gang had fled from Meadow Brook Farm.

'I hope that's not Tom. I'm not ready,' she said. She untied her apron and rushed down the stairs.

As she opened the door, she found Tom Vickers standing there in his smart grey suit with a broad smile and a bouquet of flowers.

'Tom, how lovely to see you,' she said, reaching out to kiss him on the cheek. 'And what lovely flowers. Are they for me?'

'Of course,' he said, placing them in her hands.

'Oh, Tom, you're a bit early. I've only just got back from work and I've hardly had time to do anything.'

'Don't worry,' he said, following her up the stairs. 'We've got plenty of time. Any news on the house?'

'I've just heard today. The place is mine,' replied Sunita, who had only just found time to slip into a sari.

'That's bostin,' he said. 'This is the five-bedroom place in the centre of Shawley Green?'

Sunita began to stir the noodles. 'That's right,' she said.

'After we've eaten, why don't you let me take you out on the town to celebrate?'

'That would be wonderful, Tom.'

'Great.'

'You go and sit in the living room while I sort out this meal. We're having a spicy mushroom and broccoli stir-fry, sprinkled with cashew nuts.'

'Sounds terrific,' he said. 'That's one of your signature dishes, isn't it?'

'I suppose it is. I'm also grilling some chicken for you because I know you like meat.'

Twenty minutes later, after she had served him a lager from the fridge, they sat down to their meal.

'This is delicious, Sunita,' said Vickers. He twisted some noodles round his fork.

'That's good,' she said. 'Listen, I didn't really expect to get the house in Old School Lane. There was another buyer after it and they offered more money. But they couldn't get the funds together and were forced to pull out. I upped my offer and urged them to exchange contracts *fatafat* or I would pull out as well. Lo and behold, the place is mine.'

'*Fatafat*?' said Vickers, sipping some of his lager. 'What does that mean?'

'It's a word my father often uses,' she said with a laugh while pouring herself a glass of white wine. 'It means "pronto" or "straight away."'

'There's no messing round with you, Sunita,' he said.

She nodded.

‘And because I got it for ten thousand pounds below the asking price, I’ll be able to knock down some walls and create a larger kitchen,’ she said, sipping from her glass.

Vickers held his drink in the air.

‘Well, let’s hope your move goes through *fatafat*!’ he said, clinking his glass against hers.

‘*Fatafat!*’ she responded with a smile.

‘How’s the sale of your flat going?’ Vickers asked.

‘I sold it within two weeks of it going on the market and got the full asking price.’

‘You certainly sound as though you’ve got the hang of this property game,’ he said.

‘Anyway, in the meantime, I’m very worried about the missing French boy,’ said Sunita.

‘What’s the latest on that?’

‘Well, you probably heard the Beauvais family paid two million pounds in cryptocurrency, didn’t you?’

He nodded.

‘The gang are asking for more money now. Meanwhile, the DCI’s lost his patience with Joseph Parkes.’

‘The inspector from the NCA?’

‘Yes. You know one of the gang gave himself up, don’t you? Parkes took a tough line with the guy during an interview. Now the boss is talking about adopting a fresh line on the kidnapping. He claims holding a news blackout – a strategy firmly supported by Parkes – has got us nowhere and he thinks we should hold a press conference and get national publicity.’

Vickers put the last morsel of food in his mouth, placed his cutlery down and leaned back.

‘Personally, I’m not sure that’s a good idea,’ he said.

‘Why not?’

‘Well, Parkes has a lot of experience of dealing with these situations. Silence buys time for everyone – time to pay ransoms or for the police to make a move. A high level of publicity can make hostage takers believe their commodity is really valuable. But the absence of press

coverage can knock their confidence and make them question that assumption.'

Sunita collected the plates up.

'Tom, the gang have already earned themselves two million, so they already have ample proof of how valuable the boy can be. In any case, I think the boss is right to try a different approach.'

'Don't tell him I said so, but it's a gamble, in my opinion – a gamble he might come to regret making,' said Vickers as Sunita disappeared into the kitchen with the plates.

When she returned, she brandished another can of lager for him.

'Shall we make ourselves more comfortable?' she asked.

After pouring herself a second glass of wine, the pair sat down on Sunita's leather settee. Then she turned towards him.

'Tom, let's forget about the kidnapped boy for a moment. I want to talk about us. As I've already told you, I'm really sorry I ruined our evening out at The Wheatsheaf by going on about your ex-wife. What really struck home with me was the way you expressed your feelings when you got angry.'

'How do you mean, Sunita?'

Her voice softened. 'You said you'd always loved me – from the moment we first met – and that the year we spent together was the greatest time of your life.'

He nodded and gazed into her dark eyes. 'That's right.'

'You'd never spoken so frankly before,' she said, clasping his hand. 'Your words moved me and I realised how much I'd missed you since we split up.'

He put his arm round her and kissed her on the lips.

'I've never stopped thinking about you,' he confessed. 'All the time I was over in Summerstoke, I was wondering what you were doing. I always tried to avoid going to St James Street if I could or Warwick. I was concerned I might bump into you and upset myself.'

‘Oh Tom. Poor Tom,’ she said. She kissed him – slowly at first. Then the meeting of their lips developed into a long, passionate kiss.

He was the first to break away.

‘Do you think…?’ he began.

At exactly the same time, she said, ‘Tom, do you…?’

Then they laughed together.

‘You go first,’ he suggested.

‘All right,’ she said. ‘Do you think we could begin to see each other again?’

‘Nothing would suit me better,’ he said.

They embraced again and she was about to make a move towards another kiss when she heard her phone ringing in the kitchen.

‘Leave it,’ he said.

‘It might be important. I’d better go and see who it is.’

She hurried into the kitchen and picked up her phone from the worktop.

‘It’s the DCI,’ she whispered. ‘I’d better take it.’

Pressing the answer key, she said, ‘DS Roy.’

‘Sorry to disturb you, Sergeant,’ said Roscoe. ‘But I’ve just heard some devastating news. Our key witness, Lewis Tigworth, has been found dead.’

Chapter 32

Early on Saturday morning, Sunita Roy made the thirty-minute journey from her Warwick home to the chief inspector’s house on the northern outskirts of Queensbridge. As her car drew into the narrow, tree-lined lane outside, she spotted her boss emerging from his front door. Moments later, they set off in his car to Ashwood

Vale Prison, a maximum-security, men-only jail – unofficially known to everyone as 'The Vale'.

'Do we have any idea how Tigworth died?' Sunita asked as they approached the town of Evesham.

'Not yet,' Roscoe replied. 'But it looks as though he was strangled or suffocated while he was on the phone to his mother. I've sent DC Khalid over to the parents' place in Queensbridge and I've got Dawson tracing the time of the call Tigworth made. Silas went over to the Vale last night, but I haven't been able to reach him this morning to hear his findings.'

After leaving the A46 and following country lanes for seven miles, they saw a sign saying 'HM Prison Ashwood Vale' – and realised they'd reached their destination.

Sunita gazed across at the 1960s complex, its grey walls austere and forbidding. In the foreground was a packed visitors' car park with a two-storey gatehouse behind. The main buildings were shielded by high walls and security fencing.

After he showed his warrant card and was waved through by a security guard at the entrance barrier, Roscoe chose a space in a car park for staff and designated visitors before they walked to the gatehouse, which always reminded him of a library. Once they had been signed in and searched at the reception desk, the pair were escorted upstairs into the office of solemn-faced prison governor Emlyn Griffiths-Jones.

He stood up and strode across the room to greet them, nearly knocking over a small Christmas tree perched on the corner of his oak desk.

'I remember you both from three years ago,' he said, breaking into a smile as he shook their hands warmly. 'You were investigating how one of our inmates escaped while on his way to court.'

'That's right,' said the chief inspector while Sunita gazed round at photographs on the walls of past governors and at a portrait of the King. 'You were very helpful then.

This time we're here because a man we arrested just over a week ago has been found dead.'

Griffiths-Jones nodded as he took a seat behind his desk and offered his visitors chairs.

'Yes, young Lewis Tigworth,' he said.

'What exactly happened, sir?' asked Sunita.

'Well, it was around 7.20 p.m. last night. Tigworth was on his association period and was using a pay phone in the corridor outside his cell in B Wing. He'd told his cellmate he wanted to call his mother.

'One of our warders, a man named Roland Hargreaves, was some distance away, dealing with an argument between two inmates. He heard an altercation coming from the landing where the phones are and ran to see what was happening. As he approached, he noticed a man lying on the floor and a tall prisoner with blond hair running away from the scene.

'Hargreaves examined the man on the floor, whom he recognised as Tigworth, and found him motionless. He called a colleague who was better qualified in first aid. He tried to resuscitate Tigworth with chest compressions, but it was no good. West Midlands Ambulance Service were alerted and came within twenty minutes. They carried out advanced life support procedures, but, sadly, he was confirmed dead at the scene shortly afterwards.'

'Where did they take the body?' asked Roscoe.

'The body was left by the phones because the Home Office pathologist, Dr Reynolds, was coming and requested the scene should remain untouched. After that, he arranged for the body to be taken to the mortuary in Queensbridge. It's been a nasty old business. I've had the young man's mother on the phone three times this morning. She's so upset, as you can imagine.'

'Have you spoken to Mr Hargreaves, sir, since the tragedy?' Sunita asked.

'Yes. He's devastated, obviously.'

‘Could you get someone to show us where the young man died?’ he asked.

‘Yes, I’ll ask Hargreaves to show you,’ said the governor, rising from his chair and stepping towards the office next door.

‘He’s just started his shift this morning. I realised you’d want to speak to him so I’ve asked him to come to the office and he should be waiting now in the lobby outside.’

Broad-shouldered prison officer Roland Hargreaves was a man of few words. He had been sitting on a chair directly outside the governor’s office and stood up respectfully when the two detectives emerged and closed the governor’s door behind them.

‘Morning,’ he said.

‘Mr Hargreaves,’ said Sunita, ‘the governor’s kindly explained you found the body last night. Must have been distressing for you.’

‘Yes.’

‘Can you tell us about events leading up to the discovery of the body?’ she said.

‘Yes. I was asked by the senior warder to monitor the first-floor landing on B Wing during association,’ he said.

‘That’s the association period – when prisoners are allowed out of their cells to go to the gym, make phone calls and generally associate with other prisoners and staff?’ she asked.

‘Yes.’

‘What time did you begin your period of duty on B Wing?’

‘Association begins at 6 p.m. and lasts for an hour and a quarter. It must have been a few minutes to six when I took up my position on the landing.’

‘At what time did you find the body?’

‘It had just gone 7.20 p.m.’

‘How did you come to notice it?’

‘I couldn’t see the phone booth area from my position at the end of the landing but I heard some kind of argument –

loud words being exchanged. I went to see what was going on and found Tigworth lying on the floor by the phones.'

Roscoe, who had been following every word, intervened.

'Before you arrived, you spotted a man running away,' he said.

'Yes.'

'Can you confirm that person's name?' asked Roscoe.

'Dylan Roberts, who's here for acts of violence.'

'Why are you so sure it was him?' asked Sunita.

'He's got weird hair.'

'What's weird about it?'

'I think they call it a mohawk. I'd recognise him anywhere.'

Sunita stood back and folded her arms.

'Mr Hargreaves, you immediately summoned help, presumably?' she said.

'Yes. I alerted the senior warder, Mr Warner, at 7.25 p.m. He tried CPR, but it was no good. You could see he was gone.'

'Have you tackled Mr Roberts about what you saw?' asked the chief inspector.

'I went to see him as soon as the paramedics arrived,' he said.

'What did he have to say for himself?' asked Roscoe.

'He admitted being on the landing, but denied seeing Tigworth. He just claimed he was running because he was in a hurry.'

Chapter 33

Prison officer Roland Hargreaves showed little emotion when the two detectives asked him to show them the precise spot where he had found Lewis Tigworth's body

the previous evening. Sunita tried to detect whether he was enthusiastic about returning to the scene of the crime or reluctant to be going there. In the end, she couldn't decide.

He led them up a flight of iron steps inside B Wing and along a landing until they reached a place where four phones were fixed to the wall in a recessed area. There were signs that scenes-of-crime officers from Heart of England Police had been present. A torn piece of police tape lay in a corner.

'Here you are,' he said.

'Mr Hargreaves,' said Sunita, 'where exactly was Mr Tigworth lying when you found him? Would you mind demonstrating?'

Although hesitant, the middle-aged warder agreed to cooperate. He knelt down on the floor and then lay outstretched on his stomach.

'So he was face down?'

'Yes,' he said. 'Mind if I get up now?'

The chief inspector helped him to his feet. 'You recognised him immediately?'

'I knew who he was,' Hargreaves replied.

'From among so many inmates?' said Sunita.

At that moment, Roscoe's mobile phone began ringing from an inside pocket of his dark-blue jacket.

'Would you mind holding on there for just a moment? Someone's calling me,' he explained. He could be heard answering his phone as he stepped away.

Sunita gazed into Hargreaves's eyes.

'You've already told us you spotted Mr Roberts running from the phone area,' she said. 'And you're certain it was him because of his hair?'

'Yes.

'What's Roberts inside for?'

'He beat up an old lady in Queensbridge,' he replied. 'Then he ran off with her pension money for the week. It happened only a week after he nearly blinded a young guy in a pub fight with a broken bottle.'

Two minutes later, Roscoe rejoined them.

'Can you arrange for us to have a word with Mr Roberts?' he asked Hargreaves.

'Yes, sir. I'll go and see what the situation is. Can you hold on here?'

Once Hargreaves had marched off along the landing, the chief inspector revealed his caller had been the pathologist, Dr Silas Reynolds.

'Tigworth was strangled,' he told Sunita. 'There were grip marks and red spots around the victim's neck, according to Silas. There were also tiny spots in the lining of the eyes, apparently. It seems Tigworth put up a struggle, trying to prise the attacker's hands away from his neck.'

'Without much success,' said Sunita.

'Exactly,' said Roscoe. 'Silas thinks it's possible he may be able to recover the attacker's skin cells from the victim's neck. He'll let us know in due course, but the cause of death was asphyxia due to manual strangulation.'

'It would be brilliant if he could recover the attacker's skin cells,' she said. 'Sir, I think Hargreaves is on his way back.'

The chief inspector turned to see the warder hurrying towards them, perspiring and short of breath.

'Sorry to keep you,' he told them. 'I've managed to locate Roberts and he's being led back to his cell now. Look, before we go down there, please don't mention I saw him hurrying away from the murder scene. I think he's aware that someone saw him, but I don't want to be identified as that witness at this stage. You know, in the interests of warder–inmate relations?'

'I understand,' said Roscoe.

'All right,' said Hargreaves. 'Shall we take a stroll down there?'

Roscoe nodded and the two detectives followed Hargreaves as he walked back past rows of cell doors.

Minutes later, they reached a door marked '74', which Hargreaves unlocked.

Peering into the cell, they found a tall man with a blond mohawk hairstyle on his own, lying on an upper bunkbed, reading a book. He put the book down as soon as he noticed his visitors in the doorway.

'Roberts, these are the two detectives you've been told about,' said Hargreaves.

'OK,' said the prisoner, morosely.

'Just got a few questions for you, Mr Roberts,' said the chief inspector.

'I'll leave you now,' the prison officer explained in a low voice as he began to walk off. 'But if you need me, I won't be far away.'

Roscoe and Sunita edged forward into the cell.

'You're aware that a prisoner was found dead a short distance from here at 7.20 p.m. last night, are you?' the chief inspector asked, leaning against the bed.

'Of course,' said Roberts, as he hoisted himself up on his mattress. He stared down at his two visitors with a blank expression. 'Everyone in the prison is talking about it.'

'He was found lying on the ground by the payphones,' said Sunita, who remained by the door, 'and at the time you were seen near the body.'

'Yeah, I know, but I didn't have nothing to do with it,' Roberts replied.

'Where'd you been?' asked Roscoe.

'I'd been down to the sports hall.'

'Anyone able to confirm that?' asked Sunita.

'Only about two dozen prisoners and a couple of the screws,' he replied.

'All right,' said Roscoe. 'Whereabouts is the sports hall?'

'It's on the ground floor, ten minutes' walk away, near D Wing.'

'So what time did you leave the sports hall?'

'Must have been about ten minutes past seven.'

'And what time did you reach the landing here?'

‘Around 7.20 p.m. or 7.25 p.m. I was carrying my gym gear.’

‘What happened when you reached the phones?’ asked Sunita. ‘Did you see Mr Tigworth making a call?’

‘I saw a guy there. I didn’t know who he was. I’d never seen him before,’ said Roberts. ‘Apparently, he was one of the remand prisoners.’

‘And what was this prisoner actually doing?’ asked Roscoe.

‘He was standing up, speaking on the phone.’

Sunita interrupted. ‘Can I just ask something?’ she said. ‘We’ve been told Mr Tigworth was the only prisoner using the phones at the time. Is that right? Bit unusual, isn’t it?’

‘A bell had gone, which signalled all prisoners had to return to their cells immediately,’ Roberts explained.

‘What – there was some kind of disturbance?’ asked Roscoe.

‘No. There are two bells marking the end of the association period,’ said the prisoner. ‘Maybe the guy, being new, didn’t know the rule that you’ve got to go to your cell immediately or maybe he chose to ignore the bells.’

Roscoe nodded. ‘So what happened when you reached the phone area? Did you speak to him and argue over something?’

Roberts shook his head. ‘I spoke to him but we didn’t argue. All I said was “Better get back to your cell, mate. The second bell’s gone.” He just waved his hand to acknowledge what I’d said and I carried on making my way to my cell.’

‘So, he was standing up and chatting on the phone when you encountered him?’ said Sunita.

‘Yeah. Why’d I hurt the fellow? I didn’t know him.’

‘We’ve been told you ran back to your cell from the phone area. Is that right?’ asked Sunita.

'Yeah. Well, I didn't want to get into any trouble with the screws, did I? I was late, so yeah – I ran the last part of the journey.'

Sunita was staring at a bandage on the man's right thumb.

'So, the man on the phone was alive and kicking at the time you saw him?' she said.

'Yeah, of course.'

'How did you injure your thumb?'

Roberts glanced down at the white bandage.

'Playing basketball yesterday,' he replied. 'I fell awkwardly on the court and managed to cut it. The doc put this on for me in the first aid room late last night.'

'All right. Thanks for your time,' said Roscoe. 'We might need to talk to you again.'

'That's all right,' said Roberts. 'You know where to find me. I won't be going nowhere.'

Afterwards, the pair found Hargreaves sitting on a wooden bench at the end of the landing.

'Got what you wanted?' the warder asked.

'For the moment,' said Roscoe.

'Don't be fooled by his calm appearance,' said Hargreaves, rising from his seat. 'Roberts is a nasty piece of work and, personally, I wouldn't trust a word he says. Anyway, I'll show you both out.'

* * *

'That was too much of a coincidence – that thumb injury,' said Roscoe, once the two detectives had returned to his car. 'I wouldn't mind betting he acquired it while strangling Tigworth – not while falling over during a game of basketball. He looks as guilty as hell but we need more evidence.'

'I'm not totally convinced of the prisoner's guilt,' said Sunita.

'Aren't you?'

'No, it all seems too simple and straightforward – not to mention the lack of motive. I'm wondering if there could be another explanation.'

'Well, at least we know where to find Roberts,' Roscoe said while starting the car. 'As he said, he won't be going anywhere. Listen, Sergeant, find out what you can about him – you know, family, friends, his workplace, that sort of thing.'

'Certainly, sir,' she said. 'But we surely can't rule out the possibility that Tigworth's death might have some connection with the kidnap gang.'

'I agree. That's a line of inquiry we've got to follow. The gang must have realised Tigworth came to see us and they'd have good reason to want him silenced. We're going to have to pull a few tricks out of the bag to catch this gang. And one of the tricks I'm going to use involves harnessing the power of the press. I'm going to arrange a press conference in a day or two.'

Roscoe's mobile phone began to ring and he switched to hands free.

'Roscoe,' he announced as his car travelled along country lanes towards the A46 road.

'Inspector Parkes here,' said the caller. 'Sir, I've been trying to reach you. The Beauvais family have received a new video from the kidnappers, along with full details of the new ransom demand.'

Chapter 34

Later that morning, after the chief inspector's car had drawn up outside Upper Norton Manor, the housekeeper came to open the front door.

'You're looking extremely well now,' Roscoe told Marilyn Willis as he stepped out of the car together with his sergeant.

'Do you think so, sir?' she replied. 'That's kind of you to say. I'll take you through to the family.'

Roscoe and Sunita Roy hurriedly followed her past the imperial staircase in the hallway. At the open living-room door, she announced, 'The police are here, Monsieur Beauvais,' before she went back to the kitchen.

The detectives found Jean-Jacques and Camille Beauvais sitting together on one of the three settees. Engrossed in conversation together at the dining table nearby were Katrina Drake and DI Parkes.

'Good morning, everybody,' said Roscoe with a solemn expression.

'Good morning, Chief Inspector,' said Jean-Jacques.

'Good. I'm glad you've made it, sir,' said Parkes, rising from his chair. 'Monsieur and Madame Beauvais have kindly agreed to let us watch the video on their widescreen television. Everyone here's already seen it. Here we go.'

He pressed some buttons on a remote-control device and the TV in the corner of the room sprang into life. The two newcomers found themselves seats and the video began to play.

At first, an obscure shape was seen moving around in a dark room. Then light streamed in and Marcel could be seen, sitting alone at a table, eating a sandwich. The camera rotated round the room. Then the film-maker – evidently a man standing above the boy on some stone steps, appeared to stumble. After regaining his balance, he was heard saying in a Midlands accent, 'Speak to the camera.'

Camille sobbed as Marcel stood up and approached the camera. He was unshaven and his hair was dishevelled. He still had two medallions round his neck and a nose ring. For the first time during his long ordeal, he appeared frightened.

The camera continued to pan round the room. Occasionally, the sound of nearby church bells could be discerned above the roar of passing traffic. It was clear the young hostage was being kept in a cellar. Two small horizontal windows could be seen at the top of the far wall. Wine barrels and bottles were stacked in a corner. Camille sobbed after a chain could be seen attached to Marcel's wrist.

'*Maman! Papa!*' Marcel was heard saying. '*Je suis sain et sauf.* Please do as the men say. They will let me go if you pay the money they have asked for.'

Then the screen was filled with a message in capital letters – 'TIME IS RUNNING OUT' – before the view switched to a different location and focussed on a consignment of knives, guns and ammunition.

'Would you mind, Inspector, if we viewed it again?' asked Sunita.

'No problem,' said Parkes. 'I'll run it continuously for a while, shall I?'

The chief inspector nodded as the video was replayed.

'Chief Inspector,' said Jean-Jacques, 'Inspector Parkes, he is suggesting we pay the demand for a second ransom of two million pounds. Do you have any views on this?'

'I certainly think you should enter into negotiations with the gang,' said Roscoe. 'Whether you should actually pay the money, I'm not sure. The problem is you could pay it and then they could demand even more money.'

'Chief Inspector,' said Camille, 'you have no idea how desperate we are to be reunited with our son. Our lives have been torn apart. It is like living with a knife in the heart. Every fresh message from the gang brings a twist of this knife. I don't know if there is much more we can take.'

'I completely understand,' he said. 'Look, I may as well confide in you about this now. I'm planning a press conference for Tuesday afternoon. As you know, we've been keeping a news blackout on your son's disappearance

and have been limiting publicity to the local area. But I think the time for pussyfooting around is now over.'

Parkes scowled and attempted to interrupt him, but Roscoe chose to ignore him.

'That previous approach of operating in a publicity vacuum has clearly failed. So, my inclination now is to bring matters fully into the public arena. This will hopefully encourage members of the public to come forward with information and, as a result, we may quickly find your son.'

Sunita, who had been watching the video with intense interest, crossed the room and began a conversation with Parkes.

At the same time, Jean-Jacques, who had been exchanging words with his wife, stood up and stepped towards Roscoe.

'Chief Inspector,' he said, 'if you believe this new technique has the good chance of success, Camille and I will support you.'

'Thank you,' said Roscoe. 'That's good because I'd like you both to appear at the news conference and speak to members of the press, TV and radio. Are you happy to do that?'

'Yes. If that helps to bring back our beloved son, of course we will,' he said.

'We can see from the video how tired and upset your son's become. Let's see if we can bring him back quickly with help from observant members of the British public.'

A few minutes later, Roscoe and Sunita left the house and were walking back to their car when Parkes dashed out of the front door after them.

'Chief Inspector, could I have a word, please?' he asked. 'I hope you don't mind me saying so, but I do feel you're adopting the wrong strategy. I think you're making a terrible mistake.'

'As it happens, I do mind you saying it,' Roscoe retorted. 'You say the previous approach in keeping

everything hush-hush has brought dividends in the past, but the method has clearly failed in this case.'

Parkes placed his hands on his hips as he stood beside the BMW.

'With respect, sir, this whole case has been an extremely sensitive one and lifting the news blackout could jeopardise everything. Once the floodgates to publicity are open, who knows what information is going to be printed about Marcel? News stories could place the boy in greater danger, depending on what's written.'

'I trust the press on this one, Inspector,' Roscoe insisted. 'News organisations have a duty not to endanger life or place the hostage in greater peril. In any event, we've tried proceeding without publicity and that hasn't worked at all.'

Parkes stood his ground.

'Sir, surely the value of a human life far outweighs the need for the press to freely report on absolutely everything they choose to report on.'

Roscoe frowned as he got into the car. 'Other wealthy families and their relatives may be at risk of their loved ones being snatched by this ruthless gang,' he continued. 'But, because of the news blackout, they're carrying on with their lives in blissful ignorance. We owe it to them to warn them that this has been going on and to take precautions. But our number one priority must surely be to get the lad back with his family and I sincerely believe that by changing direction in this way, we'll succeed in doing that.'

After Roscoe and his sergeant had begun driving away, Sunita turned towards him from the passenger seat.

'If it means anything to you, sir, I entirely back what you said just then.'

'Thank you,' he replied. 'Of course, your views are important to me and thank you for your support. By the way, I noticed you speaking to Parkes while we were at the house. What was that about?'

'I've arranged to have a copy of the video,' she said. 'I want to go through it carefully. I've got an idea that might help us find the gang's new hideout and lead us to the boy.'

Chapter 35

Television vans blocked part of the rainswept pavement outside Queensbridge police station on Tuesday afternoon as journalists arrived for the press conference.

The chief inspector had managed to book the station's large, ground-floor meeting room for two hours and he was making sure enough chairs were being set out.

He watched through the open door as a liveried BBC van drew up behind vehicles emblazoned with ITV and Sky News logos. Thick power cables were snaking across the pavement and weaving their way through the reception hall. Colourful posters had been fixed to the walls, showing Marcel Dubois in two different poses beneath the headline 'Missing'. One photograph showed him with medium-length hair and glasses. The other portrayed him with short hair and his two familiar medallions dangling round his neck.

Marcel Dubois, aged sixteen, went missing from Norton Prior, Warwickshire on 29 October. Marcel is French, around five feet eight inches tall and often wears two gold medallions round his neck. He was wearing a green pullover and dark jeans when he disappeared. Marcel is lately understood to have been in the Pershore area. Anyone with information should contact the police incident room at St James Street or Crimestoppers.

The sound of a gravelly voice a few metres away alerted him that DI Parkes had arrived. Roscoe stepped towards his colleague and tapped him on the arm.

'I wasn't sure you were coming,' he said.

'You know how I feel about this briefing,' said Parkes, 'but I came because I think it's important for me to maintain good relations with the family.'

'You're welcome to take a place on the podium alongside the Beauvais couple,' said Roscoe.

'Thank you, sir. I appreciate that. But, if it's all right with you, I won't be making any statement or answering questions.' Parkes then went to speak to a police colleague.

Over the next few minutes, several sound engineers climbed onto the platform and installed microphones on tables. Some colleagues set up lighting equipment nearby.

As they worked, Roscoe was disturbed to see an unexpected face appear briefly in the doorway – the face of Philippe Dubois, the missing boy's biological father.

'What's the matter, sir?' asked DC Khalid. 'You look as though you've just received some terrible news.'

'It probably is terrible news. I've just seen Marcel's other dad in the corridor outside,' he replied. 'I hope he isn't going to cause any trouble. I'd better have a word with him.'

The chief inspector found Dubois outside the police station in the high street, smoking a strong cigarette while pacing up and down the pavement.

'How are you, Mr Dubois?' asked Roscoe as he approached him.

'Oh, hello, *Monsieur le Chief Inspector*. I'm well, thank you, although I'm not sleeping.'

Roscoe frowned. 'You know there won't be any opportunity this afternoon for you to make any public statement, don't you?'

He nodded. 'I'm just here in case I'm needed,' the Frenchman replied. 'I'm glad you've invited the press to

attend. We need to move things along quickly now and find Marcel. There's no need for me to make speeches.'

'All right, sir,' said Roscoe, 'provided that's understood. We'll find you somewhere to sit.'

Fifteen minutes later, Roscoe was ready to start. He took a seat on the podium and was joined by Inspector Parkes. At the same time, PC Underhill escorted Mr and Mrs Beauvais inside and they took seats beside the two detectives.

'Good to see you all this afternoon, ladies and gentlemen,' said Roscoe, rising confidently to his feet and speaking into a microphone. 'I called this media briefing because, for three weeks, we've been investigating the disappearance of a teenage boy, Marcel Dubois. As I'm sure you're aware, he's the stepson of Aston Villa football player Jean-Jacques Beauvais, whom many of you'll recognise sitting on the platform here today, along with his wife.'

He pointed the couple out before continuing.

'I'd like to take this opportunity to thank the press and broadcasting organisations for abiding by the news blackout we requested while we maintained our initial efforts to trace Marcel and reunite him with his family.

'Because of various factors, which I won't go into now for operational reasons, we've not yet succeeded in tracing the missing boy, whom has been abducted by a gang of criminals who refer to themselves as the Matchday Boys. He's been missing since the gang burgled Upper Norton Manor on the last Saturday of October. We're going public today with details of the search in the hope that we can bring our investigation to a swift conclusion. I'm now going to ask Monsieur Beauvais to say a few words before inviting members of the press to ask questions. Monsieur Beauvais.'

Parkes whispered a remark to Roscoe while the footballer nervously tapped the microphone in front of

him. As several photographers rushed forward to take close-up pictures, Jean-Jacques gazed out across the room.

'These three weeks, they have been a nightmare for Camille and me,' he began in a clear voice. 'Marcel may be sixteen years of age, but he is not the most grown-up of boys and must be extremely frightened to be kept away from his home.'

He glanced down at a sheet of paper.

'Marcel is five feet eight inches tall. His brown hair has been cut short with what the English hairdressers call the cat scratches. He also has the nose ring. We would beg anyone with information to contact the police. Please, we need everybody to help. Marcel has never been away from his family for so long before. Help us to bring him back. He is such a dear, sweet boy.'

Camille became tearful on hearing these words. She hugged Jean-Jacques as he sat down amid a light smattering of applause from the onlookers.

Roscoe glanced around the room. 'We can now take questions,' he said. 'When you speak, please state your name and organisation.'

A tall, dark-haired man near the back raised his hand.

'Chief Inspector, John Singleton, *Midlands TV News*,' he said. 'Do police have any idea at all where the missing boy might be?'

Roscoe looked uncomfortable. He leaned forward in his seat and reached for the microphone.

'We've got firm intelligence that Marcel is still in the West Midlands,' he replied.

'But you don't really know exactly where, do you?' said Singleton.

'I think I've answered that question,' said Roscoe.

A slim, blonde journalist sitting near the front raised her hand.

'Susan Ellis-Jones, *Queensbridge Gazette*,' she said. 'The boy's disappearance obviously follows the burglary at Upper Norton Manor and the murder of Danny Jukes. So,

if members of the public come forward with information, don't police want to warn them that the gang are extremely dangerous?'

Roscoe nodded. 'Thank you, Susan. That's a highly valid point and one I was intending to bring up. You're right. We're dealing with a highly dangerous, violent gang and we're concerned that members of the public shouldn't try to be heroes if they come across them. They should report any suspicious activities to police, who'll investigate.

'At this point, I should state that we're looking for two men in particular, Kyle O'Shane and Wayne Jordan.' He described both men.

Sitting beside Susan Ellis-Jones was a fair-haired man with a moustache.

'May I ask a question, *Monsieur le Chief Inspector*?' he asked.

'Of course,' said Roscoe.

'Jerome Bernard, Agence France-Presse,' said the man. 'It's been in the news that a man was found dead in a prison ten miles from here. I'm told this may be linked to the kidnap of Marcel.'

'No comment on that,' replied Roscoe. 'Inquiries are ongoing.'

'Monsieur, can I also ask whether police are linking this gang with break-ins in Cheshire that have taken place over the past ten years? And whether an organised crime gang are believed to be behind this abduction – such as a gang from London?'

'Monsieur Bernard, it seems you're trying to ask several questions at once,' Roscoe replied. 'We aren't linking the burglary at Norton Prior with any other house raids at the moment and, at present, we've no reason to believe a major crime gang from London is involved. But we're keeping an open mind.'

After the press conference ended and journalists began to leave, Khalid approached Roscoe.

'Sir, I've just noticed the man you were speaking to earlier…'

'Philippe Dubois?' asked Roscoe.

'Yes. He's out on the pavement with an umbrella, being pestered by a group of reporters.'

Roscoe was dismayed to hear that Philippe Dubois had made himself known to the press and was making himself available to be interviewed.

'Quick. Get out there and listen very carefully to him,' said Roscoe. 'He's a bit of a loose cannon. We don't want him saying anything awkward or out of place.'

As Khalid hurried away, Roscoe slumped forward on the podium table with his head in his hands. Ten minutes later, when Roscoe and Underhill were preparing to leave, Khalid returned.

'You're not going to like this, sir,' he said. 'I caught a little of what Dubois was saying. He was criticising the footballer and his wife. He was also laying into Parkes, claiming that, because of him, he'd been barred from receiving updates on the progress of the investigation. He also claimed Heart of England officers have been at loggerheads over the right strategy to pursue.'

Chapter 36

The chief inspector strolled into the CID office early on Wednesday morning. Omar Khalid was engrossed in writing a report on his computer about a burglary in the town of Redditch.

'DC Khalid, have you seen DS Roy this morning?' Roscoe asked.

'No, sir. It's nearly half past ten and she's normally here by this time, isn't she?'

‘She called me late last night to say that she was close to a breakthrough on the whereabouts of the missing boy,’ said Roscoe. ‘She just needed to double-check some details. I hope she hasn’t done anything rash to put herself at risk. You know how impetuous she can be at times.’

‘Yes, sir.’

‘Ah. Here she is now,’ said Roscoe as a figure in a fawn coat could be seen bustling towards them.

‘Morning, Sergeant,’ Roscoe said.

‘Sorry, sir,’ Sunita said as she reached her desk, perspiring and short of breath. ‘I was just checking something.’

‘No apology needed,’ he replied. ‘You’d better come into my office when you’re ready.’

He turned to Khalid. ‘DI Parkes is by the coffee machine. Could you ask him to come and see me as soon as he can?’

Moments later, Sunita was sitting in front of the chief inspector’s desk, studying some notes, while her boss was settling into his chair. DI Parkes hurried in, closed the door and took a seat beside her.

‘Now I gather you’ve made some progress, Sergeant,’ said Roscoe.

She nodded. ‘The boy’s in Worcester,’ she said.

‘How can you be so sure?’ asked Parkes.

‘Because of the bells that we can hear on the video.’

‘The bells? They’re just ordinary church bells, aren’t they? They’re the kind of bells that ring out in any town or village in the land,’ said Parkes.

‘No,’ said Sunita. ‘Those bells picked up on the video are ringing out from the belfry in Worcester Cathedral. I’ve visited the city a few times with a friend of mine – the most recent occasion being last Easter – and it was pointed out to us by someone in the cathedral that the sound is quite distinctive on key dates. Just to be sure, I’ve played a copy of the video to the bell ringing master at the cathedral. He’s confirmed, after listening to the audio, that they’re definitely

the bells from his cathedral and he suspects the video was made within a few miles of his building.'

'Really?' said Roscoe. 'That's amazing.'

'I won't bore you with all the finer details,' Sunita continued, 'but there are sixteen bells altogether and this cathedral is the only church in the world to have a ring of ten bells in a harmonic minor key.' She glanced down at her notes. 'This special peal of bells are rung half-muffled on key dates in the Christian calendar and they've only been rung in this way once since the gang left Meadow Brook Farm, and that was on Remembrance Sunday – ten days ago.'

Parkes sneered. 'This ringing master at the cathedral hasn't by any chance given you the gang's address and postcode, has he?' he asked sarcastically.

'Don't be so ridiculous, man,' said Roscoe.

'The bells can be heard all over the city,' she admitted. 'But we've got a few other clues as to the whereabouts of the gang's hideout. I must have played the video more than a dozen times and I've been stopping and starting it. Through one of the windows in the boy's cellar you can see three distinctive blocks of flats, which are more than ten storeys high.'

'Do we know where in Worcester these flats are?'

'They're in Tybridge Street, in a suburb called St John's.'

'Any other clues?'

'The camera catches a fleeting glimpse of a lifebuoy,' she said. 'You know, a buoyancy aid, which seems to be installed by some railings. So, I'm wondering if Marcel is being kept in a building near the River Severn.'

She leaned back on her chair and glanced at Roscoe and Parkes in turn.

Parkes shook his head. 'Sounds like you're clutching at straws,' he said dismissively.

The chief inspector had a more positive attitude.

'You've done some excellent work there, Sergeant,' he said. 'I'll have a word with our colleagues over in Worcester. We need to set up a huge team to begin searching buildings on both sides of the river. We'll need dogs as well. You know the drill – calling door-to-door with photographs of Marcel, O'Shane and Jordan. We must give top priority to empty or derelict buildings. At the same time, our approach mustn't be too high profile. Don't want to cause the gang alarm and prompt them to flee again.'

'You're suggesting more of a softly-softly approach, sir?' said Sunita.

'Exactly,' he said. 'And hopefully, if your deductions are correct, we ought to make finding that lifebuoy a priority. There's a good chance Marcel won't be too far away.'

'Sir, there's one thing I'd like to point out since the river's been mentioned,' said Parkes. 'I was reading online there's been a lot of rain in the areas north of Worcester over the past week – you know, Shrewsbury, Bridgnorth and Bewdley. River levels are high and there have been warnings that some roads and farmland around the city are likely to be flooded later this week.'

'Which makes it all the more imperative we throw all our resources into finding him quickly,' said Roscoe. 'That cellar might be in a flood area and the lad could be at risk of drowning. So, if we need to supply our folk with boots and boats, so be it.'

* * *

Shortly after Roscoe began organising a team of officers to search buildings close to the river, the chief inspector received a call from his superior, Chief Superintendent Nicola Norris. She wished to see him straight away.

He made his way to her second-floor office and found her sitting in her usual place behind her desk, studying her computer screen.

'Ah, Gavin,' said Norris, peering over her reading glasses. 'Is there something wrong with your phone? I've been trying to reach you for half an hour.'

'No, not as far as I know, ma'am,' he replied, finding himself a chair. 'Oh, hang on. I took it off the hook while DS Roy was disclosing some crucial information.'

She immediately sat up straight.

'What's this crucial information?' she asked, manoeuvring her wheelchair round the side of the desk.

'There's a strong chance the missing boy is being held in Worcester, ma'am. So we're searching the waterfront.'

'That's admirable,' she replied.

'Listen, Gavin, the reason I wanted to speak to you is about this press coverage,' she said. 'Have you seen the national papers and the stuff they're spewing out online?'

'I saw a couple of the headlines when I got into work,' he admitted.

'Look at this,' she said, snatching a tabloid newspaper from her desk. 'This one says: "Cops clash over kidnap op". There's another here: "Police lock horns over missing teen ploy". Have you seen the *Queensbridge Gazette* website? Their top story is: "Father of kidnapped boy shunned by cops". What the hell's been going on, Gavin?'

'I'm sorry, ma'am,' he said. 'We've got a close rapport with the Beauvais family. DI Parkes has built up a good relationship with them, but the boy's biological father, Philippe Dubois, is in the UK now and he's a bit of a maverick. I imagine these reports are based on what he told reporters after the press conference. He was outside on the street. We weren't able to control that.'

'Well, I suggest you have a frank word with him and try to keep him sweet. The assistant chief constable's very annoyed by these reports.'

Chapter 37

A short distance from Worcester police station, in the centre of the city, two officers were sitting in their stationary BMW police car, watching passing traffic. Now and then, they would catch sight of a pedestrian scurrying from doorway to doorway along the grey, rain-lashed street.

'They say the floods this week could be the worst in years,' said PC Michael Jenkins.

'Something will have to be done about it,' said his colleague, PC Katie Smart. 'Are you going to that Christmas party at the Bank House?' he asked.

'The Abba tribute?' she replied while attempting to tuck some of her blonde hair beneath her police cap.

'Yes,' he said. 'You said you were hoping to take your boyfriend.'

'I was out of luck. By the time I phoned, all the tickets had gone,' said Smart.

'That's a shame. So have you decided where you're going on Friday?'

At that moment, a blue Nissan Qashqai swept past at thirty-five miles an hour. The speed limit for the city street was thirty.

'Look at that idiot,' said Jenkins.

He started his engine and began pursuing the car along the street. At the same time, he switched on his blue light and siren.

'You'd think, with all this rain, they'd slow down, Mike,' said Smart, as she adjusted her glasses. 'But the driver's put his foot down.'

She called the Heart of England control room on the car radio.

'Vehicle making off at 10.14 a.m.,' she announced. 'Failing to stop for traffic officers in The Tything. Speed currently five zero miles per hour.'

She gave their location and the Nissan Qashqai's registration, explained they were following the A38 road in a northerly direction and requested police back-up.

'Driver seems to be heading towards Droitwich,' she continued. 'Any mobiles in the vicinity?'

'Control room here,' came the reply. 'Inspector O'Grady. Message received. Police carrier nearby and will join shortly.'

'He's driving like a bloody maniac,' Jenkins complained as Smart ended her call.

The traffic officers sped on for another two minutes with their siren wailing and blue lights reflecting off the rain-washed street. Eventually, they began to gain on the suspect vehicle, despite its driver touching speeds of up to sixty miles an hour. They were only twenty metres behind now, but the driver – who seemed to be accompanied by a second man – was ignoring their signal to pull over.

The roadside scenery was now changing. Instead of rows of endless detached and semi-detached houses, lines of mature trees and hedges were flashing past as they entered the outer suburbs. Then, unexpectedly, a huge white refrigerated lorry emerged from a turning on their right, close to a garden nursery. Its driver was clearly unaware he was interrupting a high-speed chase.

'Look out. Look out. Look out. Look out,' shouted Smart.

Jenkins braked sharply and their car shuddered to a halt by the side of the road.

They watched helplessly as the Nissan Qashqai ploughed directly into the side of the lorry.

* * *

A few miles away, Marcel Dubois was watching a trickle of water seeping through the brickwork in the cellar where he was being held. He had been unconcerned the night before when he first heard the sound of dripping water. But now he was awake and it was mid-morning. He was becoming alarmed. The water was several centimetres deep – and the level was rising. Soon he would be unable to see his feet while standing on the floor. There was also an unpleasant smell.

He tried for a moment to reassure himself. Perhaps it's been raining, he told himself. The amount of water's built up and started flowing down the street. I expect that will end when it stops raining.

He ventured as close to the nearest window as the chain would allow, but he could see the ingress of water was continuing at a steady pace in the dim light. It was leaking in through a host of apertures. Through cracks in the brickwork. Through tiny gaps around the window.

Where were the men? He hadn't seen them since they brought him a meal of pie and chips the night before. Why hadn't they brought him his breakfast and allowed him upstairs to use the bathroom?

He tried to be cool-headed.

Calme-toi! he urged himself. One of the men must come soon. He will see there's been a leak. He will get the problem fixed and rescue me. I will soon be safe and in another place.

But a few hours later, the men still hadn't called to see him and Marcel was becoming increasingly anxious. He had glanced through one of the windows and hadn't liked the sight that greeted him. A huge expanse of water now seemed to stretch for as far as his eyes could see.

It was then that he suspected the flood was not limited to the one building he was in. He began to believe the whole area where he was being held captive might be affected by the water. Perhaps he was close to a river or lake.

Marcel remembered that the English equivalent of calling '*Aidez-moi!*' was to cry 'Help!' So, for a long while, he shouted the word at the top of his voice. And he kept screaming until he was hoarse. Then he lost faith. Why waste energy on yelling? he thought. He had tried it before when he sensed the men were absent. Nobody was coming today. Nobody ever came.

For a while, he tried, as he had many times before, to squeeze his hand out of the metal clasp that had been locked around his right wrist. His efforts were in vain. He simply made his wrist sore. Next, he repeated his efforts to tug the chain away from the metal ring, which was screwed to the wall. After all, he thought, if the water level was to continue rising, he needed to raise himself to a higher position within the cellar – such as by reaching the upper steps. If he could free himself and set foot on those higher steps, he might be able to force open the door at the top. But after a few minutes, he came to realise these hopes of breaking himself free from the chain were doomed to failure. He had attempted before to prise the chain free and he simply didn't have enough strength in his hands.

Would some leverage help? Perhaps, if he were to wrap the chain round the table and jerk the table away, the chain might break away or even snap. He tried this technique three times. Each attempt failed. Eventually, he collapsed on the bed, exhausted and close to tears.

As the minutes ticked by, he was gradually being forced to face the grim reality of his situation. He had been abandoned by his kidnappers and forces of nature were about to strike a cruel blow. The swollen river was advancing towards him and it looked as though he was condemned to spend the final moments of his life trapped in this water-logged prison. It seemed a real possibility he would never see his loved ones again.

Chapter 38

Although the front of the Nissan Qashqai had been badly damaged in the collision with the lorry, the two crash victims inside seemed unscathed. PC Smart watched as the two men both jumped out and, after a cursory glance at the stationary lorry which now blocked the entire road, raced off on foot in different directions.

The ginger-haired driver, Wayne Jordan, ran into the car park of the garden centre on the right-hand side. His passenger, Kyle O'Shane, dodged round the lorry and tore off up the road.

PC Smart pursued Jordan along with two male colleagues from a police carrier which had arrived on the scene. He was quickly overpowered and handcuffed.

Jordan scowled as Smart confronted him.

'Haven't I seen your face somewhere?' she asked.

'I don't know. Have you?' he replied.

She turned to her colleagues. 'Isn't this one of the two guys that have been in the press?' she asked.

'You don't mean the kidnapping of the French boy?' one of her colleagues replied.

'Yes,' she said, staring at Jordan's ashen face. 'I know a guy in CID who's going to be very pleased to meet you – DCI Roscoe. Meanwhile, you're under arrest for suspected car theft.'

He sneered and spat on the ground as she read him the rest of the caution.

* * *

While she was overseeing his arrest, efforts led by PC Jenkins to secure the arrest of his passenger, O'Shane, were proving a far greater challenge.

The traffic constable and a third team member from the newly arrived carrier had set off on his tail, but, unlike his associate, O'Shane was far more agile.

As he sprinted along the pavement away from the city, he darted into the front garden of a 1950s-style, semi-detached house on the left-hand side.

'He's gone down an alley at the side,' yelled a breathless PC Jenkins. 'Can one of you stay here in case he charges out of the front?'

Jenkins ran down the alley, accompanied by PC Graham Brownlow, a tall constable in his early twenties. Brownlow's colleague, PC Peter Conway, who was in his forties, remained in the drive.

'Hey, what's going on?' asked an irate middle-aged woman who was holding a basket of wet laundry when the two constables appeared in her back garden.

'Police,' replied Jenkins. 'We've been following a suspected car thief. He ran down this alley just a moment ago.'

'I haven't seen anyone,' she said.

'Do you mind if we take a look around?' asked Jenkins.

Without waiting for her response, he darted across the lawn and tried to open her shed door, but it was secured with a padlock.

'I keep it locked,' she declared.

'Where the hell did he go?' asked Jenkins, gazing out across the fields which lay behind the houses. He turned back to the householder.

'He definitely didn't sneak into your house, did he?' he said.

'I've been in the kitchen and no one came past me,' she insisted with a frown. 'Are you sure you're police?'

He handed her his Heart of England warrant card.

'Thanks,' she said, studying it and handing it back. 'You can't be too careful these days.'

Jenkins stood on a rockery that abutted the rear garden fence and happened to glance down.

'Here he is!' he shouted, staring down at O'Shane, who was crouched in the undergrowth behind the fence panel.

As the wanted man got up and careered off across the field, Jenkins and Brownlow clambered over the fence and gave chase while the lady with the washing watched proceedings with mounting concern.

When Jenkins finally caught up with the fleeing man and grabbed his shoulder, O'Shane spun round and punched him on the jaw. Jenkins punched him back and a scuffle began before the muscular man pulled away and ran back towards the woman.

Jenkins unclasped the taser from his belt and shouted a warning.

'I'll deploy this taser if you don't stop running now,' he yelled.

O'Shane ignored him. He scrambled back over the fence and onto the rockery.

'Don't come near me,' screamed the woman, who was standing on the edge of the lawn.

The two officers were approaching. They watched as O'Shane strode towards the woman. They could hear him telling her, 'It's all right, dear. It's all right.'

The woman looked down and saw he was holding a knife, but before she could turn and run back to the house, O'Shane grabbed her from behind and held the knife to her throat.

'Don't come any closer,' he hollered as the officers scaled the fence.

'Please don't hurt me,' the woman screamed.

'Put the knife down,' Jenkins demanded.

'Keep away, copper, or the woman gets it,' O'Shane insisted. While the officers stood motionless by the fence,

he lowered his voice. 'Where are the keys to your car?' he asked the woman.

'In the house,' she cried.

'Whereabouts in the house?'

'In the hallway – by the front door,' she said.

While his eyes remained fixed on O'Shane's face, Jenkins continued to hold the electronic gun by his side. He had been considering how he could use it without placing the woman in jeopardy. Then a thought occurred to him.

'I know you,' he told the knifeman. 'You're wanted for a kidnap over in Norton Prior, aren't you?'

'That's not me,' said O'Shane. 'Some other guy.'

Jenkins took a step towards O'Shane.

'Keep away, copper, or the woman gets it. I'll slit her throat unless you remain absolutely still.'

'Don't be a fool, man,' said Jenkins. 'There are police out the front of the house. You won't get anywhere. Give yourself up and make it easy for yourself.'

'That's enough lip from you,' said O'Shane. 'Right, lady. Show me where the keys are – and no games.'

PC Conway, who had been stationed at the front, had overheard smatterings of the conversation in the rear garden. He had crept down the alley and across the lawn and bravely took O'Shane by surprise. He thrust his right arm round the man's neck and the pair struggled together on the lawn for a few seconds.

Jenkins dashed forward and prised the blade out of O'Shane's hand before he could react. The kidnapper was left sprawling on the grass with Conway on top of him.

Jenkins handcuffed O'Shane while declaring he was under arrest for the suspected theft of the car.

'Are you all right?' Jenkins asked the householder as O'Shane was marched out to the main road.

'I'll be all right, dear,' she said, returning to the laundry basket which she had left on the timber decking outside her patio doors.

‘Did I hear you say that man was wanted for a kidnapping in Norton Prior?’

‘Yes, that’s right.’

‘Ooh, I say. That must be that French boy that’s been on the telly.’

He nodded.

‘They say nothing ever happens round here,’ she said. ‘I can’t wait till I get down the bowls club and tell them all about it.’

* * *

Marcel could hear the sound of water outside the building clearly now. It was lapping against the outside wall. Inside the cellar, it had been slopping over the tabletop for a while. He took a deep breath. There was a sour smell swirling around him. It was the stench of mould and decomposing matter.

Marcel was normally a calm, placid boy but he was beginning to panic. The cold, brown water was now more than one and a half metres high in the cellar and he had been forced to clamber onto the table, next to the wall.

He was cold, hungry and thirsty. His bed and duvet were saturated. The chair had drifted off towards the wine barrels. His spare clothes were floating around along with his bedsheet and table lamp.

He began to shout again through sheer desperation. ‘Help!’ he cried at the top of his voice. He repeated his call but no one came.

He thought of the men. He thought of the last time they had brought him food. The bastards. Why had they left him here? Did they want him to die? Was he no longer the valuable commodity they had once believed – the dearly beloved son of the football hero?

That was it, he thought. His parents had refused to pay the ransom and the men had grown tired of waiting for their money. He had been abandoned – abandoned to die, cold and alone, in this flooded chamber.

He watched while an object drifted past. He was unable to recognise it at first. Then he remembered. It was a red book with a yellow castle on the front. *L'Histoire de Caen.* The book that two evil strangers had bought for him on a whim, believing it would while away the hours for him while they held him hostage. How moronic those men must be to believe any book printed in the French language would serve to occupy the mind of an intelligent French teenager.

Suddenly his thoughts were interrupted. A man was shouting from somewhere outside the window. Perhaps rescuers were finally on their way.

Marcel called out for help again at the top of his voice. He repeated his cries for several minutes. But, as before, no one came and, as before, he reverted to his anguished sense of abandonment.

Chapter 39

Sunita Roy was sitting in a rain-splattered coat in the draughty foyer of Worcester police station. Beside her, by the wall, were two sets of vulcanized rubber waders that an apologetic police sergeant had handed her and DC Dawson earlier on. Realising the pair intended for her were probably too large, Sunita had decided she might try to wear them anyway, if the need arose. Milling around her just after midday were dozens of search team members. They were all due to resume their search for Marcel Dubois in half an hour's time.

Teams had already inspected many of the isolated buildings beside the river, close to the Pitchcroft racecourse and even some waterfront homes in the new developments that had sprung up in Diglis, a suburb where

the Worcester and Birmingham Canal meets the River Severn. They were now preparing to set out again.

Sunita noticed two men from the force's underwater search team carrying high-tech cameras.

Dawson had gone to the canteen to fetch some coffees and he had been gone for ten minutes.

'Come on, Brett,' she muttered to herself. 'How long does it take to pour a couple of drinks?'

To fill the time, she glanced at news reports on her mobile phone.

> *More flooding of roads and farmland in Worcestershire is expected tomorrow morning. Areas likely to be affected include Worcester and Tewkesbury. Flooding from drains may also affect the racecourse and Worcester County Cricket Ground. Further rain is expected tomorrow and river levels are predicted to remain high for some days.*

She looked up and smiled as Dawson finally emerged from round a corner and handed her one of two steaming cups of coffee he was carrying.

'Here you are, Sarge,' he said. 'You'll feel better after drinking this.'

'What kept you so long, Brett?' she asked.

'Oh, sorry. I got chatting to one of the sergeants,' Dawson explained. 'I asked about the possibility that Marcel is being held in a building close to the river. He said the city gets flooded every few years and some of the cellars by the river are notorious for getting badly flooded. He said that, if the boy was being kept in one of those places, he might not stand much of a chance.'

'I can believe that,' she said. 'Listen, did I tell you about Dylan Roberts?'

'That's the prisoner at the Vale who's a suspect in the Lewis Tigworth murder, isn't it?'

'Quite right, Brett,' she said. 'I've been talking to Roberts' family. He claimed to us he didn't know Tigworth, but one of his relatives let slip last night that the

two men did time in youth custody together years ago and fell out for some reason.'

'So Roberts may have had a grudge against Tigworth?'

'Looks that way.'

'Very interesting,' said Dawson.

The face of a slim, blonde traffic officer in glasses emerged from a corridor. She gazed round the room before heading towards the two detectives.

'You must be DS Roy,' she said with a grin. 'I've got some good news for you. We've caught two of your kidnappers.'

'Brilliant news,' said Dawson, who had taken a seat beside his sergeant.

'And you are…?' asked Sunita.

'Oh, sorry,' said the newcomer. 'PC Katie Smart, Worcester Traffic.'

'What exactly happened?' asked the sergeant.

'Just sheer luck,' said Smart. She told them about the car chase and arrest of O'Shane and Jordan.

'They're just being booked in downstairs,' she added.

'Good work,' said Sunita. 'I'd really like to interview them as soon as possible. Our priority, clearly, is to trace the kidnapped boy, and we need to get them to tell us where they've been holding him.'

'The sergeant says they'll be handed over to your CID later today. But they're both refusing to talk.'

'Par for the course,' said Sunita. 'You've obviously got their vehicle?'

'Yeah. It's probably a write-off. It's being taken to our depot so forensics can go over it. I had a quick look inside.'

'Anything that might give us a clue on where they've been staying?'

'No. Nothing. We've also got phones from both men.'

'Good,' said Sunita.

Several officers from the search team began stepping outside.

'Sarge,' said Dawson, 'maybe it's time for us to make a move.'

Sunita nodded.

'Yes. It's unlikely we're going to get any intelligence from the kidnappers for now. We'd better make tracks.' Turning to the traffic officer, she said, 'Could you call my boss, DCI Roscoe at headquarters, and alert him about the arrests, if that hasn't already been done?'

'Certainly, Sarge,' she said. 'No problem.'

One of the team leaders approached Sunita and Dawson as they left the newly built police station, clutching their waterproof boots.

'Have you any preference as regards your search area?' he asked the sergeant.

'I've an inkling that the boy could be in a building near the bridge,' she said.

'We've already done that area. Your choice is to come with me to Diglis or accompany Sergeant Banks to Barbourne.'

'I spent more time last night studying the video received from the kidnappers,' said Sunita. 'I'm pretty certain he's in the area called North Parade.'

'Please yourselves, but, as I say, that area's already been covered, as I understand it,' the officer replied before marching away.

'Looks like we're on our own, Sarge,' said Dawson.

'Not for the first time,' she remarked.

The pair walked past the city's university, skirted the edge of the racecourse and passed beneath the arches of the city's Victorian railway viaduct. At once the vast grey river – usually around eighty metres wide at this point – came into view. And it was clear it had burst its banks.

'I'm sensing that we're close to him now,' she told Dawson. 'Do you see those three blocks of flats over there?'

He gazed across to the far side of the swirling waters.

‘Yes, Sarge,’ he replied. ‘I’m guessing they’re ten storeys high.’

‘Twelve, to be exact,’ she said. ‘You can see them in the video.’

A hundred metres ahead, at the opposite end of the flooded riverside street, they could see a fire engine parked close to Worcester Bridge. A crew of fire fighters were pumping water out of a basement.

‘Time to take to the water, Sarge,’ Dawson announced.

He sat down on the pavement and began to pull off his work shoes and slip into his waders. A bemused flock of swans watched from nearby railings.

Sunita reluctantly pulled on her large waders and found, to her surprise, she could walk in them, after a fashion. They abandoned their normal footwear by the railings and began trudging into the submerged street.

As she felt the cold water slopping around her thighs, she gasped.

‘That must be the lifebuoy that featured in the video,’ she exclaimed. ‘It must have been filmed around here.’

The pair discovered they were outside the Bridgehouse Restaurant, which occupied the ground floor of a three-storey Georgian building. The Michelin-starred eatery had a sign on the door saying, ‘Closed due to flooding’.

While they were standing there, a stout, middle-aged man with grey hair opened a sash window above them and gazed out.

‘I like your enthusiasm but we’re closed,’ he announced.

‘Heart of England Police,’ said Sunita, staring up at the open window.

‘Oh, you’re not customers,’ he muttered.

‘We’re searching for that missing boy,’ she continued.

‘You still on that business, are you?’ said the man. ‘We had police round here yesterday. There’s no French boy here. They did a full search.’

‘I take it you’re the restaurant owner?’ said Sunita.

'Manager, actually. The name's Hobbs.'

'Mr Hobbs,' said Sunita, 'do you know anything about the buildings on either side of you?'

'Well, to your left, as you can see, is The Waterfront Tavern, which has been closed for three years. It was the constant floods that put pay to his business. There's no one living there. On the other side is a block of flats. As far as I know, the cops have checked out both premises.'

'There you are, Sarge,' muttered Dawson. 'We're probably wasting our time.'

She shrugged her shoulders.

'You could be right,' she admitted. She thanked the man and waded on her own towards the derelict pub next door, where the stinking river water was sloshing around its stone entrance steps.

Glancing down, she noticed two small windows which were a few inches above the level of the water. She bent down awkwardly and peeked inside the first window. Were her eyes deceiving her? Was that a human face she could see amid the gloom of the darkened cellar?

'Come and have a look at this, Brett,' she cried.

Her younger colleague followed her example and peered through the glass towards the back wall.

'Good God, Sarge!' he exclaimed. 'We've found him.'

Chapter 40

The two detectives knocked on the cellar window of The Waterfront Tavern in an effort to attract attention, but there was no response from within the flooded chamber.

'Quick, Brett,' shouted Sunita. 'Let's see if there's a back way into this place.'

At the side of the Victorian building was a narrow garden behind a six-foot-high brick wall. Halfway along, they discovered a short path leading to a solid wooden side door above two stone steps. Sunita climbed up awkwardly in her waders but the door, which was just clear of the flood water, was firmly locked.

'Are you feeling fit, Brett?' she asked.

Without waiting to be asked twice, Dawson threw the weight of his body against the door. It refused to yield.

'Stand back, Sarge,' he urged Sunita. Then he took a few steps away from the doorway and raced forward, shoulder-charging the latch with all his might. At last, the door flew open, amid the sound of splintering wood.

The detectives found themselves in a dingy hallway which led to a series of rooms. Stepping inside gingerly, Sunita found a door on the right marked 'Cellar' with a key inside the lock.

Briefly glancing at her colleague, she unlocked the door and turned the handle to find they were entering a dark basement storeroom half-filled with brown water. A chair and bedding were floating about beside other debris.

Sunita descended the first three steps of the stone stairway before her feet became immersed. Then she gasped as her eyes peered to the right and settled on the figure that they had seen moments earlier through the window.

'Marcel!' she shouted. 'Marcel!'

The kidnapped boy was somehow managing to sit upright on a table, slumped back against a wall with his head just above the lapping water. He seemed to be unconscious or in a trance.

At first, he gave no sign of life as the sound of his name echoed round the cellar. Then slowly he turned his ghostly face towards them. He was mumbling, but gradually the whispered words became clearer. '*Aidez-moi!*'

'*Nous allons vous aider*,' she called back.

‘What’s that mean, Sarge?’ asked Dawson, clambering down the steps behind her.

‘I’ve told him help’s arrived,’ she said. ‘Quick, Brett, you know the fire crew we saw near the bridge? Go and get them, and tell them they’ll need to bring underwater gear. Oh, and Brett, it looks like there’s a chain on his wrist so we’ll need bolt cutters as well.’

As her colleague retreated back up the steps, she yelled, ‘And tell them to hurry. The water’s right up to his chin. If it carries on rising, he might drown.’

After Dawson had set off on his errand, Sunita tried to reassure Marcel that he would soon be liberated.

‘Some men are coming to cut the chain and lift you out of the water,’ she told him. ‘I’m Sergeant Roy from the police, so you’ll be safe now. How are you feeling?’

‘V-v-very cold,’ he stuttered. ‘My thoughts were to die. I’m not going to die now, am I?’

‘No, Marcel. You’re not going to die,’ she said as she noticed his lips were blue. ‘Very soon you’ll be out of here and back with your family.’

‘*Merci bien, mademoiselle*,’ he said. ‘I was afraid. Where are the men? Have they gone?’

‘The men have been arrested by the police. You’re safe from them now.’

She continued talking to him in order to reassure him and help to keep his courage up.

Minutes passed. Water was swirling round his mouth.

‘Hold on, Marcel,’ said Sunita, climbing back up the steps.

‘Where are you going? Don’t leave me,’ he cried.

‘It’s all right. I’m just going to see if I can find some kind of hose or pipe to help with your breathing,’ she said.

She searched the ground floor of the premises for any kind of tube that might assist Marcel but without success. On her return to the cellar, the water level seemed to be stabilising but Marcel was spluttering and becoming even more distressed.

'I'm sure I'm going to die,' Marcel told her. 'I don't want to die.'

'Try not to worry. The fire brigade will soon be here. You'll soon be out of here.'

As these words passed her lips, she heard a rush of footsteps in the passageway and Dawson's face appeared in the doorway.

'The fire brigade have notified their water rescue team, Sarge,' the breathless constable announced. 'They're the people with underwater gear. We should have the boy out of here in no time.'

'Good,' she replied. 'We need to let the DCI know as well. We'll have to search the whole building for evidence.'

It took nearly twenty minutes for the underwater team to arrive at The Waterfront Tavern. But, once they had unloaded their equipment from a van and one of the four-strong team had donned his diving suit, the rescue passed off quickly.

While the detectives watched from the doorway above, the brigade's frogman plunged into the flood water and hacked through the chain that had secured Marcel to the brickwork. Then he carried the frail teenager to his colleagues on the steps. After they had cut away the manacle that had been fastened around the boy's right wrist, the crew handed him over to two paramedics, who wrapped him in a blanket and rushed him to hospital.

'Bloody hell, Sarge,' Dawson said as the ambulance sped away with its blue lights flashing. 'That was a close call.'

Sunita nodded.

'I know,' she said.

The detectives returned to the car park where they had left Sunita's car. Then she drove to the Worcestershire Royal Hospital, where the paramedics had taken Marcel.

Chapter 41

The whole Heart of England CID team had been waiting anxiously to hear about their sergeant's efforts to find and rescue the missing boy.

It was about two o'clock on Thursday afternoon when details of Marcel's release from the cellar came through.

Sunita Roy phoned the chief inspector to say that Marcel had been found safe.

'He's in hospital, sir, with hypothermia,' she revealed. 'But he stands a good chance of recovery.'

'That's wonderful,' said Roscoe.

After hearing a little more of her story, he congratulated her and DC Dawson. Then he rushed from his room and announced the news in a loud voice across the office.

There was a spontaneous round of applause.

'I've also been informed that two of the gang holding him have been arrested by traffic police in Worcester and they're being brought over here,' he continued. 'But none of that means our work stops. The forensic team are on their way to the gang's premises and the operation to find the gang's leader continues. But keep your chin up, folks, and I promise to put some money behind the bar at the Fleece tomorrow night to celebrate.'

As everyone returned to their desks, Roscoe beckoned DC Khalid over.'

'He was just found in time, sir,' he said. 'The family were on the point of paying another two million.'

'Yes. Very timely. Look, I'd like you to go over to the city and coordinate the search of the gang's hideout by the

river,' said Roscoe. 'It's an abandoned pub, The Waterfront Tavern.'

'I'll leave right away, sir.'

After returning to his room, there was a knock on the door and DI Parkes stepped inside.

'Ah, Parkes,' said Roscoe. 'You've no doubt heard our good news.'

'Yes, sir. I missed your announcement just now but I've been speaking to a colleague over there. Apparently, they sent out search teams today and the boy was located in a riverside building.'

'Two of our colleagues from here found him – DS Roy and DC Dawson,' said Roscoe.

'Really? I understood he was found in a disused pub as a result of a routine search.'

'Not at all. He was found as a result of the hard work and initiative of DS Roy and DC Dawson, who took it upon themselves to scour an area that the search teams claimed to have previously visited. Because of a misunderstanding, the previous teams managed to overlook the pub. If he'd been discovered any later, they'd have been pulling out a dead body.'

Parkes shrugged his shoulders.

'I wasn't aware of that, sir,' he said.

'Never mind,' said Roscoe. 'As you're so close to the Beauvais family, you need to liaise with them. I gather they're on their way to the hospital. Meanwhile I'll get the team working on the files we've got on Kyle O'Shane and Wayne Jordan. They're in the process of being brought over here under armed escort. I'm looking forward to meeting this shameless pair who've kept this young lad captive for the past twenty-six days.'

* * *

Two hours later, the chief inspector sighed as he peered through the one-way glass into the ground-floor interview room where Kyle O'Shane was briefing his solicitor.

Roscoe had been hoping for the support of a close police colleague during his first encounter with the suspect. But the only person available to sit in with him was Wendy Hopkirk, a detective constable who seemed to spend most of her time combing her hair or surreptitiously trying to listen to music on her headphones.

She was once described by a colleague as a detective who approached each job with as much enthusiasm as a vegan offered a bacon sandwich.

There was a tap on the door and Hopkirk stepped in.

'Good. We're ready to go,' he said, collecting a notebook from a desk and slipping it into a pocket.

Within minutes, the pair were sitting behind the table in Interview Room One, face to face with O'Shane. Beside the suspect, who was exhibiting a swaggering self-confidence, sat his solicitor, Dipak Sharma, a middle-aged man in glasses. On guard outside the room were two uniformed constables who had escorted O'Shane there from his basement cell.

'Right, Mr O'Shane,' Roscoe began, 'I'm just going to remind you that you've been arrested on suspicion of aggravated burglary, conspiracy to murder and false imprisonment. The caution you received earlier is still in place. First of all, could you give me your address in West Bromwich?'

The suspect stared into the chief inspector's face with an impish smile. He said nothing.

'Very well,' said Roscoe. 'I want to ask you about the events of 29 October. You and at least two other men broke into Upper Norton Manor. One of your group threatened Mrs Willis, the housekeeper, with a gun. She was then tied up and the three of you burgled the house.'

O'Shane shrugged. 'No comment,' he said.

'You'll have to speak up for the purposes of the DIR,' said Roscoe. 'This is a house where the footballer Jean-Jacques Beauvais and his family are living.

Mr Beauvais's bodyguard turned up shortly afterwards in a Bentley and was shot dead by a member of your gang.'

The suspect stared insolently at the chief inspector, who was writing in his notebook. 'I was never there. You got the wrong guy,' he insisted.

Hopkirk interrupted to say, 'We know you were there, Mr O'Shane. One of your fingerprints was discovered on a mirror in the main bedroom.'

Roscoe thought he detected a glimpse of surprise on the suspect's face. If so, it passed in a matter of seconds.

'No comment,' he replied.

'In the next phase of the crime,' Roscoe continued, 'you found the footballer's stepson, Marcel Dubois, inside the Bentley. He was abducted and held at three different addresses while someone contacted the boy's family and demanded ransom money.'

O'Shane sneered. 'No comment.'

'I want to ask about your colleagues,' Roscoe said. 'When you were arrested at lunchtime, you were in the company of a man named Wayne Jordan, who's also under arrest. What's his role in your gang?'

'No comment.'

'Then we turn to your friend Lewis Tigworth, who was found murdered in a prison cell at Ashwood Vale nearly a week ago.'

'Nothing to do with me. I wasn't there, was I?'

'I accept you weren't there in person,' said Roscoe, 'but I suggest his death is connected with the fact that he was an accomplice of yours who handed himself in. You decided he had to be silenced, didn't you?'

'Don't know the guy. Who is he?' O'Shane replied.

'So that's three deaths you're in trouble over: the bodyguard, Lewis Tigworth and – it's on the cards at the moment – the death of Marcel Dubois.'

O'Shane's face turned pale.

'He's dead?' asked O'Shane with a look of incredulity.

'He's seriously ill in hospital,' Roscoe explained.

‘If he survives, it’ll be no thanks to you,’ Hopkirk remarked.

The chief inspector looked O’Shane directly in the eyes.

‘You left him to die in a riverside building as flood waters were rising,’ said Roscoe. ‘We only hauled him out of the cellar in time. He was suffering from hypothermia and close to drowning after hours spent immersed in the freezing water. He’s still not out of the woods. He’s fighting for his life in intensive care.’

‘I know the boy’s name. Weren’t he the lad who got kidnapped in Norton Prior by some tea leaves?’ said O’Shane, stroking his chin and looking puzzled. ‘I don’t know what’s happened to him. It’s nothing to do with me.’

‘On that point, we found green Rohypnol tablets on a kitchen table at The Waterfront Tavern – some of them partly crushed,’ Roscoe went on. ‘We also found traces of the same drug at Meadow Brook Farm. Toxicology tests will tell us whether the teenager has that drug in his system. But my instincts tell me you were using that drug to subdue the boy, weren’t you? Come on, Mr O’Shane. The evidence against you and Wayne Jordan is stacking up. And it doesn’t look good for you. As things stand, that could be three deaths you’re responsible for.’

The colour drained from O’Shane’s face. He was battling to keep his composure.

‘No comment,’ he said.

‘You’re perfectly within your rights to remain silent,’ said Roscoe, ‘but it won’t look good in a court of law. With all the evidence we’ve so far collected and new clues coming in from our team all the time, there’s a good chance you’ll be convicted. If that happens, you’ll be sent down for life. However, if you cooperate with us now, the judge may well look more favourably towards you at the time of sentencing.’

The ashen-faced suspect whispered a few words to his solicitor.

Sharma cleared his throat. ‘My client would like an adjournment, chief inspector,’ he said. ‘You’ve brought forward some new information and I need to discuss all this with him.’

* * *

It had just turned 5 p.m. and Sunita and Dawson remained sitting in a waiting area at the hospital.

‘I’ll go and ask one of the nurses if they’ve got any news, shall I?’ Dawson suggested.

‘Good idea, Brett,’ said Sunita. ‘And, maybe after that, if there’s still no update, we’ll go for a cup of tea.’

‘I’m so glad we found him, you know,’ said Dawson. ‘And it was just in the nick of time. If he’d been left there like that another couple of hours, we could have been dealing with a body.’

‘That’s right,’ she said. ‘It’s amazing that he was in that dilapidated pub. It’s only a two-minute walk from the hotel where his father, Philippe, has been staying.’

‘Hell of a coincidence, that,’ said Dawson. ‘Anyway, finding that lad was all down to you. You’ve saved his life.’

‘We both played a role,’ she said modestly. ‘But I’m very glad we found him and that he’s being treated by some good doctors. He stands a reasonable chance of getting better now, although he’s still seriously ill.’

As Dawson stood up and began walking to the reception desk in the accident and emergency department, one of the nurses hurried towards them.

‘You’re with Marcel Dubois, aren’t you?’ asked the nurse.

Sunita nodded. ‘Yes, we’re from CID at headquarters,’ she said. ‘Is he going to be all right now?’

‘He’s not out of the woods yet,’ she said as Dawson resumed his seat beside his sergeant. ‘But we’re optimistic. He’s got severe hypothermia, but he’s young. He’s got a good chance.’

‘That’s good news,’ said Sunita.

'This is the kidnapped boy, isn't it?' the nurse continued. 'I'm afraid news of his presence here has leaked out. We've got a crowd of press people outside. The duty administrator's been overwhelmed with calls.'

'Naturally, we'll want to speak to Marcel and get a statement from him as soon as possible,' said Sunita.

'I'm afraid that won't be possible tonight,' the nurse explained. 'Maybe tomorrow morning. I'm afraid the parents won't be able to see him either. The consultant's said he's too weak to be disturbed.'

After she had walked away, Sunita turned to her colleague.

'Brett, you're going to have to remain on duty here overnight and speak to the parents when they come. I'll take over from you at six o'clock tomorrow morning,' she said, rising to her feet. 'No one should be allowed to speak to Marcel except his family and medical staff.'

'Where are you going, Sarge?'

'I'm going to link up with the DCI. He's yet to interview Jordan and there are a few things I need to tell him.'

Chapter 42

The chief inspector glanced up from his computer screen as Sunita Roy tapped gently on his open door. It was nearly 9 p.m.

'It's been another long day, Sergeant,' he said.

'I know,' she said. 'I've just heard that Marcel is going to be released early tomorrow.'

'That's wonderful.'

'I was wondering when we were going to be interviewing Wayne Jordan?' she asked.

'Any minute now. I'm sorry it's rather late. I'm just writing a report for the chief super,' he said, rising to his feet. 'Between you and me, I'm annoyed we didn't get any admissions from Kyle O'Shane after we restarted the interview. The evidence against him is all there, but he adamantly refuses to budge. Anyway, I'm glad you're here. Khalid's just had a breakthrough regarding the Beretta used to kill the bodyguard.'

She sat down by the door.

'I heard he'd been constantly on the phone this afternoon, working feverishly,' she said.

'Yes. It now looks as though Wayne Jordan obtained the gun used at the manor from an underworld firearms dealer. Khalid has a contact who works for West Midlands and he's learnt that a team of their officers have had their eyes on this guy for some time over a separate case. They raided his armoury in Walsall this week and seized several Berettas. One of them, a Beretta 9000S, has been tested in forensics. It's been matched to the bullets fired into Jukes's body.'

'That's brilliant,' she said.

'So shall we go and see what Jordan's got to say for himself?' he suggested.

Sunita collected two envelopes and a shoebox from her desk drawer in CID. Then the pair walked downstairs to Interview Room Two. Passing two uniformed constables who were standing on guard in the corridor, they entered to find Wayne Jordan seated at a table, engrossed in conversation with his solicitor, Salman Siddiqui.

After switching on the digital recorder, Roscoe reminded Jordan he had been arrested for aggravated burglary, conspiracy to murder and false imprisonment.

'I wanted to ask firstly about why you visited Upper Norton Manor on the afternoon of 29 October,' he said after settling into a seat opposite the suspect.

'I never went there,' said Jordan.

Roscoe sighed. 'Come on, Mr Jordan,' he said. 'Lewis Tigworth informed us you were there, before his untimely death, and we've obtained other evidence confirming this. Could you show us exhibits F and G, please, Sergeant?'

Sunita slid a colour photograph from one of the envelopes. It showed the impression of part of a shoeprint left in some earth. Then she placed the shoebox on the table, removed the lid and revealed a pair of men's black trainers.

'You'll notice this heel-print, photographed by one of our forensic team close to the front door of the manor on 29 October, contains a dark blob at the edge,' she said. 'Then we turn to the pair of trainers you were wearing when you were arrested. You'll see the right trainer has a small gouge in the rubber heel – matching up with the dark blob in the photograph.'

Siddiqui, a short, plump man of fifty-five in a navy-blue suit, interrupted. 'So you're saying that my client's right trainer was responsible for leaving the impression in the earth at the manor house?'

'That's right,' she said.

'Surely it's possible that someone in similar footwear with a gouge or cut at the edge of the heel could have left that impression,' the solicitor suggested.

'No,' said Sunita. 'The brand of trainer, the pattern on the sole and the signs of wear all point unequivocally to Mr Jordan's trainer having left the impression in the soil.'

'Loads of people have got them kind of trainers and loads have probably got holes in the heels,' said Jordan.

Sunita removed a black and white photograph from a second envelope.

'This is exhibit H,' she said.

'Yes. Mr Jordan needs to see that,' said Roscoe.

'What exactly is this, Chief Inspector?' asked Siddiqui. 'A fingerprint?'

'Yes,' said Roscoe. 'We know, Mr Jordan, that it was you that fired the gun, killing Danny Jukes. You were

positioned at a stairway window when the trigger was pulled. This is your fingerprint, which was found on the window by the stairs. Incidentally, we also found your DNA on a beer can retrieved from the house in Juniper Lane which you and your mates used as a hideaway for four days after the burglary.'

Jordan sneered. 'This is all manufactured nonsense. You're trying to frame me.'

'You had a Beretta pistol with you on that day, didn't you?' said Roscoe.

'No. I don't own one and I never have. Don't like them,' he replied.

'We now know, since West Midlands Police arrested a criminal armourer named Martins, that you rented a Beretta 9000S from him a few days before 29 October. The two bullets fired into Mr Jukes's body have been recovered by the pathologist during the post-mortem. And telltale scratches and indentations on those bullets show that they were fired by the Beretta 9000S you hired.'

'It wasn't me,' Jordan insisted. 'All right. I'll tell you the truth. It was Tigworth who pulled the trigger.'

Roscoe ignored Jordan's bogus claim.

'We've found CCTV footage of you visiting the gun dealer's premises,' said Roscoe. 'Furthermore, we have a witness – Marcel, the French boy that you and your associates abducted. He didn't see what happened since he was hiding beneath a blanket, as he'd been instructed. But nonetheless, he's just told us in a statement that he heard a man shouting, "Wayne!" just seconds before the two gunshots rang out.'

'The kid should keep his nose out of other people's business,' Jordan complained.

'Wayne Jordan, you shot a man twice from behind in cold blood. He didn't stand a chance,' said Roscoe. 'You shot him like a coward and then you and your grubby mates dumped his body behind a hedge as if he was a piece of trash. What you didn't know was that he was a

hero who'd been commended for his bravery while serving with the British Army in Afghanistan. Do you still refuse to accept your guilt?'

'Yeah. I ain't guilty of nothing.'

'You and your associate, Mr O'Shane, will appear in court tomorrow morning. And I think you should know police will be opposing any applications for bail.'

Chapter 43

Sunita Roy clung to her seat as the chief inspector drove them along the narrow country lanes that led to Upper Norton Manor on Friday morning.

Now and then, in a cottage window, she would catch a glimpse of a tree adorned with baubles and festive lights, reminding her of the approach of Christmas.

'I'm very pleased with the way the cases against O'Shane and Jordan are shaping up,' Roscoe told her.

'Disappointing that Jordan's denied even being present at the manor,' she said.

'All fish wriggle when they're caught on a hook,' he continued. 'What's this now?'

They were confronted by a throng of press and broadcasting reporters, along with photographers and camera crews, as they travelled up Ploughman's Lane. Lines of cars and television vans filled the solitary lay-by and every available grass verge.

Roscoe repeatedly hooted his horn to warn pedestrians on their approach to the gates. A police constable on duty saluted him before waving his BMW through.

After proceeding up the drive, the pair were pleased to find Camille and Marcel standing outside the front door in the mild winter air. They both smiled broadly.

'*Monsieur le Chief Inspector*,' said Camille as he climbed out. 'How nice to see you.' She hugged and kissed him like a long-lost friend.

'We were finally allowed to collect Marcel from the hospital early this morning,' she said.

The teenager had lost his pale complexion and now exuded a warm, pink glow. He muttered to his mother in French.

Camille turned to Sunita as she emerged from the car.

'Marcel says it was you that saved him,' she told the detective, greeting her with an equally effusive welcome. '*Une amie pour la vie*.'

Sunita smiled back, aware she was being hailed as 'a friend for life'.

The detectives were led into the living room, where Jean-Jacques Beauvais, DI Parkes and Katrina Drake were chatting and drinking coffee. A new bodyguard, who resembled a rugby prop forward in a suit, watched the guests arrive from a chair beside the patio doors.

The footballer rose to greet the newcomers with a broad grin.

'Chief Inspector and Sergeant Roy,' he said, 'thank you so much for helping to find our son. We will be eternally grateful.'

Parkes stood behind him, looking increasingly resentful at the praise being directed towards the two detectives.

While the family began a conversation with Parkes, Katrina Drake approached Roscoe with a puzzled expression on her face.

'It said on TV last night that two men are in custody, helping police,' she said, fondling a strand of her light-brown hair. 'Is that right?'

'Yes, they'll be in court sometime this morning,' he replied.

'Do you have their names?'

'Yes. O'Shane and Jordan. Why do you ask?'

'Oh, I was just curious,' said Drake.

The living-room door creaked open. The anxious face of housekeeper Marilyn Willis appeared. The room fell silent.

'Sorry to bother you, Monsieur Beauvais,' she announced, 'but there's a lady from the Press Association at the door. She says the press would dearly like to take some pictures of Marcel with you and your wife, now he's come home.' She quickly added, 'And Monsieur Dubois is here.'

'Marvellous,' said Jean-Jacques. 'Yes, this is the time for celebration. It's quite warm today. Let's all go outside and let the gentlemen and ladies of the press take their pictures. And let us greet Monsieur Philippe as well. Everybody should be welcome on this day of our rejoicing.'

He opened the patio doors and the family trooped out onto the veranda. Philippe Dubois marched across the lawn from the gravel drive and, totally ignoring his ex-wife and her husband, ran to his son, hugging and kissing him.

As journalists, photographers and camera crews approached, Marilyn Willis and Katrina Drake passed around glasses of ice-cold French champagne.

Shouts of 'Over here, Marcel' and 'Jean-Jacques, over here' filled the air as photographers vied for the best shots of the footballer, his wife and their son. Reporters fired questions at all three and Roscoe became concerned that the event might descend into chaos.

During the interviews, the chief inspector remained close behind the footballer like a shadow, ensuring no details crucial to the inquiry were accidentally revealed. Sunita spent her time standing near to Marcel.

'We heard you were locked in a flooded cellar, Marcel,' said Jerome Bernard from Agence France-Presse. 'You must have been terrified.'

'I can answer for him,' said Jean-Jacques. 'Marcel has told us that he never gave up hope that the British police would rescue him and he was so grateful when DS Roy climbed halfway down the cellar steps and told him he was going to be all right.'

He answered further questions about how the fire brigade cut through the chain and how paramedics rushed their son to hospital, and he disclosed that the family were buying their son several gifts – including a new skateboard – as a reward for his bravery.

After nearly half an hour, Roscoe had a brief word with Jean-Jacques and then clapped his hands to attract attention.

'Ladies and gentlemen, Marcel is obviously tired. The boy's been through a traumatic time – as have his family. I think, to be fair to them, we'd better wind this up soon.'

Despite his efforts to bring the impromptu family interview to a close, the cameras continued to flash and questions persisted until, exasperated, Roscoe ended the proceedings instantly by clapping his hands and calling, 'That's your lot, folks.'

The journalists then began to drift away.

As soon as the last one had left, a furious row erupted between Philippe Dubois and Camille.

Roscoe was talking to Katrina Drake when he heard Dubois raising his voice. He failed to understand a word since the pair were speaking in French.

'You've got a good command of the language,' he told Drake. 'What's he saying?'

'He's blaming Jean-Jacques and Camille for the kidnapping,' she revealed. 'He thinks they should have taken Marcel with them to Newcastle or they should have left him in France with him.'

'I feel sorry for the boy,' Roscoe admitted. 'He's been through an experience that no one of any age should have to suffer. Now he's back home and has to watch while his parents squabble like children. You'd think they could give up the quarrelling for just one day.'

Sunita had also heard the raised voices. When Dubois ended his tirade against his ex-wife and wandered away in a huff, she hurried across the lawn after him.

‘Monsieur Dubois,’ she called. ‘Won’t you hold on for a minute?’

The red-faced Frenchman spun round.

‘What do you want?’ he demanded.

‘I’m sorry,’ she replied. ‘I could see that you were angry with your ex-wife.’

‘Yes. All of this would not be happening if it were not for her and that big-headed footballer. My son’s life was put in jeopardy.’

‘I don’t think it’s fair to blame Mr and Mrs Beauvais, sir,’ she said. ‘They left Marcel with a security guard and no one could have predicted the events that followed. There’s been a spate of break-ins at footballers’ houses all over England and we’re unsure if they’re connected. But I can assure you we’re doing our utmost to catch the people behind the incident that happened here.’

Dubois seemed to be calming down.

‘All right, Sergeant Roy,’ he said. ‘I can see that you and the chief inspector have worked hard on this business. I really am grateful for what you have done in bringing Marcel back to us. Perhaps I should have done more to control my temper. It’s just that, being nearly five hundred miles apart from Marcel, I’m finding the situation very difficult.’

‘I’m sure,’ she said, consolingly.

‘I was amazed to discover my boy was being kept in the cellar of an auberge called The Waterfront Tavern near the city’s bridge, merely two minutes’ walk from the very hotel where I’ve been staying. You did very well to find him. So I owe you my thanks.’

Sunita was puzzled as she watched the property developer walk away across the lawn.

The chief inspector had insisted that details of the exact location of the cellar should be kept under wraps for a few days ‘for operational reasons’. They had only shared full details with the footballer in strictest confidence.

How did Dubois know it was The Waterfront Tavern near Worcester Bridge? she wondered.

Chapter 44

After the two detectives had returned to CID, the chief inspector emerged from his room and anxiously cast his eyes around.

DC Wendy Hopkirk passed by on her way to the ladies' washroom.

'Have you seen DS Roy?' he asked.

'She was in the canteen a few minutes ago,' she replied. 'I expect she'll be back in a moment.'

Shortly afterwards, Sunita hurried into the CID office carrying a sandwich.

'Sorry, sir. Did you want me?' she asked. 'There was a long queue in the canteen.'

'Don't worry about that now. I need to speak to you urgently,' he said.

He led her into his room and shut the door.

'How's Hepworth getting on with analysing the phones of O'Shane and Jordan, sir?' she asked as she took a chair.

'Not very well. Some contacts had been wiped but he's managed to find one really interesting number. It's Kyle O'Shane's uncle, Rory O'Shane. It's clear they've been speaking on the phone from time to time.'

'The guy who recently left the Vale?' said Sunita.

'Yes. He lives at Yew Tree Farm in Hartley Bishop.'

'Do you think he could be in the frame for masterminding the raid and kidnap?' she asked.

'Maybe. He's got a few buildings there and could easily be storing the Bentley that Marcel was travelling in when he was abducted so we've applied for a search warrant.

Omar should be back from the magistrates with it any time now. But listen, that wasn't the main reason I wanted to speak to you. Dawson's come up with something really interesting.'

He sat down behind his desk.

'I don't know if you remember but, when we interviewed him at his hotel, Philippe Dubois said he flew over to England on 7 November. Dawson has a good contact at Birmingham Airport. He's discovered that Dubois also flew into Britain in September and October. We've got CCTV of him arriving on one occasion, on 8 October.'

Sunita interrupted. 'He told us at the hotel he hadn't been to the UK in years, sir.'

'Exactly,' said Roscoe. 'So why did he lie?'

'It's strange you should say that. I had a brief conversation with Dubois at the Beauvais family's place. He knew Marcel had been held in a cellar at a pub near the Worcester Bridge. He even had the pub's correct name.'

'But that sort of detail wasn't publicly released until after that photo shoot on the lawn, was it?' said Roscoe.

She nodded. 'That's right, sir.'

'He's spoken to Marcel, obviously, but the lad didn't have precise information about where he'd been held. So that's a real mystery, isn't it? You don't suppose…'

'What, sir?'

'You don't suppose he had anything to do with his own son's kidnapping, do you? It seems daft to even think it.'

She leaned back in her chair and folded her arms.

'I can't see it, sir.'

'I mean, we know he abhors the footballer and his ex-wife. So is it possible he arranged for the raid on Upper Norton Manor and for the child to be abducted in order to show his ex-wife and her husband in a bad light? He might consider this a way of showing them up as bad parents in order to get his son back?'

'But to allow his own son to suffer at the hands of a bunch of criminals, sir?' she said. 'He'd have to be a fairly hard-hearted, ruthless man to do that.'

'Perhaps it was his original intention to hurt Jean-Jacques and Camille with the burglary and then it all started to unravel and he lost control of the operation,' said Roscoe. 'Anyway, I want Dawson to carry on with inquiries into these leads. Perhaps he can liaise with police in France and see if Dubois has got any form. Meanwhile, I'd like you and Omar to head off to see this Rory O'Shane.'

* * *

A man was reversing a white Isuzu D-Max pickup truck out of the drive when Sunita and DC Khalid arrived at Yew Tree Farm an hour later.

'Block him in, Sarge,' yelled Khalid.

Sunita followed the suggestion and edged her Peugeot forward in order to obstruct the man's exit.

The driver, who was balding and stocky, emerged from his car and began shouting at them.

'What the hell do you think you're doing?' he demanded as the two detectives got out.

'Mr O'Shane?' Sunita asked.

'Depends who's asking,' he replied.

'Heart of England Police,' she said, displaying her warrant card. 'I'm DS Roy. This is my colleague, DC Khalid. We need to ask you a few questions.'

'What about? I've got a meeting in Queensbridge. Can't this wait?'

'Afraid not, sir,' said the sergeant.

'You'd better come inside,' he said, shaking his head before climbing the steps to his front door. He turned his key in the lock before inviting the pair into his living room.

'What's all this about then?' he asked.

'We need to know where you were on Saturday, 29 October at around 4 p.m.,' she said.

'That's four weeks ago. Usually, I'm here with the missus on a Saturday. Hold on a minute. Wasn't that the day people broke into the footballer's place over in Norton Prior?'

She nodded.

'Look, I had nothing to do with that.'

Khalid interrupted to say, 'We've seen phone records which show two calls were made to your phone that afternoon. One was at ten minutes past five and the other at five minutes to six. They were from your nephew Kyle.'

'Yeah, I've got family like everyone else,' he said.

'Don't try and be funny,' said Khalid. 'I'm sure you remember these two calls.'

'I can't remember,' the farmer claimed.

'Mr O'Shane,' said Sunita, 'you must have heard we've arrested Kyle. Why did he phone you on those occasions?'

'The O'Shanes are a close family. We're often in touch. I expect he was calling to make sure I was OK.'

'We're going to lose our tempers with you in a minute,' said Khalid.

Before Rory O'Shane could pass any further comment, a police car, an unmarked blue Ford Focus and a large white van drew up outside.

'Hey, what's going on?' Rory demanded after glancing through his front window.

'Colleagues of ours,' Khalid told him.

'Look, what am I meant to have done?'

'Well, we've asked you for an explanation as to why your nephew called you on the day of the break-in and you've refused to give a logical answer. As a result, we suspect you of assisting your nephew in burgling the premises, murdering a security guard and abducting a teenager.'

'I had nothing at all to do with any of that,' Rory insisted.

'We're particularly interested in tracing a car belonging to the family, a Bentley,' said Khalid.

'Don't know nothing about it. You're welcome to search the whole place.'

'That's exactly what we intend to do,' said Sunita. 'And if we find the car here, we're going to throw the book at you.'

'You can't search my premises without a search warrant.'

'What do you think this is?' said Khalid, waving his court document in the farmer's face.

Chapter 45

The market town of West Bromwich, seven miles north-west of Birmingham, was masked in a veil of fog as Sunita Roy and DC Dawson arrived there at eleven o'clock on Monday morning. Dawson had visited Kyle O'Shane's parents the previous day and Kyle's father had let it slip that their son lived nearby, in Unwin Street.

After calling at the letting agents for a key, they made their way through a maze of streets on the southern side of the town until they reached the red-brick terraced house in Unwin Street where Kyle O'Shane had made his home.

'Doesn't look too impressive at first glance, does it, Sarge?' said Dawson as Sunita brought her car to a halt outside. 'But I'd give him ten out of ten for location. He's got a mini-mart next door and he's just a few steps away from a chip shop, a Chinese takeaway and a pub. Hey, how come it's taken so long for us to get an address for him?'

'The letting agent said the tenancy's in the name of Rory O'Shane. Come on,' she insisted. 'We've got a job to do.'

The key turned easily in the lock and the pair found themselves in a dark, narrow hallway. They peered into the

small front room, where there was a brown two-seater settee and matching armchair, before proceeding past a small bathroom into a large kitchen-diner.

'It's surprisingly neat and tidy compared with his parents' place,' Dawson remarked.

'Yes. It's a little strange to think that, despite his criminal background, he was a clean-living guy,' she said.

'Do you think he lived here alone?' asked Dawson as he opened one of the white, shaker-style kitchen cupboards. It was empty.

'Looks that way,' she replied. 'There don't seem to be any signs of a woman's touch. Let's take a peek upstairs.'

The pair found the house had two bedrooms and a shower room on the first floor. Once again, the rooms were tidy and had been immaculately decorated with a white finish.

'You make a start here, Brett,' she told him. 'I'll have a crack at the downstairs.'

'So what do you think we should be looking for exactly?'

'I'm not really sure,' she said. 'Anything tying him to burglary, I suppose. Any documents relating to cars and properties. Any possible proceeds of crime or drugs. Any old phones. Any names and addresses for friends and relatives. You know the sort of thing.'

'So the search for the Bentley at the uncle's farm drew a blank?' said Dawson.

'That's right, although we found a sales invoice showing the car had been sold abroad. So Rory's clearly implicated to some degree.'

'He'll probably just be done for handling stolen goods.'

'Probably. He certainly doesn't seem to have played any part in arranging or carrying out the burglary and the other offences. Come on, let's get to work.'

Half an hour later, Dawson joined his sergeant in the kitchen.

'All I've found is this small bag which smells like cannabis,' he told her, holding up a transparent plastic bag.

She took a sniff of the contents.

'You're right,' she said. 'You haven't found anything else?'

He shook his head.

'I'm wondering if he kept the place scrupulously clean just in case he got raided – you know, so there wouldn't be anything to pin on him.'

'You could be right. It looks swept clean,' she admitted. 'Hang on a minute.'

Sunita's attention had been drawn to a fridge-freezer standing in a corner, by the double-glazed back door.

Her eyes had settled upon a handwritten note fixed to the side of the appliance with a magnet.

'What is it, Sarge – his shopping list?' asked Dawson.

She removed the strawberry magnet and studied the square piece of white paper beneath it.

'It's a list of names and numbers written on the back of an envelope,' she said. 'His mother; Wayne Jordan; his sister; a woman called Sadie Mills; and a man called Josh Lyttleton. Well, there we are, Brett. We've both got something to do this afternoon. We can go through these numbers and see if they take us anywhere.'

* * *

That same cold morning, the chief inspector had decided to travel to Worcester and confront Philippe Dubois about his suspicions. Accompanied by DC Khalid, he left the CID office at St James Street and took the stairs to the ground floor. He had only just arrived in the reception hall when DI Parkes pushed his way through the doors and approached him.

'Good. I've been meaning to have a word with you,' said Roscoe. He passed the remote for his car to Khalid.

'Let yourself in, would you? I'll only be a minute,' he said.

As Khalid stepped into the car park, Roscoe and Parkes took seats in the corner under the watchful eye of the young, dark-haired constable sitting behind the reception desk.

'What have you got planned for today?' Roscoe asked the inspector.

'Well, I was going to have a chat with John Hepworth about the phones. He doesn't seem to be making much progress and I was going to suggest, sir, that perhaps one of our operatives in Birmingham should be invited to have a look at them instead.'

Roscoe shook his head.

'John Hepworth is a brilliant operator and, if he can't find any useful intelligence that could lead to us unmasking the ruthless individual that controls the Matchday Boys, no one can,' he said. 'I don't want you going over to John and making mischief.'

Parkes glared. 'I must protest at the use of that phrase, sir. I'm simply trying to overcome the challenges we're facing with this final part of the investigation.'

'DC Khalid and I are about to head off to see Dubois, who's given us grounds for suspicion over the past few days that he might have been involved in coordinating the gang.'

Parkes frowned.

'Well, good luck with that, sir. What are the chances of a father being involved with a gang who abducted his own son? Doesn't sound plausible to me.'

'Well, he's said a couple of strange things that I need to clear up,' said Roscoe.

'Sir, with respect, I think we should be re-interviewing Kyle O'Shane and putting more pressure on him to reveal who he was working for.'

Roscoe scowled. He was beginning to lose his temper with the bumptious inspector.

'Look, I've had enough of you questioning my strategy,' Roscoe exclaimed. 'You were sent here to help us, not

hinder us – and, for most of the time, you've been a hindrance. My sergeant, through dogged detective work, managed to find the missing boy but, since she did, your bitterness and hostility towards her has only increased.'

Parkes grimaced. 'Sir, that's just not fair.'

'I think it *is* fair,' Roscoe insisted. 'It's high time you took your leave of us and allowed us to conclude this inquiry on our own terms. Do you understand me? As of now, you're officially off this case, Inspector.'

On that note, he stood up and marched off to his car. Parkes, unexpectedly finding himself alone, remained on his seat with a look of bewilderment. Across the reception hall, the duty constable, who had overheard the last part of the conversation, was smiling to himself.

Chapter 46

It took the chief inspector a few minutes to calm down after his row with Inspector Parkes.

'That man's nothing less than a pain in the backside,' he muttered as he started his car and drove away from police headquarters with Khalid beside him in the passenger seat.

'Is he complaining again about something?' asked Khalid. 'I've noticed he does that a lot.'

'He thinks we're wasting our time visiting Dubois and suggests instead that we should lean on Kyle O'Shane a bit more and make him identify the boss.'

'But you've tried that and it didn't work, sir,' said Khalid.

'I know. But I suppose Parkes thinks we should use more subtle means of extracting the information from him – more psychological pressure, I suppose. But we haven't got enough leverage to do that right now.'

‘I could see through the window that Parkes was backing away from you, sir,’ said Khalid.

‘Yes, he’s off the case. I’ve sent him packing. I know I’m probably going to get a rocket from the chief super, but I’d just about had enough of that cocky inspector.’

When the two detectives arrived at the reception desk at the King’s Arms Hotel, they were disconcerted to learn that Philippe Dubois was unavailable.

‘He hasn’t checked out, has he?’ asked Roscoe.

The blonde receptionist shook her head.

‘No, sir. He’s booked to stay until the end of the week.’

‘Perhaps he’s just gone out shopping,’ suggested Khalid.

They sat down beside an elegant, ten-foot-tall Christmas tree decorated with blue and white baubles and waited for several minutes. Then Khalid spotted the Frenchman strolling through the main door with a camera round his neck.

‘*Monsieur le Chief Inspector, quelle surprise*,’ he said. ‘And DC Khalid.’ He nodded amiably and shook their hands.

‘We need to have a word with you, sir,’ said Roscoe. ‘Is there somewhere quiet?’

‘You could come to my room, if you like,’ he suggested. ‘It’s private there.’

Dubois led them to the lift and they travelled to the third floor. Then he took them along a corridor until they reached his room, number three hundred and one.

The detectives found themselves in a bright, spacious room with a double bed and a sash window overlooking Foregate Street. Its ivory-coloured walls were embellished with black-and-white prints of historic county street scenes.

‘So what’s the matter, Chief Inspector?’ asked Dubois, shutting the door and sitting down on the bed.

‘I’ll come straight to the point,’ said Roscoe. ‘When we spoke to you two and a half weeks ago, you gave us the impression this was your first visit to the UK for some

time. But we've found out you flew into Birmingham Airport in September and October.'

Dubois gave a Gallic shrug, raising his shoulders and gesturing with his arms open.

'A simple misunderstanding, *Monsieur*,' he said. 'I have been fraught with the worry over my son.'

Roscoe frowned. 'And why did you visit the UK on those two previous occasions?' he asked.

'Business,' he said. 'The UK is a good place to invest money. I'm looking for the property to buy.'

'I see. So you've been meeting estate agents in Birmingham and Worcester?'

'And property companies.'

'Your visits here are unconnected with the obsession you have about your ex-wife and son?'

Dubois glared at him. 'I don't have the obsession. My visits before my son was taken were purely for business.'

'In that case,' said Roscoe, 'you won't mind giving my colleague, DC Khalid, full details about who you called on and when, will you?' said Roscoe.

'I can do that. It may take a little time, but I can provide that information.'

'The other matter concerns something you told my sergeant while at Upper Norton Manor on Friday. You stated that Marcel had been kept captive in The Waterfront Tavern near Worcester Bridge. I believe you used the word "auberge". How did you come by that information?'

Dubois adopted a solemn expression.

'I have no recollection, Chief Inspector,' he said. 'Perhaps I read it online or maybe someone told me. I don't remember.'

'Who could have told you?' Roscoe asked. 'That information wasn't publicly available at that time.'

'Maybe Mrs Willis, the housekeeper, told me about the Worcester Bridge when I first arrived at the house. I'm sorry. I just don't know. Why is this so important?'

'Because you seem to know a lot more about the abduction of your son than you're letting on,' said Roscoe. 'Because it's crossed our minds that, since you resent your ex-wife's new marriage to Mr Beauvais, you might have arranged the break-in at the manor yourself.'

'*C'est ridicule!*' he replied. 'Who is the father who can kidnap his own son and make financial demands for his return? I'm sorry, Chief Inspector. You are at risk of making yourself ridiculous. That is not a method I would use to take revenge upon my ex-wife. So please forget that idea.'

'Very well,' said Roscoe, edging towards the door. 'We'll leave those questions there for the moment. But I must insist that you now help DC Khalid here by giving him full details of the meetings you've held in September and October – complete with times, dates and addresses. We're not finished with you yet, by any means.'

The chief inspector left his colleague to quiz the Frenchman about his activities in the UK. He took the lift down and found a seat beside a small table in the reception area while waiting for Khalid to finish his work. For several minutes, he remained there, deep in thought.

Philippe Dubois had a strong reason to dislike the footballer but, Roscoe wondered, would he have stooped so low as to hire a gang of British criminals to raid the family's home and kidnap his own son?

Perhaps the initial abduction had been a spur of the moment act. Perhaps the boy had been snatched away by the gang for fear the lad might have witnessed some of the action. But if Dubois played a part in staging the events of that late October afternoon, surely he would have used his influence within the gang to make sure his own son was quickly released?

Roscoe remained highly suspicious of the French property developer. He could see how he would relish any chance to hurt and humiliate the footballer and Camille. But it was surely improbable that he would have allowed his own son's life to be placed in peril. Wasn't it?

Chapter 47

Taking one step at a time, Sunita Roy manoeuvred her way cautiously across the office carpet in CID, carrying two cups of coffee. She placed one of the steaming drinks on the desk beside DC Dawson's computer screen.

'There you are, Brett,' she said, glancing down at the white envelope containing the phone numbers she'd found beside the fridge in Unwin Street.

After heading back to her own desk with the remaining drink, she told him, 'I want you to call Kyle O'Shane's mother and sister. Meanwhile, I'm going to tackle Sadie Mills and Josh Lyttleton.'

'What particularly are we looking for, Sarge?' Dawson asked.

'We want detailed knowledge of Kyle's personal life,' she replied. 'We need details of any close friends and associates. Did he have a job? How did he spend his private life? Any girlfriends? You know the sort of thing. But most important of all: Did he have any close links to fellow criminals?'

Sadie Mills's phone number rang for nearly a minute before the call diverted to voicemail. Sunita decided not to leave a message but to try the number again later.

She had more success with her call to Josh Lyttleton. He answered almost at once, stating his name in a deep, husky voice.

'Maybe you can help me,' said Sunita. 'I'm trying to get in touch with friends and relatives of a guy called Kyle O'Shane.'

'How did you get my number?' asked Lyttleton.

‘I found it on a list of numbers that Mr O’Shane’s been keeping.’

‘Who are you exactly?’

‘I’m a police officer. We’re just carrying out some background research. Your name’s on a list alongside his mother and sister,’ she said.

‘Exalted company,’ he remarked.

‘Yes. He obviously thought highly of you,’ she said.

‘Me and Kyle go back a long way. Look, I don’t mind talking to you.’

‘My name’s DS Roy, by the way,’ she said.

‘I’m Josh, as you’re obviously aware.’

‘Josh, you say you’ve known Kyle a while. When did you first get to know him?’

‘We grew up together in West Bromwich. We used to hang around together, although I was a couple of years older, and, I’m sorry to say, we got into trouble together. We both ended up doing a stretch in Winson Green for burglary. But those days are behind me now and I’ve started to turn my life around.’

Sunita leaned back in her office chair.

‘That’s good to hear,’ she said as, a few seats away, she could overhear Dawson speaking to O’Shane’s mother.

‘Yes. I’m training to be a church deacon,’ he said.

‘That’s quite a career change.’

‘Yes. I became friends with the prison chaplain and he helped me to find the Lord. I started reading the Bible and became a Christian and I’m now in the middle of my induction course.’

‘Remarkable story,’ said Sunita. ‘You and Kyle appeared in court together for burglary?’

‘A few times. We began with community orders and suspended sentences. In the end, we got sent down. I got three years. He got five.’

‘So you both spent time in Winson Green?’

‘Yes, but we never saw much of each other when we were inside. I tell you what, despite the years, he hasn’t

changed. He's still the same lad from West Brom trying to overcome the rough start he had in life.'

There was a pause in the conversation while Sunita wrote a few words in her notebook.

'Josh, if you were whiling away the hours reading the Bible, how did Kyle spend his time in prison?'

'He went on a mechanics course and he made a few friends. His biggest pal was his cellmate, Matt. He was a big guy, like Kyle, and serving a stretch for fraud. He's had a huge influence on Kyle – and not a very positive one. The guy had a charismatic personality and, somehow or other, Kyle fell under his spell.'

'So when were Kyle and this other man released?'

'Kyle was let out four years ago. Matt got parole a few months afterwards.'

'What happened to Matt?' Sunita asked.

'Last I heard he was running some business. Don't ask me whereabouts, though.'

Sunita frowned and shook her head.

'It must be very difficult to run a business when you've got a criminal record,' she pointed out.

'Yes, it is.'

'Any idea about Matt's surname and where he lives?'

'I've no idea where he lives,' said Lyttleton. 'I was never in his close circle of friends and I've lost touch with him, I'm afraid. His surname is something like Biddle or Beadle.'

Sunita was plunged into deep thought. She had come across the surname Biddle somewhere before. For the moment, she couldn't recall the association.

'Are you still there?' asked Lyttleton.

'Yes, sorry,' said Sunita. 'I was just thinking about something. Listen, you've been incredibly helpful, Josh. Do you mind if I give you a call sometime, if I need any further information?'

'Of course. No problem,' he said.

‘And I wish you good luck in your chosen profession,’ she added.

When she came off the phone, Dawson hurried across to her.

‘Just spoken to Kyle’s mother, Sarge,’ he said. ‘She wasn’t too helpful. Just had a string of complaints about the way he’s been treated since he was arrested.’

‘Don’t bother with that now, Brett. I’ve got details of a guy who befriended Kyle while they shared a prison cell. He might turn out to be a real person of interest.’

She phoned the governor’s office at the prison in Winson Green and, within minutes, had found details of a prisoner released on parole four years earlier. His name was Matthew Biddle.

She sent an email to the genealogist in Birmingham that Heart of England Police often used during difficult cases.

Once he had agreed to carry out some research for her into the man’s family, she moved onto the next stage of her inquiries, which involved a call to the parole service.

This revealed that Kyle O’Shane’s former cellmate was now running a car dealership in Queensbridge after having officially changed his name from Matthew Biddle to… Matthew Swinford.

Chapter 48

The county town of Warwick lay shrouded in fog when Sunita Roy rose from her bed just before seven o’clock on Tuesday morning. She glanced through her living-room window into the street outside. A white veil enveloped the racecourse in the distance like a ghostly shadow.

A growing sense of excitement had been coursing through her veins, leaving her unable to sleep. A sense that

a ray of light was about to penetrate the web of darkness surrounding the break-in at the manor.

She returned to her bedroom and slipped on her white dressing gown. Then she strolled into her kitchen and made herself a lemon tea. Within minutes, she was feeling revived and ready for the active day she had planned. But so many thoughts were spinning through her head. Was Matt Swinford, the boss of West Avon Motors, who had behaved rather brusquely towards her in his showroom, the leader of the Matchday Boys? Had he arranged for the gang to be armed? Had he sanctioned the kidnapping?

A great deal of circumstantial evidence pointed towards him. He had served a prison sentence for a string of dishonesty offences. He seemed to have struck up a close bond with principal gang member Kyle O'Shane. If he was related to the estate agent James Biddle, from Royal County Properties, that might account for the ease with which the gang seemed to find empty properties in which to take refuge. She just needed a little more information now to confirm her suspicions.

But there was a question troubling her. How could a man with a prison sentence for fraud be allowed to set up in business in the market town of Queensbridge, buying and selling cars? Had he used some ruse to get round the law?

That was not all that concerned her. The gang seemed to know immediately when the Beauvais family had called in the police. It was as though someone had tipped them off about it.

After a light breakfast, she turned on her laptop and was pleased to see that the genealogist in Birmingham had already replied to her email.

The researcher, which the police regularly used to trace the family trees of suspects and witnesses in criminal cases, had provided detailed birth and marriage information about the Warwickshire family that interested her. He had also checked records at Companies House and the probate office.

Now most of her doubts had been dispelled. Now her vision was clearer.

Delighted to receive the information so promptly, she emailed the family researcher back, 'Thank you for supplying details of those births. This has helped confirm what I strongly suspected.'

She then spent an hour on the phone making further inquiries into the case. Part of that time was spent speaking to Dr Ling in forensics.

Two hours later, she arrived at St James Street in a cheerful mood. With a confident air, she climbed the stairs to CID and, after placing her fawn coat on the back of her chair, tapped on the chief inspector's door.

'I think I might have cracked the case,' she said while entering his room carrying a slip of paper.

She was embarrassed to find she was interrupting a discussion between her boss and DC Khalid.

'I'm sorry, sir,' she stammered while backing away.

'No, it's all right, Sergeant. We were just talking about Philippe Dubois. Please come in.'

She closed the door and sat down.

'You might have cracked the case?' he said.

'Yes, sir.' She placed her sheet of paper on his desk.

'Before you go into your new theory, I should tell you that Dubois is no longer being regarded as a suspect,' said Roscoe. 'Khalid's checked the company meetings he held in September and October and his explanations stack up. Mrs Willis has confirmed that, in a fit of excitement after hearing Marcel had been reunited with the Beauvais couple, she blurted out to Dubois that the boy had been found in The Waterfront Tavern near the city's bridge – details she overheard the family discussing.'

Sunita smiled. 'I'm not really surprised, sir,' she said. 'In any case, how could Dubois successfully run a gang in Britain while based in France? And what's more, how could Dubois have found the gang empty properties to use as hideouts?'

‘Well, you say that, but Dubois is a property dealer,’ said Roscoe. ‘Anyway that’s irrelevant now. So you’ve got a new suspect?’

She nodded. ‘Yes, sir. Matthew Swinford.’

‘Isn’t that the guy who’s taken over West Avon Motors?’

‘The very same.’

He reached for the piece of paper she had placed on his desk and began studying it.

‘So what am I looking at here?’

‘It’s Swinford’s family tree,’ she said. ‘You’ll see that, in 1973, a twenty-four-year-old woman, Davina Swinford, married a guy called Martin Biddle in Evesham. They had two sons – James in 1973 and Matthew in 1975.’

‘I can see that,’ Roscoe admitted, ‘but what’s that got to do with our case?’

‘Well, Matthew Biddle and Matthew Swinford are one and the same person. After coming out of Winson Green four years ago, he decided to change his name and began using his mother’s maiden name, Swinford. Then, using inherited money, he took over West Avon Motors from Jett Lumley.’

‘I’d been wondering how a convicted fraudster could set up in business,’ she continued. ‘Apparently there was nothing to stop him. You can register as a company director as long as you’re not a disqualified director or an undischarged bankrupt. In any case, he’s made his mother managing director and he calls himself the general manager.’

‘That’s a shocking state of affairs,’ said Roscoe. ‘The law needs looking at.’

‘I agree, sir,’ said Khalid.

‘And once he’d set himself up in the motor trade, he took on a lucrative sideline,’ said Sunita, ‘organising burglaries of country houses with his former prison pal, Kyle O’Shane.’

'What about the other brother, James?' asked Roscoe, studying the family tree.

'I'm glad you asked, sir,' she said. 'I've met the guy. He's an estate agent in Queensbridge.'

'Is he?'

'Yes. As a matter of fact, I've just bought my new house through him. As we know, the gang used buildings in Queensbridge, Monkswood and Worcester. They've all been on the books of James Biddle's firm, Royal County Properties, so I've been wondering…'

Roscoe interrupted.

'If Biddle handed the keys to those properties over to his crooked brother?' asked Roscoe. 'Sounds possible, doesn't it? But there's one thing that worries me. The connection between the two prison friends is clear. But is there any more recent evidence to show Kyle O'Shane and Matt Swinford were associating together during the kidnapping?'

She nodded. 'I've had some luck there as well. Dr Ling's confirmed that a burner phone found at the Worcester pub bore O'Shane's fingerprints. It's clear O'Shane made numerous calls to a phone number in Marina Gardens, Queensbridge, where Swinford is based.'

Roscoe shrugged. 'Far from conclusive, but it gives us enough to make an arrest. Maybe a search of Swinford's home will turn up some hard evidence. We've obviously got to go and arrest this guy.'

He was still holding the sheet of paper.

'Getting back to your family research,' he said, 'at the foot of the page, you refer to Matthew's marriage to a lady called Anna Carson and the birth of a baby in 1994 called Katrina.'

'That right, sir,' she said. 'I understand that Matt Swinford and Anna are now divorced. He's now living with his elderly mother in a rambling old house in the village of Biddington. If you turn over, you'll see what happened to the little girl.'

Roscoe peered at the details on the reverse of the sheet.

'Good God!' he said. 'Katrina Drake.'

'What's this?' asked Khalid.

Roscoe handed him the page so the constable could see for himself.

'What you're saying, Sarge, is that Katrina Drake is Matt Swinford's daughter?' said Khalid.

'That's right. She changed her name from Biddle when she married Geoffrey Drake in Birmingham four years ago.'

'So all the time the Beauvais family were going through the emotional turmoil of their son's abduction, there was a spy in the camp,' said Roscoe, leaning back on his chair. 'Sergeant, you've worked exceptionally hard on this case and it's paid off. You should be immensely proud of yourself.'

She blushed. 'Thank you, sir. I suspected all the time that a person close to the family might be in league with the gang. Do you remember the Matchday Boys sent the Beauvais family a message on 9 November, berating them for bringing in the police?'

'Yes. I thought that was rather strange at the time,' Roscoe muttered. 'How did they know that police had become involved?'

'The gang's message was very specific too,' she said. 'Their message stated that police had been contacted on the morning of Tuesday, 1 November. They could only have known that so precisely if someone with inside knowledge had been keeping them informed.'

'Well,' said Roscoe, leaning forward in his seat. 'We now know who that someone was. It was Katrina Drake.'

Chapter 49

PC Derek Underhill was pacing up and down Marina Gardens in Queensbridge with a pensive look when the chief inspector's car drew up late in the afternoon. Roscoe and his sergeant got out and joined the constable on the pavement.

'It's been a while since I was last here,' said Roscoe. 'Derek, is that the showroom over there?'

'Yes,' said Underhill. 'I glanced through the window, but I could only see one person around.'

'That will probably be Michael, one of Swinford's sales staff,' said Sunita. 'Swinford is probably in his back office.'

'All right. Let's not waste any more time. Let's go and see what he's got to say,' said Roscoe.

'I heard two people were going to be arrested today,' said Underhill as they strolled together towards the nearby River Avon.

'We've got Khalid and Hopkirk heading over to the manor to pick up Katrina Drake,' Roscoe explained.

'Blimey,' said Underhill. 'You don't hang around. As soon as the cogs of the engine get turning, the old wheels spring into life.'

'Derek, I hope you're not trying to compare the CID department to the operation of an old bus,' muttered Roscoe as he walked towards the showroom entrance.

Two dark-green Land Rovers, a silver Mercedes and a blue Toyota stood on the forecourt as the salesman, Michael, emerged and greeted them.

'Police. DCI Roscoe,' the chief inspector announced. 'Is your guvnor in?'

'Mr Swinford? I think he's on the phone. Is there a problem?'

'Tell him we need to speak to him,' said Roscoe.

As Michael set off to find his boss, the chief inspector asked Underhill in a low voice, 'Is there a back way?'

'Yes, there is,' the constable confirmed. 'There's gates and a small car park for staff behind here.'

'Forgive my suspicious nature, but there's a chance our Mr Swinford might try to evade us by slipping out the back. Could you go and keep an eye on the rear?'

Roscoe soon realised his fears were unjustified. In less than a minute, Swinford, looking immaculate in a light-grey suit, emerged from his office and approached them with a questioning look in his eyes.

'DS Roy, good to see you again,' he said, 'and you've brought a colleague.'

'This is DCI Roscoe,' Sunita explained.

'I'm afraid this isn't a social visit,' said the chief inspector. 'We've come to arrest you.'

'Arrest me? Whatever for?'

While Sunita phoned Underhill to summon him back, Roscoe recited the charges.

'On suspicion of conspiring with others to commit burglary, aggravated burglary and theft at Upper Norton Manor on 29 October this year,' he said. 'On the same date, conspiracy to murder and, on various dates, to blackmail.' He recited the police caution.

'That's quite a list,' said Swinford with a scowl. 'I can't think why you're accusing me.'

'You've got a close friend called Kyle O'Shane,' said Roscoe as Underhill joined them at the showroom entrance.

'Funny. Don't remember him,' Swinford said, attempting to smile.

Sunita interrupted. 'That's strange because we're fairly sure he remembers you,' she said.

Swinford turned pale and the smile on his face faded.

'You've got the wrong man,' said Swinford. 'Arresting me is a big mistake which you'll both live to regret.'

'The keys to your house in Biddington, please, Mr Swinford,' said Roscoe, holding out his hand.

'You can't go there without a warrant,' Swinford insisted. 'In any case, my mother's in poor health. She's recovering from a heart attack.'

'We've got a warrant to search your premises,' said Roscoe.

'And we'll be careful not to alarm your mother,' said Sunita.

'Handcuff him, Derek,' said Roscoe, 'and can you arrange for him to be taken up to headquarters?'

* * *

Soon after Roscoe and Sunita set off on the six-mile journey to Swinford's home, the chief inspector received a call from DC Khalid.

'Sir, we've arrested Katrina Drake and we're on our way to St James Street with her,' the constable informed him. 'She's been charged with assisting an organised crime group.'

'Good,' Roscoe replied. 'Did she give any trouble?'

'She was absolutely stunned but didn't make a fuss, simply claiming she was innocent and that she expected to be back at the manor soon. The Beauvais family were shocked beyond belief.'

'I bet they were. Thanks for that, Khalid. We're on our way to Swinford's place and we hope to be back in an hour or so.'

The village of Biddington, three miles from Norton Prior, consisted of a church, a gastropub, a public school, three farms and around twenty residential properties.

Matt Swinford's home – owned by his mother, Davina – was a picturesque, black-and-white, eighteenth-century cottage in a narrow lane. A brick pathway meandered

down the long garden, which was mainly laid to lawn and bounded by high hedges.

Roscoe drew into a small parking area at the rear of the cottage. He and his sergeant got out and they were joined, moments later, by Dr Ling after she had arrived in her white Kia Sportage.

'Have you tried the door?' she asked as she began slipping on her white overalls.

'Not yet,' said Sunita, 'but there's a light on in the kitchen and Matt Swinford's mother is expected to be here.'

As they were speaking, a frail, grey-haired woman in her mid-seventies could be seen gazing through the window. Seconds later, she opened the heavy, oak door with a struggle.

'What are you doing here?' she asked, leaning on a walking stick.

'Heart of England CID,' said Sunita, producing her warrant card. 'I'm DS Roy. This is DCI Roscoe. Are you Mrs Swinford?'

'Yes.'

'I'm afraid your son's been taken to police headquarters and we have a warrant to search your house.'

'Why? What's he meant to have done?' asked Davina Swinford with a worried expression.

Roscoe interrupted. 'I'm afraid we can't say too much,' he said, 'but he's assisting us with our inquiries.'

'Oh dear,' she said. 'I suppose you'd better come in.'

While she had been talking, four members of Dr Ling's forensics staff had arrived. They trooped in before anyone else, followed by Dr Ling, Roscoe and Sunita.

'I suppose I'd better look at your warrant,' Davina told Sunita as she hobbled into the modern, shaker-style kitchen to fetch a pair of glasses.

Sunita and Roscoe glanced into the living-room of the Grade II-listed building. It had a marble fireplace, low ceilings with dark timber beams and traditional-styled doors.

While the chief inspector followed Dr Ling into the dual-aspect living room, Sunita remained in the sizable hallway, clutching the warrant. Once she had returned, the old lady spent a few seconds studying the document.

'It says something about reasonable suspicion there may be the proceeds of a burglary here,' she said without looking up.

'I can't comment without my boss's approval,' said Sunita. 'Why don't you go and make yourself a cup of tea? I don't suppose we'll be very long.'

'How long?'

'Maybe an hour or two?'

'An hour or two? I'm meant to be going out to the village hall in an hour,' she moaned before storming off into the kitchen and slamming the door.

Sunita stepped into the living room where the chief inspector was holding up a watch in a transparent evidence bag.

'Just found this in a drawer of the antique writing bureau in the corner,' he boasted.

'It looks like a watch, sir,' she remarked.

'Not just any watch. It's a Richard Mille watch like the one on the list of goods seized from Upper Norton Manor,' he said. 'Dr Ling's just gone upstairs. But before she went, she found a burner phone in a household bin.'

'So the evidence is starting to come together.'

'It certainly is,' he said. 'I'm just going to give this to the crime scene manager, who's in the room next door.'

After he went, Sunita cast her eyes round. The room contained two grey leather two-seater settees and a matching armchair. A rustic, solid wood coffee table stood in the centre of the room, beneath a crystal chandelier. A piano occupied the far corner. For some reason, her attention was drawn to an item lying on the mahogany piano stool.

She stepped across the room and peered down. It was a small gold clutch bag with the initials NJ.

Chapter 50

The chief inspector peered through the one-way glass into Interview Room One at St James Street.

Matt Swinford was sitting on his own, hunched over a table. He looked up as his smartly dressed solicitor, Magnus Huckabee, pushed open the door and gave the car dealer a pat on the back before taking a chair beside him.

Huckabee, a stout, balding man, was in his early forties – not much younger than his client.

Roscoe glanced across at his sergeant. 'Swinford's about to tell his brief that there's no reason he should be there and that he's the victim of police bungling.' He came and sat down beside her, shaking his head. 'This case has taken its toll on me, Sergeant,' he told Sunita, who was sipping from a cup of lemon tea. 'I think I need a holiday.'

'Maybe you'll be able to take one,' she said, 'once this is all over. But I agree, it's been an exhausting few weeks.'

He smiled at her. 'You clearly believe the murder of Danny Jukes was deliberately planned and that Swinford wasn't on his own in arranging it?'

She nodded.

'I think we'd make a mistake to assume he planned it alone,' said Sunita. 'Let me explain. When I visited Natalie Jukes the day after her husband was murdered, I noticed a gold clutch bag in her sitting room. Her initials, NJ, were embossed on it. The same bag was on a piano stool at the Swinfords' cottage. I opened it and found a driving licence inside in Natalie's name. I immediately went into the kitchen, where Davina Swinford was sitting quietly at the table, staring out of the window. I explained about the bag and asked if she knew Natalie. She revealed she was her

son's girlfriend. She said they met last Christmas and were planning to get married.'

'But you told me Mrs Jukes gave every impression of an anguished widow when you visited her in Evesham,' said Roscoe.

'I know,' said Sunita. 'She's a good actress and nearly had me fooled.'

'So your theory is that she was having an affair with Swinford?'

'Yes, sir.'

'You don't think it possible he acted without her compliance and arranged for the bodyguard to be shot?'

'I'm thinking it must have been with her agreement and I'm sure we can find the evidence to support it,' she said.

'So the burglary was used as a diversion?'

'No. Not really. Mrs Swinford also mentioned that her son and Nicola had been talking about moving abroad. It sounds like they needed money to help them do that.'

Roscoe stood up and shook his head again. 'Is there no limit to the depths of depravity some of our fellow humans will stoop to?' he said.

Sunita shrugged and shook her head.

'Did you send someone down to the Jukeses' house, sir?' she asked.

'Yes,' he said. 'Dawson's down there, but he says there's no reply at the front door and thinks she could still be at work. For the moment, I've asked him to sit tight.'

'Good,' she said. 'I think I should join him after we've spoken to Swinford, sir.'

'I'd come as well but there's no sense in all three of us going,' said Roscoe. 'By the way, you've met Swinford before, haven't you?'

'Yes, when we were inquiring about the Mercedes,' she said. 'He'd reported it as stolen – even though it was being used by the gang.'

'Cheek of old Nick,' he asserted. 'It wouldn't surprise me if he made an insurance claim. Anyway, we've given them long enough. Let's go and see how things stand.'

Carrying a small evidence bag, Sunita followed the chief inspector into the next room, where he switched on the digital recorder. The pair sat down facing Swinford and his lawyer.

'You're still under caution, Mr Swinford,' said Roscoe. 'Now, as you're no doubt aware, we've been investigating a burglary at Norton Prior on Saturday, 29 October in which a man was shot dead and a boy kidnapped. Where were you on that afternoon at around four o'clock?'

'At my business, West Avon Motors,' he replied.

'Who can vouch for that?'

'Michael Robson, one of my sales staff.'

'We'll make inquiries to make sure you're telling the truth,' said Roscoe. 'In any case, it's not being suggested you were physically involved in the break-in, the shooting or the abduction. What's being contended is that you were the brains behind what happened – that you planned and organised events, handled stolen goods and that you were responsible for the ransom demands that led to the kidnapped boy's family paying out two million pounds.'

'No comment.'

'Our team will be going through your bank statements and examining a mobile phone we found under your bed. A man called Kyle O'Shane, who's facing charges in connection with the burglary, is one of the contacts on that phone.'

Swinford glared back. 'No comment,' he said.

Sunita opened the evidence bag she'd brought with her and brought out the recovered Richard Mille watch.

'This was found in your writing bureau. It's on a list of items taken from Upper Norton Manor,' she said.

'How do you account for this being in your living room?' asked Roscoe.

'No comment,' said Swinford with a scowl.

'We've also found more than a dozen designer handbags in your bedroom which match up with bags on the same list,' remarked Sunita.

'No comment.'

'When you left Winson Green, you changed your name, didn't you?' said Roscoe. 'You dropped your original surname of Biddle and began using your mother's maiden name, Swinford. One of my colleagues has been to see your brother, James Biddle. He's an estate agent, as you're aware, and he's confirmed in a written statement that he lent you the keys to two properties – Meadow Brook Farm in Monkswood and The Waterfront Tavern in Worcester. This was done on the understanding that you were searching for suitable locations for photo shoots advertising prestige cars.'

'No comment.'

'Speaking of The Waterfront Tavern, we understand you conspired with Kyle O'Shane and Wayne Jordan to keep the kidnapped boy, Marcel Dubois, in the pub's cellar. It was here that, following the recent floods, he nearly died, having been chained to the wall. He must have been terrified as the river water rose and nearly filled the entire cellar. It's only thanks to the ingenuity of Sergeant Roy here that she discovered this location and organised the boy's rescue. If it wasn't for her, he'd almost certainly have died.'

Swinford stared across the table at Sunita, his gaze full of contempt for her. She ignored him and whispered a few words in Roscoe's ear.

The chief inspector looked their suspect in the eyes.

'Katrina Drake is your daughter, isn't she?' he said.

'What if she is?' he said.

'You encouraged her to gain employment with the Beauvais family and wheedle her way into their confidence. Then the ever-dutiful daughter used her resources to become a conduit of information for you.'

Swinford sneered. 'You'll have to do better than that, copper. Your evidence is very flimsy.'

'Then we come to your girlfriend,' said Roscoe. 'You were having an affair with Natalie Jukes, weren't you?'

'No,' said Swinford.

Huckabee interrupted to ask, 'I'm sorry. I'm falling behind here. Who's the lady you're talking about, Chief Inspector?'

'Natalie Jukes is the widow of the bodyguard shot dead in cold blood during the burglary,' Roscoe explained.

Turning his attention back to Swinford, he continued, 'Your mother's made a full and frank admission that you and Natalie Jukes have been in a relationship for eleven months.'

'The stupid cow,' said Swinford. 'Why does she have to go and say something like that?'

'Because, in the short time we've known her, we've formed the impression your mother is an honest, upright woman who always speaks the truth – unlike you.'

Chapter 51

When his phone rang at the end of his hectic day, the chief inspector was tempted to ignore it. He was eager to get home and put his feet up. But, in the end, he decided to answer it.

'They'll only call me on my mobile if I don't pick up,' he told himself.

'Roscoe,' he announced as he raised the receiver.

'Gavin, I want you in my office in the next five minutes,' said a voice he instantly recognised. 'You've got some explaining to do.'

Roscoe climbed the stairs to the second floor with an inkling about why Chief Superintendent Norris was so eager to speak to him. He suspected she had just learnt of his row with DI Parkes and how he had dismissed the National Crime Agency inspector from his team.

'Good evening, ma'am,' he said after knocking and stepping into the room.

Norris was sitting behind her desk, peering at him over the top of her glasses.

'Gavin, about a month ago, we were fortunate enough to have Joseph Parkes seconded to us to assist in the kidnapping case. I asked you to afford him every courtesy. Now I understand you've sent him packing with a flea in his ear.'

Roscoe shrugged his shoulders.

'Slight exaggeration, ma'am,' he said. 'We had a difference of opinion over strategy. I asked him to leave so that we could bring the investigation to a conclusion on our own terms. I'm afraid that, throughout the four weeks he was with us, we had several disagreements. I also felt he'd begun to become rather obstructive and a hindrance to our investigation.'

'Gavin, I'm not very impressed by your response,' she said. 'He came to us with extensive knowledge of dealing with kidnappings and ransom demands. Quite frankly, you and I don't have that knowledge.'

Roscoe shook his head. 'He wasn't shy about coming forward with all his knowledge,' he said. 'In fact, other members of the team became discouraged and annoyed by his rather arrogant attitude towards his colleagues in CID. I grant you that he developed an extremely good relationship with the Beauvais family, but he wasn't a good team player. He wanted everything done his way. Last weekend, we fell out over his continued insistence on having a blanket ban on reports in the press about the kidnap. However, as time passed and the plight of the boy became more critical, I decided, as you know, to ask for

the cooperation of the press so that we could call on the public for help. After that, Parkes started challenging every plan I came up with and became a burden to the team.'

'Is that all you've got to say?' she asked.

'Not quite, ma'am,' he said, taking a seat in front of her desk. 'I should add that, from the time he arrived, he seemed to take exception to DS Roy playing any major role in the investigation. Of course, it was only through her skill and professionalism that we located the missing boy and saved him from a watery grave. But Parkes found all this difficult to accept. Whenever he could, he downplayed her role and, in her presence, tried to make her feel uncomfortable.'

Norris leaned back in her wheelchair.

'I'm glad you've explained that to me,' she said. 'Parkes's senior officer has made a formal complaint against you. He said the inspector's told him he was denied full cooperation from your CID team and that you personally chose to ignore most of the advice Parkes gave you – despite his extensive knowledge of abductions. He also says you treated Parkes with disdain and a lack of respect and that you were constantly argumentative. However, now I've heard your side, I think I can begin to understand how this relationship between the two of you broke down.'

'Thank you, ma'am,' said Roscoe.

'It sounds as though he was trying to bully DS Roy and I don't like that at all. I'll mull over the words of the complaint and your remarks before I compose a suitable response.'

'Thank you, ma'am. While we're talking about DS Roy, are you aware of the party she's holding on Saturday? She asked me to mention it to you.'

'I bumped into Tom Vickers in the corridor yesterday,' she said. 'He mentioned something about it. House-warming, isn't it?'

'That's right. She's just moved into her new place.'

‘I’d love to come but I’ve got a prior commitment – I’m going to a show jumping event in Derbyshire.’

‘Not to worry.’

‘Gavin, will you thank her for her kind invitation and explain my situation. Oh, before you go, I need to ask you about the Beauvais case. I gather you’ve made another arrest.’

‘Yes, ma’am. A car dealer named Matt Swinford, who appears to have been running the OCG that broke into the footballer’s house. We’ve just finished interviewing him.’

‘He’s made no admissions, I’m assuming?’

‘No, ma’am, despite overwhelming evidence against him – including stolen property from the manor being discovered in his home. I’m happy to say I’ve just come off the phone to the CPS. They say there’s enough evidence for a case against him. Swinford’s due to appear before magistrates in a few days, along with the two men I told you about last week, O’Shane and Jordan.’

‘Good. That’s excellent news. So how did you find out Swinford was the boss of the gang?’

‘DS Roy discovered Swinford and O’Shane were close friends while in prison together,’ said Roscoe. ‘Then she found out the gang’s hideouts were being chosen with help from Swinford’s estate agent brother and they were being fed inside information by the Beauvais couple’s personal assistant, Katrina Drake – who happens to be Swinford’s daughter. But DC Khalid’s also been a great help. He discovered that Wayne Jordan, who shot Jukes, obtained the Beretta he used from an underworld firearms dealer that Swinford got to know while in Winson Green.’

‘Excellent teamwork, Gavin,’ she said.

‘We’ve come up with one more suspect – the bodyguard’s widow, who seems to have been having an affair with the car dealer.’

‘Really? So the murder of Danny Jukes may have been planned?’

'It looks as though the gunman served two goals at once. He took out the interfering guard but also got rid of a hated husband.'

Chapter 52

The countryside around the town of Evesham was swathed in the same veil of fog that had been blighting the rest of the West Midlands as Sunita Roy travelled there just before 7 p.m. that evening. It seemed as though wisps of vapour were almost tickling the tranquil waters of the River Avon. At times, cars or lorries would startle her by looming unexpectedly out of the silvery haze, and she was relieved when, at last, she reached the town's southern suburbs.

As she entered Primrose Way, she found DC Dawson sitting in his red Ford Focus. He had parked a short distance back from Natalie Jukes's house, number forty-three, in the hope the bodyguard's widow would not notice him.

For a second, as Sunita approached on foot, she wondered if he had fallen asleep. Then she realised he had lowered the back of his car seat in order to relax and was listening to some music.

She surprised him when she tapped on the passenger window.

'What's happening, Brett?' she asked, glancing towards the house. There was a light on in the kitchen and the grey Ford Fiesta she had seen on her previous visit was parked in the drive.

'I was going to call you,' he replied. 'Mrs Jukes arrived back a quarter of an hour ago. I don't think she's seen me.'

'All right,' said the sergeant as she began to shiver in the cold early December air. 'It's time to confront her and see what's she's got to say for herself. By the way, Hepworth's been through Swinford's phone and found some interesting material. I'll tell you about it later.'

They locked their cars and Dawson followed as Sunita strode up to the front door.

Natalie Jukes took more than a minute to respond. Then she drew back the door in a blue sweater and jeans, looking red-faced and flustered. Her dark hair was shorter than Sunita recalled from her previous visit over four weeks earlier.

'Oh, it's you,' she said, staring at Sunita. 'What do you want? I'm in the middle of getting changed to go out.'

'Just need to bring you up to date with the investigation,' said the sergeant. 'Is it all right if we come in? This is my colleague, DC Dawson.'

'I suppose you'd better, but you can't stay long,' she said.

The detectives stepped into the hall, walked past the open kitchen door and entered the living room. There was an open suitcase on the floor and a pile of clothing on the carpet beside it.

'Going somewhere in a hurry?' asked Dawson.

'I've been packing for my holiday,' Natalie said while gesturing for the pair to sit down. 'So what's all this about?'

Sunita settled down on the settee beside her colleague. 'Have you heard about Matt?' she asked Natalie.

'Matt?' said Natalie, whose face was turning red. 'I don't think I know anyone called Matt.'

'Yes, you do,' the sergeant insisted. 'You've been seeing him since last Christmas, according to Matt's mother.'

Natalie shook her head. 'No.'

'Well, we were round at his house in Biddington earlier today and I found your clutch bag. I don't know if you remember, but when I came here to see you on

30 October, there was a gold bag with your initials on your sideboard. That same bag was on the piano stool at Matt Swinford's house a few hours ago. Your driving licence was inside.'

'Oh God,' said Natalie, slumping down into an armchair.

'You *do* know him, don't you?' said the sergeant.

Natalie crouched forward with her head in her hands. When she removed them a few seconds later, her mascara was running. Her eyes were filled with tears.

'What's happened to Matt?' she asked.

'He's been arrested,' said Dawson.

'Listen,' said Sunita, 'our investigation's moved at lightning speed today and I've been making some inquiries about you.'

'Oh my God! This is so ridiculous. I think I'd better tell you what I know. Then you'll see that I haven't done anything wrong.'

'If you want to talk, that's fine,' said Sunita, taking out her small, black notebook. 'The law looks more favourably towards those that cooperate.'

Natalie took a box of tissues from a nearby table and tried to compose herself.

'All right,' she said. 'I expect you'll be talking to the neighbours, so I may as well tell you the truth. Danny and I hadn't been getting on for a couple of years. I think he was cheating on me. There were a few times when I'm fairly certain he was with another woman, but, when I asked him, he always insisted he'd been doing security work. We were always arguing and I was very unhappy. What made matters worse was that I couldn't seem to get pregnant, no matter how hard I tried.

'Then Matt came into my life. I was looking for a new car for myself and called round at several dealers. Matt showed me the Fiesta you saw outside and it suited me down to the ground. He took me out for a run in it and we didn't stop laughing together the whole time. He asked me

out for a drink and I thought, why not? It was round about this time last year and, the day before, Danny and I'd had a massive row. I thought, what's the harm? It's only a drink.'

'Where did he take you?' asked Dawson, as Sunita continued to write furiously in her notebook.

'He took me to the Old Pheasant pub in Queensbridge, and do you know he was every bit as charming as he'd been during the test run? Afterwards, we went for a curry before he took me back to my car at the pub and I drove home. From that moment, I was hooked. We began seeing each other regularly and I began thinking seriously about getting a divorce from Danny.

'Then one night I came home very late from seeing Matt. Danny was here and I got the impression he'd had a lot to drink. He wanted to know where I'd been. I told a lie. I said I'd been out for a drink at a pub with my friend Sarah. But it was a stupid thing to say. He knew I kept Sarah's phone number in an address book by the television.

'He phoned her there and then – although it was after midnight – and asked her where we'd both been. Of course, she didn't know what to say. It was obvious I'd been lying. He put the phone down and then launched into a ferocious attack on me.'

'He attacked you physically?' asked Sunita.

'Yes. He left me with bruises all over my face, arms and legs and I couldn't go to work the next day. I had to call in sick.'

'That's appalling,' said Sunita. Dawson shook his head in agreement with her.

'I knew then that my future lay with Matt and I went to see a solicitor with a view to getting a divorce.'

'So then what happened?' asked Sunita.

'Life just carried on as before,' said Natalie. 'I somehow managed to tell Danny I was divorcing him without getting too much of a battering. The legal letters started and I moved into the spare room. I stopped going home until

late. I wanted to avoid seeing Danny and I was planning to move out.'

'To live with Matt?' asked Sunita.

'Well, yes. Either that or I could have moved in with my sister. Anyway, we reached the end of October and Danny spent that Saturday in Queensbridge with the boy Marcel. And, of course, you know the rest.'

Sunita leaned back on the settee. 'That's not the whole story, is it, Natalie?' she said. 'You played a part in your husband's murder, didn't you?'

'What?' said Natalie, putting her hands to her face. 'You must be joking.'

'We've found certain phone messages,' said Sunita while standing up.

'Messages?'

'Natalie Jukes,' the sergeant continued, 'I'm arresting you on suspicion of conspiracy to murder Danny Jukes.' She recited the rest of the police caution.

'I can't believe you think I had anything to do with Danny's death,' said the startled woman.

'I'm afraid you'll have to come with us,' said Sunita. 'Can you fetch your coat?'

Sunita beckoned her colleague to one side of the living room while Natalie began sorting through a rail of coats and jackets in a hallway cupboard.

'Before I came down here this evening, I received a call from one of our digital forensic specialists,' she whispered to Dawson. 'They'd been examining Matt Swinford's phone. Among the stream of messages on his phone from Natalie, there was one text in particular that stood out which was received on the day of the murder. It had been deleted – presumably by Swinford – but the forensic guy managed to retrieve it.

'It said, "He's definitely driving the silver Bentley Continental. Make sure they are ready at 4 p.m. Nat."'

Chapter 53

Tom Vickers stopped his white Audi A3 outside Sunita Roy's new home at midday on Saturday. He got out and opened the two wrought-iron gates before driving onto the gravel forecourt and parking. The new owner of the five-bedroom house emerged through the wood-panelled front door in a bright-green sari as he clambered out and she rushed to greet him.

'Thanks once again for all your help over the last two days, Tom,' she said while embracing him.

'I wish I could say it had all been a pleasure,' he replied with a grin. Then, lapsing into his Black Country jargon, he added, 'But after lugging all those boxes up your stairs, I was absolutely zonked last night.'

'Never mind. Come in and I'll make you a cup of tea. My friend Rupa's here and my sister, Tulika. They're helping me prepare the food. You met Tulika once, didn't you?'

'Yes, once,' he said, 'and I've met Rupa several times.'

The sergeant led Vickers through the hallway, which she had decked in holly, paper snowflakes and twinkling lights. She led him into the large, bright kitchen at the rear of the house. Rupa and Tulika were working on a long oak table beside an ancient Aga cooker.

The two women both said 'Hi, Tom' and waved as he was shown in. He glanced out of the picture window which afforded views over the landscaped rear gardens. Then, while the aroma of a rich Bengali curry wafted across from the Aga, he watched for a moment as the pair placed samosas and other Indian delicacies on plates.

'Looks like you're both doing a grand job,' he said before turning to his hostess.

'Sunita, I couldn't help noticing that you've come up with a new name for your house,' he said. 'I saw the sign on the hall floor.'

'Yes, it arrived this morning,' she said. 'I decided to call the place Ashiyana, which means beautiful home, and, before you say anything, I see that as a long-term goal rather than a reflection on what the place looks like at the moment.'

'Fair enough,' he said with a smile. 'If you like, I can come round with my drill and screw it to your front wall for you.'

'Tom, you are sweet,' she said. 'Thanks for the offer but I'm quite capable of fitting a sign onto a wall. But I tell you what you can help me with, Tom. I'm not very good with drinks. If we go next door, can you tell me if I've missed anything out?'

After she had put a kettle on to make some tea, she led him into the generously sized living room, which had a wood burner and a Christmas tree at the far end.

He followed her past the two brand-new cream leather settees that he'd seen delivered the previous day until they reached a dining table where, for the moment, Sunita was keeping a selection of wines, beers and spirits.

'Do you think I've left anything out?' she asked.

He smiled. 'You've done magnificently, Sunita, as you always do. No, you've got gin, whisky, rum, lagers, real ales and cider, as well as red and white wine and soft drinks. That little lot should suit everyone. How many people have you got coming?'

'About fifteen,' she said. 'I've invited the DCI and his wife; a handful of folk from CID; Derek Underhill and the Listers because they live nearby; and some of the neighbours.'

She glanced at her watch, which showed it was half past one.

‘The first people should be arriving around now,’ she said.

Right on cue, she heard footsteps outside and the doorbell rang. She went into the hall and drew back the front door in delight to find the chief inspector standing there, clutching a present. Helen Roscoe was beside him.

‘Here you are, Sergeant,’ he said, handing her the gift-wrapped box. ‘Something I hope you find very useful.’

‘Thank you so much, sir,’ she said. ‘I’ll unwrap it immediately. I don’t often get presents.’

‘I’m sure that’s not true,’ he said. ‘By the way, this is a wonderful part of the village. The gardens here are beautiful.’

‘Come and look at this, Tom,’ Sunita called out, as the Roscoes followed her into the hallway.

The inspector appeared from the living room and greeted the newcomers as Sunita tore back the fancy paper to reveal a set of wine glasses.

‘I know you’re not much of a drinker, Sergeant,’ said Roscoe. ‘But I thought these might come in handy for all the parties I expect you’re going to be holding now.’

‘Very thoughtful,’ she said. ‘Thank you, although today’s event is just a one-off, I can assure you.’

‘You’ve done very well for yourself, Sunita,’ Helen remarked while gazing around. ‘But this is such a big house for one person, if you don’t mind me saying. Maybe you should find others to share it with.’

Helen smiled across knowingly at Tom Vickers while making her last comment.

‘I’m certainly not thinking of having lots of children, if that’s what you’re suggesting,’ Sunita said hurriedly. ‘I’m a career girl.’

‘We know that,’ said Roscoe.

‘Come on,’ said Sunita. ‘If you come into the main room, I’ll get you both a drink.’

While they all sipped from glasses of wine, the chief inspector took his sergeant aside.

'While you were off work yesterday, we arrested Roland Hargreaves at the Vale,' he said.

Sunita's eyes lit up.

'So my theory that the prisoner Dylan Roberts didn't kill Lewis Tigworth was proved right,' she said.

'Yes. Your instincts have been vindicated, Sergeant. The prison governor held his own inquiry into Lewis Tigworth's death and the details Hargreaves gave about the times he was on the landing didn't match with what other warders were saying. So the governor became suspicious and ordered a search of Hargreaves's locker.

'A pair of gloves were found which were handed to Dr Ling and yesterday afternoon she rang me to say Tigworth's DNA had been found on them. That comes after Dr Reynolds recovered Hargreaves's DNA from under Tigworth's fingernails. We've also found £25,000 in one of Hargreaves's building society accounts and he hasn't been able to give a rational explanation as to how the money got there. The payment came from a company which is no doubt linked to Swinford.'

'So it looks likely Swinford paid Hargreaves to shut Tigworth up?' Sunita asked.

'Looks that way,' he replied. 'Apparently, Hargreaves was a warder at Winson Green while Swinford was an inmate.'

Helen stepped towards her husband and touched his arm.

'Come on, darling,' she said. 'Let's have a break from your work today. Sunita, why don't you show us round your new place?'

Sunita smiled. 'I'd love to take you round. But I think the food's nearly ready. Can we do that afterwards?'

Roscoe put his arm round his wife's shoulder.

'I promise not to go on about work today,' he said, 'but I must just mention one more thing. I received a phone call last night from Jean-Jacques Beauvais. He said he's so grateful for the way the sergeant and I handled the

kidnapping that we're both welcome to come and watch Aston Villa with free tickets from him.'

'That's a lovely gesture, sir,' said Sunita, 'but, as you know, I'm not really interested in a lot of sweaty men running round a field chasing a ball.'

Helen laughed. 'Me neither,' she said.

'I know you're not, Sergeant,' said Roscoe. 'I believe you once said you'd rather watch your uncle's iron gate rusting in the rain than watch a football match.'

'I think I did say something like that, sir. So will you be taking Monsieur Beauvais up on his offer yourself?'

He shook his head. 'Unlikely,' said Roscoe with a smile. 'I'm a Blues fan, through and through.'

THE END

If you enjoyed this book, please let others know by leaving a quick review on Amazon. Also, if you spot anything untoward in the paperback, get in touch. We strive for the best quality and appreciate reader feedback.

editor@thebookfolks.com

www.thebookfolks.com

More fiction in this series

MURDER ON OXFORD LANE (Book 1)

A budding chorister doesn't return home from practice but his wife doesn't appear concerned. DS Sunita Roy becomes convinced he has been murdered but she has her own problems in the form of an ex-boyfriend who won't take no for an answer. Will she keep her eye on the ball when all expect her to fail?

THE CROSSBOW STALKER (Book 2)

When a serial killer armed with a crossbow terrorises the West Midlands, Chief Inspector Gavin Roscoe suspects a motive of jealousy and revenge. But as the number of victims increases, the connection initially established between them wears thin. DS Sunita Roy has a different theory and resolves to pursue her own instincts, come what may.

MURDER OF A DOCTOR (Book 3)

Police search for the identities of people seen near the scene of a doctor's murder. And it seems like an open and shut case when a father with a grievance against him can be placed nearby. But DS Sunita Roy wants to dig deeper, and with an internal affairs investigation ongoing, she'll have to tread carefully.

OUT FOR REVENGE (Book 4)

There's a noticeable change of atmosphere in the city when a dangerous prisoner is released. He has plans to up his drugs business. But someone will quickly put an end to that, by putting an end to his life. Detective Sunita Roy has the unenviable task of hunting down the gangsters who were likely responsible. But when the cops close in, they'll have an even bigger problem than they first imagined.

HEIR TO MURDER (Book 5)

Miles Kenworth makes the lives of others in his apartment block a misery with his loud music. One day the woman next door hears a commotion and enters Miles' flat to find him lying dead in a pool of blood. The man from upstairs is standing over him. It looks like a straightforward case until DS Sunita Roy opens a can of worms…

All FREE with Kindle Unlimited and available in paperback.

More fiction by Tony Bassett

SEAT 97

Journalist Nick Colton lands the scoop of his career when a concertgoer sitting next to him is shot dead in front of his eyes. But the gunman escapes amidst the chaos, and Colton's investigation into the murder will see him treading a dangerous line through London's unforgiving streets.

FREE with Kindle Unlimited and available in paperback.

Other titles of interest

CATFISH by Sadie Norman

It is not without some malice that rookie detective Anna McArthur is called "crazy" by her colleagues. She certainly tends to act first and think later. But when Anna discovers the body of a murdered woman who has "catfish" carved into her chest, she feels a personal duty to do everything she can to up her game and find the killer.

Printed in Great Britain
by Amazon

47407567R00148

CPSIA information can be obtained
at www.ICGtesting.com
Printed in the USA
FFHW011943190519
52544355-58010FF

9 781643 675183